Two Spies Reach Out from the Grave

by

CHAD HUSKINS

Reviews of Chad Huskins novels

Psycho Save Us

Zephyr Book Reviews - an amazing tale! It is filled with layers of wonderful prose

Ana Q Crow - disturbing, powerful, gritty and grand

Jen - Huskins knows how to create characters that live and breath and he knows how to shape drama and keep a reader on the edge of their seat

Amber Marie S. - Huskins writes in a way that definitely draws you into the story and does not let you go until he is through

Christi S. - Wow. What a page turner.

Zero Star

John Grimes – Relive the birth of Science Fiction. Thought provoking and still fun.

Ann Engel - the scope and depth of this story puts it up there with the sci fi classics of the 1970-80's authors

Humble Frog - This was a fantastic hard Sci-Fi tale that interestingly enough was not only about the science. There was genuine character development, great action, moral dilemma, pure emotion. I loved it.

Daniel Clark - every once in a while I stumble upon a great work that is definitely not in the canon of classics, but it blows me away with its unique greatness.

Liz P - The story is, of course, delectable. But it is the delivery that has given me such excitement. I've never read anything quite like it. Read this book. See how a master creates a story with such a unique ability.

Sol Ascendency

Fernando - Amazing book. Incredibly good read. I honestly don't think I've read anything this good in quite some time.

Imaginos - creates a universe and does a great job at keeping the motivation of the parties secret or ambiguous

Ron Baker - Science fiction on a grand scale.

John Bales - Definitely a page turner, couldn't put it down once I started.

John Bell - a truly great story and value for money, a yarn that will rattle your cage, and leave you feeling somewhat uncomfortable.

Khan in Rasputin's Shadow

Kevin S. - I have never read a story quite like this one and I recommend it to anyone who likes suspense or military fiction.

Shelly Dawn T. - action-packed and incredibly detailed.

Diablo5050 – Fascinating …Chad Huskins' intimate knowledge and description of stalking, reconnaissance, weaponry, stealth, surveillance, mediation…

Chad Huskins

All characters and events in this book are fictional. Any resemblance to real people and events is purely coincidental.

Two Spies Reach Out From the Grave

Copyright 2018 by Chad Huskins

Edited by Thomas Fruman

Cover Art by: Micah Champion

Published by Nine Dusks Entertainment, LLC

www.9dusks.com

ISBN-13: 978-1-7325641-1-4
ISBN-10: 1-7325641-1-6

Also by Chad Huskins:

The Psycho Series

- Psycho Save Us
- Psycho Within Us
- Psycho Redeem Us

The Phantom Series

- The Phantom in the Deep
- The Immortal Game

The Sol Ascendancy

The Shinobi Conspiracy at Izu Harbor

The Devil in the Dust Bowl

Kinjin

Zero Star

Waves Crash & Seas Split

Lady of Drith

Khan in Rasputin's Shadow

Just a Phase

Chad Huskins

For Melissa, Tom, and Will, and the support you've given me.

Contents

PART ONE

The Asset

1

See these hands. See them. Lined and cracked. With tracks etched jaggedly across aging flesh, channels cut by the rivers of time and use, avoiding only the hardened knuckles. Pronounced veins that begin to press against the skin, a roadmap with no beginning or end, no destination at all. Hands that might've built a house, might've held the hand of an admiring daughter, might've thrown the baseball to an adoring son. Might've. Those are all possibilities.

These hands didn't do that. They were put to other use.

These hands clutch the weapon they were told to clutch. These hands know it well. The cold steel that is more familiar than a lover's touch. Feel it. The weight of it. Its purpose. A cold, inanimate object that will do nothing ever again unless it is acted upon. Unless the trigger is squeezed. Unless the hammer falls. The mind is at ease with this, both knowing and not knowing. The mind and the hands are aware of each other and not aware of each other. Acting with both autonomy and concert. The gun presses to its victim's head.

The hands have been here before. They don't tremble like they used to. Not even age can make them tremble. Not yet. That will come later. Along with the doubt, but the doubt is the mind's burden, not the hand's. The hand has to do the pointing and the squeezing, but it doesn't have to do the suffering and the doubting.

"Please," he whispers. Down on his knees like this, facing away from me, he resembles a person giving prayer. Total surrender often looks like prayer. I've seen it enough times to know. Is that what prayer is? Total surrender of the self to a higher power? Asking for forgiveness? If so, the moment is appropriate. "Please. I have children. I have three children."

He doesn't know that this doesn't matter. It can't matter. The mind has already decided this. It did so long ago. Every person the hand has killed at the behest of the mind has been someone's child. That being true, many children have been slain by the hand. It can't matter now. If it matters now it should have mattered then. And that the mind *cannot* bear. Besides, the mind says, most people over a certain age have children. If we spared every evil person because they had children, then evil persons would only make sure they had several children, as insurance. We can't let children be shields for them.

The mind knows this. The mind has rationalized. The mind has decided.

"Please."

"Make the call," I tell him, handing him the cell phone. With shaking hands, he takes it. With shaking fingers, he dials. His hands have not been here before. Neither has his mind. He thinks that dialing the number for me might postpone this, grant him a reprieve. Maybe his killer will have mercy on him for it. Appreciate it. I won't, but he is free to think that if it gets him through the next few minutes.

"No codes," I tell him. "Nothing to let him know you're under duress. No codes," I repeat. "Or I'll know."

He holds the phone to his ear. I can hear it ringing. I hear someone pick up. He speaks quickly back and forth. The words are not my native tongue, but I understand them well enough. And I listen for any obvious codes. I can't detect any. He tells the person on the other end that everything is okay, the shipment was received, and that they should carry on with their plan. Then he starts speaking faster, and mutters *wabakhai* a lot, which in Pashto can mean either *excuse me* or *I'm sorry*. Slightly different meanings. If it's the latter, he may be trying to apologize for his betrayal.

Can't take the chance he's about to say that. He's speaking faster and faster, I'm having trouble keeping up. I take the phone from him and hang up. The person on the other end will just have to assume the call was dropped.

"Good," I say, and place the phone in my pocket.

"Please," he says once more, now sobbing. "Please. I'll just…I'll disappear. I did what you said! Please let me go. I'll disappear, I promise. It will be just like I was dead. You'll never hear from me again. Please. Please."

The silencer makes the pistol's shot a whisper. Brain and skull fragments splatter against the wall. His head snaps forward. The body crumples into a heap. The air smells sweet with cordite, and the coppery aroma of fresh blood. It's a strange thing. Someone taught him how to walk, how to talk, how to read and write, how to add and multiply. Someone was there at his graduation. He had someone who loved him. Probably lots of someones. People he wanted to reconnect with, people he wanted to apologize to. Once the trigger is squeezed, you take all that away from them. Grocery lists forever unbought, apologies forever unspoken. You do that. *You.* When you pull the trigger.

Now I'm replacing the pistol in my tactical hip holster. Now I'm taking one last look at the body. Cool embers of confusion and hatred still live in those dead eyes. I don't linger on it. Stepping away, I make my way out of the building. Same way I came in.

No searchlights. No raised voices. Just the dark, unending fields of takirs. Dried crust that forms with huge cracks on the desert surface. Behind me, the half-crumbling stone house rests quietly. A couple of lights in the upper floor. The children he spoke of. They'll find their father in the morning, in the basement, a hole in his head. They won't know why. The mind says this is normal. It says that I was also confused when my father died of a heart attack, also asking why.

The mind says a lot of things.

The fields are seemingly unending. Only a single oasis grants the eyes any reprieve of the dry ugly sameness. I pause here. Take a look around. One hand goes to my ear, the other to the radio clipped to my vest. "Nest, this is Ageless Fox. Target neutralized and the dove is in the air. Repeat, *the dove is in the air.* Ready for evac. Over."

Silence.

I'm out here with nothing and no one besides the wind. The bushes all around the oasis whisper conspiratorially. Crickets chirp, searching for mates, warning off competition, fighting a battle of survival that came before Man and will surely outlast him. I try calling the Nest again. No answer. Just me and the wind and the crickets. The house is now a glowing dot in the distance, resting atop a small hill and beneath a starry sky. Nothing like an Afghan sky. Zero light pollution. Orion is climbing over the eastern horizon, so I can tell without looking at my watch that it's a little after 2100 hours.

I give the Nest another call. Nothing. Still silence. This could get dicey. If I can't contact the Nest, then I'm alone. Comms between me and my people at the Nest are like the tether that keeps an astronaut from drifting too far away from the spacecraft. Left out there too long, that drift may become extreme. You won't be coming back. Lost with all the other detritus under the sand left by other wars, tanks and jeeps abandoned when a sandstorm proved too problematic, piles of arrows and bullets and even artillery left in deserts and mountain ranges because it was cheaper than shipping them all back.

It can be easy to be left behind. Any tool can be left, if it outlives its usefulness. Not like it would be hard. They pick us for our disposability. Toss one of us to the side, who's really gonna care? They made sure no one would care before they picked us. Part of SOG selection. Probably the number-one criteria. They don't let you know what all the criteria are, but that's probably one.

A soft chime deep in my ear. I touch the radio on my vest. Tap the button twice to send the acknowledgement. I hear a soft ping. Then a kind of living silence, like when a television is left on but with the volume muted. A new link being established. Finally, a voice comes in. A terse male voice speaks. "Ageless Fox, Nest. Do you read? Over."

"Nest, Fox. I read, five-by-five."

"Say status."

"Target neutralized. The dove is in the air. Repeat, the dove is in the air. I'm safe away, two mikes out from target zone and ready for evac at rendezvous Charlie."

I wait to hear the verdict. Am I alone, or is there a hawk coming to take me away? Never can tell. Situations are always fluid. There *was* a hawk ready when I first set down, but things change. Between then and now, a sandstorm might've been conjured up in the west, something could've gone wrong politically, might be an enemy bird materialized out of nowhere and is scanning the whole region, or some idiot forgot to clean the sand out of the hawk's engines.

So, I wait. Am I hoofing it, camping out in the desert mountains, eating snakes and goats for weeks on end? Or do I have help coming? I'm prepared for either.

"Copy that, Fox. Got a hawk in the air for you. ETA twenty minutes."

"Fox copies, Nest. That's good to hear. Fox out."

And now it's a waiting game. And so I wait. I wait with my back pressed against a boulder that's probably been here since the last Mongol invasion. This boulder's seen it all. I'm nothing new. Just another passerby. Just another participant in a war beyond reckoning. I wait with Orion. With Rigel, the star that's his foot. Rigel, nine hundred light-years away. Older than both me and the boulder. It's just us guys out here. Me and Orion and Rigel and Betelgeuse and the boulder. A dead body is two mikes east of me. A body I made dead. Just us guys out here.

I hold up my hands. See these hands. See them. Still not shaking.

When I hear the *whup-whup-whup* of the helicopter, I hunker down, and prep for a quick take off. It's over fast, and without ceremony. I'm inside my steel angel and it is delivering me from this wasteland of contempt and age-old vendettas. I get a pat on the back from the gunner. I'm inside the steel angel with other men who have been sweating and living inside their body armor for weeks. I've never met them before. They don't know me. They came to give suppressive fire in case I needed it. I strap in.

Sunrise. A ribbon of fire ignites the eastern horizon. We head for it. And now we're landing back at base. And now I'm at a preliminary debriefing with the colonel and others. CIA rep is there, too. A new Homeland guy, as well, overseeing my operation and others for the Secretary of Defense, who had direct operational control the whole time. The power to pull the plug on it if necessary. To cut ties with me and leave me out there, too. The whole time I was out there, there were other people deciding my fate. Even the president had involvement. My name fell on his ears. Well, not my real name, just "Ageless Fox." He and I will likely never meet, and he'll never know which American's life he held in his hands for Operation FAST SPIN.

Now I'm being asked to write up a report, which will be included in my team's after-action review. The purpose of an AAR is to let my team and others reflect on lessons learned, so we can all do better in the future. I'm lying in my bunk during my first reading of my team's AAR, where I discover that there was a moment when the whole operation was almost scrapped. While I held my gun to the head of the American defector, while his family was upstairs not knowing he was on his knees pleading for his life, while my mind was justifying the kill, while all that was going on there was a hiccup from our PAG. The Political Action Group hit a snag trying to get permission from the Afghani government to allow the Chinook to take flight on what was deemed "standard reconnaissance." It was a close thing, it all very nearly fell apart. Then one of our Afghan informants called in a favor for us. No one is clear what happened, whether a threat was made or not, but the Marines got their go-ahead and I got my steel angel.

And now I'm on another helicopter, heading to Forward Operating Base Arian in Ghazni Province. Now we're sweeping over the arid lands and crossing the Kabul-Kandahar Highway, flying low enough to frighten a man and his children and their herd of goats. One of the children waves at me. I wave back.

Now I've landed at the ISAF base. It consists of Polish and U.S. Army forces. I nod amiably to everyone, but I don't salute. I don't know any of their faces, and I won't try to remember any of them. Because I'm not here to stay and after only a night's rest I'm off again. On a C-130 with cargo, medical supplies, and a group of Marines headed to the ancient city of Bagram to relieve some of Task Force Phoenix stationed there. I don't know any of these guys, either, but they see that I'm alone and guess what I am. They don't ask questions. They know not to. My job has me bouncing around like this, and my peripatetic lifestyle means I encounter people in small doses, getting little vignettes of their lives and never the full novel. We chat about baseball. I'm from Atlanta and there are two other Braves fans among the soldiers. One of them thinks the ol' Bravos have a chance this year. I'm skeptical.

We touch down during a windstorm. Not a bad one, but the crosswinds buffet us down the two-mile-long runway. When I step off the plane, I can just make out the control tower and the two snipers stationed up there. Now I'm reporting to the CIA handler on site and shaking hands with the team that's been fighting on my behalf behind the scenes to grant me windows of opportunity, and creating an environment in which I can operate. U.S. Army Colonel Gibbs and CIA analyst Aaleyah Omar headed up the Nest this time, and coordinated with various branches to both insert me and extract me.

There are other CIA spooks here to greet me, and a medic to ask me about my health, and someone from Homeland Security I've never met. These names and faces I will have to know, even if our relationship is short-term. They've read the AAR and my personal summary. They say they're very impressed. The Secretary of Defense is happy that the operation went off without a hitch. They're going to let me rest a night before filling me in on other matters I need to know about. Which means I probably won't hear many more details about the mission. My part is done.

Now I've got my own room, about a quarter-mile away from Bagram Airfield. Every few hours there's a plane landing, bringing supplies or reshuffling soldiers around the country.

Next to my room a couple of soldiers are laughing, I think playing cards, and blasting Dr. Dre's *The Chronic*. I was, what, twelve, thirteen years old when that album came out? Heard it for the first time riding in the back seat of Sid Baker's car on our way to a Falcons game. We ran out of gas on the way home that night, had to call Sid's parents. We joked all the way home. I smile, remembering.

Wonder where Sid is now? Think last I heard, he got married to Debbie Gilmore. Hard to see him as a family man.

Nightfall.

I walk outside, sand whipping around me. There's Orion. Rigel and Betelgeuse are brightest. It's just us again. Just us guys. That's nice for a while.

I go back inside and lie down on my bed. It's comfy. I remember the first time I laid on a bed like this one in Afghanistan. I thought to myself, *This makes it permanent*. When they start shipping you super-comfy beds to bases in the middle of nowhere, you know the occupation isn't going to be a short thing. They're in it for the long haul. Like Orion and me.

In the distance I can hear the *pop-pop-pop* of guys at the gun range. Putting the time in. Killing boredom. Tomorrow I'll be on a plane headed for Dubai. The day after that, I'll be on another plane for the States. I try to think on that as I wind down for the night. Home. It grants some small peace. I can still hear Salam's plea before I shot him. *I have children. I have three children.*

See these hands. See them. Steady as a rock.

So why does the idea of killing myself seem so appealing?

2

"Quit tomorrow," he said to me. I remember that. Phase One training at Great Lakes was my first wake-up call. Before that, I remember thinking I could do anything. For a time, though, it seemed I might not be cut out for life in the SEALs. I couldn't make things work. My quals were okay, but not great. Once or twice it occurred to me to quit. You can do that, you know. Just quit. People think that because you signed a contract with the United States government that you're now trapped, that you *have* to serve. But if you want to just lie down and quit, you can. The SEALs don't want someone who is *eager* to quit. They'll gladly send you home. But if you wash out that way, you can never go back. Not ever.

Some of the people that quit, you'd be surprised by. Some of them look like the all-American super-jock, with square jaw and biceps that have biceps. And some of the people that make it all the way through would surprise you, too. Skinny guys. Short guys. Even some heavyset nerds make it through. Quitting occurs to everyone. People that say it doesn't are lying. It crosses your mind at least once or twice. No escaping that. The trick to staying in? A drill instructor told me: "It's telling yourself, 'I'll quit tomorrow.'" Just keep saying that. And when tomorrow comes, say it again. "I can make it through today, but then I'll quit tomorrow." Eventually, it becomes a mantra, a new program you've written in your head.

Tricks like that are how lone operatives like me make it when we're out there in strange lands, when we've got no more MREs and we're eating insects, when things are tough and it looks like we're not going to make it.

We quit tomorrow.

I'm not the most dangerous man in the history of the SEALs or CIA. I'm not even the smartest, or the wiliest, or the most fearless. What I am is a man who figured out a way to make it work. I have a series of mental tricks that keep me motivated and moving. Quitting tomorrow, mnemonic devices for memorization, accepting that I'm already dead (*bushido*), muscle memory from hours upon hours of mindless training—these things have kept me alive and moving on a dozen missions where I was alone, hurting, even a little scared. Quitting tomorrow helps.

My drill instructor couldn't have guessed that when he advised us to quit tomorrow, he was giving me the very tool that would keep me alive. I don't know if I can explain what I've been going through, but I can try. I've been experiencing the melancholy, the signs of which we've all been trained to recognize, both in ourselves and in others. Psych evals reinforce this self-awareness. Thank God for those.

I look at evaluations as a means to bounce around my ideas about my job, to hear my own voice say the words. But I don't share everything. I know we're supposed to, but I don't. The sessions are like a pressure-release valve to some extent, allowing some kind of stoppage in my chest to finally become freed, but there are also things I feel are better kept in the pipes. Those things are for me, for those deeply introspective 1 AM sessions with myself and the stars. I know this is wrong. I know the better way is to share these thoughts with someone. But I can't and I won't. I have yet to tell my counselor that I'm thinking about quitting tomorrow.

*

I'm back at CIA headquarters at Langley. Got my own room. My day starts at 0500. I wake up, do a twenty-minute session of transcendental meditation, then do a slow ten-minute yoga workout to loosen things up, then grab some coffee, usually black, even though the people at Langley have just about every kind of coffee accoutrements a connoisseur could ask for. I take one look at myself in the mirror and decide to finally shave the beard that grew during my deployment. Take a look at the lines in my face, etched like canyons from ancient rivers long since dried up. The pale green eyes stare back at me, asking me something. It's strange. I don't often look in a mirror. Not really *look*. In fact, I do it rarely enough that I'm surprised by the face I see. Didn't expect to see *him*. That's a little eerie.

I've got to give a talk, kind of a lecture. That's the last thing I'll do for the CIA before I go on leave. I was asked months ago to prepare a speech to give to a group of SOG operatives who will be deploying soon to Afghanistan. I go over my notes, sip my coffee, and rewrite parts of the speech. Satisfied for the moment, I pull on my sweats and head out, nodding to the interns that haunt these hallways at all hours.

This morning, I'm one of five using the agency's gym. I get in some quick cardio with a two-mile run, then hit the weights. When I'm done, I'm in the steam bath, then a quick shower, then back in my room getting dressed. It's 0730 when I head to the briefing room, bringing with me notes I've been prepping over the last week and a tablet for taking more notes.

I'm not the first to arrive in the briefing room. There are two assistants already at their seats, as well as a secretary walking around the long oak table, placing classified report packets in front of each chair like a butler preparing the table for guests. No assigned seating here, only don't take the chair at the head of the table, that's for the DDO. It's never been specifically said that that's where she sits, everyone just knows. Just like it's understood that she can be late, but no one else can.

Everyone starts filing in. I smile and shake hands. They give me that look. The one that says they're appreciative of everything I do. It's an admiring look, but also one that's just a little bit curious as to what the hell goes on inside my head. A lot of them must wonder what it's like. How could they not? Paramilitary Officers are often talked about but not seen. By now they've all read the AAR and know about my actions, but here I am, clean-shaven and well-dressed, not a scratch on me. Maybe even some part of them thinks I'm a work of fiction. Until they shake my hand.

Joint Special Operations Command have some people here. These are guys I usually never meet, but they're operating behind the scenes on a grander scale, often greasing the wheels of communication between the various military branches. Sometimes they don't even know what sort of operation they're facilitating, they just get everybody talking to each other.

A couple of people from CIA's Special Activities Division are present. These are my people. I don't know any of these particular faces, but they're the ones who fight for their operatives behind the scenes, surrendering weekends and holidays as they fight tirelessly against both bureaucracy and their superiors to get me what I need.

Sometimes that includes weapons and supplies, but usually it's just buying me time and permission to do things.

Deputy Director of Operations for CIA Susan Halbach sweeps into the room with two assistants in tow and a single tablet, which she tosses onto the table before sliding into a seat. "Good morning, everyone." She doesn't acknowledge me like all the others have done. Everyone says good morning back. "All right, everyone's here?" It's a question, but the tone is a command. She's late, but no one else can be. "Okay, let's get started. Tony? The door?" One of her assistants leaps up from a seat he's just taken and softly closes the door. "Morning all, morning all. George, good to see you. How's your wife?"

"She's fine, ma'am," George says. When we shook hands earlier, he said he was with the Ops Center.

"Somebody told me she was pregnant? Or did I hear wrong?"

"No ma'am, she's not pregnant."

"Well, maybe you can do something about that?"

Good-natured laughter around the table.

"Yes, ma'am, I'll get right on it," George says.

More laughter.

I smile because I'm supposed to. It would be weird if I didn't. The icebreakers over with, she puts on her glasses and gets down to it. "Okay, so, I've been over the report, as I'm sure you all have. Today's meeting is to discuss Operation FAST SPIN and its successful execution. It's—pardon me, I just realized I've been awfully rude. Mr. Adamson, welcome back." They all turn to me with friendly smiles.

"Thank you, ma'am. Good to be back," I say.

"Right up front I'll say your handling of this operation was terrific. You and your team did a great service, and I applaud your skills and professionalism. Exemplary work."

"Thank you, ma'am."

She smiles briefly. With that out of the way, she looks down at the report that was laid out for her, and opens her tablet. "So, the operation went about as well as expected, and 'the dove is in the air,' I see. Now, Mr. Adamson, there are one or two people in this room who I've only recently brought in on this, to help us develop this intelligence lead further. They've assured me they've read all the reports, but I would like you to clarify what it is that went down in Ghazni Province, exactly. And its significance."

Everyone looks at me again.

I lean forward. Hands clasped on the table. Clear my throat. "Well, seventeen days ago I was stationed at Bagram Airfield, overseeing some of the training for three new POs that SAD had flown in. A hundred miles away, a tip reached a unit with Special Operations Group, actionable intelligence from HUMINT, saying there was a local informant that had a bead on Farooq Salam's location. Salam is—*was*—one of us. A military intelligence officer, working clandestinely with Doctors Without Borders in the region some years ago, but then left when he got mixed up with some people there. People with connections to Islamic extremists. No one's sure how exactly it happened, but Salam became radicalized. He sent for his family, who joined him there, but it doesn't seem they knew what he was really doing.

"And what he was doing was feeding information to terrorists, giving them the movements of American military personnel, as well as suggesting locations of attack on Doctors Without Borders clinics. About thirty dead soldiers and a dozen dead doctors can be blamed on Salam's actions.

"From what I understand, after a standard psych evaluation, Salam broke all contact and fled, possibly became paranoid, suspected his bosses were about to start an investigation on his unit to see if there was a leak. No one could find him for weeks. CIA finally zeroed in on his location five years ago, almost got him, but then he fled to Syria and was not seen for a while. Then intel emerged linking him with ISIS in Syria. CIA tried to nab him there. Missed again. Then, eighteen days ago, an informant in Ghazni dropped us a clue. Salam was there, but maybe not for long. There was a window. He was a high-value target specifically because of the information he could continue to share with our enemies, information on how the U.S. military works, which has been beneficial to ISIS in training new recruits.

"There were thoughts on how to do it. An airstrike, or a SEAL team insertion. But all those would leave a large footprint in a region where we're trying to pull back from. Either blowing the hell out of

Salam's residence or putting that many boots on the ground would undo a lot of the trust we've been gaining from the Afghan government, letting them police their own back yard and all."

To my right there's a woman named Tara Yarwick. Before the meeting started she introduced herself as a psychologist for JSOC team analytics. She's watching me closely. Taking notes as I speak. There's nothing I'm saying that's not in the report for her to review later. That means she's not taking notes on what I'm saying. She's taking notes on me.

"I was brought in at the last minute as SAD floated the option of a one-man insertion solution to the deputy director," I nod towards Halbach, "and was flown to Forward Operating Base Arian in Ghazni and placed on standby, until we got the go-ahead from both Deputy Director Halbach and the Secretary of Defense. Both agreed that, should the operation go sour, a single Paramilitary Officer could be easily disavowed."

That last sentence hangs in the air a moment. It won't spur anyone to guilt—they've all had that part of their souls surgically removed—but it does create a solemn silence as we mourn our innocence.

"Fourteen days ago, I deployed from Arian and was dropped off during a nighttime insertion by Chinook in the westernmost region. I made my way through the hills and reached the desert plain the next day, spotted the house at around oh-seven-thirty, monitored the house from afar for twenty-four hours to get an idea of the baseline. It was exactly as the satellite images showed. A two-story rock house in the middle of nowhere, owned by a Syrian businessman with ISIS sympathies. No security, and no sign of anyone coming or going. I took my time figuring out ingress and egress points.

"I remained in contact with the Nest the entire time. I was told I had discretion. Main ingress point was a cellar door I had scouted that first night. I was planning to go upstairs to find him when nightfall came. But I lucked out. He came to me. A late-night visit to his wine cellar. Just luck. Otherwise, his wife and children might've gotten involved. But he was alone. That's when I ambushed him and made him make the call."

"Can you explain the significance of that phone call for those who aren't fully up to speed?" Halbach asks.

I nod. "While I was out there, new intel came in stating that the people who had put Salam in that house had actually included him on another operation being planned fifty miles away, and that Salam was checking in with these people every few hours so that they knew he wasn't dead or captured. That way, his ISIS connections had ensured that their networks hadn't been compromised. My mission objectives were then changed somewhat. I was to neutralize Salam, but not alert those abetting him, for at least six hours, because a SEAL team was being assembled to take them out after I had Salam. So, I had to wait around for Salam's check-in time, so that he could make the call and give his ISIS pals the all-clear. I then exfil'd the same way I came in, and was picked up a couple hours later by—"

"Sorry. You waited *six hours* while the man knelt there in front of you in the basement?" asks a gentleman on my left. Jamal Fowler, he said his name was, also with JSOC, and it's obvious what his real question is. He's in awe, probably mildly disturbed that I stood there over my intended victim, him knowing he was going to die in six hours once the call was made, him praying his family or someone would come down to the cellar and discover us and distract me and give him a chance to escape, and me having to wait all that time with my gun out and knowing that I'm going to kill him. And me knowing that he knows.

"Yes," I say. "I did."

Please. I have children. I have three children.

"So you sent the message," Fowler says. " 'The dove is in the air.' Message sent and Salam's people were none the wiser. SEALs hit them around the time you were being extracted, did I hear that right?" he asks the room.

"Yes," I say. "That's right."

Yarwick has stopped taking notes. Her gaze lingers on me a moment longer until the deputy director picks back up. "Mr. Adamson is here to answer any questions we might have as we go along. The end of this meeting will bring to a close this chapter of the operation. So, whatever develops afterwards will not be within his purview, so you'd better ask whatever you have to now, he'll be going home for a

15

few months. Some R&R I'd say he's earned." She smiles at me. It seems at least partially genuine.

"Damn straight," someone mutters.

"Yeah, it's damn good work, Agent," someone else says.

"Would you do it again?" Yarwick asks. Everyone looks at her. "Right now, if you had the choice, would you go back out there?"

A pall comes over the room. It brings a strange silence. This kind of question usually means something. It presages an offer for future work, something she's developing on her own.

"If I was needed, Ms. Yarwick, I absolutely would." It's no lie. Because it's not just "quitting tomorrow" that keeps me going. There's also the fear. The fear of letting someone down. Letting the country down. It's why people like me don't do too well with too much downtime. You have to stay frosty, on the edge, or else your mind and your skills become soft. Can't let that happen.

But Yarwick does not disclose what she's thinking.

Director Halbach clears her throat, and continues with the meeting. She outlines what the operation's success means for other operations going forward, and recommends FAST SPIN be used in future analyses on how such ops ought to be done. She congratulates department heads and the people from JSOC for liaising between CIA and the military groups that helped pull this off. I get another "good work" tossed in my direction, then the meeting is adjourned.

Nobody asks me any further questions. I've been brought here as a formality, and now my use has ended.

*

I let her approach me first. That's part of the tradecraft they teach you. The part about attracting informants, potential recruits. The habits never really leave you. There are signs that someone is about to approach you, or that they want to. Your job is twofold: to not look too eager, and to create the opportunity for them to make their move. She exits the conference room and sees me at the water fountain. I time my final sip so that I can turn away from her just as she sees me. I walk over to the elevator, hit the button for the bottom floor, and wait. I hear her high heels clicking against the tile. Smell her perfume, some expensive kind. I know it's expensive because it's subtle. And natural-smelling. Rose petals.

"Adamson," she says.

I look at her in mild surprise. Mock mild surprise. "Ma'am?"

Yarmick smirks at that. Either because she suspects I'm playing coy or she finds the use of *ma'am* quaint. Can't tell. "Got some time to spare?"

I check my watch. "Got a talk to give in a couple hours. Other than that, yeah, I've got time. What for?"

"I want to pick your brain about something."

"All right. Early lunch downstairs?"

"Lead the way."

We don't talk in the elevator ride down. Instead we stand in the awkward silence as others get on. The cafeteria of the Original Headquarters Building is wide enough that, though nearly full, everyone has their space. Laptops on tables, people leaning in for discussion, people making their case on an issue. A lot of operations are born and die in this cafeteria.

I grab a tray and a salad and tell Yarmick I'll get us a table. When she sits, I take one look at her meal—brown rice, spinach, feta cheese, a bell pepper and shrimp—and match it with the gray suit and skirt, the toned legs and auburn hair, the black briefcase and the tiny American flag pinned to her lapel. The shirt is white and stylish, surrounding the neck without depriving the viewer of her neckline. No rings. No bracelets. The only jewelry is a necklace, barely suggested beneath the collar. Fingernails immaculate. Sleeves ending just where they're supposed to. All things in their place. Measured. Like regs for navy uniform.

"Benefits of being back home, right?" she says, taking off her jacket and laying it on an unused seat beside her. "Some decent food."

"Actually, chow's pretty good at Arian," I say, digging into my salad.

"Huh. You lucked out, then. Things didn't run so smoothly at Lion. We had supply problems like you wouldn't believe. Food was shit."

I glance up, pause mid-bite. "You were in Afghanistan?"

17

She nods. "Panjshir Province. Camp Lion was a good place to indoctrinate new recruits and hide informants for a while. Not so much these days. They're getting some use out of the old base, though. Turning it into a women's college." She brushes her hair to the side and scratches her long neck. A deliberate action. Might be she wanted my gaze to go there. Might be I'm looking too much into it. There are few women in the places where I'm deployed. Might be my man parts are just too eager.

"What are you doing these days?" I ask.

"I do team analytics. I go places and see how well teams are working together. Then I break the teams down to their component parts—the individuals themselves. I find out what makes them tick, sometimes recommend them for reassignment if I feel their skills are being wasted in a particular field, or if I feel they'd be better suited on another team."

"Ah."

Now it's her turn to pause mid-bite. "Ah?"

"The question you asked back there. Whether or not I'd be eager to head back out immediately if I had to."

She smiles. "You caught me. It's hard to turn off, especially when you're good at it."

"I know the feeling."

She smiles at me. I smile back.

We eat in silence for a while. She breaks it first. "What's your speech about?"

"SOG's work in Afghanistan. Things to look out for while you're there. How things are evolving in Kabul and surrounding regions. Things like that."

"A heads-up for the guys going out there."

I nod.

"Your whole career with the Company has been in Afghanistan, hasn't it?" By *Company* she means CIA. "Doing recruiting and some capture-or-kill ops as a solo operator within Special Operations Group, right?"

"I'm sure you read my file," I say. "You would have to before you make the sales pitch you're about to make."

Yarwick smiles. It looks good on her. I check her hands again. No rings. "Your mother was half Russian. She taught you to speak the language, I understand?"

I take another bite of my salad, wash it down with a sip of my water, and nod. "My mother's father was Russian, she spoke it fluently, and she taught my and my brother to speak it. We had to speak only Russian when around my grandfather."

"Your grandfather was from southern Sakha, right?"

I nod again.

"Still keep up with it?"

"What, Russian? Some. Why?"

"Because I need to know."

I shrug. "I had a girlfriend in college who was Russian, that helped. Never had use for it again until I went through final quals at Great Lakes, they were looking at putting together a special unit that could operate jointly with Russian special forces in certain embattled Islamic regions. Spetsnaz and those guys. I was going to be adopted into that, I was put through a crash course in their economics system, their relationship with Europe and Asia, their military deception tactics, their spies, *kompromat*, all that. But it got scrapped for whatever reason, and I wound up with another unit."

"Say something."

I purse my lips, and shrug. "*Odnogo jazyka nikogna nedostatočno*," I tell her. *One language is never enough.* Something they drilled into us in Special Forces. Your education is never over.

She considers me. Her face is chiseled from granite. I have no idea if I've passed her test or not. I know my Russian is pretty solid, but it's southern Russian, with variances, all the *g*'s having a soft velar fricative, kind of sounds like hocking a loogie. She's probably wondering if the Russian is the kind she needs for the mission she's putting together.

Taps the table with her forefinger. Considers me some more. "You were with SEAL Team Seven for five years?" she finally says.

"Four years operational, the last year was instructing at Great Lakes."

She nods, considering me some more. "And who approached you about recruitment into SOG?"

I think back to that day. Could've been yesterday. Kind of scary how quick the invitation came, how fast I accepted it, and how soon I was swept into an entirely different lifestyle. "It was a woman. I don't know her name. Never seen her since. She was on base with other CIA recruiters when we returned from an op. I don't think she was there for me. She and the other recruiters were trying to develop contacts in Khost Province. I think our team just happened to be there when she heard about what we did."

"Operation FAREWELL. I've only been allowed to read the overview. Mind if I ask what you might've done to attract this woman's attention? Without getting into specifics of targets, I know all that's classified."

I shrug. Take another bite of my salad. "It wasn't anything heroic. I was spotter on a sniper team. We were advancing forward into a village where our targets were." Even as I say it, I feel the hot wind on my face. "It was a mess. The village was made of bombed-out buildings shoddily put back together." Smell the dry air. "We were just scouting, but we hit a snag. Intelligence said our target was in a two-story building, and that there was only *one* two-story building the area. But when we got there, there were *two*." See the stars, and the clouds spread thinly like cotton candy across a wide Afghani sky. "We weren't sure which building the target was in. It was impossible to tell, they looked almost identical." And the moon, crescent like a bitten-off fingernail. "Then...I heard this noise. A boy. He was singing. Somewhere on the other side of the hill from where we were hiding." The boy's voice. Beautiful in the night's virgin silence. He could carry a tune. "I recognized the language. I was getting good at Pashto back then. His voice was getting closer, and it sounded like he was about to be right on top of us anyway. The only way for me and my partner to go was over a cliff, and we couldn't do that, so I decided to stand up and approach the boy."

"You just sprang up from hiding and talked to him? In the middle of the night?"

"No. If I had done that, it would've scared him. I stood up before he could crest the hill, and put my rifle away. Took my helmet off. I started walking in the direction of his voice. Just like I was on a stroll. When I saw him, he stopped singing. I waved to him, and smiled. I passed by him like I didn't care if he saw me or not."

"That put his guard down," Yarwick says. "He's thinking since you're not making a big deal out of it, then it must be okay."

I nod. Take the last bite of my salad. Push the tray away. "As he walked by me, I heard him start singing again. So then I know he's comfortable with me being out here. So I turn back and I say, in what I'm guessing was passable Pashto, 'Hey kid, you from around here? What's this village called?' He's a little hesitant, but answers. I start chit-chatting with him. I tell him a joke I heard one of our interpreters tell another of the locals—I had it memorized in case I needed to break the ice with anyone. The kid laughs." Hear his laughter. A child's laughter. A welcome thing in that god-awful place. "We get kind of chummy. After about twenty minutes, I straight up ask him if he's seen a man with a trimmed black beard and missing an arm—our primary target. The kid nods and points to one of the two-story buildings in the distance. I thank him. I radio to my partner which building it is, and keep chatting with the kid to make sure he doesn't run back to the village and tell anyone we're here looking for someone."

"And you got your target?"

"Later that night, we did, yeah." See the target through the spotter scope. Hear the report of the rifle. Watch his head snap back, the wall behind him painted with his brains. The woman next to him opens her mouth in horror. A scream muted by distance.

I down the last of my water, and stare at the empty bottle.

"And the CIA woman, she heard about this and figured you might be worth bringing in to Special Operations Group?" Yarwick asks.

I shrug. "I guess she saw potential in me as a recruiter. A gatherer of local informants. My CO said she wanted to speak with me in a tent. Alone. We talked maybe twenty minutes." See her no-nonsense gaze, the cold professionalism. "She made it clear that SOG operatives are those guys you hear about that get disavowed if they get captured or killed, that it was even more dangerous than the work I was already doing. I gave her my answer right then and there. She left that night, her and all her people."

Hear the sound of the Chinook as it took her away.

"Next I heard about it was two months later. A phone call when I got home. Two months later I was at the Farm." Remember the Farm. Camp Peary. A place of third birth, they called it, the second being INDOC at Special Forces training. The Farm is where I learned tradecraft and the rules of solo operations. Even back then I was thinking of killing myself, but I maintained the philosophy of quitting tomorrow. "I've performed a few different kinds of operations in the region, usually just recon, usually with the same Nest team."

Her hand is on her glass. Index finger lightly tapping it. The soft eyes see me clearly, and they don't patronize me with either a sad or admiring look. They just look.

"You're right. I've seen your file," she says. "Looked it over pretty good, too. You were a painter, did a semester in college for it, but you don't do it much anymore. Your father was a judo instructor, he won bronze at the Olympics and you were brought up in his school. You became a martial arts fanatic. Your first black belt was in judo, and you competed in championships. Your best judo throw is *o goshi*. You briefly considered a career teaching martial arts with your dad, you got black belts in…um, let's see…Indonesian silat? Right? And kali? With some jiu-jitsu mixed in there. Brown belt, right? You could've had a happy life helping your dad teach and run the school. But you decided to go Navy. Your mother was an engineer in the Navy. She liked life at sea. You did, too. You got a degree in oceanography." She chuckles. "Then ended up in Afghanistan, about as far away from the ocean as one can get. You dove hard into prepping for SEAL training. Full steam ahead. You've been like that ever since."

I look at her frankly. I nod. "And so."

"Your pattern is to stay active," she goes on. "You don't like a lot of downtime. You don't own a home, despite having saved up plenty of money to buy a couple of them. You rent an apartment, put a lot of your stuff in storage, most of your connections in this world are military buds. Well, there's *Sophia*." She has indeed read my file thoroughly if she knows about Sophia. "You prefer staying in the field. It's practically all you know now that everyone else is gone."

"Are you asking me to go to Russia, Ms. Yarwick?"

"If I did, and if my team allowed it, and if I could arrange it with the upper brass, would you be okay with the transfer? I know Russia would be a different environment than you're used to."

"I have some working knowledge with the region, but my team is almost exclusively outfitted for Middle East operations."

"You would have a whole new team, a whole new Nest," she says with a magician's hand wave. The flourishing gesture doesn't match everything else. Cute. I want to smile at it, but I keep professional.

"What's the op?"

"Might be a series of ops. We don't exactly know right now. It's all in its very nascent stages of planning."

"Can I at least get a hint?" I persist.

The edge of her smile twitches. She squints a little. Something's been bothering her. The table vibrates. The cell phone she placed next to her tray is going off. She silences it without looking at who it is. She's laser-focused on me. Got me in her sights. Can't allow any distractions. "There's something going down in Amur Oblast, around Vostochny Cosmodrome."

I search my memory. "The new spaceport?"

"That's it. There's a lot of military personnel moving in to act as security there, more than usual. Couple that with the rumors we're hearing…we'd really like to know what's going on there. The Vostochny Cosmodrome is far too conspicuous to drop lots of boots on the ground, and spy drones can't get anywhere close. Also, some people in JSOC and SAD aren't even convinced of the intel my team has received. But if the intel *is* accurate, then it could be big. It's taken a while to gain traction with this operation. I've just started scouting for assets, you're first on my list. We've gotten tacit approval from the White House to insert one asset—"

"*Tacit* approval. Not approval?"

She answers confidently. "I've convinced almost everyone that matters that we need an asset in the region. We'll get approval once we have a full packaged plan to put in front of the president, I'm sure of it."

I mull that over. Look around the cafeteria. Look at the flatscreen hanging on the far wall. CNN says a train derailed somewhere in Connecticut. Twelve dead. "Targets?" I ask.

"No targets. Just reconnaissance. All weapons and gear OSP." She means on-site procurement. Basically I'd be naked.

I mull that over. "What's this intel? What's the rumor?"

"Can't tell you the specifics just yet."

I mull that over, too.

She continues. "But I can tell you how it started. Connections we've made between Iran, Syria and North Korea, pertaining to an exchange of funds. Possible future projects being arranged, some new deal between Putin and Kim. One of those projects being the finishing of the link between the Trans-Siberian and Trans-Korean railways. SIPRI's reported lots of Buratino platforms going from Russia into Syria, and that Syrian nuclear scientists have been invited to areas of Russia we think need exploring."

I nod. "Go on."

"SIPRI also reported more mobile weapon platforms moving into Amur Oblast, specifically around the closed town of Tsiolkovsky, via that Trans-Siberian Railway." She looks at me meaningfully. "My team thinks there's something big here. Something new on the board."

"What?"

"Give me your answer and I might tell you."

"You expect me to give you an answer right here and now?"

A knowing smile. "Pardon me for being so presumptuous, but you don't read like a guy who needs to think about what he wants. You certainly didn't with the CIA recruiter in Khost. You're trained to make snap decisions. It's either this or downtime. You've already decided."

I glance across the lobby. I watch a CNN reporter on TV interviewing a survivor of the trail derailment. She's right. I'm not getting any younger. I have the experience. If I can help, I will. If I can work, I prefer to. I'm not unmarried and childless by coincidence.

"What do you say, Mr. Adamson?"

"You know, what you're doing is called poaching. Or it's damn close to it. It's not considered good form to poach agents."

"You'll still be with SOG. I'm not stealing you from anybody, except your usual Nest team. I just work with facilitating joint operations. There's an operation that could use a man like yourself, and I'm facilitating it. That's my project. And after it's over you can go back to your old familiar stomping grounds in Kabul or wherever. So, what do you say?"

I take another look around the cafeteria. A dozen other similar conversations are happening all around us, someone trying to convince someone else of some plan, some project, some new intelligence. A quiet hall of whispered secrets and offered favors and carefully worded pleas.

"How soon are you wanting to move on this?" I ask.

"With you attached, I imagine we might get approval as early as next week. Two months at the latest."

"I'd need at least a week to decompress. I don't like a lot of downtime, but I do like to let a little steam off."

"We know you do, and we prefer it that way."

I'm sure you do, lady. You know all about me and you know about Sophia. So I'm sure you do.

She checks her phone for the time. Or maybe to look at the message. "I gotta run," she says, standing up and taking her jacket and purse in one hand, her tray in another. The handling is expert. Guessing a waitressing job when she was working her way through college? "You won't hear from me for a few days at least, I've got other items to put in place."

"Understood, Ms. Yarwick."

"I'll have my people speak with the division director about borrowing you from the Afghan field office. If all goes well, I'll have a briefing ready for you in forty-eight hours. In the meantime, I'll have my office send you maps, files, and relevant information about the area where you'll be deployed. Study them."

"I'm good at cramming for exams."

The knowing smile again. "We know you are. Good luck with your lecture."

*

The lecture goes well enough. I've given enough of them to know my audience. I'm not there to outline how Middle East operations work, they know that already. Some of them have been deployed with SOG before. All of them have served there in Special Forces. What they need to hear is my personal experience. A couple of anecdotes, and my perspective on what I did right and what I could've done better.

There are a few questions. Direct and to the point. The men and the women in this room are not bullshitters. They don't believe in wasting time with gossip or chit-chat. They want to absorb what they can, while they can. Every bit of information I can share might bring them back home to their families.

I tell them about the importance of keeping their heads in the game, staying focused on the mission and trusting in their Nest. I tell them all that, knowing full-well that I'm compromised. I keep my little secret. Even Yarwick doesn't know. She may have read about me and Sophia and my psych profile and my time at the Drifting Place, but she doesn't know that I'm quitting tomorrow. Nobody knows that. Nobody but Sophia.

I shake hands with the SOG boys after the lecture. Answer questions. Listen to one or two of their anecdotes. Them I'm off campus, leaving Langley behind for a few days. I need to decompress. I need to throw someone.

3

Life has a push and it has a pull. There are moments—mere moments—when there is a yield, a slight let-up in the pressure it's giving you. If you've had enough experience, you learn to sense those moments *before* they happen. When that occurs, you seize the moment, and make your move. You use the momentum of adversity against itself. You slam it to the earth. That's judo.

Feel the sweat. The heaviness of the *gi* around the body. The opponent's hands on your wrist and collar. Smell his breath. What he ate for lunch. *Hear* his breath. How close is he to exhaustion? Feel which way he's moving. Be aware of your own base. Sense which way he's going to tilt you. Sense the misdirection as he tries to push you left while he sets up the throw on the right. Watch those feet. He'll try to sweep your feet using *sasae* techniques. If you pull too far away from that, he'll dive his hip in for the throw.

This is part of the decompression. Friendly competition, not a fight for survival. That push and that pull. Judo is the art of throwing someone, even if they're larger than you. There are only forty throws in all of judo—that's it, just forty—just like how you have only sixteen pieces in chess. But it's how you use them. How you piece them together in combinations. You only have sixteen pieces in chess, and yet there are more possible combinations of chess games that can be played than there are atoms in the universe.

Judoka believe that judo is "full-body chess."

I'm at O'Grady's Judo Studio. I've been here before. I like to visit whenever I'm at Langley. Master O'Grady is eighty years old, he competed in the Olympics, just like my dad. He's old school. Things are rough at his gym, he doesn't baby anybody. He wants you to be tough. Yet he's incredibly technical, and stresses technique above strength and youth. I've never seen anybody throw him.

Tonight I am paired with a few brown belts and a couple of black belts. It has been a long night. There are some big sharks present in this session. I get slammed twice by the same black belt with the same move: *o guruma*. But I manage to keep my feet more often than not. There's a brown belt who is a clear prodigy and he's giving me a run. He's tall and lanky, and favors *sasae tsurikomi ashi*. I manage to get him with *o goshi* twice. The whole time we're feeling each other, sensing what our opponent is made of, what *we're* made of. Hearts pounding. Every synapse firing in the focus of each move and counter-move. We give in order to take. Find those sweet spots. It feels good, this push and pull.

Afterward, we wipe sheets of sweat off our faces and gulp water and swap notes about each other's technique. Always the best way to end a session. I hit the shower and head to my apartment just outside of Langley.

Home is not a word I usually equate with my apartment. I've lost a connection to home, the way you lose touch with an old friend. Too few visits make it easier to have even fewer visits. I had lots of friends before Special Forces. I had Blake and Jerome, old judo partners. Blake moved to California and teaches judo in a small studio there. Jerome got drunk, hit somebody with his car, and is doing a couple years in prison. I had Scott and our weekly *Dungeons & Dragons* sessions at college. He's married with kids, moved to New Hampshire for a job. I sometimes talk to him on Skype when I'm back in the States. A bunch of other friends that I shared so much with, and now we're all scattered to the four corners. Some of them stay in contact with each other, but they all left me behind. Or I left them.

I haunt my apartment like a ghost that belongs to another house. I catch up on current events. There's been a massive power outage at Atlanta's Hartsfield-Jackson Airport, the busiest airport in the world. Planes grounded, others circling the runway, waiting for landing instructions.

I can't help but read the latest from Kabul, a place I've been deployed before and might again. A car bomb killed a dozen people yesterday. The Taliban spokesman Zabihullah Mujahid has claimed responsibility. He's been a high-value target for a while now. We'll get him. Maybe I'll be the one.

But I need to decompress. That means leaving work alone. I check online for things to do, see what's going on at the local cinema, if there's anything good I'll go catch a flick by myself. Love those Marvel movies. I make a few calls to Tomlinson and Fitzgerald, SF buddies who I know are still out there somewhere. Their wives tell me they're both deployed at present. It's usually that way. Our schedules rarely line up.

There's Sophia. I'll make a point to chat with her later. That's essential for decompression. Essential for the push and pull.

Steady workouts and judo sessions and reading. Those give me new goals to reach. Twenty minutes of meditation when I wake up and before I go to bed are mandatory. Also putting out the milk for Edward, the neighbor's cat. He seems to know whenever I'm back in town. I find him a lot on my patio, meowing like *where've you been*, and I give him a little extra love. He's old, he's got some fresh scars across his belly. It didn't make him timid, though. Wears the scars like a champ.

"Been fighting, Eddie?" If so, he must've done all right to still be around. Edward understands the push and pull. I feel like he does, anyway.

The books I'm reading are all on Russia, the Kremlin, the current political climate. I've found a few articles online about the Vosochny Cosmodrome and the planned launches of the Angara rocket. It's a new style of rocket that's going to put about twenty-five tons' worth of "special satellites" into space in the next decade. Nobody's sure what those satellites are going to be doing, and the fact that the Russian's aren't being clear about it is making intelligence agencies nervous.

Yarwick also mentioned Syria, North Korea and Iran, so I've got some audiobooks on those that I listen to during my morning jogs. She said that Russia had sent TOS-1 "Buratino" launch platforms into Syria. Those were first known to intelligence agencies in 2014, and were uniquely designed with thermobaric warheads that explode in the air above a target, spreading a flammable liquid that ignites instantly. It can kill thousands of people and destroy several city blocks at once. They were used against the Ukrainians at the airport in Donetsk in 2015 and they annihilated almost everyone there.

Russia's being ridiculously bold if they're sending those to Syria. It means an agreement has been reached behind closed doors. But what kind of deal?

"What've we got here, Eddie?" I say when I first sit down on the patio to read the latest news reports out of Russia and Syria. Edward is lying down near my feet, eyeing me suspiciously. "Just what have we got?"

It's all very difficult to follow, with things staying fluid as ever, and my focus has been on Iraq and Afghanistan. That's been the bulk of my ongoing training. While I understand the overall architectures of the Russian-Syrian issue, there are finer details I'll need to iron out.

What I do know is this. Syria is bound to Iran, mostly out of religious and strategic ties. But Iran's support, while significant, is not alarming. What *is* alarming is that Russia is backing Syria. What you *don't* hear much about on the evening news is this: There is a riddle as to *why* exactly the Russians are helping Syria in the first place. It is a riddle being asked by every major power on the planet. It doesn't make a whole lot of sense, what with Russia and Syria having had no special love for one another in the past?

So why is this happening now? Why is Putin supporting Syrian President Bashar al-Assad so stalwartly? What is going on?

There are theories. The first is that Russia is protecting Syria because Syria buys so many Russian arms. The problem with that theory is that, yes, Russia does get a lot of business from Syria, but not nearly as much as they do from their top customers: China, India, Vietnam and Algeria. The second theory is that the Syrian port of Tartus is an important base of operations for Russia's dreaded Black Sea Fleet, which has risen like a phoenix from the ashes in the last decade. But that base is hardly huge, and is only really good for operating surveillance.

There is some weight to the theory that Russia is simply afraid of Islamic extremism gaining a foothold in the region, extremism that has long been pouring over into Russia, and if Assad falls it may mean that southern Russia will be overrun. It's just a day's drive from Syria, through Turkey and Georgia, to Russia. But if that was the only reason, why didn't Russia react long before? This pressure cooker has been building for decades.

So, what gives? What does Putin stand to gain by helping Syria and putting himself at odds with much of the rest of the world?

An emerging new theory is that Putin simply wants to make a point. A strong point. America has sent humanitarian groups into Syria, and he has often held that American-led humanitarian interventions are just a cover for the U.S.'s plans to use its vast power to reshape the whole planet, spreading its gospel of democracy and overlooking its own criminal deeds. Russia and China both claim that humanitarian interventions should only be approved through a vote at the U.N. Security Council—where Russia has the power of a veto. America has often circumvented the UNSC, making Russia appear to be irrelevant, weak, fangless. In short, Russia's actions in Syria may very well be Putin taking a stand. Nothing more.

Yarwick also said that there was reason to believe that Russia was sending lots of extra military personnel to act as security around the Vostochny Cosmodrome. Yarwick said that SIPRI has tracked the movement of weapons platforms around there, as well. The Stockholm International Peace Research Institute keeps track of arms exports the world over. They're rarely wrong. If they say the Russians are putting lots of military security there, they're probably right.

And that's bad.

Yarwick made it sound like she wanted me to deploy in Amur Oblast, where all this increased activity is happening. It seemed important to her that I had the southern accent. So I need to know everything about it.

First thing I notice is the terrain. It's in the southeastern part of Russia, between the Stanovoy Mountain Range and the Amur River. Vast stretches of wilderness. It's a mixed bag. There are vast plains and forests, but also hills that rise in such altitude that the biome has no trees, just alpine tundra, with dwarf shrubs for miles upon miles, and the occasional dwarf Siberian pine. Along the river plains there are forests of larch and pine. But all that greenery comes to a sudden halt, forming bald patches of rock for dozens of miles. The land is bountiful until it's not. Green until it's not.

Varied terrains. Lots of vegetation in places. Zero vegetation in others. Lots of cold. With advanced security installations around the Cosmodrome. The city of Tsiolkovsky has literally been built up around it. The core of Tsiolkovsky was once living quarters that served the Soviet's nearby ICBM base, then shut down for ages after the collapse, and recently reworked to serve the spaceport and the people who work in it.

Tsiolkovsky comes with houses and apartments crammed with state-of-the-art tech for their scientist and military residents. A "closed town" as they're called—a settlement where travel restrictions are such that they require special authorization to come or go. A luxury residential area for Russia's top researchers, and it's in the middle of nowhere.

Christ. This is what Yarwick plans to penetrate? It's an entirely different approach than Ghazni. An entirely different problem than Farooq Salam.

Please. I have children. I have three children.

I put all this reading material aside and tell myself it's not even a sure thing that I'm going. Like Yarwick said, the plan is still in its nascent stages. A lot could change from inception to actualization. I need to remember that. How many times have I been put on standby and then sent home with blue balls?

I have three children.

I need to speak to Sophia.

It's raining when I leave to go see her. Edward's meowing from my patio. I'll feed him when I get back.

*

The drive through the Virginia hills reminds me a bit of my life on the farm. Not *the Farm*, where my third birth took place, but the farm of my first birth. The rolling hills peel back the layers of years and show me the places where I played hide-and-seek with my father and brother. With the windows down, I can smell the telltale signs of spring in the air. The roads, dilapidated by the twin powers of time and neglect, are also familiar. Not paved and flat, but the kind of roads pocked randomly by holes that form staccato rhythms on the tires of my Ford F-150 as I drive. The kind of roads that led me back home from school, college, and from basic.

These roads don't lead back home. Most arteries to that ancient past have been severed, and what few have remained open are closing fast. Where did everybody go? Where did the time go? See these hands. See them gripping the steering wheel, just as they gripped the gun pointed at Salam's head. Just as they gripped the bat in junior-year championship. Just as they gripped Tyrone Zelby's hand when we won it. Where did ol' Zelby go? Where did everybody go?

These roads don't lead back home. These roads lead to the small town of Thomasville, where the trees suddenly give way to dominating green fields of grass, which sweep right into the horizon. Dappled across its greenery are residences, some big, some small, some of them farms and some of them not, all of them with at least one garden. On the outskirts of Thomasville, down a long, straight hardpan road, is Rose Lawn Retirement Home.

Entering, I pass by an old man being wheeled around by an orderly. An elderly woman waves at me, calls me Sam, thinks I'm her grandson. I smile at her and the nurse attending her, I play along for a moment and then head inside. At the front desk there's a woman whose long fingernails click against a keyboard. Beside her is a TV switched to the news, more about the power outage at Atlanta's airport, one plane nearly crashed, dozens injured.

Upon seeing my approach, the woman at the desk pulls down her glasses and lets them hang from her neck. "Oh, hello. Mister…Adamson, wasn't it?"

"It was."

"Good to see you again. And I'm sure Sophia will be glad to see you, too."

"What kind of mood is she in today?"

"I'm not sure, I haven't seen her. She's been having a good run these last couple of weeks, I hear. Not so fretful or forgetful. An orderly says she's been asking about someone named Isabella."

Isabella was Sophia's second daughter. Dead at birth, strangled by the umbilical cord. She never talks about Isabella, and I only found out about it after taking a look at her records years ago. Not easy to get a file on an ex-SDECE agent, especially one with a career that reaches back to the Second World War, but I had some help.

"Well," I say, "I guess I'll take my chances. She can be feisty."

The woman behind the desk laughs. "Yes, she can."

I thank her again and go searching for my Sophia.

I stumbled upon Sophia de Marenches quite by accident. A therapist some five or six years ago suggested I do some volunteer work to diversify myself and raise my spirits. Giving back to the less fortunate often gives soldiers something to do when they come home, makes them feel useful. I think the therapist meant soup kitchen work, feeding the homeless, shit like that. But a posting online said there was need of people willing to spend time with aging veterans at Rose Lawn. I got in contact with them and they gave me five options. I selected Sophia because she was the oldest and she wasn't an American veteran. She was part of the French resistance against the Nazis during the German occupation of France. After the War, she went on, so the old hen claims, to be part of French intelligence services.

At first, I wasn't so sure I believed this story. I mean, the woman had to be nearly a hundred years old to have had a career at the time of Hitler's push through Europe. How could such a hero from a mythical age be forgotten, alone, fading away at a retirement home in the middle of Nowhere, U.S.A.?

But I met with her. Found her interesting. Then I had her checked out. She was legit. As legit as I've ever seen.

It's mind-boggling. If not for Sophia, Hitler would have trampled the globe. Maybe conquered it. She sacrificed a comfortable life and decided not to be satisfied with keeping her head down and looking the other way. She opted to put her life on the line. Some people survived that god-awful period by keeping their heads down the entire war. They also survived because of Sophia. The organizations she ran stood against one of history's greatest tyrants. Many of her own people told her to keep silent. She would not. Many of them told her to stop fighting and just accept the way things were. She did not. She risked capture, rape, torture, and execution. She risked everything. And she emerged victorious.

She defeated the tyrant.

And here she sits, in a wheelchair facing a lake where an orderly left her, watching videos on an iPad of a laughing baby, which I'm assuming is another video that her granddaughter sent her of her great-granddaughter. Someone's put a quilt across her lap to keep her warm. She's in a white robe with a red scarf around her neck, upon which is stitched *I'm With Shit-head*, and in parentheses *(That's You)*. It is not de rigueur, but as I understand it Sophia has never been a slave to what's fashionable. Also, according to what few family members I could contact, Sophia always liked English curse words and inappropriate humor.

It's only a little chilly out. The rain that started when I headed out has now stopped. The clouds remain gray and still overhead. Thin blades of sunshine peek through.

"*Bonjour, Sophia,*" I say.

She stops laughing at the video and freezes, like she's been caught masturbating, and turns to me slowly. When my hand touches her shoulder, she looks confused for a moment. Then, slowly, she brightens, and reaches up to touch my hand. See those hands. See them. How many secret messages have they carried? How many copies of *Défense de la France* did they hand out to spread the real news to the French people? How many times did they hold a sensitive package that won the war, or a gun that was only there in case she was captured?

Respect those hands.

"Shit, you scared me," she says. There is very little trace of her mother tongue. "So, you haven't quit yet."

I smile back and shake my head. "I know how to follow instructions, *mademoiselle.*"

"I'm glad you're starting to listen to me." She tries to pause or stop the video on the iPad. She can't manage it.

"I always listen to you, Sophia. I wouldn't dare ignore advice from a nonagenarian."

"I'm only a nonagenarian one more month."

"Really?" I raised my eyebrows. "A hundred years old in another month? I had no idea your birthday was around the corner."

Sophia watches me carefully as I walk around her wheelchair and take a seat on the bench across from her. "You're a good liar, Nathan, but you're full of shit. Where's my gift?"

I feign obliviousness another couple seconds. I smile, my cover is blown. Then reach into my jacket and pull out the fist-sized box. "It's all I could find." I lay it on the quilt in her lap. She reaches out with those old delicate fingers and opens it with some mild shaking.

"Oh, you shouldn't have." She takes out the bags of French coffee grinds. "And they're Fiones! How did you know that's my favorite?"

"You told me, Sophia."

She blinks. "Did I?"

I smile at her. "Yes, you did."

She blinks again. "Oh...oh...yes..." She smiles to cover her embarrassment. Or is it embarrassment at all? "Is this an apology for being gone so long?" she asks, recovering masterfully.

"I hear that cognitive functions slow down significantly after sixty years old. I also read that coffee can help counter that, keep you alert."

"Why do I need to stay alert anymore?"

"I dunno. All these horny old men around here ogling you? Need to be on your toes if you wanna keep them at bay, you old hen."

"And who says I want to keep them at bay, you little bastard?"

"Have it your way, then," I chuckle.

Sophia smiles wider, revealing a mouth of mostly missing teeth. "That laugh sounds good on you, Nathan. The smile looks good, too. Where were you this time?"

"The usual. Afghanistan. I told you that before I left, remember?"

She points her finger at her head and makes a twirling gesture. "My memory. You know how it is. Or you will someday."

"I doubt I'll make it to your age, Sophia. Few of us do. Especially in this business."

"What business?" Is it her turn to feign now? Is she getting back at me, having fun at my expense? Or does she *really* not recall?

"This work we do," I say. "Dangerous stuff."

"Your work is much more dangerous than anything I ever did."

I look at her.

Bullshit, I think. I know what you did. You may forget, but I met your oldest daughter once, you old hen. Chloe. The story she gave was that you ran all over the French mountains in the dead of winter, sneaking Jews and British POWs out of the country during the German occupation. You had never fired a gun in your life when you shot a German patrol officer that tried to stop you and your fellow resistance pals at the border. You later learned that German died in the hospital, and you never shed a tear. You seduced another German soldier and slept with him twice to get intel out of him before slitting his throat in his sleep. The girl that you were had a passion for freedom and ice in her veins. After the tyrant was defeated, you returned to your pre-war work as a filing secretary at a law firm. You would've stayed there, too, totally content with leaving it all behind, but your country came calling again in 1946 when the French government formed the Service de Documentation Extérieure et de Contre-Espionnage, their version of the CIA. They wanted you to teach other women to do what you did during those hellish years. How to operate clandestinely, make and translate secret messages, and use uniquely feminine guiles on the enemy. Tradecraft. And you caught two double agents working in SDECE. You were present when Faustine Dubois, the woman you caught selling government secrets to Russians, was put in front of the firing squad. You spat in her face before she was shot. She smiled back at you. You hated yourself for not being able to see her deception sooner, and swore you'd never do it again.

I could say all that to her. But I'll let her have her modesty. Or perhaps it's not modesty at all. Perhaps it is all beginning to fade. Or maybe she *wants* to forget. Maybe she wants to recall the good parts and edit out the bad parts. Will that be me someday? Am I now living a life I'll ultimately want to erase?

"I'm surprised to see you still coming around," she says, trying to pause the baby video but having difficulty. I lean forward to tap the button for her. She doesn't thank me, just snaps at me. "What are you doing here? Shouldn't you be unwinding at some singles bar, finding a woman? Don't people still do that?"

"They do," I say. "But I gotta admit, none of them are like you."

"Like me? What about me?"

"I like talking to you, you old hen. It's like a…I don't know. Like a recharge for my batteries."

"A recharge? Batteries? What are you talking about? Talking to an old woman that time forgot is *refreshing* to you? You need more excitement in your life."

"I get enough of that elsewhere."

Sophia smells the coffee, then looks at me critically. "How was it?" she says frankly. "You don't have to give me any details, obviously." She laughs. "Although if you do, you won't need to worry about me sharing them with anybody."

It takes a moment to gather my thoughts on it enough to summarize. "It went…smoothly."

"Smoothly," she says.

I nod. "No glitches. Pretty much by the numbers."

"Well, I'm glad you made it back, you little bastard."

I smile. "I might not be back for long. They've got another thing they want me on."

"What other thing?"

"Just some new thing. You know how it goes."

"Not really."

Bullshit. But I let her have that, too. "Let me ask you a question. It's about your time in the resistance. I mean, if you can think that far back."

She eyes me some more. Taking me in. Assessing me. Yeah. I see it in you. You know what's up, you old hen. The old Sophia is still swimming around in there somewhere, gazing out at the world through an old woman's eyes, but the instincts are still there. "If I can recollect that far, I'll certainly try to help."

"Did you ever think of quitting? I mean, when you were in the resistance. Did it ever occur to you to just give up, let someone else do the fighting?"

"Never." She says it with ironclad rigidity that is incongruous with her previous foggy memory.

I nod. "And what about after the war, when you joined French intelligence?"

She gives a bony shrug. "I thought about quitting *that* sometimes, sure."

"Why? What was the difference?"

Sophia sighs, and smooths out the quilt in her lap. "The difference was, in the resistance, our enemy was plain as day. We were fighting pure evil. The lines could not have been drawn more clearly, and the stakes were just as clear. But afterwards…our enemies were everyone and no one. It became so hard to tell. The Cold War and all that business. It was…" She makes a scattering gesture with her hands. Those hands that pulled the trigger at the French border and drew the blade across that German soldier's throat. There are men in graves somewhere because of her. "What's wrong? Why do you ask me these things?"

"Nothing's wrong." *Please. I have children. I have three children.* "Just wondering if I'll know the signs, you know? When it's time to quit. The agency, not the other thing." I'm referring to quitting at life, just packing it in and killing myself, and only she knows this about me. Sophia knows, even if she sometimes pretends she doesn't.

"You'll know," she says. "Even if everyone else around you doesn't know, even if they try to convince you you're wrong, that you just need a little downtime, you'll know." Sophia leans forward fractionally, as much as her bones will let her. "Just don't quit on *me*, Nathan. You hear me? You don't let the darkness win. Look at me." I obey, and stare into those brown eyes, one blinded by glaucoma, yet still penetrating. I obey. "Fuck the darkness." She always liked English curse words. Her and her daughter both. Hence the scarf with the vulgarity written on it, which I'm sure she didn't sew.

I nod. "You've got my word on that, Sophia, you know that."

"No, I don't know that. I don't know anything with you." She now takes me in with another critical eye. An evaluation, like a principal's pose. "How many are you going in with?"

"So far, it seems it's just gonna be me."

"Where?"

"Russia."

"*Mm.* Cold. Familiar territory?"

I shake my head. "Never been there before."

"That's not good. What kind of operation?"

"Reconnaissance."

"Any targets?" Old habits die hard, it seems.

I shake my head. "Not so far as I know."

"What kind of tools are they sending you in with?"

"To be determined."

"Tactical entry or undercover?"

"Also undetermined."

She leans back in her wheelchair, ruminating.

"Were you ever scared out there, Sophia? When you were alone in the mountains?"

"I suppose so. At first. But we all learn how to deal with that. We all have our own Drifting Place, I suppose." She shrugs. "There were times I was gone away from home for so long that people thought I was dead. My family thought I was dead. The people in the resistance thought I was dead. The world thought I was dead. I might as well have been."

I want to ask her what she means by that, but I sense I should leave it alone.

Sophia ruminates some more. Then she shifts in her seat. She looks uncomfortable.

"You okay?" I ask.

"Yes. I believe I may have just shit myself."

I snort out a laugh.

She stabs a finger at me. "You remember this. Sixty more years and you'll be in *my* position." Then she chuckles, too. "If you're thinking of quitting, Nathan, you do it now. Quitting the agency, I mean, not the other thing. If that's why you're asking me, you do it *now*. Don't hesitate."

"I'm not hesitating on anything, Sophia. In fact, I think I'm excited to go on this next mission. I was just asking."

She nods slowly, suspiciously. She starts to say something else but just then my phone twitters. I check it. It's a text from an unknown number: Hey, this is Yarwick, is this a good time to talk? I look up at Sophia. "I think I have to go, Sophia. Sorry to cut this so short—"

Sophia waves a hand. "No, you go. Go. Do what you have to." If anyone understands, it's her. How many conversations did she cut short when she received a letter or a phone call from a fellow resistance member? How many times did she end a discussion because of raised voices coming from down the street? How many times?

I touch her hand before leaving. "See you after your hundredth, Sophia."

She pats my hand. "Take care." I walk away. I don't get five steps before she calls out, "Nathan?"

I turn to her.

"Don't take too long deciding," she says. "Don't wait until you're too old and everything has passed by. Don't wait until everyone is gone but you. At least I have a daughter and grandchildren, you don't even have that."

Harsh words to leave someone with, but then at her age I doubt she cares anything about mincing words. And the icy bitch always speaks from her icy heart.

I nod and assure her I will do as she says. I'm not even to the parking lot when I text Yarwick back that I can talk when she's ready. She calls me when I'm jumping in my truck. "Hey," she says. "We've gained some traction. You ready for a preliminary briefing?"

Sophia's words are in my head for two seconds, maybe three. "Tell me the time and the place."

"It'll be next week, but I thought I'd give you the heads up. Things may start moving very fast, and if they do I need you to be ready. There are some things the upper brass want you to do."

"Name it."

The truck is cranked. I'm backing out of Rose Lawn and headed out of Thomasville when the rain starts up again.

4

The kill house at the Farm sees use at all hours of the day and night, but it's usually filled with teams of four to eight operators moving through the halls, armed to the teeth with rifles loaded with simunitions while they practice CQB. Close-quarters battle has traditionally been a thing of teamwork, with a point man, a second man, a breacher, and the rear guy covering the team's six. They practice stacking on corners and hand signals and coordinated shooting. That's how CQB training is typically done.

But there is specialized training that the boys at the Farm have been cooking up over the last decade. It's called Lone Wolf CQB, and they've been refining it year after year as they get feedback from operatives using it in the field. It's based off the same tactical movements as standard CQB, only with zero reliance on teammates and a concentration on all the weaknesses and strengths that being a lone operator affords.

Ever since leaving the SEALs I've been drilling Lone Wolf CQB exclusively. The three basic elements are the same: surprise, speed, and violence of action. Only now I'm far more mobile without my teammates, I have to check my own six with a glance, and I have to keep focused on moving forward, forward, forward, always forward, with little delay. I don't have the luxury of backup or counting on buddies to grant me suppressive fire, so aim and prioritization of targets have to be finely tuned. Pushing forward continually means that I have to pull sneak-and-peeks much faster— eyesight for a Lone Wolf CQB trainee has to be 20/20. If they don't have that, they have to be able to get surgery that grants them such vision, or else they cannot be recruited. Reflexes are timed. Weapon transitions are timed. An operator has to be able to switch from rifle to pistol and back to rifle in under three seconds, all while firing bursts from each weapon.

Hand-to-hand techniques must also be at peak conditions. A lot of judo, ju-jitsu, kali and muay thai blended with weapon retention techniques, in case someone grabs the barrel of your rifle and sweeps it away, or tackles you while you're reloading. The operator must be able to transition from pistol to knife and back to pistol in under three seconds, with knife thrusts to critical points in between.

Eight hours a day, with water breaks every two hours, and lunch at the four-hour mark. Five days a week. This is life for a lone SOG asset. I'm one of only fourteen people that have completed the Basic, Intermediate, and Advanced Lone Wolf CQB training courses. At almost forty years old, I doubt I'll be able to hold on to that spot much longer, especially with my performance today.

It starts inside of you. You notice a difference in yourself, even if others do not. They see a polished operator, but you can feel things are just slightly off, not as clean as they were five years ago. However, what you lack because of age you can cover up with experience. My improvisation is better, for instance, even if my cardio is waning a little.

Advanced LWCQB isn't necessary to remain in SOG. As I said, almost no one can do it, since the requirements are having a certificate to teach military martial arts programs, as well as at least two other black belts in separate martial arts. But for the Russian op, Yarwick tells me the brass want to see me renew my subscription, as it were.

That's my first cue of what kind of op this is going to be, and the risk level they've attached to it.

So I move through the kill house, sweating, doing what are called flow drills, repeatedly rehearsing scenarios, wearing different types of gear, from heavy battle armor to civilian clothing and even once barefoot and shirtless. I check around corners, "slicing the pie" as we call it, then move quickly down the corridors with my weapon aimed in the direction of travel, but slightly down, for unobstructed vision.

There's no time for the agency to put me through a full SERE course—a standard course of Survival, Evasion, Resistance and Escape takes months to prep operatives on surviving in the wilderness, sheltercraft, firecraft, traps, snares, and methods of evasion such as stealthy movement and blending in with crowds, as well as escape from bondage, lockpicking, and resisting torture. We went through all this in Special Forces, but the brass want me to go through a miniaturized two-week course on these things at the Farm. I get the feeling I'm still auditioning.

There's a reason operatives are called assets. A single man or woman that's undergone this level of training will, over the years, cost the U.S. government hundreds of thousands of dollars, perhaps even a million dollars by the end of their career.

I have not seen Yarwick in all this time. She and I have been communicating via text and occasional phone calls. It is a relief when I'm finally called into the office to speak with her and a few JSOC and military intelligence officers.

*

When I step into the room I'm dressed business casual. Everyone else has their war paint on. Pressed suits and briefcases. The conference room where this little op is being born is not much bigger than my bedroom, but I happen to know there are piezoelectric oscillators embedded in the walls and white-noise generators to prevent electronic surveillance from outside sources. There's a coffee machine in the corner and a flatscreen on the wall and that's about it. Humble settings such as these are often where clandestine operations are built.

As I come in, the security boys who do their daily sweep for bugs are coming out. The folders are all laid out on a long black marble table by an operations officer, and on the flatscreen there is a frozen image of what I now know are the wooded mountains of Amur Oblast. It's like coming to class early and seeing what the assignment's going to be. There's a laptop open in front of Yarwick, and she's leaning forward and squinting while running her tongue over her teeth, sussing something out. When she sees me, she brightens a little and stands up to shake my hand.

"Hey there, Adamson," she says. "Good to see you." I'm surprised at her tone and how genuine it sounds. More personal. She's glad to see *me*, not just an asset willing to do the job she needs done. Or maybe I'm reading too much into it. "Have a seat."

"Any particular place?" I ask.

"Nope. First come, first serve."

As I remove my jacket and move towards a seat, a tall thin man walks over and shakes my hand. "Hi. Emil. Emil Drucker. I'm the systems man on your Nest." *On my Nest.* Meaning this really is moving forward.

"Nathan Adamson. Pleasure. Worked a Nest before?"

"Once before," he says eagerly. "I was working the Atlanta thing before I got reassigned to this?"

"Atlanta thing?"

"Yeah. The power outage at the airport."

I raise an eyebrow. "Is that considered an attack?"

"Uh, maybe? Heh. There's evidence that foreign actors may have found a way to hack into the airport's main generators and influence its PLCs—those are programmable logic circuits—and effectively sent them into overdrive. They overheated and one of them caught on fire, turned all the power off." He shrugs. "Probably Kim and his assholes, we're still looking into it."

I want to inquire more, but then an Indian woman in a flawless white suit reaches across the table to shake my hand. "Amrita Tigga. Regional research."

Beside her, another woman rises, this one small and anodyne, but with a firm handshake that surprises me. "Harriet Kozner, Russian political liaison, on loan over here from PAG." Political Action Group. SAD's subdivision that handles all covert activity that influences politics, economic warfare, and psychological operations. These are the guys who try to figure out how to infect the enemy's leadership from within, and let it rot itself from the inside out. These were the least happy people in American intelligence when we learned what Putin's people had done to influence our 2016 elections. They really let their guard down on that one. "It's a pleasure to meet you." Kozner's voice has a slight Russian accent. Southern, like mine and my mother's.

A large, thickset guy also shakes my hand, half black, half Asian. "Al Wainwright, SIGINT." He's not built like the typical signals intelligence guy. Not wiry or nerdy. Huge. Looks like he could pick me up and throw me across the room. When he claps me on the arm, it bumps me sideways. Maybe they ought to be sending him in instead of me. "Heard a lot about you," he says. "I read the report from Kabul. Excellent work up there."

"Thanks, Mr. Wainright—"

"Call me Al."

"Okay, Al. Then I'm Nate to you guys."

"Nate it is."

"Samuel Isaacson, DARPA," says a fellow stepping up beside him. Looks half Asian, half white. Thin, but in good shape. "People call me Sammy. Glad to meet you." He's wearing an expensive suit, and he would blend in just fine with the other suits in the room if not for the half-unbuttoned shirt that reveals an undershirt that says SAGAN IS MY JAM.

Deputy Director Halbach sweeps in with her two assistants in her wake. She says a curt hello to everyone and favors me with an abnormally sincere smile when she shakes my hand. She remembers me, she's been hearing more about me, and she knows what they're asking me to do. That puts her ahead of me because I still don't know what all this is about.

Behind the deputy director are two navy admirals and a CIA analyst named Bob Oebecker, whose specialty is Kremlinology, he says, the study of Russian intelligence methodology. Also present are Solomon Tant, the Army Vice Chief of Staff, and Donald Peters, the Division Director of SAD. I've met the latter only once before, at a ball. Let's see if he remembers me. We shake hands.

"Mr. Adamson. It's been a while," he says. "You look the same."

Very good for an old spook. Still remembering names and faces. "Thank you, sir. I haven't heard back on all my quals, but I feel good about them."

"I've already gotten word from your instructors. Some of the best scores we've ever seen, particularly the Lone Wolf stuff. Excellent, excellent." Peters waves me to the seat I've already selected, and I take it. "Let's all get settled in. We're about ready to get started here, aren't we, Tara?"

"Yes, sir," Yarwick says. She nods to someone behind my back and a guard closes the door. "All right, so, first thing's first. Everything I'm about to tell you is classified top-secret, and you won't discuss it with anyone outside of this room unless given permission, not even your coworkers out there. We're keeping this operation extremely close to the chest. Yatta yatta, you guys get it."

Everyone smiles and nods.

"We've received a greenlight from the Secretary of Defense and the president, ladies and gents. That go-ahead came through because of a few things, but chief among them were my report and the level of talent I've assembled. That's you." Points at all of us. "Now, all of you have heard *parts* of what I'm about say, but *none* of you know the whole story. So, without further *adieux*."

No one says anything as Yarwick clicks a few things on her laptop and the image on the flatscreen transforms into a four-way split-screen. Top left: satellite image of Tsiolkovsky, with its vast green forests and mountains and roads etched across the landscape like varicose veins. Top right: satellite infrared pic of the Vostochny Cosmodrome, with heat blooms showing over key areas, and lines drawn to certain buildings—administrations annex, rocket propulsion lab A, B, C, etc. Bottom left: a ground-level photograph of Vostochny as it was being built, with President Vladimir Putin standing there with shovel in hand as if he is going to build it himself. And bottom right: a wider shot of the facility that was released to the press once it was completed.

As Yarwick speaks, her cursor moves over the photos. "This is Amur Oblast, home to not much besides the city of Blagoveshchensk, which is the administrative center and the oldest city of the Russian Far East. Amur Oblast is famous for just one other thing, and that is the site of the emerging Russian space program." Her cursor touches the bottom-right pic. "It's been up and running for years, but it's getting better upgrades every day, better equipment, and now there's tighter security around it. Security that both IMF and SIPRI agree is rather alarming.

"In recent months, my team has picked up information from multiple sources inside the Kremlin that say there's something going on down there. There's been an influx of Russian rocket scientists and physicists into the area, more so than we would expect, taking up permanent residence in Tsiolkovsky, a town that facilitates the spaceport.

"If it was five or ten physicist a month going into Tsiolkovsky, it would be business as usual. But our estimates say it's around thirty a month, many of them students being pulled right out of university and dragged there."

I raise my hand. *"Dragged.* As in forced to go?"

"Yes. They are taken care of while they're there, every need attended to, and their education is continuing, but there are signs of some young bright college kids becoming conscripts into a new Russian project that they didn't ask to be part of. The image you see here," her cursor floats over the infrared pic of the Cosmodrome, "was taken six months ago by one of our spy satellites, and it shows an increase in heat and energy signatures in and around the buildings. The heat signatures inside the building confirm an influx of new staff, and you can see many of them arriving by bus here, here, and here. There's a road that leads out to Tsiolkovsky, and our spy satellites are picking up significant increases in traffic.

"Energy signatures, you said?" asks Wainwright, raising a hand.

"Getting there," Yarwick says. "Our people have been over these pics and the readings with a fine-toothed comb. Pentagon scientists concur, the energy spike levels are a concern. Sammy?"

She nods to the guy wearing the SAGAN IS MY JAM shirt, who is currently slumped in his chair. Bad back posture. The price of a lifetime sitting in front of computers.

"We tasked another spy satellite to do a sweep of the region," Isaacson says. "A satellite that's more suited for detecting telltale signs of nuclear weapons production—uranium, plutonium, all that— and it came up nil. Then we expanded the search to include different parameters, and we found something interesting. When we looked at just one of the buildings, we found that the heat was transferred rather quickly. It was cyclical, kind of in a wide ovoid shape that wrapped around the length of the building. Another building showed that same heat transfer circuit happening, but in an area as small as this room. Our conclusion was that the Russians are developing a powerful new particle accelerator."

I wince at this. "Those are usually huge, right? Like, twenty, thirty miles long?"

"Scientists at the National Accelerator Laboratory in California proved you could make one as small at eleven inches," Isaacson says.

I raise my eyebrows. "Eleven *inches*?"

"Sure. As long as you have the right metamaterials. And it could probably propel particles five hundred times faster than modern particle colliders. Usually you need a long tunnel to throw the particles through and have them pick up speed, but the way they get around that with an eleven-inch model is by having the mini-accelerator fling particles through a chamber filled with superheated plasma of hydrogen gas, where clouds of electrons get zapped by a laser and then pass their energy off, one to another, picking up speed with each pass-off."

Everyone just nods like we understood all the jargon.

"Right," Yarwick says, picking back up. "And normally this might not alarm anyone. So the Russians want their own particle accelerators. Fine, let them have it, right? Nothing wrong with advancing science. But when coupled with the forced recruitment of so many physicists…we had to ask, 'Why such urgency to recruit, and step on people's human rights?'

"Well, that's what JSOC is for. My department in particular liaised with various agencies to see if any of them happened to have any intel they were sitting on that they hadn't shared with anybody, intel that might not have seemed so significant when they got it, perhaps filed it away somewhere, but could help shed some light on what's going on at Vostochny when all the information is put together."

Yarwick hits a button on her laptop. The screen goes blank for a second, then the picture of a large, fat man with a bald head and thick black beard appears on screen. It looks like a candid picture. He's jogging across a snowy street, dressed in a heavy coat and wearing a black *ushanka* that doesn't quite fit his large, round head.

"This is Boris Jablonski," Yarwick goes on. "He's ex-SVR, Russian foreign intelligence, used to be an assistant *rezident* at their London Station, now defected to the U.S. for reasons I'm not allowed to share and working for us. He's been advising us in all matters of Russian intelligence work for five years now."

She flips to another pic, one where ol' Boris is hunkered down in a van, looking filthy, with what looks like a U.S. Special Forces team surrounding him, protecting him. All their faces are blacked out.

Presumably the team that rescued him from something terrible and helped him to escape to the U.S.

"Before he fully defected, Jablonski was working with some of your people," Yarwick says, pointing to the deputy director. "Apparently during that time, he fed a CIA handler lots of intel on a civilian scientist that had been recruited into something simply called the Program. These civilian scientists were reportedly black-bagged by a Russian agent we know as 'Karambit,' along with a special squad of SVR operatives known only as the Unit." A picture of this "Karambit" pops up on screen, a blurry color photo taken from a mobile phone. Blonde hair, icy blue eyes, a strong jaw and muscular build. He's smiling.

In the photo, Karambit is smiling at a man standing in front of him. That man looks afraid.

Director Peters speaks up, "We've known about Karambit for a while. But mostly by reputation—we've run his face and his profile, it doesn't show up in any of the data mining we've done. He and his Unit run operations inside of the Motherland itself—covert ops for the regime, *mokroye delo*, 'wet work,' spying on its citizens, interacting with the Russian mafia, and we *think* he's been behind some of the assassinations of Putin's enemies—politicians, journalists, outspoken military leaders—although we have no proof of that."

"A very bad man," Yarwick tells us. "Specializes in torture. Allows his Unit to rape their captives. Used to teach the Indonesian martial art silat to SVR recruits, hence his codename, after the karambit knife silat uses. Under his command, the Unit has worked with some of the worst of the worst—PLC assassination squads, and killers-for-hire like that German sniper Innick Fardün."

Kozner makes a look of disgust. "You mean that guy who shot that one guy's wife in the knee, left her out in the open so the husband would come out to help her and he could tag him?"

"That's the son of a bitch," Yarwick says.

"So, Karambit does the conscripting for the Program," I say, "and may provide security for it with SVR units? Particularly *the* Unit?"

"That's right. But the head of the Program, Jablonski told us, was a woman named Olga Daziyr. We did some digging and discovered that Daziyr is a particle physicist, one of the foremost in her field." Yarwick now looks at all of us meaningfully. "And, if the papers she's written for *The International Journal of Physics* are any indication, she's got some pretty bold ideas for using particle accelerators as power sources for fixed-focus beams."

The room goes quiet.

In case nobody got it, Yarwick says. "Yeah. She thinks you can make a DEW system that can fire from a few hundred thousand miles away," she says, referring to a directed-energy weapon. "That's farther than the Moon, and she believes you can hit a target with pinpoint accuracy. That phrase 'pinpoint accuracy' is usually just an approximation. But a narrow, fixed-focus particle beam could *actually* hit a target as small as a flea from space, incinerate *just* the flea, and leave everything else around intact."

Sammy steps back in. "Or, if you can dial the power up enough, *just* a tank, or *just* a building, or…well, we don't really know what kind of power yields Daziyr's talking about, but you get the idea. We could be talking about a weapon that fires fifty, sixty terajoules of power, about the amount of power released at Hiroshima, from space."

I raise a hand and wait for the lady to acknowledge me. "Yes?" Yarwick says.

"Is there any DEW on earth that we know of that can come close to that kind of power?"

Yarwick looks at the man from DARPA. "Naturally we've theorized it's possible," Sammy says. "We've had people thinking about it. Sure. But no current projects are moving forward."

I turn back to Yarwick, who resumes. She clicks over to another slide, which shows a stone-faced woman in black dress, speaking to a man holding a briefcase. Neither one of them look happy. Behind them is a building that's a little blurry in the distance. "This is Olga Daziyr. You probably can't make out the structure behind them, but there's a blue logo at the upper right that should tell you what you're looking at." I squint, and notice the blue logo showing a man in a spacesuit smiling. Below it are Russian letters I can easily read: VASOCHNY COSMODROME – MAIN CENTER. "This picture was taken two months ago by someone we have living in Tsiolkovsky. Daziyr is there."

Well. This doesn't look good at all. A mini-accelerator being built at a spaceport where they launch satellites, and the physicist who theorized about weaponizing particle beams is there, too. Scary, but also interesting. In this moment, I'm very glad I decided to quit tomorrow, and not yesterday.

"Mr. Oebecker?" Yarwick says, pointing to the CIA analyst sitting beside me.

"All of this separately doesn't seem remarkable," he says, leaning forward. "But when you put it all together—the forced conscription of scientists and high-achieving university students, the increased military presence around the Cosmodrome, the transfers of money from North Korea and Syria to Russia, seemingly in exchange for the weapons platforms Russia has been sending, and Daziyr's presence and DARPA's theory that these heat blooms are mini-accelerators...well, you see where this might alarm us. And the methodology of conscripting and keeping it all under wraps and out of the eye of human rights groups is typical of the Kremlin."

"Not only that," Yarwick says, "but Russia and North Korea are now linking their railways through these regions. If part of the deal is that the Kim regime gets to have a look at the new weapons tech Putin's people are cooking up, we could also be looking at a budding alliance. An important one. A total gamechanger on the geopolitical board."

"Tara's JSOC team was the first to raise alarms about all this," Director Peters says. "It seemed a little farfetched to some people in the agency at first, but after listening to Tara and her people I became convinced, even though there's nothing conclusive."

"Right," she says. "There's nothing conclusive. Nothing concrete at all. No smoking gun to prove beyond a shadow of a doubt that the Russian military is attempting to build a superweapon on the scale that Daziyr dreamed, much less that they're thinking of putting such a weapon into orbit around the planet. No evidence at all."

She looks at me.

"Which is why Mr. Adamson is here today, hearing this for the first time along with the rest of you. I've spoken with all of you individually about the parts that might pertain to you, but this is the first time—here in this room—that we're laying it all out. JSOC listened to me and allowed me to pitch the idea to the CIA, the Secretary of Defense, and the POTUS, and they've given us a greenlight on a reconnaissance mission."

Here, Deputy Director Halbach finally chimes in. "One-man entry. Get in, get proof of what's going on there, and get out. A single man to go in virtually naked, in case he's captured."

Total deniability.

Everyone mulls that over. Almost everyone's eyes steal a glance over at me. They know what's being asked of me.

I raise my hand again. "Russia, Syria and North Korea all in bed together, sharing weapons tech, hiding it all from the West, and possibly forging a stealth alliance to create high-tech weapons to use against us. This all seems very fast. Why the sudden urgency?"

It's small, mousey Harriet Kozner from SAD's Political Action Group that answers. "The fear for a while has been that these three would find common ground. Honestly, I've felt for a while this was bound to happen, an alliance formed over one major project or another, and by mutual interest."

"What mutual interest?"

"The rise of their regimes and the collapse of America," says Director Peters bluntly.

Yarwick nods. "Honestly, that's about it in a nutshell. There are complexities and nuances, sure, but in the end the Russians and the North Koreans are run by egomaniacs, their egos only kept in check by the fortunate fact that the men in charge of each regime are in charge *now*, at a time when both their nations are hurting, even floundering, and they can't do much more than spread propaganda and spy on us. Both of which they do exceptionally well."

Kozner says, "Kim and Putin want nothing more than their two nations to rise, and to be the victors that *caused* their nations to rise above all others. Heroes. Gods. Whatever. Putin also has self-preservation as a motive—if he's ever overthrown, you can bet he won't see trial. Any number of his enemies will execute him. He needs a win. He needs it in a big way. Right now, he's keeping public opinion on his side by propaganda and staging 'great moments,' like having his picture taken while diving into a sunken treasure ship, then having Russian media run with the headline 'PUTIN DISCOVERS AN

ANCIENT SHIP ON HIS OWN,' like he's the Chosen One or some shit. But it's been working. From 2013 to 2016, Putin has been *number one* on the *Forbes* list of the World's Most Powerful People."

I tap my chin with a forefinger. "And what about Syria? President Al-Assad? I mean, an alliance being forged this fast was bound to send up red flags. Why risk this, especially now that he's got help from both Russia and U.S.?"

"Our read of him is that he's content running his small pond. I mean, he'd definitely rule the world if you *handed* it to him, make no mistake, but that's not his current goal. What al-Assad wants right now is stability in his region and total dominion of his country without having to lean on the West for intervention against ISIS and his other enemies. The only way he can get that is with Russia's help, and if Russia has dealings with North Korea, then so will he."

"And wherever North Korea goes, Iran follows," says Oebecker, the analyst. "They go way back to Iran's Islamic Revolution, when their new republic was strapped for military hardware and North Korea came to the rescue. Then in '93, Iran bankrolled North Korea's nuclear program with half a billion dollars, with the understanding that they would share the nuclear technology that resulted from it."

"PAG's been thinking that things may be escalating faster than previously thought," says Kozner, our political action expert. "Their ties have been getting stronger ever since the U.S. started backing out of the Iran nuclear deal, and of course since the U.S. started saber-rattling at North Korea."

Yarwick says, "Our enemies are bonding over their misery and one simple philosophy: *Fuck the U.S.* This could be the tipping point, folks." She watches us, gauges our reactions.

The mousey PAG lady adds, "It's also a fact that, historically, whenever two or more nations begin a friendship over the buildup of their arsenals and weapons manufacture, it's almost always a sign of a war in the not-too-distant future. In fact, we've had *two* major incidents you might have heard of where this was the case."

Nobody comments on that. I think of Sophia and the tyrant she overthrew. Here we are again, you old hen.

Yarwick clicks a button. The slides on the TV screen change, revealing an overhead layout of what looks like a multi-story complex. "These are not blueprints of Vostochny Cosmodrome, we haven't got our hands on those, but this is as close a composite as we've been able to put together using the intel from spy satellites and our informant on the ground."

Halbach leans in and interlaces her fingers on the table. "Our major concern is the weapon and the project itself. Our main objective will be to ascertain whether or not there is any validity to all of this. Adamson is here because he was selected for the one-man op, primarily because, of all our capable solo SOG assets, he's the one who speaks southern Russian most fluidly, and should things go wrong he can pass for a local."

Is that true? Did it really come down to just that? Was the only tiebreaker the fact that I can speak the local lingo? As much as it might hurt my ego a bit to think I wasn't always the man for the job, it shouldn't surprise me. Every mission must be planned down to the last detail. Putting me through all that requalifying of Lone Wolf CQB was probably for that reason—most likely, it was down to me and a young buck whose southern Russian wasn't quite as good as mine, and people in offices I'll never see were haggling behind the scenes. *My guy can do it. No,* my *guy can.*

I have a feeling Yarwick fought for me.

"What's happening in this room right now," Yarwick says, "is the formation of the operation Deputy Director Halbach is talking about. The thirteen of us are going to plan this operation together, down to the last detail. I'm the chief coordinator through JSOC but CIA has primacy. I'm here to get whatever you need, whether it's gear, favors, or time. Adamson is going into Amur Oblast and he will infiltrate the buildings we think have the highest probability of containing the weapons project."

She nods towards the military boys.

"The admirals here are going to be in charge of the missions that will plant Adamson there, including any diversionary tactics. The Army Vice Chief of Staff will apprise the president of every move we make, and basically be our representative to the POTUS. The analysts and intelligence officers in this room will work with Adamson to make sure he has everything he needs and knows everything he needs to know, and will also form the Nest for the entirety of the operation, for however long that lasts, be it three days, three weeks, or three months. The deputy director and HUMINT will also get us in contact with the CIA handler that's been working with our informant inside the Cosmodrome," she says. HUMINT refers to human intelligence, actual people on the inside feeding us information.

"Why would HUMINT give us their informant's name?" I ask. Since those things are always kept close to the chest.

"Part of the op may entail making contact with her."

Her. The informant at the Cosmodrome is a woman. "About that informant," I say. Yarwick looks at me. "Why aren't we using *her* to get the proof we need, instead of sending in me? Don't get me wrong, I'm all psyched for this, but she seems like the most logical way to go." I shrug. "So, what's her deal?"

"The informant's codename is 'Talon,' and she is a resident of Tsiolkovsky as an on-site journalist writing for a science publication, but has very limited access to the Cosmodrome itself, so she can't get into the areas we need to get into. I can't tell you much at present, because I've only been allowed to know a little, but I can tell you that Talon is a native Russian and she's risking a lot by helping us."

Risking a lot is putting it mildly. A lifetime in prison and a lifetime of torture, without a doubt. If Talon's ever caught spying for us, she'll be lucky if there's a quick execution, but that's not likely. The Russians don't fuck around with traitors.

I wonder why this Talon betrayed her country. I can't know that till later. Maybe never. CIA handlers are notoriously tight-lipped about their informants, and for good reason. Just writing their name down could be dangerous, since hacks happen all the time, both large and small, and you'd be crazy to think the Russians don't have spies in our networks as well. To be a traitor in a regime like Putin's requires balls so big you need a wheelbarrow.

Yarwick checks the time on her phone. "We've got an hour before the deputy director here has to report to Director Riley, so let's go ahead and start the conversation while we have her. I have a plan that my team's come up with, but I'd like all of your input on fine-tuning." She turns off the computer, and the flatscreen returns to the seal of the Central Intelligence Agency. Then she hands out folders marked TOP SECRET. "All right, let's go over it all. From the top."

Oie

Some things are stable. Other things are not. Some things are easily remembered, kept on an ice-covered mantelpiece deep inside the mind, on a hearth adorned with familiar portraits. Other things are not remembered, but rather felt. Sometimes, in the dead of night, when a random thought from the past recurs, it's easy to think that Then is Now. Cold winds. A tap on the window. Four taps, with a pause between the second and third. A signal. Someone is coming. Time to run.

Someone is always coming. There is never a time when things are safe. Whether on the cold mountaintops or in the cafeteria, where the damned air-conditioning always blows way too hard, and the orderlies ignore the complaints of the residents.

There's reason to believe it's Then, but there's also reason to believe it's Now. Easy to believe either. And neither.

Some habits die hard. Like parking one's own wheelchair against one wall facing the door, so that one can see who enters and who leaves. Counting the heads. That never goes away, the counting. Like what they call OCD. Count the heads and as they come and go, do the mental addition and subtraction. Remember persons by clothing colors, keep track of them in the periphery.

Pale, decrepit hands work on knitting. Not as keen as they used to be. Never will be again. Alternating wales of pink and white knit stitches gather in the lap. Each stitch in a wale is suspended from the one above. The hands operate slowly, having to think about what they're doing. Not as dexterous as they once were. They tap and consider. Sometimes they come to a full stop, and they flex slowly, using the Hammond hand exercises they've been taught. That relaxes them fractionally. The payoff for such exercises decreases year after year. Still, better than nothing. Better than ending up one of the old fucks around Rose Lawn that never move again, crumbling statues barely held together by wire, sinking deeper and deeper into their chairs with each passing day.

Better than nothing. Better than *that*.

Still, the hands struggle. So much so that when the yarn is given a testing tug, the loops of the knitted course begin to come undone. Time to start over. It's not the first time, probably won't be the last. But the act of undoing and restarting a stitch has a therapeutic side that is undeniable. It is a permissive act, allowing the mind to be focused on one thing and not worrying about the past or the intervening years between Then and Now.

When sleep comes, so does the confusion. Waking up is occasionally terrifying. The space all around is vacant of familiar items. Like waking up in some ancient pharaoh's dark tomb, artifacts of that person's life strewn all around. Sometimes not even the photographs on the nightstand ring any bells. Sometimes legs are moist from a midnight self-wetting. Sometimes the body cannot even sit upright on its own. Sometimes an orderly needs to be called. The button beside the bed summons them.

Some things in the mind are stable. Some things never waver. The mind can always remember its granddaughters. But the daughters? Those are another matter. Sometimes those names become confused. Sometimes the mind doesn't know them at all. Sometimes the mind doesn't know anyone at all, leaving one as a nameless prisoner adrift inside themselves.

But those are only sometimes. For the most part, things are clear. Or clear-ish. The mind understands it has lived a life and understands there is something wrong with the body. Most times it even knows who the president is and what he's been fucking up. But these things don't matter. The mind has a difficult time assigning worth to anything besides family. All the mind can recall before family is a hurricane. Deceptions and close calls and torrid love affairs and cold mountaintops and dead friends and friends that were never seen again after stepping out for milk and eggs.

It's obvious what happened to them. They went out for milk and eggs and were picked up by the goose-steppers who stalked them always. But nothing can be done about that. Too much time separates Then from Now. The line between the two may be blurred inside the mind but the linear reality is very clear. Time moves only in one direction, it's our perception of it that bounces around. The mind knows that, too.

If the mind could ever find those goose-steppers, the ones that had hurt old friends, then these decrepit hands would find more sport than knitting. Oh, yes, they would. But for now there is knitting.

And the telly. There is always the telly on, in almost every room. Lots of gameshows. Those are the favorites, as they are interactive and (typically) inoffensive. Something to watch while you knit. In common areas where the men gather without the women, there is often the news shows. Around the clock. Well, at least until bedtime. Usually FOX News. Lots of shouting heads. Hard to say why the men care so much and the women care so little. Don't the men realize that it's not their world anymore, that the news being reported no longer has anything to do with them, that their opinions are outmoded and no longer relevant to modern conversations on the topics of sex, crime, patriotism, the Constitution, and politics? They have to know they don't matter, those old perverts sitting in their chairs wetting themselves. They have to know. Maybe it's like being in a zoo for them, watching through the screen at the outside world, raging impotently at how it's all going wrong, that everything these old perverts fought for is now going down the shitter.

Shitter's a funny word.

While knitting, these half-blind eyes gaze deeply into their knitting. These ears, mildly touched by the distant ringing of tinnitus, focus almost solely on nothing at all. But the ears do hear someone say, "Oh, isn't that just horrible?" and when the half-blind eyes look up, they see what is so horrible. A train derailed in Connecticut. Almost twenty now dead, dozens more injured. These half-blind eyes keep watching until the train derailment story wraps up, and they linger on the telly as these brittle hands continue knitting by memory.

The next story is horrible, too. Two young black girls abducted off the streets of Atlanta have finally been found, but they are badly damaged, suspected of being taken by human traffickers but somehow they managed to escape. An APB is out for a white man named Pelletier, suspected of being involved. These old eyes look at the mugshot of the suspect, memorizing the face the way they were once trained to. Mark the pale complexion, the slight crook in his nose, the thin neck and pointy jaw.

Then the next story pops up. The eyes blink. The mind goes back to knitting, half paying attention to the news. There, the rheumy eyes see a photograph. Seven people in formal wear, dressed in pressed suits and skirts, some of them African and some of them are Caucasian. It's there and it's gone, but for a moment the mind remembers. One of those faces was familiar, but now the picture is gone. The news reporter lady says the picture was from an embassy in South Africa, a meeting of politicians from several nations. Some kind of bomb went off during the meeting.

"Rewind that."

All eyes turn to look at the old woman knitting in the corner. One of the men, Albert, he says, "Sophia, it's the news, not a VCR, you can't just rewind it."

The other men laugh at her, and go back to watching the news.

These old hands put down their knitting and slowly, slowly, press the wheels on the wheelchair forward, carrying this old body around the edge of the room. The hands shake as they pick up a controller, point it at the telly, start winding back the footage.

"Hey!" Albert exclaims. "What the hell—"

"It's Comcast DVR, you dumb fuck," these old lips say. "I can play back any goddamn thing I like."

They all stare like I'm some witch with a wand, conducting live TV like I am the master of time and space. If only winding back time was as easy as winding back video. Now I look at the footage, and these old eyes strain themselves to find the photograph. When I find it, I hit pause. There it is. I scan the picture for what it was I sensed before. It's like something was off before. What was it? What did I see…?

There.

A man stands at the back of the ground, off to the right. An old man. A very old man. White, but with a severe tan. Sweating. He isn't used to the heat. He stands in a gray, two-button Brioni suit, with a white shirt and a black Marinella tie. I know my suits. Up until about thirty years ago, I used to be quite the fashionista. Ever since then, I follow fashion trends only through catalogues. The years of silk dresses and sleek business skirts are behind me, but not forgotten. Just like the left droopy eye on the well-dressed man is not forgotten, nor the large forehead.

But who is he? I both know and don't know. It is strange, being two minds in one body. One mind forgetful, fretful, somewhat afraid. The other mind young and focused, capable, a caged animal trying to get free of its cage. I'm both and I'm neither. From moment to moment, I am one, and then I'm the other. One part of me remembers. Screams out what it is I'm seeing, like it's so obvious. The other part of me says that's just silly.

A shiver comes over me. The visitation of a ghost. I'm both scared and exhilarated. I may have pissed myself. I have pissed myself. I feel the warmth spreading in my diaper.

These old hands do something they have not done in an age. Thumb and forefinger come together, and lightly start rubbing together, like they're rolling a cigarette. I close these rheumy eyes, and I can smell his cologne, and the dark room filled with smoke and loose boards that creak beneath his feet as he walks overhead. I'm wondering if he's going to see me, going to find me hiding under the floor—

"You gonna hit play anytime today, Sophia?"

My eyes open. Only one of them can see the old bald *caca boudin.* "Eat your own dick, Albert," I say, and toss him the remote.

"I don't know how to use this!"

"*C'est ton, problème, idiot.*" I back out of the room. I leave the ghost behind me and go down to the cafeteria. It's lunchtime, and I'm hungry.

5

When I was a boy, my parents would take me and my brother up to my grandparents' farm in Wyoming. The neighbors had some kids who liked to come over and play whenever we were there. My grandparents had such large fields and so many different barns and silos that it was only natural kids would end up playing a little hide-and-seek. There was this kid, Kenny, really big and kind of a bully. Whenever he was "it" he always seemed to find me. No matter which direction I went, no matter how far I ran, he seemed to know exactly where I was hiding. I was a slow learner. Naïve. Took me a while to realize Kenny was cheating, peeking through his hands while he was counting.

So, one night, I got to thinking. While Kenny was counting, I would run *past* him, stop, and turn back towards him, facing his back. If he wanted to see where I went, he would have to turn around. He couldn't be too obvious about it and turn around fast or it would be obvious he was a cheat. He would have to do it slow.

So, I gave it a try. As he turned around slowly, I tiptoed right around him, timing my footsteps with his. If he saw me while he was counting and called me out for not playing the game right, no big deal, since calling me out would only reveal that he had been peeking all along. And when Kenny opened his eyes, I was right there behind him, already close enough to touch base. The first time I did this, he ran off looking for me, confused as to where I'd gone.

I did that a few more times. I'm pretty sure Kenny turned fast enough to catch me a couple of times, but he couldn't outright lunge at me as soon as he stopped counting—no, he had to *pretend* he hadn't seen me pulling my trick. And so he went off after the others. Kenny and I shared a secret. We both knew he was a cheater, but never spoke of it.

My father used to be "it" on occasion, and he was really good at finding people. He knew his sons well. Always found us wherever we hid. That's when I realized I had to stop thinking like me, and think like someone else. I had to go to those places he would never check, the places he knew I was forbidden to go, the places he knew I was scared of the most.

If I wanted to beat my dad at hide-and-seek, I needed to go under the front porch. Everyone knew I was afraid of the porch, ever since one summer when I was playing under there with my brother and a rattlesnake bit me. A hospital visit I'll never forget.

So I mustered all my courage. I even cried as I crawled under the porch. That's how badly I wanted to finally beat my dad. I went where I was most terrified. While I was under there, I imagined I heard slithering things all around me. Was probably nothing, but I didn't think so at the time. I was so scared I started sobbing, but then I covered my mouth so that I wouldn't make a sound. That's how bad I wanted to win.

And I did.

And each time I went under the porch, I had to face that fear. I closed my eyes and went to the Drifting Place—that's how I thought of it, because of an episode I saw of *The Twilight Zone*. The Drifting Place was where I went when I shut my eyes and let myself slip away into another dimension. Not under the porch, but wherever I wanted to be. At home playing with my dog. Flying in the sky next to Superman. Anywhere.

The Drifting Place helped me through a lot. When people started figuring out my spot under the porch, I hid inside the old wellhouse, which Grandma had made it clear was crawling with black widow spiders and that I was to *never*, under *any* circumstances, go in there. Nobody ever found me there, because I was always a good boy, so well behaved, and no one suspected I would break the rules and go inside the wellhouse. I hid there several times, aware that if any of those poisonous spiders killed me, I could die, and it might be a while before anyone found my corpse. But I sat there and dealt with the fear. I closed my eyes and I drifted.

I learned a lot about hiding on my grandparents' farm. I learned that in order to win, you sometimes have to go places you fear most. I learned that sometimes if a person spots you, they can't always *admit* they've spotted you, for fear of outing themselves. I learned that if you go to places forbidden by others, most will not seek you there. I learned that the Drifting Place is always there if you need it, you just need to relax and focus. I also learned how to be alone with my own thoughts and fears. A useful skill in my line of work. Just like in the wellhouse, if anything happens to me out in the field, no one's going to find me for a long, long time. Maybe never.

Look how far those lessons have taken me. I doubt my parents, grandparents, or Kenny could've guessed those games would build the foundation for a career with CIA.

Oh, where life takes us.

I've only told two people in the world about the Drifting Place: Sophia and Dr. Thomas, my evaluator. I told Sophia because I wanted to hear how she dealt with fear. It turns out, Sophia visited there, too. She didn't have a name for it, but she said that whenever things got dicey, and it looked like she might not make it across the border with her POWs, she would make-believe that this was all a story, that she was dreaming, and that dying didn't really matter.

Like I said before, you need all sorts of mental tricks to keep yourself moving, not panicking, focusing. In judo, we learned about the samurai who developed the art, and we learned about *bushido* and how a facet of that belief system meant accepting that you're already dead. Even ancient warriors understood that you needed these mental tricks.

Looking at the terrain I'm going to be dealing with in Amur Oblast forces me to perform another mental trick. Mnemonic devices. Tricks to help me memorize the names of every valley, every mountain, every river and tributary. I'm standing in an ops room on the second floor of the Langley facilities, poring over a large table that has a huge interactive touchscreen as its tabletop. I use my fingers to move the map around, tapping in areas to change from topographical settings to true-color settings.

It's godlike. You know something no one else knows. You know you're going into an area you're not supposed to and doing things you're not supposed to. Nobody but you and your team know that. You have this overview of everything, and you get to decide how a lot of it's going to play out. Not all of it, but a lot of it. You can never decide all of it. The best laid plans and all. But there's nothing like it. The stakes at their highest and it's all on you.

This is why I hate downtime. This is why I love operational time. Moments like these, I don't even think about quitting tomorrow.

Behind me, Yarwick and Oebecker are at a similar table as mine, only they're looking at the latest satellite footage from the Cosmodrome. It's old footage. They can't risk sending their spy satellite for another pass, it seems, for fear of it falling victim to one of the Russians' hunter-killer sats, so all the footage they're looking at is at least months old. "—maybe ingress points here and here," Yarwick is saying. "And an egress point over here. Let's run that by him." By *him* she means me.

They're bringing me all their notes, seeing what my experience has shown me to work and not work. I check the satellite footage of the Cosmodrome and look at the ingress and egress points they've selected. Some of them look good, others are no-gos because not enough alternate routes close by in case I need to change course. They listen to me patiently, accept my feedback, and offer alternatives.

They run me through my options for if I'm discovered. I have fake IDs and passports claiming I'm Sergei Prokhorov. I even have a background story, what we in the spy world call a "legend." Part of my legend is that I'm a swimming instructor from Khabarovsk, with a work history and a living address on Pushkin Street. Went to college for oceanography in Blagoveshchensk, never finished, drove a taxi for a number of years before I fell into teaching swimming to kids.

Everything is being ironed out. Nothing can be left to chance.

*

The operation has an official name now: NARROW VOID. My codename for the op will be Ares. The POTUS has been informed by the Army Vice Chief of Staff of our plan thus far, and the POTUS is all in.

I'm in constant contact with the Army Vice Chief of Staff and the two admirals who will be conducting the U.S. Naval fleets in the Pacific Ocean around Japan during the time of the op. The plan they're working on is getting me on board the *Virginia*-class submarine USS *Colorado*. My cover, in case any sailors aboard ask, will be a Navy public affairs specialist conducting a study on life aboard a modern submarine. Then, during a scheduled exercise in the Sea of Japan, the sub will surface and I will go topside and hop aboard the JS *Hayabusa*, a patrol boat for the Japan Maritime Self-Defense Force.

Hayabusa's standard operation is to patrol the Strait of Tartary, which divides the Russian island Sakhalin from mainland Asia. I'm gonna hitch a ride. Once through the strait, I'm supposed to hook up with a group of Japanese smugglers that Yarwick says JSOC has used twice before to drop off assets. I'm promised these smugglers will ask no questions, simply carry me safely to where the Amur River dumps into the strait. I'll go ashore, walk for two days along the shoreline, then come to Rendezvous A, which is a ferry service owned by a Russian family, who will grant me passage the rest of the way up the river. From there, I'm on my own until I can make it to Blagoveshchensk, the capital city of Amur Oblast. If I can make it through there, I move on to Rendezvous B, a gas depot just outside of Tsiolkovsky, where I will meet up with the asset codenamed "Talon." Meeting Talon is *sine qua non* for the mission, since she alone may have information about where the Russian's new weapon is being kept, and what else is going on inside the Cosmodrome.

That's Plan A. Plan B is a HALO jump from 28,000 feet that everyone seems nervous about. No one wants to go that route, as it means passing through a *lot* of Russian airspace, no matter which direction we approach from.

The components are there to build an insertion plan, and we begin to assemble them, all of us conferring with each other, checking and rechecking, searching for where the snags are going to be, and what to do should each snag occur. As the month wears on, we circle closer and closer to a workable plan.

During this time, I visit Sophia again. She doesn't remember our last conversation. She remembers some of the ones before it, though. And she also seems troubled. She's distracted. Can't even focus on her knitting, or on me, or anything but the wall on the far side of the room. I speak to her for half an hour before I finally ask the old hen what's got her mind so far afield. She waves me away. "*Je suis en train de travailler.*"

"My high school French ain't so good."

"I'm working on something," she says.

"What are you working on?"

"I saw someone recently. Someone I remember."

"Family? Friends?"

She shakes her head.

"Who, then?"

She waves her hand, and I drop it.

As I talk, she slowly comes out of her reverie and we begin discussing some things. I mention how my training has seen an uptick. She makes a brief allusion to her own training and how hard it was, some of the men getting grabby, how she put those in their place. When I bring up the topic of going out again, she says only, "Watch your back out there. Don't trust anyone you haven't seen naked."

I chuckle at that and ask the old hen how often she got in trouble doing that.

"Too often," she says seriously. Adding, "If something smells fishy, break and run. Whoever gets in your way, kill them. Come back to me." I'm not smiling anymore. I just nod and tell her, "All right, *oie*." *Oie*. Goose. Her old codename at SDECE.

I'm back at the Farm, moving through the kill house, but only for an hour a day. They don't want me overtraining, that can cause injury or a kind of brain meltdown. You want your assets right on the razor's edge, but not going over it. I spend two or three hours a day speaking Russian with native-born Russian men and women who joined CIA, practicing the conversational flow, which I haven't experienced in a while. I'm studying maps and pictures of the local flora and fauna in Amur Oblast, reading up on what's edible in the region and what's not. Amur Oblast is mostly wilderness, with the one city of Tsiolkovsky surrounding the spaceport, so I may have need of hunting for my own food.

They also put me through refresher courses in vehicle dynamics, defensive driving, breaking through barricades with a vehicle, and basic road evasion techniques, since I will briefly be in a couple urban environments and you never know what might go wrong.

Meanwhile, the Nest team has had another task to complete. The Nest has a room all to themselves at the Farm, where I visit and exchange notes with them on the op, and watch them run through their coordination exercises. Their computer room and surveillance setup are a simulation of what they'll have in the field. While I'm deployed, they'll be at a safehouse just across the border in China, in the Heilongjiang Province. From a rented flat in Harbin, a gleaming city that's a bastion for tourists, they'll be surrounded with their computers and other electronic miscellany, giving me support and waiting to receive me once I'm extracted.

It's all coming together.

*

I pay one more visit to Sophia. This time she remembers our last discussion, but she doesn't mention it much. Instead she talks about her daughter and granddaughter and great-granddaughter, she mixes up their names sometimes, and there's one point in the conversation where she thinks her husband Jim is still alive. She transitions seamlessly between knowing and not knowing things. I kiss her head before leaving. An orderly pushes her along, following me to the door so she can see me off. Before I walk out the door, she says, "Nathan?" I turn to her. "Remember what I said. If something smells fishy, break and run. Come back to me." She stabs a finger at me. "But complete the mission. Do. Not. Let. Them. Win."

It's an order.

"Yes, *mademoiselle*." I give her a smile because she says it looks good on me and I turn to leave. I have an appointment with a doctor.

My final physical before I head out is handled by a man almost half my age. He checks me out top to bottom. Heart rate's good. Joints and mobility all good, although the interphalangeal joint on my right index finger is slightly arthritic, probably from a lifetime of pulling the trigger, doc says. I had no idea. The pain's been creeping up on me so slowly. But it's no big deal, he says. All else checks out. Visual acuities good, reflexes good, BP is 124/83. When I head out of his office, I catch a look at myself in the mirror hanging from his door. Looking good, Adamson.

Now I'm off to the range to practice weak-hand shooting. On the way there, Sophia's words keep echoing in my head. *Do. Not. Let. Them. Win.*

Two Spies Reach Out From the Grave

*

The surgery to have the cochlear implant is noninvasive. I've heard of them, but never had one inserted into my ear canal before. It takes five minutes, and all I ever felt was a tickle. I'm lying back in a chair under a light. The CIA technician handling the procedure pushes away from me and his roll-around chair carries him to a computer across the room. He picks up a headset, taps it twice. I hear a scratching in my ear, crisp and clear. He speaks into his mic. "Testing. Testing. Can you hear me?"

"Yeah," I say. "I can hear you." His voice comes through clear as a bell.

He then lowers his voice to a whisper, so that I cannot hear his voice carry across the room but I can hear his voice in my ear. "Elephants love beautiful red flowers. What did I just say?"

"Elephants love beautiful red flowers."

"Okay, I'm just going to test the frequency settings. This won't take but a few seconds. To turn it on and off, just bite your teeth hard enough to click. The device can pick up the sound and knows what it means. You will only be able to switch between the main channel and the emergency channel, in case your main channel is picked up by enemy actors. You do this by snapping your fingers in your ear three times very fast, then saying 'Switch channels.' The earpiece can hear your voice command and it will do the rest. Give it a try."

I do as he says, clicking my teeth and receiving a click in my ear. The device is on. I snap my fingers beside my right ear and switch from one channel to the next.

"And presto," he says. "Now you can receive transmissions sent from the Nest without anyone else around you hearing them. Optimum EMSEC." Emissions security. Protection against someone picking up any radio emissions that are either purposefully or accidentally emitted.

The way I understand it, the implant will transmit an encrypted signal to a relay the CIA has stationed near the border between Amur Oblast and Mongolia. The relay machine will transmit that signal in super-high-frequency burst in the Ka band, up to a satellite, which will send a reply back to the relay machine on earth in the Q band. In all, I shouldn't experience more than two-second delays.

"You can also speak in a low voice and the Nest will pick up what you say quite clearly." The techie chuckles. "Only make sure you're alone when you do that, or else people will get suspicious, or think you're talking to the wind. And the Nest can also hear what's going on around you, but only if you have it switched on."

"Got it. What's the range on this thing? And battery life?"

"Range is about eight hundred miles. Battery life is about four weeks."

"Eight hundred miles?"

"Welcome to the twenty-first century. It's the very latest in covcom," he says, referring to covert communications equipment.

I wag my head left and right to see if I can feel anything rattling around in there. Nothing. I feel no different. It's about this point when Yarwick steps into the room and asks how it went. "Pretty good," I tell her.

The techie puts in, "He's showing all green. Optimal reception."

She nods approvingly. "All right, then let's grab some lunch. After that, we're going to run a field test between you and the Nest."

*

Yarwick oversees every aspect of our preparation, pushing us through one exercise after another. I have moved through the kill house nine times now, each time with my Nest team in my ear. I have practiced moving down the corridors and neutralizing targets while accepting directions and commands from the Nest, intermittently switching channels the way I've been taught. But today we're doing something different. Today I'm not indoors. I'm outside, running through the dense foliage surrounding the Farm.

"Head south, five mikes," says Amrita Tigga in my ear. She's head of regional research for this mission, and will be my guide through whatever terrain I come to.

"Copy that. Ares is on the move."

She conducts me through the forested hills, across a river I'm somewhat familiar with from past exercises on the Farm. Yarwick chimes in, "We've got an update on your objective, Ares. Second story, east-facing side, an office marked Room two-one-five."

"Ares copies. Second story, east-facing side, Room two-one-five."

"Also, SIGINT says your comms might be experiencing trouble. You'll be in total blackout soon, completely on your own."

"Copy blackout."

There is no real blackout, it's all part of the training scenario. The blackout was probably dropped on Wainwright as part of signals intelligence training and adaptability, and passed on to Yarwick in real time as a surprise. It'll train them to find the source of the comms problem, and test me in being completely alone on a dangerous solo infiltration.

Before, when I was running through the kill house, that was basically seeing if I had what it took to shoot my way out of a sticky situation, should the need arise. Today, I'm moving through the 9,000 acres of wilderness surrounding the Farm and having the Nest feed me information on buildings they want surveilled. It is a whole-day exercise, going into the night, and I've been listening to them give me cues on when to move west, now northwest, now east, all while avoiding being spotted by the agents who are roleplaying as guards.

After a couple hours of constant movement, I come within sight of a compound of five buildings, all done up to look like office buildings. I survey the area, find the building I've been tasked with infiltrating.

Wait for nightfall.

A few things to remember. The first is chiaroscuro, the study of the interplay between light and shadow. Watch the perimeter lights come on as night descends, see how they cast shadows and where. Watch for overlapping shadows, which will naturally be darker and safer. Also, try and keep a light source between you and a patrolman. If there's a streetlamp nearby, see if you can't keep it between you and one of the guards, because seeing *through* a light source and *into* shadow means the person in shadow is virtually invisible to the viewer.

Watch for shift changes. Look for openings. A lazy guard. A patrolman who's gotten bored with complacency and has let his mind wander a bit. Two or three guards gathered in clusters, chatting to pass the time. Wait for a loud noise, like thunder or a car starting, to mask the sound of your movements.

The objective for my team is inside a place simply labeled Building B. It's in a mock office on the second floor, east-facing side. I'm to make my way in by whatever means, kill no one, be seen by no one, grab a ream of papers, and get back out. To keep things realistic, the roleplayers have not been told exactly what they're out here to do, only that they are to guard this place. For all they know, it could be the CIA testing out a new stealth surveillance drone on them, or they might come under attack by a mock enemy force. It could be anything. They're being tested, same as me.

I get the feeling this is my final exam, though. Complete this, and the mission is fully go.

So I take my time. I have twelve hours to achieve my goal, and I think I can do it. I start my approach from a mile away, gathering resources I think I'll need along the way, tearing strips of bark off of trees and ripping them apart until they're frayed. I'll have need of them later. I pause here and there to look for drones. Just like the roleplayers don't know what they're looking for, I don't know what the people running this exercise are going to spring on me.

I make it through wooded hills by 2300 hours, and as I lay behind a fallen tree, I surveil the perimeter of Building B.

Eight guards around the perimeter, with two agents patrolling. Four men on the roof, snipers with their spotters, northeast and southwest corners. Streetlights on each side, with double halogen lights attached to the walls. Decorative bushes all around the building. There's a storage shed on the west side and three patrol vehicles parked helter-skelter. A door on each side, with a fire escape leading down from windows.

I watch the patrols. Every so often one of the patrolmen hops inside one of the jeeps and does a circuit around the building, drives up into the woods with his high beams on, returns five minutes later, having scanned the macadam roads leading to Building B.

I'm going to need all night to do this. A lot of what I use comes from the scoutcraft I learned in the SEALs, but there are techniques specific to lone operator work that were drilled into me when I entered SOG. I come out of the forest slowly, inchworming along the ground, watching the patrolmen, seeing which one is least attentive. I pause and lay prone whenever I feel I'm inside their cone of awareness. I'm still more often than I'm in motion. The first thing the human eye sees in its periphery is movement. Next is color. After that is contours, shape. If you don't want to be spotted, best thing is to sit still. You'd be amazed how many times just laying still can get you not noticed, even in broad daylight without camouflage. So, I just lay here. In the Drifting Place.

I've selected an approach vector on the west-facing side because the guards there are engaging in more chitchat than the others, and because neither rooftop sniper appears to be watching that side much. And they're certainly not watching it when the fire starts in the woods.

When one of the guards sees it, he alerts the others.

It's an old trick. Misdirection. I used the strips of bark I gathered during the day as kindling, spent a bit of time with a wooden stick and a fireboard I made from a dead tree branch, and worked it just enough to get an ember going, then put it deep into the kindling. The fire is building now. Not big at all, but bright enough to be seen at night.

The guards aren't stupid. They know this could be a diversionary tactic. But it also might be something they're supposed to look into. The drill they're running is to literally expect anything. *So, they're thinking, maybe we're only supposed to deal with a perimeter fire while not letting our guard down?*

It doesn't matter, because it serves its purpose. All the guards are alerted, and they're only human. They can't help themselves, they have to at least look in that direction. That includes the snipers, whose spotters turn their scopes towards the woods.

This is how you create openings. It's a small one, but that can make all the difference. So now I'm doing a fast fox-walk, keeping to the darkest shadows, where the shadow of one of the patrol jeeps overlaps with the shadow of the storage shed, creating a darker shadow. There's also a bright streetlight between me and one of the guards. Chiaroscuro to the rescue. There's a moment when no patrolman is looking my way. I crawl out from shadow, do a push-up into a crouch, and I scuttle across the lawn.

The fire's out now. Doesn't matter. Did its job. I'm crawling inside the bushes now. Wait for the patrolmen to carry on their way. I peek through the window behind me. A dark mockup office. No one inside. I try to open the window. Locked, of course. That's okay. Planned on it. I take off my charcoal-gray jacket and wait. And wait.

And wait.

An hour later, I have my opportunity. One of the patrolmen climbs inside a jeep again, and I get set. When no one's looking I press my jacket against the window behind me, and when the jeep grumbles to life and smash the window with my elbow. The jacket helps muffle the sound a bit, and also keeps me from getting cut. I reach inside and unlock the window, open it, climb inside, and shut it back. It all happened in less than eight seconds. Once inside, I find that I'm lucky and there are window shades. I pull those down. Should help mask the fact that the window's been broken.

Now I wait three minutes for the rhodopsin in my eyes to naturally adjust to the darkness of the room, giving me my nighteyes. Now I can move through the office without bumping into anything. I press my ear to the door. Listen. No footsteps, no voices. I open the door a hair, and see only dim hallways lit with soft orange lights hanging from wall sconces. I open the door a couple of inches. It squeaks on its hinges. That means I need to open it fast. The faster you open a door with squeaky hinges, the less sound it makes. That's something most people know, but gets drilled into you in lone operations training.

I step out into the corridor, drawing my pistol and putting it at low-ready position. I'm not supposed to take anyone out, but if I have to I will. Better to survive the exercise and get out with what I came for than to die and totally fail.

The hallways are all dimly lit, with no one in them. I don't hear anyone inside any of the rooms. Could be no one's in the whole building. I don't believe that.

Need to find the stairs. My objective is on the second floor. When I finally come across them, I stop when I hear footsteps echoing from the other side, coming down an enclosed stairwell. I turn to look for places to hide. Shit. Nowhere. I start to bolt back to the end of the hall, back to the room where I started…when a thought occurs. I check an office door next to me. It's unlocked. I open it halfway, leaving it ajar, then run back to the stairwell and wait on the left side of the door.

When the door swings open, a man walks through, dressed in full SWAT kit. He might see me as the door slowly swings closed. He *should* see me. But he doesn't. Because he's an animal and he sees the door I left standing ajar just a few feet in front of him and he knows that's not right. It's out of the ordinary. Doesn't fit the system of other closed doors lining the hallways. He's psychologically locked into it, his eyes and brain fixed as he approaches. No choice, he's bound by the need to investigate the door that's been left slightly open. As he does, I step inside the stairwell he just exited, let the door shut on its own, then start up the stairs, my pistol up and looking for work.

I climb the stairs with supinating, heel-to-toe steps to diminish the sound. At the second floor, I press my ear against the door and listen. Nothing. Silence. Then, I hear a voice loudly over a radio say, "Unit Two, this is Command. Check in and say status."

Someone else answers. A man with a deep voice. "Command, Unit Two. Finished a floor sweep, nothing unusual. Over."

A bit of static. Then, "Copy, Unit Two."

By the sound of it, the guard is down a corridor on the right. The door opens on the right, so I can't get a peek at them, but what I can do is wait. Wait for an opportunity. At least until the guy downstairs comes back up. Or someone on the other side of the door decides to suddenly come through.

I stand away from the door, so that if it opens, it will conceal me. Two minutes later, that exact thing happens. The door swings open and covers me, as a SWAT-kitted guy steps through. He doesn't see me behind the door. I reach out and hold on to the doorknob, keeping it from swinging shut. I sneak a peek through the crack between the door and the hinges. I see no one down the hall. I have a choice to make.

I take the chance.

While the SWAT-kitted guard is stepping down the stairs, I train my pistol on the back of his head, step through the door, then enter a hallway. My pistol is up and at the ready, sweeping left and right. No one in the hallway. I move down the hallway, come to Room 215, press my ear to the door. Silence. I test the doorknob softly. Locked. I could pick it, but that takes longer than the movies make it out. I pull out one of two pieces of tech I bring with me on runs like these: a lockpick gun. It's worth a hundred times its weight in gold. I spray it with graphite to lubricate the keyhole, insert the key, pull the trigger. There's a slight hum as it goes through hundreds of combinations, figuring out the puzzle.

Then there's a small but satisfying *click!* and I turn the knob.

A voice from the other side of the door says, "Dalton? That you?"

Shit. Someone inside, after all. Must've been sitting quietly, guarding the objective.

I have no choice now.

I push open the door before he can react. My pistol is a modified airsoft gun, and it fires two tiny red paint pellets into the chest of the man standing up, and one to his helmeted head. He squeezes off a burst from his own airsoft rifle by reflex and tags me in the leg and arm.

"*Shitfuck!*" he says.

This happens all the time. You get one of the "bad guys" in the scenario but they shoot anyway, just out of instinct. But we have to agree who got who first, or else the exercise cannot continue. Cameras planted all throughout the buildings keep us all honest.

"All right," he huffs, sitting back down. "Fuck. You got me. Right in the head. No way I would've got my shots off."

"We agree I'm still good?"

"Yeah, you're alive."

"Thanks. And sorry about that," I say, and glance over at the desk across from him with a manila envelope sitting on top of it, holding a ream of papers. The objective. I scoop it up, and head out.

"I'll get you next time, haus," the guy swears.

I give him a companionable smile. "I don't doubt it."

I'm lucky on the way out. Very lucky. The stairwell is clear all the way down, and an application of my lockpick gun opens a door on the northwest corner, which I had selected earlier for a primary egress point because of its closeness to the woods and overlapping shadows of two jeeps still parked close by.

But then the alert goes up. Someone found my dead roleplayer upstairs. He's not allowed to tell them which way I went, as per the rules of the game (dead men tell no tales), but they know he's been shot so now there's shouting over radios and a scramble for a search.

There is a different kind of psychology at play when people go into search mode. In stealth training, they teach you that there are generally four states of the mind: oblivious aware, oblivious unaware, alert aware, and alert unaware. The most unpredictable is oblivious unaware, where a patrolman can literally do anything because they aren't aware of any threat. Alert aware is considered the most dangerous for a sneak, because the guards are aware of your presence, yet it's also the most predictable, since there will be certain patterns that you can trust people to follow when organizing a search, especially if they're police or military.

In this way, the alert aware state can actually be beneficial, if you know when and where to take action. You watch for them to group up and exchange information, quick updates about who was found dead and where. You watch them stare into their radios and wait for responses. You see one or two become just a little confused, with certain directions from their supervisors conflicting with the directions coming from Central Command. Tiny hiccups in communication may result. You watch them begin a sweep, see how they move.

You watch and you wait.

Part of this is luck, and part of this is skill. Like poker. I could probably shoot my way out of here, using the vehicles and storage shed for cover as I make it home free to the woods. I consider this, but before I can act I see another opening. Just a moment when no one's eyes are looking in my direction. I run in a low crouch to cover behind one of the jeeps, wait a beat to make sure I wasn't spotted, then bolt for the woods.

Two hours later I'm knelt on the extraction point, snapping my fingers in my ear to switch to an emergency channel, and calling it in. "Ares is out with the package. Waiting at extraction point A. Over."

"Copy that, Ares," Yarwick says in my ear. "The Nest has your back. Sending extraction team to you now. ETA fifteen minutes. Good job." I can hear the smile in her voice.

*

I have had almost zero time to actually sit down and get to know Tara Yarwick. Here's what I've got so far. Grew up in Atlanta, Georgia, went to Emory on a chess scholarship and competed internationally. That's where she first developed relationships with Russians, since Russki chess players are world-renowned. She dated two Russian players and learned their language. At GSU she took a semester of computer programming and discovered she had a knack for it, then refocused on that, did well enough that when the university sponsored an event for Army Intelligence she got to meet some interesting people who really wanted to recruit her for computer forensics.

She went through basic, which was a hard thing because of her asthma, met a guy in the Army that she married, divorced a year later, and stayed single for the next seven years as she proved herself in Iraq and Afghanistan. Whenever soldiers in Kabul busted a terrorist cell and found any tech or computers in their hideout, they brought the gear to Yarwick and her team to analyze and hopefully extract intel from. She was the only woman on a special team that was assigned to assist 1st Special Forces Operational Detachment-Delta (Delta Force). Four years of that, all while gaining an education in computer and political sciences.

She worked with Intelligence Support Activity for a while. Used her cover as an old chess player to enter into the country and do some clandestine activities. Wrote some of the first papers on how terrorists were starting to use Bitcoin to pay for weapons and gear on the downlow, which helped a lot of the old-timers in the military understand how cryptocurrency worked, and how it was changing the war on terrorism. I looked into it, and found that those papers really helped modernize U.S. defense strategies for finding terrorist bankrollers. Yarwick is humble about it, but it seems she's really helped shape intelligence policy in key areas.

After ISA, she jumped around a bit. Ended up with JSOC and apprenticed under some big fish who taught her how to liaise with agencies. Learned to grease the wheels of bureaucracy to get black ops moving. Apparently, she picked it up quick. Been doing it ever since.

I learned all that from the numerous lunch meetings we have, but I don't know much else. I don't know what drives her, where she sees herself in twenty years, her life's regrets, all the DNA of a human spirit. Usually that's fine. Just like with my training, it's best to be on the razor's edge with all your professional relationships in CIA. You want people to know you well enough that they can trust you, but not so much that it disrupts a working relationship.

Ten days before mission launch I meet up with Yarwick again, this time over breakfast. We're in the cafeteria again, where all this started between us. I wonder if she feels the significance, too, or if such symbolism means nothing to her. The TV on the wall is showing CNN. They're doing a story about a new missile system being installed on U.S. destroyers at sea. I can't help but feel this demonstration was arranged for the press as part of a greater ploy.

One sword keeps the other one sheathed. Sophia said that to me once.

"So," I say, "any idea of when we launch?"

"I've been talking with Tant," she says around a mouthful of eggs. She doesn't cover her mouth when she speaks, probably a habit of eating in so many mess halls while deployed. "Insertion A is looking like a go. The fleet in the Pacific have permission to conduct a defense exercise in the Sea of Japan, which includes an emergency ballast blow and surfacing. And JSOC said the boatmen at the Strait of Tartary are prepped to go."

I take a sip of my coffee and shake my head in wonderment. "A lot of moving parts."

"Takes a lot to get into a place like this," she says. "Nothing can look obvious, like we or our Japanese allies are going out of the way to conceal something. The Russians are bound to get wind of the sub's exercise, so it has to look like it was on the docket to begin with."

I nod. "How much of the taxpayers' money do you think is getting spent on this? When it's all said and done, I mean."

She snorts. "God only knows."

"Submarine fuel cost. Personnel being moved around and retasked. All the training they're putting us through. And the Japanese smugglers I assume are being paid via a slush fund or dummy account in another country."

"Starting to feel a little sorry for the taxpayer, hotshot?" She smiles at me over the rim of her coffee cup.

"I'm not saying I feel sorry for anybody." *Please. I have children. I have three children.* "But it does give one pause. Or it should."

"The upper brass believes in you and believes in our team. Even more, the president has come to view this mission as a priority. Seems we're now officially on the PDB," she says, referring to the president's daily briefing. It's a top-secret document given to the President of the United States every morning. "Everything we do from here on out will be under the highest scrutiny. No room for mistakes."

I suppress the need to remind Yarwick of the old saying about how no plan survives first contact, but I'm sure she's aware. *No room for mistakes* is just a thing she has to say. "You've been spending a lot of time on this, and once we're in action, you're going to be holed up in a room in China for at least a week, on call around the clock with the rest of the Nest, giving me support. You got anyone that will miss you?"

"You mean family?" she asks. Her face is a mask, hiding everything. But even that is a tell.

I nod.

"Not really," she says. "There's a guy I've been dating on and off for about a year, but he's NSA and he knows the drill."

"No one else? No parents or siblings?"

"I've got three sisters. I keep in contact with one of them, but she understands that sometimes I gotta be incommunicado. The other two…I dunno, they're off somewhere. The youngest was in jail, but she just got out and God only knows where she went. Mom's passed away, and Dad vanished several years ago with my stepmom. They travel around Europe. I get emails sometimes. Postcards." She holds her coffee cup in both hands, stares down into a void. Then she shakes off the past and looks at me. "What about you? No girlfriend?"

"Don't pretend like you don't already know," I chuckle.

She lifts an eyebrow. "It might surprise you to know, but we don't keep up with everyone's private life."

"You knew about Sophia."

"That's because I had access to your psych profile and you mentioned her as someone you can talk to to recharge. That was seen as a check in your positive column, by the way. A good agent needs to not be a total loner. Being completely alone raises a few eyebrows."

"Why's that?"

"An asset needs a reason to come back. A reason to come in from the cold." Her eyes lock on to mine. There's a depth to them, she's searching and feeling searched, too.

"A reason to not betray his country?"

"Pretty much."

I smile, and down the rest of my coffee. I glance over at the TVs on the wall. One is on CNN, they're covering yet another train derailment, this one is Kentucky. Seven dead. It's like déjà vu, the last time I was in this cafeteria eating with Yarwick and discussing the mission there was a derailment in Connecticut. "So what's yours?" I ask.

"What's my what?"

"Your reason. What sort of leash keeps the upper brass confident that you're not going to go AWOL someday?"

Yarwick shrugs. "I have a few reasons. I guess the main one is my nephew. My sister—the one who's in and out of jail?—she had a son that she's seen maybe five, ten times since he was born. He's with his dad. He's smart, but they're dirt poor, so the kid's got no hopes of a decent education. But I visit with them every month. They're a good family. I help out with their bills."

"That's nice of you."

"I guess I got the same advice from my evaluator as you did. If you don't have much investment in the real world, you'll get detached from it, and then you'll forget what you're fighting for. You donate your time to retired veterans, I donate it to my nephew."

I nod. "Anything else?"

"I have a cat."

"No shit? Me, too. Well, it's my neighbor's cat technically, but he likes me better. We should introduce them to each other."

Yarwick smiles. "Maybe we should."

"It's a date, then."

"I'll bring the catnip, you can bring the—" She's cut off by her vibrating phone. She lifts it from the table, and frowns at the message.

"What is it?"

She grabs her jacket. "We gotta go," she says.

"Why?"

"Something's come up. Something new."

I gather both our trays, toss the contents into the trash, then follow Yarwick out. She's practically running.

6

"What the hell am I looking at?"

The room we're in is huge, almost as big as NASA's mission control, and constructed similarly. It's a room for signals interceptions and the control of reconnaissance satellites. There are concentric rings of desks arranged like stadium seating and arrayed around three huge TV screens. At each desk is a signals analyst with a headset staring into a monitor. All around us, we hear commands being issued into those headsets, messages being relayed from station to station.

Up on the central screen is an image. In the top-right corner there's a string of numbers, as well as the satellite's designated code and number. It's a KH-11 recon satellite. The timestamp says the image is two hours old. Deputy Director Halbach is present, as is the Lead Signals Expert William Yu. Yu is explaining how he received an order from operations to change the KH-11's orbit and retask it to look at a specific set of coordinates over the Vostochny Cosmodrome.

"The coordinates came from a CIA handler with reliable HUMINT," he says. "I was told it was top priority."

Halbach looks at me and Yarwick. "I approved the retasking of the satellite. We got word from Talon. She said something was going on at Vostochny that we should see."

"What the hell am I looking at?" Yarwick says again.

I'm trying to figure that out, too. Up on the screen, there's an overhead view of one of the many buildings that make up the Vostochny complex. Above that building are two small gray dots that seem to be hovering. A slide show reveals pics taken over a span of several minutes, and when played in sequence they make a little movie. The gray dots move around like flies. For size reference, there are military vehicles surrounding the buildings, and a few dots that are obviously humans standing atop the building. The gray dots look to be about the size of a human being, maybe a little bulkier, and yet they fly around like gnats.

"We think," Halbach says, taking out her mobile phone, "you're looking at this." She shows us a picture, this one taken at ground level and looking up in the air. "It was taken by Talon a few hours ago. Or so she claims."

83

Yarwick takes the phone. We both look at it. It looks like a bulky machine with of gunmetal-gray armor, shaped like a comma and about as big as an elephant. From its sides extend two long robotic tentacles, kind of like a squid's tentacles, only about eight feet long and made of steel. We cannot see the pilot's face for all the armor, or even if the machine *has* a pilot, but it looks menacing in its alien appearance.

"It's clearly flying," I say. "But I don't see any obvious propulsion system."

Stunned, Yarwick looks at Halbach. "Have we ever heard of this kind of tech?"

"I'm told someone has," the deputy director says. "He's on his way here now."

*

"It's called the Tianshi," the old man says. He's Chinese. His English is a little broken. I'm not allowed to know who he is or how the CIA came to be in possession of him, but what I gathered from Halbach on the elevator ride up to the top floor is that he was a weapons designer for the Chinese military up until four years ago. I'm assuming he defected for one reason or another. In exchange, he gives us insight into what weapons programs the Chinese might be cooking up.

"What does it do?" Halbach asks, sitting across the table from the beleaguered-looking man.

He adjusts his glasses, and shrugs. "I cannot speak to its full capabilities, I was not privy to every aspect of its design phase, but I do know that it never made it past proof-of-concept. I never even saw a working piece of tech myself, I only read the theories on paper—"

"Well then, what can it *theoretically* do?"

Adjusts his glasses again. "As you see. It creates a propellerless lift system, meant to be capable of carrying weapons platforms and equipment over long distances without much fuel."

"Propellerless lift system," Yarwick says.

The man nods. "A repulsor system."

"You mean levitation. Without any expulsion of air to create the lift?"

"There's *some* expulsion of air, through a downward-pressing jet system. It's not complete levitation. The Tianshi suit was meant to generate a fixed-focused electromagnetic lensing field, which magnifies the planet's magnetosphere and produces a reciprocal effect. It's not a strong effect, but combined with the jets it can maneuver very fast. It was still a work in progress." He looks at Halbach gravely. "But its twin propulsion systems happen to render it virtually silent."

I glance over at Isaacson, who sits beside me. "Sammy? You boys at DARPA got anything like this?"

The DARPA man is chewing on a stick of gum, but he's doing it slowly, thoughtfully. He shakes his head. "Nah. Nothing like this. There's been some advances in things like quantum levitation, but you usually need some kind of rail beneath the vehicle, usually coated in frozen nitrogen."

"And you're sure it's a *Chinese* design?" asks Yarwick.

"Yes," the defector says. "Positive."

I ask, "What are the tentacles for? Those steel grapplers dangling from the sides."

"If they follow the initial design that I saw, they're meant to be manipulators—they can carry very heavy equipment over long distances, or handle powerful weaponry that gives off massive recoil, or scoop up injured people on the battlefield."

"This is a *huge* leap in tech," Isaacson says. "Far beyond what we know of modern scientific knowledge."

The defector gives the ghost of a smile. If a smile could be said to contain dread, his does. "The futurist Ray Kurzweil calls it the Law of Accelerating Returns. He has been speaking on such quick advancement for years, and been warning the military about it. A technology explosion is coming. The Internet has accelerated communication, and thus accelerated collaboration between scientists and designers." He nods grimly. "In the next twenty years, you're going to see a terrifying acceleration of weapons tech."

Everyone in the room exchanges looks.

Minutes later, we're standing outside the conference room. The defector has been taken somewhere. I'll probably never see him again.

Yarwick, Halbach, Isaacson and I stand in the hallway and digest what we've just heard. Yarwick says, "A Chinese weapons platform being tested or used to patrol a Russian spaceport where they're about to cook up a particle-beam weapon. If this is all true, it might mean..." She stops.

Halbach nods. "The Chinese are either sharing tech or they're directly involved with the Russians in this weapons-building endeavor." She shoots a look at Isaacson. "Sammy, what're we looking at with those Tianshi drones? I mean what're we *really* looking at?"

"It's the leap in tech that's worrisome," he says, still jawing on his chewing gum. "If they're that far ahead...well, it's not good. Also, what the guy said about the tentacles being grapplers, and how they can handle massive weapons and absorb all the recoil? That's...it makes a lot of sense if the tentacles are as loose as they appear to be. Really kind of brilliant. Nothing rigid to jolt the platform off-course, just let the tentacles fire something huge and then go limp. And those satellite photos made it seem like they're zipping around pretty fast. And I imagine they are heavily armored. I could see them being used to sabotage helicopters in the sky. And being so small, they'll be hard to target. This could be a gamechanger on the battlefield, right along with the particle-beam weapon and God knows what else."

"Don't forget he said they're very quiet," I put in. "That would make them perfect for stealth operations."

"Right," Isaacson says. "All our propulsion suits and drones have been loud, expelling heated air for thrust. A weapons platform like that Tianshi opens up whole new avenues of warfare."

"Jesus," Yarwick says. "Russia, Syria, North Kora, Iran, and now China? If this is all happening, they're really getting in bed together. It's a budding eastern alignment, possibly with the foundation being built around shared advanced arms programs. And with a propulsion system like Tianshi, their war machine could be more mobile than anything we've got."

Halbach looks me dead in the eye. "I hope you understand what this means for NARROW VOID." I do. The importance of mission success just went through the roof. To Yarwick, she says, "I'm increasing the budget on your mission. If there's anything else you needed and were afraid to ask, now's the time." That shouldn't be too hard, since Title 10 of U.S. Code says operations like ours don't have to report our budget to anyone—not Congress, not the president, not anyone.

Yarwick nods curtly. "This certainly makes me believe that the security at Vostochny is going to be more intense than we even initially believed. A *lot* more intense." She looks at me. "We were planning on sending you in clean, just fake passports and MREs and papers to pass you off as a local in case you were seen. Now..."

I nod. "A stealth infiltration," I say. "I'm going to need a kit. A damn good one. Something that includes heat masking. But it can't be bulky, because I gotta be able to move."

Isaacson says, "We might have something that'll work. Loose clothing lined with a new insulator sheet. Has a thin layer of nanofiber armor, too."

Halbach looks back at Yarwick. "Give him whatever he needs." Back at me. "You leave in one week." She turns to go give her report to the Director of CIA.

Yarwick turns to me. "Well, there's your answer. Operation NARROW VOID is go. Get ready, hotshot. You're about to take a dive into the unknown."

*

I'm ready to die. No, more than ready. Perhaps *eager* is too strong a word? I don't know that it's a *want*, either, nor is it a *need*. It's not that I think I deserve death. It's not guilt that impels me to consider checking out for good. Let's call it "prepared and waiting." I don't know why the thought is there, but there it is. And it's been there for a while. It's not depression. Depressed people are rarely as motivated as I am—it's sort of their defining characteristic. Or perhaps I *am* depressed, just without the symptoms? Can you be depressed but asymptomatic?

The thought is there, regardless. And who cares who or what put it there? There it sits and it's not going anywhere and I have to deal with it and no one else. Maybe all operatives carry this with them.

Maybe it's the secret we all share. The final secret in a career of secrets, filed along with private regrets and apologies unuttered.

There are things that I know. I know that you cannot do this job without love of country, but there has to be something more, too. There has to be Another Reason—maybe fear of dying in a useless office job, maybe only pure professionalism, maybe something else—and that reason must be so white-hot in order to become an operative in the first place that it basically burns away all permission to kill oneself. Perhaps it's when that white-hot flame becomes nothing but an ember when the secret, that "prepared and waiting" feeling, metastasizes to the mind and heart before evolving into what it was all along. Melancholy. Or whatever.

Maybe that's how it goes. How would I know?

Maybe it all piles up. Like debt. Where did this bill come from? Maybe it's like that. The secrets you've kept, the family you've sacrificed, the people you've killed. Here's one. Here's another. Maybe that's how you end up like Sophia.

Age doesn't help. Age robs you of so much. Not just your youth and vitality, but of friends. *Where did everybody go?* you say. Astonishing how fast they can vanish. And it's more critical than you conceive when you're young and only *thinking* about getting old. There's all the inside jokes that are meaningless now, because the person who speaks for the other part of that joke is gone. You try to tell the joke to others but end up saying "You had to be there." And slowly the world fills up with people who had to be there. Because they weren't there. And so neither were you. A lifetime erased. Like all of Sophia's heroics and acts of bravery.

So, if we were never here, who or what are we?

We're people who quit tomorrow. Because fuck the darkness. Like Sophia said.

That's what clears my head when I wake up in the middle of the night. It's the day before I leave, and I have to unravel my own feelings about the mission and my role in it. The stakes have been upped. What I'm being asked to do is see if there's reason to believe another World War is on its way, one with new advanced tech.

I have to unwind. Put it all aside. I can't think about the monumental things, not tonight. So I get out my favorite book, *The*

Hitchhiker's Guide to the Galaxy, and lose myself in the ridiculous antics of Arthur Dent and gang. I remember the first time I read it. I remember being introduced to it by Scott, and we would discuss it over pizza and movie night, or during our *D&D* sessions. It gives me an unexpected sense of renewal. All those old friends of mine are out there living their lives, oblivious to what I do for their country and way of life.

It gives me something besides Sophia to fight for. Like Yarwick with her nephew. Fuck the darkness. I'm not quitting today.

I fall asleep and wake up to the alarm. I meditate, stretch, take a shower, get dressed and grab my gear bag. My room at Langley will be some other agent's now. I step out into the hall, nod to all the interns doing the work for Uncle Sam, and I head for the black sedan that's waiting outside. Waiting to take me to Langley Air Force Base.

I show my ID at the base entrance and after that I'm ushered to where I need to go by an army colonel I'll likely never see or speak to again. He takes me straight through the base, saying nothing, asking me nothing. He's been briefed. He knows I'm a spook and he can't ask anything. He's probably done this countless times before.

Yarwick's waiting for me on the tarmac beside the airstairs. It's a beautiful day. The sun is shining. Spring is fully upon us. She's dressed in a black pantsuit and is just hanging up her phone when I approach. "You ready, Mr. Adamson?"

"Call me Nate. We've been formal for too long."

There's a slight smirk as she looks up at me, a momentary glimmer of both formal and informal respect. A tease of something. "Okay. Then I'm Tara. You ready for this, Nate?"

"As anyone can be, Tara."

"I just got off the phone with Halbach. Latest update from Talon is that Karambit is now on site at the Cosmodrome, along with his entire unit." The SVR hit squad. Run by an agent who approves of rape in torture tactics. About as horrifying as it gets. And they're going to be all over my objective.

"Shouldn't be an issue," I say. "Long as I stay invisible."

"I just thought you should know. We also got confirmation from both the ferry boat owners at Rendezvous A, and the handler in charge of contacting Talon. Everything's go. Talon's been notified to be ready to make contact with you at Rendezvous B. You'll just let the Nest know when you're arriving, I'll contact Halbach and she'll make sure Talon gets the message. When you meet, you'll ask her 'Where is the green fortress?' She'll respond with 'Under your bed.'"

"Green fortress. Under the bed. Got it."

"The rest of the Nest is on a plane for Harbin as we speak. I'm hearing the weather's good all the way there, so they should be set up in forty-eight hours. I'll be there a day after them, just got a few things to finish up here."

"Sounds good."

"Your naval uniform and kit are all on board the plane." She pauses to let the pilot and copilot head up the airstairs into the Gulfstream. She looks at me. "This is it."

"This is it," I say.

She offers her hand. "Good luck out there, Nate."

I take her hand. "You too, Tara."

"Keep in touch."

"You do the same."

I head up the stairs. I stop just before stepping inside and turn to watch her go and see her glance over her shoulder at me. She's halfway across the tarmac when the absurd notion occurs to me that I should've kissed her. It makes no sense. I have no connection with her outside of our professional relationship. But I've been in Afghanistan for a year and I've been alone for a while and it's been just me and Sophia and a man is an animal with needs. And there's always the chance of never coming back.

But now the engines are cycling up and she wouldn't hear me if I shouted and it would seem ridiculous and the moment is gone. For a man trained to seize opportunities, I'm good at missing them. I step inside the plane and get my head in the game.

*

And now it's like it was when I was in Afghanistan. Things move fast. People shuffle me around, and I'm a leaf on their wind, going where they carry me. Now I'm in the air, dressed in naval fatigues though I'm no longer in the Navy. Now I'm landing at

Miramar Air Force Base in San Diego, California, where I shake hands with another colonel who has been told to escort me where I need to go without asking questions. And I wait no longer than thirty minutes before I'm ushered over to an HH-65 Dolphin, the twin-engine helicopter of choice for the Coast Guard. One of the pilots reminds me to buckle up. Other than that, they say nothing until I reach the rendezvous.

The rendezvous is a spot of ocean just fifty miles out at sea. We land on top of the aircraft carrier USS *Theodore Roosevelt*. Now I'm taken to the captain's quarters and introduced to the man in charge. We speak for no more than five minutes as he receives my papers and gets proof I am who I say I am, and that no mistake has been made. I tell him I'm a public affairs specialist and he knows I'm lying and now I'm walking to my quarters.

We change course.

Now it's two days later and it's midnight and I'm on a skiff that's carrying me over to a submarine that's just surfaced. The *Colorado* awaits.

And now at the place of my second birth. The Navy. The sea. This brings back memories. The gentle swaying. The narrow corridors. The smell of sweaty men kept in too close proximity for too long, an odor you can never eradicate and is practically a component now of the alloys holding this ship together. I spend most of my time either in my bunk or in the fitness room, with regular visits to the galley, of course.

No one talks to me.

I talk to no one.

Not that I'd mind conversation, but it's usually best to keep my head in the game. Stay focused. I keep up my usual rituals: wake up, meditate, stretch, work out a little, and study Amur Oblast terrain on a paper map. I feel at home. Maybe more at home than I've ever felt. Though I can't see the water from in here, I'm in the ocean, and the ocean is where I first felt a real calling to do more.

Two weeks later, I actually get to lay eyes on a wide open blue sea, when *Colorado* surfaces and rendezvouses with the *Hayabusa*. I don't speak Japanese, but luckily many of them speak English, and I'm accepted on board with smiles and bows. I return both.

Now I'm done pretending to be a Navy man and I'm moving through the Sea of Japan and pretending to be an oceanographer that has been allowed to come along to conduct a study of the Strait of Tartary. Lucky for me I got my degree in oceanography. Perhaps another reason I was a candidate for this mission? It'll certainly make it easier to explain my presence on a Japanese vessel once we get into waters with more Russian vessels. The Russians wouldn't dare board a foreign government's vessel, but you never know which of these Japanese sailors might turn out to be a blabbermouth.

Now I'm passing through the strait. Now we're boarding a Japanese vessel that I and the captain happen to know is a smuggling boat, but *Hayabusa*'s crew thinks is only a random check. I go aboard with a team of *Hayabusa*'s security force. The security force goes back to *Hayabusa* twenty minutes later, after having finished their search. I remain aboard the smuggling boat.

Now I'm on a boat with a dozen filthy men posing as fishermen, all of whom give me an unreadable look. Distrustful, I think.

Two days with these unwashed bodies. Two days with smugglers who have been paid secretly through a dummy account by my bosses.

Now we're within sight of shore. We find where the Amur River dumps into the strait. They don't dock, but send me on a row boat to land, with four guys rowing for me.

Now they're rowing away.

I'm alone on the shore.

I'm seven thousand miles away from home, and there's no way back. All that training, all that planning has led to this. Time to go to work. Commencing Operation NARROW VOID.

Oie

Walking hurts, but these old legs can do it. And if one is capable of doing something, one should make the effort to do it. The mind believes, on an instinctual level, that that's the key to how this ancient body has stuck around. I carry myself forward whenever I can, usually under the watchful eye of an orderly. If I fall, I'm likely to break ten different bones. But I have to stay moving. Everyone in this place that dies at sixty or seventy or eighty or ninety, they were all non-movers. That's something I've noticed in my time at three different retirement homes. An object at rest stays at rest, while an object in motion stays in motion with the same speed and the same direction unless acted upon by another force. I remember someone smart said that. I used to know their name. I can almost remember it...slippery, like a fish...*Newton*. That's it. Smart man. I am in motion now because I have remained in motion. A healthy diet will do it, too. And the coffee. That's where I'm going now...I think. I may have had a different destination when I first started walking but now I feel like coffee so I'm getting coffee.

They let me make my own coffee. Not because they trust me (they don't), but because these new coffeemakers have basically made it idiotproof. Which means it's old-people-proof. I use the Fiones that Nathan brought me. There's a tiny hole in the top of the bag where I've been sniffing it occasionally, anticipating making a fresh pot. I resealed it with a pink potato-chip bag clip with a My Little Pony logo on it that Henrietta left when she last visited. I smile thinking of her.

I smell the coffee. Launches me back to the fields in Martinique. That boy Jean-Luc chasing me through the morning-damp grass for ages, trying to get a peek up my skirt. I finally let him, in exchange for a peek inside his pants. A fair exchange, I think.

When it's finished, I pour it in the thermos so I don't spill it. Clumsy hands.

I take another good long whiff. Take a sip. That's authentic Fiones, all right. Good boy, Nathan. Wonder where he's at. He visited a week ago, said he'd be back. Or was it two weeks ago?

These old legs shuffle down the halls gingerly. One hand holds the coffee, one hand touches the wall on the left for safety. Have to be careful. Three spills in the last thirteen years have not only brought great pain, they've also brought admonishment from a stern daughter, an even sterner granddaughter, and a weeping great-granddaughter who says she doesn't want *Soso* to die. That's what she calls me, *Soso*. Henrietta's memory brings a smile. No matter how confused my days get, I somehow always remember her. Hard to believe I lived long enough to see them all grow.

How many men did I prevent from seeing their own children? How many children are left unborn because of me?

Let's not think on that. Let's think on Nathan and Jean-Luc and this warm coffee. Yes, let's think on that. Too much darkness when thinking on those old things.

I glance over my shoulder and see Orson, the fat orderly, still following me. He's new, still green, just here for the paycheck. He has been assigned to help some of us walk around a few times a week. My daughter pays for such extra care. That includes that nurse, Kristin, to check and make sure I'm taking all my pills. *Kristin.* She looks so much like that cunt Faustine in Department IX, the one who fucked all her agents, and, in the end, fucked us all by betraying us.

Walking can be troublesome. I am blind in one eye, no depth perception. Orson is supposed to watch me closely. But he is absentminded, always playing on his phone. I've been keeping track of him out the corner of my eye. I wait for my moment. It'll come.

When it does, it comes in the form of Wade Barrett, the grumpy fucker who always complains that someone's stealing his alprazolam pills. He's right. Someone is. I know who, too. But I'm not telling. Holding on to secrets is like holding on to stock, its worth may go up and its worth may go down, but when it goes up it's capable of opening doors.

This time, Wade assails Orson the orderly, barring his path with his walker like he's still the Nashville detective he used to be. Orson and Wade get into it. I keep walking. I wait until I reach a pillar near the cafeteria. I round it, breaking line-of-sight. I keep walking. I'm out the door. Orson's and Wade's voices fade behind me.

The cobblestone path is lined with rosebushes. My slippered feet make soft scraping sounds as I make my slow way along the path. A robin shoots by and lands on a branch beside me. I stop and look at it, wondering if it's real. Sometimes I see things that aren't really there. I decide that it's real. It bobs its head up and down, turns its head to look at something. Maybe me. We share a moment, both wondering what the other one is all about. Perfect strangers. I smile and it flies away. What a gift from God you were, little robin.

My feet keeping moving. The mind is drifting. Out for a stroll. But the mind also has a goal. What goal is that? I knew before I stepped out here. Now I'm moving more on instinct, like an ant that doesn't understand its greater place in the universe but still knows it must follow the line of its kin to somewhere deep, deep inside the anthill, to deliver something important. Is this how ants feel all the time? Is this how my own grandmother felt when I visited her in Ars-en-Ré, when her feeble hands held my young, soft ones, and pushed my hair out of my eyes like she was trying to see through curtains at something that was supposed to be familiar? Grand-mère was long-lived, too. Ninety-two when she died. Guess it's in my genes.

Where am I going?

I chuckle to myself. Where, indeed? That always seems to be the question these days. I'm both losing my mind and aware that I am. I'm incredibly fortunate that I've lasted this long. God has given me this life, though I don't deserve it. Or perhaps I do. Perhaps it's the ones I left in the cold Aquitaine forests that deserved to have died, the ones in shallow graves dug in haste.

Remembering them summons them, like always. I see them walking beside me. Phantoms. The doctors say it's finally the beginnings of dementia, exacerbated by the Lorazepam I no longer take—though the staff doesn't know I quit taking the pills. Dr. Willard says he has ways of finding out whether I've been taking my pills or not. Smelly old Dr. Willard, *mes couilles sur ton front.*

In any case, I see them. The people I killed or who think I killed them. The ones in the shallow graves. They don't judge me. They don't cast accusatory faces at me or issue threats. In fact, they never even speak. Their uniforms are sometimes crisp and sometimes filthy from where they climbed out of the graves. I have sometimes become so confused that I think I'm dead and that they are alive, and that I am a spirit doomed to follow them forever. It is sort of disorienting just now, to the point that if I don't focus I may become confused again. I may have one of my episodes. I've only had three of those. No…four. Or has it been three?

Now I remember. I came out here to find what it is I left inside the hole in the willow at the other end of the back yard. I wave to Henry Griggs as I head that way. He's seventy years old, thirty years my junior, and walks around just fine most of the time. He has eyes for Jennifer Swanson, and she has eyes for both him and Geoff

Stanton, the little minx. Ah well, let her have her fun. God knows I had mine.

My dead spirit friends follow me to the willow. Wait…wait…why am I here? How did I…?

And now the familiar fear sets in. Where am I? How did I get here? Who am I talking to? Who are you?

Wait…yes. *Oui…oui*, I know where I am. Placing my hands on the willow roots me. Foolish Sophia, you know who you are. You know who you're talking to. You're talking to yourself. And the ghost friends who may or may not know you. Complete your mission. Do what you came here to do.

My hand slips inside the tiny hole underneath the lowest-hanging branch. I feel around for it. Got it. I take the orderly's cell phone and I put it in my brassiere. If they search me like last time, they won't go near my tits. James the orderly's phone has been missing for several days and I overheard suspicion that one of us took it. I remember wondering who it could've been. Now I know. Maybe I'll forget again later. Forget why I have it hidden in my brassiere. But my instincts will be to hide it. Hide it long enough for me to remember again.

"Sophia!" Orson. *Peau de zob.* I turn to him smiling, looking mildly confused. Not difficult to pull off. "Sophia! Jesus. You can't just run off like that."

"I don't run anywhere, Orson," I say.

"What're you doing out here?"

"I don't know." And that's the truth. I know I had a mission, and I know I completed it, but I also know that it's kind of slipped free again. A wet fish in my hands. I sort of remember. I look at my ghost friends. If they know anything, they're not saying it.

"Let's go back inside," Orson says.

"Of course, Orson. *Je te chie dans le cou.*"

"What does that mean?"

I say nothing as I and my dead friends follow him back inside. There's something in my brassiere. Uncomfortable. I adjust it. I'll check it later. Not out here where everybody can see me fiddling with my tits. That would be unladylike.

PART TWO

The Promise

7

I open my gear bag and go through the kit. It's all very slack, not a combat soldier's kit. Camouflage pants and jacket, black shirt, all very snug where it needs to be, and loose where it counts. Black ski mask and night-vision goggles. Tactical gloves and boots. For CQB I've got a simple Glock with sound suppressor, and a compact SA58 Mini OSW rifle with EOTech scope and stock that folds to the side, in case I have need of close-in, one-handed use.

Woven into all the cloth is a layer of heat-masking insulation, as well as a layer of an advanced thin fiber-weave for bulletproofing. There are also pouches with ration bars, spare ammo clips with subsonic rounds, three flash-bang grenades, a spotter's scope, a small medical kit and survival kit, a radio in case my cochlear implant fails, five thousand dollars' worth of Russian rubles, a fake passport that has me as Sergei Prokhorov the swimming instructor from Blagoveshchensk, and a mobile phone with high-definition camera for snapping pics of my objective. I've got bottles of water and purifier capsules for when I need to refill from the river.

And there's one tiny, clear plastic bag that has only one pill. One teeny, tiny pill. It's a capsule of succinylcholine, to be ingested to save myself from torture if I'm captured. It's quick, I'm told. Be dead in seconds, and it looks no different than cardiac arrest.

A quick inspection of everything shows it's all in order. I dump my civilian clothes in the gear bag, then snap my fingers three times next to my ear to open a channel. The GPS transmitter in my clothing should let the Nest know that I'm in position. They will have been tracking me ever since the *Colorado* surfaced.

"Nest, this is Ares. Do you read? Over."

Silence.

"Nest, this is Ares. Come back. Over."

Silence.

I take a look around. I'm on a river bank slushy with mud and littered with cracked stones. It's cold out, a few degrees above freezing. It's midday, the sun is peeking cheekily from behind clouds. I walk a distance into the woods, just to be clear of any patrol boats that might come along. Hunkering down, I try the Nest again. No answer. I peel off my clothes and change them out for my kit wear. Once fully decked out, I try the Nest one more time.

"Nest, do you read? This is Ares. I'm dry. Over." Dry means I'm finally on land. They should know that, but maybe there's more than one glitch going on here. "Nest, this is Ares. Not sure if I'm in the blind here. If you're reading me, I can't hear you. I'm dry and awaiting the go. If I haven't heard anything from you by morning, I'll commence. Over."

It's going to get colder as the temperature drops, so I build a shelter. Takes three hours to make a small one-man-sized debris hut. I use two Y-shaped sticks and stab them into the ground, run one long stick between them, then lay down a latticework of dead tree branches to act as the roof. Toss on some leaves for both insulation and waterproofing, in case I get surprised by rain. Building shelter occupies my mind, kills boredom.

The temperature's dropping. Now around twenty degrees Fahrenheit. The stars begin to come out, tiny white dots peeking through the forest canopy. Pretty soon it's just me and Betelgeuse and Rigel again. Hello old friends.

I'm halfway through an MRE when a scratching noise sounds in my ear. I pause. Listen. It's faint. Then, a distant voice calls out. "Ares...est...you read? Over."

"Nest, this Ares. You're coming in choppy."

A few seconds pass.

"How's this, Ares?" says Yarwick in my ear.

I breathe a sigh of relief and the tension that I didn't know I was holding in my chest releases. "Much clearer. Five-by-five, Nest."

"You're coming in clean, too."

"Had me worried there for a bit."

"Sorry, there was an issue with the signal bounce from the satellite. Looks like we've got it worked out. Say status."

"I'm dry and alone. Shelter's built. I was just about to tuck in for the night when you called. Pretty cold out here. I was thinking of starting my run at oh-four-hundred, use some of this darkness while I can. You agree?"

A few seconds. Then, "That sounds like a plan to us, Ares."

Always best to confer with your team. This whole thing is part improvisation on my part, and part orchestration on theirs. I'm a tool that they direct, but a tool with a brain.

"Get some rest. We'll let you know if there's anything in the area you need to know about."

I look up at the sky again. Somewhere up there, between me and all those stars, there's a KH-11 moving around in orbit, risking getting spotted by Russian hunter-killer satellites, and feeding info back to the Nest to give them a greater overview.

"Copy that, Nest. Ares is counting sheep."

It's a tight squeeze into my debris hut, but that's on purpose. I shoved as many leaves inside as I possibly could to create a cocoon that, combined with my insulated clothing, will keep me warm throughout the night. I roll my ski mask over my head, and pack more leaves around my head like a pillow. I settle here, close my eyes, and try not to think about the Kamchatka brown bears that live in the region. They mostly stay up in the mountains, I read, but if food gets scarce in those rivers they have been known to drift down this way.

There are few night sounds. No animals stirring. Too cold for that. Only the wind pushing through the forest and the trees whispering conspiratorially and the dead leaves rustling.

*

Morning. Still dark.

The tactical watch on my hand wakes me up with a vibration, not with a beep. A beep might alert others around me. I keep my eyes closed for a few seconds, listening, pretending to be asleep in case I've been taken prisoner without knowing it. Another habit instilled by tradecraft training. Once I'm certain I'm in the same place I fell asleep, I climb out of my shelter and take about ten minutes to totally destroy it. If they really looked, a person would be able to tell that someone slept here, but at a glance it just looks like some animals had a fight around here.

"Nest, Ares. I'm awake and on the move."

The response comes from another woman's voice. "Copy that, Ares." It's Amrita. Yarwick must be asleep, or simply out of the room at the moment. "Be advised of a heavy thunderstorm moving to your area. Should be hitting you in about two hours. It'll be good cover should you need it."

"Copy, Nest. Thanks. Ares out."

And so it's onward. Starting through the woods, I move at a steady pace. I keep under the forest canopy, and stay away from any clearings. These hills are not yet mountains. It will take another million years or so for the natural tectonic motions to encourage them to ascend to the heavens. Far in the hazy north, though, are the true titans. The Stanovoy Mountain Range. If all goes well, I won't be driven in that direction. Those mountains are frigid and mostly lifeless. Practically a death sentence this time of year.

Following the Amur River is easy to do from afar. I can stay well within the concealment of the forest while also keeping the water within sight. I see no one, I hear no one. There is a bitch wind coming from the west, portending the storm. The day wears on.

A few times I stop, listen, look at the sky for drones, and then push on.

The storm Amrita promised hits, and it hits hard, just as the sky is beginning to lighten. The dark clouds are the harbingers. They bring with them a cold, severe wind that bends the trees all in one direction. Thunder builds in the chest of the beast. Arcs of blue lightning sketch themselves across the sky for a split second. No rain. Just wind and thunder and darkness. Amrita was right. No chance anybody sees or hears me out here in this. So I figure it's safe to pick up my pace.

Three hours later, the storm moves on. No more lightning or harsh winds. There's distant thunder in the east, a report from the monster in retreat. I come to a dirt road that doesn't look well-traveled. I cross it quickly. Keep following the river.

Twice I stop to rest and eat, but not for too long, the constant movement keeps me warm. I check in with the Nest along the way. Yarwick is back. She checks in every hour to hear how I'm doing physically. She says my GPS signal is still broadcasting loud and clear, they know exactly where I am. Monitoring me like gods in the sky.

Up one hill, down the other side, one mile after another. My legs feel good. My watch shows my heartrate. All good. Water consumption is on schedule. Won't need to scoop any up from the river to purify it for at least another couple days.

I keep checking in. A couple of times, I hear a distant scratching sound in my ear. I report this to Yarwick, and pray it's not a malfunction of my cochlear implant. "We're showing green on our side, Ares," she says. "But we'll keep looking into it. If LOS then you know what to do." With a loss of signal, I'll use the radio they sent me. Not as secure, but better than nothing.

One hill after the next until sundown. I build another shelter, far enough away from the river that any patrol boats passing in the night won't see me. I lay down, I sleep, I wake up at 0400 hours to my watch vibrating, I climb out of my shelter, destroy it, and move on. It's a brighter, warmer day, almost fifty degrees Fahrenheit. Good day for a hike.

Check in with the Nest. "Good morning, Ares," Yarwick replies. "Everything's good on our end. You're making good time."

"Affirmative. At this rate, we should be able to make that kitty-cat date by the end of the week."

"I told Persephone about that. She's holding you to it."

"You named your cat Persephone?"

I can hear the smile in her voice. "At least I *have* a cat, and didn't have to steal my neighbor's."

"Me and Eddie have a special bond."

"I'm sure you…hang on. Update coming in from SIGINT."

While I wait, I finish my meal. Breakfast is a prescribed meal of flavorless paste and half a ration bar, washed down with a quart of water. Everything has been planned out, down to the last calorie. The Law of the Six P's: Pre-Planning Prevents Piss-Poor Performance.

I look over at the Stanovoy mountains. The tops are snowcapped. I have a sudden mental image of Sophia traversing mountains just like that, escorting POWs out of France.

Then Yarwick is back in my ear. "Ares, Nest. We've locked down that transmission problem, I think. SIGINT says there was a solar flare earlier, he thinks it caused the distortion, maybe the noises you've been hearing." She means *Wainwright says*. He's in the room with her, but we use no real names over comms. "The satellite was having a problem, but we're showing green now."

"Copy that, Nest. Tell SIGINT I said thanks. Ares is on the move. Out."

Put the water bottle away. Take a look at my surroundings to make sure I haven't left any traces of my presence. Then I move on. Hill after hill, mile after mile. Yeah, it's a nice day for a hike.

*

At dusk, I finally come within sight of the ferry service. It's a boat dock along the widest part of the Amur River. I keep in concealment beyond the trees and scan the area with my spotter's scope. The dock holds two leisure yachts, both of them Lazzara 80 Sky Lounges. Big enough for eight passengers each, a small deck at the rear and sides for sightseeing. I see a sign that reads *Tidov Obsluzhivaniye Lodok*: Tidov Boat Service. There's a refueling station attached to the dock, as well as a small house, presumably the offices of the family that owns it. There's one gravel road leading up to the place, and an old silver Toyota truck parked at the entrance.

I see only one person out and about. It's a tall, skinny, bald man. Looks like he's refueling one of the boats. Someone hollers to him from behind the house where I can't see. He nods, and walks away from the dock.

"Nest, Ares," I say. "I'm at Rendezvous A."

"Copy, Ares. We see that," Yarwick says.

"I've surveyed the area. Looks clear."

"Copy that. You are good to make contact. We have called the boat service and let them know you are en route and they are prepared to take you to Rendezvous B."

"Understood, Nest. Moving to make contact. Guess you can go ahead and tell Talon that all's well, and I should be at Rendezvous B in forty-eight hours as planned. Over."

"Copy that, Ares. Will do."

I've been on my stomach for twenty minutes, surveilling the area. Now I do a push-up and come up to a kneeling position, giving the area one more looksee. I see a group of steel barrels marked as fuel all clustered together near a supply shed. Six of them. I mull something over.

Never walk into a situation you can't walk out of.

I scout crawl over to the barrels, smell their contents to make sure they actually contain fuel. They do.

Ten minutes later I move out of the forest and step onto the road. I walk right up to the house. The Russian family inside knows I'm coming, CIA handlers ought to have contacted them, so they should expect a guy in full tactical kit. The handlers say they've used these guys several times before. Their services are above reproach.

Night is setting in when I walk up the steps and knock on the door. A curtain in a window to my left is parted, and a face peeks through. Then the door opens and I'm facing a rough-looking woman with gray hair, half as tall as me, with a scowl that shows disapproval for all that she sees.

"My name is Sergei," I say.

"Of course, it is," she snorts. The quickness of her reply indicates to me that my Russian is as smooth and conversational as I hoped.

"I understand you can help me."

She sizes me up, then pushes the door open wider. "Come in. We have coffee if you want it."

"Thank you," I say, stepping inside. "I would like that."

Inside the house, there are three men. One is a gray-headed fellow in a lounger watching an old box TV. He looks at me critically. He could be the old woman's husband or brother, can't tell. There's a man about my age on a sofa, and next to him is a boy, looks about sixteen or seventeen years old. The sofa they're on looks like it came from the eighties, plaid, it's frayed and with stuffing poking out of the cushions. On the floor is a dog, a mutt of some kind that was panting when I walked up, but is now holding its breath and staring at me. They're all staring at me. My rifle hangs from its sling, and I slide it around to my back.

"Hello," I say.

None of them speak to me. The boy waves at me.

"Get us some coffee," the woman says to the man on the sofa. To the old man, "Vladimir, get the boat ready. And take your medicine." To me, "This way."

She conducts me into a kitchen with split linoleum floors and cracked walls. Smells like a slaughterhouse. Through the kitchen and into a door on screaming hinges, then into a cramped office with a small desk. Probably the place where she tells tourists her prices. There's a calendar on the wall that's up to date, and beside it a newspaper with Putin's face on the front page with the headline NEW TROUBLES FOR PUTIN. Someone has drawn a clown face on Putin. Other news clippings around it are highly political, many of them about Putin's most recent political adversary.

A backwoods Russian family with strong political leanings. They obviously despise the current leadership. The CIA probably didn't have trouble getting their help. Wonder how the CIA found— oh. I think I have my answer already. The old woman sits at her desk and pulls a cloth off of an expensive computer monitor. She takes a seat at a keyboard and starts typing away. Seems this old dog knows new tricks. CIA probably found her on some online forum bitching about Putin. I've heard of that brand of recruitment. Never seen it, though. When I recruited in Afghanistan, it was always in the field.

"Have a seat," she tells me.

I obey. There's only one other seat in the office, and it's on the other side of the desk from where she sits. And there's a cat sitting on it. I push it off and take the seat, feeling strangely like I'm at a job interview. I drop my gear bag to the floor beside me.

Just before she starts talking, there's that distant scratching in my ear again. Guess Wainwright didn't lock it down, after all.

Then, I hear a distant voice. No, *voices*. Sounds like shouting. It's all inside my ear, so the old woman can't hear it. It's there and then it's gone.

"I can take you up the river seventy kilometers," she says flatly. She turns the computer monitor a bit so I can see it better, and she points to the map. It looks like it's from Google Earth, and she scrolls up the river using a wireless mouse. "After that, you're on your own. My husband and son cannot risk going farther."

"Why not?" I ask.

Someone steps into the office behind me and my hand slips to my pistol on my hip. But it's only the middle-aged man from the sofa bringing me my coffee. I accept it with thanks, and he hangs out by the door. I don't see a gun on him, but his shirt is untucked and hanging over his waistline, so it could be concealed. The woman doesn't appear afraid. Not of me, and not of getting caught helping foreign spies. They're either very good at this or very stupid.

"Because," Grandma Tidov goes on, "there are increased patrols that now extend out from the town of Tsiolkovsky. Farther than ever before. And drones."

"Do those drones ever come up this way?"

"Rarely. And they're not a problem for us as long as we're just ferrying tourists. But when we have delicate packages such as yourself, we must be extra careful. Even the *stal'noy'os'minogi'lyudi* have been known to push that far."

That one word catches my ear. Must be a local portmanteau, like blending *breakfast* and *lunch* to make *brunch*. Takes me a second to work my head around it. "*Stal'noy'os'minogi'lyudi*. Octopuses…of steel?"

"The Steel Octopus Men," she simplifies by speaking slowly and choosing different words. "That's what my grandson calls them. The flying men with the two steel tentacles hanging from their bodies."

I look into my coffee, then up at her. "Flying men."

"Yes."

The Tianshi drones. I suppose they might look like men in suits from high in the air. "How often do you see them?"

"All hours of the day."

"Do they ever come down this way?"

Grandma Tidov shrugs fractionally. "Only once before, at night. Vladimir saw them outside our window with his night-vision scope. Three of them."

Conducting test flights? Or are they already completed and they're running reconnaissance missions? A bit of both, maybe?

"And seventy kilometers is—" I wince at the scratching in my ear. It's followed by a high-pitched whine. A voice. Yarwick's voice. There and gone. I thought I caught the word *coming* in there, but there was too much static. I'm a bit alarmed, but I try to keep my face even while I look at Grandma Tidov. "Seventy kilometers is the absolute farthest you can take me?"

"It is. My son here," she points to the man by the door, "and my husband have risked a lot for your people in the past, but this is really pushing it. I have a business to tend to, and it doesn't take a genius to realize if people want to get in and out of the country from this region, *this* is the easiest way to do it, up the Amur River. It leads all the way to Blagoveshchensk."

I nod. "Well, I'm grateful to you and your family."

"Just make sure your bosses show their gratitude. The last time, our payment came very late. I would appreciate—"

I don't hear the rest of her words, because there comes another loud screech inside my ear canal. I try to mask my discomfort so neither the old woman nor her son will see it on my face. There's static. Harsh static. Then, it clears up. Just a little. And through it all I hear Yarwick's alarmed voice. "—you hear me? *Ares, do you read!* You have to get out of there! We're burned! Repeat, we are *burned*! They will be coming for you!"

Now I can no longer be discreet. I interrupt Grandma Tidov by standing up and calling out, "Nest, this is Ares. Say again. Over."

"What's going on?" asks Grandma Tidov.

"We are burned! Get out of there!" Yarwick screams. "They may be coming for you! We...*shit!* Wainwright, run! Get the fuck—!"

"What's going on? Nest? *Nest!* Say status!"

Grandma Tidov rises slowly from her chair. "What is happening?"

I start to answer, but just then the window behind Grandma Tidov shatters and her head explodes.

8

Her skull fragments and brain matter spray across my chest and her son's face. I drop to the ground. Her son screams and runs for his grandmother's corpse. I yell at him, tell him to get down, but he doesn't listen and before he even reaches her he dances like a puppet when the bullets rip through him. He drops on top of his mother.

Bullets tear through the walls, the desk, the ceiling. The world erupts into chaos and the walls are shredded by high-caliber rounds as I crawl on my stomach out of the room, through the kitchen, and into the living room, where I find Grandpa Tidov on his knees, holding his grandson in his lap and screaming while windows shatter all around him. The grandson's throat has been opened wide by a bullet, and one of his eyes has exploded. The grandfather doesn't seem to notice the bullet wound to his own arm, nor the bullets ripping through the walls, nor me shouting at him.

"Vladimir!" I scream. He's sobbing, kissing his grandson's forehead, combing the poor boy's hair like he's got to groom him for some important event. Maybe a school dance. "Is there another way out of here? *Vladimir!*" But he's not listening. The bullets are shattering his whole world. I don't hear the report of the rifles, probably because they're all silenced.

They want me alive, but they'll take dead if they have to, I'm sure. They're not tossing in grenades because they need proof. My corpse has to be relatively intact so they can show it to the world. I don't know who they are exactly, but I know what they want. Yarwick said we're burned. We've been found out. We sprung a leak somewhere. They knew I was coming and they struck at me and the Nest simultaneously to make sure we couldn't warn each other. An amazing coordinated attack in two separate countries.

The old man continues weeping and I stay on my stomach with the sofa between me and the wall. Thirty seconds after the assault began, the barrage finally ceases. No more bullets, no more smashed windows or walls, only the wail of a heartbroken grandfather. I wait in stillness, trying to listen to my approaching enemy, but I can't hear it over Vladimir's screams.

"Vladimir! Be quiet!"

He's not listening. Who can blame him. His world is ending.

I've got my assault rifle in hand and it's aimed at the front door. I'm trying to listen to the footsteps of the enemy that I know must be surrounding me. Vladimir won't stop wailing.

"Vladimir! Hush! Please! They're coming—"

Suddenly, he flings his grandson's corpse to the ground. He struggles with bad knees, gets to his feet, and runs into another room. He's in there rummaging around for five seconds, then comes running out, double-barrel shotgun in hand, screaming like mad and going for the door.

"Vladimir! Stop! Don't go out—"

He flings the door open and I hear him get no more than five steps before the shotgun booms. He's still screaming. I can hear his voice jump as silenced bullets tear through him. He's still screaming. He fires again. Still screaming.

I take advantage of Vladimir's sacrifice. As soon as he dashed outside, I began looking around for something flammable. I have the lighter from my survival kit already in my hand. I grab a shirt from a dirty laundry hamper sitting by the sofa. I put the lighter to it, wait for it to catch fire. Outside, Vladimir has just stopped screaming. I stuff the flaming shirt halfway into an empty beer bottle I find on the coffee table and take one look out the nearest window. I don't have to shatter the windows, they did that for me.

First, I toss out a flash-bang grenade. Wait for it to go off. As soon as I hear the bang, I fling the flaming shirt out into the night. I wait to hear it shatter. It's a distant sound, just barely there. I think my aim was correct.

Now I spring up to one knee, take aim in the general direction I threw the bottle, and let out a short, controlled burst. Then a second burst. Now a third. On the fourth burst, it finally happens. The fuel barrels sprung a leak and at least some of the fuel hit the flaming shirt. The resultant boom shakes the floorboards underneath me and sends red and orange flames into the treetops. My enemies should all be wearing night-vision goggles this time of night, they're probably blinded by both the flash-bang and the flames, and even if not they'll be rocked by the sudden explosion.

Surprise, speed, and violence of action. I've given them the surprise.

I wait five seconds for the flames to simmer down, then pull my own NVGs over my head. Switching them on turns the whole world into monochrome green. I sweep out the front door in a low crouch, see my first two targets, who were closing in on the dead Vladimir when the explosion went off. They're kitted up, full combat gear. They're tearing off their NVGs, struggling to regain their sight as I plug the first one in the chest, center mass, then tap him in the head. The next one gets his gun up but my bullets tear through his rifle, arm, hand, and finally his head. They both drop like marionettes with their strings cut.

Voices behind me. Someone shouting into a radio. I turn, sweep the barrel right to left, and tap another operator ten yards away, also blinded by the explosion.

I sweep my rifle around, scanning the rest of the yard. The docks. The corners of the house. Ignoring the intense heat coming from the destroyed barrels. I see movement. I turn and fire at the guy coming around the side of the house. His silenced MAC-10 machine pistol fires wildly as he twists, and drops to the ground. The partner behind him gets tapped next, and drops similarly.

A gnat zips by my ear. Someone firing on me from an unknown position. I've made it across the yard and take cover behind a tree. I peek out from cover. I see two enemies running to take cover behind the Toyota. They have goggles on. Must've been on the opposite side of the house from the explosion when it happened, because they don't seem blinded, they're moving just fine.

I let the rifle hang from my side, and transition to my pistol. It has a suppressor and subsonic rounds, it'll be more difficult for them to pinpoint my location. I extend the pistol at arm's length and hug the suppressor against the tree for greater stability. I see them sneak peeks around the side of the truck. I don't fire. They've lost me. I need them to come out from cover so I can tap them. One of them comes running out from cover while the other one props his rifle up on the hood of the truck, waiting to give his partner cover should I reveal myself.

I take aim at the guy behind the truck, squeeze off a round. The bullet shaves his head on the right side, snaps him backward, and he drops. The guy running ahead has no idea his backup man is dead. There's too much noise between his own footsteps and the flames crackling in the tree branches. He has no hope of hearing my silenced shots. I tag him five seconds later, just as he's taking cover behind a woodpile.

I'm shaking. Watching the world from outside my own body, letting the training and muscle memory do the work, visiting the Drifting Place. I look for any sign of movement. The wind rattles the branches. Above me, clear skies. Orion watches on in silent approval. Nothing, no other movement. I stand up slowly—

And that's when I hear it. Footsteps. They're trying to move carefully. I turn, just in time to see him. An enemy, coming around a tree. He knows I'm out here and he's looking for me. He's turning in my direction. We see each other at the exact same time. He's faster with his aim. His weapon goes from his left and sweeps right, coming around to my face. I bat his pistol away, let the shot whisper past my head. He wraps a meaty fist around my pistol's suppressor and pulls. I let go with one hand and hammer-fist his face and his NVGs go flying off. He grunts, but hangs on, and smashes my hand up against a tree trunk and then expertly twists the weapon from my hand.

Disarmed, I wrap my whole left arm around his gun hand while delivering elbows into his face. I pry his pistol loose. Try to catch it. Lose it in the darkness. Now we're scrambling, pushing and pulling at each other's clothing. At some point he rips off my goggles, flings them away. I head-butt him. His hand goes for something. Another weapon probably. I wrap my arms around him, pinning that arm to his side, then throw one leg out in front of him for *o goshi*. I send him flying to the ground. He lands on his back and I scramble to get on top of him.

He's stronger than me. Pushes me off of him as soon as I try to get into mount position. We roll on the ground, clawing and punching and elbowing. No one's coming to help him, and we're making enough noise to attract attention for fifty yards around, so I'm assuming I've got all his pals. It's just us now. Just him and me.

We slide downhill, rolling end over end, then come apart. We see each other in the moonlight. We both scramble back to our feet. I trip over a log and he gains the advantage, wrapping his arms around my neck in a clinch and delivering a knee into my gut. All my wind leaves me. I'm dazed. But the training takes over and I press my fists into his hip to prevent the next knee, which I know is coming. I let him attempt two more, then reach over the top of his arms, grab his left hand, and yank it into a wrist lock. I yank it hard enough that I hear a crack. I've snapped his wrist. His knees buckle. I kick one of those knees until he's knelt down in front of me, with his back facing me, then I seize his neck in a rear choke.

I know the feeling of a good choke. I know when I've got it sunk in properly. I have this one. He must know it, too. In a last desperate attempt he's reaching back to claw at my face, but he can't reach it. I squeeze tighter. Tighter. See these hands. See them. They know their work.

Finally his body sags. One more spasm of resistance, and then he goes completely limp. I drop his lifeless body to the forest floor.

I'm shaking even more now. Panting heavily. And I'm sitting and watching and listening. I don't know if I got them all. No way to tell from here. Based on their operations and skills, they're not amateurs. These weren't thugs. My guess is Spetsnaz. Russian special forces. This is bad. This is so bad.

"Ares to Nest. Come in."

Nothing. Silence.

I snap my fingers beside my ear three times and say aloud, "Switch channels." I hear a click. "Nest, Ares. Do you read? Over."

Nothing.

I wait and I listen to the forest. I check my body, making sure I haven't been hit. It's totally possible to take a critical hit by a bullet and not know it until you faint. Then you bleed out and die, never knowing what happened. I find a single tear in the flap of my jacket where a bullet smacked into it, mushrooming and embedding itself in the middle layer of armor.

But I can't wait forever. There has to be a backup team waiting to hear from them, probably no farther than half a mile from here. I can't take either of the boats, they'll be looking for that. Grandma Tidov said there were drones in the area these days, and Steel Octopuses in the skies.

That means I'm on foot for now.

I don't have time to give the Tidovs any kind of respectful burial or sendoff, or to search my enemies' corpses for anything useful. I have to move now.

I scramble back up the hill, do a brief search in the dark for my pistol and NVGs. I stumble upon the pistol, but not the goggles. Can't stay and look for them any longer. I rush back into the house, pass the bloody bodies of the Tidovs, who sacrificed everything for me. Maybe for some money, too, but also for me. I pick up my gear bag and I turn away from the macabre scene, leaving all the dead and all the ghosts where they are, and head deeper into the woods.

*

"Nest, this is Ares," I say into the emergency radio. "I'm on the move. Was ambushed at Rendezvous A but I made it out. Eight enemies neutralized. Require instructions. What's your status? Over."

No reply.

I'm not even trying to keep silent, just trying to create distance between me and the Tidov docks. Crashing through branches and vines and bushes. I pause every forty or fifty yards to take cover behind a tree, aim my weapon at the darkness, listen for enemy footsteps or drones or anything else. I look up at the stars through the forest canopy. The Chinese defector said the Tianshi suits were nearly silent. If they're above me right now, I probably wouldn't know it.

Then I turn and dash again. I check my watch, it shows I've traveled two miles. Not nearly enough. The perimeter will be at least five. And there aren't many roads to cover. Drones can do the searching for them in the forested areas. At least five miles. Gotta make it outside that radius. Time to really move. No stops, no meals or water, and no checking in with the Nest. If they're there, they'll get back with me. If not, it's all the same. Gotta make distance.

Come back to me, Sophia said to me. It was not a request.

It's hard to see without the NVGs, but my eyes adjust to the darkness well enough, and moonlight guides me. I think I hear an engine grumbling in the distance, and some shouting, but I can't be sure. No time to stop and listen, just keep moving. One foot in front of the other. Muscles burning from the sustained effort. No time to worry

113

about cramps. One foot in front of the other. Up one hill after another, glancing up at the skies, looking for Steel Octopus. Lungs burning from the cold air. Temperature has dropped to about thirty-one. Can't worry about that now.

One foot in front of the other.

At one point I pause to send a message using my watch. It allows me to send e-mails to a fire-and-forget account set up for this mission. It also has a function that gives me a special connection to the CRyPto-DEX, a specialized instant-messenger for CIA use only. It posts messages on an encrypted forum. I have one link, and that's to the Nest. The second after the messages are seen, all traces of it are instantly scrubbed, and will not be hosted on any other server between them.

No response. I move on.

There's definitely an engine grumbling somewhere nearby. Probably a road off to my right somewhere, beyond a row of hills. I won't be going in that direction. My legs are really burning now, but I will them onward. The alternative is death. And I'll quit tomorrow.

It's just after midnight when I finally reach the goal I set for myself. Five miles. I made it five miles at a steady run, moving up and down hills, pushing through briars and brambles, and now I kneel beside a tree to catch my breath. And listen.

I check my watch for any messages or e-mails. Nothing.

"Ares…to Nest," I pant. "Come in. Come in, Nest. Do you read? Over."

I'm alone. Not even Orion is in the sky now. He's moved on to other business.

And now, because good enough is never good enough in SOG, I have to keep moving. Five miles was the minimum I set for myself. Now I have to get up and push farther on. I don't have to run now, I can be slow and calculating, watchful and careful. I just have to keep moving. I've gone sixty hours without sleep before. It's crushing, and it makes you far less alert, and you will hallucinate, but if I have to do it I will. I'll move until I feel safe enough to build camp.

"Get up, Adamson," I huff. "You're not done yet. Sophia's waiting." I push myself up, and get to it.

There are no more sounds of grumbling vehicles. After an hour of careful movement, I come across a bubbling brook. I take the opportunity to refill all my water bottles and drop purifier capsules into them, then put them in my gear bag and keep moving. I see a blinking red light far up in the sky, a plane so high I can't hear it. Still, I take cover, just in case it's been deployed to scan the area for me. It wouldn't surprise me. They have to have found their dead pals by now. They know they're not dealing with an amateur. They won't make any mistakes the second time.

I can't let there be a second time.

One foot in front of the other. Onward and upward, until 0300 hours. I come to a tree that's been uprooted. It's fallen over a rocky overhang, dead branches and leaves have accumulated around it, forming a kind of cave. I slip inside, deciding this is better than a debris hut. This I don't have to build or break down. So I just sit and listen.

"Nest, this is Ares. Do you read? Over."

Nothing.

"Nest, do you read? Come back."

I keep trying until I fall asleep.

Oie

Fini à la pisse. That is what you are, Orson. *Fini à la pisse.*

These old hands can do nothing. These old words spoken from these old lips can do nothing. As Orson removes the last of the drawers in my armoire—the armoire my husband bought me fifty years ago, and has been following me from one retirement home to another—I look on helplessly. The bags of secret treasures, which are the representation of the last vestiges of control I have in this world, are seized. Honestly I don't even know why I have them. Ziploc bags of soap bars and tiny shampoo bottles taken from the restrooms when the orderlies were looking away to let a lady piss with some dignity. Bags of unused syringes and empty pill bottles palmed when Lizzy, the pharmacist, was talking to someone on the phone.

"How many times, Sophia?" he says exasperatedly. Orson holds one of the bags in front of my face, like holding up the evidence to a dog that's been digging into the trash. "How many times we gonna do this same song and dance?"

"Those are my things," I say defiantly.

"No, they're not. They belong to other people who—"

"They weren't using them."

"Not at the time," he says.

"Just leave it, Orson. It's not hurting anyone. Just leave it."

Orson starts to say something, then sighs and shakes his head. He tosses the last of the bags into a cardboard box and picks it up. Heads for the door. "I'll have to report this to your daughter."

"Threatening to tell on me? Like I'm some child."

"She pays the bills, Soph. Gotta tell her what's goin' on. Don't take it out on me. Now, it's past bedtime."

"Like I'm some child," I say again.

Orson gives one of those *why me* looks and surrenders. He asks if I need help getting in bed and I say I can manage. The bed lowers and raises with the press of a button. I'm tech savvy and he knows this. Even so, he helps me onto the bed. I hug his neck reluctantly, and as he lowers me onto it, he does not feel the feather-light touch of my hand at his hip. I palm his magnetic ID card.

He says he'll be back to check on me in an hour. He flips out the light and steps out into the hallway and shuts the door, taking my goodies with him.

Orson only flipped off the main light, there's still the bedside lamp that's switched on. I press the button beside the bed and lower it. Slowly, gingerly, I raise up and sit on the corner of the mattress. I stare at the black-and-white checkered tile floor for I don't know how long. My head is clear. It's been clear for a few days now, in fact. I still have good days. Lots of them.

Been wondering about Nathan. Been thinking about Henrietta's birthday. Wonder if Chloe and Zoe will bring her by. Wonder when they'll start skipping visitations because they know I'll just forget a lot of them anyway. Then I'll be alone and I won't even know it. Somehow that's worse than the other.

My hand has already slipped underneath the mattress and pulled out the cell phone. Orson the *sous-merde* didn't find that. Got lots of caches, and not all of them are in this room. Some are in the willow trees and the rosebushes, some are hidden inside the hollow metal legs of the Naugahyde chairs in the theater room. One is in a metal lunch box I dropped just three steps into the lake, behind the big boulder where George and Eloise go to smooch. That was eight years ago that I planted the lunch box. Wonder if it's still there.

I flip open the phone. It belongs to James the orderly, and I've seen him use it plenty enough times, punching in the password right in front of me without a care. And why should he care? I'm just the little old hen that few people like and no one besides Nate and my family visits.

The phone has a quarter battery life. Better use it wisely.

The iPad is mine, there's nothing wrong with me having it, so Orson left that. Chloe and Zoe spent an afternoon teaching me how to use it so I can Skype with them, marveling at how well I do with modern tech, perhaps not realizing my mind was trained to adapt to changes in technology. Once I showed I was proficient, they started Skyping me all the time. Potentially more reason to suspect they will stop visiting me in person altogether? It requires more investigation. I make a mental note to make light inquiries when next I see my daughter and grand-daughter. A mental note I will, in all likelihood, forget.

I connect to Rose Lawn's Wi-Fi and I pull up Google. I try a search. My fingers don't always obey—the ring finger keeps jumping out, unbidden, tapping the screen and ruining my search. Eventually I pull up what I want. Reports on the embassy attack in South Africa. I find the same picture as before, download it to my image file, then spend time zooming in on the man in the gray, two-button Brioni suit, with the white shirt and black Marinella tie. The man with the large forehead and droopy left eye, with a slightly wolfish grin. Yes…that grin.

Then I do another search. It takes me ten minutes to find the right national archives—every major country has their own online, all of them detailing the official records of veterans, missing in action, draft records, casualty lists, D-Day footage, all that. For a moment, I am confused by all the options, and temporarily forget what I'm doing. Then it all comes back to me. I have been to the British archives before, and I now scroll through the section on operations that involved aid from the French Resistance. A picture of Paris the day the Germans marched into the city and took over the Louvre. There is a picture I have never forgotten. A picture of a man with a wolfish grin. Besides one scandalous video, this is the only one I've ever seen of him.

I compare the two pictures: the one in my image file and the one from the archives. One blind eye and another one going that way is not exactly ideal for making a match, but you would be a fool if you didn't see it.

The old man at the embassy and the young soldier in the Paris picture are the same person.

Now I look at the embassy story again. I try reading it, even though reading from a computer screen often gives me a headache. The story, which FOX News did not detail in full on the telly, is elaborated online. A multinational group of surveillance techs, assembled from China, Russia, Ukraine and the Philippines, were injured during a stay at a Russian embassy in Pretoria. The men and women in the video are part of that surveillance team, called Arumush.

I compare the photos again. I look at the seventeen-year-old soldier, who would be ninety-five if he survived this long, standing next to a Panzer III tank, smoking a cigarette and laughing at the general mayhem he and his friends caused by invading Paris. He would go on to rape women, girls, and boys.

But it was not during this time that I encountered him. When I first caught on to him, I was already with the Service de Documentation Extérieure et de Contre-Espionnage, hunting down Germans who had worked in the camps and escaped justice for the horrors they did there, and who might be involved with other nations in postwar profiteering, using their skills as mercenaries.

Herr Wilhelm Vogel came from a wealthy family, and was using both it and the skills he learned in the War to undermine operations the world over. A security firm, mercenaries, freelance terrorists at times. He disappeared three times during the decades that SDECE hunted him, and when I left the agency, he was still missing.

"I always assumed you were dead by now, Herr Vogel," I say to the room lit only by a single lamp. "But I guess you are like me, still hanging on. Except you're still working, aren't you, *Bite Molle*."

Soft Prick. I forget who gave him that nickname, but I remember the grainy surveillance video, provided by a Russian mole working for us, that showed him in a Moscow hotel, unable to get an erection with two prostitutes, yet when they left was able to masturbate furiously by slapping himself while looking into the mirror and fingering his asshole.

I giggle at the memory.

Herr Vogel. You knew we were on to you. You knew we were getting close. And every time you smelled us, you went dark. Twice I came close to you. Once you spotted me in the alley as you darted away into the winding streets of Marseille, vanishing into the fog and the wafting smells of Merguez from the street vendors. You sent a taunting note to us later. What was it you called me? Ah, *oui*, "that French tart who sniffed my ass as I slipped away." Very bold of you to put it in writing, and in your own cursive, no less. Our analysts made a lot of that.

"How is it you're still operational?" I ask the face on my screen.

How is that possible? And why would you be, after all this time? For God's sakes, you're almost a hundred, what else could you possibly want? The world is for young people, not us. We had our time. We had our War. What could possibly motivate you to keep going?

Is it your soft prick? Was it never able to give you a family? Without family, were you left with no adored ones, no children, no one to inherit the wealth of your parents, so you make your work into your family? Poor man. Poor, poor *Bite Molle*.

A knock on the door. Orson steps in without waiting for my response. I hide the phone under my ass just in time. "Sophia, time for bed. I already said."

I nod and turn off the iPad. "All right," I say.

Orson gives me an *attagirl* smile and shuts the door.

I lay here a moment, thinking about what I'll do about Herr Vogel. What *can* I do?

I suddenly wish Nathan were here. I could tell him this. He would understand. My girls wouldn't. They never lived the life. They never played the Game. But Nathan would understand. If only he were here.

There's something else I can do, though. It is a bit bold, but then, that is how the Game is played, is it not? I take out the phone and lie in bed. I turn the iPad back on and go searching for a number. Doesn't take as long as I thought it would. I dial the number. A man answers politely and in the most elegant French. He asks how he may direct my call. "*L'oie comme son gander,*" I say.

"*Pardon?*" he says.

I repeat it once more, then hang up. Will it reach the right ears? Is it even possible?

I look at the phone. I had better hide it before I fall asleep and wake up in the morning forgetting why it's here. I stuff it under the mattress, then shut my eyes and listen to the wind against the window and the shouts of someone losing their mind down the hall. Sounds like Ethel Gruber having another episode. Wonder where Nathan is.

Who's Nathan?

9

"Ares, Nest. How do you read?"

The voice comes from far away. At first I think I'm dreaming it, but as I rise up through the levels of sleep and become increasingly aware of where I am, the voice gets closer. I was having strange dreams. I was in an ocean that was only knee deep, and I was trying to move silently through it because I knew that somewhere in those waters was a large creature that swims fast and attacks things that move. And Mom was there. And Derek, my brother. They were crying out to me. They needed me to hurry before the creature in the black waters found them, but if I hurried too fast, it would find me.

Now the dream drains from me. I recognize its absurdity. I'm awake, but I keep my eyes shut in case I've been captured, and then slowly open them to see bars of sunlight coming through the trees. And I hear the voice calling out again. Yarwick's voice. Not from my emergency radio, but from inside my ear. "Ares, do you read? This is the Nest. Come back. Over."

My head snaps up from where it's been resting against the cave wall and I sit up straight. "This is Ares. I read you, Nest. What's going on? Say status."

"First say yours. Are you okay? Are you safe?"

"I'm free and clear. I was ambushed at Rendezvous A by a special forces unit. My ride is burned, everyone at Rendezvous A is dead. Repeat, our local contacts are dead."

"*All* of them?"

"Affirmative, Nest. I barely got out myself. Eight enemies neutralized on the way out. It was a close thing. Over."

"Jesus Christ, Ares…" I hear relief, sadness, and amazement all woven into her voice. Glad that I'm alive, sad about the Tidovs, and astounded I made it out of there. "What's your present location?"

"You mean you don't have it?"

"Negative. Your GPS signal was unique and logged only at our original Nest site. All that's gone now."

"What the hell happened?"

"We got raided," she says. "Can't discuss it all now. Suffice it to say I got out alive, along with SIGINT, politics and systems." She means Wainwright, our PAG specialist Kozner, and our systems man Emil Drucker. "We lost everyone else."

"Lost?"

"Dead. The guys raiding our hotel were a hit team. We had two guards stationed in plainclothes downstairs at the lobby, one of them got a warning up to us before the hit team came up the stairs. We grabbed a bit of our gear on our way out. It was a close thing for us, too. Took us a while to make sure we were safely away and reconnect with the satellite relaying this signal."

I'm thinking about the members of our team that didn't make it. See their faces. "Are we sure *this* channel is clean?"

"We are. We've jumped to a different satellite and we're using a different coding sequence—different satellites, not the Company's— and bouncing the signal around a bit more, so you may experience some delay in our responses."

"How did this happen?" I ask, looking around at the forest, up at the sky, searching for any sign I've been spotted.

"The team's location was somehow leaked. We're not sure how, but there are people looking into it. The interference you've been hearing was likely them hacking into our satellite link with you, listening in on comms and waiting for you to signal us when you were at the rendezvous. We've moved to an alternate location, that's all I can tell you right now."

"Sorry to hear all that, Nest. What are my orders?"

"It depends. What's your overall condition?"

"I'm good. A little tired. Lost my NVGs." I look at the hole in my jacket where the bullet came close. "But otherwise good."

"Then you are to continue as planned," she says. "Make it to Rendezvous B by whatever means and make contact with Talon."

I blink. Certain I heard that wrong. "Nest, say again? You want me to continue as planned?"

"That's affirmative, Ares." Her voice is rigid. I can tell she doesn't like it, either.

"Nest, I'm burned. I'm exposed out here. My ride upriver is gone. And I should tell you that before our pals at the boat service got aced, they informed me that there are patrols of drones and what they call 'Steel Octopuses' around the area." She has to understand that if I keep going to Tsiolkovsky, there's going to be increased security around the Vostochny Cosmodrome. We've been burned. They didn't get all of us, and that's the problem. They know I'm still out here. Or that multiple someones are out here.

"We understand that, Ares," Yarwick says patiently. "But Command has made it clear that you are to complete your objective. They've stressed that we need to know what's going on there." Then, after a few seconds, she says, in a confidential voice, "The people that raided us were Chinese. If yours were Russian special forces, then there is definitely collusion between the two actors on this. We may have been penetrated from all sides, exposed to all of them. We need to know how far this goes and what they're cooking up there, and how much we need to be worried."

I fight the urge to give the counterargument, to tell her that my presence here is a violation of international law. If I'm captured or killed, my body is evidence that the U.S. is conducting something they shouldn't be in areas they shouldn't be. Such an international incident could prompt Russia to show me off as proof to their allies as to why they *need* to be allied so close. It could increase their bond. This entire mission might actually backfire on us.

It was always a risk I would be captured, but we had the advantage before, when we thought no one knew I was here. Now that they know...

But it's not the job of someone like me to argue with my superiors. It's my job to follow orders. And besides, Yarwick's got enough trouble on her hands with at least three dead agents, worrying if she's going to be compromised again, and conferring with SAD and CIA directors on what the hell is going on. She doesn't need me adding another problem to the list. "Ares copies, Nest. I'm going to grab a quick breakfast, then drink a lot of water and massage my legs a bit. I did a lot of running, don't want a cramp. I should be under way in ten minutes."

"Copy that, Ares." She adds, "It's really good to hear you're okay."

"Can't give up, Nest. Still gotta have that kitty-cat date."

I hear a chuckle, but it dies quick. In a much more serious tone, she says, "There's something else."

123

I snort out a laugh. "Yeah? What else? I'm all ears."

"We've received intel that Karambit is in your region. He's left the Cosmodrome and been flown into an airfield near you, along with the rest of his Unit. His SVR hit squad."

I heave a sigh. "Beautiful."

"Are you still up for the op?" Yarwick asks. There's a part of her voice that makes me want to believe she wants me to say no, I can't take it, please extract me. That might be a fantasy on my part, an illusion from the masculine ego that wants to know a beautiful female somewhere cares about me.

"Ares is up for it, Nest."

A moment. Then, "Good to hear. Contact us once you' re on the move. I'll let you know how fluid things are on our end. Good luck out there. And…be careful, Ares."

There's a distant click, and now Yarwick is a thousand miles away again. Might as well be a million. I eat my breakfast, get good and hydrated, massage my legs thoroughly, then open up a map on my watch and review the terrain, the roads, the nearest settlements. Not much out here, just a few farmlands and small work towns built up around gold mines. There are two roads that run parallel, a dirt one and a highway. They both intersect a major railway. All of them cross over the Bolshaya Pyora River ninety miles ahead, where my goal, Tsiolkovsky, rests.

Now I'm up and on the move. Sophia speaks from a million miles away. *Do. Not. Let. Them. Win.*

Yes, *mademoiselle.*

*

The journey takes two days. Two days of hard going. Two days watching the skies, watching my six, waiting in hiding whenever I hear a plane or helicopter. I follow the highway for twenty miles. Twenty grueling miles through hills and brambles. The mountains in the north slowly grow larger. I check in with the Nest every couple hours. A rainstorm comes through and soaks me to the bone. I build a shelter in the rain, and sleep until my watch wakes me at 0400.

At dusk on the second day, I come within sight of a roadblock. I'm ensconced within shadow a quarter mile away from the highway, viewing it all through my spotter's scope. Three military jeeps with Russian Army markings block the road and are inspecting nine civilian vehicles. Two of the soldiers have search dogs sniffing around the cars. There's very few places in Amur Oblast for a person to go, just vast stretches of land separating one small settlement from another, and so they know I have few arteries through which to travel.

I slip deeper into the woods and move on. I check in with the Nest. They have nothing new to tell me, no news about our leak or what else is going on. This far out in the middle of nowhere, the world could be ending and I wouldn't even know it. I think of Sophia and remember what I'm fighting for, to maintain peace in the world she saved from the tyrant.

An hour after I discovered the roadblock, hear a blaring horn. The sound carries throughout the hills. A train. When I top the next hill, I look away in the north, and scan with my scope. A train is cutting straight through the forest, traversing a long unbroken ridge. The Trans-Siberian Railway, the same railway the Kim regime wants to connect their Trans-Korean Railway with, and which supposedly has been bringing conscripted scientists, military personnel, and advanced tech to the Cosmodrome.

I have a clear and easy path to follow now. Just have to keep out of sight.

It's a hard push west now. I make it another mile before full dark sets in. I find an outcropping that produces a natural overhang, so I don't have to build a shelter. I sip my water and eat my food. I sleep. I wake up at 0400, open my eyes slowly, and discover I'm exactly where I went to sleep. I stretch for a couple minutes, eat a quick meal, and try to cover any traces that I was here. I start to get under way again, and that's when I hear it.

It starts as a distant hum, but soon grows louder. Now it's a buzzing, like a swarm of bees moving all around me, just out of sight. I know that sound. I've heard it before in training. I look up, and at first there's nothing there. Then...movement. About twenty yards to my right is a drone, maybe half as long as I am tall, sweeping low over the treetops.

I grab my gear bag and haul ass around the nearest tree and press my back against it. I peek around the tree to see the drone's course. It's coming right towards me. My suit has layers that cover body heat, so my only concern should be movement. Movement will get you spotted every time, whether it's a machine or a human viewer. But I know that a surveillance drone has to have software to search for the human form. My camouflage may confuse that programming, and it may not. In wilderness training, when sneaking around solo, we're taught that you have to break up your human form to make it not so noticeable—both humans and machines are built to recognize the connections between head, chest, torso, and limbs, basically the cartoon outline on restroom doors. To thwart the human eye and form-seeking software, you have to not be in that shape.

When the drone sweeps nearby, I move slowly, slowly around to the other side of the tree. Just in case it suddenly zips overhead and gets a good angle on me, I turn my shoulders in the direction of the drone, tilt my head down, and put my left leg directly in front of my right leg, making myself a straight line when seen head-on or from above.

I calm my nerves by visiting the Drifting Place.

The drone does zig and zag around the area, and finally moves on, heading north.

If I had been spotted, it probably never would have left me alone, just climbed a hundred feet and hovered there and monitored me until the enemy converged on my location. Even so, it's time to make serious distance again. Time for another jog. Five miles at least.

*

By noon, I'm seven miles from where I started. No more drones, and no bad guys converging on me. Everything seems good. I'm still fifty miles away from Blagoveshchensk, the capital city, and I'm now seeing fewer and fewer trees to hide within.

This is where it gets very dangerous. I'm coming to the alpine meadows, where the altitude is too high for any trees to live and temperatures can drop below zero this time of year. It looks like those open places where they filmed *The Lord of the Rings*, when Aragorn and his pals were tracking the orcs that abducted Merry and Pippin. But with the bad news comes some good news. Zero trees means zero obstructions, and if I'm going to be out in the open anyway there's no reason to go slow and steady. I can move fast at night, sleep in low valleys during the day, and make it to Blagoveshchensk in two days.

So that's what I do. My suit keeps me warm enough while I'm traveling. And if Sophia could do it, I can do it. I'm lucky that the weather is with me, though. Temperature never dips below forty degrees, even at night. Maybe Orion is watching over me, after all.

The loneliness cannot be understated. It is a vast, beautiful, unending sea of silent hills, some of them green with stubborn grass and moss, but most of it just bald rock. These parts could pass for Mordor. I remember playing *Dungeons & Dragons* with Scott, and how whenever he was Dungeonmaster he would describe areas just like this for our characters to walk through. I used to think it was so romantic, just a band of merry adventurers in the middle of nowhere. Not so romantic when your balls are frozen stiff and you don't have a mage handy.

It seems as though the hills will never end, and every moment is another when a night-vision-equipped drone could spot me, and this has all been for nothing. I wonder about the people that helped plan this op with me that are now dead. I'm fighting for them now, too. I won't be quitting today.

Eventually, I come down in elevation, and there are a few more trees now. Saplings at first, then dwarf Siberian pines, then larger pines.

Lungs burning, I pause, and scope out a village in the distance. Grodekovo is an ancient settlement, they've been there since explorers first found this place, and archaeologists say there's reason to believe the settlement was first established a thousand years ago. That's what I found in my research, in any case. I give Grodekovo a wide berth, staying well away from the cattle that are fenced in around the outskirts.

It is almost morning the second day when I surmount the final hill, and come within sight of thin white lights that dot the horizon. Blagoveshchensk. I made it. Thank Christ.

127

Chad Huskins

10

Time to switch it up. I change into my civilian clothes, blue jeans, black shirt and brown leather jacket with hoodie, and stuff my tactical kit into my gear bag. I keep only the Glock, sound suppressor removed, and I tuck it in my waistline. From the medical kit I take out a tube of New-Skin. Liquid bandages that dry clean and clear and, if placed on the fingertips, leave no prints. It works well in places where tactical gloves might look out of place. My facial hair has gotten kind of scraggly over the last few days, so I use a razor and a mirror from the medical kit to trim it—I don't shave it completely off, just spruce it up into a bit of stylish scruff.

I click my teeth and open a channel. "Nest, Ares. I'm within view of the city and beginning approach. Is there any indication that the people that burned us released a picture of my face?"

"Ares, Nest," Yarwick says. "We have no confirmation one way or the other on that issue. You are advised to proceed with caution and conduct SDRs." She means surveillance detection runs, sometimes called dry-cleaning runs, because old spies used to pretend to get some dry-cleaning done while really watching their backs and trying to get any surveillance to reveal themselves. "And avoid cameras wherever possible."

"Copy," I say, shouldering my gear bag. "Moving in. Ares out." I click my teeth and end the transmission.

I stuff my passports into my jacket pocket and head into a city that's almost as old as the United States. The main highway leading into it is spotless, sleek, and clean. The city is one of the oldest in the Russian Far East, and yet it's well kept, very modern. Sleek low buildings, no skyscrapers, but they're all gleaming and reflect the greenery peppered throughout the city. There are plenty of well-manicured parks and benches, flourishing trees next to shimmering glass buildings, a perfect blend of quaint and contemporary.

There's a preponderance of classical Russian architecture, churches built with the famous onion-shaped domes and stone buildings that look as cold as fortresses. But there's also a subtle Chinese influence creeping in, what with a growing expatriate community and the city's leaning on border trade with China. The Amur River finds me here again. It cuts the land in half, and in the far,

far distance I can see the Chinese city of Heihe resting on the south bank. Looking at this place, with the two nations having two cities in such cozy proximity, facing each other across a slow-moving river, it's easy to see why this region may be chosen for a Russian-Chinese coalition program.

The Manchus conquered this whole area in the 1600s. The Russians fought back in bloody wars, and it only ended when the Manchus were pushed back and the Russians finally recognized their sovereignty over certain areas of the Amur in 1689. Those same Manchus helped form China. Once great enemies now powerful allies. The slow tide of history makes us all into strange bedfellows at one time or another.

My watch gives me a city map, complete with hotels, train schedules and bus stops. I wait for nightfall and catch a ride in a double-decker bus, paying with rubles and sitting quietly at the back. It takes me to a hotel called the Mechta. Small, family owned, nothing special about it besides a sauna and room service. I show my ID and the lady behind the counter puts it into her computer. I get a key and go to my room and lock the door. I don't stay long. I go right to the window and sneak out.

I walk a quarter-mile away to a public park and sit watching the Mechta from afar. Thankfully the temperature is about fifty degrees, quite pleasant. I watch the hotel for several hours through my scope, and I never once see a patrol car or any suspicious persons go in or out.

My fake ID is in the clear, I guess. And my face hasn't hit the police wire. For now.

"Nest, Ares. Completed an SDR, looks like my ID hasn't been leaked. I'm packing it in for the night. Over."

"Copy SDR, Ares. Get some good sleep. You'll need it."

I find a different place to stay, just in case there's a delay on my ID, the bad guys will have me registered at the Mechta first. I stay at the Hotel Asia and everything goes smoothly. So far, my Russian doesn't seem to be raising any eyebrows.

I give myself time to take a shower, just so I don't look like hell run over. I keep the scruff, just in case the mole at CIA did indeed spread my picture to SVR or FSB; the scruff might throw a few people off. Then I prepare the room. I put a chair up against the door, and pull the curtains to. All lights are turned off. I get dressed in full kit, just in case I'm ambushed in the night, and sleep beside the door with my weapons on me.

In the morning my watch wakes me up and I change back into civilian clothes and I'm out the door. "Nest, Ares. Checking in. Any updates for me? Specifically about the people that hacked our satellite and comms?"

"Good morning, Ares," Yarwick says. "That's a negative. SIGINT and systems are working on figuring out the attack vector, so far they've only found how the satellite was manipulated by someone infiltrating a Company computer—they used a complex spoofing system, though, and bounced their connection from one proxy server to another all around the globe, so it's gonna be difficult to pin down a source." Meaning it's pretty much never going to happen. "But that's not your concern right now. Something else has changed."

"Oh?"

"Yeah. Talon says Rendezvous B is compromised. Change of plans. She's coming to you. A hotel called Ichavoi, just outside of the airport. She's reserved a room there, number one-one-seven. ETA eight hours."

A check of the map on my watch shows my proximity to Ignatyevo Airport. "I can be there in two, depending on traffic. Gives me plenty o' time to complete a couple of dry-cleaning runs. Ares is mobile."

*

Dry-cleaning runs are essential parts of tradecraft. You have to make sure your trail is clear of all unfriendlies. The most common method is to hop in a car and circle the block, look in your rearview mirrors and see who keeps up with you. Also, look at the vehicles ahead of you. A good grab team will have a vehicle out in front of you, slowing down to keep you from going through stoplights while the other vehicles catch up, controlling where you go and when without you ever knowing it.

My watch directs me to a car rental shop, and I do exactly this. After circling the block in my rented Civic a few times, I hit the highway. It's a cloudy day. I don't hear thunder and I don't see rain, but the promise of both are there.

I stop at a restaurant to eat. I walk a shopping plaza, doing some window shopping but really looking into the windows to see the reflections of the people behind me. Checking to see if anyone's watching me. I'm all clear. Back in my car. A few circuits around the block, then I head south on a road called Shatemako. I waste time stopping and getting out, window shopping. Then at about 1100 hours, I finally head to my destination.

Planes roar overhead as they come in for a landing at the airport. The Ichavoi Hotel is a five-story building across from it. I survey the hotel from a parking deck across the street. Looking through my scope, I see all the exit points, all the means of approaching the parking lot, the public park on its south side. I need quick escape routes. There's always the chance Talon has become compromised and is being used as bait. It's possible I'm being set up. If so, I need to know ways out. An advance team could be at the Ichavoi Hotel already, but if they are, I see no signs.

I check my watch for nearby car rental shops. As you might expect being this close to an airport, there are several. I rent two cars from two different shops, drive them to exit points around the Ichavoi Hotel and park them. I leave the doors unlocked and the keys in the glove compartment. The Civic that brought me here I park at the far end of a marketplace called Anvoyev, near a train station. The gear bag with my tactical kit I leave in the trunk.

Now I walk over to the Ichavoi Hotel and step into the lobby. I nod curtly to the man behind the counter and rent a room. I specify that it should be room 116, because that's where my wife—God rest her soul—and I spent our honeymoon and I'd like one of those rooms for old time's sake. The man says 116 isn't open but 118 is. Close enough, I tell him.

*

I'm waiting inside room 118 for two hours with the door slightly cracked. Whenever I hear footsteps, I peek out into the hallway. Pistol in my hand. See these hands. Steady as a rock. Breathing is steady. Controlling my anxiety by occasionally visiting the Drifting Place. I check my watch. She's late. Never a good sign when a contact is late.

Then, I hear the familiar *thump-thump-thump* that is the sound of a woman's high heels on carpeted floors, every step punctuated precisely, moving fast. Sounds like she's in a hurry. I peek out into the hall and see a blonde woman in blue dress and red scarf approaching 117. Her face is one of concern. Can't tell what that means yet. She is so focused getting her magnetic key out to shove into the door's scanner that she doesn't see or hear me step out. Right as she starts to turn the knob, I press my hand around her mouth and yank her backwards. She tries to scream.

Press the gun to her temple. "Say nothing. Come with me."

Thankfully the hallway is clear. I guide her into my room and kick the door shut with my heel. I keep her facing away from me.

"Hands up where I can see them." She does as she's told. "Drop the handbag." She does. "Don't move." She doesn't. I pat her down, top to bottom, not caring about propriety. I'm wearing gloves, just in case she's been dusted with so-called "spy dust," the chemical compound nitrophenyl pentadienal, or NPPD. The Russians call it *metka*, they've been using it since the Cold War. Coat someone's hands or clothing in NPPD, and anything they touch also gets coated. Some varieties appear under ultraviolent light. Basically, if you're ever caught by Russian intelligence, and they look at your hands, they can tell if you've been in contact with someone they've marked. Which means you're their enemy.

This woman may have been coated with *metka*, with or without her knowledge, and that could in turn mark me.

"Turn around. Slowly." She does. I keep my pistol trained on her. "Talon?" She nods. The woman in front of me is tall and slender, with high cheekbones and a finely carved chin that would make her look regal if not for the trepidation in her eyes. Her lips are slightly parted. She's trembling.

"Sergei?" she says.

I don't respond to that. Always assume the person you're talking to knows more than you. That's kind of a taxonomy of conversational types, and a useful one.

"Aren't you…supposed to ask me something?"

I consider her a moment longer, gauging her mien. "Where is the green fortress?" I ask.

"Under your bed," she replies without hesitation.

That doesn't mean much on its own. Not now that the whole mission has been compromised and we've sprung a leak. There's always the chance this isn't her, that the real Talon is in a torture camp somewhere and she gave up her codename and the passphrase to SVR. I could be talking an SVR operative. But there's something honest about the fear in the woman standing in front of me. She was afraid on the way in here. Afraid before she ever saw me. An SVR agent would have trained to keep such fear off her face when rendezvousing with the enemy.

"Sorry I had to change meeting spots," she says. Her Russian places her origin somewhere in the north. "It was…" She starts to lower her hands. I aim the gun at her head. She raises them back up. "It was necessary…because the gas depot outside of Tsiolkovsky has a new security detail they've put there. Extra men swarming around the place since four days ago. Drones everywhere. New security cameras. Something's going on. Something's changed."

That's because they know I'm here, I think, but don't say. "We can't talk here."

"We…why not?"

"We have to keep moving. You might've been followed."

"I wasn't. I was careful—"

"I'm sure you were, but careful's never careful enough. Let's go. Out the window."

She blinks. Tilts her head curiously. "Out the…?"

I don't give her time to articulate the rest. I grab her by the elbow and escort her over to the window, which I left unlocked just in case I need to bail out fast. I let her go first, then I'm right behind her. We step out into a noon sun. The clouds from before are beginning to part. The weather is kind of nice. Warm and bright. Talon starts walking fast ahead of me. Too fast. I touch her elbow to slow her down. I hide the pistol in my jacket and wrap my arm around her waist. Just a couple of people in love, that's all we are. Out for a stroll across the hotel's east lawn.

We are almost a block away when I know something's wrong. Two cars pull into the hotel parking lot behind us. They're moving a little too fast, and come to a halt at the entrance. The doors open and men in plain clothes jump out. Even the drivers get out. Six men walk fast through the hotel entrance.

"Move faster."

"Why?" she asks.

"Because," I say, "you're made."

*

They've got a perimeter set up all around us. It's a big one, and a tight one. I spot a police vehicle driving by quick, it's siren turned off. It joins another patrol vehicle up ahead and blocks off a road called Uzkiy Put'. There's no way the two cars I parked close by earlier in the day will be of use—we'd just be stopped at a roadblock and captured. But there's the one at the Vavilov train station.

I tug my girlfriend slightly in another direction, down a small path I spied earlier in the day from the parking deck across the street. It leads us right to the marketplace. Lots of people shopping at one o'clock in the afternoon.

"Nest, Ares. I've made contact with Talon and am on the move. She's been followed. I don't think I'm made yet. Can you give me instructions from Heaven?"

"Negative, Ares," Yarwick says. "We don't yet have a satellite positioned to give us a look at your area. We will monitor local police channels, however, and give you updates as we receive them."

"Ares copies." I leave the channel open so they can hear everything that's happening around me.

"Who are you talking to?" Talon asks.

"Just keep moving."

The Anvoyev marketplace is a busy place, filled with a variety of shops spread over several cobblestone paths. It's a hodgepodge of Russian and Asian clothing and cuisine. There's a fat man cooking *shashlik*, lamb on a stick. Right next to him is an Asian woman with a mobile restaurant serving steamed rice with sweet and sour chicken. Beside her is a stall where two Russian women sell *matryoshka* dolls and other knickknacks. There are street performers, guys plucking guitars and women doing some kind of mime act. It's like that down every lane, on both sides, with locals and tourists bouncing around like pinballs.

There's a policeman up ahead. His head is craning over the crowd. He's looking for someone. Talon sees him at the same time I do, and she does good masking her alertness. She's already turning down another lane before I can pull her by her waist.

"I don't understand," Talon says. "I was careful."

"Like you said. Things have changed. They upped their security, which means they've probably been watching certain people closely. You've been stationed at the Cosmodrome how long?"

"Almost a year."

"Uh huh. And you're just a journalist. The first kind of person to be suspect. They've probably had a file on you the whole time, might've even seen some strange activity from you, monitored your emails, things like that. When they saw you taking an unexpected flight to Blagoveshchensk, it brought up a red flag."

"What do we do?"

"First thing is strip those clothes off."

"What?"

I take her scarf off her and toss it into a nearby bin. Then I nod towards a clothing stall. "Grab something. Anything. Whatever's your size. Just no bright colors. Browns or dull greens. Not blue. They may already know you're wearing a blue dress, they might be looking for that."

She does as I instruct. We go right up to the clothing stall and she points to a beige sundress hanging on a wall behind the stall's proprietor, who starts to get it for her. "No," I say. Talon looks a question at me. "Sundresses are too sexy. Something plain." I point to a pair of brown slacks and a grey T-shirt, as well as some tennis shoes that look like they'll fit her. I purchase them and walk away without waiting on a receipt. Look around for somewhere to change. There's a unisex porta-john ten yards away. I guide her over to it. "You've got thirty seconds," I tell her.

She's in and out in twenty, her hair a little bit in disarray.

"Let's go," I say.

"Hang on." She tears off a tag hanging from her sleeve. "Okay."

We walk arm in arm at an even pace. Twice I have to slow her down. She's too eager to get away, trying to move too fast. I see two men walking fast and purposeful right towards us. They don't see us yet. I pull Talon to a stop in front of a stall that sells antique vases. "Pretend to shop. Ask questions. Lots of them."

"Excuse me," she says to the shop owner. "Are these *real* antiques? Who's your supplier?"

I keep track of the men in my periphery. One of them puts a hand to his ear, listening to commands in his earpiece. They keep moving on. To my right, there's a view of a street called Blagoyeva, and I see another roadblock has been set up there. I scan the sky for drones. There's one hovering high over the market, but it's moving east, away from us.

The bad guys will know I'm here. The fact that I'm connected to the Nest means that there will be spikes of encrypted radio traffic. They know Talon is here and that she's met someone. A foreign agent.

I grab Talon's hand and tug slightly, and she gets the cue and breaks off her conversation. We move down the lanes, weaving around stalls and pretending to shop. Two uniformed policemen are coming our way. Probably they've got a description of Talon.

I grab my girlfriend's ass and pull her in close. "I've just said something funny."

Talon looks puzzled for only a second, then starts laughing. I laugh with her, and pull her in for a kiss. It's like new lovers, giggling at every little thing the other one does. Giggling between kisses, and kissing between giggles. It feels almost real. The smell of perfume intoxicating. For a microsecond I recall how Sophia slept with an enemy and then slit his throat in his sleep. The things we do to stay ahead of the game.

The two officers walk right by us, and I grab Talon's hand and lead her towards the south entrance of the marketplace, where my Civic is parked.

"Ares, there's a massive influx of law enforcement in your area," Yarwick says. "They haven't yet sealed off the streets on Boldaya and Orostovich."

"Copy."

We cut down a lane of the marketplace where there isn't much foot traffic. Not many places to hide now. I try to keep us to what few groups there are. Four serious-looking men turn down this lane, heading our way. And I immediately recognize one of them. Blonde hair, cold blue eyes, a well-built frame. Karambit. I saw that one photo enough times to never forget it. It's his hit squad. The Unit. We're fucked.

I glance left and right. There's a street performer showing a magic trick with cards. He's talking to a group of six people, explaining something. I direct Talon over to him. "Aleksei?" I say. The performer turns to me. He smiles and cocks his head, wondering who I am and why I'm interrupting his trick. "Aleksei, it's me. Boris." I stick my hand out.

"Um...I'm not Aleksei," he says. But he shakes my hand anyway. Because he has to. Because it's etiquette and it's been trained into him.

I laugh like he's just said the funniest thing I've ever heard. Talon follows my lead. We're two laughing idiots looking at a street performer who's slightly perplexed and a group of people all engaged with us expectantly. Karambit and the other three serious-looking men barely give us a glance as they sweep by, continuing their search.

"My apologies," I say, waving goodbye to the performer. "I must've been mistaken."

Judging the baseline of crowds and finding your moments of opportunity is key, but we can't keep this up forever and we're running out of people. The farther we get from the nucleus of the marketplace, the fewer people there are around us.

"This way," I say, conducting my girlfriend to a set of stone steps that lead up to an outdoor café.

We're approaching the street, seemingly beyond the search perimeter. We round a kiosk with multiple ATMs, and then step around a few benches of an outdoor bar and grill. There are more people here. Doing good. We're doing good.

That's when we round the corner and our luck runs out. There's a man coming right for us. A big man, head shaved, with no partner and no reason to be there at the outdoor bar and grill because he's not eating and he's not standing in line. He's got a searching look. Scanning the crowd. We're just ten feet away from him. He sees me. I see him. He knows. And he sees that I know.

To my girlfriend, I mutter, "Vavilov train station. South entrance. Run. Now."

Talon looks at me. "What—"

She doesn't finish the question before it happens.

My enemy's hand moves fast as an adder, going for the gun inside his jacket. I lunge forward, grip the pistol around its slide, my thumb finding the hammer and preventing it from firing. Using my free hand, I form a yoke grip and strike my enemy in the throat. I do this several times to make sure I crush his trachea, then ram a knee into his groin. My enemy's grip on the gun melts, and his knees buckle. I rip the pistol away and toss it into a nearby potted plant.

Talon is gone. Just like I told her.

It all happened within the span of seven, eight seconds. The man collapses, trying to breathe, but I catch him and hold him up like a man helping out a drunk friend.

Two witnesses are nearby, they saw only the final moments of the altercation. I look at them both, feigning concern. "He's about to have an attack!" I look at the nearest witness, an elderly woman. "My friend suffers from epilepsy, he's about to go into a fit. Can you please go and find help? *Please!*"

The elderly woman nods and rushes away. I look at the other witness, a young punk kid with purple hair. "Please go with her, make sure she finds help." He obeys without question. They both may have seen the last strike I delivered to my enemy, they might even have reservations about what they saw, but the stress in my voice overrides any confusion. Whatever they saw, they know this man needs help.

It's important to know how to control a crowd. It's not that difficult, as long as you say your words with confidence.

I drag my choking enemy down the alley between shops. I pass half a dozen people who give us queer looks. I hold my enemy's left arm around my neck while he clutches at his trachea with his right hand, and gurgles, and drools. He is dead when I bring him into a public restroom and drop him in the handicap stall. I sit him down on the toilet and search him for a radio. It was up his sleeve, tiny, easily concealable. I take his earpiece and plug it into my ear.

"—changing location now," a man's voice is saying over the radio.

Another voice says, "This is Tiger. Team Two is mobile, heading east by the candy shop. No visual on target."

I leave my dead enemy and make my way down a narrow lane of smaller shops, which are formed in a circle around a fountain with the statue of the Virgin Mary. An onion-roofed church is nearby with two nuns standing outside taking donations.

"Raven reporting," someone else chimes in on the radio. "No sign of target. My location is north entrance. Mobile."

"Copy," says a man with a distinctly northern Russian accent. "Stallion, Coyote, report."

"Stallion here," comes a gruff voice. "Stationary at west entrance. No sign of target. Four policemen are guarding this spot with me."

After that, there's silence. Then a terse voice says, "Coyote, report. Coyote?"

No response from Coyote. I'm thinking Coyote is my dead guy. "Coyote here," I say, trying to sound like I'm panting, hoping that will disguise the fact that my voice isn't their comrade's. "I have visual on target. I'm by a shop near the center where the lady is selling *matryoshka* dolls. She's with two men, one of them is armed. They don't see me yet. I'm alone, request backup."

"Coyote, this is Raven. I read you and I'm on my way to your location."

I continue on, hands in my pockets, walking casually.

Then the man with the northern Russian accent comes back on. "Stay where you are, Raven. Coyote, say your destination again."

"At the center of the marketplace, near the doll shop," I say as I pass the fountain and head up a short flight of stairs.

A long pause.

Then, the man says, "Coyote, what is your grandmother's name?"

I don't respond immediately. I know what he's doing. When I finally respond, I try to sound confused. "Say again. I did not read that." Trying to buy time.

"Your grandmother's name. What is it?"

"I don't understand," I reply. "Please clarify."

Then there's a long, raspy laugh from the man. In English, he says, "Well, hello there, Ares. I figured you made it this far. You gave us a real run in the woods. But to have made it this far in so few days...*phew*, you must've really been...eh, how do you Americans say, 'U-Haul ass?' Is that how you say it?"

"Hauling ass," I say, now heading for an alley between two office buildings. "But close enough." Ahead of me is the street, but three cop cars are parked along the sidewalk, so I'm not going that way. The alleys probably aren't covered. At least not as well as the streets are. So I head that way.

The man laughs. "Yes! That's it! Do you know, that was my favorite thing about learning English. Such colorful expressions."

I hear a helicopter. I look up and see a police chopper hovering over the area. The SVR has really pulled out the stops. It seems all the police in the district have been told to swarm this place.

"You guys have got a few that I like, too."

"Oh?"

"Yeah, like *ida na hui*. That's a good one."

The man laughs loud. Incredibly loud. He's not faking it, he's thoroughly enjoying this. Even as he laughs, he says, "You didn't kill my poor Coyote, did you?" Before I can answer he says, "What am I asking? Of course, you did. Or else *you* would be dead? *Da?*" I don't respond to that. "Do you know who I am?"

"I have some idea."

"Let me guess. *Karambit*? Is that still the name your CIA friends are calling me?"

"Among other things."

Karambit laughs again. "You know, I'm going to enjoy watching my dogs rape you. And by dogs, I mean literally dogs. We've worked out how to make that happen, you know. Kind of like Caligula and Nero back in Ancient Rome, when they fixed those mounts to put women in, so that the bulls could fuck them to death."

"Yeah, well, sorry to spoil your fun, but that's not gonna happen today." He's trying to get under my skin. Make me lose focus. Two can play that game. "You know, you SVR guys are pussies. Your Coyote pal really screamed when he died. It was kind of pathetic. A sad way to go."

"Well, I'm sure he's waiting for you in hell. That's where we all go, you know? People like us?"

I start to respond, but then something occurs to me. He's talking to me. Continuously. Takes me a second to realize I've been stupid. Really stupid. I was confident enough using Coyote's radio, but as soon as I was found out, Karambit started tracking me. *Through* the radio. It clearly has a GPS so they can all track one another if need be. "It's been nice talking to you, Karambit. See you around." I give him a smooch, then rip the earpiece out just as he's saying something, and I throw it and the radio into a trash receptacle.

There are sirens echoing all around me, but I don't see any flashing lights.

The alley leads to Orostovich, where the Nest said there weren't any roadblocks yet. It's a narrow cobblestone street, a quaint piece of Blagoveshchensk that's left over from its historic roots. Small buildings hug each other close like old friends. Tourists are taking in the sights. The sun is shining overhead. I hear a buzzing sound. I know that sound. I glance up. About fifty yards ahead is a drone. I have to get off the street. They have my codename, so maybe they have my face?

I turn into a tattoo parlor, nodding to the two artists working there, who look at me puzzled as I head out the back door and step out onto a wide-open street. I glance behind me. I'm beyond the last police roadblock. No one's looking in my direction. The Vavilov train station is three blocks up. If Talon listened to me, and if she hasn't been caught, she ought to be there.

I make it two blocks before I realize I've got a grab team on my tail. No, not just on my tail. They're in the street ahead of me, on the sidewalk across from me. They're all around me.

I'm found.

*

Whoever gets in your way, kill them, Sophia said to me. *Come back to me.*

I'm trying, Sophia.

The best thing to do when you're spotted is to not let on that you know. Carry on nonchalantly, keeping track of your followers in the reflections of cars parked curbside or shop windows. Slow down. Speed up. Pause to ask a stranger for directions so that your followers will wonder if that stranger is on your side, a potential threat, and also so that you can catch glimpses of your followers under the guise of following the stranger's gestures. Don't let yourself be alone where they can attack you easily. Watch for operatives on perches. If you can, create a diversion. Lead them to where *you* want them. Corral them. Look for an opening. Then separate them.

Then start vectoring them how you want them.

The team appears to be made up of five people. Four men, one woman. The woman is across the street, wearing a black suit, moving at a leisurely pace. She's window shopping but without a purse, that's what drew my attention first. The second thing that caught my attention was the phone she's holding to her ear. Now she's keeping pace with me, glancing in the windows but never for very long. She's the lead in this chase, staying ahead of me in case I run, conducting the others with feedback.

The team of two guys trailing me were easily spotted when I stopped to ask a newspaper vendor for directions. Two no-nonsense men, faces grim. One's wearing a blue-jean jacket and the other a gray trench coat. They can't grab me just yet because they're not sure about me. That's one of the reasons you never react when you know you're being followed. If they haven't got a clear look at you and they're not sure, then if you're nonchalant they'll wonder if you're really the guy they should be after.

Second team of guys I spot when I pause at a pastry vendor, buy a *cheburek*, pay for it, and chat with him for a few minutes about how good it is. I see them just over the vendor's shoulder, only fifteen feet away, both of them wearing heavy jackets. It's warmed up today, those kinds of jackets are out of place.

There must be half a dozen grab teams just like them deployed all around the marketplace and beyond. But Coyote's radio signal led them to my vicinity, then their drone identified me as suspicious. They're still not sure, but they're feeling like I'm a good candidate for Ares.

This team can do it all—trailing, leading, parallel, and leapfrog. They mix it up a little as we walk, adapting the way jazz players do.

I obey the no-walk sign before crossing the street, both so I don't look in a hurry and so that the team behind me can catch up. I nibble on my pastry. There's a hot twenty-something girl standing next to me at the corner. She's waiting on the walk sign, too. She's wearing tight pants. I pretend to scope out her ass. I even nudge a guy standing next to me and smile, nodding towards it. The guy nods appreciatively, and then the walk sign changes and we cross the way.

My grab team must be very confused right now. They're not closing in, but they're remaining equidistant and never letting me out of their sight. This can't last forever. They're professionals. You don't get to their level being so easily manipulated. They're just a little unsure right now. I've only stalled them, bought myself time to look for opportunities.

There's a cab pulling up to the curb. I could try to slip inside of it, but I'm pretty sure they would throw all caution to the wind and descend on me, and then I'd be trapped in the back of a cab. I'd have to shoot them, cause a scene. Even if I managed to force the cabbie to drive at gunpoint, it would be impossible to evade drones and police helicopters.

I finish my pastry and toss the wrapper into a bin. The train station is up ahead. I might have enticed them now. If they suspect I'm heading for Vavilov, they might back off and let me go on my way, waiting to see who I rendezvous with. As I get closer, it seems that's exactly what they want.

I told Talon to meet me at the south entrance. I head for the north entrance. The station is a wall of glimmering, reflective glass. As I approach the front door I can see my followers behind me. The woman in the black suit is ten yards ahead of me, walking through the turnstile.

Inside, there are hundreds of people moving about, feet clicking on marble floors. The ceiling is a transparent dome and the sun is now fully out and beaming. There are potted plants lining the walls and sticking out of small islands. Bubbling fountains give the whole place a radiance on par with a five-star hotel. Lots of places to take cover.

I stop at a gift shop to look behind me. They're all inside now. I've corralled them.

I waste no time using my environment to divide them. I scouted this place when I dropped the Civic off, so I know the layout.

Moving fast, I exit the gift shop through a rear entrance. The lead woman loses me first. I go down a flight of steps, down a short corridor where I know there's a large marble column right before the restrooms. I dip behind the column. Listen for their hurried footsteps. And they *are* in a hurry, having lost sight of me. I round the column slowly, letting the first team run ahead of me, then I double-back and go back up the stairs.

Turn left at an information kiosk and come into the atrium. Pause behind a large potted weeping fig, and search the crowd.

There's the second team, the guys with the too-big jackets. They're stationary, spread out about twenty feet from each other, covering the atrium's exits and scanning the crowd. Perched, we call it. I wait for an opportunity. About forty-five seconds later, I see both their heads turn in the same direction, away from me. I take off my jacket and toss it in the tree pot, then move into the crowd. In a crowd, human beings typically seek one another out by their height. Bend your knees a bit, dip your head just a little, and you will be about five to six inches shorter. Keep the back straight, so you don't look all weird and hunched to others around you.

Weaving surreptitiously through the crowd, I make it to the far side of the atrium, in plain sight of my pursuers but they don't seem to see me. I'm doing good until up ahead I see the black-suited woman again, coming right for me. I dip into another gift shop, hoping she didn't spot me. I hide behind a postcard stand, my hand slipping under my shirt for my pistol.

She walks by.

I relax a fraction. Step out of the gift shop. Glance left and right. Looks clear. The woman is heading north, which is where I need to go. I step right in behind her, following from fifteen feet away. So far, she doesn't see me. I'm passing the restrooms when I feel it. Something's not right.

Do this job long enough, and sometimes things just don't *feel* right.

I turn just in time to meet the man in the blue-jean jacket. He's rounding a pillar. He figured I might be trying to separate them, come in behind them, so he fell back and waited for me to do exactly that. He's pulling his weapon out from his jacket.

Time slows.

The average human being can close twenty-one feet before a trained police officer can draw their weapon (law enforcement calls it the 21-foot Rule). The man in the blue-jean jacket is less than fifteen feet away, but his hand is already on his gun. I take two quick, wide strides, and on the third I lunge, slam into the man and send him backward. We struggle with the gun briefly, but thankfully I'm better at this. The gun is disarmed easily in a kali-style strip, and then I smash my enemy's face with a head-butt, then another, and another. The man's nose is broken on the first one, and a waterfall of blood cascades over his lips and chin, down his shirt. I grab my enemy by his collar and rotate him so that he is a shield against the woman, who I know has to be preparing to attack.

I'm right. Her hand is up, but she holds only a stun gun, not a pistol. She's running towards us.

Someone screams.

I grab my enemy in a *puta-kapala* hold, underhooking one arm and overhooking the head. I sling him about, kneeing him in the chest multiple times, then finally fish-hooking his face, yanking his head back, and delivering two quick hammer fists to his throat. He is probably dead from the first, the second only seals the deal. As his body falls to the floor, I realize I'm about to lose my human shield.

The woman is rushing me, about to stun me. I grab my shirt by the bottom and stretched it out, like a net. When the woman fires her Tazer, the electrodes are caught in the shirt like a net, thousands of volts snapping just inches from my chest.

Someone screams again. Someone else calls out for the police.

I tear the electrodes out of my shirt, rush her, just as she's drawing her pistol. I bring my hammer fist down on her wrist, breaking it. I feel more than hear the snap. She screams. The scream is cut off when I knee her groin, grip her long hair in one palm, and smash it against the wall. She's tough, she doesn't go out. Instead she lashes out with a knife she's drawn from somewhere. I catch her wrist, but not before the blade drives an inch or two into my ribs. I head-butt her, then smash her head into the wall again. This time she drops like a sack of potatoes.

I turn immediately and walk away, pressing my hand against my side, putting pressure on the wound. I make it down a set of stairs with two station guards rushing past me. I put on my most panicked face, shouting, "Officers! Officers! Oh, God! There's a man in a gray trench coat, he's waving a gun! Oh, God! I think he may have shot someone back there near the bathrooms!"

They don't ask for any further details, they bolt away, hands on their pistols.

I have no doubt that someone in a security booth somewhere has already pinpointed me on a camera. I need to confuse the search. I'm looking for opportunities everywhere. I find one as I slip through a small cafeteria. An abandoned tray and plate sitting on a table, plastic utensils dropped into the food. I lift the plastic fork. Pocket it. Check my side. Still bleeding. Bitch got me good.

Seconds later, I emerge from the cafeteria into a short hall and see another opportunity. A fire alarm, fastened to the wall near a customer service desk. I sweep right by it, smash the glass protector with my elbow, and yank it. The alarm goes off.

I follow the map in my mind. Heading north. Praying to God that Talon is there and is safe. The alarm is blaring. A voice comes over the intercom advising everyone to move in an orderly fashion. It takes turns in multiple languages.

Glancing behind me, I catch sight of one of my pursuers, becoming lost by the tide of panicking travelers, people frightened by the alarm, by the prospect of a terrorist attack. I cut through an evacuated restaurant, dip behind a kiosk, watch the two heavy-jacketed pursuers run by. Wait to make sure the coast is clear. Step back into the fleeing tide.

North entrance dead ahead. Almost there. I scan the area for anyone else on their perch.

Just as I'm rounding a doorway leading to baggage claim, the man in the gray trench coat suddenly appears around the corner. It's just coincidence. We see each other at almost the same time. And he is fast. Fast enough that he deflects the plastic fork I try to stab into his neck and holds onto my wrist as he goes for his gun. My hand shoots for his, pinning it there, keeping the gun in the holster. He head-butts me, rocks me back. I chop him in the brachial plexus, that shocks him, loosens him up. Then I do something you won't see in the UFC. I step on his foot, pinning it to the floor, then, with my other leg, I drive my knee into his knee. His foot pinned, his knee can't go anywhere. It snaps sideways. He screams. I probably just blew out his ACL.

He drops to the floor screaming. I stomp his head into the marble. He stops screaming. The flood of evacuating people around me see it, keep panicking, and keep running. I join them.

Once outside, I look for Talon. If I don't see her, I'll keep running. I cannot be captured. I'm looking all around for any other pursuers and for Talon. I'm almost completely away from the station when I see her, standing near a statue of Mikhail Gromov, a Soviet aviator and hero. I walk right over to her. She sees me. Relief floods her face. Still clutching my side with one hand, I grab her wrist with the other, direct her to the far end of the parking lot, and we hop into my rental.

"What happened in there?" she asks.

"We'll talk when we're clear." I pull out of the parking lot and onto the 202 Highway, looking in my rearview mirror the whole way out of the city.

11

We're twenty miles away before I'm certain we're clear. I keep pressure on the stab wound, occasionally having Talon take the wheel. Then I pull into a shopping center parking lot and park the car. Watching the skies, I grab my gear bag from the trunk and head to a different end of the lot. I find an old black Corolla, pre-2000's, because those are easier to hotwire. I make sure no one's around and smash the window with my pistol. "Keep a lookout," I tell her. Talon nods. She stands in front of the car while I sweep out the glass and use a knife from my survival kit to strip away the plastic from the steering column. I touch the ignition wire and the battery wire easy enough. Dashboard lights up, but it takes a while to get the starter going.

As soon as I get it revved up, I call to her, "Get in."

We drive five miles further, I pull into another shopping plaza and park. "Keep lookout again." She does so without question. I use the survival knife to unscrew the license plate and switch it with the plate of the car parked next to us. We're back on the road and out of the city ten minutes later.

By two o'clock we come to the small outlying town of Dorzorensk, and I park us under a bridge. When I turn off the engine, Talon and I sit there for several seconds. Just listening. I've had the radio on, listening for any news alerts. There was one quick report about the Blagoveshchensk Police searching for a fugitive that the FSB has been chasing, but there are only scant details.

I turn the radio off and look at the gauze I've been pressing against my side. Soaked pretty good, but looks like the bleeding has stopped, thanks to the QuickClot from my med kit. It's going to need stitches, though.

I look at my passenger. "What's your name?"

She looks at me. "My name?"

"Yes. Not your codename, your real name."

"I'm...I was told by your people that I should not divulge that to anyone. It's...whatever your people called it. PERSEC?"

"Personal security, yes, but I need to know who I'm talking to and that I can trust you."

Talon looks at me with supreme incredulity. "After all we just went through—"

"Your name." My pistol is out, resting on my chest, the business end aimed at her. "I won't ask again."

She looks at the gun, sighs, and shakes her head ruefully. "Tatiana."

"Tatiana what?"

She glares at me. "Tatiana Kantorovich."

I take out my mobile phone and look up the name on the Internet. All I was ever allowed to know about her was that CIA says she's a journalist stationed at the Cosmodrome. Let's see about that. A search pulls up articles Tatiana Kantorovich wrote for *The Moscow Times* before she went freelance, focusing on stories about advances in science, exposing the methods of Russian hacker groups like Shaltai Boltai, and the political implications of new technologies. She's on a list of trusted Russian journalists that the Reporters Without Borders puts out, so she's not considered one of those journalists that publish only Kremlin-prepared stories. That's probably why the Program was initially happy to have her reporting from the Cosmodrome, since she had credibility. There are plenty of photos online that prove it's the woman in my passenger seat.

I look at her with fresh eyes. I look at her delicate hands, unblooded surely, but her actions have placed her in a game with those that deal in blood. I look at those blue eyes. Cold. Zero humor in them. There might be fear, but like most Russians she hides it well.

"Well, Tatiana Kantorovich," I say, putting the phone away. "You understand that you're a fugitive now, and can never go home?"

She nods.

"You're going to have to run. Do you have ways of doing that safely?"

She nods.

"You know you can't call anyone or talk to anybody by email or Skype or anything like that, not until you're clear."

She nods.

"I take it you prepared for this day, just in case?"

She nods. "Your people gave me instructions."

"I imagine they did. I wish you'd followed them a little more closely. Now your life is over and they probably have my face on some camera somewhere. It'll be released to the press soon, then there'll be nowhere I can go."

"I'm sorry. I did everything I knew to do. I did the dry-cleaning runs, I always checked who was following me—"

"Why did you change the meeting place?"

"Why?" She looks confused. "Because the gas depot outside of Tsiolkovsky is overrun with fresh security. I told you that."

"And you didn't think that would mean the few journalists living inside Tsiolkovsky would be under extra scrutiny? You're a journalist. You didn't think SVR and FSB would be going all over your records, your e-mails, your travel plans? When's the last time you left Tsiolkovsky?"

"I...maybe six, seven months ago?"

"Then there it is. You don't frequently leave. You should've been preparing for something like this, taking occasional trips outside the city so that you could develop a pattern, and that pattern wouldn't be broken by you taking a trip around this time, when an American agent is loose in the region and security is being upped. You—"

She looks at me stone-faced, then turns away. And I know I've gone too far. Her whole life just ended and she's getting rebuked. And she couldn't have known. This isn't her world. This isn't her normal job. She was recruited. Hell, as careful as I was, I didn't even have all the bases covered. Made a few mistakes myself. A few too many assumptions. I think back to the Tidov's, and how safe I felt once I was in their home.

"I'm sorry," I say.

She keeps looking out the window. Clouds are moving back in, covering the sun. The world goes dim. A soft rain starts.

"It's fine," she says stoically.

"No, it's not. You're in a bad spot, you're scared, and you don't need me lecturing you. Besides, what's done is done. Can't take it back. Spilled milk and all."

She looks at me. "Spilled milk?"

"It's an expression. Forget it." I hear a helicopter. Glance out the window. It's a mile or more away from us, heading away. "Nest, Ares. Have you been hearing all this?"

"That's affirmative, Ares."

151

"Instructions on exfil?"

There is a long pause. Finally, Yarwick comes back with, "Uh, Ares, you are not to exfiltrate. Repeat, you *are not* to exfiltrate. Your orders are to carry on with mission."

I can't believe it. "Say that again, Nest. Because it sounded a lot like you're asking me to continue with a mission that is beyond salvaging."

"What's going on?" Tatiana asks.

I hold up a silencing hand. "Did you hear me, Nest? I'm burned. Bad. As bad as it gets."

"Ares, the situation is fluid here, but all I'm authorized to tell you is that there is evidence of a…a *mobilization*. By multiple foreign actors. There's been another power outage, this one at LaGuardia."

"Power outage. You mean like the one in Atlanta? Someone's shutting down our airports?"

"They may have been doing it for a while. A slow, steady push to destabilize us. Airport outages, train derailments—"

"Train derailments?" I think back to the train wrecks I saw on the TV in the cafeteria at Langley. "You mean those weren't accidents?"

"I can't say for certain at this point, Ares," Yarwick says. "Like I said, it's all very fluid. But the upper echelons are worried, they need to know the weapons capabilities of our enemies."

The hairs on the back of my neck raise up. "What did you mean when you said, 'mobilization?' Are we…are you suggesting that we're about to enter a *shooting war*?"

"NAVSPEC-WARCOM says there's reason to believe the Black Sea Fleet is deploying deeper into the Atlantic. For years they've been looking for the telecommunications cables we've got buried in the oceans. And SIPRI says they're tracking LVTP-7s moving into islands in both the Atlantic and Pacific. The Russians have been buying up spares in Ukraine and Syria for years, and now we know why."

LVTP-7s (Landing Vehicle, Tracked, and Personnel-7s) are 30-ton amphibious tanks that can roll on land and move over water. In use since the 1970s, the 7s were equipped with grenade launchers, .50

cal machine guns, radar, stealth packages, and can carry twenty-five troops to their landing zone.

LVTP-7s were not built for defense. They were built for invasion.

"There's no way," I say. "No way they're considering an outright *invasion* of the U.S. or our allies."

"PAG and the uppers don't think so, either," Yarwick says. "Doesn't seem realistic, not at this stage, anyway. The likely tactic for now is to act all indignant that we've pushed our navies far across international waters, claiming we've moved into Russia's territorial waters at times. They'll use this stunt to gain ground in the Atlantic and Pacific, knowing we won't risk a shooting war at this point, since Putin's got North Korea in his pocket, and, in the past, China has made it clear that in a war between the U.S. and North Korea, they'll side *against* whoever instigates it."

I sigh. "What a fucking mess."

"You can't focus on that right now, Ares. Your orders are to carry on with mission. Is that understood?"

I want to yell at her. I want to tell her that she's insane and that all her "upper echelon" bosses are insane. But I can't do that. For one, it would do no good. When the command comes down from that high up, there's no talking them out of it. And secondly, it's not her call. Never was. No more than it is mine. "Understood, Nest. But I'm gonna need some serious help."

"What resources do you need?"

"I'm still kitted up," I tell her. "I just need a clear way into the objective destination, because right now all roads seem like they're going to be sealed off."

"Not all roads," says Yarwick. "I'm told Talon knows of one or two alternate paths through the hills, particularly something called *Staraya Gryaz'*, or something like that."

I wrestle with the strange pronunciation. "Old Dirt?" I look at Tatiana. "Does the phrase *Old Dirt* mean anything to you?"

She sighs heavily, and nods. "It's a road that leads through some farmlands, winds its way through the Kreshvoyev Hills for fifty miles. It's a dirt road the whole way, mostly hardpan, with thick trees and paths that cross over rivers. I used it just once, the first time I met with Donovan, my CIA handler. It gets you close to the Zeya River, and from there you can follow the tributary of the Bolshaya Pyora River. But there are *no roads* that way, only wilderness."

"Is it safe?" I ask.

"I've never seen anyone out there besides me and a couple of fishermen."

To Yarwick, I say, "Talon has the way, Nest."

"Copy that, Ares. Sorry to put you in such a sorry position, but the leadership needs to know what's going on there and they want eyes on that installation and its weapon. We really need this one."

"Copy that. I'll let you know when I'm mobile again. Out." I click my teeth to end the connection, and look over at Tatiana. "You're driving."

"Me?"

"Yeah. I've got some stitching to do."

*

Quitting tomorrow has been such a good mantra for me. It encompasses everything, and reminds me that whenever I feel like things are falling apart and I'm not going to make it, I'm just being a pussy. See these hands. Steady as a rock. How can that be? Watch as the fingers weave the needle and thread so delicately through the flesh. So expertly done. How can that be? I ask that question knowing the answer: Because they're steady when I need them to be. *Please. I have children. I have three children.* And they falter when the mind is satisfied that the mission is done and gives them permission to tremble. The mind serves the mission. It's weird to think of oneself as a tool, as utilitarian as a wrench, but tools are necessary. Tools serve a purpose. But whenever the darkness begins to seep in—

Fuck the darkness. Come back to me.

—it's good to know you at least have the *option* of quitting tomorrow. That's what quitting tomorrow is really all about. You can always move forward as long as you know you have the choice to lay down and quit. It's when you lose all control that you become desperate for even a morsel. That's when you'll do anything for an ounce of it. Just one ounce of control.

I need to control this mission. I need to not think about the nonsense keeping me here and how insane it is to move forward to the objective, and just get to it. I tell myself I have the option to quit, and that keeps me moving.

The stitches look like a true professional did them. I daub the bruised flesh all around it with disinfectant on a cotton ball while Tatiana drives, then pop two ibuprofen and an antibiotic. We stop only once to fill up on gas. By nightfall, the rain is really coming down. That's good, it'll mask the headlights from a distance, but it's getting my driver soaking wet, since I smashed in the window.

We're moving into some higher elevations now, passing farms in the alpine meadows. The only two people on Earth and we're pushing ahead on some mission of importance we don't understand.

"You do this work often?" Tatiana asks.

"I do it enough," I say.

"How long have you been doing it?"

"Ten years."

"And before that? Military?"

I nod. "Yeah."

"I don't know how you people do this. I haven't even made it a year and already my mind is going."

I look over at her. A beautiful woman. She could have had a modeling career but she chose journalism. And then she chose traitor. "Can I ask why?"

She glances at me, but keeps her eyes nervously on the road. "Why what?" She dials up the intensity of the windshield wipers.

"Why did you betray your country?"

"When there is evil in this world, you expose it," she says without hesitation. "Even if it comes from your own country. You cannot be loyal to your country above all humanity. Putin and his people are worse than scum. The people that make friends with him are scum. The world leaders that praise him and ally themselves with him are scum."

"Aren't journalists supposed to be unbiased?"

"It's not biased to call scum scum."

I shrug. "Fair enough."

"The choices I've made are difficult, but I've settled up with the guilt."

"I suppose we've all made tough choices."

"Really?" She glances over at me again. "You really think you've made difficult choices?"

"You have no idea," I tell her.

"I have some idea. And the choices you've made, I can guarantee you they aren't choices like we have had to make."

"*We?*"

"Russians. We have to make choices about how to view our leaders, and ourselves, on a daily basis." She shakes her head ruefully. "You Americans don't know anything about hard choices. You've been sheltered from having to make the big ones for too long." She slows down when we hit a bumpy patch of the road. She glances at me again. "What would you do if I told you that the world was going to explode, and that the only way to save it was to rape a child?"

I look at her. "What the hell kind of question is that?"

"Just humor me. What would you do? Would you rape a child to save the world?"

"Fuck no."

"No? Even if the entire planet was going to explode, killing everyone, *including* the child?"

"Jesus, lady," I say, wincing at the sore spot on my face where I was head-butted. It's tender, somewhat swollen. "You have a dark fucking mind."

"It serves a point. You don't know how to make an impossible decision like that because you can be *certain* that you will never be presented with that choice. You are sheltered from ever having to think like that because it can *never* happen. Since it can never happen, you never have to exercise your brain in that way, to weigh the pros and cons, your morals against the logical choice, which is to rape the child."

The car slews a little to one side and she gets it back under control, straightens us out.

"That's what it's *really* like when you suddenly have to decide between your country, your family, your career, your *whole life*, and doing what's right." She looks at me. "You Americans have never had to honestly think like that. It's going to be scary for you."

"I've got enough on my mind right now," I reply. "Don't need more bad shit filling it up."

She doesn't seem to hear me. Or if she does, she doesn't care. She drives on, saying, "We didn't think Putin could happen till he happened. Look at Kim. Look at al-Assad. Look at your own leadership. The world is filling up with monsters who are in control. We worship villains now. Like you Americans with your Tony Soprano and Walter White and Dexter and Scarface and all these psychopaths you watch every day on television, rooting for them to win. You've gotten used to rooting for the bad guys. You *like* rude men who are bullies, who insult people openly, who have no manners, who are crass and loud and destructive." She snorts. "It's only a matter of time before you get your Putin. Then who will survive? The world, or the child's innocence?"

"Can we change the station?"

"Change the station…? Oh. Ha! Like I'm a radio. I get it."

"Talk about something else. Something that can help me."

"Like what?"

I raise my seat up straight. Move around a little bit to test the flexibility with the stitches. Not bad, if I do say so myself. "Tell me about the Cosmodrome. What's it like there? What can I expect? That kind of thing."

Tatiana purses her lips, thinking. "The Cosmodrome is a wide campus of mostly two-story buildings, with one very large command center that's eight stories. The place is very well kept, very clean, lots of streetsweepers and guards around the clock. The population largely consists of volunteers, but there are plenty of conscripts, students and professors black-bagged and forced to conduct their research there. They are paid, they are free to walk around, but make no mistake, they are prisoners in what is basically an open-air prison."

"Tell me about the type of security. How many drones? Is there a curfew?"

"There are always drones in the sky. It differs throughout the day. There is a curfew: nine o'clock for children, ten o'clock for adults. Unless you're working late-night at the Cosmodrome."

"What happens if someone who's not authorized is outside after curfew?"

"Then they will be stopped and questioned."

I nod. "Anything else?"

"Mm...they installed a tall electrified fence last month," she says. "Separating the main road to the Cosmodrome from Tsiolkovsky. Not much else is new."

"And what about the Steel Octopuses?"

Tatiana makes a weird face. "Steel...? Oh, you mean the men in the Tianshi suits. The *Bespre 'del*."

I vaguely know this word. It's one of those words that's untranslatable in English. In Russian it somewhat means "without borders or limits." It usually denotes a chaotic state. Lawlessness. When in this state, a person is said to be totally unpredictable. An ordinary person is at the mercy of a *bespre 'del*'s whims. "Why do you call them that?"

"Because they are some of the Unit's worst men," Tatiana says, her voice growing cold with ire. "At least, they seem so. Maybe it's just the suits that make them feel invincible, like such...how do you say, *hotshots*. I've seen them do terrible things."

"Like what?"

She looks troubled just recalling. "Two scientists tried to escape. They were spotted by the *Bespre 'del* trying to get over a perimeter fence. They descended on them, and they...those steel tentacles that extend from their suits, I've seen them lift a small car." She looks right at me. "They used them to tear those poor scientists apart, rending flesh from bone, like...like a child plucking the wings of a butterfly. The scientists were screaming, and the *Bespre 'del*, they just...they just continued. They laughed. Karambit was nearby. He was laughing, too."

"Matveyev?"

"Sorry. I think you know him as Karambit."

"You know his name?"

She nods. "The Unit mostly goes by codenames, but I heard one of his people slip." She looks back at the road. "Another time, late at night, a woman was out after curfew. I didn't see it, but I heard two of the *Bespre 'del* descended on her and lifted her up into the air, tore her clothes off, and dropped her in an icy pond. The woman was screaming in the air, one of her breasts was torn half off in the struggle. By those tentacles. She survived. The pilots were reported. Nothing was done about it."

Tatiana looks at me again.

"If the *Baspre 'del* spot you, best to put a bullet in your head."

I nod. "What about the objective itself? This potential particle-beam weapon?"

"There have been movements of large materials and scientists on the outskirts of the largest residential area of Tsiolkovsky, near the main research center. I think that should be your main target."

"Why?"

She puts on the brakes, slows us down as we pass by a broken pine. We are once more decreasing in elevation, coming to the first trees we've seen in miles. "I saw the weapon. Yesterday."

I turn to her. "Wait, you *saw it*?"

"Yes. I saw them loading it onto the rocket they plan to send it up in."

"The Angara?"

"Yes. They placed it on the Angara rocket and tested the rocket's thrusters. Then they shut it all down, took the weapon off, and brought it back to a hangar at the research building."

"What does it look like? The weapon."

"I couldn't tell all the details," she says. "It was mostly covered in a kind of black aluminum sheeting. It's about twice as large as this car, though, I can tell you that much."

"Did you get a picture of them placing it on the Angara?"

"No. Too much security. We're not allowed to take pictures of anything in that area. I wasn't even supposed to be there to see it, but I've been dating one of the scientists, who will pretty much do whatever I ask." She shrugs like this is no big deal, just a way she has with men. I can imagine, especially among scientists cooped up in a sterile place like that.

"What's this scientist's name?" I ask.

"The one I'm dating? Aleksandr. Dr. Aleksandr Gogol. Why?"

"Doesn't hurt to know a name. Tsiolkovsky, tell me about that."

"It looks like a quaint little city, lots of clean roads and trees and parks. Families walking their dogs. There's a school and sports teams. By looking at it you wouldn't know it was a city specifically built to facilitate a spaceport."

"How's the security there?"

"More relaxed. It gets much tighter as you approach the Vostochny Cosmodrome."

I nod. Mull that over for a bit. "And what about Karambit—er, Matveyev? How much do you know about him?"

"Nothing."

I look at her. "You mean you don't know *anything* about the guy in charge of security around that place?"

"He's SVR," she says, just as she slows us down again. We are now passing through a forest, with large, gloomy trees that lean from each side of the road. "They wouldn't pick someone who was so easily researched. He's a ghost. The only thing I can tell you is that he is a bully and proud of it. I've seen him and his team take people right off the streets, and a few of them have never been seen again. One of them was Aleksandr's friend Mikhail."

"What was Mikhail's last name?"

"Bondarchuk."

I nod. "Nest, Ares. You get all that?"

"Copy that, Ares," Yarwick says. "Sounds like they're farther along than we thought."

"Yeah. They're not just testing the tech anymore, they're getting ready to launch it."

"Copy. We're sending the information up the ladder. I'll let you know what the uppers think about it. In the meantime, how are you holding up?"

"I'm good. Just need a little rest." I look at Tatiana. "How far away are we from where you can safely drop me off?"

"Maybe two hours?"

I nod, recline my seat, and shut my eyes. "Wake me in two hours, then." She nods, keeps her eyes on the road. By reflex, I leave my hand on the butt of my pistol inside my jacket. Though my eyes are shut, I can see the flash of lightning. Hear the report of thunder.

The storm rages all around us. I try to relax, go to the Drifting Place, and not think about children plucking butterfly wings.

*

The sleep is not deep or thorough, but it's enough to bring my senses back to where they need to be. Tatiana doesn't have to wake me up. I somehow sense we're there. Maybe it's the finality of the car coming to a stop. Maybe it's something about the way she sighs once we're there, the way a person does when a long journey is finally done. Whatever it is, I once again keep my eyes shut for a few seconds, then slowly open them, making sure I'm where I'm supposed to be.

The storm has passed, though dark clouds do linger. It's nearly nightfall. I raise my seat up quickly, and Tatiana is startled. She was just about to reach over and wake me. I look around at the wilderness. We're on a heavily wooded hill, no sign of civilization anywhere, not a powerline or rest stop to be seen. Through the trees, I can see a valley ahead of us. And just beyond it, the Zeya River.

"This it?" I say.

She nods. "The road goes on, but this is as far as I think I can take you. If we go another couple miles, there might be roadblocks. We're awfully close to Tsiolkovsky now."

I take one more look around, searching for signs of ambush, drones, or *Bespre 'del* who like to pluck people apart. "All right," I sigh. "Let's do it."

We step out onto a muddy road. Tatiana slips and falls. I walk around to help her up, still watching the forest. "Thank you," she says. I pop the trunk and take out my gear bag. Without thinking to ask her to turn away, I strip naked and get kitted up. Takes me about three minutes. I check my pistol, and pop its suppressor back on. Check my SA58 rifle, make sure it's good to go, sling it across my back.

"Guess this is it," I say to her. "Time to get mov—"

She cuts me off with a kiss on the cheek. "Thank you," she says.

"For what?"

"For saving me." She takes my hand. "God knows where I would be right now if you hadn't…"

I look down at her hand. Her hand in mine. The kiss was abrupt but not unwanted by any means. The ape part of my brain considers it. It actually considers stripping off every part of my kit that I just put on and throwing myself on her. If she rejects me, let her reject me, at least I'll know that I tried. I look at her. There's sadness there, but also something else. Or am I imagining it? We only just met. But now I realize that we're two of a kind. We are two people that this whole country wants dead. We are the same now. That's our connection. Our only connection. Still, people have fucked for less.

So the fantasy continues. Maybe I could kiss her, test her out, see if she's up for it. Just look at her neckline. Smell her scent. Feel those hands. Feel them. Think how good it would feel. It's been a while. Grab a handful of ass. Clutch it. Know that feeling again…

But then the logical part of my brain realizes how stupid this exercise is. Imagine a road patrol drives up on the very fugitives they're after, caught literally with their pants down.

"And thank you for driving me," I tell her. "I needed the rest."

Tatiana nods. Is there disappointment there? Or am I reading too much into it again?

I pull up a map of the region on my watch, zoom in on our coordinates, and then show the map to her. "Show me which direction. And then explain to me the exact layout of the streets leading up to the main research building."

*

Quarter till midnight. The storm has subsided and the clouds are beginning to disperse. To give Tatiana a better chance on her own, I smash the Corolla's taillights. "Okay," I say. "Drive only at night, with the headlights off as much as possible. That'll mean driving a lot slower, but it'll be worth it. Moon's coming out soon, looks like, so it shouldn't be too bad. Do you know anybody who lives out here in the country?"

Tatiana shakes her head. Now she's looking really scared. No longer able to hide it. I'm leaving her alone and there's nothing she can do.

"Then once you get past the border, hitchhike as much as possible. Only use cash to pay for buses and trains. Keep away from cameras. If you're out walking and you hear helicopters, head into the nearest public building and exit out the back way. Also, first chance you get, change your hair. Cut it, dye it, shave it all off, whatever, just make it so that your own mother would have to do a double-take. You know this place better than me, so I'm sure you know a way across the Zeya?"

She nods.

I pull some of my rubles out of my gear bag and hand it to her. I press her fist around it to make sure she holds it and understands. "You can't use your credit cards. Once you're across the border into China, exchange these for Chinese renminbi, and take buses and taxis to an American embassy. The closest one is in Chengdu. Tell them who you are and that you've been working with CIA handlers. Your codename will reach the right ears. Understand?"

She nods. She's fretting with her hands now. Now that she's going to be alone, it's starting to really sink in. I hate myself for doing this to her, but there's no place for her on my mission. Now that she's made, anyway. I have to move forward, and she's got to run. She seems bright enough. As long as she's careful she ought to be able to make it clear.

"Thank you, Tatiana." On a whim, I lean forward and give her a kiss on the cheek. "If you're ever in the States, look me up."

Tatiana gives a weak smile. "I don't know your name."

"It's another expression."

Her jaw tightens. She swallows. "So, in other words, I'll never see you again."

Might as well be honest with her. "No, probably not." I see her shivering. "You gonna be okay?"

"I can't help it. I keep thinking…what if they capture me? I've heard what Karambit and his Unit does." Her eyes gleam, and for a second I think she'll spill tears, but she doesn't. She holds them back. Strong girl. "I'd rather be dead than…" She trails off.

I look at her seriously. Then, a thought occurs to me. I don't know if it's charitable or not, but the thought does occur. So, I follow it through. I reach into a pouch on my left side, and pull out the teeny, tiny bag with the teeny, tiny white pill inside it. "Take this," I say.

"What is it?"

"If you're serious about you'd rather be dead…it's a pill. You take it, you don't wake up. Ever." I put it in her hand, adding, "It's quick."

She looks horrified. Then a strange thing happens. Her face turns stony, and she gains a resolute posture and countenance. She nods, but says nothing.

I hold out my hand. She takes it. Then, slowly, she pulls herself in and hugs me. "Thank you again. And I'm sorry I caused you so much trouble."

"It's fine." I hug her back. That feels good.

We stand there in the night, embracing, until one of us—I don't know who—finally releases first. We pull away, look at each other for a moment. "Do whatever it takes," I tell her, quoting Sophia verbatim. I squeeze her hand one last time. Don't want to let go. Some atavistic compulsion to protect her. Then I let go. She watches as I turn away. She's trapped on her island of fear now, cast away.

I grab my gear bag, now stuffed with my civilian clothes, and head into the woods. I'm fifty yards into the brush when I hear the Corolla start. It snores away from me, and then it's just me again. Me and Betelgeuse and Rigel and all the stars that have watched me do this work countless times before. Hello, old friends.

12

It doesn't take me long to make it to the Zeya. I am worried about patrols intensifying up ahead, so I move slow once I reach the river bank and follow it two miles north, where the waters go from calm to a soft, foaming roar. Here's the divide, where the Bolshaya Pyora branches off from the Zeya. The waters get a bit calmer, the river a bit narrower. Tatiana said it was safe to cross here, said it was waist deep most places, but some places I may have to swim. The water's cold, but not nearly bad enough to risk hypothermia.

On the other side, I jog quickly to the nearest trees and duck down, listening for the buzzing of drones, looking for any sign of the silent *Bespre 'del*. Nothing. I move on.

It only takes me another mile before I see them. Something silent and fast, moving low over the trees on the opposite bank, where I just swam from. Soaking wet, I run for cover, hiding behind a pine and peeking around at the cluster of dark spots. Wish I had my NVGs. I'm only able to see them because the moon has decided to come out and my eyes have adjusted. I can't make them out clearly but I know what they are. Something that size, flying that fast and silently? Sure, I know what they are.

I watch the *Bespre 'del* glide quietly over the trees to the east, following the riverbank, and then disappear from sight. My heart is pounding. I'm getting close to it now. In the thick of it.

Click my teeth to open a channel. "Nest, Ares. I think I just had a close encounter with our Tianshi flyboys. They're moving east, away from me." I glance at my watch. "I'm on course for final destination. Gonna push for a small forest I see up ahead, maybe catch some shut-eye if I can. Over."

"Copy that, Ares. You didn't by any chance snap a pic of the flyboys, did you?"

"Negative. Too dark, too far away. Ares is mobile."

"Copy that. Stay frosty. Nest out."

I make it to the tree line a few minutes later. I build a rough shelter, not nearly as good as the others, but I don't want it to be too much of an eyesore when seen from the sky. Between my suit's insulation and the leaves, it's enough to keep me warm. I drift to sleep wondering what Sophia's doing right now. I wonder what my brother

Derek is doing. Haven't spoken to him in six, seven years. Where did everyone go?

My sleep is not perfect. Several times I wake up to a twig snapping, or something moving in the underbrush close by. My watch wakes me at 0400 hours. I slowly rise, and even more slowly slither out of my shelter. I wait on one knee, rifle in hand, listening. Once I'm satisfied I'm not being watched, I tear down my shelter and hide my tracks.

Click to open a channel. "Nest, Ares. I'm up and mobile."

"Good morning, Ares," Yarwick says.

"Any news for me today?"

"Camera footage has been released of you at Vavilov train station. It's blurry, but it's good enough to ID you if law enforcement gets close, especially with a police sketch that's been going around. It's safe to say you won't be visiting Moscow ever again."

"Believe me, if I get out of here, I'll never even eat borscht again," I chuckle. I walk to the edge of the trees, kneel, and scan the landscape ahead of me with the spotter's scope. "What about the other thing?"

"You mean the conflict?"

"Yeah. We at World War Three yet?"

"Not quite. But Navy Intelligence is reporting that several of our submarine commanders are spotting Russians testing previous no-go zones. They're moving into waters that are red-flag comms areas."

I take my eyes away from the scope. "Telecomms links?"

"That's the theory. They may have zeroed in on our cables."

That's not good. That's not good at all.

Beneath the Earth's oceans there is a secret world, one made of ancient volcanoes and still rock, where sunken ships rest quietly all across the seafloor, silent monuments visited only by the sharks and crabs and other life-forms that swim through or scuttle across them. But in that hidden world are also crisscrossing power cords and fiber-optic cables, lines dropped along paths made as far back as the 1860s. Telecommunications links between nations. Most of those cables are in easy-to-find areas, clearly delineated on maritime charts available to the public, placed there so that repairs were easy to make, according to longstanding agreements between nations.

But there are those that aren't so easy to find. Special fiber-optic cables, hidden away in secret locations and at incredible depths, have been commissioned by the U.S. and other countries for military use. These cables show up on no maps. Ever since 2013, the Russians have been searching for them, but to my knowledge, have found only two.

It's estimated that cables like these carry around *ten trillion dollars'* worth of global business each day, and carry ninety-five percent of all daily communications. Severing just one of these, and at such a depth that only military vessels could go and repair it, would be like putting a pin into the Western economy's balloon. And if a war were to ensue, NATO nations would have serious difficulties trying to communicate with allies.

"Is it what it looks like?" I ask.

"Too early to tell. Probably just strutting. But you know that strutting has been known to lead to hotheads doing what hotheads do." I hear a quiet a sigh from her end. "But there is some good news. We've managed to get some eyes on your region from Heaven's perspective."

I look up and smile. It's a small thing, but having a satellite watching me, lending what support it can, is never a bad thing. "That's good to hear, Nest."

"Stay sharp out there, Ares."

"I copy, Nest." I put the scope back in its pouch. "Ares is doing his part. Mobile now. I'll contact you with any updates."

"Same here. Nest, out."

*

On the other side of the planet, nuclear submarines from two or three different nations are playing peekaboo with each other. Meanwhile, hackers are apparently looking for easy ways to disrupt the U.S.'s transportation and economy. That might as well be happening on Mars, or Jupiter, or Betelgeuse. It doesn't influence how I operate. I'm aware that my mission plays a part in all that, but there must be dozens of others—hundreds, most likely—happening all over the planet.

But I have to remember that it's for the home team. That keeps me going. Keeps me quitting tomorrow. Keeps me putting one foot in front of the other, mile after mile. I think of my dad. He always said my brother was the better athlete, but about me, he said, *There's a whole lotta Don't Quit in you. Sometimes that's a bad thing, most times it's good. Your problem will be learning to tell the difference.* I think about Mom, who was furious when she found out I put myself at risk in the wellhouse with all the black widows. If she could see the kind of trouble I'm in now...

I think of all these things but focus on none of them. The submarines, the hack attacks, Sophia, the brother I haven't seen in years. They're a collage. A swirling mass of detritus gathered over a lifetime. Several lifetimes. Through three separate births. My first birth, my naval birth, and my CIA birth. What was it all for if I don't accomplish my mission?

That's motivation for you.

The hills keep rolling on, the sparse woods give me adequate cover, and when I spot two drones flying high in the air, I just take cover and let my mind slip away. To the Drifting Place. When they've gone, I'm up and running again.

The sun rises at around 0800. I can see more details to the landscape now. There's a road in the distance. Pretty sure it's 61 Highway West, leading towards Tsiolkovsky. Glance at my watch for reference. Coordinates are right. I'm about two hours away from the city. Almost there, Adamson. Almost there.

*

The city is not walled in. It doesn't look like a prison. It looks very modern, very beautiful, the kind of place you'd want to move to with the wife and kids to let them go to a better school, in a safe neighborhood away from gangs and crime. It's exactly as Tatiana described it. Quaint and green, with perfect roads dividing groups of houses into subdivisions. From two miles away, I observe. I face west, so that the sun doesn't cause a glint on my scope. Kids walking about. A church bell rings. Someone jogs with a small Pekingese on a leash and checks their pulse. There's even a park with a young couple enjoying a picnic. A few outlying farms orbit the entire town, some of which look like they jumped right out of a Thomas Kinkade painting.

The only thing that mars this happy little scene is the strange presence of uniformed men, jeeps, three guard posts at the town entrances, a roadblock with a tank and armed guards stationed at it, and the six—make that *seven*—drones hovering over the town and farmlands.

Thomas Kinkade, as imagined through the lens of George Orwell.

And beyond all this, the Vostochny Cosmodrome. It sounds like something out of the Mad Max movies, but there's no great dome or Colosseum-like arena to be seen. Rather, it's a vast complex that looks industrial in places, and like a stock-trading business center at others.

And that's where I see my first Steel Octopus.

It's just one, but I'm arrested by its elegance. It's too far away for me to make out much detail, it's weaving in and out between the Cosmodrome's tallest buildings. I take out my mobile phone, zoom in as much as I can, and take videos. Every little bit of intel helps; even from this far, CIA analysts will get an idea of the Tianshi platform's mobility.

"Nest, Ares. I'm within sight of final destination."

"That's good to hear, Ares. Best news I've heard in a while. Send us your coordinates and we'll give you an eye in the sky."

"Copy, Nest. Stand by for coords." I get the coords from my watch and send them to her via the CRyPto-DEX messenger.

"Coordinates received, Ares. Stand by."

And so I stand by. It's going to take them a while to find me from orbit, for the same reason that the drones and *Bespre 'del* haven't spotted me from up high yet. My kit masks my heat signature, and my camo is perfectly matched for my environment. But they ought to be able to get a view of my general area and let me know if I'm safe, if anyone has come up behind me, or maybe surrounding me.

Minutes later, Yarwick reports, "We're on top of you, Ares. We have visual of the area. We don't see anything, not even you, so I guess that's a good sign."

I chuckle. "Yeah, I'll take it over the other. Also, I'm sending you a video now. Check your e-mail."

Seconds later, Yarwick says, "Jesus, those Tianshis move fast."

"That they do." And they pluck people apart like butterflies. "Listen, I'm going to take tonight to reconnoiter the perimeter, get a look at their movements. If all goes well, do I have your permission to proceed tomorrow night to the objective?"

"Affirmative, Ares. You are clear to use discretion."

"Copy that, Nest. And thanks. I'll leave the channel open but I won't be saying much. Let me know if the situation changes around me."

"You bet, Ares. Happy hunting. Out."

The day wears on. I watch for a bit and then retreat into the woods behind me. I get prepped. I leave my gear bag inside a rotten tree trunk that's hollowed out, then I eat a big meal, a full MRE and two energy bars, and a whole bottle of water. I wait for nightfall. As soon as I see Rigel and the gang, I'm moving.

*

I run in a low crouch, using cover that I selected earlier in the day while scanning the area with my scope. I crawl whenever I want to get close, and close is never closer than fifty yards from an outlying farm or building. I scuttle back to hiding whenever I come upon areas with searchlights. Now, at nighttime, with these bright lights strafing the area, Tsiolkovsky does begin to look like a prison. A helicopter buzzes overhead. Two Steel Octopuses come flying out of the Cosmodrome fast at a little past 2300 hours, racing silently away towards the Bolshaya Pyora River. I see no indication that anyone knows I've made it this far, and the Nest has only given me the updates of where the drones are moving to and when. So far, those appear to cluster around the Cosmodrome and rarely ever search outside its perimeter.

That's all fine and dandy. What's worrisome are the out-facing cameras attached to the walls of every building I've seen so far around the Cosmodrome. Studying them, I see that some of them pan and some are stationary. With security cameras, there are three basic designs for the overall network: regular, offset, and random offset. Random offset is the worst, with cameras set up everywhere irregularly. There are holes, though. There always are. And I mark them. The cameras are more concentrated around the Cosmodrome, though, which does have some chain-link fencing with barbwire topping, but the town of Tsiolkovsky doesn't have so many cams.

The curfews seem to follow what Tatiana told me. No one besides the armed guards is on the street after ten o'clock. The guards patrol in dark-green jeeps and black vans. The ones in the jeeps are your typical soldiers, wearing fatigues and carrying assault rifles slung over their shoulders. A few of them are in much heavier gear, though. Spetsnaz would be my guess. The guys in the vans are dressed more casually, mostly in black, but a few of them I can see wearing body armor. Karambit's Unit. Is he here?

Helicopters come and go, taking off from a landing pad inside the Cosmodrome's main compound. There's a small airstrip out there, I see only three planes parked, all Gulfstreams. The spaceport's main launchpad stands tall above everything else, bathed in spotlights, empty at the moment, awaiting its next rocket. There's a tall hangar half a mile away from it, inside of which I assume is the Angara rocket.

Very little traffic on the roads besides large delivery trucks, and even those are infrequent. And they all come from the northwest, picking up supplies from the Trans-Siberian Railway.

By two o'clock in the morning it's already abundantly clear that the best way into the Cosmodrome is going to be through Tsiolkovsky itself, through its picturesque neighborhoods and Orwellian curfew patrols, making my way towards the central core of the Cosmodrome's compound step by careful step. I can see the research building Tatiana was talking about, as well as the hangar where she said they're keeping the weapon.

By four o'clock in the morning, I've done a full circuit of the entire Cosmodrome and its adjoining town, and returned to my gear bag. "Nest, Ares. I've got what I need. I'm go for tomorrow night. Repeat, I'm go for twenty-two-hundred hours." No response. "Nest, do you copy? I'm go for twenty-two-hundred hours." No response. "Nest, do you copy?" For a second I'm worried.

We've been compromised again. Men with guns are soon to descend on me.

Then, I hear a click. "Sorry, Ares, just…just grabbing an update for you. Copy twenty-two-hundred."

"What's the update?"

Yarwick takes a second, then comes back. "Looks like your mission objectives have just been updated, Ares." I listen intently. Last-minute changes are rarely good news. "As previously planned, the upper echelons have determined that you are to take pictures and/or video of the weapon, and transmit it to us. Only now they want you to destroy it. By any means necessary."

"Any means." I sigh. "I wasn't sent out here to do that, Nest. My kit didn't come with any explosives."

"I hear you, Ares. That's why the 'any means necessary.' You have guns. Shoot it to shit if you have to. Set it on fire. Whatever, just do it. The uppers don't want to see that thing find orbit."

I give it some thought. That means getting awfully close to the weapon, not just snapping pics from afar. I'll have to get right up to it. Unless someone around here has a rocket launcher handy, which I doubt. Their security seems to be about keeping things out, not fighting a war in their own streets, not causing serious property damage to themselves. "I copy, Nest. Anything else?"

She sounds hesitant. "Yes. I've, uh…I've also got some good news and bad news here concerning the op. Good news is you should have some rain tomorrow night. Could help with the infiltration."

"Good to hear. And the bad?"

There's more hesitation. It must be bad. Really bad. You can sense that in a person even from thousands of miles away. "It's Talon. She was captured."

A stone sinks in my gut. "What? Where? How did it happen?"

"Near the border. The others thought I should keep it from you, but I thought it'd be better to let you know. In case she told somebody something. Something about you. If you see any sudden strange activity in your vicinity, that may be the reason."

I close my eyes, and let out a sigh. My hands close into fists. See these hands. See hers in mine. Feel her. Feel her embrace and see the fear mounting inside of her. "Where is she now?"

"Unknown. They've already moved her body."

"Her...body?"

"Yes, we only found out when our systems man said that Tatiana Kantorovich was admitted into a hospital. She was brought in by black-suited men and armed soldiers," Yarwick says. "We're not sure how it happened, but she went into cardiac arrest. She's dead."

Oie

The man in the black jacket standing on the patio is waiting for my family to leave. I don't pay him any mind. I don't really care about him right this minute. Nor do I care about the dead people who hover around him, the ones from the shallow graves. My life is lived in the tiniest of moments, I'm scarcely able to hold on to them. So I don't try overly hard, I just soak it all in. I enjoy hearing Henrietta's laugh and listening to Zoe talk about going back to college and Chloe telling her she best be serious this time otherwise she's wasting money and time.

They argue a bit. Not fighting, just arguing. They ask me for my opinion, which I'd give in full if I wasn't so captivated by Henrietta, her youth a window into a time I can barely recall even on my best days. Henrietta is a time capsule, something brought into this world to show us what we once were. I'd just as soon sit here all day, looking into brown eyes that still see nothing but potential. It gives me satisfaction knowing she won't have to have a life like mine. My sacrifices bought her this chance at a life without burdens such as I knew.

But Chloe and Zoe are persistent, they want to know what I think Zoe should do. I explain, at length, that I am proof that life, while it may stretch out to a hundred years, is limited, and there are things that can only be done in blocks of decades. Once you're beyond the twenty and thirty blocks, you're no longer fit to be a ballerina. Once you're in your fifties and sixties, you're never going to be able to start a job as a nurse, no matter how smart or good you are. Know what block you're in, and do everything you can in that block. Everything.

They make peace with some overall pledge to help Zoe achieve her goal. I tell them that's my girls, and they're off. Henrietta cries when she's taken away from me. I cry, too, though I hide it. When they're gone, Orson comes to wheel me away. I wave him off. "I believe the gentlemen over there is here to visit me."

Orson looks at me quizzically, then at the man in the black jacket thirty yards away. "You know him?"

"No, but you can go over and tell him I'm ready for him now."

Orson looks a little confused but shrugs and does as I say. The man in the black jacket steps away from the ghosts from the shallow graves and approaches with an avuncular smile and a confident stride. *"Bonjour, Madame de Marenches."*

"Bonjour," I return. "I should thank you for waiting until my family left. Most wouldn't in your place."

"In my place?" His accent is Marseille, or I'm a three-dicked pig.

"Yes. I imagine you came here with many questions."

"Actually, I'm not sure what I'm doing here at all. My superiors sent me on a fact-finding mission of sorts. But your file is long since closed, more than five years before I was born, so of course you're not operational and no one expects much from this. That's why it's just me, and that's why I'm curious."

I nod. "Not questions, then. Curiosity. Study. I suppose I am a relic. You might put me up for auction to museums, see what sort of price you could fetch."

He smiles, and extends a hand. "I'm Baudelaire. Very good to meet you."

I accept his hand. He's gentle with mine. "Investigator?"

"Researcher," he says with a shrug. "Nearly the same thing."

"Have a seat, Monsieur Baudelaire," I say, gesturing to a bench. As he sits, I roll over to him. "Now then, tell me, how did you finally work out who I was and where I was?"

Baudelaire smiles a smile that I'm sure has given him more cunny than he can stand. "I'm sure you remember all the channels, how it all works." He snorts. *"L'oie comme son gander.* Quite remarkable you remembered it after all this time. I have trouble keeping all the different passphrases straight in my head, they're always changing."

"I suppose it was recorded like every phone call," I say. "Probably seemed enigmatic to the junior officer who answered the phone. Probably got tagged yellow, semi-intriguing, potentially a threat, perhaps an agent in the field phoning in a tip. Only when the message reached the ears of the department heads, no one knew of any agent using that passphrase. Think maybe then it went to Department Fifteen. Records?"

"Records is Thirty-two now," he says.

I nod. "Ah, yes. It's not the SDECE anymore, it's the *Direction Générale de la Sécurité Extérieure*. Did the DGSE do some kind of word-search of the older SDECE documents?"

He nods. "Took several days, but there was finally a hit. Everyone thought the computer must be mistaken. Far too old of a code to be in use today. And there was nobody to ask because..."

I nod again. "Because no one's left that would remember me. I outlived them all."

"Yes, *Oie*. Goose. It is a remarkable thing, you being alive this long. I mean no disrespect, but all records of you stop twenty years ago. The agency has not been tracking you since then. I guess they thought..." He shrugs. "Well, if not dead, then forgetful and forgotten."

"So nice to meet a Frenchman again, I enjoy the bluntness, Americans like to feign politeness. And yes, I imagined your superiors would not care enough about me to keep tabs this long. Plus if all my allies are all dead, so too must my enemies be, so who's going to come looking for Sophia de Marenches and torture her for outdated information?"

Baudelaire nods, and keeps an enigmatic smile on his face as he looks at me. He's soaking me in, I can tell. Wondering how the fuck I ended up here. "Since you're probably wondering, no, I didn't try to evade anyone, I didn't go dark, I didn't do anything special to go off the grid. I just got old and your bosses—my bosses—forgot about me. I moved to the States in 1983, the same year *Return of the Jedi* came out. It's the first thing I did when I came here, I stood in line with my daughter for three hours to see it. I got paid three visits from SDECE Station Chiefs over a period of five years, just old friends still at the agency checking in on me. They once tried to recruit me back, I said no. I imagine they kept tabs on me for another decade, then lost interest."

Baudelaire smiles, gives a curt nod. "It is as you say, Sophia. May I call you Sophia? I've looked over the follow-up files. The last time anyone filed a report on you was 1998. I believe you were just entering your first retirement home then. That's what the report says, anyway."

I nod. "And after that, I suppose I was considered as good as dead."

The young pussy magnet looks around at the grass swaying in the breeze, the willows hissing at one another. "It's beautiful here."

"I'm surprised you came. I really didn't think it would work."

"There were some who said I shouldn't, and others who thought it worthwhile."

"I'm sure. Probably once they figured out who it was who called DGSE headquarters, they had to go through old SDECE files, wondering if it was possible I might still have knowledge important to national security, any old French codes still in use. They were afraid I called because I'm getting senile and I'm thinking I'm back in the War, spilling secrets."

"That was a concern. But talking to you now, you seem cogent, completely aware of who you called and why."

"I am."

"So why, Sophia?"

I consider him for a moment. Drinking him in. I look at his manicured nails and his sharp Henry Arlington cufflinks. Framed ovals, the color of pearls. Black Aubercy button shoes and white St. George's pants. He's a Frenchman, all right. His eyes and jaw remind me of Nathan's. But this one is prettier. A preening, posturing male. I used to have a thing for these types. I would have this strange urge to suck their cocks. No sex, no foreplay, no reciprocation from them. I'd just get on my knees and swallow them whole, and spill not a drop. Wind the clock back seventy years—*merde*, even fifty—and I think I could do things to this boy to make him quiver and follow me around like Jean-Luc did. But now he sees me as nothing more than a relic, perhaps a minor puzzle that needs to be solved.

"The Direction Générale de la Sécurité Extérieure succeeded the SDECE around the time I left. Are things much different since the changeover?"

Monsieur Baudelaire shrugs. "I wouldn't really know, would I? I wasn't even born when the changeover happened."

"Ah, *oui*, of course. But let me ask this, is there still a department called *Héritage*, or some such? Are there still Legacy files?"

He taps a hand on his knee. I look at those hands. I see no rings. "Why do you ask, Sophia?"

I consider him some more. I decide I can trust him. Besides, I'd better get it all out before I forget again. "I was watching the news recently," I tell him.

"Oh?"

"*Oui*. And I saw a familiar face pop up. At first, I thought I was crazy. But then I became increasingly convinced." With clarity of both thought and movement, I reach into my handbag, which I set beside my wheelchair. I put it in my lap and go rummaging through it. I produce the iPad, and pull up the saved images from the news sites and the British war archives. "There."

Monsieur Baudelaire takes the iPad and looks between the two pictures. At first he just winces in consternation. He stares at the twin wolf grins. Then, slowly, his brow resolves. He looks up at me in mild appreciation. "You think they are the same?"

"They are the same," I say. "His name is Wilhelm Vogel. We called him *Bite Molle*. He held many different ranks throughout the War. We chased him for many years. Not just for the sake of revenge or to satisfy the people working in Legacy with the Israelis, but because after the War he continued activities against both France and her allies, always for remuneration from our enemies." I gauge his reaction to my next words. "He was one of those Wiesenthal named."

Baudelaire looks up at me sharply. "The Wiesenthal List?"

"*Oui*. Part of Action T4, under Stangl."

He watches me for a moment, judging me. "How come this man was never neutralized?"

177

"The French and the Israelis founded Legacy together, but only the Israelis kept up the hunt. The French were very committed at first, but as time went on it got harder and harder to chase these people down, or to even prosecute them in court."

"May I ask why?"

I shrug. "Witnesses grew older and were less able to provide clear testimony. Nazi fugitives grew older and changed their names, their looks, we didn't have facial-recognition software like today, nor was the media ever utilized to spread their faces all over like they should've done, and some became so old they were deemed 'unfit to stand trial.' So, as long as these Nazis kept a low profile for long enough, they were usually safe. Funding for the trials fell off, and Austria and Germany became less cooperative, preferring to forget their Nazi past. Interpol picked up some of the cases, as did the OSI for a time, the 'Nazi-hunting branch' of the U.S. Justice Department, as did their Human Rights and Special Prosecutions Section. But this one, Herr Vogel, he evaded them all. Now he apparently runs a multinational surveillance-group-for-hire called Arumush. God alone knows what he is doing."

And he's still watching me. Still judging me. He's thinking how he may have guessed wrong, that I may still be senile, or at least sad and lonely, looking for attention, conjuring this story up so that I have someone to talk to. I can tell he sees no hint of the fog I occasionally exhibit. He looks back at the iPad, and nods appreciatively. "The *Département d'Héritage* will have a look, I can promise you that. Your country owes you that much." He shrugs. "The world, too, for that matter."

The man is sincere. I can tell. Nothing better than a sweet, sincere man. *Oui*, I would have sucked you dry, Monsieur Baudelaire. I might still, if you're curious enough to try. "I would be grateful."

"We should at least be able to spare one or two investigators to look into the embassy thing in South Africa, see what this Vogel might be doing there. Meanwhile, I'll give you my personal e-mail, so that you can check in with anything you may recall, anything that might help."

"*Merci.*"

He stands up and shakes my hand. "Thank you for all you've done."

It feels good to hear someone say it. I did not think I needed to hear it, but I did.

He turns to leave.

"Monsieur Baudelaire?" He turns back to me. "I have a granddaughter about your age, recently divorced. Very beautiful. I believe you saw her leaving?"

He smiles. "Zoe. Yes. We did our research. Lovely family you have."

"I could give her your e-mail also."

His smile widens. He blushes. I would have eaten him alive. Spanked him until his ass cheeks were rosy red and then devoured him. "Thank you, but Claire might have a problem with that."

I arch an eyebrow. "Oh? You're married? I didn't see a wedding ring."

"Not married yet. But we're engaged."

"If anything should go wrong, keep Zoe in mind."

He turns beet red. "I will. Good day, Sophia."

I watch him go. He moves like a Frenchman. Forgot how much I missed men from my country, hearing the language the way it's supposed to be spoken.

The day wears on. A wind chases leaves up the cobblestone path, rustles the rosebushes.

Already, I feel the memory of our meeting fading. It's like fighting off sleep when you've been up more than twenty-four hours. You just can't shake it. I *will* forget. Then, later, I will remember. What a lovely day. Focus on that, Sophia, you old hen. Focus on that, and on Nathan making it back, if God is as good to him as He was to me. Don't focus on the dead men from their shallow graves. Focus on the sun and the clouds, and on the three young adventurous Brits who bathed naked with you in the Rhine when the pamphlets fell from the sky announcing the end of the War. Oh, the fun we had.

13

My sleep is about like it was the night before. Intermittent. I come and I go from the waking world, visiting the dreamscape every so often. That dreamscape is a composite of forests and rivers, some dark creature chasing me, my mother and brother Derek calling out to me from somewhere. When I step into the dark river, Tatiana reaches up at me, fear in her eyes, the pill I gave her on her tongue. Someone's begging for their life. In the shadows. Someone's begging for their life and saying *I have three children* over and over again.

It goes on like this. Anxiety follows me through all of it.

But there's also peace. There's the Drifting Place, given more solidity now than ever before. There's home. There's Mom's bacon sizzling in the kitchen. There's me watching Saturday morning cartoons and eating Fruit Loops. There's me and my SEAL team brothers, running at night, watching each other's backs.

There's a collage of a life here, tossed before my eyes like clothes tumbling in the dryer, one piece folding into the other, separate but moving together.

My watch wakes me. It's morning, but not sunup. I eat a meal and crawl to the same spot that I spied on the town from yesterday. I watch the town and the compound around the clock. Nothing much different than yesterday. Delivery trucks in and out. Drones coming and going. Only one Octopus moving around the Cosmodrome. He's carrying something large—a bundle of long steel bars. A test, maybe? Maintenance? Or is it helping with construction of something I can't see inside the compound?

I feel a speck of rain on my hand. Look up. There's an overcast that's been settling in for about an hour.

"Nest, what time's that storm supposed to hit?"

"Uh, around nineteen-thirty hours, Ares."

I check my watch. That's an hour away. The world is already dimming. With overcast and rain, it's going to be a dark night. Be a lot easier if I had my NVGs, but if I'm careful, and follow Tatiana's directions through the streets to the hangar—

Tatiana. It's hard not to think about how I left her there in the middle of nowhere to fend for herself. I barely knew her. I thought of kissing her, taking her, and now she's gone. It's like I dreamt her.

"Ares? You there? Come back."

It's only now that I realize Yarwick's been asking me something. "Yeah, I'm here, Nest. Say again?"

"The clouds are too heavy in that region now. We're not going to be able to give you a bird's-eye view. I've been thinking about it. You sure you don't want to wait for clearer skies, so that we can monitor the drones for you?"

I think about it for a second, then decide. "It's either the advantage of knowing where all the drones are, or the advantage of optimal concealment. I think I'll go with concealment. I think I'm well-insulated against infrared. Besides, in that kind of weather, I doubt they'll want to fly drones much. Maybe they'll even keep the Steel Octopuses indoors. It might actually work out in my fav—hang on. Someone's coming."

I hear the buzzing of an approaching helicopter. I look up. A dark-green Kamov Ka-60 *Kasatka* is coming in from the east, looking to land. I track it through my scope. There are three Steel Octopuses trailing in behind it, maneuvering as easy as you please. I take out the mobile phone and take video of it. The Kamov doesn't land where I expect it to. Rather than on the Cosmodrome's helipad, it lands along the highway, near a security checkpoint. The Octopuses land beside it, for the first time I get to see them operating in broad daylight.

The Octopuses walk around somewhat awkwardly in their steel suits, and the two steel tentacles that reach out from their large collars and helmets curl themselves into a tidy ball and are then reeled in, storing themselves inside a large hunchback-shaped casing on their spines. The pilots' arms maneuver pretty well. I notice they each have small rifles. Can't see which type, though.

Then the side of the helicopter opens. I expect to see troops step out, maybe some high-ranking general. But instead it's men casually dressed, some of them with chest armor showing through open black jackets. And then, I see him. Bright blonde hair. I zoom in, needing more details, but already feeling sure of it. I can't see his blue eyes, but it's him. I know it is.

"Nest, I'm sending you a video now." I send the video to Yarwick's e-mail. "Look who steps out at the end. You seeing what I'm seeing?"

"Affirmative," she says. I hear the tension in her voice. "Jesus, Ares…"

"He doesn't know I'm here. Yet."

"How do you know that? Talon could've told him your direction, and that you were on foot—"

"Talon didn't tell Karambit anything, Nest. I made sure of it."

"You…?" It slowly dawns on her. "You gave her…?"

"I gave her a way out, Nest. She must've taken it as soon as they laid hands on her. Must've had it in her hands as they were chasing her. If not, she would've been handcuffed and never would've gotten to it. So yeah, there's no way they got a damn thing from her."

It takes a few seconds for her to digest that. "All right," she says. "But he knows what your goal is. He has to. If our operation was compromised from the moment we got hit in China, and if they were listening in, then I'm sure they know where you're headed."

"Oh yeah, they know. That's why he's here. He knows if I met with her, then my mission has to do with this place. And he knows I have to come through here." I nod to myself, resolute. "I have to go soon."

"You're going at twenty-two-hundred—"

"No, I'm going in now. I can't wait."

"There's still light out, Ares."

"I know. But he's going to make sure I can't make it inside. It's dark enough. The storm's coming. I'm beginning my approach now and I'm going to get in and out while Karambit's still settling in and issuing orders, telling everyone to be on alert, maybe shuffling guards around to reduce complacency. There'll be excitement, some confusion. A good time to move. Maybe the last small window we get."

Just then, a few more drops of rain fall on my hand. Then a few on my arms, my legs. Now my head.

"Ares, I highly recommend that you wait for the predetermined time we agreed on."

"Sorry, Nest," I say. The forest around me now sighs with the oncoming rain. It's getting heavier, and heavier, and heavier still. "But I think I just received the go-ahead from a much higher power." I can't hear her response for the torrential downpour that ensues.

Two Spies Reach Out From the Grave

*

When I was in Sunday school, I remember learning about Noah and the Ark from our teacher, Mrs. Masterson. Something I was always curious about: Was Noah joyous when he saw the rain because he knew this was the Big One, that his time had finally come, and that all his hard work was about to finally pay off? Or was he happy because, all that time, he'd been secretly wondering if he was just crazy and hearing voices that he called God? Did he endure the mockery of others for years upon years, and when finally the Big Rain came, he was vindicated? If that's so, then it occurred to me that Noah could still have been wrong. The rain might not have been providence at all. He might still have been crazy, it's just that, by total fucking coincidence, a world-changing flood happened just as he was finishing up his massive boat.

I wondered that up until I was sixteen or seventeen, when atheism began to take its roots in me. Even then, the question kicked around inside me. A lot of religions have stories about a huge flood. Enough that we can guess that it's happened multiple times to multiple cultures. And we know that many stories survive by oral tradition, passing mouth-to-ear for generations, and that many have been proven to be right. So the question still remains: If there was a Noah, was he both crazy and lucky to plan for such a deluge?

Crazy or not, he knew when to take advantage of a bad situation. He saw the rains, and seized his moment. Noah and I have that in common.

I've never seen such rain. Or if I have, it's been decades. It comes down in great sideways slashes, communicating a roar across the world. There's heavy winds but I hear no thunder, I see no lightning. Pressed firmly against the ground, I become soaked. Then I'm up and running. I scuttle in a crouch, then crawl, then inchworm towards the perimeter of Tsiolkovsky. There is a checkpoint with five screaming men outside. Soldiers. Two of them are in rain jackets and the other three are fighting to get theirs on. The searchlights sweep the area. I watch them carefully, gauge their trajectories, and move closer.

I avoid the road and the checkpoints altogether, coming up to the first group of houses. I sidle up to a wall and press my back against it. Watch the skies. Listen for voices. There's nothing but the slashing rain and the roaring wind.

The real advantage I have is that this whole place was never *meant* to be any kind of military installation. Tsiolkovsky is a leftover from a town that serviced the workers of the former Soviet Union's ICBM base (now gone), and the town has been spruced up with the opening of the spaceport. The Vostochny Cosmodrome itself was constructed to be much like NASA, simply there for exploration and scientific advancement, not to conduct top-secret weapons test. Tsiolkovsky and the Cosmodrome were not meant to be fortresses, and outside of basic security considerations, they don't have the infrastructure or layout that you would expect to find in a place built to prevent invasion. They were meant to be wide, expansive, even inviting. This original thought towards aesthetics gives me opportunities. Lots of openings, lots of gaps.

I exploit these gaps. Open parks and ornamental gardens, outdoor theaters and gazebos, a golf course and tennis court, retail outlets and parking lots that are dead after curfew. I follow the map in my head, and the one Tatiana detailed for me.

I move between the houses, into the front yards. I scuttle along in a low crouch, first through a playground and then into a wooded park. Soaked to the bone, I crawl through the mud of a construction site—looks like someone's installing an inground pool. There's a road nearby. I hear a jeep snore past. I see its headlights moving left to right in front of me, maybe forty feet away.

There's a large, rickety storage building up ahead that could take me around a huge roadblock. I sidle up to one of the doors. It's locked. Takes my lockpick gun two minutes to figure it out, but eventually there's a satisfying *click!* and the door opens. I step inside, walk thirty feet to the other side of the building, and step out the back door. I'm ten yards beyond the roadblock.

I keep it moving.

Passing through a small wooded area, I hear a trio of armed guards out walking a patrol. They're ahead of me. I freeze and dip my chin, turn my shoulders towards them, breaking up my human form. I see one of them through the trees. One of them looks right in my direction, then immediately looks away. I hear them talking about some woman they know with a huge ass. They never even look back at me.

I move on.

There are a few guard towers all scattered about. Each one has a searchlight, but most of them are pointed outward, towards the wilderness. One of them is an old castle, once belonging to the Donetski clan, placed here to prevent invasion from one ancient enemy or other. Thanks to Tatiana, I know that its baroque façade conceals much of the area's central command.

There's a concept in the study of the "psychology of the search" that every operator must know. It is very dangerous to sneak towards an enemy that is actively searching for you, yes. However, once you are *within* their perimeter, it's actually quite easy to move around, since the majority of their focus is outward-facing. Just don't make any stupid moves. So as I make my way around the old Donetski castle, I feel quite comfortable moving underneath its intense out-facing spotlight.

The rain intensifies, if that can be believed, and it continues to cover me as I dash from house to house, avoiding the patrols that appear sporadically on the streets. The combined glow of the streetlights helps me catch glimpses of Steel Octopuses moving gracefully through the sky, apparently unfazed by the rain. They're beautiful. Like jellyfish gliding through a turbulent current.

As I'm crossing a street, a patrol vehicle suddenly rounds a building on my right, and is turning my way. Its headlights are going to rake across me, no doubt. There's a sedan parked along the sidewalk. I dive behind it, barrel roll to its side, and wait to see if the driver saw anything. The vehicle keeps going. It was a close one.

I sneak around an armored troop-carrying truck. There's only a driver hanging out inside the cab, no one else around it. My pistol is now in my hand at low-ready. The Cosmodrome is up ahead, many of the buildings bathed in light like monoliths made by gods, but still barely noticeable through the downpour. I make my way towards the Cosmodrome, towards a tall, chain-link fence topped with razor wire. Tatiana said that fence was newly installed, and electrified. So there's no way over or through it. But there's a weakness. There's always a weakness. Running along the fence for a few minutes brings me to a fence gate. I look at the muddy ground. No footprints. Doesn't look like this gate gets frequented.

I move along.

Then I come to another gate, identical to the first. There are two sets of fresh bootprints in the mud. Nearby is a guard shack, its walls are ringed with wide windows for 360 degrees of view. The lights are on inside and I see a TV on. Someone's watching *Friends*. I see the back of their head. They're sitting down and not moving. That's all I see for guards. A small gravel road leads up to the guard shack, but no vehicles are approaching.

Then, I pull back behind the cover of a power generator, and kneel. I wait for an hour. As the rain begins to subside, I become worried I've wasted my chance. Then, I see through the chain-link fence a man walking my way. He's waving a flashlight left and right. I crouch low, pull up my pistol, and get ready. When he opens the gate, I see him wreathed in the light of a nearby streetlamp. He's a black-jacketed man. One of the Unit, I presume. He takes a moment at the fence gate to fiddle with a key. And once he's through, he keeps walking, letting the gate shut itself behind him. That's when I make my move.

I come out from behind the generator, moving in a careful hurry, pistol aimed at the back of the guy's head. I predict he'll turn right, because that's the only direction in which there's a gravel path. He does so. And as he does, I lightly grab the latch, slow the door's closing, slip through, then lightly shut it. If he had turned around, I would've shot him. If it had looked like he was going to shut the door himself, rather than let it close by itself, I would've let him go and looked for another opportunity. Such are the hard decisions we operators make.

Rain's letting up a lot. Gotta keep moving while I have it.

I'm now in the heart of the Cosmodrome. Tall, sleek buildings are on all sides of me, some of them separated by a football field of length, with nothing but landing pads and staging areas filling them. I don't see many roving patrols, but there are jeeps that remain stationary at key areas. Cameras are on most corners of the buildings, but it's dark, and it's raining, and it's easy to stay out of their field of vision. And what're the odds anyone's looking at the exact camera I'm passing, anyway? Maybe that's foolish thinking, but then Noah was foolish, too. He counted on the rain, and when it came, he seized his moment.

The rain remains steady as I move through narrow lanes, keeping to the perimeter, where there are still some decorative trees. I move in closer when I see all that's guarding the rear of the main research hangar is a group of soldiers in two jeeps who don't want to get wet, I guess. So they're staying inside, looks like.

I inchworm towards them. It takes the better part of an hour to get behind their jeeps, but then I do a push-up and come up to kneeling. I scan the perimeter of the hangar. The main bay doors are closed. There are doors all around the side but they're closed, probably locked. I see only two guards in rain suits walking a patrol. There's a guard tower nearby with a searchlight moving lazily all around the gray, hundred-foot-long slab of concrete, where I imagine they roll out the weapon on occasion to get it prepped for attachment to the Angara.

Now I spot a guy stepping out from one of the doors on the side of the hangar. He's about fifty yards from me. He closes the door, swipes a card in front of an electronic keypad, and it beeps and flashes green. There's a moment while I ponder going over to him and forcing him at gunpoint to let me in. But then something occurs to me. It comes quite out of the blue, and while it seems strange, there's no reason it couldn't work.

I stand up, remove my facemask, and walk right over to the man. I approach him from the front, so he can see me plainly. I can see he's middle-aged, with thinning black hair, dressed in plain gray slacks and a blue button-up. One of the scientists? A late-night janitor? It doesn't matter. He has a means to get in, and that's all that matters.

When the man sees me, he looks momentarily startled.

"I need to get inside," I say.

The man pulls up short.

"Eh…?" He stares at me.

There's a name sewn into his shirt: *Tabakov*. "Tabakov, right? It's a random nightly inspection. Increased security protocols. Something's going down, I'm sure you've heard?"

The man stands in the rain, looking puzzled. His brain tells him this doesn't feel quite right, but I'm fully kitted up, I've got a rifle and a pistol, I'm walking around like I belong here, and I'm speaking the language fluently with a local accent. So another part of his brain is telling him it's fine, just another security protocol someone forgot to inform him about.

"Come on," I say, not giving him the option. I start walking towards the door.

He follows me for two steps, then stops and says, "Eh...don't *you* have a keycard to get in?"

I turn to him, and say in an exasperatedly tone, "I didn't *plan* on having this patrol tonight. This order came from my commanding officer and one of your people, Dr. Aleksandr Gogol. Ms. Daziyr approved it. Now come on, before the *Bespre 'del* show up and we both end up like Mikhail Bondarchuk."

It takes a moment to register, and then he nods. It helps to know a few names. Names are like magic. They can open so many doors. I could have forced him to help me at gunpoint, and if he hadn't complied, shot him and taken his card. But this is easier and cleaner.

Tabakov waves me to follow him. I follow, glancing around for spying eyes.

He runs his keycard by the keypad, there's a double beep, and then we step through into a huge, open hangar bay, with steel crates stacked along the walls, a small single-engine plane parked at the far end, and forklifts all around. And, dominating the center of the bay, is a thing as large as a truck and covered by a black tarp.

Looking around, I see only a single camera mounted high in a far corner, with a view of everything in the bay. There are no guards in here, no researchers or late-night workers at all. Except for the pitter-patter of rain on the metal roof, it's totally quiet.

I thank Tabakov, and ask, "Do you mind terribly walking me over to the weapon? I need a witness to know I inspected it thoroughly. It's what *they* want now. For redundancy, you understand."

Tabakov sighs. Now he's the one exasperated. "Of course," he waves me on. I follow him over to the large, mysterious object sitting on a platform at the center of the room. Wrapped in that black tarp, unmoving, and so large, it somehow looks ominous, dreadful. Like the monolith in *2001: A Space Odyssey*. Scott showed me that movie after one late-night *D&D* session.

"Remove the tarp," I tell Tabakov.

The man looks at me strangely. I can already tell this is not exactly in line with protocol. But he's already come this far and he wants to get this over with. He reaches forward and grabs the tarp. It takes four strong tugs for the whole thing to come off, puddling to the ground like a woman's dress puddles around her feet when she undoes the shoulder strings and lets it drop. The thing I'm looking at looks like a large, silvery, octagonal donut, with a gigantic transparent lens in the center hole. There's black webbing all over it, keeping its retractable arms hugged close to its body.

I walk around the Great Donut, trying to imagine the destructive power that Isaacson, the DARPA representative at CIA, said it was capable of. While I'm doing this, Tabakov walks over to a workbench beside it, and waves at something. "Do you need to see the *Kop'ye*, as well?"

Kop'ye. Meaning *spear*. It's a strange pronunciation. I don't ask what the Spear is, or else it'll raise a red flag, so I walk over like I know what he's talking about. It's a small, black, handheld device, roughly in the shape of a pistol. It even has a handle big enough for one hand, and a trigger, with an elongated barrel that almost looks like a suppressor. It's inside a case made specially for it, with three small panels open on its side, revealing complex inner workings.

"My research team left it here so that we could start work on it first thing in the morning," Tabakov says. "I hope that isn't an issue? The lensing is almost finished. And the gas feeder ought to do well enough for five, maybe six uses?"

"Uses?"

"Yes. The deuterium-fluoride laser should create a greater wall of concussive force, if we've amplified it correctly."

I nod as if giving my approval. I have no idea what I'm looking at. Some new type of pistol? What's it got to do with a satellite that fires a particle beam from space?

I walk back over to the Great Donut, take out my mobile phone, and start recording.

"What the hell are you doing?" Tabakov asks. He looks at me in supreme astonishment, and instantly I can tell that I've broken a major protocol. Everyone in the Program has likely been told that all pictures of the weapon have been strictly forbidden.

I consider trying to lie further, but at this point it would only waste time. I take out my pistol and aim it at his head. He gasps, his eyes go wide, but he doesn't move. "Hands up." He obeys. "Turn around and get on your knees." He's in shock, doesn't move. I repeat the order and he slowly obeys. "Now get on the floor, arms and legs spread out." He obeys.

And now I don't have much time. The camera may be monitored by a guard at that very moment, or the guard might be looking away, or he might be on a bathroom break. Whatever the case, I have to assume I'm being monitored right now. I use a set of rollaround steps to get up close to the Great Donut. There are panels all over it. Some of them are easily openable, others are locked tight. I open the ones I can and take video of their inner workings.

I move fast, giving myself only thirty seconds, counting in my head. The tech guys at DARPA and Langley can slow down the footage later and dissect what it is.

I have to assume men with guns are on their way right now. I have to complete my objective before they get here. I e-mail the video file to Yarwick, then say to Tabakov, "See that forklift over there? Run over and lay down beside it. *Move!*" He doesn't need to be told twice this time.

My rifle already has the sound suppressor on. I take aim. Let her rip. The 7.62mm armor-piercing rounds tear through the Great Donut, no problem. I empty an entire clip into it, and when I'm finished, there's smoke coming out of one side of it. I dump the clip and pop in a fresh one. Then I take one of my flash-bang grenades and drop it inside one of the open panels. I hear it dropping into the inner guts of the Great Donut, and I run far away, hide behind a forklift, and plug my ears with my fingers. Five seconds later, it goes off. For what it's worth.

The smell of smoke and potassium nitrate is thick in the air. My ears have only a distant ring, otherwise I'm good. I walk over to the *Kop'ye* on the table, take a picture, and e-mail it to Yarwick, then I scoop it up and find it's easy to disassemble. It comes apart in three pieces, which I stick in one of my pockets.

I run over to Tabakov. His hands are around his ears and he's having trouble standing up. Of course, he wasn't blinded by the flash-bang, but the 175-decibel explosion disturbed the fluid in his ear, making him partially deaf and without perfect balance. I grab him by his shoulder to help him up, then lead him toward the nearest exit, one that, if my internal map is correct from the previous night's scouting, should help us emerge onto a narrow concrete path that leads to a little-used helipad on the west side of the Cosmodrome.

"Can you hear me?" I ask.

Tabakov looks at me, eyes wide with fear. He winces. I can tell he's wondering if I just said something. His ears must be ringing something fierce. I can only gesture him to the door. He staggers like a drunkard, but manages to open the door. He doesn't need his keycard to get out, it seems, just to get in. I hold Tabakov back and peek outside. I see only a jeep parked thirty yards away. Headlights are on, the guy in the driver's seat is talking to an armed soldier standing outside in the rain, which has all but died off.

I make Tabakov look at me, and I put a finger to my lips. Even through his fear, he gets the message, and nods. I walk out with him, my hand on his belt to help keep him straight. We walk like two people with no concern in the world. We reach the edge of the hangar and we turn. We're almost out of sight of the jeep when it happens.

A long, loud banshee wail goes up all around the base, filling up the air, filling up the world. A voice comes over an intercom that I don't see. It's like the voice of a disembodied god, crying out, *"Alert! Alert! All units alert! We have an intruder on base! Section Three, hangar bay! We have a saboteur! All units converge on Section Three and reinforce—"*

Shit. Someone either saw me in action shooting holes in the Great Donut or else saw the smoke coming out of it and wound the footage back to see what happened. Doesn't matter. It was a bit of luck that I got this far, and now—

"Hey! You there!" a voice calls from behind us. One of the guards from the jeep. Approaching fast from behind.

There's no point in pretending anymore. The jig us up, or is seconds away from being so. So I grab Tabakov by the arm, pull him close to me like I'm asking him a serious question. He stares at me, confused. When a flashlight beam hits us, I maneuver so that Tabakov is between me and the guard.

"Hey! You—"

Then I slip the pistol out and fire over Tabakov's shoulder, just six inches above the flashlight beam.

I'm temporarily blinded, but the guy holding the flashlight is dead. Now the guy in the jeep is screaming, and driving fast towards us. I turn and bolt, leaving Tabakov standing there, looking around in shock.

I'm around the building and dashing behind a row of parked forklifts and some kind of huge tractor. The jeep's headlights are bouncing around behind me, sometimes catching me, then losing me. I bolt into the shadow of a building marked for maintenance equipment, dash through a small parking lot at its rear.

"Alert! Alert! The Cosmodrome has been infiltrated—"

There's an eight-foot chain-link fence topped with barbwire. An unattended Miata is parked right beside it. I leap onto the hood of the Miata, then onto the roof, and jump halfway over the fence. My jacket gets snagged on the barbwire, but my momentum gets me to the other side and rips the jacket open. I land awkward. My ankle buckles, but thankfully doesn't get twisted. Not so graceful as in my youth.

The sirens are still blaring and the disembodied voice is still shouting over the intercom when I make it back to the tall electrified fence. Thankfully, coming from this direction, no key or code is needed, I push on the door's horizontal bar and dash through it, emerging back onto the Tsiolkovsky side of the compound and looking for the nearest deep shadow. Found one. A tall statue of a naked angel at the center of a fountain overflowing with rainwater. It sits on the lawn of a building marked COMMUNITY CENTER. A streetlight nearby is causing the statue to cast a long shadow, which I merge with.

I lie here listening. I hear raised voices. Men shouting into radios all around me. Fifty yards ahead of me, two jeeps go streaking through the rain-soaked streets, wheels splashing through immense puddles.

Suddenly, behind me, I hear voices approaching. Footsteps splashing through mud. I turn to look. Ten yards away, from behind the community center, I see multiple flashlight beams. I've got nowhere to go.

Spring up to one knee, transition to my rifle, and take aim. Four armed men come swiftly around the corner, moving as a stacked unit, the flashlights on their rifles sweeping left and right.

I take aim at the second guy in the stack, squeeze off a short, controlled burst, and his head snaps back. As he drops, the guys behind him stumble over his body, and the guy in the lead searches for the source. In the confusion I tap the lead guy, then the third guy. The guy at the rear knows what's good for him and backs up to take cover behind the community center's corner. He fires wildly around the corner, not even looking, and I move in a low crouch behind the angel statue. I wait for him to reload, then move to the end of the street, keeping the statue between me and my enemy. Once I'm clear, I make a mad dash across the street.

Just in time, too. Multiple jeeps and vans are converging on the community center. I hear them slewing to a halt as I leap over a chest-high fence into someone's back yard. Lights come on. Motion sensors. I jump another fence into the neighbor's back yard, then dart across a community playground.

A van comes splashing down a road on my left, headlights sweeping towards me. I dive to my stomach, crawl to cover behind a row of bushes. The headlights rake over me, but the van comes to a halt half a block away. I do a push-up, peek over the bushes. There are two vans there, and black-suited Unit guys come piling out of the sides and back, forming groups of four and five and splitting up.

One team is coming my way. Can't tell how many because they're passing in front of the van's high beams.

I crawl away, reach another house. The homeowner is stepping outside with an umbrella, looking around at all the commotion. I sidle up next to the house, watch a jeep go speeding by. The siren is still going, the disembodied voice has stopped shouting. An APC goes driving by, stops a block away, then the back opens up and it gives birth to twenty troops.

I start to slip around the house, to the wooded area in its back yard.

Then, lights from the heavens. I look up and see half a dozen Octopuses streaking fast overhead. They're coming from the Cosmodrome, splitting up in all directions. I count four drones escorting them. They know I've made it into Tsiolkovsky.

I'm pretty sure I'm going to die tonight. The thought is there and resolute. I can't be taken alive. I'm comfortable with that, I think. Like I said, it's never been a desire, just a state of prepared-and-waiting. I don't have the succinylcholine pill. I gave the gift of its mercy to Tatiana. I'll have to do mine the messy way, when the time comes. But I don't quit yet. Quitting is for tomorrow. Or when I know capture is inevitable.

"Nest, Ares," I say.

"Ares, Nest. Go ahead."

"Pretty sure I'm not gonna make the kitty-cat date. Tell Sophia…tell her I tried to make it back."

"Ares…" But there's nothing for her to say, and she knows it, not at this juncture.

I move into the forest, watching multiple lights play and dance all around me. Beams coming through the trees, from multiple vehicles moving along the roads, from porchlights, from everywhere. The shadows shift and elongate, shrink then grow. The whole world is becoming light, and the dark world where I do my business is shrinking, shrinking, shrinking. I emerge from the forest and dash across the street, and just as I do, a search team of eight comes from behind a house not thirty feet away.

There's no cover, no more shadows left, at least not nearby. I toss my last flash-bang grenade at them, just as the lead man sees me. I shoot him, dive to the ground, and roll to make myself a more difficult target. Three seconds later the flash-bang goes off. Their helmets insulate them somewhat, because they use flash-bangs themselves, but only when tossed through a room they haven't entered yet. When it goes off amidst them, they are dazed. Two of them drop to the ground like they've been shot.

I prop up to kneeling, move with soft knees to the house for cover, firing into their group. I tag three of them, then run behind the house. Make it two blocks before another vehicle slews to a stop ahead of me on the street. I know the headlights swept me. They saw me. I leap over a hedge and run into the woods, just as bullets smack into the trees all around me. One or two rounds whizz by my head.

I'm on another street, then moving through someone's back yard, then more woods, then dashing across the empty parking lot of a shopping plaza. As I run past the storefronts, I check their doors. All locked, of course, and none of them have the kind of lock my lockpick gun can hack. Except a side door! Someone left it propped open with a small bucket—God knows why—and I run inside and move into a stock room filled with boxes. Looks like a toy store, lots of teddy bears, water guns, and video games on the shelves.

I move in through the front of the shop, behind the checkout counter, facing the two large bay windows that look out into the parking lot. I see nothing. I hear only the sirens. All around me are shelves of toys hanging from pegboards.

I kneel behind the counter. Catch my breath. Focus. I can't stay here long, but I can give the search some time to cool down. If I shook them a couple of blocks back, then it'll take them a while to spread their resources, cover more ground. And maybe if I'm lucky the rain will start up again.

"Where's a fuckin' biblical flood when you need one?"

The sirens are still going. A voice is now shouting something that I can't quite make out. Sounds like a warning to residents to stay indoors.

A searchlight sweeps by the front window. I peek out from behind the counter. Nothing there. I get my rifle ready. I eject the magazine, and reload. My last mag. Then…a sharp pain in my side. I look down. I'm shocked to see blood. It's coming from my right side. By the dim light it looks like a bullet nailed me. The armor stopped most of it but something got through. Not good. I don't even know which encounter it was, I never felt a thing.

Then, the searchlight returns, brighter than the sun. I look up, and see something fast approaching. Soundlessly, smoothly, stealthily. I know what it is even before it crashes through the bay windows.

Chad Huskins

Through the light, I see two long steel tentacles reaching out.

14

The world is a shower of glass and wood. The Steel Octopus smashes its way inside, raping its way through the hole that its made, one tentacle slamming against a toy shelf and sending it crashing to the floor, the other one pressing down on the countertop in front of me, crushing it, sending splinters flying everywhere.

I don't hold back, I let loose with a salvo from my rifle directly into the body of the Octopus. Let me have this before I die. Just this. Fuck the star on the wall at Langley, let them put on my tombstone that I killed an Octopus.

The Octopus reacts, jerking to one side, then reeling both its tentacles back in quickly, fast as a rattlesnake, and covering its front. Its searchlights are aimed right at me, trying to blind me, but I lay on the trigger to keep it covering itself with the tentacles, hoping one of my armor-piercing rounds gets through as I dash out of its beam. I find a toy aisle filled with tricycles on both sides, move fast in a crouch to the far end, listening to the Octopus tear the store apart looking for me.

I peek around the corner, see it levitating over to the split wooden counter where I was hiding a moment ago. I can hear it making some kind of chatter, almost like a voice. I fire into its back, and watch it jerk like a deer that's been shot in the ass. It spins, coils in the air, reeling in its tentacles again to cover its main body. It's got a rifle attached to its hand, and it sprays the air.

I dip into an aisle filled with small lit aquariums. The bullets tear through it, shattering aquariums and sending water and fake goldfish splashing to the ground. I emerge from the other side, get a clear shot of its main body, pull the trigger—

A linebacker tackles me. Or feels like it. One of the tentacles randomly rakes the aisle, smashing through the shelves like they're made of balsawood and nailing me in the ribs. I'm slammed against the wall like I was hit by a car doing thirty. I land beside a small toy desk, the wind knocked out of me. Coughing. Gasping for air. Somehow I managed to hang on to my rifle.

The tentacles keep sweeping the store, tearing into the walls, the shelves, the ceiling. In all his thrashing about, I don't think the Octopus realizes it hit me. Growling at my own weakness, I force myself up onto my knees. My ribs are screaming at me as I raise my weapon. Probably cracked a rib, or broke a few.

"Ares! Report! Say status! Ares!" Yarwick's voice. A million miles away. As far away as Rigel.

I take aim. I know I can't have many rounds left in the mag. Have to make it count.

The Octopus continues thrashing, fires randomly into walls, shelves, everywhere. I wait for the tentacles to clear. Watch its movements, how it bobs up and down, up and down, so graceful, so effortlessly. I take a breath, let it out slowly, and squeeze the trigger.

Its whole body snaps sideways and he goes flying to the left, almost flipping over, crashing into a far wall. It's dead, but it floats there in the air like a jellyfish, those tentacles now lightly waving around. Limbs without a brain to conduct them. I'm up and limping. I also may have sprained my ankle.

I'm breathing heavily. Test my side. Not broken, I don't think. But probably cracked. And now I'm bleeding more from the bullet wound. Fuck me.

Check my mag. Rifle's dry. I drop it, and move through the stock room, where I entered. Behind me, I hear tires screeching. Vehicles arriving in the parking lot. I'm out the back door and running, despite the pain in my ankle. One foot in front of the other.

Fuck the darkness. Come back to me.

"I'm trying, Sophia."

Behind me, there are spotlights. I glance back and see three Steel Octopuses converging on the toy store. I smile when I think about them finding their dead pal. That's for you, Tatiana. For you and comrade Mikhail Bondarchuk.

I cross the street into more trees. The city of Tsiolkovsky now seems to be never-ending, just a continuous stream of shadows and Orwellian homes and sirens and searchlights. A constant loop of this. Maybe I'm going in circles. I don't even know anymore.

There's a dog park up ahead. I cross it, trip down a set of steps, then hide behind a tree when I hear a van go zooming by. I look north. There's a farmhouse just a hundred feet away, and beyond that the open grasslands go for another hundred, and then there's the first trees in the forest.

"Almost home, Sophia," I say, knowing I'll never make it. There's already a drone buzzing around that farmhouse, moving slowly towards me. I don't have many places left to go.

The van that went by has stopped somewhere down the street. I peek around the tree. It's parked about thirty yards away. Someone's getting out of the driver's seat. I see only their silhouette in the high beams. It's a man. He kneels and inspects something on the ground. I hear the buzzing of drones. And a helicopter has now topped a building a hundred yards away and is scanning the ground with a searchlight.

The drone's buzzing is getting louder. I've lost sight of it over the trees.

I turn and run in a low crouch, over to a public restroom at the far end of the dog park. Inside, there's only a sallow white light to illuminate the two stalls and the urinal. I shut the door and press my back to it. I take deep, deep breaths. I clutch my side. Now the pain is mounting. My ribs and my ankle. There are ways of dealing with that. I shut my eyes and go to the Drifting Place, where nothing matters, where I give myself permission to be afraid and then to let it all go.

I'm going to die, and that's fine. That's just fine. But I'm not going to make it easy on them. I press my ear to the door and I hear the helicopter moving farther away. I can't hear the drone, either.

Maybe I'm finally beyond the search perimeter. Maybe the helicopter and the drone have other ghosts to follow. Maybe I'll get lucky and some homeowner will report something suspicious in his back yard that has nothing to do with me, and all search teams will converge there. Maybe I'll have my opening.

I hobble over to the sink. There's a fluorescent light blinking on and off indecisively overhead. By that flickering light, I wash my hands, my face, and my side. I rip off my jacket and body armor, toss them to the ground. I'm losing blood, gotta deal with that. I take out my medical kit and scramble for the QuickClot and apply ample doses. Don't have time for stitches. I spray it with disinfectant and put a compression bandage over it. I'll deal with digging out bullet fragments if there are any later.

Outside, I hear the rain picking up. Doesn't sound like a deluge anymore, but still pretty heavy. That'll help.

I've been about ten minutes in here. Need to get moving. I wince bending down to pick up my body armor. I'm just about to put it on, when I hear something. A splashing noise. Just outside. I look at the door. A voice is coming from the other side. I look down at the floor and see my own goddamn blood trail. Idiot. How did I not realize I was leaving a fucking trail of crimson blood?

The door opens, I draw my pistol right from its holster, and I tag the first guy through. He drops to the ground, bullet went straight through his skull. A black-suited man. A Unit man. I keep my gun trained on the door. Approach it slowly, one step at a time. I see no one else. I hear no one else. But I know I heard him talking to someone before he made it to the door. That means he was telling someone about the trail that he found. That means—

Just I as cross the threshold, my gun aiming outside, a hand reaches through the open doorway and grabs my wrist. The hand jerks me forward, and I'm too weak to stop it. But I know what's coming and I reach out with my free hand to smack away the pistol that's going to be aiming at my face. It fires wide, ringing out fivefold in the confines of the bathroom. I'm rushed by a shadowy figure who comes in through the doorway, both of us tripping over the dead body of his teammate before he slams me against the first toilet stall.

My pistol is being gripped by its suppressor, giving him a better handle to wrench it free. It goes flying. I put both my hands on his pistol and eject the magazine, then pull the slide to eject the round in the chamber. He drops the gun and shoulder-butts me against the stall again. A blade comes out, slashes me across the arm I've put to my face. I shuffle away from the second attack and towards the sink. When he steps into the light, I see the karambit blade before I see his face.

"Ares," Matveyev chuckles, like I haven't just killed his teammate behind him, like he's bumping into an old friend at a party. "There you are."

*

The knife lives. It's here and it's there, and behind it is a gleaming smile. The knife lives. It's got a mind of its own, moving intelligently and deftly through the air, hissing like a snake's warning. The knife lives. My eyes and hands can barely keep up, between the horizontal slashes of the raptor claw-shaped blade and the thrusts at my face. The knife lives. As organic and hungry as a creature evolved to seek the flesh of another. The knife lives.

My hands are detached from me, operating without my consent, doing what they know to do, checking the forearm to stop a slash and batting away the wrist. I'm keeping up, keeping pace, keeping focused, visiting the state of no-mind. My future is uncertain and unlived, my past never happened and I'm in this moment. I was born here, not anywhere else. I'll die here, not anywhere else. My hands keep moving. They keep up. They're doing well.

But the knife lives.

The karambit feeds on my limbs, tasting morsels of my left forearm, then my right elbow. It nicks me above my right eye. Rivulets of blood cascade down my sweating face. I catch the wrist. Total luck, but I caught it. But my grinning enemy delivers a knee into my guts, close to my cracked ribs. I stagger back and he gives a spinning side kick to my waist. The kick glances off, but still keeps me going backward. He comes at me and he's smiling and there's blood everywhere and the knife lives.

Waste nothing. The voice comes out of nowhere. Like a ghost. Why is it there?

My mind is a million miles away, watching all these events unfold, watching the glimmering blade fade in and out of existence, in time with the flickering fluorescent lighting. Blood sprays across the mirror above the sink. My blood. The karambit slices me good across the right forearm.

Waste nothing. There it is again. A voice. A man's. Familiar.

The grinning man comes at me and the blade lives. He's not backing off. He doesn't know how to. He doesn't need to. He and the knife are one and they are close to achieving their goal. He comes at me, testing high and low, slashing at air, keeping me in check, keeping me from getting close.

Waste nothing. And now I recognize the voce. And I know why it's there. A self-defense instructor from eons ago at Camp Peary, telling me that in a fight, you waste nothing. Use everything at your disposal. Weaponize your environment. *Waste nothing. Use everything. Turn the enemy's strength against them.*

I grin.

The blade lives. But I know a secret.

Blood is draining down my arms. I back away from the next slash, and the next, and the next. My back is to the wall. Nowhere to go. When the grinning man comes at me again, I fling my hands at his face, and the blood that pooled there goes directly into his eye. His next slash goes wide. I rush forward, wrap both my arms around his knife-holding arm and clamp down. I do not let go. I will never let go.

He delivers punch after punch into my side, my ribs howl at me, but I hold on to that arm and I'll never let go. Because for now, the blade is dead. If I ever let go, the blade will live again. That can't happen. It won't happen.

I head-butt my enemy, then drive him backwards, back through the doorway. He trips over his dead friend and I was waiting for that. When we make it outside, his balance is off, and I set him up for *o goshi*. He's good. He prevents that throw. Then I sweep his front foot with *sasae*, but he hops on one foot, keeps his balance, but then slips in the mud and I transition to his side and a kick a leg across his midsection, using *o guruma* to throw Matveyev to the ground.

I've done judo long enough to know when the throw is executed right. And when it's executed right it's devastating. He hits the earth with a thud that must've been heard in the heavens. I feel his grip on the knife melt. I twist his wrist, and yank it away. My hands are too slippery with my own blood, though, and in the struggle I lose my grip on it. It falls away into the mud, lost in the darkness.

The knife is dead, but my grinning enemy has recovered. He spins around in the mud, kicks out with both feet, and knocks my legs out from under me. I fall to my knees, and he leaps at me. I wrap my legs around him and control him in guard, and we roll once, twice, and on the third time I end up in mount position. I wrap my left arm around his neck and press my right fist into his throat.

I have him. I almost have him.

But he bridges his hips off the ground, and sends me rolling off of him. We both scramble to our feet. He's first up. My ankle slows me down. He delivers a punch directly to my temple. "You don't have it, Ares!" he shouts. "You don't have what it takes!"

I stagger backwards, slip on the mud, and drop down to one knee. There's a takedown from here in judo, I've never been a big fan of it, but I have no choice. I throw myself into his legs, and he trips over me and faceplants in the mud. Now I'm the first one back to my feet. Just as he's standing, I give an ineffectual hook to his head. Karambit's still coming. I reach out and grab him by a wad of his blonde hair, yank his head down, and deliver a knee into his face. I hear the crunch of his nose, and he collapses to the ground, moaning. He tries to stand. Collapses. He's rocked, practically unconscious.

I'm sucking wind hard. This has gotta be it. There's gotta be enough tactical teams around me to kill me easily now, right out in the open. But I don't hear anything. No drones, no helicopters, no vans or jeeps. The sirens are still going in the distance, though.

I stagger over to the bathroom. I grab my body armor and jacket, scoop up the medical kit, and take off. I don't have time to look for my gun in the dark. I grab the pistol out of the hands of the first guy I shot. I step outside to finish Karambit, but just then, a searchlight hits the ground fifty yards away from me. I look up, and see an Octopus sweeping the area. He doesn't see me yet, but an unsilenced gunshot would attract his attention.

I take one last look at Matveyev, then turn and dash for the farmhouse a hundred yards away. The whole way, I keep thinking a searchlight will land on me. Even as I run and struggle to tug on the body armor and jacket. Even as I stumble and fall into the mud. Even as I climb back to my feet and bleed and stagger into the woods.

And as I run blindly through the trees, a single thought recurs, on a constant loop. *I should've killed him.*

*

One foot in front of the other.

The machine is somehow able to move. It's surprising. Even when it's damaged and it's leaking and the brain isn't functioning properly, the body, the machine, keeps working. It's stubborn. There's old programming in there that won't let it quit. Not till tomorrow.

There's also a primitive creature deep inside that rages against the concept of defeat. *Fuck the darkness.* With fluids leaking and the body screaming to stop, the machine-brain won't let it. It's not quitting time. Not until the machine-brain says so.

One foot in front of the other.

I don't know how many miles I've crossed. I no longer sense time the way I should. Adrenaline is still too high. I don't hear anything. Just the rain. I'm bleeding but I can't do much besides stop on occasion to throw some QuickClot on it, but that's not going to do the trick forever. My feet are always moving. How are they doing that?

"Ares, say status," someone says.

The sun's coming up. How long have I been running? The clouds have dispersed. The world is wet and there's the sound of water droplets dropping from one leaf to the next. It's cold. I'm carrying my jacket but I'm not putting it on yet. Not until I've done something about the blood.

One foot in front of the other.

"Ares? Do you copy? *Ares?*"

My feet go splashing into a narrow, knee-deep river. I don't know if it's a tributary of the Bolshaya Pyora or not, but its cold, bracing waters give me the first jolt I've had in a while. I wade to the other side, find cover in the woods, and sit down with my back against a tree. I rummage through the medical kit for an adrenaline shot. Jam the syringe into my thigh. Hellooooooooooo there! That'll wake you up. I feel an exhilarating force rushing through my veins. My vision clears up. Didn't even know it had gotten foggy.

A voice slips through from another time and place. *The world thought I was dead. I might as well have been.* Sophia's voice. I look around for her. She's not there. I keep moving.

Now I've got some work to do. I apply the last of my QuickClot, then take a look at the injuries. Seven cuts, three of them deep into the flesh. The bullet wound is bleeding again. I've got some needlework to do, maybe some surgery with scissors and pliers. Think I've got plenty of disinfectant spray left. Hope so. I have to live. I have to keep going. I have to make it to tomorrow so I can quit.

15

I don't remember giving myself permission to fall asleep. Maybe I didn't need permission this time. I wake up slowly, looking up at a sun way past noon. I'm sore all over, but especially my side. I vaguely remember digging for bullet fragments, feeling around inside the wound with the tip of the scalpel, looking and listening for any metallic clicks. If they're in there, I didn't find them.

Trying to sit up straight hurts, but I make myself do it. I look at my naked ribs. I wrapped them as tight as I could, first with bandages, then by tying my jacket around my midsection really tight. I slept on my side. Best way to sleep with cracked ribs. Got to keep breathing, even though it hurts. Biggest problem with cracked ribs is pneumonia. Still remember that from combat medicine training. What was the guy's name that threw up in that class? Higgins? Hodgins? He didn't like the sight of blood. He thought he could handle it, but then they cut open that dead goat in front of him and he upchucked.

I smile at that. And laugh. Big mistake. The laugh causes my ribs to scream at me in protest. Where the fuck is Hodgins now? Or was it Scoggins?

Time to get moving. Gotta make it to tomorrow so I can quit. I force myself up onto one knee. Then onto my feet. I take a few testing steps. Ouch. The ankle was pushed to its limits by all that running. I limp in a circle for a few minutes, testing it out. Maybe it's a minor sprain, maybe it's not. Either way, compression ought to help, so I wrap it up tight. As I do, I look to the sky for enemies: drones, helicopters, and *Bespre 'del*, oh my.

Heh. I seem to have developed a sense of humor. Probably the adrenaline and post-battle euphoria.

Once I'm done wrapping the ankle, I walk around a bit more, getting used to it. I check the pistol's clip. Full. It's a SIG Sauer, and it fits okay in my holster. I've got two ration bars in my vest, so I devour those. No water. All my bottles were with my gear bag, and I'm not going back for it. Doubtless, it'll be found in a full sweep of the surrounding woods. My fake IDs are in there, so they'll have a better picture of me to float around to the media.

But I need water. I need it bad. I limp over to the river. Water looks pretty clear. I kneel and take large gulps of it. Hopefully I don't get a Giardia infection or other contamination. I have to take the risk. I need the hydration right now more than anything else. We'll worry about diarrhea and stomach cramps later, if they come.

I click my teeth. "Nest, Ares. Do you copy? Over."

There is a long silence. Then a male's voice responds. Sounds like Drucker. "Uh...uh, yeah, Ares. Copy. We copy! Uh, hang on while I get..."

"Ares?" Yarwick. Sounding flustered, relieved, and angry all at once. "That you? Say status."

"Affirmative, Nest. Not dead yet, that's my status. Damn near it." I look at the stitches on my arms, across the back of my wrist. One of those slashes was close, came close to some major veins.

"What's the damage?" she asks hurriedly. "Specifically, what's hurt on you?"

"I'm stitched up for now. I'm hurt bad enough to slow me down, but I can walk. Cracked ribs, a bullet wound that's not so bad. I've got no gear besides my main combat kit. Lost both of my weapons, procured an enemy's. Lost a lot of blood. Dehydrated. No food. It ain't lookin' good."

"You hang in there, Ares," she says. It hasn't slipped my notice that she hasn't asked about mission success yet. She's only concerned with me. "You just hang in there, we're going to figure out a way to..." She trails off. I get the feeling someone cut her off, maybe asking her a question or telling her something. "Ares, what is mission status? Did you complete the objective?"

There's someone from higher up the chain of command in the room with her. Doubtless, they're chomping at the bit to ask me questions about what I saw, what happened, if it's all finished.

"Mission success, Nest. I tore the weapon a new one. I don't think it's going to be functioning, at least not without a major overhaul." I wince, touching my ribs. "Also, I picked up something else. I sent you a picture. Don't know what it is, but they call it a *Kop'ye*. I think it's supposed to fire some kind of laser? A deuterium-fluoride laser, I think." I touch my pockets where the pieces of the pistol-like object are tucked, making sure I didn't lose them. "Did you get the files I sent?"

"Affirmative, Ares. We got them. Great job. Now let's work on getting you home."

"Sounds like a plan."

"Skies are clear, we've got satellite view of your region. We're monitoring a new influx of troops coming from the railway. There's been a lot of activity outside of the base. Looks like roving search parties. Wherever you are, you need to make distance."

"I'll send you my coords." It takes fifteen seconds to e-mail my coordinates to her. "I'm gonna head north for a day, then cut west. If I'm lucky, I'll make Zabaykalsky Krai in three or four days."

"It's mostly wilderness that way, Ares. And mountainous. And cold."

"You got a better idea, I'm all ears."

There's a long silence. Then Yarwick says, "I've, uh...we've got a new regional expert on the team, Ares. He's knowledgeable of that area and says that's actually not a bad way to go, if you're thinking of heading south eventually into Mongolia, and *if* you can endure the cold. There's likely to be snow soon. Lots of ice. And you'll need to procure food and supplies as you go."

"I can do that, Nest."

There's trepidation in her voice. "Then you have our blessing, Ares. I'm sending you the coords for a town called Simenga. Our regional guy says it's your best bet."

"Copy that," I grunt, bending down to pick up a dead tree branch that I think will make a decent walking stick. We'll see how it helps with my limp. Might have to fashion crutches later if it gets any worse. "Ares is mobile. Out." I click off, and then pop two pain pills and put one foot in front of the other. I glance back to see if anyone's following me, then look up at the sky to make sure it's clear.

I walk until nightfall. I see nothing and no one. The darkness gathers and the temperatures drop. And all I think about the whole way, even as I build my shelter, is *I should've killed him. For Tatiana, I should've killed him.*

*

On the second day, I see an Octopus in the far south. He doesn't come anywhere close to me. A helicopter on the third day sweeps nearby, but the searchlight never comes close. The fourth day finds me wandering into the foothills of the Stanovoy Mountain Range, the same mountains I saw my first day here, when the Japanese smugglers dropped me off. The same mountains I'd hoped I wouldn't have to go anywhere near. It takes me two extra days before the Nest informs me that I've technically crossed the border into Zabaykalsky Krai. Still in Russia, though on the Siberian outskirts.

The temperatures are dropping drastically. My gloves keep my hands warm enough, but only so long as I keep moving.

I'm making slower progress than I thought I would. The first reason is because of my foot. My man-brain overestimated what my body could actually do. I ended up having to take more pain pills and rig a splint for my ankle, as well as fashion a crutch from a dead tree branch.

The second reason this is taking longer than I thought is because it's more uphill than I had conceived. There are no easy paths that aren't roads—the roads have been carved through these foothills, but I cannot go near roads any more than a virus can go near a white blood cell. I'm an infection in this region, crossing through the body of Russia, and if I go through her main arteries I will surely be seized by her antibodies that have learned my tricks.

I subsist off of what I can grab. The Nest e-mails me pictures of edible plants in the region, but I only come across a couple of pea shrubs, and they direct me to rivers and creeks where I can gather water, which I boil over a fire using a pot I stole from a cabin I passed, along with a couple of chickens. At night, I check the dressing on my wounds, spray some disinfectant, and just hope everything heals the way it should.

I fall asleep in my shelter and have a nightmare where I realize I'm strapped to a bed in Karambit's torture chamber. Then I wake up, and think, *I should've killed him.* I destroy my shelter and get under way again.

Along the way, I check my pockets to make sure I still have the disassembled *Kop'ye.* Tabakov said it was some kind of laser. And the Great Donut was supposedly a kind of particle-beam weapon, the first of its kind. I recall what the Chinese defector told us at CIA headquarters, about the Law of Accelerating Returns and how war technology was about to see a boom.

Mile after mile, the temperature drops. On the eighth day, there's the first flakes of snow falling from the sky. The next morning, when I crawl out of my shelter, I'm met with a winter wonderland. Two feet of snow covers the forest floor, the trees are icy sculptures, and the skies are as gray as my mood.

One foot in front of the other, Adamson. Let's go.

*

On March 13, 1993, a blizzard hit Georgia. It was called a once-in-a-hundred-years thing. I was twelve years old at the time. People make fun of Georgians for panicking during snowstorms, but there's good reason. It's like the old folks have PTSD, remembering the '93 storm that came through and shut everything down. All the power, all the phones, all the roads. Since Georgia gets so few serious snows, the state doesn't keep a lot of salt trucks year-round. So when a big one hits, you can bet that the whole state shuts down. The roads are solid ice, coated in snow, and trees, heavy with the burden of all that snow and ice, are prone to collapse in the wind, smashing cars on the roads.

When the '93 blizzard hit, us kids didn't understand the severity. We were running outside, playing in the snow, delighted that school had been cancelled for a *whole week*. We were building snowmen and snowfortresses, we were sitting inside the cold house around a crackling fireplace, roasting marshmallows, we were using our sleds to go flying down traffic-less hills. We were in heaven.

But the grownups knew a secret. A secret they weren't telling us. There was trouble all around us. Serious trouble. They tried not to let it show, and some of them were successful. The problem was we were limited on food. The pipes were frozen, so no water was coming out. We'd heard that snow was coming, but no one at the time had predicted *this level* of snow. No one was prepared. With the power out, a lot of food couldn't be prepared correctly. I heard later that some neighbors shared food with one another, but at the time we didn't have any close neighbors.

People were freezing to death in their homes. Literally, people were found dead in their homes, having no heater and no fireplace. People with medical conditions, who normally would have been all right since they could just call 911, found their phones didn't work. Stroke victims had no one to call. People who fell down the stairs had no one to call. And for the few people whose phones *did* work, the ambulances couldn't get to most of them.

All over the state, cars were left abandoned on the side of the road. Even military vehicles, which had been brought in for disaster relief, slid off the roads and got stuck in ditches.

Our closest neighbor was a man named Dee Fortenberry, and he lived a mile away, and the storm was too heavy those first two days to reach him. You'd get lost in the snow if you tried, might wander onto the highway, might get hit by some random idiot who was trying to be a hero in his four-wheeler. Mr. Fortenberry lived with his elderly mother. They were both freezing to death and we didn't know it. On the third day of the blizzard, us kids were outside playing when we heard a gunshot. Then another. In the silence of the snow-covered world, we heard it quite well, and told our parents. My dad trudged over to the Fortenberry house, and discovered they were panicked, freezing, starving to death, drinking only what water they could bring in and melt.

Stories like this were happening all over the state. Kids having fun. The grownups panicking like the End Times might've come. Whenever I see a heavy snow, I always think about that. The innocence of youth. To children, the snow is for play. But adults hold a secret truth. They know what it can be. For those who have seen Nature's full fury, they know what it can mean if you are not prepared.

I'm currently not prepared.

My suit keeps me pretty warm, but as temperatures continue to drop to the single digits, I'm facing a challenge. I don't have much food left and I don't have adequate shelter. The Nest is directing me towards a settlement five miles south. Place called Simenga, near the Nizhnyaya Tunguska River. I head there stubbornly, forgetting my hunger and my pain and the cold. I do this by visiting the Drifting

Place, accepting the hunger, pain, and cold, even welcoming it. I decide that I like the cold. Another mind trick to keep myself going.

Come back to me.

At one point I stop to catch my breath. Just one minute. I rummage through my pockets and take out the three pieces of the *Kop'ye.* I wonder what the hell it is, then put the pieces back and keep moving.

I see the first lights of a settlement at dusk. I head right for it. I don't care what I look like, that I've grown a scraggly beard and I'm dressed in bloody armor and camo and carrying a gun. I just need the warmth. And food. And water. And everything.

I toss my crutch away and limp into town. I pass a pharmacy that's closed and a café that looks open, though all the lights are off and there's only candles lit at each table. Only two people are inside, both are employees cleaning tables. I take a second to look at my reflection in the window of a car parked in the lot, try to make myself look decent. I've removed my tactical vest and hide it beside a Dumpster. I'm just wearing my camouflage gear. Hopefully that doesn't raise any suspicions. I tuck the pistol in the back of my waistband and walk inside.

The two waiters turn and see me. One of them says something to the other, who heads behind the grill. I take a seat at the bar, trying to appear nonchalant. When the guy approaches me, he looks at me askance, but only for a second. "What do you want?"

I look at the menu on the chalkboard behind him. There are a mix of Russian and Chinese meals. I'm near the Mongolian border, so no surprise there. "The Stroganoff," I say. "And water. Lots of water." The guy nods and goes to the grill. He tells the other waiter to bring me a pitcher of water and a glass. I try not to guzzle it desperately, but it's hard. My body wants it.

I sit there quietly basking in the warmth of the restaurant, my foot thanking me for the break.

When the Stroganoff comes, it's like heaven. When I'm finished, I get up and approach the counter to pay. I pat myself down, looking confused. "I forgot my wallet in the car," I tell the guy looking at me expectantly. "Mind if I go get it?" He nods, and shrugs.

I step outside and grab my vest and walk behind the restaurant and slip behind a barber shop. I walk two more miles before I spot a gas station. There's only one or two customers inside. I wait from across the street, looking in through the windows to see when the woman behind the counter looks occupied grabbing something for a customer. I jog across the street, step inside, scoop up a handful of candy bars, a loaf of bread, and a jug of water before I step back outside. I don't think the lady noticed a thing.

I'm another mile away when I sneak in through the back of a sporting goods store. It's closed right now, but an application of my lockpick gun gets me in. I don't hear an alarm as I move quickly through the store, but there might be a silent one, so I have to move fast. I only grab a heavy jacket, a pair of black khakis, a T-shirt with a roaring lion on it, an *ushanka*, and a large brown duffel bag to stuff it all in. I'm out in two minutes.

Five minutes away, I see flashing lights. Cops racing towards the supply store.

I take refuge behind a supermarket. Night has fully fallen, and now I'm keeping warm by a fire I've started inside a small plastic bucket. There were some papers and scraps of wood from a busted pallet that I tossed inside the bucket. I used the lighter from my survival kit to start the fire. There's a small wooden supply shed with a lock that I broke off, and brought the bucket-fire inside with me. I eat one of the candy bars and sip at the water.

"Nest, Ares. I'm subsisting. No sign of increased police or military activity. I don't think the Unit knows I'm here."

"Copy that, Ares. Good to hear. How are you feeling?"

"Tired. Gonna catch some shuteye here in a few." I sigh. "Hey, boss? Now that I'm away from all the mess, care to give me an update on what's going on on the global scale?"

"No one's shot anybody yet, if that's what you mean," Yarwick says. "The Black Sea Fleet is mobilizing more subs from the shipyards in Polyarny. Spy satellites have picked up more than a dozen heat blooms. They don't seem large, most likely subs that have been sitting there rotting for over a decade but have been reoutfitted."

"How many are mobilizing?"

"Hard to say. The North Koreans and Russians are putting their strong subs into the Atlantic and Pacific theater. The Russians are advancing their *Dolgorukiy* subs, but are keeping their older war vessels closer to home for defense. Iran's only got three *Kilo*-class subs, sold to them by the Russians years ago. We've kept track of those for years, they're not very stealthy, and now they're moving to the Gulf of Oman. They're just sitting there, possibly to attempt sea denial operations."

I sigh heavily, and take another bite of my candy bar. Caramel. Not a big fan of caramel. "And no one's taken a swing yet, you said?"

"No. No one yet. But our sources are telling us they're hearing rumors out of Tsiolkovsky. They know something went down there. Something bad. Something that's going to set back operations for years." I hear the smile in her voice. "Looks like you really did a number."

"Glad to do my duty," I say, and mean it. Why do this job if you don't love your country?"

"PAG predicts the Russians will spin this as reason for their new aggressions, getting ahead of the accusations they know are coming their way concerning the hack attacks, airport blackouts, and train derailments. News outlets are just starting to pick it up that we've upgraded to DEFCON Three."

DEFCON 3. "Round House" they term it. All U.S. Armed Forces are put on alert, with the Air Force specifically ready to mobilize in just fifteen minutes. Usually things don't slow down until DEFCON 2 is reached, and our enemies realize we're ready to mobilize in half that time. DEFCON 1 has never been reached. If it had, the world probably wouldn't exist right now.

"What are the Russians saying right now about all this mobilization?"

Harriet Kozner comes on the line. "A lot of their usual political rhetoric, a lot of whataboutism," she says. "Every accusation NATO makes about how they're breaking maritime laws by moving into protected waters, they say 'what about the American fleet?' and 'how come they get to move so freely?'"

"Stalling, huh?"

Kozner snorts. "Yeah, it's their usual bullshit. For them, whataboutism isn't just a short-term defensive strategy, it's a long-term strategy that aims to instill in the American people, among others, super-cynical beliefs that 'everybody's doing it' and reject any expectation of Russian leaders to act with good conscience or virtue."

"It's been working well for them for a decade now," Yarwick says. "They never accept responsibility for anything, they just find a hair-thin story about how the U.S. kind of did the same thing one time, usually a defensive operation or a politician's words taken out of context, and make it seem like they're doing the same thing, so it's no big deal."

Koznzer says, "Unfortunately, studies show that more and more Americans are falling for it. Even politicians who make policies that govern trade with them. It looks like that might've all been priming us to be underprepared. Our latest penetration seems to confirm that."

No one ever accused the Russians of not being crafty, or having short-term goals. They never die, they never quit, and the current regime desires respect and domination at all cost. "Anything from Russian news outlets about me?" I ask.

"The same stuff, but more of it," Yarwick says. "More circulation by the hour."

"No clear picture of my face? Nothing from my passport?"

"Negative, Ares. You're not Condition Red yet."

I nod. "Hey, Nest?"

"Yes, Ares?"

"I'm gonna get some sleep now. Try to, anyway. Let me know if anything changes."

"Understood, Ares. Goodnight. Nest, out."

*

The watch wakes me at 0400. I'm lightly covered in snow, and my fire is smoldering out. It's twelve degrees out, but inside my little living space it's warm enough I don't freeze. Just barely. Ice has gathered on my eyebrows, around my nose. My mouth and chin are tucked inside my collar.

My ribs protest as I sit up. A dream is just fading, one where I was shoplifting at the gas station, only I was just a boy, and the cops caught me. One of the cops was Karambit, and he was taking me away to some dungeon. Mom was there. So was Yarwick. Yarwick was screaming for me to help her. They had already amputated one of her legs, and were about to take another one.

"Nest, any updates?"

"Good morning, Ares. Negative, no updates right now. Roads in your area still look clear, all the way to Turung Highway South. That'll lead you to the Tseng Wilderness Area and into Mongolia."

"Copy that, Nest. Ares is mobile."

I roll up my blanket and step out of the shed slowly, searching for Steel Octopuses and their ilk. Then I start my hike across town, dressed in my new clothes and limping as I go. My combat kit is stuffed into the duffel bag, and its slung over my shoulder.

Simenga seems a quiet town at all hours. Not much traffic. At sunup, I actually see a kid riding a horse, a man—I'm assuming his father—leading the animal on by the reins. Like most Russians, they don't acknowledge strangers with a curt nod or a wave, so I don't acknowledge them. There's a convenience store at the far end of town that I step inside, warming my bones one last time before the long trek south. There's a TV hanging on the wall. It's turned to a news station, where a stern-faced woman is talking to her audience in most serious tones. The headline beside her says *World on the Brink?*, and at the bottom, there's scrolling messages from social media, people giving their two cents.

I use the restroom, and refill my water jug from the sink. When I step out, I head right for the door. But I stop when I see a familiar face on the TV. My own. A picture of me from the day I posed for the fake passport pic.

A quick glance around the store shows that no one else is paying attention. I head out before they start.

"Nest, Ares," I say, heading away from the town, trudging through knee-high snow towards a farmhouse that's just outside of town with a dozen huge windmills, capturing wind energy. "Do you copy?"

"Ares, Nest. Go ahead."

"I just stepped out of a convenience store where my face was clearly plastered across a television screen."

A moment. "Yeah, we're just getting that, too. Looks like this happened within the last hour. It's trickling down through different stations. We hadn't had it confirmed until a few minutes ago."

"This can't be good, Nest. They'll find out who I am. Who I really am. I was hoping I'd be far from here before that happened, safe at home." There's any number of ways the Russians can figure this out. Facial-recognition software could match my face to anything they've obtained from old military photos and catalogued in FSB or SVR databases. Any agents they have in place in our intelligence community could possibly look it up. The mole that warned them about Operation NARROW VOID, for instance, but who evidently didn't know the name of the agent assigned to carry it out, could call in a few favors, figure it out, and give the Unit my name, home address, everything.

Or, even more easily, social media mining could do it. Such a clear picture of my face is bound to show up on the web. American news outlets will pick it up. They might be warned by the government not to show my face, but the picture will make it to certain websites. Somebody from my high school will say in a chatroom, "Hey, I remember that guy." Might be Scott, recalling our *Dungeons & Dragons* days. Could be an ex-girlfriend, Natalia, the Russian. Could be anything. It'll trickle into the Russians' web. They'll eventually find out.

This could hit the U.S. very hard. I'm sure after she learned I lost my passport, Yarwick already communicated to her superiors that this could happen. Probably Deputy Director Halbach sent it up the chain. Right now, there are conversations happening with my name—my *real* name—being communicated to the POTUS, and the topic of how to distance themselves from me is coming up.

I know what's coming. It's what every SOG operative has to understand when they take this job.

"How much time do I have to disavowal?" I ask.

"It depends," Yarwick says, her voice conveying a barely contained stress. I can tell she hasn't slept well in days. "Depends on whenever the Russians finally drop your name to the press, and say that you're an agent and known Navy SEAL. After that…I'm guessing two to four hours before the president has to make a statement saying he has no idea what the Russians are talking about, that he and the CIA have no connection to you, that you officially retired from the military years ago."

"I'm sure the Russians will buy that," I say sardonically.

"There is a backup plan in play," she says. "I started forming it as soon as we found out you were about to head for your objective. It's not much, but I had my sources do some looking and it turns out an Islamic fundamentalist group was taken out by Russian troops about a hundred miles from you. Suspected terrorists. They were trying to sneak into the region."

"So what's the play? Blame the Tsiolkovsky attack on them?"

"Like I said, it's a small thing, but I asked Halbach to activate propaganda agents in the area to spread the story that three or four of the Islamists got away, and were seen trying to sneak across the border into Amur Oblast. The story's been circulating for days now. Didn't pick up much traction. But it might once the president issues his statement of disavowal."

Statement of disavowal. Never thought I'd hear those words in relation to myself.

"Let me know the second my name hits the airwaves," I tell her. "And when the president issues the statement."

"Of course, Ares. Ares…"

I don't know what she wants to say. I don't think she does, either. So I make it simple for both of us. "Nest, I'm gonna be hustling for the next little bit. Gotta make distance. I won't be saying much. Over."

Yarwick sighs. "Understood, Ares. Be careful out there. Please. Nest, out."

I trudge through the snow, knowing I'm leaving an easy-to-follow trail in my wake. My injured foot is screaming at me. My ribs are, too. Doesn't matter. None of it matters. Gotta make that distance. One foot in front of the other.

Come back to me.

16

Disavowal is not like it is in the movies. It's not the end of the world. When an asset is disavowed, he or she does not automatically become Public Enemy No. 1, and he or she is not forbidden from ever entering the United States again. What it means is that the asset cannot receive any help of any kind from any U.S. official, be they military or political. The reason for this is, should a disavowed asset get captured, no persons connected to the United States can be charged with aiding and abetting him. So, the asset is cut off, so that there can be no confusion about the U.S.'s lack of involvement.

The asset is alone, out in the cold, as they say. And so the asset's only choice is to run.

There are plans for this. A lot of a mission's preplanning involves how to help an agent after he's disavowed. That includes a couple of other fake passports placed in key locations that he alone can access, or money set aside in case he needs to rent a cottage out in the middle of nowhere, or planting weapons for him in predetermined areas.

So, while I maneuver through the frozen forests of southern Siberia, and I receive the call from Yarwick saying she's given me a "window," I know what she means. "The bug-out package is going to be dropped off within the next forty-eight hours," she says. "At the Daichin train station in Bulgan. I'm e-mailing you the coords now. There'll be a locker at the train station, number two-four-four. The key is going to be placed on top of it. We have an agent in the area who will know when you've arrived. The challenge code will be *surreptitious*, response if clear is *dolphin*, response if under duress is *guppy*."

"Got it. What about the *Kop'ye*? I'm sure DARPA would like to get their hands on it. It looks high-tech as hell, Nest."

"We'll work out a dead drop for you somewhere, a bridge or park bench where you can stash it for one of our assets to pick up later, but first we're working on getting you clear before disavowal protocols set in. We're moving fast on this one, Ares, trying to get ahead of the shitstorm that's coming our way. But after it hits…"

After it hits, I'm cut off.

"Yeah," is all I say, between breaths and trudging onward. I'm not staying on the road, of course, but I'm within sight of it. I kneel when I see a roadside sign in the distance. I look through my spotter's scope. The sign says Turung Highway South is a mile ahead. "Found my artery, Nest." I look up. "Skies are clear of unfriendlies. I should make it over the border by nightfall."

"Copy that, Ares. Good to know."

Hours later, when darkness descends, the skies clear and the stars come out, and so does a gibbous moon. I trudge on, stopping only once my watch's GPS says I'm suitably across. I drop to my knees, give myself a moment to rest. I eat my last candy bar and drink some water, which I've kept from freezing by keeping it next to my chest and zipping my jacket. My clothes feel a little loose. I'm losing weight. Almost two weeks on the run with irregular meals will do that to you.

"Nest, Ares here. No longer mobile. Looks like I made it across."

Relief floods Yarwick's voice. "Nicely done, Ares. Only a little farther to go. Time to get some rest for now."

"Ten-four," I say.

I build a shelter and a fire. I clear out some snow, then lay down some of my gear to act as a barrier between me and the frozen earth. I set my watch to wake me every thirty minutes to toss more wood on the fire, then head back into the dreamscape, where dark waters and strange voices are waiting for me.

I wake fully at 0400 hours as always. I destroy my camp out of habit, even though I should be well outside of the Unit's search radius. But who knows? The world is changing far from here, whole armies are being mobilized, nations are doing more than just saber-rattling.

I let the Nest know I'm under way. There are no new updates, just same as yesterday. But I make it about two miles from camp when I come to a paved road—not a highway, but a residential road—and just as I'm about to inform the Nest of this, I get a call from Yarwick.

"Ares, Nest." I can tell by the dread in her voice. I know what this is. "The statement's being issued now, and I just got the call from Halbach. Operation NARROW VOID is officially over. You are formally disavowed."

I come to a halt. "Well. Shit."

"Yeah. Look…we're going to have to wrap it up here. My team is going to have to get pulled out soon. Halbach says money and resources can no longer be spent on…"

On me, she wants to say.

"Understood, Nest. Is this…the last time we're going to speak?"

"Negative, I'll still have communication through satellite link, and your cochlear implant's battery is good for…" She pauses. Probably checking the power readout on a screen. "Just two or three days, I'd say. But remember, Daichin train station, Bulgan, Mongolia, locker two-four-four. The asset said he's close, he should be dropping off the bugout package now."

There ought to be some money in it, new IDs, passports, maybe a gun. And almost certainly another succinylcholine pill. "I copy, Nest. And thank you for moving a package to me on such short notice. I know it must've been a bitch to work out."

"Not a problem, Ares. You're worth every bit."

"So…that kitty-cat date. Guess it's on hold for now."

She snorts out a laugh. "You and Edward aren't off the hook yet."

I smile. "If you say so, boss lady," I say. "Hey, if I don't see you for a while, will you give Sophia a visit? Just give her someone to talk to. I think you'd like her."

"It would be my pleasure, Ares."

"Thanks." A car comes swishing by, it's headlights cutting through the dark forest. "Time to get moving, Nest. Ares is mobile."

"Copy that, Ares," she says, in a voice that comes sealed with finality.

And maybe it is final. Because if I can't ever find my way home, Ares may be mobile forever. Until someone finds him. Until Matveyev or the Unit or the Steel Octopuses close in.

I follow the road through winding hills and thick forests, coming into areas where the snow did not fall as heavy. It takes me a day to come to proper civilization, a small village with no road signs, and just one bus stop. I check the price for a bus ticket to Bulgan on a sign hanging outside.

But I'm not getting on a bus without money. Easy fix for that. I walk right up to the first person I see, which is an elderly man of mixed Mongolian-Caucasian race, and I offer my brand-new sports jacket to him for enough tugrik to purchase a bus ticket to Bulgan. Thankfully, he speaks Russian. The man looks me up and down, and, I suppose out of charity, just gives me the money I need and walks on.

There's only two buses a day, and I have to wait four hours for the next one. A little after three, an old, rusty, short bus comes grumbling up to the stop. Six people get off. Me and eight others get on.

We drive for two hours, encountering almost no other cars on the road. The snow begins to disappear, now it's just thin powder, a few desperate threads clinging to trees.

Finally, we come to the volcanoes.

*

The temperature rises incrementally, mile after mile. We cross the valley between the main extinct volcanoes of the Khanuy-Gol. Tall giants surround us, great flattop mountains with crumbling sides. Beasts that haven't erupted since the Pleistocene era and probably never will again. Dead. Their snowcapped corpses stand as silent monument to the slow march of time. They invite mortals to consider their teensy lives and the teensy amount of time they get to live them, and the teensy impact they have on the imperceptible geological engines that form the surface of the planet we inhabit. If some mortal gazes back far enough, that mortal can see when all continents were one. Russia and the U.S. were once joined territories.

Such crushing amounts of time separates us from that period. Three hundred million years ago, before Man was even a dream conceived by Nature. We act out our plays of life and death across the geography that these engines have shaped for us. If those engines had shaped these lands in a different way, the borderlines would have been drawn differently. We wouldn't be having this particular war, we'd be having a different one. We are governed by them, and they don't even realize, and wouldn't care if they did. Neither do we realize or care. It's strange, for neither us nor Nature to care about our connection in

221

this way. We just go about, like on automatic pilot. Nature has her engines, and we have ours.

The long bus ride lulls me almost to sleep, puts me in this philosophical mood. I watch endless fields of white and green glide by slowly. One house after another. Then groups of them. Neighborhoods. Now gas stations and stores. Now buildings tall enough that I can no longer see the Khanuy-Gol giants.

Bulgan is a city almost as small as Simenga. Somewhat modernized, surrounded by open green pastures but very few farms. At the bus stop, I ask the driver for directions to the train station, then hop off. Twenty minutes later, I limp into the station and head right for the lockers. I find 244, then reach on top of it, feel around for a second until I find the key. Glancing around the station for watching eyes, I open the locker.

Yarwick really came through. Whoever she sent out here to do the drop-off left me with a dark-green backpack with two changes of clothes, a jacket with a hoodie, five thousand dollars' worth of Mongolian tugrik, a brand-new medical kit, a laptop, and two separate sets of IDs. The IDs have me with blonde hair. Digging through the backpack, I find blonde hair dye. In a side pocket is a surprise: a modified M1895 Nagant revolver, with a single box of rounds. My first thought is, *You have got to be kidding me.* The Nagant is an old Russian classic, pretty much just a collector's item these days. My dad's brother Saul had one of these, modified it a lot. Whoever set up this package must've been scrounging for whatever they could reasonably get across the border.

I check to make sure it's loaded. No other bullets in the bag. Must've really been scraping the bottom of the barrel to get me this.

And finally, there's a keycard for a hotel room in Ulaanbaatar, the capital city of Mongolia. About an hour drive east.

"Nest, Ares. Package received. Thanks."

"You bet, Ares," Yarwick says. "Listen, we're just about wrapped up here. Getting ready to shut everything down. We're being asked to break comms with the satellite relay and the encrypted channel. Your implant only has about a four-week battery life, and it's been close to that long since you had it inserted. Battery life is showing very low on our end."

"I get it. We'll be outta contact soon."

"That's affirmative, Ares."

"Well, I better not stop here. I'll head into Ulaanbaatar and see what kind of suite you got for me. Ares is mobile."

"Nest copies," she says.

I check the train schedules, which thankfully are in multiple languages, and look to buy a ticket to Ulaanbaatar, but one's not coming through for another five hours. I don't like hanging around such a public place that long. I might be recognized here. Doubtful, but it is possible. I'm still close to Russia and the media may have hyped it enough that locals are talking about some fugitive on the run. I am one of about four Caucasians I've seen since arriving. So I pull on my *ushanka* and hoodie, and walk over to an information center where thankfully one lady speaks Russian. She tells me there is a bus to Ulaanbaatar every two hours just up the block.

Thirty minutes later, I'm asleep on a bus. I don't even know we've arrived until the bus driver nudges me. I come awake too fast, startled, and grab his wrist and pull him into an armlock. He yelps. I let him go. Apologize. I don't know if he understands me. I step off the bus, shaking off the dream where I was fighting with some tentacle monster in the dark.

It's night, and I'm in a city of lights and action. However, it's sprawled out, with very few high-rises and a couple of industrial centers marked by huge smokestacks in the west. Most streets have few enough tall buildings that you can see the mountains encircling the city. From the bus stop, I receive a commanding view of the docks along the Tuul River. Bathed in lights at this hour is the 130-foot-tall Genghis Khan Equestrian Statue, which sits atop an enormous visitor center.

It's freezing out. I plunge my hands into my pockets and limp with my backpack and duffel down the street, asking strangers where the Hotel Tikina is. I don't speak Mongolian, and most of them don't speak Russian. I finally find a guy who recognizes the logo on the hotel keycard I hold up, and he points me towards the river. So I walk that way for twenty minutes, still asking people. Another guy recognizes the keycard and directs me down a street. I see the sign in bright lights.

"Nest, Ares. I'm there."

No response.

"Nest, this is Ares. Do you copy? I'm at my destination."

No response.

"Nest?"

Nothing.

So that's it, then. Battery's dead. I'm disavowed and alone. Where did everyone go?

I could try sending an e-mail to Yarwick, but that would be in violation of disavowal protocols. I'm meant to break all direct contact, at least for the foreseeable future. It would be especially dangerous since there's apparently a mole within the agency. I have to be careful with communications now. So, so careful. Any mention of me in any CIA documents is being scrubbed right now, or redacted, so that any moles can't glean my true station within the Company, and if I slip up and provide the Russians with proof I am, in fact, an agency operative—proof that they could wave in front of the entire world—I will have compromised everything.

Yarwick must remain incommunicado. Indeed, she's probably already been ordered to delete the e-mail account, and to deny me access to the CRyPto-DEX messaging system.

I limp towards the Hotel Tikina, all the way thinking about Karambit's last words to me. *You don't have what it takes.* "The fuck I don't," I mumble.

I'm so exhausted, time seems to jump.

Now I'm checking in at the front desk. Now I'm taking the elevator to the sixth floor. Now I'm in my room. Now I drop my backpack and duffel bag on the floor and make sure the door is locked. Now I'm propping a chair against the door and shutting the curtains. Now I'm popping two ibuprofen and falling asleep on the bed and vanishing into white sheets and the most gorgeous sleep you've ever known.

I don't even think to remove my clothes.

Somewhere amid those comfortable swirling sheets and all that darkness and the kaleidoscopic dreams I hear a voice. It echoes down through the halls and caves and empty buildings. *You don't have what it takes, Ares.* It continues to echo, a sourceless voice that means nothing, and slowly fades into the dim cave I've fallen into.

And then, another voice. "Nest to Ares, do you copy?" A female voice that also fades into nothingness. The last thing it says is a single word. A strange word. *Fardün*, it says. Such a funny word.

Oie

The news isn't good. It never is. I don't know why all the men prefer gathering around the telly like it's their golden idol and watching it. I keep to myself and knit and try not to hear all the negativity.

"—demanding a stand-down of all Russian military forces and their allies'," Anderson Cooper is saying. "The president's speech made mention twice of an 'Eastern Alignment.' CNN has obtained a copy of an earlier draft of that speech that seems to indicate that the term 'Eastern Alignment' came specifically from intelligence officials, who have branded the five countries under this new umbrella."

At the bottom the screen, the ticker-tape news scrolls by, saying "RUSSIA AND NORTH KOREA MAKE SHOW OF FORCE; IRAN, SYRIA, AND CHINA VOICE THEIR SUPPORT, VOW TO LEND MILITARY AID IF RUSSIA'S NAVAL FORCES ARE ATTACKED."

I half pay attention, thinking about Nathan. Him and his people will all get mixed up in this.

On the screen, there's footage of angry people. Mobs in the streets. Riots.

"—Putin claims that American interventionism is to blame for most of the world's problems today—"

You come back to me, Nathan. Wherever you are, you do whatever you have to do, you kill whoever you have to kill, and then you come back to me. Us old spooks have to stick together. Nobody else knows what we go through, and I need someone to talk to me about it, even if we do not directly address everything we have done. Come back to me. I might even let you marry Zoe.

"Sophia," says James, the orderly whose phone I stole and he still doesn't know. I look around. He is just stepping into the common room. "Time for your bath."

"Yes, it is," says Albert, fanning the air and laughing with the other man. "The ol' cunt is starting to stink!"

"Oh, hush, Albert, you limp-dicked ass-nugget." I heard that one on one of the movies on my iPad. Chloe doesn't know I know how to download those illegally.

The other men in the room whistle and laugh. Albert tries to laugh it off, but he is also turning red, barely hiding his ire.

James pushes me down the hall. As we go, I happen to spy Janette Oakes being put onto a stretcher. She is having a fit again. I see a doctor pulling out a syringe from a fanny pack filled with syringes and other medications. A lot of the orderlies wear these. On a sudden inspiration, I look over my shoulder at James, still pushing me along. I time it just right. "James, did you see that woman behind us with the knife in her hands?"

"What?" Alarmed, he immediately stops pushing me, turns for just two seconds to look behind him. When he does, my hand slips inside the fanny pack of the orderly helping Janette. I nab a small bottle of something. Pills, I think. I do not know what kind, but I palm the bottle just in time. When James turns back to me, he says, "There's nobody there. Who did you mean, Sophia? You saw a lady with a knife?"

"I…I don't know. I get so confused, you know. Perhaps it was just…" I make a twirling gesture around my head. He smiles and nods, and pushes me on. I hide the pill bottle under the cushion in my wheelchair, and go to have myself washed and scrubbed like an animal.

In my bedroom, I am given fresh clothes and I'm left alone. James promises to come back for me at lunchtime. I thank him. When he is gone, I take the pill bottle out from underneath my cushion and read the label. Sedatives. Strong ones. Nothing really exciting, but it adds to my treasure trove, which I have to rebuild since Orson's last shakedown.

I hide my new treasure and then pull out my iPad. Of course, I check my e-mail first. No word from Monsieur Baudelaire. It's been how many days? I don't really know. I am at the point where weeks might have passed. Months, even. Monsieur Baudelaire might have been a dream all along.

Where is Nathan? I need to speak to him. Oh…*oui*, he's on assignment. Well, he needs to come back. I need him. He will make the DGSE pursue my inquiry and not dismiss it as just some old woman's rantings.

I spend the rest of the day napping and knitting, knitting and napping, in no particular order. This is how much of my time is wasted now. I stand up and walk around when I can. Whenever an orderly isn't looking, I try to nip something from the cafeteria—a spoon, a fork, anything—if only to have a goal, something to do, someone to defeat, even if it is just the orderlies.

I go through my hand stretches as I walk. My dead friends from the shallow graves are nearby. One of them is waving at me. I ignore him. Orson is always hovering around, too. I see he has got a new ID card with the magnetic strip. Probably thinks he lost the other one. Doesn't know I took it. It is the little things that keep me moving. Quitting tomorrow, as Nathan says.

I am walking over to the bay window in the game room, looking out at a rainy day, when someone lightly touches my arm. It's Henrietta! "Soso!" she exclaims.

"Well, look who's come to visit," I chuckle, looking up to see her mother, Zoe, and Zoe's mother, Chloe, walking up with smiles for me. We embrace. But Chloe looks troubled. It is a face I have seen on her countless times before, when as a child she saw me checking all the doors and windows in the house twice to make sure they were locked, when she locked herself out of her college dorm and discovered I could pick locks, and when she first saw me flirting with another man after her father's death. It is an inquisitive look, but one that suggests she ponders the depths of my secrets.

"*Mère*," Chloe says. "There is a woman here asking about you."

"A woman?" I ask, playing a slow, old-lady version of pattycake with Henrietta. "It's not that bitch Faustine, is it?"

"No, *Mère*. Faustine is dead, remember?"

"Good." I look over at her. "Then who is it?"

"I don't know. We were just signing in the visitor's log and we heard her mention your name to one of the ladies at the front desk. They stepped into some office. I didn't hear what she wanted."

"Mm. Well, I don't know about that, dear."

She gives me that look again. A daughter trying to fathom the secrets of an ancient mother with more secrets than she has hairs on her head. In truth, I do not know who it is, but I might have one or two ideas. Perhaps three.

Later, while we are strolling outside, I notice a raven-haired woman in a tight black business skirt and no-nonsense look step out onto a patio and look in our direction. She has a nurse with her, explaining something. I take out my iPad and pretend to fiddle with it. I set it to record Henrietta. I tell her to dance for her Soso. She does. But I do not focus the iPad's camera on my great-granddaughter. Rather, I make sure I catch the raven-haired woman before she turns away.

Wait…why was I recording? Why am I not focusing on Henrietta when I record? It is not until time skips and my family has left me and I am alone in my bed that night that I remember who I was recording and why. I take the iPad out, find my glasses—sometimes I need them, sometimes I don't—and pull up the video of Henrietta dancing. I pause it when I get a good shot of the raven-haired beauty. I take a still picture, then zoom in. She is a dark-skinned woman with hard eyes. She is looking right at me as I record. Does she know?

"Who are you, Raven?"

I check my e-mails again. No response from Baudelaire. Did I dream him?

Did I dream it all? Jean-Luc, Herr Vogel, the cold bitch wind that bit into her bones as we crossed the lower Alps, the family I have, the joy I knew, the horrors I experienced, the dead men staring at me from the corner of my room?

My hands are shaking. Nathan. I need Nathan. Nathan will understand. Where is he?

"Nathan?" I call out. "*Nathan!*" Only the darkness hears me. The darkness and the dead people from the shallow graves and the raven-haired beauty staring up at me from my screen.

Then I fall asleep and time seems to…not skip…but blur. And now I am outside, sitting across from the raven-haired woman. I vaguely recall how I got here and I vaguely believe that she is not an illusion. She's more solid than the dead men. "Sophia, do you understand what I'm saying?"

We have been talking. I remember now. We have been talking but not for long. I told her she can call me Sophia and she said I can call her Abijah. She is not smiling, but she seems friendly. Her briefcase is snapped open and she is taking out a yellow legal pad to take notes.

"Yes," I say. "You're Mossad, Department Six, what's left of the Israeli component of Legacy. My ears work just fine, young lady." That came out more barbed than I had intended, but I get cranky when I suddenly come out of the fog and find myself in a place I only barely recall arriving at.

All the details are rushing back at me. Waking up that morning. Orson changed my diaper. Went for a short walk, got tired, he pushed me around a bit. Then Vincent Conroy, the eighty-year-old former football coach, pushed me around. We ate strawberry cake. I asked where Nathan was and Vincent didn't know who that was. Then this lady came to visit me. She introduced herself as a colleague of Monsieur Baudelaire. He made the friendly phone call to her people at Mossad, and so here she is.

"Yes, that's right," Abijah says. "I'm one of the last remaining people with an interest in the Nazi-hunting aspect of Legacy. Most everyone else is just interested in archival work."

"That's because there's no one left to hunt," I say. "Or wasn't."

"My superiors are only marginally willing to admit that there is a similarity between the two pictures you showed Baudelaire. Facial-recognition is strong but inconclusive. Most of my colleagues believe you are right. It is him. Wilhelm Vogel was a particularly nasty subject on the list Wiesenthal made before he died. He is one of only two I am sure is still alive. The other one is probably somewhere in Papua New Guinea, but I'm not sure."

I look her over. "Why would you be interested in hunting these old antiques down? Surely they're all almost dead."

"Why do *you* want to hunt them, Sophia, when these men could easily die any day?"

My thumb and index finger rub together slowly. "Because they've lived to nearly a hundred while they raped and killed children that never saw eight. And because they deserve to have their lives cut short, even if it is only by a few more days. I want to rob them of those days, few as they may be."

The Israeli woman arches an eyebrow. "And so you have it."

I nod.

"I'm going to ask you some questions, Sophia. Questions regarding your case against Vogel throughout the fifties, sixties, and seventies. Every detail may help to better understand what it is he's been doing, and help us vitiate his activities if they are still proving harmful. Of course, if you choose to answer my questions, it will be a serious violation of the oath you took to never speak to a foreign agency about matters concerning—"

"Will my answers help you catch him?"

Abijah inclines her head. "Perhaps. Mossad is still very much committed to Legacy, even if our partners in *Héritage* are long past caring."

"Then ask your questions, girl, and stop wasting time. Every breath Wilhelm Vogel draws is another I don't get to rob him of. I've suffered that wolf grin in my dreams long enough."

The Israeli smiles fractionally. "Let's get started."

PART THREE

The Disavowed

17

My watch wakes me at 0400 hours. I shut it off. When I finally wake up again, it's almost noon. My back aches. My knees and ankles have tiny needles in them, or feel like they do. Getting old. The years just keep coming on. I slept almost thirteen hours. I stand up and walk stiffly over to the curtains. Open them. A fresh snow has just blanketed the whole city. Some of it is still falling. *Fardün*. The name echoes down a corridor of fog and shadow. I search for its meaning, but it's fast receding into that place where all dreams go once you wake.

I click my teeth. "Nest, do you copy?"

Silence.

It's weird. It's almost like it was all a dream. All of it. From my life growing up in Georgia to the Navy to the SEALs to meeting Sophia to the CIA to Operation NARROW VOID. All of it just a fantasy, and I just woke up from it, here, in the Hotel Tikina. Cut off like this—and *knowing* just how severed I am from all those things— makes me feel alone like I haven't ever felt before.

I'm disavowed, and yet I still have a job to do. That job is don't get caught.

"I'll quit tomorrow." I say it aloud, as an oath to both myself and Sophia.

Fardün.

I close the curtains and strip off my stinking clothes. I check my wounds. All of them seem to be healing well. Then I jump in the first shower I've had in weeks and watch the brown water run off my body and spiral down the drain. From the transparent door, I can see the mirror above the sink, and I see the bruising around my ribcage.

Fardün.

When I'm out of the shower, I dry off and put on my new clothes. I trim the beard to just barely more than scruff, keeping it stylish, and dye it and my hair blonde to match my new IDs. Then I try on my new clothes and check on my gear. I check on the *Kop'ye*. At some point, someone will contact me about a dead drop, someplace I can dump the *Kop'ye* for a CIA asset to pick it up and take it back home to be dissected by DARPA and maybe reverse-engineered. I don't even know what the fuck it is. Looks like a gun, but no gun I've ever seen. Weird-looking.

I sit on the edge of the bed and turn on the TV. It's some Mongolian gameshow where people wear blindfolds and try to run a maze with their spouses giving them directions on a microphone. I change the channel, looking for a news station that speaks either Russian or English. To my shock, I find CNN.

And the news ain't good.

"—demanding a stand-down of all Russian military forces and their allies'," Anderson Cooper is saying. "The president's speech made mention twice of an 'Eastern Alignment.' CNN has obtained a copy of an earlier draft of that speech that seems to indicate that term 'Eastern Alignment' came specifically from intelligence officials, who have branded the five countries under this new umbrella."

At the bottom the screen, the ticker-tape news scrolls by, saying "IRAN, SYRIA, AND CHINA VOICE THEIR SUPPORT OF RUSSIA, "TOGETHER WE AIM TO PUT AN END TO AMERICAN INTERVENTIONISM."

On the screen, there's footage of angry people in the streets of all nations involved. Russians holding up signs saying the West has it coming. Americans doing a march for peace and reason. Syrians holding up signs saying the West needs to burn for its sins.

"—Russian president has made it clear he does not wish to attack the U.S. or its allies," Cooper goes on. "He claims he's only pushing back against the navies of the U.S. and its allies, who he says have extended their reach far beyond international waters and into Russia's own territorial waters—"

Fardïn.

I'm watching all this, thinking about my old buddies in SEAL Team 7, and how some of them are still out there serving, and how my actions have helped move all this along, placing us all on the brink. I know there are other factors, but NARROW VOID certainly played a role here. Now that the CIA has informed the president of what I found, and shown him the pictures, and explained to him the gravity of a particle-beam weapon and what the Russians were attempting, there's no choice but a show of force. And maybe more.

There's footage of soldiers and sailors hugging their spouses goodbye as they are called back from leave, getting ready for a deployment in case it's needed. I walk over to a desk near the window and open my new laptop. The code to get in is written on a sticky note placed on the screen. I hook up to the hotel's Wi-Fi and check the Internet for options.

There's an American embassy in the city, but obviously I can't go there. Disavowal protocols are strict about that, I can't put the embassy, and thus the U.S., at risk. Also, anyone at the embassy will think Nathan Adamson is a fugitive from justice, a rogue ex-SEAL, so I'd probably just be arrested.

So I use Google Earth to go over all the streets, all the neighboring provinces. I scan a few articles about how foreigners are treated in Mongolia (mostly they are ignored), what the politics are between Russia and Mongolia (I'll need to know that to understand how much danger I'm in at any given time), and just what kind of law enforcement they have (not exactly crack teams, but they've been beefing up their police in recent years, particularly in the capital).

Fardïn. Fardïn. Where do I know that name from?

I try to do the same morning ritual I do back home, a ten-minute warmup stretch to really get the day going. Can't. My foot and my ribs still aren't fully cooperating. I take two ibuprofens (don't want to abuse the morphine-based painkillers) and watch online videos about how to say basic Mongolian phrases.

I close my eyes and breathe evenly, going through transcendental meditation.

Then, it hits me. *Fardïn.* It's been nagging me since I woke up, and I've been dismissing it as part of a dream. And now, like a dream, parts of it come floating up to the forebrain. There's dust and muck on the memory, and it takes me a second to clean it off, but then I have it. I think…yeah…yeah, I think I heard Yarwick say it. Didn't I? While I was sleeping?

I click my teeth. "Nest, this is Ares. Do you copy?"

Nothing.

Maybe it was one final transmission, something she was able to get through just as the battery was dying. Is it a place? Why does it sound so familiar? It takes me a second. And then, clarity. It comes to me like a final piece of a puzzle. "Innick Fardün," I say aloud, making it real. I remember now. Yarwick mentioned his name just once, during our very first briefing, when I first met Wainwright and all the others. Innick Fardün. Hungarian sniper. Killer-for-hire, known to have worked jointly with the Unit.

But I heard the name again last night as I was going to sleep. Was it a dream, or was Yarwick really talking to me?

I look over at my curtains, making sure they're shut.

What did Kozner say about Fardün? A killer-for-hire. Shot some guy's wife in the knee, left her lying out it the open, screaming, so that the guy would go out to save his wife and get tagged. Something like that.

I stand up and walk over to the window. I part the curtains slightly, and look around at the cityscape. I'm on the sixth floor. Ulaanbaatar is laid out before me, draped in virgin-white snow. Lots of shopping centers, a few low-rises, three high-rises in the distance, a church with green palatial grounds surrounding it, a webwork of main streets and side streets and blind alleys.

Fardün. Did I dream it? Or did Yarwick really give me a final warning, but I was too exhausted and too consumed by the first comfy bed in months to realize it? *Shit!* I can't remember. Was it a dream or was it real?

I step away from the window and look about the room. The SIG Sauer I brought all the way from Russia is on the desk. The Nagant revolver is on the bed. The TV is still on, showing Russian President Vladimir Putin saying something at a speech given at the Kremlin. Might be old footage, might be new. He looks stoic as always.

Fardün. If he's out there, and if he knows where I'm at...if that's what Yarwick was trying to tell me...

"He'll be angling for a shot right now."

I do another glance out the window. A sniper's spotter is basically an apprentice position for the lead sniper in a team. I spotted for two years, took out four enemy combatants in Kabul during that time. I know how a pro shooter thinks. But it's been a while. I've been firing mostly pistols and assault rifles for the better part of a decade now. Besides, I don't have the kind of weapons to—

235

The Nagant.

I walk over to the bed and pick up the revolver. Inspect it. It's been modified, similar to the way Uncle Saul modified his. It's been too long—I must've been nine, ten back then—so I don't remember the exact process, but this one's been given a handle similar to the C96 "Broom Handle" Mauser. I can work with that. Maybe.

I go to the Internet to check the gun laws in Mongolia, because I genuinely have no idea. Turns out, you can carry sporting rifles and some pistols meant for sport—ah, that explains how Yarwick's operative managed to get the Nagant to me; with its modified C96 handle, it can be fitted with a stock for long-range shooting. But a Nagant isn't good for anything more than a hundred yards. A football field length at best.

A quick search for sporting gun shops in Ulaanbaatar pulls up just three. They have an online inventory, and I see what I want, available only through one shop. Two unique stocks for a C96 Mauser. I tuck both pistols in my waistline and head out.

*

I can't take the main exit out of the lobby, there might be a spotter there, someone inside the hotel whose job it is to signal Fardün that I'm leaving. I take the stairs, find my way to the kitchen, and exit out the back door with only a few staff giving me odd looks.

I step out into the cold, the snow crunching underfoot. I don't know where the shot might come from, but I have some idea. I've gone on plenty of sniping forays in urban areas before. I note the parking decks two hundred yards away, a high-rise just behind that, the church's bell tower beside it. I wait for a long red bus to come to a whining halt right in front of the lobby, slewing a little in the snowy slush and dumping two dozen passengers out. I merge with them, and jog alongside the bus for a block before turning away.

I jog two more blocks, hail a taxi, and ride to the gun shop across town. It takes some time to explain to the shop owner what it is I need, he doesn't understand a lick of Russian or English. I finally have to show him a picture on my mobile phone. He goes and grabs the two stocks. I choose the short one, easily concealable inside a trench coat, as well as a roll of duct tape and a screwdriver. Then I find the nearest clothing store and buy a long black trench coat, thin gloves, and a black, short-brimmed Stetson hat.

I return to the Hotel Tikina through a side exit, buy a 16 oz. bottle of water from the cafeteria, and go right to my room, all the way checking behind me. Once inside my room, I briefly ruffle the curtains. I do this so that, should an enemy sniper be watching by window, he'll know someone's inside. It'll keep him focused and not thinking about the fact that I'm on to him.

In the bathroom, I use the screwdriver to attach the stock to the Nagant revolver, just like Uncle Saul did with his Nagant, and use the duct tape to affix the water bottle to the end of the barrel. Sound suppression from water bottles is not impressive, but they do okay in noisy urban environments, and it's all I've got.

Then I head back out into the street from the kitchen again. This time no one sees me. I'm wondering if I'm being overly paranoid. I've got on my trench coat. My SIG is tucked in my waistline. The trench coat I wear over my shoulders like Lando Calrissian wears his cape, with my arms outside of the sleeves and tucked inside, the Nagant's stock pressed into my right armpit and my finger around the trigger guard.

I weave through the urban foot traffic. My room's window is on the hotel's west-facing side, so now I head west, looking at the tall buildings and structures and bridges where a sniper might set up. Time to go hunting.

18

If there is an assassin out here, he has lost the advantage. A sniper's best weapon is secrecy, and if Fardün is resting in his nest, he thinks only one of us is aware of the game that's afoot. I have the marginal advantage of knowing what he doesn't: that I'm aware. I can make maneuvers that he doesn't know I can or would make.

Then again, I could have Fardün's spotter on my tail, telling him where I'm moving and when, and I wouldn't even know it. I have to keep a good eye out, double-check my six, and move surreptitiously through the crowds, cut through shops, step out the back door.

Six blocks from the hotel, I stop to buy a couple of sandwiches from a vendor and check for followers. I hop into a taxi, concealing my makeshift compact sniping Nagant within my coat. I have the driver drive in circles, acting like I'm looking for a friend but forgot where he lives. While he talks to me in broken Russian, I devour one of my sandwiches. When I finish the dry-cleaning run, I hop out of the taxi near a Sheraton Hotel, but not before I ask the driver where the tallest parking deck is in the area. He tells me four blocks south. I tip him extra and head out.

The parking deck is for students at a local university. I limp all the way to the top, move slowly around each car, making sure my enemy hasn't selected this as his nest. I'm now south of the buildings I feel are the top candidates, buildings I scoped during the dry-cleaning run. I head to the north corner of the building and take my spotter's scope out from my coat.

One building at a time, floor by floor, I eliminate the possibilities. An open window midway up the Sheraton? No, someone closes it after I study it for a minute. How about those workers on the office building rooftop about four hundred yards away? Nah, they look like maintenance guys, not moving tactically at all. There are several windows open on the east-facing side of an apartment building—the side that would face the Hotel Tikina—but I find it doubtful that a sniper would be able to rent an apartment that fast, or would kill a resident just to have access to a window facing my room. He'd have to be not only ruthless, but stupid, as the family of the resident could come home any minute.

So I keep scanning.

As the sun drops lower on the horizon on my left, the temperature continues to drop. It's freezing out. My breath comes out in clouds. I zero in on two final candidates. One is a four-story shopping mall with a wide roof and lots of cover from power generators and elevator control boxes. The other is a four-level parking deck about seven hundred yards away from me. Both have a great view of the Hotel Tikina's west-facing side.

While I monitor the parking deck across from me, I swallow two more ibuprofens and eat my last sandwich. At one point, I think I found my guy. There's someone moving covertly along the second level...but then he jumps on top of another guy, scaring him. They both bust up laughing. Just a prank. I keep scanning.

Then, my scope happens to rake over something interesting on the shopping mall rooftop. It was there one second, gone the next. Something long and thin and shiny, like a needle from this distance. It was poking out from behind one of the elevator control boxes, which is in the foreground and is about three times bigger than a refrigerator...

Then I see it again. I zoom in. It's a shiny black barrel, all right. The hairs on my neck and arms raise up. I can't see the shooter, his body is hidden by the control box. I zoom in to the max my scope will allow, and I see a black sound suppressor on the tip of the barrel. Now I lower my scope, and look at which way the barrel is pointing. Directly at the Hotel Tikina.

My Nagant is accurate to about a hundred yards, which is pretty good for a revolver, but my enemy is over five hundred yards away, at a slightly higher level than me, and his entire body is hidden. I couldn't make the shot from here even during the best of weather, and it's getting pretty windy out.

Gotta get a better angle. Gotta get closer.

I run as fast as I can with a hurt ankle to the elevator that takes me to the bottom floor. Policemen are on the street, writing someone a ticket, so I can't move too fast. I walk calmly across the street, careful not to slip on ice, making my way north, never letting the shopping mall out of my sight.

Once I'm there, I walk all the way around it, getting an idea of his exits. He'll have thought that out well in advance. There's a side door propped just slightly open with a tiny rock. It's a good bet he did that, and that the stairwell inside is his primary exfiltration plan. I move steadily up, up, up, until I reach a door that has a sign on it written in Mongolian and I'm assuming says something like *Staff Only Beyond This Point*. This door, too, is propped slightly open with a block of wood.

Open the door a smidge. Peek outside. The rooftop is a labyrinth of a power generators, electrical boxes, AC power units, elevator controls boxes, and three separate skylights. Before I left the parking deck, I marked as much of the layout in my mind as I could see from that vantage.

I step through the door. The rooftop is covered in gravel with a layer of brittle snow, so my steps are anything but silent. I look to my right, where the sun is setting in the west. My elongated shadow is cast hard to my left. I have to make sure that doesn't cross into his field of view. I keep close to one of the power generators, so that my shadow is up against it, not spilling over onto the gravel.

With each step, the gravel and snow beneath my feet, and my gut tenses.

Peeking around the corner of a generator, I see the edge of a man's foot, just barely visible around a large control box. I move slowly to the left, seeing more and more of his body, until finally I see all of him. He's at the far end of the building, about eighty yards from me, maybe more, kneeling on one pad-covered knee, taking aim at the hotel almost a mile away with his Barrett M82 rifle.

I slip the Nagant out from my trench coat. Press the stock against my shoulder. Gauge the direction of the wind. East to west. Take aim. Breathe in deep, let it out slowly, and squeeze the trigger…

When the shot goes off, it makes a sharp *pop!* like a firecracker, and when the bullet hits my enemy, he jerks. Grunts. He abandons his rifle immediately and barrel rolls away, moving to cover. Not dead. Gotta be wearing body armor. Has to be. I aimed for his arm, but for whatever reason the round hit his shoulder, and he's moving spryly.

I take cover behind the generator, and just in time. A semi-silent *spat!* sounds out, and a bullet tears into the corner of the generator. He fires twice more. With my left hand, I take out my SIG, aim it around the side, and fire twice blindly in his direction. The SIG's bark is much louder than the Nagant, but the SIG's got more penetration power.

Footsteps. Moving fast. Away from me.

I peek around the opposite corner of the generator, just in time to see my enemy going over the side of the roof, down a ladder. I take aim. Too slow. He's already sliding down and I pull my hand back. Can't take the shot, the bullet could carry on and kill some innocent a block away. I rush to the side of the roof, try to get an angle on him as he goes down the ladder, but he's already stepping inside a door. His Option B for exfil, I'm guessing.

Before he slips through, I see he's carrying some kind of silenced machine pistol. I fire down at him, but hit the edge of the door just as it closes.

I wait a few seconds, just watching the door, waiting for him to come back out. He doesn't. I can't go that way, because if I do, he could be waiting on the other side to take me out. I run back over to the opposite side of the roof, from whence I came. I ignore the pain in my ankle and run down the stairs, back to the bottom floor, and I run far away from the building. Turn back to look, to see if I see anyone racing away from the mall—

And there he is. Fifty yards away. Stepping out of the rotating door of the front entrance, jogging across the street. He's bald, with alabaster skin, wearing a brown jacket and blue jeans. He doesn't see me yet. I can't shoot him right out in the open. Too risky. Besides, I might want this one alive.

The SIG is tucked back in my waist, I keep the trench coat over my shoulders like a cape, my arms outside of the sleeves, hidden, and the Nagant tucked and ready at my right side.

Twenty yards behind him. Not much foot traffic. If he looks over his shoulder right now, he'll see me. There's a bus stop ahead with a wide billboard ad for some kind of perfume. I dip behind that, and watch him walk fast, glancing behind him. I don't think he spotted me. He continues on. Thankfully, there are no taxis for him to slip into, but I imagine he's got a getaway vehicle parked nearby. I've got to drive him away from that, or else nab him before he reaches it. I step back onto the sidewalk, move into the street, walk parallel to the sidewalk he's on while keeping the vehicles parked on the curbside for cover.

Then, he turns. His eyes sweep the street. He sees me. Several things happen at once. I duck and fire through the rear windshield of a parked Honda. My rigged suppressor makes the shot into a firecracker shot again, and I dip the weapon back into my coat as the rear windshield shatters. The bullet passes through the front windshield and misses my target cleanly. He fires at almost the exact same time, not so surreptitiously as me. He wields the machine pistol with one hand, and the suppressor whistles as his bullets tear through the Honda.

A couple of passersby see this and react in shock. One man runs away. Others hear the noises but weren't paying attention where it all came from, they appear more startled than anything, and look astonished as the Honda's windows come apart. I stay ducked and press my back against the tires, peek over the top, and see him running on. When he rounds a corner, I take off after him.

I stop just short of the corner. Peek around. I don't see him. Lots of people in the crowd. Can't tell where he—

I see the barrel peeking out the side of a bakery on the opposite side of the street, and duck my head just in time as bullets go whizzing by my head. I peek around the side again, let my Nagant slip just outside of my trench coat. Squeeze off a shot. Sounds like a firecracker again. A few people look around, but I've dipped back to cover. My bullet misses my target. I peek out again, fire again. He does the same. Our shots zip past one another. His are silent, mine are loud enough that people are starting to realize something's up.

The next time I peek around my enemy has stopped firing. I think he's run on down an alley. I bolt across the street, make it to the corner of the bakery and peek around the side. There he is! Bounding up a set of stone steps. When he's at the top, I take a shot. I see him jerk. I got him. But he's still running. The *pop!* of my gun alerts two or three people around me. One of them sees me pulling the Nagant back into my trench coat and screams. I run after my enemy.

The blood trail starts at the top of the steps, which lead onto Sukhbaatar Square. It's not a lot of blood, the droplets are only every twenty feet or so, but they stand out starkly against the fresh snow. I must've just nicked him. Then I see him walking up another set of steps, to an overpass for trains. There's a crowd of people in the town square between us, people loitering on street benches or taking pictures next to a fountain. He's looking right at me, but doesn't fire. I guess because there are too many people all around him on the steps. I jog after him.

That's when he fires. Directly into the crowd all around me.

There are screams. I duck behind the fountain, peek around the edge. Just as he's about to disappear again, I slip the Nagant out and take a shot. No one hears the pop of my gun this time. Too much screaming. I slip the Nagant back into my coat and keep running.

I bound up the steps, taking two at a time. Once up there, I cast around. I don't see him. But there's the blood. Looks like he went into the train station.

As soon as I'm inside, I see him. Twenty yards ahead. He's not limping or running. He looks completely calm. Then I see why. He's hidden his pistol inside his coat, and shouting to a pair of security guards. He looks over his shoulder, and gesticulates towards me. The second the guards lock eyes with me, they start after me. I calmly but quickly turn around, and step back out of the station, even as they shout at me. Once outside, I run for it.

Their shouts follow me as I round the station. I've got to make it there before he exits out the back and disappears. I'm in another town square again, surrounded by another crowd. Takes me a second, but I spot the bald, alabaster head moving ahead of me. I slip into the crowd, using a large stone column and the statue of someone that looks like Genghis Khan to block the view of my pursuers. I hear them coming, hear their voices, and move to the opposite side of the statue in sync with their footsteps. When they're beyond me, I turn my attention back to my enemy, who is approaching two dozen pedestrians standing at a crosswalk with a no-walk sign.

I hear sirens. Ambulances for the people he shot. Police for me. That's just a guess, but a pretty good one, I think.

There aren't many places for me to hide if he turns around...except...

A public bench. A woman and her daughter are sitting there feeding birds. I walk right over to them, take off my Stetson, and take a seat, putting them between me and my enemy, who is forty yards away. The woman and her daughter look at me strangely, but I ignore them while I eye my enemy. He's looking over his shoulder. Looking for me. Doesn't see me. I keep still. Let him think I've been tackled by security or police.

I can hear the shouts blocks away. People still hollering for help. People dying because of my enemy.

The crosswalk sign changes to walk, and my enemy follows the crowd. I let him get ahead, then slip off the bench and continue following.

From fifty yards away, I see him. He's walking a sidewalk parallel to mine, and slightly ahead. The pedestrians peter off. Not many places for me to hide now. I dash across the street when there's a break in traffic, come up behind him, about twenty yards back. Now fifteen. Now ten.

Suddenly he turns. Sees me. My weapon is up first and I shoot him. Center mass. Son of a bitch fires wildly, almost hits me, I take cover and he keeps running. Around another corner. Definitely wearing armor. I chase after him, my body getting exhausted from the sustained effort.

This new street is busy. I've lost him for a second. I look at the crowd. I look at the ground. A few droplets of blood lead me towards an arcade, and when I step inside, the lights are flashing bad enough to cause epileptic seizure and they're blasting a techno version of "Hold Me Now" by the Thompson Twins. They played the original version at my junior prom. I went with my friend Kirk Lipscomb. We ended up dancing with each other's dates more than our own. He married mine after graduation.

Where did everybody go?

My enemy is pushing through a bustling bunch of kids crowding around different video games and pinball machines or else clogging the lanes by standing and chatting. I lose him entirely. I walk around the edge of the room, and see him at the far end, passing a stage where some kids have jumped up to show off some dance moves. He doesn't know I'm here. I could tag him easily, but I might hit a kid or two in the process.

So, I follow. I move around a huge interactive gaming stage where teenagers and twenty-somethings are playing against each other in a dance game. The lights are still flashing, the music still pulsing (*oooooh, hold my heart*) and my enemy intermittently vanishes and reappears. When he spots me, I think I see him grin. I take cover behind a steel beam that seems to support the ceiling, and when he fires, no one hears a thing. But the bullets tear into the side of a large Mrs. Pac-Man game and shuts it off. The kids playing it are totally baffled.

I peek around the beam. See the enemy stepping through an exit at the rear. There's a clear shot, and I take it. This one nails him in the back. He falls through the door. I rush over, kick open the door, and then kick the pistol away and stomp on his wrist, keeping the weapon pinned down. I aim the Nagant point-blank at his head.

"*Fuck you!*" he shouts above the music still pumping through the half-open door.

"Innick Fardün?"

"*I said, fu—*"

"Two choices. I end you here and now, or you cooperate."

He snarls at me. He's breathing heavily. I can tell my last bullet penetrated his armor. How deeply, I don't know, but I see more blood dribbling from his backside.

"Your choice," I tell him.

*

After a pat down, in which I find only a cell phone, I scoop up Fardün's pistol and help him to his feet, then direct him down the alley behind the arcade, and then behind a supermarket. I tell Fardün to man up and walk straight. He does. And he laughs. Like some drunken idiot. I direct him into a public bathroom. I shove him inside, where he collapses to the ground, bleeding profusely and still chuckling. Then I shut the door and lock it.

"All right," I say, rounding on him with the SIG. "I want it. I want it all. Your sources, who you're working with, all of it. If I don't get what I want, you don't get a hospital."

"I'm bleeding out."

"Don't care."

"It hurts."

"Deal with it."

"I'm kind of a pussy when it comes to pain."

"Probably shouldn't have become an assassin for hire, then."

"You sound like my mother," he laughs. For a moment, I'm befuddled. His accent is bizarre, sounds like a mix between Hungarian and German and Spanish. Never heard anything like it. Fardün tries to stand, falters, then puts a hand up against the wall and slowly stands up. He looks at me and smiles. "First time in Ulaanbaatar?"

"Who sent you?"

"Word of advice, avoid the deep-fried *khuushuur* on Gidong. It'll give you the runs. Or 'mud butt.' I had an American friend who used to call it that." He laughs. "*Mud butt.* It made me laugh—"

I cut him off with a backhand across his face. "You seem to think I'm playing around here."

"Aren't we? Aren't we all just 'playing around' here?"

"You got a real sense of humor for a man that's about to bleed out."

"It helps to have a sense of humor about these things." He spits out a gob of blood. "If you don't have that, you won't last long." He chuckles, then walks over to the sink, like he's not my prisoner, like he's not really concerned about me putting a bullet in his head. He even turns his back to bend over and splash water on his face. He spits out another red gob. "A sense of humor is all that's got me through this."

"Through what?" I ask, aiming my SIG at him.

"How do you think I ended up like this? How does a man with my skills find this kind of work?" Fardün grabs a towel from the dispensary, wipes his hand and his face, then tosses the towel into the bin. He turns his back to the mirror, and turns his head to get a look at the wound in the mirror, the one on his back. It's not deep, but it must be causing insane spasms and pain. Then he looks at the gunshot wound in his side, presses a hand to it, then turns to face me. "How do you think it ends this way?"

"I don't know, and I don't give a shit about—"

"You don't just go hunting one day and someone says, 'Hey, you're pretty good with a gun. Want to be an assassin?' You know that. We go through training, we gain—" Winces in pain. "We gain experience in killing people, and then, sometimes, we are disposed of. Left to fend for ourselves. We cannot find work because our only skills are infiltration, shooting, and killing, so..." He shrugs, and smiles, holding up a blood-covered hand. "You may be looking at your future right now."

"Did the Unit send you?"

"Yes, but they didn't have to. There is a general contract out on you."

I narrow my eyes at him. "Contract? What are you talking about?"

"On the Dark Web, in certain corners where only me and a few others know to look, written in secret code, there are contracts placed on certain people. The Kremlin knows how to reach me. We are...ah...BFFs?" Fardün laughs again And winces. And laughs. "Or is it Bae, now? So hard to keep up with American slang, it's always changing, and too fast. I'm old, I despise that kind of quick change?"

"How much?"

"I despise it *this much*," he says, holding his hands a foot apart. And laughs again.

"No, I mean how much is the contract?"

He chuckles again, coughs up more blood. I don't know if it's from my punch or the bullet. If it's the latter, he's a goner. "One-point-five million U.S.," he says. "Dead or alive, but only if there is clear proof of death." I imagine he sees the surprise register on my face, and he laughs harder. "You didn't think you would ever be worth that much, did you?"

"Why a contract? What's done is done. Whatever happened at the Cosmodrome is being dealt with by politicians right now. The war is already kicking off. Bringing me in won't—"

"The war. You helped create that. But then, so did I," he adds with a shrug. "A lot of wars happen because of the games we play in the shadows." He shrugs, adding, "And there's also the matter of something you stole."

"What do you mean?"

"You did more than just destroy some weapon," Fardün says. "You took something. Something very precious to them."

I start to ask him what he means, but then I remember. "The *Kop'ye*?" I'd completely forgotten about it. These past twenty-four hours have been a hurricane of other concerns.

"I don't know what it's called, I just know that something serious was taken, and I gather…" He trails off, wincing in pain. "I gather it was you who stole it."

I imbibe that, and nod. "Who else knows I'm here?"

"No one."

"Bullshit. You told *no one* that you found me?" I say skeptically.

"Finders keepers."

My instinct is not to believe him, but the man seems downright honest. Blunt, even. He's older than me by about ten years. He may be approaching that age where he just doesn't give a fuck anymore, and where he knows the deal. He's been waiting for the bullet that'll get him. *Bushido*. He long ago accepted that he was already dead. As soon as he stepped onto his first battlefield, he made peace with it. Thirty or forty years of that will develop a fuckload of gallows humor and bluntness. I've seen it before. Everybody deals with it in their own way.

Even so, his instinct will be to survive, to look for a way out. Even as he stands there bleeding to death, even as much as he may hate himself for some of the things he's done, he's not quitting until tomorrow. And not before. Can't let my guard down with this kind of animal.

"How were you going to collect this reward?" I ask.

Fardün spits out another gob, then shrugs like I just asked him who he thinks the Falcons will draft this year. "There are different ways. Secure ways. It varies. I would have to make contact with the right people, and they would let me know the method for payment transfer. Usually I shoot them a text, they send a string of numbers that goes to a local bank or some lawyer they have on retainer, yatta yatta."

"Who would you contact? Karambit?"

Fardün smiles his biggest smile yet, his yellowing teeth coated in blood. "You mean Matveyev?"

I cock my head to one side. "You know him?"

"Your intelligence people call him Karambit. His codename with SVR is *Smeyushchayasya Sobaka.*"

"Laughing Dog?" I ask.

"That's it. But his real name, I discovered, is Fyodor Matveyev."

"What do you mean, 'discovered'?"

"I like to know the people who employ me. I did some digging."

"Not even the CIA knows his real name."

"I have different sources," Fardün says with a wink.

"Sources better than the goddamn CIA?"

"I didn't say better, I said *different.*" He smiles another bloody smile. "Okay, yeah, better. Just a little bit better. But let's not get into a shitting contest about who's got better sources."

"*Pissing* contest," I say.

"I like shitting contest better," Fardün says.

"Who are these sources?"

"Now why would I give you those, when the very next thing you're going to do is kill me after you have them?"

That's not necessarily accurate, but it's not inaccurate, either. I haven't decided yet exactly what I'll do here. I can't let him leave, he might warn others where I'm at. At the very least, I can probably count on him to come after me even harder next time, and it won't just be for money, it'll be personal. I could plug him right here, right now, and be done with it. But if I could get something out of him…"If I can contact my people, perhaps get you to an embassy, they might be willing to help you. They have medics. In exchange for those sources—"

"Oh, fuck you, Adamson," he chuckles.

I aim the pistol right between his eyes. "I know you want to live, Fardün."

"Yeah? Think you know me so well?"

"I know enough."

"Tell me, then. Tell me about me."

Jesus. He's acting like we're long lost cousins or something, just catching up with each other. How's the family? What have you heard about Uncle Saul?

"I know you shoot women to draw out their husbands and kill them. I know you're not above the grossest fucking tactics. I know that much."

At this, Fardün acts as if I've just made a strange callback joke, something inappropriate but still funny. Then, of course, he chuckles. He's always chuckling. "Ah, you're talking about the Dadalia family."

"I don't know their names."

"Well, maybe you should," he says. "Maybe you should know Devan Dadalia and his wife Sasha. They worked for Doctors Without Borders. You know them, of course?" He nods as if I answered. "They were health inspectors. They worked with children. Some of those children went missing. The Libyan JSO thought there was something suspicious about these disappearances. They occurred just days or weeks after the children had gone to the Doctors Without Borders for a checkup. All of them. It's the only thing these missing children had in common. After an investigation, what the JSO operatives discovered was that the Dadalias—both husband and wife—were helping a local human trafficking ring select the healthiest children for transport out of the country, to be prostituted in Sierra Leone." He winces, puts more pressure on his wound. "The Dadalias were given a heads-up by their colleagues in the trafficking world, and they ran. They did pretty well. Got all the way to Zurich, beyond extradition." He smiles wide. "But they couldn't run from me."

"The Libyans *sent* you to kill them?"

Fardün nods. "The government wanted to avoid a scandal. They didn't want people thinking less of their country than they already did. So, they kept the trafficking ring under wraps, executed all the main players, and put a contract out on the Dadalias. The world did not know why the Dadalias died, but it did somehow leak that I was the one who killed them." He shrugs as if to say this is all part of the job, and spits out another red gob.

"You're telling me this so I'll think you're innocent. Not such a bad guy, after all."

"Oh, fuck you, Adamson," he laughs mirthlessly. "There are no innocents in war, at least not after the first year or so. I've killed innocents and I've killed bad people. So has the Unit. So has Karambit. Sometimes we do good things, sometimes we do bad things. Like you. How many men just doing their jobs did you kill while in Russia? Mm? How many people have begged for their lives just before you pulled the trigger?"

I have three children.

"We're all a bunch of assholes," Fardün concludes. "Today it's my turn to be an asshole to you. In a minute, you will shoot me and then you will be the asshole again. It's like a...ah! Hot potato?" He chuckles. "We pass it around to each other!"

"You do what you do for money. It's not the same with me."

"Oh, fuck you, Adamson. Would you have *ever* done *any* dangerous work for Uncle Sam if you *weren't* getting paid? Mm? Risked life and limbs for free? You've been getting paid since the day you entered basic training." Another chuckle, this one filled with liquid. "Different kind of employer, but you're still employed. I just get paid better."

I don't like this kind of talk. It's getting us nowhere. "Let's get back on track, buddy. Karambit. Does he have a general idea where I'm at right now?"

"SVR figures you've made it into Mongolia by now, and the Unit has been tasked to follow you," Fardün says. "But I'm the only one who tracked you this far." And now, for the first time, he looks at me in surprise. "How did you know I was here?"

"Got a message from a friend in CIA."

"Ah. Before you were disavowed?"

Now here's something interesting. "How do *you* know about that?"

"The Unit. Apparently, they have people inside your agency."

"What people?"

"I don't know, but I once overheard them refer to this person as Alpha Source, and I understand this source is never wrong."

I look him over. Consider him. "How the hell would you know about all this? They'd never tell a hired mercenary about a mole, much less mention them by name."

"They didn't tell me. I told you, I overheard it."

"How?"

"I've met with members of the Unit more than once. I usually scope out our meeting places long beforehand, plant recording devices around the area before anyone shows up." He shrugs. "I've caught my employers talking about a lot of things when they thought no one was listening."

"Where are those recordings?"

"Safe."

"Where?"

"Safe."

I take a step closer. "Where?"

"Oh, fuck off, Adamson," he chuckles.

"No," I say. "You fuck off." I backhand him with the pistol, sending him to the floor. I stand over him, press the pistol to his head. I'm about to pull the trigger when something occurs to me. A thought. Something that Sophia once said. *The world thought I was dead. I might as well have been.* And then I realize there's a way I might be able to help my people at CIA. A way to find the mole.

"What are you waiting for?" Fardün asks. His voice is not so confident now, not so mirthful.

I take a step back, and look him over. "What if I had a way," I say slowly, working the plan out even as I speak it, "of helping us both out?"

He looks up at me. "If I bargain with you, if I give them my sources, it won't matter if you let me live. They'll know. They'll find me and kill me anyway."

I sit down on my haunches next to him. "What if I'm dead already?"

Fardün looks at me queerly. Then he smiles, and shakes his head. "I see what you're thinking. But they would find out. Eventually they'd find out. They always do."

"But not for some time. By the time they find out, you can already be long gone. With one-point-five million U.S. Even if they do come after you, it's better than dying here, now."

Fardün looks away, shaking his head. "It'll never work."

"Is there a way for you to contact Karambit directly? A phone number you call when the job is done?"

"Yes, there is, but…it'll never work," he repeats.

"It's either this or you die right here, right now. I gave you the same choice back in the alley and you chose to come with me. I think you still wanna live. What's it gonna be, Fardün?"

The mercenary stares at me at length. With an exhausted sigh, he says, "Ohhhh…fuck you, Adamson."

Oie

My interviews with Abijah have awakened something. A feeling that no connection to family has ever been able to satisfy. I love my girls, I do, but Abijah sits and talks of operational movements, she asks questions concerning operational history, and she speaks using operational nomenclature. She knows who and what I am. Like Nathan, she gets it. Only with Nathan I sometimes held back, not wanting to reveal my true self. Maybe it is Abijah's feminine nature, knowing that she has been the underdog in only the way a woman can be in the intelligence-gathering world, expected to use her cunt to make her way, one way or another, through the spyscape. There is a coldness in her wrought-iron eyes, one that bespeaks commitment to an end. I respect that.

On those days when she knows my family won't be coming around, we meet over coffee or tea. We quickly become old friends, shaking hands as professionals and leveling with one another about this or that. She asks her questions. I lay it all out. She asks for greater background on myself and my time in the War and with SDECE. Occasionally we discuss family. She has four boyfriends. I like her even better. She does not brag and she is not ashamed to have men waiting for her in Israel, Britain, Ukraine and Egypt. I get the feeling she would never give such an admission if I had not bluntly told her about the many men in my life.

Mossad could not have sent a better fit. Yet still, I watch her for deceptions, as I am sure she watches me, knitting, divesting myself of a hundred or more secrets that have been locked inside the vault for ages. The vault has been strong, ironclad, its combination never divulged. Not even Nathan could get into it. But Abijah is a woman and our goals are aligned and DGSE apparently does not care as much as us about finding Herr Vogel. I guess it is true what they say, monsters like Vogel simply need to live long enough that their crimes become legend, myth. When a person reaches a certain age, it does not matter how monstrous they were in their youth, the world simply moves on. If that maxim is true—if Abijah and I *allow it* to be true— then that means being a rapist or a murderer or a thief has an expiration date. These monsters are simply running a marathon, and if they keep themselves from getting caught for long enough, they get to live and die peacefully.

This is insufficient. In the Resistance, when it came to such monsters, we required blood. In SDECE, in *Héritage*, we required blood. In this wheelchair, I require blood. In this wheelchair, I am called to manifest. To bring about. To plan. Abijah has a similar calling. From here, inside the lobby of the Rose Lawn Retirement Home, we will be the architects of Herr Vogel's end.

But just like any operation, we must be patient. We must be clear about the facts. We must know the realities, what we used to call "ground truth," meaning that the higher-ups can make their own plans all day, and tell us what we ought and ought not to do, but at the end of the day there is a different truth on the ground where the troops are.

So I relate what I can recall, and I am honest about where things get fuzzy.

Wilhelm Vogel would have been an unremarkable soldier in the German Army, had it not been for a combination of his ruthlessness and a bit of luck. During the War, he bounced around between units, supporting tank brigades and reinforcing roadblocks throughout France. But it was not until there was a personnel shortage in Alkoven, near Linz, Austria, where the Nazis had started Action T4 at the Hartheim Euthanasia Centre, that Vogel found his calling. Once transferred there as part of a security group, he soon showed his superiors he was willing to do anything to maintain order among the Jews in the camp.

He advanced quickly in rank. Stories from a number of Jews who survived there said he liked to perform what he called "last rites" on women, meaning he selected one or two to rape the night before they were executed in the gas chambers.

Vogel became fast friends with the lead staff. There are pictures of him dining at the camp with Franz Reichleitner, the criminal policeman who was later commandant of the Sobibor extermination camp. In the picture, they're both smiling and toasting the cameraman with their coffee cups. Both men were eating eggs at the time. In the background were two Jewish women serving others in the cafeteria.

Vogel also made friends with Criminal Commissar Christian Wirth, later commandant of the Belzec extermination camp, and Franz Stangl, Gestapo deputy and later commandant of Treblinka. There is one file from Georg Renno, the camp's lead psychiatrist and deputy head of euthanasia, where he said of Hauptmann Wilhelm Vogel in a letter-of-recommendation for promotion, "There is no finer man to keep order in a place like this. It is like keeping dogs in a kennel. And like any decently run kennel, you must have someone to teach the dogs who is master. No man exemplifies this better than Hauptmann Vogel. He has the right attitude for dealing with the Jews and gypsies who do not yet understand their place. He also stirs the other soldiers to work hard. An exemplary leader with a gift for directing even the most stubborn men to follow his example."

The Gestapo must have liked him very much, too, for at some point between 1942 and 1944, he was recruited to return to France and help hunt down Jews in hiding. He was made *Kriminalsekretär* and according to reports at the time he raped most of the people he found before sending them off to die in camps. He raped women, boys and girls. There was one report, I tell Abijah, that I recall quite clearly, of how Herr Vogel once castrated a man, then cauterized the wound and made him wear his own penis by a rope around his neck, like a necklace, as he was marched off towards a camp. He was made to do this in front of his wife.

For six months, Vogel was put in charge of selecting candidates from among their prisoners at Dachau to be part of experiments that placed them inside low-pressure chambers, to determine from what altitude crews of damaged aircraft could parachute to safety. He also selected a few women to be part of a freezing experiment that allowed the Nazis to test treatments for hypothermia. A few children he and the Gestapo sent off to be part of an experiment to test methods for making seawater potable. Many of these subjects he made sure to rape before he sent them away. There are at least six children who were fathered by this monster, and possibly as many as twenty-three, the Jewish mothers who somehow made it through the War were forced to raise the life he seeded in them. How disgusted they must have been.

Here is the kind of man who, in peacetime, would have wandered about with nothing to do. Probably been a clerk in his father's hotel, like his brothers, and lived with a wife who despised him and whom he despised until the day he died. He would never have been able to ascend to the level of monster he became in the War. War invites the beast inside us to come out to play. Those without discipline, those who secretly *want* the beast to come out, delight in wars. I sometimes think about what I became in the War. Was I a monster, too?

It is unclear how Vogel managed to escape capture after the War, though records indicate he was in areas where the Allies came through, seriously killing and capturing every German they could find. This is the beginning of an era in his life when French intelligence first became aware of him, and fully realized just what a slippery *sous-merde* Wilhelm Vogel can be.

The monster only came across our intelligence radar because of Simon Wiesenthal, the Holocaust survivor who, after the War, became a Nazi hunter for a time, releasing his famous "Wiesenthal List" that began the hunt of more than a hundred Nazi officers, Gestapo operatives, and doctors. The List was taken to heart by Israeli intelligence officials, who, with five French Jews working for SDECE, began assembling the quasi-official Nazi-hunter group Legacy, called *Héritage* among my superiors.

In truth, Mossad pulled most of the weight in these hunts, never limiting their prey to just those on the Wiesenthal List. The numbers are unofficial, but, as Abijah knows, there is substantial evidence that her Mossad predecessors clandestinely killed scores of Nazi war criminals on the run the world over.

At the same time Wilhelm Vogel was making his way through the ranks and wallowing in debauchery and barbarism, I was maneuvering my way deeper and deeper into the Resistance. It took a couple years for me to finally make the plunge. I was first a clerk, and then a paralegal, and then nothing at all when the Nazis took France. I briefly considered prostitution like my cousin—very briefly, in a moment of despair when I thought the world was crumbling. It *was* crumbling.

But then I met a man. A Brit by the name of Zachary Karkus. Dashing and handsome, he spoke fluent French and appeared to be a scholar who became trapped in France when the occupation began. At first, I did not like him. He was recruited to help some of the Gestapo with their French, to understand the nuances of the language, certain ways Parisians spoke in code. I heard about him. Saw him two or three times at the Calrum market near my house. One evening while out shopping, I bumped into him. He introduced himself and I spat in his face. He laughed. I hated him for that laugh.

Three nights later I came home to find Karkus and another man waiting in my house. Just sitting in the dark. I screamed. I thought the Gestapo had come for me, thinking I was Resistance. He said to me, "You know, you could be severely punished for what you did. You knew it when you did it, but you did it anyway." I was dead. I knew it. Then, he bade me sit down at my own kitchen table, and listen to him and his friend speak.

And that is how I found out the truth of him. He was British intelligence, sent into France to help. A lone operative in France to find what rebels were there and lend them support, sometimes money, sometimes supplies, in order to undermine Nazi operations in the region. Karkus said he and his friends wanted to recruit me, to help them rid France of the Nazi *fini à la pisse* once and for all. I was shocked. Certain that it was a trap. Seeing my reticence, like any good recruiter, Karkus sat down and spoke with me all night, elaborating on their methods. He said he knew he could trust me because he had had his friends inquire about me in the area, had other agents speak to my mother in Marseille and my uncles in Chartres. He said he knew my sentiments against the Nazis were that they were vile abominations, creatures from some dark region of hell. His approach to me at the market had been planned. When I spat in his face, he knew.

He asked me to show a little faith, to come with him the next night to meet some of the people he had already recruited, see what kind of operation they had going. I wanted to say no, thinking it would be my end. But my heart coerced my lips, and they said yes.

I did not sleep that night, still half afraid that it was all a trap, that I had agreed to sign my own death warrant. But the next night I went to a dress shop on Rue Cler and met Pierre, and Sarah, and Emma, and Louis and Paul and Gabriel and Raphael. Brits and French, working together. I had heard the rumors. We all had. French people helping Allied pilots who had been shot down escape the country, so that they could return to service and keep fighting the good fight against the Nazis.

That first night, I just listened. They told me stories. Some were funny, some were tragic, and some dealt with what was going on inside Austria and Germany, what was happening to the Jews being taken away. I had never heard such horrors, and could scarcely believe it. But they had pictures.

At the end of the night, Karkus asked me, "Sophia, will you help us?" I asked him what exactly he needed me to do. "Anything and everything you feel comfortable with," he said bluntly. Somehow, I sensed what he meant, but I do not think he believed I would ever go as far as I did. I was introduced to local leaders of the Resistance, and I only ever saw Karkus twice again, at the end of the War.

I passed around secret newspapers at first. That's it, just flyers. I became the number-one distributor of *Défense de la France* in all of Lorraine and its surrounding provinces. I dispensed newspapers that told of the victories against the Nazis, victories the Germans would not speak of or let be known. After six months of this, and after the Resistance leaders saw how deft I was at maneuvering across the provinces, I was given the job of dropping off messages and packages. Dead drops. I learned about brush passes and secret codes, surveillance and countersurveillance, how to disappear in a crowd and know when I was being followed, handling "cut-out" agents and the art of "limited hangout." That last I was particularly good at. It entails admitting to partial wrongdoing, which shuts down further inquiry about one's true deception, usually something embarrassing, i.e. telling authorities that the reason you are traveling without papers is because you are fucking a married man in the next town and you do not want your name getting around, lest it get back to your own husband. Admitting that you were a slut usually did the job, you just had to ignore the wry smiles and knowing nods as you confirmed their theories on French women.

But apparently my true calling was in the honey trap. I lost count of the Nazis I sucked off to get what I wanted. When my friends in the Resistance began to suspect that this was why I was so efficient at gathering information, some of them intervened, telling me I needn't go this far. When I stared them in the eye and said I enjoyed putting men through ecstasy, especially when I secretly knew I would be their undoing, I got some worried looks. God, what must they have thought of me? But they let me continue. How could they not? God only knows how many undercover Gestapo agents I discovered, how many planned strikes on secret Resistance hideouts I gleaned, and how many Jews who were secretly feeding the Germans information on their own people that I outed.

So, it did not matter how many of the enemy I sucked off.

"No one argues with results," I tell Abijah. She nods knowingly.

As the days go on, I try not to elaborate too much more on my time in the Resistance. I do not tell her I gave birth to Isabella, the offspring of a Nazi named Heinrich who was soft and tender and I actually sort of fancied. Nor do I tell her that I lost Isabella at birth.

I do not keep these things from Abijah because I am ashamed (I'm not), but because the reason she came here was to hear how I came to be on Wilhelm Vogel's trail. And that begins just after the War, when SDECE was founded as a successor to the Bureau Central de Renseignnements et d'Action. Karkus had been approached by the new SDECE leaders to help them locate all the French Resistance fighters and agents he and his people had worked with. They asked him to put together a list of the best operatives.

This was how I once again met Karkus. Apparently, he had been hearing about me during the War through our intermediaries. I had already returned to work at my father's friend's firm, and was dating two men at once, trying to decide which one I would marry, when I was approached by a man named Verlaine, like the French poet. We talked in person twice, then over the phone once. I made my decision and left for Paris to go through a recruitment camp. I did not marry either man.

I was assigned to Department XV, Records. And here is where Herr Vogel first came into my view. I, along with seventeen other women, were given the onerous task of sorting and cataloging all papers seized from camps. We went through deportation papers from Dachau, prisoner lists from Bernburg, disciplinary forms from Buchenwald and Le Vernet, we even read food order forms from Stutthof and Sachsenhausen, so that we could track ex-Nazi's movements by their signatures on the orders.

Three years of this, and I did this happily. Thanks in part to those of us in Department XV, 127 war criminals were identified and dealt with in various ways. Then someone found reason to bring me back into the field.

My work in Records was good, they said. But they were starting something new, called *Héritage*, in conjunction with the newly-founded Israeli intelligence service Mossad. Started because of the Wiesenthal List, and then expanded because of the almost 4,000 depositions given by concentration camp survivors throughout Europe, *Héritage* was fast becoming a priority to some of the higher-ups who did not wish to be viewed as forgetting the horrors of the past.

They needed agents in the field. They had plenty of men, but few women. Women might be able to glean information in ways that men could not. They never said I had to fuck anybody, but I would not have cared if they had. Somehow, this does not bother me, fucking men whom I planned to kill or capture. Perhaps something is missing inside of me that makes me not revolted enough by their despicable crimes to keep from enjoying it. Somehow it is okay that I fucked them, it was even occasionally enjoyable.

I was given my codename: *Oie*. Goose. I was asked to show a few of the female recruits how seduction works, and how they may go as far as they are comfortable going. Then I was in the field. And thus began my operational history. I used any means. "Slutting it up" as one *sous-merde* agent put it before I spat in his face and slapped him.

I tell Abijah, "Once, I overheard two agents in a breakroom talking. One of them said, 'There she goes, the one that half of Germany has fucked.' The other agent replied, 'Yes, but *she* fucked *all* of them in the end.' I thought that was clever. I even laughed." Abijah gives her fractional smile, and the days continue to drain and I forget how much time has passed and now I am being visited by family and now Abijah is back and we are talking again.

Vaguely, I am aware that there is a new war stirring on the television. I wonder if Nathan is safe.

Now it's tomorrow and I am sitting in front of Chloe. She came alone this time, no Zoe or Henrietta. Chloe looks troubled. The look on her face is like when she had to tell me something had happened to Daniel. The look of a bearer of bad news. She tells me there's been an issue with Nathan Adamson. She knows about him. She knows he is a nice man who was in the Middle East during all those dreadful wars and that he has been talking to me, one veteran to another.

"He's been in the news," she says.

"Nathan? In the news? What for?"

19

"I'm his brother," I tell the nurse at the front desk of the ICU. Thankfully, she speaks Russian well enough. "I'm the one who brought him in. I should be on the visitors list. Can I see him?"

The room she leads me to is tiny, with one hospital bed and a tiny window. It's on the fourth floor, so I know the patient can't jump for it even if he wanted to. I stand over Fardün, who still appears unconscious. Doctors say he will be for a while, perhaps days. He was bleeding badly when I brought him here. It's weird to be here now, standing over an enemy and hoping he doesn't die, but that's exactly what I'm doing. If he dies, our little plan doesn't work.

While he was under the knife, getting my bullets taken out of him, I took the liberty of heading back across town to the Hotel Tikina, gathering all my gear, and storing it in a rental car I parked downstairs. I took the *Kop'ye* and hid it in a locker at Chinggis Khaan International Airport, in case I'm taken prisoner later and need a bargaining chip. Fardün's sniper rifle I retrieved from the shopping mall rooftop after some consternation, but I decided it might come in handy at some point. I disassembled it and packed it in with my backpack. I'm ready to go mobile. But for my next move to work, Innick Fardün must survive.

He's breathing evenly with plastic tubes in his nose. There's a steady beep from his vitals. He's under a quilt, wearing nothing but a hospital gown, and so I get a look at his body. Tanned and starting to look brittle, like old leather. There's a spot on his arm where crisscrossing scars have marred an old tattoo of some woman. He's also missing the last knuckle of his left pinky finger.

The lead doctor comes in to speak with me, and the nurse is there to translate. Looks like Fardün is going to make it, but there was some minor nerve damage, he might have trouble standing and sitting for a while, maybe forever. Hard to tell right now, the doc says. I thank him. When I'm alone again with the sleeping Fardün, I pull up a chair and sit next to his bed. I turn on the wall-mounted TV, switch it to the news with English subtitles, and watch the world lose its mind.

*

The Korea Central News Agency is reporting that the Kim regime has denied talks with the South Korean leadership. The South Koreans are trying to intervene on the U.S.'s behalf, talk the Kim Regime down, let them know that should North Korea go to war with us, they won't have allies from their neighbors in the south. This hasn't slowed North Korea's actions one bit, and their subs continue to buffer certain key areas at sea between the U.S. and Russian vessels.

There has been a tenuous ceasefire in Eastern Ukraine for a year, but it's starting to get tense again with a few potshots being taken by Moscow-supported local militias against Kiev forces. There has been a slow collapse of the Ukrainian government, and Vladimir Putin seems eager to take advantage and grab more territory in the country.

And now my photos of the Great Donut have hit the web. It's not the first time my actions or the actions of my SEAL team have made the news. In fact, that happens quite often in this line of work. Even if no one knows it was a SOG operation—which they never do, the government doesn't release the details of our ops—the repercussions of our actions are usually felt in either direct or indirect ways. Maybe an assault on a jihadist hideout leaves destruction and debris that looks good on al Jazeera, or else there are political ramifications that stem from our work. But never have I seen photographs that I took myself appear on the evening news.

The Great Donut is now on display for all the world to see. The pics are selected stills from the video I took. I'm not sure what the strategy was in releasing the photos, except maybe to get any of the U.S.'s NATO allies that are still on the fence to realize that particle-beams fired from space is really, truly, *genuinely* on Russia's list of things to do this year.

The BBC has two scientists on a split-screen from Berkley talking about the rumors of a leaked memo from Homeland Security that says these pics have to do with some kind of directed-energy weapon. They sit there explaining the DEW and the possibility of excited particles being blasted towards Earth from orbit and how many terajoules of destructive power that could yield, while I sit here smiling to myself because I know that the memo was leaked to cause exactly this kind of discussion. Homeland was ordered to do it, most likely by the POTUS, who was himself urged by the Director of National Intelligence to give the world a reason to reevaluate how serious the Russian threat is.

And then there's China. They've mobilized all their subs and begun sea denial operations around the South China Sea. The rumor is Taiwan is being surrounded, and that China is getting ready to reabsorb what they've wanted for decades. Since they've got their sea denial operations going on, it's going to be difficult, if not impossible, for Taiwan to get any help from other nations.

Even if we don't go to war, the Chinese are expected to take this opportunity to change things on the ground so fast, and create such a new geopolitical landscape, that the rest of the world will have no choice but to accept it. No one will *let you* wipe out a tribe of people on protected land, but if you completely massacre them before anyone can stop you…hey, what's done is done.

It's unofficially being called the Conflict With the Eastern Alignment: Russia, China, Syria, Iran, and North Korea.

Conflict. Not a *war.* Not yet.

Just before midnight, the pics that I and Tatiana took of the Steel Octopuses appear in the news, as do rumors of a new "deuterium-fluoride laser" the Russians have been developing in tandem with the Chinese. All my efforts in Russia are bearing fruit right before my eyes.

My face pops up a few times, as well as my name and the president's disavowal of former U.S. Navy SEAL Nathan Arthur Adamson.

And now the story turns to the U.S. and its battle-readiness. All forty-eight attack submarines have been fully deployed and made ready, it seems, as opposed to the usual twenty, and all eighteen *Ohio*-class submarines have been dispersed to secret locations. If these rumors are true, this is looking like DEFCON 2 to me. The news goes on about the U.S. Navy's warships with their abundance of missiles and terrifying new lasers purchased from Lockheed Martin back in 2017. The lasers produce beams up to 400 kW and can destroy missiles and boats from miles away, and cost almost $200,000,000 each.

Then there's the U.S.'s newest drone tank, the Hammer-1. It's a hovercraft twice the size of an Abrams tank with a huge railgun jutting out its right side. The railgun is an electromagnetic projectile-thrower, which flings a football-sized hunk of steel at Mach 6, more than 4,500 miles per hour, and has a range of 125 miles. Once fired, it basically becomes an asteroid, annihilating everything in its path. And unlike bullets that lose speed once they're fired, projectiles from a railgun *gain speed* as they go along.

The Mongolian newscasters are obsessed with all this new tech being revealed. And I remember the CIA's Chinese defector again, talking about how fast things were moving technologically, how it's outpacing our ability to understand it all or use it wisely.

I need a break from all this. Pacing for a bit, I find my ankle is doing a lot better. My ribs, too. I'm almost breathing normally.

When I go down to the cafeteria, it's all that's on the TV there. I take my meal back to Fardün's room and eat it there. I don't like to let him out of my sight for long. Another reason I stick to his room is because I don't want too many people getting a regular look at my face. I've got blonde hair and a well-manicured beard, and I walk with drooped shoulders and a downcast head, but my other passport picture is still occasionally on the news. Thankfully, though, the DEW is taking up more coverage.

I go to the restroom and stand there looking into the mirror. "Nest, Ares. Do you read?" Nothing. I check the old e-mail address to see if Yarwick's sent me anything. Also nothing.

I return to Fardün's room and sleep in a recliner facing his bed. My watch wakes me up at 0400 and I switch it off to catch up on some sleep. I've earned it.

*

One day when I was six years old, I woke up to someone screaming down the hallway. I jumped out of bed and ran to my brother's room, where my parents had already convened around my brother, who was lying on the floor, terrified, tears streaming down his cheeks. He kept shouting over and over again, "I can't feel my legs!" My father was scared. So scared he kept yelling at Derek that he needed to quit fooling around, that this wasn't funny anymore. My mother already had the phone in her ear, dialing 911. Derek just kept screaming that his legs wouldn't work.

Dad ended up carrying my brother into the family van and driving us all down to the hospital, where they gave my brother a full physical. Derek was nine years old, my big brother, and I saw him shaking and crying like I'd never seen anyone do before. Mom was praying. Dad was leaning intently towards the doctors, arms crossed, eyes wide with fear.

Derek was diagnosed with Guillain-Barré syndrome, a rapid-onset muscle weakness than happens when one's own immune system attacks the peripheral nervous system. It can come out of nowhere. Back then, no one knew what caused it. These days, there are theories that it can be triggered by certain strains of flu virus. GBS is not as deadly as it used to be, thanks to some advances in medicine, but back then it was close to a death sentence, and even if Derek lived he was not expected to ever walk properly again. They said he'd never run and play like normal kids.

I remember sitting next to Derek's bed. Day and night. I watched my big brother cry and look angry and be scared. I saw him getting skinnier and skinnier. I went back to school, life went on for me, but Derek had to do homeschooling. He missed all of his friends, while I got to run around and play with mine.

One night, I'll never forget, I woke up in the hospital room. Mom was asleep on a couch next to me. Dad had gone out to get something to eat from the hospital's kitchen, I think. I saw Derek's eyes were open. I stood and walked over to him. I touched his arm, and smiled at my big brother. "You want me to get you anything, Bubber?" I asked. *Bubber* was what I called him, a leftover from when I was very small and couldn't say *brother*.

That's when my brother looked at me. No one else heard what he said, and I never told Mom or Dad. "This should be you," he said. I stared at him, not understanding. "This shouldn't be me. This should be *you!*" It was the coldest thing anyone ever said to me.

Dad came back to the room before I could say anything back, and we never talked about it again. I don't even know if Derek remembers saying it. Maybe it was some kind of medication they had him on? Whatever the reason, over the next two years, Derek went through treatments and then physical therapy, and became one of the two percent of GBS sufferers who make miraculous full recoveries.

But I never forgot what he said to me. I never forgot it. I even thought about it at Derek's wedding. *This should be you.* He was walking just fine at his wedding reception. Smiling and dancing, trying to get me laid with a bridesmaid. It was an important lesson. When people are on top of the world, their hearts are filled with nothing but joy, contentment, and goodwill towards others. But when the chips are down, even a sibling can turn on you.

I think on that as I watch Fardün's chest rise and fall rhythmically. The sterile smell of the hospital room evokes those memories of long nights around Derek's bed, wondering what he meant by his vicious words. I can't help but recollect that moment when I felt ice flood through me after I heard those words. *This should be you.* I expect the same level of viciousness when Fardün's eyes flutter open for the first time, and I walk over to him.

"Hey there, buddy," I say, smiling down on him. "Looking good. How you feeling?"

His lips move, but no air comes out.

I lean a little closer. But not too close.

With an effort, Fardün pushes air from his lungs, and in a whisper, he says, "Oh, fuck you, Adamson."

Essentially the same sentiment as my brother at nine years old. People in their hospitable beds can't be trusted to be on their best behavior. Or maybe it's when we're our most honest. I don't know if I can take an *even more* honest Innick Fardün.

I chuckle. "Doctors say you're gonna be more or less fine. Some minor nerve damage, maybe. I'll go grab them, let them all explain it." At the door, I freeze, smile, and shoot two finger pistols at him. "Hey, don't go anywhere."

"Fuck you, Adamson," he wheezes. And laughs.

I retrieve the docs, and stay in the room while they give Fardün the rundown on his health. I only need to be here for one reason: to make sure he doesn't pull some stunt, like tell the hospital staff that he actually doesn't know me, that I'm the guy that shot him, that he's in serious danger and only came with me to the hospital under duress.

267

When the doctors are finished speaking with Fardün, we get some alone time. I pull up a chair beside his bed, and have a seat. "All right, let's talk about how this is going to work."

"It won't work," he says. "Not in the long run."

"We discussed this already, remember? We only need it to work long enough for me to get what I want and for you to get clear. I'm assuming you have a nest egg set up, as well as a bank account for rainy days?" He doesn't say anything. "Plus, you got the one-point-five mill comin' your way for killing me. If you can't have a little plastic surgery done and vanish into a small town in Italy or Switzerland with all those resources, then you're a shit assassin."

Fardün looks at me and sighs heavily. "Like fucking SpongeBob. Always up to fucking hijinks. Fine. What exactly are your plans to make this work?"

I pick up the remote control to the TV, and turn it on. The news is on. "First, let me bring you up to speed, just so you know where we stand." On the screen is a Mongolian newswoman with an image of the American flag and the Russian sickle-and-hammer right next to her, with flames boiling up between them. Very dramatic.

"The Russians are really pressing it now," I tell him. "North Korea's all in. Iran and Syria are mostly providing support, but they're pretty solidly joined at the hip. So far, China hasn't pressed subs into U.S. territory, or even our allies' territory—at least, no more so than usual—but China *is* using this to their fullest advantage. While Russia and North Korea pull mostly sea denial campaigns, China is blockading Taiwan and now maybe even Hong Kong, trying to reclaim both into a new unified China. And, oh, hey, look at that," I say, just as pictures of the Great Donut and the Steel Octopuses appear on screen.

Fardün squints at this. Is it possible that, even though he knew what his employers were so upset about, he's never actually *seen* this tech before with his own eyes?

Next is a series of images of the U.S.'s Hammer-1 hovering over a lake, making one-eighty turns, and firing its railgun. It's footage taken from a test at Lockheed Martin some years ago.

"This is it," I tell him. "The world on the brink."

Fardün sighs. "And so what? War is good. Good for business. At least for men like us." He chuckles. It turns into a heavy cough. "This is the way the world evolves, Adamson."

"Not anymore. Now if we have a World War, everything ends. Everything collapses."

"And so what if it does? It was bound to eventually."

"So, you're a nihilist, then."

"Are you surprised, Adamson? I'm a fucking assassin."

I shrug. "I guess you're right. I shouldn't be surprised." I sigh and mute the TV, but leave it on. "Okay, so, you don't give a shit about what happens to the rest of the world. Fine. Let me put this in context for you, and explain how it relates to *you and me*." I toss the remote control onto a table. "Right now, the world thinks this might be it. Doomsday. And it might very well be. And to the Russians, and their 'Eastern Alignment,' this just reeks of opportunity. And that's all they want. *Opportunity*. Nobody wants a war. Nobody's that stupid. But it may come to that if they can't get the U.S. and its allies to back down.

"The Chinese are with the Russians and North Koreans for right now because they just want to take back Taiwan and expand their strength in the East and South China Sea, like they've always wanted. The North Koreans want to increase their clout in a world that's mostly considered the Kim regime a dinky little country run by a madman. Iran and Syria just want a little more over the Middle East landscape, and, if they can get it, a means to permanently banish the U.S. and its allies from meddling in their business. That's all any of these fucking countries are after in this, just a way to gain a little ground. It's posturing. But as you and I both know, posturing can turn into fighting if someone doesn't back down.

"And the way the Russians get everyone to back down—at least *one* of the ways—is to pull this whataboutism bullshit. If they have me as proof of stealing something, of conducting espionage in their country, of *killing Russian operatives* while I was Amur Oblast, it gains them a little bit of credibility. No one will care about the details, that Russia was developing a weapon they fully intended to launch into orbit without telling anyone—not NATO, not the United Nations, nobody. And no one will *really* care that I was just there to take pictures, and shot those people along the river because they killed the Tidov family and came to kill me.

"The only thing that will matter is that I was where I wasn't allowed to be, and that I destroyed their satellite and stole the *Kop'ye*. It's enough for the Russians to deflect responsibility, deflect accusations of readying for war, deflect any notion that they're doing anything that other countries wouldn't do. Deflect, deflect, deflect. That's all my dead body means to them, a means of deflection."

I shrug.

"After they have that, and pull some other political bullshit, and boast and point fingers at the U.S., there will be some discussions between world leaders, then a gradual stand-down of forces from all sides. But by then, it'll be too late, China will have what it wanted out of all this, it will have taken Taiwan and asserted control over the China Sea while everyone else was posturing, and Russia and the others will have what they came for. *Clout. Respect.* They made America flinch. And this goes from being a potential World War III, to the Cold War II. Not much better, but better."

Fardün purses his lips. "And so..."

"And so, that's why this will work. The Russians need me dead. A reason to show the U.S. that I was, in fact, present in their country. And they'll pay you anything and everything you ask for to get to me."

He raises an eyebrow. "What I ask for?"

I nod. "You're going to ask for double the normal payment, because not only do you have me dead, but you also have something else they want. And you're going to send them a picture to prove it."

"And what is that?" Fardün asks, as if he doesn't already know.

"The *Kop'ye*."

He chuckles. And wheezes. "And what do you get out of all of this, Adamson?"

"The world thinks I'm dead, and you get to arrange a meeting with Karambit. A meeting I'll be at."

"Why?"

"Because I want to know who Alpha Source is."

And I want to kill Karambit, I think, but I don't say. For Tatiana, I want to kill the son of a bitch.

Come back to me.

20

The doctors want Fardün to remain in the hospital for another three days to keep a watch on him. He's out less than twenty-four hours after I spoke with him. We're staying at a small hotel together on the outskirts of the city, on Khasbaatar Street, near the Gandantegchinlen Monastery. It's in a part of the city that still looks historic, almost like traveling back in time, except for the ATM machines and billboards and bustling traffic.

In our room, I allow Fardün a couple hours to lie down, relax for a bit, and watch some TV while I prepare everything. It's not hard to make fake blood. Some corn syrup and food die will do the trick just fine, or you can just buy pig's blood, which is easy to do at markets in this area. And there are tips online from indie horror filmmakers on how to make realistic-looking exit wounds on a body.

Faking being dead, though, is something I've never had to do. It's strange and morbid, but I draw inspiration from all the dead bodies I've seen, all the people I've killed, and how they looked just moments after death. That lazy, glossy-eyed, somewhat dumbfounded look, like you're confused about something while falling asleep.

Fardün and I set the stage, flicking blood about the room, along the walls, like we're Dexter Morgan trying to get just the right kind of blood spatter. "Time to go into makeup," he laughs. "Showtime in five minutes!"

I put on my "makeup" while keeping Fardün within my sight. Don't want him backing out now, running out of the room and telling Karambit what I plan to do.

I lay beside the bed, and place the SIG just underneath the bed where the camera can't see it. The pistol is in case Fardün tries to kill me while taking my picture. I make sure he knows the pistol is there. Fardün takes my picture from several different angles. I go through his camera, decide on the best ones, and delete the others. "Those are the ones you'll send to Karambit," I tell him. "Now take pictures of the *Kop'ye*'s pieces."

He does so. And when he's finished, I prepare a text message to send to Karambit, so that I know that Fardün can't warn him in any way. Then, once I'm satisfied the ruse is as complete as we can make it look, I hit SEND.

"You know," he chuckles raspingly, "you've basically just killed me. Even if Karambit finds out that I betrayed him under duress, I'm either dead, or, at the very least, not reliable enough to use anymore. My reputation will never recover. Word will get around that I make compromises with whoever points a gun at my head. Professionals like me are supposed to be above that kind of coercion."

I toss his phone on the bed. "You're a mercenary, Fardün. Consider this one last job."

Slowly, Fardün pulls off his shirt, and looks at his bandages. He peels one off, and takes a look at the stitches. "You've been disavowed by your own government, and you still want to help them find this mole?"

"I do."

"You think it fucking matters at this point?" he says, pointing at the TV.

"It matters."

"And you're sure this is all just for your country? Nothing else?"

"I'm sure."

But I see Tatiana's frightened blue eyes. And I hear Karambit's voice.

You don't have it, Ares! You don't have what it takes!

Fardün shrugs. "Fine, then. What do we do now?"

"Now," I say, "you help me clean up this mess. Don't want to be rude to the hotel staff and leave them with a crime scene, now do we?"

Just then, Fardün's phone dings. I snatch it up from the bed before he can reach for it, and I read the text message.

"Well?" he says, wincing as he touches his stitches. "What does it say?"

"Seventy-four Wangfujing Street."

"Where the hell is that?"

Takes me a second to look it up on my watch. "China." I look at him and smile. "We've got a meeting place."

*

273

The Ulaanbaatar Railway leads away from the city, cutting through scenic squares to make sure the tourists see them and avoid any of the more run-down areas. The office buildings and parking decks slowly give way to the ice-covered countryside, where nomadic tribes ride atop their horses, traveling vast distances to hunt in the south. I'm struck by Mongolia's mix of the tribal and the modern.

The meeting place is in Beijing. I decided not to use Chinggis Khaan International to travel, as Ulaanbaatar is still a mostly modern city and my face might be recognizable. Also, I'm bringing all my gear with me, weapons and all, and an X-ray machine would spot that right away. A quick search of TravelMasterExpress.com tells me that the eastern border security checks are no trouble at all. So, we're heading east, for Inner Mongolia.

The whole way, I never let Fardün out of my sight. He stays in the same train car as me, in the same compartment, and once when he goes to the restroom, I go with him. I keep his phone on me in case Karambit calls and I need to tell Fardün what to say, but that never happens.

The train takes us into Urdna, a small town on the edge of Mongolia, where we hop off and take a bus to Inner Mongolia, an autonomous region of China, and from there we take yet another bus to Ordos City. We travel into a place as clean and modern as any high-class metropolitan area, past another huge Genghis Khan memorial, past sleek-looking Ordos Ejin Horo Airport, and then, ultimately, passing through a border patrol that barely even looks at us askance.

Fardün eats a lot. I guess he lost a lot of blood and needs his strength back. He talks a lot as we travel. It's all nonsense, nothing at all to do with our mission. He says things like "The first movie I saw in theaters was *The Empire Strikes Back*, and I remember thinking, is this supposed to take place in America? Is this what America is like?" and "I had my first and only orgy in China" and "I don't understand this *Rick and Morty* show. Gibberish."

It's like this all across Inner Mongolia. I don't respond with more than a grunt of acknowledgement.

Then we're in China proper. We exchange our Mongolian tugrik for Chinese renminbi, then we're in much warmer climes. Not an ounce of snow. Sixty-two degrees with the sun shining. Enormous rocky hills surround us, but eventually give way to the most emerald-green landscapes I've ever seen. We're in Hebei Province, about eighty miles from Beijing. It's a starry night when we finally come within sight of the city. It's a haze of light that's threaded thinly across the eastern horizon, but as we approach, that haze begins to come into focus.

You see such beautiful things, and such ugly things, Sophia once said to me in regards to the kind of work we do. Yes, we do get to see the world, just not always in the way we'd like.

*

"It's time we had a serious talk," I say, just as the day's first light paints an orange ribbon on the dark horizon. A small village slides by my window. A woman and her son are outside wrestling with a stubborn goat. They're in my window and gone within the same second.

Fardün opens one eye. He's been sleeping—or pretending to—in the seat next to me. "Talk?" he says.

"Yeah. We need to get some things clear."

"But I already know what you're going to say."

"You do?"

"Yes. I'm surprised it took you this long." He touches his side, winces. "You're going to tell me that I have little choice here but to help you kill the Unit and take Karambit alive." He shrugs, and chuckles. "You're right. If I don't help you, I don't get paid. My reputation will be ruined, true, but that will happen regardless of whether or not I help you, because now people know it's possible to get the drop on Innick Fardün, that perhaps I'm getting too old for this, and that I can be coerced. No employer can trust my work now."

"At least if you help me, you get paid, and can go on the run to wherever you want. And if Karambit lives, he'll know you're still out there somewhere. He'll keep looking for you until he has—"

"Oh, fuck you, Adamson. You already know my answer."

*

We pass monastery after monastery, the office buildings climbing higher and higher all around them until at last we arrive in the Dongcheng District. The bus lets us off at 74 Wangfujing Street, right in front of a wide stone courtyard with ornamental trees that lead up to St. Joseph's Church, one of four historic Catholic churches in the Roman Catholic Archdiocese of Beijing. It's built in Romanesque Revival style, with a mix of European and Chinese architectural design and lots of statues, archways, high windows, shrubs, and a towering sanctuary that can provide lots of cover.

It's noon. Nine hours before we're supposed to be here.

Once we step off the bus, we stand amid a hundred sightseers, all marveling and taking pictures. I'm one of only five Caucasians around. I'm not sure what Fardün is.

I look at him. "Time to get to work."

The old sniper looks around at the square, at all the people, at the buildings surrounding us. "Not many high spots," he says. "You're going to be firing from relatively low to the ground. Unless..." He points to a few buildings east of us. "Those four buildings. And I believe that's a water tower I see in the distance?" He takes out his binoculars, the same ones he was using to spy on my hotel room, which I scooped up when I grabbed his Barrett M82 sniper rifle. "Yes. That would be nice. But we won't know until we see what the view is like from there. Let's go have a look."

We inspect a parking deck, but it's too far too busy. It seems to service a very popular outdoor shopping mall nearby. As we ride in a taxi to the next possible position, I ask him, "How many does Karambit usually bring with him?"

"Three," Fardün says. "Always the same three. His most trusted men. I call them Larry, Curly, and Moe." He laughs. "But those are just the ones he will have stationed nearby, perhaps in a car or walking the park." He winces, touches his side. "A fourth man is always stationed as a sniper from far away."

"We need to find the most likely position for that guy, too."

"Indeed."

"And we're in China now. Russia and China are both in the Eastern Alignment, so the Unit may have support from locals."

"This is true."

The prime spot for me, as the assassin previously mentioned, is a water tower nine hundred meters away, with a clear shot to St. Joseph's. It's a perfect vantage point. But there's a problem. While on the sniper team, I didn't train very much beyond eight hundred meters before I was recruited into CIA, and so I never had much experience dealing with the Coriolis effect—that is, the deflection of the bullet due to Earth's natural spin. "I'd like to keep it within seven hundred meters," I tell Fardün. "No more than eight hundred. That's where I'm best."

"Something closer, right," Fardün says. "But remember this spot, it may be very attractive to the sniper that Karambit brings. But for you..." He points to two spots. "There, those two buildings. Perhaps one of them."

We start to head in that direction, but then I stop. I hear a distant ring. A bell. I turn and look back at St. Joseph's. "Wait, maybe we're overthinking this."

"What do you mean?"

"Look there." I point towards the church, at a bell tower maybe two hundred meters away from the meeting place itself.

Fardün makes a face. "*Mm*, that's a little too close."

"Your rifle has a suppressor."

"It does, but it's a little too obvious."

"Why would it be obvious? The Unit thinks I'm dead."

"But they might think I have another partner in play. One of them may come to search the bell tower."

I nod. "Maybe that's a good thing. They come to search it, I'll hear them coming, maybe hide and wait for them to set up. You give me the call that Karambit's arrived, I take out the sniper and search for the rest of his team from his own nest."

He sighs. Thinks about it. "It's a matter of access, Adamson. We don't even know if you can get inside without raising suspicions, or how often priests or nuns go up into the tower to check things out."

"There's probably a quick way to find out. We go ask for a tour. I hear nuns and men of the cloth are very trusting."

Fardün looks back at the church, then turns around and around, surveying the surrounding area. "It might actually help if you were closer," he allows. "In case things go wrong, you won't be too far

277

away to run in close and give me support. Maybe keep a rental car close to the bell tower, so you can hop in and come pick me up?"

"Exactly what I was thinking."

He nods approvingly. "We'll call that exfiltration plan A, then. Assuming we can even get proper access to the tower. Let's look at some other options."

"We need to hurry. It's getting late, and soon he'll have his own advance team down here to look it all over."

21

There are no guards and no security cameras all around the church and its bell tower. That's because there's not much to steal from St. Joseph's Church. There are, however, many iron gates topped with pointy iron prongs. I climb over these with ease, and pass through the small chapel undergoing restoration, and pass under cover of darkness into the rear courtyard. I'm dressed in a black shirt and jeans, with a balaclava over my head and face, all of which were purchased just hours ago. I've got the Nagant tucked in my waistline. The SIG I gave to Fardün; he'll need it more than I will. His rifle is still disassembled in the case I carry on my back.

It's cold out. Temperature dropped fast when the sun set.

The lockpick gun makes short work of the door at the rear of the church, and I step inside easily, my revolver now pulled out, ready to take a nun hostage and tie her up should she see me. But the thirty-minute tour we got earlier from a Chinese priest informed us that the bell tower is a brand-new addition and has only been rung a handful of times in recent weeks to let the town know of the new building. They don't ring it or go near it after eight o'clock.

Climbing the cobblestone stairs feels like I'm back inside one of Scott's *D&D* adventures, raiding a castle to look for a dragon's gold kept high in the keep. Jesus, Scott, how the fuck did I end up here?

Come back to me.

I'm trying, Sophia.

At the top of the tower I come to a trapdoor, slowly raise it and peek around. All clear. I come up through the hole, and round the large, 1,200-pound bronze bell that hangs there in the darkness, dormant. I move around it slowly, my Nagant up and at the ready, in case Fardün's prediction is right and one of Karambit's own people is up here. But it appears I'm alone.

I open the case at once and assemble the rifle. After I pop on the scope, I place the empty case on top of the trapdoor, so if anybody comes up I'll hear them fighting the weight of the case and then hear it slide off. There's a tall wooden table, thankfully, which means I won't need to unfold the cardboard box I brought with me to support the rifle. I set the rifle up on its bipod on top of the table, back away from the window, so that the barrel doesn't stick outside, and I scan the courtyard two hundred meters away.

"Ares is with the angels," I say.

From the one earphone in my right ear, I hear Fardün say, "Copy. Moving to Position A." Position A is near the large stone bench beside the statue of Father Lodovico Buglio, the man who established this church in the 1600s. We delineated five different position points around the main square, and assigned the church and the three restoration sites around it with numbers, so that I know where he's at if he starts running for cover.

We're still almost two hours away from the meeting, but the Unit should start setting up soon. I look through the scope's red and green mil-dots, scanning the passersby. There are only a few people stopping to take pictures and selfies, but most people are passing it by. The church isn't so majestic at night, I guess, even with all the streetlamps lighting it up.

I find Fardün, standing right where he should be. "Anything?" I ask. Through the scope, I see his right hand hanging by his side, and it does a little wiggle. That means negative.

I take my eye away from the rifle scope and use my spotter's scope to scan all neighboring rooftops, using both night-vision and infrared settings to check the spots Fardün and I talked about earlier in the day.

Been a while since I've operated like this. But old training and experience begin to resurface. Rifle feels both strange and familiar in my hands.

I delicately maneuver the scope over Fardün's head, less than two hundred meters away. Then I scan Wangfujing Street, which is busier than I'd like it to be this time of night. A lot of flashing

279

headlights casting moving shadows, made all the more complicated by a net of fog that clings to the ground. No, not fog. A bus is nearby, pumping warm exhaust out into the cold air, rolling right off the street. Cars parked along the curb also present a possible hiding spot for Larry, Curly and Moe.

Now I rake the reticle over one of the Chinese flags flapping in the breeze. Flags are good for estimating wind, especially in urban environments where wind is the most chaotic. I'd say wind is one-quarter value right now, east to west.

In my ear, I heard Fardün cough. That's my cue to look back at him. Light foot traffic moving all around him. He's doing something with his left hand. I focus my scope on that. He's tapping his thumb and forefinger, asking me if I've got anything yet.

"Negative," I say. "No sign of targets."

My scope grazes over people on the street. The Unit is probably made up of Russians, which means probably Caucasians, but that's not a guarantee. Like I mentioned to Fardün, the Unit could have help from the Chinese at this point. So I watch everybody carefully, even little old Chinese ladies in wheelchairs. Anything could be an act, anybody could be a spotter or backup. You just have to watch body language, see where their gaze goes to naturally.

Another cough from Fardün. I look back at him, and he's scratching his chin. The finger is pointed up, which means something directly ahead of him. I slowly pan the rifle up, gaze intently through the scope. There he is. Blonde-haired and blue-eyed and smirking. Hands in his pockets, Karambit approaches from about twenty yards beyond Fardün. I can't tell where he came from, whether from a vehicle that drove by or simply came walking up.

But I can't watch him for long. Earlier in the day, Fardün gave me a good piece of advice. "The angle at which Karambit approaches will probably give you an idea of which direction his sniper is planted," he said. Makes perfect sense. Karambit would want cover the instant he walked into an area like this.

While I scan the buildings with the spotter's scope, I listen to the two men greet each other.

"Well, hello again," says Karambit.

"Mr. Matveyev," says Fardün.

There's a long pause. Then Karambit says, "You know better than to use that name in public."

I look through the rifle scope, and see both men standing right next to each other. Fardün's back is to me, but he has wisely stepped to one side and is leaning slightly to his left, allowing me a clear shot to Karambit if I need it. I see Karambit's face is taciturn, his humor now drained. "My apologies, comrade," Fardün says.

I keep the rifle trained on them while I scan the rooftops again. I'm just grazing over the water tower when I spot the first one. Infrared setting shows him to me. He's stationed exactly as Fardün said he would be, up high on the water tower, facing Karambit. I switch to night-vision setting. I can see his hazy outline, but his rifle comes through crystal clear. I switch to true-color, and he vanishes in the darkness. I move the rifle away from Fardün and Karambit and train it on the water tower. Switch the scope to night-vision, and focus on my breathing.

"Was it difficult?" Karambit is asking.

"Not too bad," Fardün answers. "The hardest part was finding which room he was in."

"He had everything on him? Even the *Kop'ye?*"

"No. I searched him afterward, and found a key for a locker at the airport. I checked the locker and found the device there."

"Let's see it."

Fardün chuckles. "Not so fast. First let's discuss price."

"Price?"

"For the retrieval of the *Kop'ye.*"

"You've already been promised—"

"That was for neutralizing the target. I was thinking of a bonus."

That's it, Fardün. Keep him talking.

My reticle is aimed on the hazy black-green outline of the sniper. But as I told Fardün earlier, this might be troublesome. I never trained much beyond eight hundred meters. The water tower is about nine hundred meters away. I've got a lot of mat to deal with. I check the wind again. Still about a quarter value, east to west.

When a round is fired from that kind of distance, everything becomes a factor. To compensate for this, the round must be fired at an arc calibrated for temperature, distance of the shot, how far the round is going to fall, wind, humidity, and even the curvature and rotation of the earth. I'll have to fire a little high since I'm facing west—bullets fired to the west always travel somewhat low.

I don't have to get a perfect head shot. Almost anything will do, since the round is powerful enough to finish anyone.

"Why are you haggling over this now?" Karambit is asking.

"Because it's important to *you*," Fardün answers. "And because I'm thinking of retiring soon. I think the *Kop'ye* is worth a little extra bonus, don't you?"

Karambit sighs. "My superiors don't like sudden changes to plans. Neither do I."

"I'm sure you can afford it."

"What were you thinking?"

"Double," Fardün says.

See these hands. See them. Steady as stone. I exhale slowly. Squeeze the trigger. The rifle makes a muffled *thunk!* that is lost amid the swishing cars and pedestrians gabbing into their phones on the street. Less than a second later, I watch through my scope as the body of the sniper twitches once and violently. His rifle falls. He doesn't move again.

"Sniper neutralized. We need to move fast before they figure out they're down a man."

"*Double?*" Karambit asks, even as I sweep my rifle scope back over to him. "You want me to pay you double? You want me to transfer three million dollars to your account right here and now?"

"I think it's only fair," Fardün says casually. "It was a very risky job, and I performed the cleanup perfectly. You can see the body yourself and where I stored it. If you have people in Ulaanbaatar, you can call them right now."

"The package is not with you?"

"You think I would drag a dead body all this way? Are you fucking insane?"

"What about the *Kop'ye?*"

Fardün sighs and scratches the back of his head. His bird finger is a sign he's spotted one of the others. Then he juts his thumb out, indicated somewhere to the south of him. I pan slowly that way, past a father walking hand-in-hand with his two daughters, beyond two teenage girls taking selfies in front of a lit fountain...and then I see him. A short, stocky Caucasian man who sticks out like a sore thumb, dressed in a business suit, talking on a phone and walking in circles. It's Curly. I won't take him out just yet, not until I've found the others.

"Got eyes on Curly," I say, panning back over to Fardün. "See Larry or Moe?"

"The *Kop'ye* I brought with me," Fardün explains, and shrugs his left shoulder. That's a no. "It's in three separate pieces, so I was easily able to get it across the border." There is a long pause, and Fardün finally adds, "That is the reason I think I'm in the position to ask for the bonus."

"Double is not just a bonus. It's fucking *double*."

"Your people must've spent a lot on the weapon," he says. And there it is. Our two-word code phrase: *the weapon*. Any time Fardün says it, it means he's spotted someone else. "I'm sure you can spare a bit more to get it back."

I pan my scope back over to him. This time he doesn't scratch his head—that would be too obvious a second time. Instead, he wiggles his left hand, makes a fist, and sticks out only his left pinky. That means east of him. So I pan that way. Karambit and Fardün continue haggling, talking about what's fair. It takes me thirty seconds to see the guy he's talking about. Caucasian guy. Moe. Stocky, bald, dressed in jeans and a brown leather jacket, hands jammed into his pockets. I see him say something into his wrist. He looks around worriedly. Is he contacting his sniper? If so, he's not getting an answer, and that may be a problem soon.

"Got him," I report to Fardün, who is drawing out the negotiations. "But he's talking to someone. Looks kind of worried. I think he knows something's wrong with their sniper." I take my eyes away from the rifle scope, look through the spotter's scope, survey the area quickly for the third man. Fardün said there's always three hovering around Karambit. Got Curly and Moe, so where's Larry? Over by the church? No, not there. How about in one of the cars parked along the street? Impossible to tell from here, but it wouldn't be a bad spot for a getaway man to sit and wait.

"I want to see it first," Karambit says. "Where is the *Kop'ye*?"

"No, no, no," Fardün laughs. "That's not how this works, and you know it."

"How do I know you still have it?"

"I sent you the picture. And how could I have lost it? And why would I lie to you, when you know where my family lives?"

Family? Fardün never mentioned a family. Never mind. Focus.

"I want to see it," Karambit says. "I want to—" He stops talking. I look back through the scope, and zero in on both men. I see Fardün taking a step back, looking uncertain. Then, Karambit looks up and around, towards the surrounding buildings. He finally looks at Fardün and says, "What have you done?"

"What do you mean?"

I know it's happening now. I quickly pan over to Curly, then over to Moe. I see them both on the move, quietly stepping away from their stations. Time to act. I zero in on Curly, give him a bit of a lead since he's now jogging. Take a breath. Let it out slowly. Squeeze the trigger. Another *thunk!* and Curly's head snaps back. The round ripped through his throat. I don't even wait to hear the screams, which I know are coming. I pan immediately over to Moe. Can't find him. There he is...no, wait, lost him behind the statue of...there!

Squeeze the trigger.

The bullet drops more than I thought. Tears through his right shoulder and sends him spinning to the ground. Not dead.

Now there are people screaming.

I hear Karambit say, "What the fuck have you—" He's cut off when I hear the gunshots. My scope is just landing on the two men when I see it. Fardün must've panicked, pulled his pistol, and went for cover. Karambit pulled his own pistol and fired, I take it, just as Fardün landed behind the statue of Father Buglio. They both fired at each other. Looks like they missed. I try to get a clear shot of Karambit but he's running for cover. Fardün keeps firing at him, forcing him to duck behind a car parked at the curb.

I abandon my rifle right where it's at, pull out my Nagant, and run for the trapdoor. I can hear the *pop! pop! pop!* of gunfire as I race down the stairs. Hear the screams of men and women. Tires screeching.

By the time I get to ground level and bolt out the door, the gunfire has stopped. That's either very good or very bad. "Fardün! Talk to me! Say location!" He doesn't respond.

I haul ass, climbing over the fence and pulling the balaclava off my head so as not to alert anybody. I never timed myself on how fast I can run two hundred meters, but tonight I clear it so fast I don't even notice the cold air burning my lungs. Nor do I pay attention to the crowd of people fleeing the courtyard of St. Joseph's. I feel a twinge in my right knee. Pain. Getting worse. Don't know where it came from. That's age. Random pains starting for absolutely no reason.

At the courtyard, I leap over a row of hedges and I take cover behind a stone plinth with some bronze scroll on it. My knee is now singing with pain. I look around for Karambit or Fardün. I see a blood trail where Moe fell to the ground and then crawled away. I move with my gun up. Almost no one is around to see me.

I hear sirens approaching.

When I finally round the statue of Father Buglio, Fardün is lying on the ground, clutching his bleeding leg beside a car with shattered windows where he took cover. I see two people standing over Curly's body. One of them is taking a pulse, the other one is taking a picture with his cell phone. Next to Fardün is one dead man. A Chinese man, dressed in business casual. As we feared, the Unit had help from locals.

"That way," Fardün points. "I think I nicked him. Fucking Larry got out of a Lexus across the street and came to help Karambit! They went that way!"

"Do you need—"

"Oh, fuck you, Adamson! Get him before he tells anyone what—"

I don't hear the rest. I'm rounding the vehicle and going where he's pointing. I'm standing in the street, which has become choked with cars that veered off the road, I imagine, to escape the chaos of pedestrians racing away from St. Joseph's and into the streets. With nowhere else to go, the traffic behind them came to a grinding halt. I jump on the hood of someone's BMW. The driver has abandoned it. I look over the crowd, gauging the baseline of people running with generally no purpose…and then I see two men running with *great* purpose. They're running towards a black Lexus.

I hop off the hood of the BMW, wince at the shards-of-glass pain in my knee, and move in a fast crouch, weaving my way between vehicles parked with their engines still going and white plumes of exhaust wafting in front of me like lost ghosts.

I ignore the pain in my knee. I can see Karambit. I can see the son of a bitch. He's hobbling, shot somewhere on his body, and Larry is helping him to the Lexus. Karambit flings himself into the back seat, and when Larry turns to look at me, we lock eyes. I freeze. He freezes. A second later, we both throw down. My hand comes up first.

See these hands.

I fire. The bullet rips through his throat and he fires wild. The second bullet thumps his chest. As he drops, I dash for the Lexus, but Karambit must've climbed into the front seat, because when I'm just five strides away, the car peels off. I fire, aiming at its tires, but I seem to have missed and then the Lexus rounds a corner and is gone.

I leap over Larry, who's spread eagle on the pavement, gargling up blood and staring up at the night sky like it's done something terribly unfair to him. Running around the corner, I come across a silver four-door Nissan that Karambit cut off, and came to a screeching halt. I open the driver's side door and grab the driver, a middle-aged Chinese man with wild gray hair like Einstein. I point the gun at him. He gets the idea and backs away.

Sirens and flashing lights are behind me.

My knee is screaming at me now. I climb into the Nissan and floor it.

Do. Not. Let. Them. Win.

*

Follow the flow. Like a river flowing down the mountainside, there is a rhythm. One branch of the river smashes off of that rock, flows around it, creating another branch. Leaves and other forest debris drop into the river, and then obey the river's logic. They go where the river says to go. They flow as the river says to flow. The rivers carry sediment down, down, down the mountainside, picking up speed as they go, but then they slow down as they approach a lake or the sea. When that water slows down, the sediment is deposited, forming deltas. There is a logic. If you're paying attention, you can predict where all the parts will flow next.

When the Toyota Camry in front of me puts on his brakes, I splash left, interrupting the flow in the other lanes. I get ahead of the Camry, then dart in front of it. I follow the flow, even as the flow is being disrupted by the Lexus a hundred feet ahead. I see its taillights weaving in and out of traffic, those blood-red lights slashing left and right, leading me on.

Check the rearview mirror. Red and blue lights approaching fast. Sirens blaring.

Follow the flow. That's what they teach in vehicle dynamics. Following a person in a car is different than following a person on foot, and evading police in a vehicle is ten times harder than doing it on foot. Eventually, the police win. The police always win. Unless you keep the chase short, so they don't involve multiple units. Beijing Police are top notch, too. I know that much.

The first bullet hits the hood of my stolen Nissan. I swerve around to the right side, the passenger side, to keep Karambit from getting a clear shot. There's a stoplight up ahead, which he blows right through. A rusty old van barely misses him, comes to a screaming halt right in front of me at the intersection. I can't go left and I can't go right. I aim for the rear of the van, and floor it. I smash into it. The force of the hit sends the van spinning around its heaviest part—its engine in the front. My speed is barely cut by ten miles an hour, and I keep going more or less straight.

Some people get hurt in this game we play. Sophia's words, reaching back from ages ago, when I first revealed to her what I did. And, because she's always with me, *Come back to me, Nate.*

The Lexus is dead ahead, maybe sixty yards, only one car between us and it's moving out of the way, the driver sensing something is wrong. Up ahead, another intersection, cars coming off an overpass and flowing onto Xingdong'an Plaza. Fardün and I scouted through here earlier, but only briefly—

Follow the flow. Watch what it does.

Karambit glides through it, just before the flood of traffic hits our street, disrupting only one car. Then other cars cut around it. The cascade spreads. I honk my horn several times, trying to stall others around me. A couple of cars heed this, and come to a halt before I ever reach them. I swerve around a Corolla, skip off the side of an eighteen-wheeler's rear wheel, and narrowly avoid slamming into a Ford Focus.

The Lexus hit a car up ahead. Rear-ended them. Now he's slowed down, trying to get around. Karambit turns hard onto a sidewalk, and cuts through the huge courtyard of Xingdong'an Plaza.

Late-night shoppers dressed in their best mall clothes dodge out of the way when they see us coming. I honk the horn constantly, waking a few phone-gazers out of their reverie and applying my brakes liberally. Karambit does not care so much. He's plowing straight ahead, and God help anyone in his path. To my left, driving *around* the perimeter of the plaza, are the Beijing Police. Three patrol cars are keeping to the outskirts so as not to add to the chaos, but their plan is to head us off at the pass. They won't get there in time.

When the Lexus emerges onto Kun Street, I'm right behind it, narrowly missing its tail end. That's what I'm aiming for. I mean to fishtail it into a spinning dead halt. But Karambit knows this. He knows exactly what I'm trying to do. And he's not letting me have it. He turns hard into oncoming traffic, forcing me to slam on the brakes and swerve away from him. I ride on the right side of the road and follow parallel to him until he cuts through another intersection, crashes through a bus bench, and crosses back into the right side.

Knee is killing me...

Follow the flow. Watch how it moves. See the truck almost hit him, put on its brakes, and drive side-by-side with him.

I pull to the right side of the truck, keeping it between me and the Lexus. My target can't see what I'm up to from here. I'm not sure what I'm up to, either. I'm keeping clear of his shots for now, looking for my opportunity. Up ahead is yet another intersection. The light is green, but there's traffic in the middle lane, where the truck is. When it slows down, I speed up, emerging back into the Lexus's sights. I go up onto the curb and honk my horn. There's only two people on the sidewalk, thankfully, and they get out of the way.

Follow the flow. Watch how it moves.

You don't have it, Ares. You don't have what it takes.

Up ahead, there's another highway offramp dumping more traffic onto the street. A street with no streetlights. I look to my left. The Lexus is in the far-left lane, now slowing down. I get ahead of him. At the offramp, I shut my headlights off and I slow down and merge into the traffic. I see the Lexus coming up from behind me, still in the far-left lane. I speed up, get close to a work truck in front of me.

Then, I swerve suddenly in front of the Lexus.

Karambit knows it's me, but by the time he starts slowing down, it's too late. I throw the Nissan in reverse, making sure to keep my head straight as I watch my mirrors. I let off the gas while cranking the wheel as hard left as I can. The Nissan spins and I hang on for the ride, until my front is facing the car behind me. Until I'm facing the Lexus. Then I flip on my headlights, blinding him just as I figure he's about to try and take the shot. His front end runs into mine. I hear a shot fire, but it apparently goes wild.

I fire twice into the windshield.

He keeps coming. He has me just off a little, starts plowing into my Nissan's right front tire, causing me to swerve back around. As I become parallel with him, I stick the Nagant out the window and fire three times into the Lexus's left front tire.

The Lexus turns away from me, and I slow down even more, firing into the left rear tire. He's got double flats, and though he floors it to get ahead of me, he can't get far. He can sense it. The Lexus's steering isn't answering like it should. He makes it two more blocks, struggling the whole way, then drives up onto a curb, smacking a man with his front end and knocking the fella down. But he's still trying. He's almost made it.

That's when I reach into my waistline, and pull out the other weapon I brought with me. I don't know if it works, but Tabakov said it did. Said it had five or six shots' worth of propellant. I press the gas pedal to the floor, come up alongside the Lexus. I see Karambit through the passenger window. He sees me. He starts to fire. But I have the *Kop'ye* in my hand, all three pieces assembled. I'm not even sure it will work, but I brought it with me because I knew I had limited ammo. I aim it like a pistol at his passenger-side door. I pull the trigger.

There is zero recoil. It's like a toy pistol. Nothing happens.

Then…

The air all around the Lexus warps. The passenger door caves in like an invisible giant has kicked it in. All windows shatter as the Lexus flips over, shoved away from me like a Kansas tornado is lifting it off the ground. It flips twice in the air, smashes into the ground, rolling onto its side and skidding along before finally landing upright.

When it finally comes to a halt, the Lexus scrapes the side of a jewelry store.

I come to a stop beside it, climb out of the Nissan and jump onto the Lexus's hood, my right knee hating me for it. I leap onto its roof. Karambit is just now scrambling out the passenger-side door, staggering. He looks left and right, but doesn't think to look up as I drop down on top of him, smacking him hard in the head with the butt of the *Kop'ye.* The revolver is empty, so it's only use now is as a melee weapon.

He falls forward, but rolls, recovers, and springs back up. He's about to fire on me when I wrap my right arm around his weapon hand. His pistol is underneath my armpit, the barrel spitting out bullets behind me while people screaming and run. He fires and fires, trying to create havoc, but as I smash him in the face with the *Kop'ye* repeatedly, he realizes his best option.

My knee…my knee is singing…

My enemy lets go of his pistol so his hands can free themselves from my armpit. Then he reaches behind him. I know what he's going for even before the moonlight and city lights catch it.

The knife lives.

I deflect the first attack, accept a slash across my right sleeve, then jab him in the face with the *Kop'ye*'s barrel. I keep pressing forward, deflecting, parrying, sidestepping, shuffling, evading. My body's not as tired as it was when last we met. He's weak, bleeding from a pair of gunshot wounds—one of them mine, I'm guessing, and one of them Fardün's.

I keep coming. The knife lives and I deflect and the people around us are screaming and the knife lives. My knee still hurts. Feels like glass shards getting deeper. I keep coming at him, swinging with my gun. When my barrel catches him in the jaw, I see I've got him. He's rocked. Like a boxer that's taken the magic punch from his opponent, he staggers backward, legs like water.

But still the knife lives. He's trained with it, clearly. Trained with it as much as I've trained not to give up until tomorrow. Because the karambit never leaves his hand, and it keeps moving intelligently and in deadly arcs. Even as he struggles to stand, the knife lives.

Sirens approaching.

My enemy is determined, but he can't keep up the pace. He lunges forward one last time. I wrap the wrist with my right arm. Jerk him to one side. Smash his jaw again with the revolver. I hear the sharp *crack!* and his whole body crumples.

The sirens are almost here.

It's nearly impossible to lift an unconscious man. There's only one way I know to do it. While a few people around me watch in shock, I roll my enemy's body over and pry his karambit knife from his hand, then spread his arms and legs out. Then I back up to get a running start, dash at the unconscious body, dive on top of it, tucking my head down and rolling over him, catching one of the legs quickly as I go, hugging it close, then use my momentum to finish the roll and bring myself, holding my enemy in a fireman's carry.

I stagger. My right knee absolutely killing me. Haven't done the rolling fireman's carry in a while, my balance is off. I hold tight to him and run down the dark street ahead of us. At best I can only run one-quarter my normal speed like this. The cops are close, fifty yards behind.

I turn and aim the *Kop'ye* at my stolen Nissan and fire. Once again, there is zero kickback, but the Nissan's front end collapses like a beer can and flips backward into the road, smashing against other cars abandoned by people running from their cars when the shooting started. The barricade of smashed cars forces the cops to come to a halt.

I cut through an alley, hoping there's a way out. If there's not—

There are several ways I can go, it turns out. I pick the way that seems to lead directly away from the sirens. I limp in that direction. hear tactical-sounding shouts, calls for positioning. Men with badges are on their way, spreading out, covering ground. I emerge onto another dark street. Not a lot of foot traffic. There's a highway up ahead, and on the other side there is a park. Beyond that, I see a monorail station.

Karambit mutters something incoherent.

I move to the side of the highway, wait for it to be clear both directions, and hustle across. Now I hear a helicopter. It doesn't sound very close, but that doesn't mean its searchlight can't sweep over me at any second. I make it through the park, which only has a single lone jogger as far as I can see. A jogger that, thankfully, is running ahead of us and never looks back to see the one foreigner carrying the other one.

Before I get to the monorail station, I drop Karambit like the burden he is and watch his eyes flutter open. His eyes look around in search of meaning.

In all the excitement, the earphone and mic fell away from my ear. It's hanging from the collar of my shirt. I put it back in my ear, and say, "Fardün? You copy? Talk to me."

Sounds like static. Then I realize it's heavy panting. "Adamson…"

"Where are you, Fardün?"

"Where the fuck are *you*?"

I look at the station sign. Thankfully, it's in three languages. "We're at Sun Hung Kai Station."

" 'We?' You mean you got him?"

"Yeah. What about you? Did you get away?"

"What do you think, I answer my phone in prison?"

I would laugh if I wasn't so exhausted. "Think you can make it to our rental car at exfiltration point A and come pick us up?"

"I'm bleeding from my leg here, Adamson."

"Bad?"

"I'll live."

"So can you pick us up?"

"Oh, fuck you, Adamson!"

*

When Fardün arrives at the station, he looks drained. He pulls the car to a halt in front of me and stares at me like he'd like to see me dead. Probably would. I've already pulled zip-ties from one of my pockets and bound Matveyev hand and foot. I toss him in the trunk and we get underway. "Where are we going now?" Fardün asks desperately, as I take the blood-soaked driver's seat. I tell him where we're going and he doesn't like it. I don't really like it, either, but it's got to be done. If we went to any hospital in the city, he would be found by Moe, who dragged himself away from St. Joseph's Church and doubtlessly contacted the rest of the Unit. Not only that, but the Unit clearly has help from Chinese forces, probably agents of the MSS, Ministry of State Security.

There's nowhere else to go.

When I pull the car to a stop and look across at the well-lit building, Fardün says, "I don't know about this."

"They've got medics inside," I tell him, massaging my knee. It feels a little swollen.

"There's an unconscious Russian operative in our back seat. You really think they'll just welcome us with open arms?"

"It'll work."

"You've been disavowed! You can't go in there!"

"All I've gotta do is mention a name. Names are like magic. They open doors."

"What the fuck are you talking about? Magic doors?"

I ignore the question. I listen for sirens. I open the door.

"They'll know who I am," Fardün says, grabbing my arm. "They won't like you bringing me in there."

"Then we won't tell them who you are."

"But they can—"

"Wait here."

I get out and cross the street. I look both ways, listening for sirens. I walk towards the tall steel poles topped with American flags snapping in the breeze. There are two guards out front, and two on the other side of the gate. When they see me coming, one of them starts forward. Before he can say anything, I say, "I'm an American citizen."

"Okay, sir," the soldier says. "Do you have papers?"

293

"No, I don't."

"Your name? Your business?"

Can't give him my name. I'm disavowed and technically a fugitive. But my presence does have to reach the attention of certain ears. "I can't tell you that, soldier. But I can tell you this: Sigma, alpha, sigma, bravo, bravo, delta, bravo, sigma."

He straightens a fraction. He's been taught to be ready for this. Probably never had to do it in his life, but as an embassy guard he'll know certain things other guards don't, key phrases to listen to, including sigma-entry codes.

His hand starts to raise to his radio.

I tell him, "Codename Ares. Tell the embassy consulate that name. Ares. And tell them to send it to Tara Yarwick at Joint Special Operations Command. Tell Yarwick our kitty-cat date is still on if she's good for it. *Ares. Tara Yarwick at JSOC. Kitty-cat date.* And tell them to hurry, I've got two men who need medical attention. One of them is a friend, and one of them is an enemy combatant of the United States with actionable intel that is vital to national security. You tell them that, soldier."

22

Tap-tap-tap. The man sitting across from me has been doing this rhythmic tapping of his Rolex for a while now. He's from the embassy's Office of Military Cooperation, and he looks at me like I'm some kind of specimen. The two guards posted at the door look at me like I'm something that might need killing. The OMC guy is dressed in business casual, the yellow legal pad on the table in front of him hasn't been touched, mainly because I haven't been answering his questions. The audio recorder has been going for a while now, recording only silence. And the tapping. *Tap-tap-tap.*

Tap-tap-tap. He makes a *tsk* noise, looking me over.

"You know," he says with the tone of a man trying a new tact, "this might go faster if you just told us a few things."

"I'm sorry, but I can't tell you anything," I tell him.

"Not even your name?"

"Not even that."

"We could easily run your fingerprints to determine—"

"No, you can't."

"I can't?"

"No."

"And why not?"

"Because you've been contacted by JSOC and I'm guessing they told you not to do that," I say. "That's why you haven't taken my fingerprints yet. You have your orders, sir, and I have mine."

Because I've broken disavowal protocols and the only thing that might fix this is men like this OMC guy listening to *his* superiors. He doesn't know who I am, but he's been told this could be a potential shitstorm and, for the love of God, *do not* take this man's fingerprints, and *do not* run his face through facial-recognition. Because OMC cannot know I'm Nathan Adamson. No one at the embassy can. If they do, and it got out that the embassy knew who I was and that they harbored me, it's as good as a confession to the world that Nathan Adamson was, in fact, conducting espionage in Russia on behalf of the United States government.

I have to remain quiet for Mr. OMC's own good. I have to let him have plausible deniability.

But he has to do his job. He has to question me, make sure I'm not some terrorist pulling a fast one. He might even have encountered something like this before, a CIA agent on the run. Or maybe he's heard about it from one of the senior embassy guys. But he's part of the checks and balances, too, like internal affairs for embassies. He needs to make sure that any military or intelligence operation passing through his embassy cannot bring him or the consulate any blowback.

It's a tense game when you can't even trust your own countrymen with your secrets, but compartmentalization exists for a reason.

"So, you're not going to give me anything," he says. "No reason for visiting Beijing? Not where you've been or what you've been doing? Not gonna tell me why two men were in your car with bullet holes in them?"

I drum my fingers on the table.

"You know, we got word of a shootout around St. Joseph's Church. By the sound of it, three or four guys were killed, a couple of armed Chinese guys and some white dudes with Russian IDs. Know anything about that?"

I drum my fingers on the table.

"You said the blonde-haired guy is an enemy combatant of the U.S., and has information that could be vital to national security. Who is he?"

I drum my fingers on the table.

"What is this vital information that he has?"

I drum my fingers on the table.

"What's the 'kitty-cat date'?"

I scratch my nose. And I drum my fingers on the table.

The OMC guy sighs in frustration, and he's just about to ask me something else when there's a knock at the door. He gets up and goes over to answer it. The two guards keep staring at me. Someone at the door whispers something into the OMC guy's ear. He comes back over and stands next to me. "There's a room prepared. You'll stay there until your pal gets here."

"Pal?"

"You asked for Tara Yarwick. Whoever she is, she's on her way. I've been ordered to tell you that, and to give you a message."

"What's the message?"

" 'Don't say another fucking word until I get there.' Her exact words, apparently."

I snort out a laugh, and nod.

As the guards guide me out the door, the OMC guy calls after me.

"Oh, um, Mr. Ares? You haven't brought my embassy a storm of shit, have you?"

I shrug, but keep my mouth shut, as per Yarwick's last orders.

*

The next day, there's a knock on my door, and two soldiers step inside, along with a tall man in an Army colonel's uniform. He tells me to say nothing and conducts me to a parking garage. I know what this is. They drive me off site, away from the embassy, ten blocks away, then escort me into a small hotel in a traditional part of Beijing, complete with pagoda rooftops and lots of ponds. The skyscrapers of the business center are towering in the distance like looming gods watching over everything.

The colonel leads me into the hotel, the armed guards remain in the car. The main entrance has two huge wooden doors, but I'm guided to a side entrance, which takes me across an indoor pond that you can only cross by either walking on the small stone steps or swimming. The CIA must have some kind of arrangement with the people who own this place. Other places might be inconspicuous, but this is classic hiding in plain sight. Whole operations might run out of here.

I'm led to a room on the second floor, which has a balcony overlooking the indoor pond on the first floor. The colonel opens the door, and waves me inside. Yarwick is standing there at a window, overlooking the palatial gardens that surround the hotel. She turns around once the door closes, and looks at me, arms folded.

"Tara," I say.

"Nate." She smirks, but it doesn't look entirely friendly. "Thought you were dead."

I cock my head to one side. "Dead?"

"We have our own people in the Kremlin. We heard a rumor that the Unit was excited about having the final proof to show the world the U.S.'s hypocrisy. We took this to mean they had you. Which meant you were probably dead, because I know you wouldn't let yourself be taken alive."

I nod. "They *did* think they had something. They thought they had me. I, uh…well, I had someone try to kill me, but I got the upper hand and, well…I convinced him to sell them that story. Karambit and his people bought it, just long enough for me to bring him in. I've also got the *Kop'ye*. Handed it over to the embassy guys." I add, "It packs one hell of a punch. Zero recoil, and an immense amount of damage. Smashes cars like soda cans."

Yarwick nods thoughtfully, then says, "The man that helped you, the one with the bullet in his leg, he's not saying anything but I'm guessing that's Innick Fardün?"

I nod.

"And you got the drop on him?"

"Yeah."

"How?"

"A little voice in my ear tipped me off."

She smiles. "So, you heard that. I was wondering if the transmission got through before the battery died."

"It was the last thing I heard. I was asleep at the time. Wasn't even sure it was real. How did you know he was coming for me?"

"HUMINT came through with a tip," she says. "They have a group monitoring the Dark Web at all times, one of their technicians has been working contacts on a job site for journeymen killers, posing as a would-be employer looking for would-be assassins. They found out Fardün had taken the job, passed it to SOG and Directorate Seven. SAD tracked the passport of one of his known aliases, saw that he was in Mongolia." Yarwick looks down at her feet. "I know why you broke protocol. You had Karambit and you thought maybe he could tell us who the mole is."

I nod. "That was the hope. As soon as Fardün told me he'd heard the Unit talking about 'Alpha Source,' I figured this was something I needed to pursue."

"Even though you are disavowed and no longer fighting for this country."

I snort. "I'm always gonna be fighting for this country, Tara. If I'm not, then what the fuck was my whole life about?"

For a while she just looks at me. Then she sighs again, and smiles. "It's good to see you, Nate."

"It's good to be seen." I smile back. "But I take it I can't actually be seen with you out in the public still, right? That's why I'm here, and not at the embassy?"

"Yeah. The president said the disavowal still stands."

"He's aware of where I'm at."

"He's aware that I'm aware. But you're not his biggest concern right now."

"Right. The war."

"Among other things. I don't know if you've seen the news this morning, but there's a problem with a Russian sub that went missing. Now, the Russians claim they suspect we blew it up, that we got too close to their task force in the Atlantic and got trigger happy."

"What's the real story?" I ask, walking over towards her.

"We don't know. The sub might not be missing at all. They might only be reporting that it's missing because they want the POTUS to be in denial mode again, constantly reeling and apologizing and looking for answers, so that he can't focus on decisive military action. Putin is trying to *make* us worried about being the ones to fire the first shot of World War Three. More of their *maskirovka*," she says. *Maskirovka* is the Russian military doctrine developed in the twentieth century, and it literally means "disguise." It is the philosophy of military deception, from camouflage to denial and deception techniques.

"So in other words," I say, "the Russians sent their sub into full stealth mode, and when it disappeared off our scopes, before we could say, 'Hey, where'd your submarine go?' they said 'Hey, where'd our submarine go?'"

"That about covers it." Yarwick sighs, and looks out over the city. "And then there's the near failure of NARROW VOID, and the fallout from that."

A beat of silence.

"What about Wainwright and the others? Have their bodies been...reclaimed?"

She shakes her head. "You know the U.S. can't acknowledge they know who any of those bodies belong to."

"What happened in Harbin?"

Yarwick lays it out. They were set up nicely at the hotel—Wainwright from SIGINT, Isaacson from DARPA, Kozner from SAD's Political Action Group, Drucker working systems, and Amrita for support with regional research. They had all their gear set up with covcom and burst-transmission hardware for communicating with CIA Deputy Director Halbach and SAD Director Peters via satellite. Back in the States, the Secretary of Defense had her phone on her at all times, waiting for any updates on NARROW VOID. Everything was set. From the moment I emerged from the submarine and joined the *Hayabusa*, the Nest was tracking me via the GPS in my gear. Not even twenty-four hours later, it all went to shit.

SIGINT noticed some unusual spikes in bandwidth, interference with encrypted channels. Things seemed okay at first. Then Yarwick heard that I was hearing strange things in my cochlear implant, and told Wainwright and Drucker to run a systems check. Again, everything seemed fine.

They didn't know it, but at the same time I was being surrounded outside the Tidov residence, their signals were being tracked from within China. A team of a dozen or so operatives raided the hotel where the Nest was staying. The two guards stationed downstairs made enough noise that the guards outside the Nest's room heard it, and gave Yarwick and her team enough time for half of them to get out. All guards were killed, one of them while leading Yarwick and the others down a stairwell.

"Isaacson was killed trying to take cover," she says. "Three shots to the body from a rifle, dead instantly. Amrita took two to the gut, died in transit to a hospital in a vehicle one of our guards had parked out back for a quick escape. The guard also bled out from a chest wound."

"Jesus," I say, shaking my head. "I'm sorry, Tara. That must've been..."

"Skin of our teeth, Nate. Just like you."

"I'm sorry. They were all good people. How's that investigation coming along?"

Here, Yarwick looks at her feet again, troubled by something, then looks up at me. "It took our data-flow analysts ten days, working in shifts around the clock to suss it all out."

"What went wrong? How'd they penetrate us like this?"

"If you can believe it, it all started three years ago. At least, that's what it's looking like. Some Chinese hacker, it seems, found some exploit in a Windows server component, then wiggled their way into a few minor networks among government contractors, and found their way into the U.S. Department of Defense, then executed an upstream attack to all military intelligence agencies linked to them. They laid a few 'cuckoo's eggs'—malware that laid dormant and hidden—and waited years to let them hatch into our systems."

"They couldn't have known about Operation NARROW VOID that long ago, unless they can tell the future."

"No," she says, "they just laid the cuckoo's eggs in our systems and waited for a time when they absolutely needed to attack our systems and control a particular comms satellite or network. They most likely activated the malware when our mole told them NARROW VOID was going down, and that he was pretty sure when and where it was happening, just not exactly who the agent in question was." She shrugs. "Probably an MSS operation. Our systems people found some of the code, and matched it with other code we've seen from their cyberattack divisions. Code like that is like a fingerprint, pretty much one of a kind."

"If it's MSS, that means they helped the Russians."

"Right. Just seems to confirm the Eastern Alignment was already a thing before we really knew about it."

I nod. "They let us carry on with the operation, and wanted to catch me in Russia, and you and the rest of the Nest in China, to show us off to the world as proof the U.S. is a bunch of assholes."

She nods. "Adding more fuel to Putin's whataboutism propaganda campaign."

"What's the battlefield look like? Any plans for boots on the ground somewhere?"

"Maybe. Putin is bringing up old wounds, like the accidental killing of a hundred Russians back in late 2017. If you remember, more than two hundred Russians that Putin sent to fight on behalf of Bashar al-Assad tried to take an oil refinery held by U.S.-allied forces, but they were killed by our people. It was called an 'accident' because the Russians claimed it was just a rogue group, a bunch of mercs that weren't really Russian military, but now Putin's claiming we spread disinformation in order to 'lure the mercenaries in,' tempting them to attack when we knew we would slaughter them."

"So, we might be going to reinforce U.S.-held refineries in Syria?"

"Yes, but that's not all. The Iranians are using all this chaos to threaten Iraq over control of the Persian Gulf oil fields. The Russians seem intent to help out, out of the kindness of their heart," she rolls her eyes and makes a jerking-off motion that is weirdly sexy, "but really we know that they'll want their fair share of the oil when it's all said and done."

"More soldiers headed to the Persian Gulf, then?"

Yarwick nods. "And maybe Taiwan. The Chinese have their blockade of Taiwan and Hong Kong in full swing. Japan has vowed to help, but there's been a snag. Apparently, the Russians have something on the Japanese president. Something lurid and embarrassing."

I nod. The Russians call that *kompromat*, their playful word for compromising material.

"It's pretty bad, sources say. That's the rumor, anyway. Russia wants Japan's neutrality in this, and now they're sweetening the deal by offering to give back the Sakhalin island."

"Russia's offering Japan both the carrot *and* the stick," I snort. "North Korea?"

"North Korea's being North Korea, boasting a lot, flexing, acting like hotshots and getting the world stage like they've always wanted."

"Sounds like everyone in the Eastern Alignment is getting what they want," I say.

"Not totally. The only weakness is Syria. They're not happy that all of this has, so far, not brought about any serious talks to have the U.S. and its allies pull troops and all American-led humanitarian groups out of their country. The focus of these last few days has involved four of the five Eastern Alignment nations, but not Syria."

I pull out a chair from the room's only desk, place it beside the window, and take a seat. "Sounds like a new war is comin' on."

"It does seem that way. A cold one or a hot one, who's to say?"

"I've been through two of them. Three, technically. I guess three's a good number to go out on."

She looks down at me. "Go out on?"

"Yeah. I mean, I think it's safe to say I'm not going to be involved in any SOG operations anymore. Probably nothing CIA-related ever again."

"I don't think it's safe to say that," she says. "I don't think it's safe to say that at all."

"Why not?"

Yarwick gives me a look. There's humor there, but also cunning. It's a look I saw a lot while poring over details about the mission. "Do you forget who we are, Mr. Adamson?" she says mockingly. "I'm Joint Special Operations Command, and I do work with your Special Operations Group, and under Title Ten of U.S. Code we don't have to tell anyone what our budget is. Shit, we barely have to report to anyone. As long as the job gets done and there's no blowback, who asks questions? The POTUS is even on a need-to-know basis on some things, like the actual name of agents."

I lean forward in my chair. "So...what are you saying?"

"There might be room for an agent that's been publicly disavowed," she says. "If the whole world thinks you're a fugitive, and some in the intelligence field believe you're dead, you might be able to do things others can't. Deep cover things. A man without a country can do lots of things, like..." She shrugs, and lets my imagination fill in the rest.

"But I'll never set foot inside Langley again."

She shook her head. "No, probably not. Not even Halbach or the director can know you're alive."

Now I'm astonished. "Hold on...you mean...you mean you didn't tell *anyone* it was me you were coming here to see?"

"No," she says. "Your message got to JSOC, but no one there knows who 'Ares' is—that was your CIA codename, and I was their only liaison. I never told your people at CIA that I received the message. They've all heard the same rumor I did, that the Unit probably found you and that you're probably dead. I came out here on my own and set up this little meeting through a JSOC rep inside the American Embassy. He doesn't know who you are, either. He may suspect, but he's not going to say anything."

I shake my head. "Then how can I ever work for CIA again?"

"By working for me," she says, and smiles sadly. "Your skill sets are worth millions in training, I'm not just going to toss you out into the cold because *we* fucked up and let a mole inside CIA."

That feels good. That feels really, really good. Just hearing someone say that they're still in your corner, still fighting for you…it means the fucking world.

"There's strong feelings that some kind of war is about to break out, Nate. Rapprochement is pretty much off the table here. And a few people inside JSOC have been tasked to do whatever it takes to make sure America wins. I've been promoted to Covert Team Operations Leader, given permission to put together a few teams. Off the books, wetworks, shit like that. The people I use can vary, and I don't have to report who they are. Kind of like the recruits you worked with in Kabul, and the rebels the U.S. has armed throughout the Middle East."

I look at her. "No names required?"

"We don't keep ledgers with the names of every single one of those rebels. You could just be another one."

This almost seems like a dream, or like I stepped inside someone else's life. "I'd be NOC," I say. Non-official cover, an operative still working for a government but with absolutely no formal ties, and little, if any, aid from my countrymen.

"Yes, you would. And it'll be more dangerous for you now, since the Russians will have a *liternoye delo* on you now," she says, meaning operational file.

"And…my old life?"

"Over. Though, I'm sure you could visit the States from time to time to visit Sophia."

A beat of silence passed between us. Neither of us knows what to fill it with.

I break it first. "Listen, about Karambit. Or Matveyev, I guess I should say. I know we can't keep him here. He's probably already told the consulate he's SVR, which isn't a crime, and so the embassy will want to know why I brought in an unconscious SVR agent with two gunshot wounds. They haven't said anything about it to me. Have they said anything to you?"

Yarwick nods. "You handled it right. You called him an enemy combatant, and that gets people's attention. When he woke up, he admitted he was SVR. Those two things raised eyebrows, especially now that I'm involved and telling the embassy it was part of a joint operation between military and CIA. And considering what's going on in the world right now, they're taking it very seriously."

"Is that enough to hold him?"

"It is for now," she says. "Especially since I've told them there's reason to suspect he collaborated with a mole inside CIA. Now everybody's getting involved and I suspect we can hold him for a while."

"But not forever."

"No, not forever. But we can make him *think* he's not ever going to see the light of day again. With enough isolation, and letting him get the feeling no one's coming for him, we might be able to get the mole's name from him."

"And if not?"

"If not, if he's smart and clams up for weeks on end, and survives the isolation…we let him go."

That is unacceptable, and it infuriates me to no end. The idea of such a man getting loose, of Tatiana's captor going free…"I want to see him."

"You know I can't let you set foot back in that embassy."

I fume for a second. "Where's Fardün?"

"Still at the embassy clinic."

"Is he under arrest?"

Yarwick shakes her head. "Believe it or not, for all his terrible deeds, Innick Fardün hasn't done anything that the United States government wants him for. So far as we know, he's never killed an

American or any of our allies. He's a son of a bitch, but he's a son of a bitch that hasn't fucked us the wrong way. We *are* holding onto him right now, though, dragging our feet with his release."

"Can I talk to him?"

"Why do you need to talk to him?"

"Because our ruse didn't work long enough for him to get paid, and because of me he's unemployed."

She shrugs. "I might be able to get him out of the embassy for a short visit. Say...take him for a stroll in his wheelchair to a café around the corner? Meet you there?"

"That'll work."

"What are you going to say to him?"

*

"Oh, fuck you, Adamson."

As soon as Fardün sees me, he's rolling his eyes. He is sitting in the middle of the café and being kept under guard by two plainclothes soldiers sitting at a window a few feet away. His leg is elevated in a cast and he looks angry enough to eat nails. One hand still has the pink ring around his wrist where I imagine he's been handcuffed to a hospital bed for two days. "This is how I'm greeted?" I ask, standing up from the table I've reserved for us in the corner. "After all I've done for you?"

"Get the fuck out of here. Nobody told me I was coming to meet you—"

"Listen—"

"You ruined my life."

"Yeah, sorry about that. How are they treating you?"

"Like a prisoner. Funny," he says, "since you told me they probably wouldn't even know who I am, or have any interest in me."

"Yeah, well, here's the thing. I've talked with my boss, she says they don't actually have any reason to detain you. You've never done anything against America or her allies, at least as far as we know." I walk over and grab the handles on the back of his wheelchair and roll him over to my table. "*But.*"

"Oh, here we go."

I take a seat across from him. "There is one little problem. You know that I'm alive."

He winces in confusion. Shrugs. "So?"

"Karambit probably told his superiors I'm dead, Moe got away but he never saw me, so right now it's beneficial that the intelligence world be unclear whether or not I'm dead. It'd also be nice if no one knew I was being aided by this embassy."

Fardün winces again, but then he brightens, and smiles sardonically. "Oh. Of course."

"Now you see the problem."

"Well, what are your bosses going to fucking do? Are they just going to keep me locked up forever in that embassy?"

"They can't, really. There would be too many questions from the consulate that runs this embassy. We're black ops, we don't have to tell anybody about our operations, but we can't just force embassies to hold prisoners without telling them who, what, and why. That's that renditioning bullshit that we all got in trouble for back in the Bush years."

"So, what do we do?"

I prop my elbows on the table and cup my hands. The waitress brings us over some waters. "My boss can detain you here for a while. Or…she could let you go immediately, under your own care. It's really up to you now. But, seeing as how we're in China and the MSS is helping out the Unit, and we know that Moe survived and has probably told his bosses what went down at St. Joseph's, you probably won't get very far." I add, "Without some help."

Fardün eyes me cautiously, the way he might if I were cardboard box someone has set in front of him. And inside of that box he can hear something hissing and rattling. "Some help," he says slowly.

"Yes," I say, knocking a knuckle on the table. "You can walk out of here today—or *roll*, I should say—and nobody will stop you. Of course, nobody will help you, either." It's a spiel I've given in Afghanistan a dozen times or more to guys whose backs are up against the wall, and who I know are primed for recruitment. "*Or*, you can come work for us. With me. Get paid that way."

Fardün looks incredulous. "Come work for you?" he chuckles.

"You said it yourself, your reputation is shot, and you didn't get the payment you wanted from the Russians. What other options do you have, now that you're likely a wanted man?"

"Fuck you."

"I'll give you twenty-four hours to think about it. It'll be steady pay, even when you're not working. All expenses paid for. I'm being brought in to help the U.S. but in a slightly different capacity, and I've given permission on limited recruitment of skilled people. You were my first pick."

"Fuck you." He sips his water slowly, eyeing me over the rim of his glass. Then he says, "What kind of jobs?"

"The kind you and I are best suited for," I say. Then I get honest with him, just the way we were taught to do when recruiting. Find what motivates them, and then appeal to their needs and wants. "When we first met, you said guys like us gain skills and then get tossed aside for one reason or another. You seemed pretty bitter about it. At least this way, your skills wouldn't be a total waste." Now I appeal to his ego. "You're clearly very good at what you do, and you would've gotten me in Ulaanbaatar if I hadn't been tipped off by my people. Whatever sources helped you find me would be invaluable to us."

"My sources," he says with a smile. "*That's* what you're hoping to get out of this. The sources that led me to you."

"Those would be very helpful in fieldwork," I admit. "You would be handy in more ways than one. You're clearly very good at what you do. But now you need allies, someone to watch your back."

"Because of you!"

"Yes, because of me. But you forget, you tried to murder me for money, so I think that makes us even."

"Even my fucking ass!" But I see it in his eyes. I see the barriers coming down. Innick Fardün is a logical man. He couldn't be a successful assassin and have a messy, illogical mind. He sees opportunities and he recognizes logistical truths. He props an elbow on an armrest, and scratches his chin distractedly.

"Like I said, you have twenty-four hours." I reach inside my jacket and pull out a slip of paper. Slide it over to him. "That's the number to call, and an e-mail. Her name is Yarwick. If you come along for this, we'll be answering to her. And only her. Think about it." I stand up to leave. "Order whatever you want, it's on me."

He says nothing as I exit the café.

23

There is no way for the United States government to arrange for me a way out of Beijing. Even if Yarwick did it on her own, it would put both her and the country at risk. Can't do that. Yarwick meets me at a hotel room she's set up for me, a slummy little place off of Qianmen Street. Here, I sit and I wait. I've convinced her not to risk herself anymore. She's agreed, but she's also been in contact with someone else. Not sure who, but she says the people she's sending have helped her out before. *Allies*. That's the word she used. I take that to mean either mercs or else a friendly nation's intelligence officers; MI6 or Mossad.

I'm waiting forty-eight hours when I finally hear the agreed-upon series of knocks at the door.

I don't peek out the peephole. I'm not that trusting. Instead, I take a magazine and wave it in front of the peephole. No bullets come flying through. "I didn't order room service," I say.

A man's voice responds, "Someone told me you might want what we're serving."

The agreed-upon passphrase.

Pistol in hand, I open the door an inch. The person standing on the other side is not who I imagined. I don't know who I expected exactly, but it certainly wasn't a fifty-year-old Jewish man with a bowl cut and a scraggly beard that makes him look homeless. He's dressed kind of schlubby, too. Like a guy who got pulled away from watching the Super Bowl and he's unhappy about having to miss the fourth quarter.

"Can I come in?" he says, looking half bored.

I let him in. As he steps inside he glances at my pistol. Doesn't seem to bother him. He looks around at my digs. He seems to both see it and not see it. He looks at me. "Okay, there's an airplane waiting. If you're ready, we can leave now."

"Where are we going?"

"We'll move from here through Dazhalan. It's another slum. Beyond there is a private airfield. It's used by local businessmen who sometimes help us out. For a stipend. From there, we'll take you first to Japan, hold you there for a day or two, then take you someplace safe. Right now, we're thinking Denmark."

"Denmark," I say. "Okay. And…who are you?"

He shakes his head. I don't get to know that. "We leave in five minutes, assuming you're ready, and assuming my driver says it's all clear outside. You'll receive instructions from Yarwick when you're safely in Denmark."

"All right, I'm ready."

"Then pack your things, Mr. Crenshaw." He reaches into a jacket pocket, and hands me a complete set of IDs. I'm Gerald Simon Crenshaw now, with an Idaho driver's license and passport to prove it. I don't know who these guys are yet, but Yarwick really came through.

*

The trip is a quick one. In under twenty-four hours I'm in Tokyo, waiting. My mystery Jew is with me the whole time. At the airport the security guards and Customs guys check his ID, and it says he's Emil Goldberg, but I'm sure that's not his real name. I have time to eat some sushi at Haneda Airport, use the restroom, and take a shower. While we wait on our plane to board, I watch two wall-mounted TVs, one showing an old *Power Rangers* episode and the other showing a tank brigade crossing into Ukraine, with a flock of Steel Octopuses gliding over them.

Then we're on a plane for Denmark. We're flying nearly eight thousand miles nonstop. My mystery Jew sits next to me, saying nothing the whole way. He puts in earphones and listens to Yo-Yo Ma, and sometimes naps. I try to relax. Massage my ribs and wonder about Fardün. And Yarwick. And Eddie the cat.

And Karambit.

And Sophia.

I go to the Drifting Place. That seems to help. Apparently, the Drifting Place is useful for all kinds of stress, not just when I'm being shot at or hunted. I shut my eyes and imagine it. It's always a little different. Sometimes it's a hill with tall grass hissing in the wind, other times it's a meadow of flowers with a swift sunrise dead ahead. Right now it's a soughing sea beneath a black sky, stars twinkling.

The moon's out and I can see across forever. I have no body here. No brain. I am nothing. Empty.

I fall asleep at some point. The Drifting Place is better than counting sheep. When I wake up, we're almost there. The pilot is telling us Denmark is experiencing some rough winds. There's a bit of turbulence. I hear one lady yelp. The mystery Jew looks like he's angry about being late for a meeting.

When we land, he conducts me swiftly into a white Nissan outside of Aalborg Airport. I've been given a smartphone, and I use it to do a little research on Denmark. I happen to stumble on the fact that Aalborg is a dual civilian/military airport, and that we happened to land on one of the military runways. Is he from PET, Denmark's national security agency? Or does he just liaise with PET?

The driver of our Nissan also looks Jewish. This is confirmed when he and my mystery Jew start speaking to one another quickly in Hebrew. They speak it in whispers, conspiratorially, each of them checking their mirrors.

We drive slowly down the busy streets of Copenhagen, then onto the cobblestone of an area called Købmagergade, a major place for shopping, according to the Wikipedia on my smartphone. Now we're pulling into Nørreport Station, and stepping into the underground railway. A twenty-minute ride takes us to Østerport Station, and from there we take a bus to the district of Hellerup. I'm not sure if we're performing an SDR or if my Jewish friends are just trying to confuse me.

We end up in a small town I don't know the name of, in the middle of nowhere, with melting snow on every side of the road. We pull around to the back of a small cottage that looks like it could come out of a child's fairy tale, with a partially thatched roof. I'm taken inside, into a house that is spartan. One couch, one bed, a window facing nothing but a flat, open field of nothingness.

My two Jewish friends have spoken maybe ten words to me on the whole journey, just directing me places.

Now the driver steps outside to go do something, and "Goldberg" says, "You want something to drink?"

I look around at the living room, then nod. "Sure."

He heads into the kitchen, comes back with bottles of water for each of us, as well as a bottled beer and a glass to pour it in. He waves towards the couch and I take the hint. I sit on the couch and he sits in a recliner across from me. "So," he says, after taking his first sip of water, "how long have you known Sophia de Marenches?"

I pause just as I start to pour the beer. It's maybe the last thing I predicted him saying. "I'm sorry, what?"

"Sophia. That's her name, right? How long have you known her?"

"How do you know about her?" I ask. "And why are you asking about Sophia? Has something happened to her?"

"Nothing's happened to her, Mr. Crenshaw."

"Then why—"

The door opens. The driver steps in and says something in Hebrew to Goldberg, who gets up quickly. "You stay here," he says to me.

I shoot to my feet. "What's going on? What's happened to Sophia?"

"Just drink your beer, everything will be okay." They both step outside and shut the door. Through the front window I can see them talking quickly about something. It looks like an argument, maybe. Then, up the driveway, I see a car pull up. Black Prius. Goldberg walks out to meet it. The Prius comes to a stop and out of the back seat steps a white man with bright blonde hair, wearing an Armani suit and carrying a briefcase. He looks young. He starts talking to Goldberg. They smile and shake hands like old friends.

Goldberg and the white guy enter the house. Goldberg says to me, "Mr. Crenshaw, it seems your friends came through much sooner than expected."

"What do you mean? What's going on?"

They white guy steps forward, offers his hand. "Mr. Crenshaw, I'm Agent Jim Davies, I'm a junior unit director with SAD. It's an honor, sir." He knows who I am, he's using the fake name for the sake of practice. I shake his hand. "Langley sends their regards. And now, if you're prepared, we can bring you home."

"Home?"

"Your disavowal still stands, but you are no longer *persona non grata* to the United States, as long as you keep a low profile and follow certain protocols when you return." I stare at him blankly until he puts it more bluntly. "You're going back to the U.S., sir."

*

"How did you pull this off?" I ask.

Yarwick's voice comes over the phone. "I didn't do it alone. A lot of pieces had to be moved around. A letter from myself and Halbach to the CIA director explained how we could probably pull you in from the cold without attaching ourselves to you, by using allies in Mossad or elsewhere."

"It must've been one hell of a letter," I say, watching Agent Davies and Goldberg discuss something at the far side of the room.

"It also helped that the story PAG's been circulating about Islamist extremists near the border of Amur Oblast at the time you were there has finally started taking root—a lot of people have dismissed your actions as those of terrorists. It's enough to take some of the heat off." CIA's Political Action Group worked their magic, then. There's a beat of silence before she adds, "Plus there's just too much going on right now for you to matter much, the political discussion has evolved, we're in a whole new news cycle."

"Still, thanks."

"You're welcome."

"So…Davies said something about coming home with a provisional return of my status with the Company?"

"We'll talk more about that when you get here. But obviously you can't just return home as normal; some old college buddy might see you walking around town, mention it on Facebook, and then the Russians would have reason to open this whole can of worms again."

"What about work?" I ask, pressing her.

"You can't be operational in areas where you'd be easily grabbed. No more jobs in Russia or in its allies' territories. But we may have other work for you."

"Like what? I can't show my face at Langley, any one of those people there could be the mole. They'd out me fast. So what kind of work are we talking about? Don't tell me office stuff."

Yarwick sighs. "Like I said, we'll talk about it when you get here. Right now, let's focus on the positive. You're out of the doghouse. You can come home. You don't have to live out in the cold anymore. You can see Sophia."

There's another silent beat, one longer than before.

"And you and I can introduce our cats," she chuckles.

I think about that for a second. I smile. That's not a bad thought. "Okay. I'm sure Eddie would love to meet Persephone."

"It's a date, then. Oh! One more thing. I got a call from your friend."

"My friend?"

"Yeah. Fardün. He accepted your offer."

"You're shitting me."

Yarwick snorts. "No. Apparently you haven't lost your touch when it comes to recruiting agents in the field."

"What kind of work will you use him for?"

"I don't know. I'm sure we'll think of something."

I walk over to the window, look out at the world. It's different now, knowing I don't have to run. Knowing I'm going back to the Nest, with friends, with colleagues. What few I have left. But then I recall that there's reason to suspect at least some of those friends betrayed me. Betrayed us. "What about Karambit? Has he said who Alpha Source is yet?"

"No, not yet. And I'm afraid we can't hold him much longer. The Russians either knew or suspected that we're keeping him. They knew he was in Beijing and that he went missing while going to meet with Fardün. They knew the Chinese don't have him, because the Chinese are part of the EA. And when they asked the Embassy, the Embassy officials had no choice but to be honest and tell them they were holding one of their SVR agents under suspicion. Motions have been filed by the Russians. He'll be out soon. He doesn't know that yet, so we're still trying to keep him in the dark, squeeze him."

"Keep trying. Don't stop. Fardün swears Karambit knows who the mole is and they're codename is Alpha Source."

"We're doing everything we can." Another long beat. So long I think she may have hung up. Then she says, "It's good to know you're in the clear, Nate."

*

I spend two nights in Denmark, then I'm on a plane for the U.S. We touch down at Langley Air Force Base, but before anyone can see me, Agent Davies guides me into a black sedan that's waiting for us on the tarmac, and off we go. It's an eight-hour drive to Connecticut, to a safehouse that I'm sure has been used to hide other agents and CIs who were too hot to be walking around. It's a little cabin on a private stretch of land in the middle of the forest, with brick walls, an iron stove, and a deer's head hanging over the fireplace. Otherwise, it's pretty modern, with TV, stocked fridge, Internet connection, and a laptop that I've been supplied.

It's so strange to be home. I've been weeks away, but it feels like a lifetime. Just stepping off the plane in Langley felt surreal. Now that I'm here in this cabin, on friendly soil…I feel like I stepped out of one dream and into another.

I walk over to turn on the TV. My knee suddenly jolts with pain. I hiss. Take a seat and massage it. Damn, where did that come from? I stand up again, testing it. Seems fine. I walk over to turn on the TV and see coverage of the Conflict. Syria is sending troops to their borders, getting ready to fight off any invasion.

"You won't be here long," Davies promises. "Ms. Yarwick told me to tell you that. And you'll have visitors, and have the right to pay visits to certain people. Not right away, of course, but in time. There's a car around back, the keys are in the glovebox, but you are encouraged not to go anywhere unless it's an emergency."

"Understood. Thank you, Agent Davies."

"You bet. Oh, also, Ms. Yarwick thought you should know, a friend of yours named Sophia had an episode?"

My heart skips. "What do you mean, 'an episode?' "

"I'm not sure about the details, but apparently she fainted. From what I gathered, it was believed she was dehydrated. But she's fine now, Yarwick says. She just wanted you to know. Said she didn't want you left in the dark about it."

He shakes my hand again. Tells me what an honor it's been. I watch him leave. From the front porch of the cabin I see the trail of dust his sedan leaves behind. As soon as he's gone, I'm out the door, in the Camry he left for me outside, and driving eight hours back the way we came, headed for Rose Lawn Retirement Home.

24

Sophia's chest rises and falls slowly, almost imperceptibly. The IV drips soundlessly. Her breath is half gargled. Feels like I'm trespassing on someone's most private moment. This might've been a bad idea. I could startle her into a heart attack. But I had to come here. I had to see her.

The hospital room is dark. If she wakes up, I might appear like a specter of death. Will she remember me? If she does, will she want to see me? Maybe she'll be resentful that I wasn't here when it happened, or that I'm still in my, relatively, young body while hers is collapsing. It's probably stupid to be thinking like that, Sophia's not that kind of person, but childhood fears have a way of lingering forever, and as her eyes flutter open and the glaucoma-less one stares at me, I can't help but think of Derek's words when we were boys. *This should be you.*

"Nathan," she rasps. "You...mother...fucker."

I snort, relieved. "Hey, old hen."

"What...what're you..." She trails off, swallows a dry mouth. There's a juice bottle someone left on the table beside her bed with a straw. I help her take a sip, then she waves it away like it's a swarm of gnats. "You're not here."

"I'm here, Soph," I tell her gently. "I made it back, just like you told me."

"You're...still in Prussia. Or...*Russia.* They told me. On the news, they said...they said..."

"I know, Soph." I pull up a chair from a group of chairs. Looks like her family was sitting in them all day. They might still be here, but I doubt it. The halls were quiet, mostly empty, just one nurse at the front desk and a guard on an occasional patrol. It was easy infiltrating Rose Lawn. It ain't no Vostochny. "I know. I'm all over the news. Been disavowed. Don't worry, it's not as bad as it sounds, just means I can't work right now and I can't show my face to anybody."

Suddenly, Sophia gives a raspy, gravelly cough. "What does that make me? A nobody?"

"Something like that. We're a couple o' nobodies, you and me."

"Speak...for...yourself...asshole."

I chuckle. "So, what happened? Someone said you had an 'episode?'"

"Just haven't been getting enough sleep, that's all. They keep saying it's because I've been overexerting myself, but these fuck-clowns forget I was a nurse in the War, too. Sometimes I was, anyway." She lets out a short cough. I offer her more juice and she resists at first but then sips it and nods. Waves me away like a swarm of gnats.

"Why weren't you sleeping?"

"I've been thinking about this thing. This *thing*. This thing, it's…"

"What thing? Soph, what is it?"

She looks at me. "Oh, Nathan…Nathan…I don't know what's real anymore. I've been talking to a woman…and I don't even know if she's real or not. And I see things sometimes…people from shallow graves."

I touch her brittle, cold hand. She's getting poor circulation. "It's okay, Soph. I'm real. I'm right here."

"I wish I could believe that. You don't know what this is like. Pray you never do."

I kiss her hand. She smiles. "Who's the woman?"

"W-woman?"

"The woman you've been speaking to."

"Oh. Her." Sophia looks to her right, as though she sees someone there, then looks back at me. "I'm pretty sure she's real, Nathan. The only weird thing is she doesn't feel real. Nothing feels real anymore. Not even Chloe or Zoe. Not even…oh, God…" She puts a hand over her face. She doesn't weep. Once upon a time she might've, but this woman has put people in graves and seen her friends vanish and twice saw the remains of her friends who had been tortured by Gestapo. No more tears left in this one. Nothing but ice and steel. She looks at me now, her cracked face filled with supreme resolve. "I'm being silly. It doesn't matter what's real, only that this is real now. And I've been selfish. *Mon Dieu*, how have you been? Nathan, thank God you made it back. Thank God."

"I made it back, yeah. Thanks to you."

"What did I do?"

"You were with me, Soph. The whole way."

"Tell me."

And so I tell her. I don't give her specific names or locations, I just describe the submarine ride and being dropped off. Before I left I told her I was going to Russia, but now I elaborate and she listens. I see something in her eyes. Interest. Genuine interest. It's like she's in on the operation, hanging on every detail and demanding I report more. Whenever I pause she encourages me to go on, or asks for clarification. I'm worried the security guard might come by to check on her. What will I tell him if he does? Who cares? This is Sophia and I'm surprised how much I missed her so I keep talking. Probably stupid, but Sophia commands me and I obey.

I cover the gunfight, the mission, taking pictures of an unspecified Russian weapon. She smiles. She likes to hear that I was successful. Makes her feel good, like she's on the side of good again. She's in on the secrets. She thrives on secrets. They bring her nourishment.

When I'm done outlining my escape and how I wound up on the news, she chuckles. "I never fucked up so badly I wound up a celebrity," she says.

I make a pained face. "Hey now, be nice."

"I'm dying. I don't have to have manners."

"Dying? What're you talking about? You're Sophia de Marenches, you're immortal."

"I wish. Then I might live long enough."

"Long enough for what?"

"To see *him* get what he deserves."

"Who, Soph?"

She shakes her head. Swats nonexistent gnats away again. "I don't even know if it's real. I don't even know if you're real."

"Talk to me. Tell me. Let's find out together."

There is a moment while she looks at the wall and I'm not sure she heard me. Has she lapsed into some kind of waking coma? Is she having a stroke? Then she looks at me with her one good eye. And she starts talking.

*

"Do you believe me?" she asks, once she's finished.

The night has worn on, well past midnight. She's been talking for an hour and no one has come. Feels like it's just me and her and that it always has been. In the whole wide world, just us, nobody else, no wars or conflicts or romance or anything. The life and anima has drained from the world and there is only the two of us. Her words came out haltingly at first, but picked up speed and confidence as she went along. She held my hand like she was afraid that upon letting me go she'd watch me evaporate.

But I didn't evaporate. I stayed right here and listened. Because it's Sophia and she's earned that. And I didn't just humor her. I listened. I imbibed. I processed and even asked questions here and there. For the most part, though, I just let her get it all out. She dumped it all on me and when she's done I'm left sitting here wondering what kind of hell it must be living inside a skull with that many secrets and with the fog of advanced age obscuring half of them. And then I wonder, of course, *Is this real?*

"What do you think?" she asks, after I've given her another sip of juice.

"I think it's a hell of a story, old hen."

"But do you believe me?" Her eyes are beseeching. Her hand is on my wrist.

"Sophia, I respect you enough to give you the truth, so here it is. I believe that you believe it. And I'm inclined to think that at least some of this is true. You're still pretty sharp, even if your mind is going, day by day."

"Her name is Abijah."

"That may be true. But it could also be a scam. If she's even real, that is. I don't know the angle. Maybe life savings. Maybe someone playing a prank on an old woman. It's cruel, but people do that kind of shit."

"She's genuine. I can tell. I was trained to tell the difference, Nathan. So if she's real then the whole thing is real."

I pat her hand. "I'll make a few calls tomorrow, see what I can find out."

"She didn't give me her last name. I never thought to ask." That last part seems to bring her great shame.

"Wouldn't have mattered if you did," I say. "If she's real, Abijah might not even be her real name. But I know people. There are cameras in this place and that stuff's usually backed up on the cloud these days. So if I can get the cam footage pulled and do facial-recognition on it—"

"Do it," Sophia says.

I nod. "I will."

"Do it," she repeats. "But don't stick your neck out too far for me. I know you need to keep a low profile."

"Hey, for you, old hen, I'd draw mustaches on Mount Rushmore."

She squeezes my hand. With more strength than I would have given her credit. "Help me find him, Nathan. I need this one. This one last thing."

I squeeze back. "I live to serve, *mademoiselle*."

*

The journey back to Connecticut takes longer than the journey to Rose Lawn. I hit some roadwork, lots of traffic. After finally reaching the cabin, I lie down and finally sleep. I've been up almost twenty-four hours. Sophia's voice is still in my head. When I wake up I start in on a bit of stretching. I put on the news and make myself some breakfast. CNN says Ukraine's outer regions are officially warzones. Russian forces haven't reached Kiev yet. I cook some eggs, biscuits and hashbrowns. Americana. It tastes good. And I mull over everything Sophia told me.

Wilhelm Vogel, formerly Hauptmann Vogel of the German Army, formerly *Kriminalsekretär Vogel* of the Gestapo. That shouldn't be too hard to look up, especially since Sophia said there are records, and of course the famous Wiesenthal List. I take a shower, thinking on it, then dry off and put on new clothes and go to the computer. I search for the Wiesenthal List, most of which was made public ages ago. And there he is, right in the old archives, just like she said. Sophia was telling the truth about Vogel, right down to the large forehead and droopy eye.

There's a flash from the TV. Missiles being fired into a Ukrainian border town. The Russians are using their TOS-1 "Buratino" launch platforms, firing their thermobaric warheads, which explode in the sky and spread their flammable liquid that ignites instantly. It's beautiful at night, watching the sky come alive in white-orange light that ripples outward, and a split-second later the cascading liquid flame that paints the sky in a horrifically gorgeous show.

Several blocks are destroyed at once.

Russian TV cameras catch it all and CNN replays it over and over.

What about Abijah, and the information Mossad has been providing for the sake of Legacy? How much is truth and how much is fiction? Is *any* of it true? I do a Google search of Arumush, and I find both the story Sophia was talking about at the embassy in South Africa and a website for a security firm that has no picture of Vogel and makes no mention of the company's founders.

My phone rings. I know who it's going to be before I answer it. "How's things?" I say.

"I was going to ask you the same thing," Yarwick says. "Congratulations on making it back to home soil."

"Thanks. It's good to be back."

"So," she says. "What are your plans for tonight?"

"I'm pretty open. Why? Have something in mind?"

25

When I open the door, I feel like I've severely misjudge Tara Yarwick. "Hey," she says, stepping inside wearing loose khaki pants and a motorcycle jacket unzipped down the front. Glancing outside, I see her ride. A Harley-Davidson Switchback, with long handlebars and gleaming chrome wheels. She catches me giving it a look. "You ride?"

"Not in a while," I say. "You drove here on that? Eight hours?"

"Weather's supposed to be good the next couple o' days. Figured I'd take advantage." She smiles. "Something wrong?"

I shut the door. "Nah, I just...I guess my spy senses are off, I never pegged you for a rider."

"It's kind of a new thing I'm trying out. Got a wild hair up my ass, I guess you could say. About six months ago I started doing all this research on bikes."

"You joined a gang yet?"

"Not yet, but I'm still looking," she laughs. "You got anything to eat?"

"Well, you're a little early, but if you're starving I can heat up the meatloaf dinners in the fridge. And some wine called Woodbridge somebody left."

"Sounds like a plan."

The meatloaf is passable and the wine is terrible. I think we both know that but neither of us comments. We don't talk at all for a few minutes, and when we finally do, it's about her bike, not about work or Putin or our dead colleagues lying in a morgue somewhere in China.

This isn't a date. I don't know what this is. An informal meeting? A casual get-together? It was her idea. After we both narrowly survived murder and capture, is this just how agents like us cope? The Tidovs are dead somewhere in a forest by the river, and Wainwright and the others haven't had their bodies reclaimed by the U.S. because our people denied to the Chinese government that they had anything to do with them being in Harbin.

That could've been Tara. That could've been me. Two unclaimed bodies. We're eating meatloaf instead, and drinking cheap-ass wine and talking about bikes.

"How's it running for you?" I ask, taking a sip of the Woodbridge and wincing at the rancid taste.

"Good, I guess," she says, using the plastic fork the meal came with to push around the mashed potatoes. "I don't have much to compare it to. I'm actually having a lot more fun with the maintenance."

"Maintenance?"

"Yeah. My uncle was a mechanic. He had a really technical mind. I used to help him in his shop. I hated it at first, but then I got to liking it. I kinda miss working on stuff, so I got something I could tinker with" She takes a bite, wipes her mouth with a napkin. "Thing about this type of Harley, it came with a problem. It uses plastic 'shoes' riding on the cam chains. The shoes rub against the two chains and the plastic shoes wear out. Fast."

"Wow."

"I'm learning to disassemble and inspect the inner and outer shoes. I have to watch for them to shave off, clog up the oil pump, which would destroy the engine."

"Sounds like a lotta work."

"Keeps me busy."

"Is that what you do to relax?"

"Relax? What's that?"

I chuckle, and wait for her to give a real answer.

"No," she says. "I like to read by the pool whenever I get the chance. Visit my nephew, see how he and his dad are doing."

I nod, taking another sip of wine. Terrible stuff. After a sufficient silence, I decide to ask the hard questions. "So, tell me about these cuckoo's eggs. Our enemy had them hidden in our systems, then decided to enact them to take over a satellite, and listen in on NARROW VOID's progress, but they couldn't have even known of its existence without someone inside telling them. So, who told them?"

"It's a short list of suspects," Yarwick says. "Including the POTUS and V-POTUS, there were only sixteen people privy to the enactment of NARROW VOID. Not even the submarine commander or pilots that carried you that way knew what your ultimate destination was, or what you intended to do once you got there. And you never mentioned the name 'Tidov' over comms to us, you stuck to mission protocols and referred to it as 'Rendezvous A' the whole time, which means the Russians didn't learn where you were from just tapping into comms."

I nod. "And none of it was written down? They couldn't have hacked any computer and discovered NARROW VOID's purpose?"

"No. NARROW VOID was only mentioned in PDBs, and presidential daily briefings don't have specifics like that. Any specifics pass from mouth to ear—from the Director of National Intelligence's mouth to the POTUS's and V-POTUS's ears. That's it. NARROW VOID *was* mentioned in a memo to both SAD and CIA directors, but in name only, there were no details. Any and all details were delivered mouth-to-ear."

"That settles it, then. Not a hack or an accidental leak. A mole. Somebody spilled it." I drum my fingers on the table. "But how could they have thought they'd get away with it? If only sixteen people knew, the mole would have realized that there would be an investigation into everyone up the chain who knew about NARROW VOID."

Yarwick shakes her head. "Not necessarily. If all of us had died—even if only *you* had died, or been captured—a lot could have been chalked up to incompetence on our part. Maybe it could be suggested you were a defector, that you had gone over to the Russians and that your capture was only the cover story they fed. Or that we messed up in the Nest, somehow failed at PERSEC or OPSEC. But enough of us lived that now they don't have a choice."

I nod. "They're going to have to move quickly to cover their tracks. They might even be considering defection at this point, to get ahead of the charges of treason."

"That's probably true."

We don't say anything else for a while. We both just sit and think and consider the room and mull everything over. We did our job. The mission was a success. Barely. And considering everything that went wrong it's a goddamn miracle. But we did it.

But now there's another problem; a series of them, actually. I'm still disavowed but I'm only provisionally back in action and might very well be under suspicion, especially if the mole tries to shift blame. There may come pressure from somewhere, someone on the inside suggesting that Ares's return is suspicious.

Isn't it interesting that Ares survived, even against such odds? Isn't it possible that his wounds were self-inflicted? How do we know that he destroyed the Great Donut? Isn't it possible that he's working *for* the Russians, or that they got to him somehow, suckered him with a honey trap, blackmailed him, offered him a fortune to disappear forever? Think about it, Nathan Adamson has no family, no real friends, no one to return to in the U.S., just some old lady in a retirement home. No wife, no children, nothing. Wouldn't it be easy for him to take an offer from the Russians? Wouldn't he be a prime target for their recruiters? How could he have survived such trials in Russia? It defies belief.

My paranoia has me thinking of everyone as a suspect. Even Yarwick. Just out of healthy skepticism. As I'm sure she's probably given some serious thought to me. We can all be deceived. But Yarwick has gone out of her way to keep me alive, and I can't see an angle where that would be good for her if she's the mole. She's had ample opportunity to kill me. Could've let Fardün kill me in Ulaanbaatar.

And maybe she realized she could trust me, too. Because if I was a Putin puppet, I wouldn't have stayed inside the Hotel Tikina, exactly where she put me, never leaving, never making a phone call, obeying her every instruction. If I were the traitor, smartest thing would have been to stay in Russia and collect my reward.

Thinking about that, I just realized that bringing me back to the States isn't just a charity, it's also a good idea for Yarwick. Me coming back is proof I didn't vanish off the grid, so I can't be the mole. Unless I'm stupid. And my return also means there's cover for Yarwick. If she's the mole, and not me, why would she come tip me off in Mongolia when killing me and making me disappear would be the better option for her Russian masters? My disappearance would make me look suspicious, take the heat off her.

So that makes her an ally. Probably. But I have to remember that she works in intelligence. Intelligence people think dynamically, in 4D chess. I remember Farooq Salam (*please I have children I have three children*) and how that operation was meant to kill an enemy combatant while ensuring his people thought he was alive and uncompromised, so that a SEAL team could later catch Salam's friends in the act. These operations are a balancing act, and a traitor's or defector's escape plan will invariably be planned the same way.

Shift the focus of the investigation. Confuse the data. Shift the blame.

I look at her. She's looking back at me.

"What are you thinking about?" she asks.

I shrug. "Just how good it is to be home."

She nods, smiles, and sips her wine.

"Truth be told, I'm also thinking of something else."

"Yeah? What?"

I muster up the courage. "I have a favor to ask."

*

We're standing in the living room now and I'm looking across at her stern gaze. I don't think I've ever seen this look on her before. In fact, I'm positive I haven't. It's the look of betrayal. Of incrimination. Strange to see it on a friend's face. I think we're friends. Aren't we?

"You went out?" Yarwick says. Her arms are crossed under her breasts. "You went out without asking me? Without clearing it with me first. You drove all the way to see Sophia, with your face on the news."

"You said all that had died down—"

"I did not say it had all died down, I said we had taken some heat off of you. Those are not the same things."

"Okay. You're right. I'm sorry. It was stupid. I won't do anything like that again without your permission." I sigh. "Now, can I tell you something? Something that Sophia told me?"

"What?" she says tersely.

"It's something I'd like you to look into. If you could."

"Something for Sophia?"

"Yeah."

"What is it?"

I lay it all out, just as Sophia did for me. Abijah, Vogel, some guy named Baudelaire from DGSE, everything. Yarwick listens patiently, even leans against the wall and cocks her head to one side inquisitively. When I'm finished, I go to the stocked fridge and grab a couple beers and return to hand her one. She sips it. "Well? Am I crazy?"

"You're definitely crazy. You snuck out of a safehouse and risked exposure to infiltrate an old folks home to talk to a nonagenarian who's slowly losing her mind. Now you're taking her story seriously and want to do an investigation? Am I hearing this right?"

I take a swing of beer. I wipe my mouth with my wrist. It's not great, but better than the wine. "I just want to do right by Sophia. She's never really been this off before, and so far her story checks out. I'm not asking for a lot of time to be allotted to this, just...maybe find out who the woman is visiting Sophia? Find out about Abijah, if she's even real. That should be easy, just go up and ask the Rose Lawn staff. I'd do it, but they'd probably recognize me."

"And if she's not real, Nate?"

"If she's not real, we drop it. Simple. If she is real, though, I want to know if she's really Mossad. If so, reach across to our Israeli colleagues, find out her real name."

"And then do what?"

"Arrange a meeting."

Yarwick is midway through a sip. She spills a bit down her chin. I grab a Kleenex from the coffee table and hand it to her. "A meeting? For what?"

"I don't know. To see what they want with Sophia's story."

"And *you* want to be in on this meeting?"

"Is that a problem?"

"Uh, yeah, just because the U.S. is harboring you now doesn't mean you're not supposed to be incommunicado with the rest of the world. You can't be in on a meeting with Mossad."

I sigh, and look at her.

"You want to go after a hundred-year-old Nazi?"

"Got nothin' else better to do," I say. "And it's Sophia."

"You have a job and a commitment to the United States government to remain off the grid—"

"Technically I'm disavowed, no longer bound to that commitment."

"Horseshit. Disavowal's just a political tool to let politicians dodge blame, it doesn't mean you're out in the cold."

"And yet here I am, with only you and a handful of Company men knowing where I am."

"Because we don't yet know who the goddamn mole is or how he might use you if he got his hands on you."

He. She assumes the mole is a man. "I want to look into this," I say adamantly. "Sophia's scared. She's all I've got. Like you said before I left, she's the thing that keeps me grounded to this hunk of rock called the U.S. She's the reason to come home. We're...I don't know...*partners.*"

"Partners."

"Look, contact OSI. The Nazi hunters in the Justice Department. See if any of them have ever liaised with Mossad's Legacy division before. Gotta be one or two of them know Abijah if she's real. The U.S. has had hundreds of Nazis turn up here over the years, there's at least one new one every year."

"How do you know that?" Yarwick asks.

"Read it on the Internet."

"You do a little research and now you're an expert?"

"Didn't say that," I say, and take a final swig of my beer. Yarwick finishes hers off, too, and I take the bottle from her. Our hands touch briefly. There might've been a lingering there, a moment when we instinctively held contact. I toss both bottles in the trash and look at her. "Have you got anything else for me to do? Any real work?"

Yarwick shrugs. "Not yet."

"Then humor me. This might be a way for me to help."

"How?"

"If it's something worth looking into, Mossad and OSI might want our help. Tell them you have someone. An operative. Say that JSOC can coordinate—that's what you guys do best—and that you can give them a NOC. They don't need to know your NOC is disavowed."

"My NOC is a disavowed A-list celebrity on the world stage."

I curl my bottom lip. "C-lister. B-lister at best."

"This isn't funny, Nate."

"I'm not laughing, Tara. Sophia's got business to finish, and I want to help her."

"I can't let you go after some ancient Nazi! Jesus Christ, are you serious right now? Nate, you're a witness to everything that went on at Tsiolkovsky. I helped you escape after disavowal so you couldn't be caught. I brought you *here* so you wouldn't be done in by SVR operatives in Beijing or by some sweepers the mole sent."

As she speaks, it sinks in. I've been entertaining a fantasy. I've been nursing a secret wish that I can be the one to help Sophia finish her unfinished business. But leaving the country again isn't an option, it would literally jeopardize national security and potentially many lives, Yarwick's among them. I'm disappointed by my shortsightedness, but not as much as I'm disappointed by the realization that I can't help Sophia.

"Then will you at least look into Arumush? Will you look into Vogel and Abijah and all this? I'll stay out of it if you want me to."

She heaves another exasperated sigh. "If it'll calm you down, sure, I'll ask around to see if we have any reliable Israeli liaisons who can touch base with this woman."

"Thank you."

"*If* she exists," she adds. "And Nate? Don't make me sorry I gave you back your personal freedom again."

331

26

The next several days I sit and meditate and exercise and watch TV and think about home and Yarwick and Tatiana and Sophia. I also wonder about Deputy Director Halbach and everybody back at Langley. I wonder what they're doing, how much of a shitstorm I created for them by doing the job they sent me to do. Theoretically I made the world a safer place, but that's hard to see from inside this cozy cabin.

Images of a new invasion flash across the screen. I'm barely keeping up with it all. I don't feel connected to it, watching it like a television show, just like everybody else in the world. Video footage of night attacks are constantly repeating. Tracer rounds shoot out into the black Ukrainian skies like needles of white fire. Missiles and gunfire can be heard but rarely seen. Night-vision cams catch the mobilization of the EA's forces the world over.

There are officially PRC boots on the ground in Taiwan. Kim has sent troops to the border, facing his old enemies in South Korea. Bashar remains mostly quiet, merely voicing his occasional support while demanding all U.S.-led humanitarian groups leave the country.

Rumor is, a North Korean sub has been sunk, and an unnamed American frigate is limping into a port along the equator to conduct repairs and resupply. There was some kind of unfriendly exchange in the Atlantic, that's for sure, but nobody's saying what happened. This is a strange "conflict," it's not a cold war or a shooting war—not totally, anyway. Anderson Cooper is calling it the Quiet War, a new kind where you hit the bully on the playground but neither of you admits to it because you're afraid of what will happen to both of you if the teacher finds out.

My face has kind of drifted out of the public eye, which is good. There are way more things to concern reporters with than my face and name and Putin's conspiracy theory that I was an operative sent into Amur Oblast to destroy some new satellite that he claims was innocuous.

I get one phone call from Yarwick every day, just one to check up on me. After a week, I get a call from her saying that she wants me to meet some people. Her JSOC bosses. These two are above suspicion, she says, because while they knew of NARROW VOID's implementation, they were not privy to any of my locations, or where exactly I was going to be inserted, and only one of them knew what my objective would be. For the sake of operational security, they were each kept in the dark about different details.

I agree to meet with them, mostly because of Yarwick's faith in them. I get myself cleaned up for a noon meeting. All three of them are on time. Yarwick is dressed smartly in a black Varoni suit and matching heels, her hair pulled back in a tight bun, and the two black-suited JSOC guys look like Secret Service.

Yarwick gives the introductions. "Nate, this is Division B Director Rinaldo Matthews," she says, as I shake the hand of a tall Hispanic man with broad shoulders and a buzzcut so shallow he might as well be bald. "And this is Director of Facilitation Victor Hames." Hames is a pale-skinned blonde man that kind of reminds me of Karambit, with skinny hands and skinny fingers that no less take mine in a bear-trap grip. "Gentlemen, let's have a seat."

"I have some leftover pizza, some beers and some water," I say. "Pizza should be easy to reheat."

"Thank you, but I'm good," says Matthews.

"I might have a sip," Hames says.

We all take a seat at the only table in the room. The curtains are closed. I see Hames look that way, probably making sure of the window. I sense an old spook. Matthews plops a briefcase on top of the table and snaps it open, but he doesn't take anything out yet. "Mr. Adamson, I'd just like to say off the record, thank you. What you did was a tremendous service to your country and I'm damn proud to be seated across from such a patriot."

"Damn straight," Hames says. He smiles fractionally. I watch them all. Their hands. All married. Erect posture. Both seem like former military men. Most likely they were, most likely in intelligence. That's a fast track in JSOC and such agencies.

"And as a token of that appreciation..." He reaches into his briefcase. I know what it is even before I see it. A plaque with a light-blue ribbon and red stripes is placed on the table and slid halfway across. "We would like to honor you in the appropriate way, with the Distinguished Intelligence Cross, for valor in the field." I reach across to touch it. The closest I'll get to the Medal of Honor for now, since the Medal of Honor has to come from the POTUS, and right now he has to publicly denounce me.

I look up from the ribbon and into each of their faces. "Only CIA gives these. You're all JSOC."

Yarwick nods. "Halbach wanted us to pass this along."

I nod. "Make sure Amrita Tigga, Samuel Isaacson, and anyone else on your team gets a posthumous medal," I tell her.

"Of course," Yarwick says. "Halbach says it's in the works."

We sit in silence a moment. Then I ask, "Does the POTUS himself actually know I'm alive and back at home?"

"We've all decided to keep it out of the PDB for now. If your name is mentioned in the presidential daily briefing it could start to spread. I'm trying to get you help from inside, Nate, while still keeping knowledge of your whereabouts contained to those above suspicion."

"Above suspicion," I say.

"Deputy Director Halbach asked us to relay this to you," Hames says. He retrieves the plaque and puts it back in his briefcase. "But, of course, we'll have to hold on to it for now. You know how it goes."

"Yes, sir, I do." I look at all of them in turn, then splay my hands out on the table. "Okay, so, to what do I owe this visit? You didn't come down here just to say thanks."

Maybe my tone had a bit too much edge, because Matthews and Hames glance at each other, then at Yarwick, who takes the lead. "Directors Matthews and Hames have both been asked to develop clandestine agent-handling operations in Ukraine, and I've been pegged to draw up the initial plans, since I have both Russian and Ukrainian agents in Kiev. And Kiev is where Putin's people are going now."

I wince. "Are you here to recruit me for that? You can't possibly be thinking about sending me in. I mean, no offense, but you went through a great deal getting me free of the Russians, sending me into Kiev would be risking having me be caught by EA forces once they reach the city." I shrug. "I mean, you know me, you know I'll work, but it just seems—"

"No, that's what *I'm* tasked with, Nate, not you. I'm being reassigned, which means I won't be able to spend any more time cleaning up NARROW VOID or hiding you. Which was one of the reasons why I had to bring in others on this secret. I couldn't just leave you stranded here while I move on."

A stone drops in my gut. I don't like hearing her say "move on" in relation to me. Don't know why it hurts, but it does. "I see." Hames and Matthews look at me critically. I know that look. Sizing me up for something, gauging my mien, wondering where my head is at. "Well, then, what are we here for?"

"I did what you asked," Yarwick says. "I put out some feelers at the Justice Department. Said someone from Mossad might have been snooping around an old folks home, that there might be someone there interviewing a former French intelligence officer. That didn't blow up many skirts." She gives me a weird smile, one I haven't seen on her before. "But then I mentioned the name Abijah, and I got seven phone calls from seven different people in OSI in twenty-four hours."

"Yeah?"

She nods. "They wanted to know how I know her, where I'd seen here, what all I could tell them about her. I described her as you did to me. That got me on the phone with the OSI Director. He demanded I tell him exactly where I had seen Abijah Zurer."

"Zurer? That her name?"

"I'm guessing. Apparently, they have a file on her. They call her the 'Last Lady.' While Legacy is still technically open, few people still pay it much attention. OSI still persecutes Nazis, but only as a matter of records and to trace illegals. The French gave up on *Héritage* a while ago."

"Okay. Then what's Zurer doing here?"

Zurer is the granddaughter of Holocaust survivors. Her grandfather died in 1994, screaming his head off, thinking he was back in Buchenwald where they probed him anally with a hot fire poker and cut off all his brothers' fingers while he watched. For Zurer, it's about prosecuting evil, no matter how old. She won't stop until the last Nazi kicks it.

I'm taken aback. "Jesus. And she came all this way to see Sophia?"

"That's what we want to discuss with her when you meet."

"When *I* meet?"

"Yes. OSI sent out an invitation to Mossad's Director of Special Operations and we had ourselves a conference call. Just five minutes long. But in that time it was decided."

"What was decided?"

"Mossad has no operatives to spare on this, but I told them I had an operative that could go where others could not." Yarwick looks at me with a raised eyebrow. "Now, I know what you're thinking, I said you were in danger if you left this cabin too soon, but Directors Matthews and Hames both agreed your skills are too priceless to waste away inside this place. And Halbach agreed that we owed you for your service and your public disgrace."

I wince at that. Never thought about it as disgraceful. I guess I should have, though. Wow, that's a new spin on it, Nathan old boy.

"It seems a good fit," Matthews says. "Right now, working with Zurer would be the smallest of operations, and she wouldn't even need to know who you really are. You could communicate purely through intermediaries. Mossad said they've spoken with her and she's all for it. She needs operatives in the field to make arrests, and her people aren't interested in giving her any, what with everything going on right now. And OSI really needs another win, another reason to keep the Nazi-hunting branch funded, so…" He shrugs and smiles.

"And Langley is okay with this?" I say.

Yarwick says, "You won't be exposed directly to EA forces, so yes. You would just be helping with research, and perhaps the final approach on the target."

Target. They've already decided. It's strange to think that all of this came from an old lady losing her mind in a retirement home. Still, I lean forward, eager to hear more. This is getting interesting. "What do we know about the target?" I ask.

"Zurer has more information than we do, and she's not sharing just yet. Says she wants Vogel's 'final end' to come from his Jewish enemies."

"So, I'm to capture him, then bring him back to Mossad?"

"The planning is still in its nascent stages, but yes, the tacit agreement right now is that a safehouse will be set up near the strike zone, and you'll extract Vogel—who's living under the name Krause now—and bring him to the safehouse to be taken out of the country and back to Israel to stand secret trial. If he's proven to be who Sophia says he is and who Abijah now believes he is…well, you can imagine."

"OSI will still want credit though, right?"

"Mossad will write a public commendation for the U.S. Justice Department, saying they were instrumental in bringing a Nazi to justice, and they might even commend Sophia publicly, but they won't name the Nazi. Vogel will just vanish."

Hames leans forward, elbows on the tables. "Arumush is also of interest to us, Mr. Adamson," he says. "They're kind of becoming a major player in the private security field, and most of their clients recently have been our enemies. Namely the nations in the Eastern Alignment."

Matthews says, "We'd like a look at their full client list, what they've been doing, their connections to the Dark Web, things like that. Mossad has assured us that they will share what intel they get out of Krause. Er, *Vogel*."

Oh. I see. JSOC's got to get something out of this, too, as does CIA. Everybody's gotta win. Besides Abijah, nobody is doing this out of the kindness of their heart or for the sake of honoring an aging hero of the French Resistance. That War was too long ago for anyone to care anymore. The new Conflict is all that matters. "What exactly has Arumush been up to?"

"This is where it gets a little interesting," Yarwick says.

"Yeah?"

Hames nods, and says, "The Iranians have been developing their nuclear program, you know that. I'm sure you also know that a primary reason for the Iranians being held back is that they've lacked sufficient uranium hexafluoride feed stock. Until now."

"Okay."

"There was an investigation into Arumush several years ago by CIA, as part of a larger operation against multinational security firms. CIA did a secret audit. Arumush's books were clean, but their clientele list included a couple of shell companies run by Iranian politicians."

"Okay."

"Not long after that," Hames says, "a few documents from an Iranian nuclear scientist who defected to Britain suggested that Arumush was brought in to act as security after the Stuxnet computer virus nearly destroyed Iran's nuclear program. The defector also claimed Iran has been getting the materials they need, and that Arumush has been the supplier of the feed stock."

I squint, working that out. "Where would Vogel's security firm be getting uranium hexafluoride?"

"I'm sure CIA and Mossad would be happy to ask Vogel if they get the chance," Yarwick says.

I drum my fingers on the table, thinking. "Okay. So, the old geezer's still a player on the world stage and we need to grab him. What would my part in this be, exactly?"

"Covert deployment to Vogel's current location," Yarwick says. "Abijah's the one who discovered the name he's currently going under, and she's also pinned down his whereabouts. It's actually far more cut-and-dry than NARROW VOID, with a lot less moving parts."

"Snatch-and-grab?"

"That's about the size of it. You may have to rendezvous with Mossad NOCs, but that'll be the limits of your contact with anyone. And you won't be going into any nations friendly to the EA, so your exposure shouldn't be a problem while traveling."

I give it some thought. Think about Sophia, alone and afraid inside her own dwindling world. "All right, I'm in. Just tell me when and where."

"Okay," Yarwick says. "But understand, *if* you are chosen to be the one to actually do the grabbing, you won't have a crack team of government elites, nor will you have the assistance of local law enforcement. You'll have Mossad helping you plan but that's it."

"I understand."

"So any team we assemble for you must also be off-the-grid, just like you. And we can't afford to send elite units on this, since Special Forces and SOG operatives are going to be needed soon in places like Ukraine, Taiwan, maybe Russia and China." She adds, "God help us."

"Who did you have in mind to help me, then?"

Yarwick looks at me. "How much do you trust Innick Fardün?"

I snort. Then I laugh. "You're kidding?"

"Not in the least. I told you before, JSOC's assigned me the task of coming up with NOCs and disposable mercs we can use in the field. He's already agreed to help in Kiev. Fardün is Hungarian, right next door to Ukraine, and his history indicates he's had lots of work there."

"But in Sweden? And so soon? The guy's probably barely healed up."

"The two of you won't be seeing any action for at least a couple weeks. Plenty of time for him to recuperate."

"He and I tried to kill each other," I chuckle. This is a trip.

"But you saved him, got him to a hospital. You even worked together once already to grab Karambit."

"He wasn't exactly helping out of the kindness of his heart."

"No, he was helping out self-preservation. And that's a motive I think we can use. And he works for pay."

"He's used to much larger paychecks than I think *you're* willing to write him."

"He's a beggar right now, and beggars can't be choosers." She shrugs. "We've also pinned down where his family lives. They need help with lodgings. We intimated that we might be able to help them, if he helps us. He seems eager to move ahead."

I shrug. "I mean...*possibly.*"

Yarwick nods. "We can discuss mission details after we've spoken with Zurer." She hesitates. "One more thing you need to know. It doesn't have anything to do with this mission, but just so you are aware, Karambit's people couldn't be held back any longer. He was released this morning, taken in a car by a Russian ambassador and his team. We have no idea where he is now."

*

It's night but the stars aren't out. Clouds have moved in, obscuring even the moon. The world is tomb-quiet, not even any cicadas are out singing. It's like everyone senses something coming.

There's no thunder or lightning yet, but we all sense it. It take a sip of my beer and watch Yarwick give Hames and Matthews a final handshake and a wave. When their driver has taken them away, Yarwick walks up onto the porch with me, and takes the beer that I offer her.

She leans against one post, and I lean against the other. "How many agents you reckon have come through here?" I gesture at the cabin.

Yarwick looks at the old brick walls. "God only knows."

"Think anyone's ever been rolled up in there? Like maybe a traitor was brought here, made to feel right home, lulled into a sense of safety, then killed as soon as he admitted to what he'd done?"

"I don't know. Why?"

"Just something I've been thinking about. How many people come to a safehouse and find out it's not so safe. Is that weird?"

"I don't think so," she says. She takes a sip. "Matthews is eager to move forward. His department could use a score like this one. It looks minor right now, so no one else is on it, but he smells something bigger with Arumush."

"What about you? You smell something?"

She smiles at me. "I gotta admit, it has that flavor."

"Not so crazy, after all, eh?"

"No, it's crazy. But it's a kind of crazy we can work with."

I nod, finish off the beer, stare at the bottle. "You headed home tonight?"

She shrugs. "Kind of a long drive. I don't have to be in the office tomorrow. Maybe I should, though. You know?" She looks at me. Now I'm certain of it. She's giving me the opportunity. Here it is. But this still doesn't feel right. This is all still business. Has to be. We never finished our first date-or-whatever-it-was because I brought up Sophia and her story about Nazis. And we've still got a job to do. I remember dating women that I worked with. That's never good.

This would've been easier if I had been removed from all active duties.

"You can stay here tonight," I say, meeting her halfway, hoping she sees that. Not rejection, but not throwing caution to the wind, either. "I can sleep on the couch."

She smiles, and looks down at her beer. "Yeah. I can do that." She takes a swig.

*

I fall asleep on the couch. Gentleman that I am, I don't try and take advantage. I'm not sure that there's an advantage to be taken. Yarwick sleeps quietly in the bedroom. I wake up once to hear footsteps. Is she coming, approaching? I peek over the back of the couch and look towards the bedroom. The door has been left open.

I lay back down. Shut my eyes. Go to sleep.

In the morning, we barely say anything to each other. She reminds me about PERSEC and to keep to myself and to not go visit Sophia. I smile and say I won't. She hops in her rental car and drives away. That's it. Chance missed.

27

Yarwick moved me closer to Langley. A log cabin this time instead of brick. There are places like this all around Langley and its satellite towns, most of them with decent surroundings to go out jogging, with some workout equipment, computers, Internet, maybe a swimming pool.

I'm in the woods on the outskirts of Loudoun, the neighboring county of Fairfax. God knows how many defectors and informants in need of political asylum have stayed here, too. I'm given a gun and there are targets here to practice on, most of them with bullet holes already in them. Gives me something to do. My skills are going to be a bit rusty, considering what my body went through on the last mission, followed by a whole lotta sittin' around on my ass. Never a good combination.

I'm trusted with another vehicle but it's only for emergencies they say, and I'm asked, politely, not to visit Sophia or anyone else for now. Just stay lowkey and let JSOC and Halbach work out the machinations with Mossad and OSI behind the scenes. Eventually Yarwick will come over and both of us will have a teleconference with Abijah Zurer and her division director. Zurer has stated she wants to meet me in person. Yarwick and Halbach denied the request, they don't want anyone knowing who the operative they're lending is going to be. Zurer then insisted. It's still being negotiated.

Now that I have more room to move, I take advantage. I'm jogging every day, taking in the air of the coming spring and prepping my mind for the mission ahead. I don't know any specifics and I won't until I speak with Zurer. She still wants to meet me in person and JSOC still says no. This could all still fall apart if she proves intransigent.

Two weeks of lonesome training, with only occasional visits from Yarwick, and it occurs to me it's been a while since I've thought of quitting tomorrow. Maybe it's because I got a chance to see Sophia, or that I'm working again, or that Yarwick's face is close enough to a friend's. Maybe it's all of that.

Yarwick and I enjoy one late-night discussion over drinks that has nothing to do with work. We've improved our alcohol situation— she prefers IPA and I prefer Budweiser. We talk about those preferences, among other things. She was ready to move on from JSOC when the Conflict began, now she's not so sure. "The agencies all need good people," she says. "And I'm good at what I do." I agree. "That's why I hope we can still use you," she adds. That's as close as we get to complimenting each other. She then tells me she's going to help arrange the first teleconference between me, Mossad, OSI and the Justice Department. "After that," she says, "I doubt we'll see much of each other." It gets late. She's in no shape to drive home and I offer her the bed again. I take the couch. I keep thinking I should make a move, walk into the bedroom and just make a fucking move. I don't. In the morning she gets up and we speak only of professional matters. Then she's gone. Was I a gentleman or a loser to not make a move? I don't know. Either way, opportunity missed yet again.

When the day finally comes to speak with Zurer, Yarwick and I sit in front of a microphone that connects us to Langley, which routes the call through to us, ensuring it cannot be traced. Don't want any enemies knowing where the CIA keeps its safehouses. They're seven hours ahead of us, so when our conference starts at five o'clock in the afternoon, it's midnight in Tel Aviv.

"Ms. Yarwick," says the voice of a female techie at Langley. "You are now on with the director and Ms. Zurer."

"Thank you. Hello, Director Dayan, Ms. Zurer."

"Good afternoon," a man's voice says. Deep and resonant, without severe inflection on any syllable.

"How do you do?" says a woman with near zero accent. Zurer. She sounds poised, no-nonsense, supremely professional, just as Sophia described her. Yarwick pulled security camera footage from Rose Lawn Retirement Home and I've now seen what Zurer looks like. I match the voice to that stoic Israeli face.

"I'm here with my operative. He won't be speaking, but I assure you he's here and he's eager to listen. Deputy Director Halbach will be listening in remotely, as will OSI Director Vosberg and JSOC Division Director Matthews."

Director Dayan says, "That is all satisfactory, Ms. Yarwick. Thank you for arranging this meeting."

"Yes, thank you," Zurer says. "On behalf of Legacy, we thank you for giving this your attention. And for Sophia, I also thank you.

As we discuss, I would encourage all who are listening to imagine her here in spirit."

"Of course," Yarwick says, and looks at me. "It's because of her that we're all here today."

"Then let's get straight to it. I am not interested in wasting any time as Wilhelm Vogel's time draws shorter each day, and I would like to apprehend him as soon as possible. Sophia has given us a lot to help in research, and our investigations into Arumush, as well as its founders' movements and investments and training, have given us a greater profile."

"I understand you have some idea where he's at," Yarwick says.

"Arumush does not have a single headquarters, they like to keep mobile. A habit Vogel picked up decades ago, I assume, and reinforced by skills taught to him by intelligence agencies."

She avoids saying it was *our* intelligence agencies. Is that diplomacy, letting bygones be bygones, or just politeness, or is it politics? She does not seem like the one to let bygones be bygones, or else we probably wouldn't be here talking about a hundred-year-old war criminal.

"Right now, however, we feel confident that Vogel has moved on from South Africa, and that he is staying at a villa in a village called Porjus, in Sweden. From there, we think he oversees a computer security firm in Helsingborg."

"Is he very active in the business?" asks Yarwick.

"He is in semi-retirement. He has a golf course at his villa and stays on it pretty much the whole time. He does, however, enjoy coming out from time to time to put a personal touch on all his operations. He does not seem like a man who likes to be left out of world events, so he does what he can, even at his advanced age."

"Is this where you would want to implement the operation?" Yarwick asks.

"Again, with people of his age, time is of the essence. Plus we do not know when he might travel elsewhere again. We would include Swedish authorities in this if we could, but in Sweden extradition only applies if the act for which extradition is requested is equivalent to a crime that is punishable under Swedish law. Things like murder, rape, that sort of thing, and only if it is not beyond statute of limitations. But Sweden no longer prosecutes World War Two criminals, so this will not help us, especially since it appears Vogel has been generous with donations to Swedish politicians for the last twenty years."

"Trying to get him out would be muddy," says Mossad Director Dayan. "And Vogel would probably only get a heads up from Swedish authorities. Even if he didn't, the struggle over extradition would give him time to either wiggle free using lawyers, or else die under house arrest. In which case he never answers for his crimes."

"And that will not be tolerated," Zurer makes clear.

"Understood," Yarwick says, casting a look over at me that says *This bitch means business*. "Well, let us talk about what an operation like this might look like, and what resources we would each have to lend. Sweden is a friend to all of us in many ways, so we have to be delicate here. And I would request that, in the interest of maintaining good relations, we at least let the government of Sweden know that we have extracted Vogel, but only *after* the fact. And we let the Swedish prime minister know *why* we acted clandestinely inside his country."

"That is politics, and I leave that to you, if you wish. Just as long as no one outside of our joint operation knows what we are doing beforehand."

"You have my word on that, Ms. Zurer."

The OSI Director chimes in next, introducing himself and saying that he will be taking over for Yarwick, as she has other obligations towards JSOC. Yarwick assures Mossad she will still keep an eye on the operation and can be reached should they need further liaising with U.S. agencies, but after today she will take a back seat. The operation is now in Mossad's hands. I am on loan to them. No one currently on the phone—not OSI, not Mossad, not even Halbach— knows that I'm friends with Sophia, and that I brought this to Yarwick's attention. Yarwick said she told Mossad they had simply tracked Zurer's passport upon arrival and investigated her activities while in the States. Whether they believed that or not, the subject never comes up.

The POTUS, having been told in a PDB that Arumush should be considered a component in the Conflict, has agreed to greenlight a single team of trusted mercs to go after Vogel with Mossad's assistance. He does not know that the leader of the merc team will be Ares.

After the conference, Yarwick and I shake hands. She says she'll see me around, maybe pay me a visit when she gets the chance. Now she's off to check on the operations she's about to put into motion in Kiev. "OSI has the number to this phone," she says, handing me a new cell. "Keep it charged and on you, they'll be in touch."

She leaves the safehouse, and I'm left there thinking, *That's it, my last shot. There it goes.* Her Harley leaves a thin trail of dust on the road away from the safehouse. Never did get that kitty-cat date.

*

The guy they send to talk about Operation WOLFCATCHER with me is named Connor. That's all he goes by. He's short and slim, mocha-colored skin, well groomed, dresses in a jogging suit, like those guys in *The Sopranos* who show up on short notice to bury a dead body. Has the look of a utility man. He may or may not know who I am. I'm betting no one told him, and that Halbach or someone at the Company brought him in from another branch. A lone operative in SOG, like me, only his job is running agents, defectors, and informants, not infiltrating foreign nations. Right now I'm his agent, and though my dyed hair and beard change my appearance significantly, I get the feeling he slowly works it out over the next few weeks.

Connor showed up in a beat-up Ford F-150 and immediately commenced preparing me. He brought guns and body armor and radios to simulate a lone operative's communications with a Nest. He sets me up with a training regimen, to keep my skills sharp. He's a pretty good grappler, brown belt in Brazilian jiu-jitsu, and he and I spar two hours a day, five days a week.

See these hands. See them get back to work. See them work with surety. Feel them. Feel the bones and the marrow inside. Be aware of the mind commanding them.

My knee occasionally gives me problems. God only knows what I did to it over the years. Guess it's just the mileage.

Connor also happens to have an instrument capable of snaking inside my ear, attaching to my cochlear implant, and recharging the battery. I barely feel anything as he does it. Once he's finished, he says, "It'll stay off until you click it on in the field, so save its battery life for the op."

"Will I have a Nest?"

"That's what I've been told," he says.

WOLFCATCHER's success is dependent on how well Connor relays what Mossad is planning. I've never been to Sweden, and honestly never planned to go there as long as I lived, but it looks beautiful and Connor sure paints a picture of the obstacles our operation faces with Swedish law enforcement and citizens. "They don't like interference of any kind," he says. "Lots of wealthy people there, lots of vacation homes and getaway spots, lakes, canals, archipelagos, and big wide skies that glow with the Aurora Borealis."

Helsingborg is a coastal town filled with modern roadways and waterways and Medieval towers. A mix between old and new, with mild winters, a health-conscious population, new pollution controls, and an extremely low crime rate. A slice of paradise for those wanting to get away from it all.

"You can't be inserted by any legitimate means," Connor tells me bluntly one day when we're in a small study, which has probably been used to brief dozens of operatives before me. It occurs to me that I'm part of a secret club with a secret membership list, people who have come and gone from this safehouse and will never know who preceded or succeeded them. Life in the intelligence world is like that all the time. Like the DIC medal I was awarded. It can never be awarded publicly, I can never wear it publicly, and will in all likelihood be kept in a vault with others just like it, with no name written on it.

"Mossad wants you on site as quickly as possible, but I've been told by Ms. Yarwick you can't risk any more encounters with Customs, TSA."

"Okay, so, I won't be flying United," I joke.

"That's for sure. Got a special bird in a hangar just for you. You leave in one week, and you'll land on the island of Gotland— we've got people there—and then hop on a tourist boat in Visby.

Don't worry, Mossad assures us the captain is one of theirs, so nobody will ask you any questions, you'll get your own private quarters and be left alone. I've been told you're used to this kind of thing."

"I'm familiar, yeah."

"Good." He pulls out a USB drive and waves me over to the kitchen table. "Got the layout of your target's villa outside of Porjus on here. The contents are for your eyes only, not even I know what you're doing, for OPSEC's sake. Everything on here is the op as it stands right now. Names, streets, districts, ingress and egress points, all that." He drops it beside the laptop I've been provided. "Study it well. When you're done, destroy the drive and call me on the phone. Got it?"

"Got it."

"All right. I'm gonna head out soon and buy some more groceries for you. Need anything special, make a list now."

"Just the usual stuff, I guess. Bacon, eggs, bread, cereal. I do have a request, though. One maybe you can send up the chain of command."

"Uh oh."

"Uh oh?"

"I don't like requests that have to go up the chain," Connor says.

I smile. "It's nothing too obscene. I'd just like to visit a friend before I leave."

*

Yarwick wasn't okay with me meeting Sophia at night like I did last time. Though she trusted my skills, she didn't want to risk me getting caught. And I can't just walk in there and request to speak with her, since the staff knows me well enough that even this beard won't fool them all. So, Connor does his homework and sees that there is a day trip planned for some residents of Rose Lawn. A drive into the Thomasville Art Center. Connor said he got a message to Sophia, asking her to make sure she signed her name on the list of residents going on the trip.

When the three vans arrive from Rose Lawn and let loose their passengers, I at first think she didn't make it, something went wrong. Eighty-year-olds are moving with ginger steps out from the vans, and none of them are Sophia. Then, the van at the back slides open its side door, and a ramp slowly descends. A robot arm slowly lowers her down the ramp.

It's a beautiful sunny day. A lot of locals have come out to look at artwork put up by other locals, mostly middle school and high school students. I stalk Sophia and the orderly pushing her through the tents. She finally does as Connor asked her in the message, and tells the orderly she wants to be left alone near a fountain with a statue of some Civil War hero riding a horse that's come up on its hind legs. She shoos the orderly away like he's a gnat, her signature move, and I'm close enough to hear him say he'll come back to check on her intermittently. He goes off to watch the other residents, and I make my approach.

My limp is almost nonexistent, but it's there. The knee's really giving me problems. When I sit down on the bench by the fountain, Sophia gently nudges her wheelchair's right wheel to turn and face him.

"Hey there, old hen."

"Hey there, you little bastard."

We smile at each other. Behind me, water trickles out of the mouth of the horse.

"So, you're going somewhere."

"How'd you guess?"

"You've got your goodbye face on."

I snort. "Can't hide much from you."

"You never could."

"Yeah, well, you guessed right. I'm heading out soon." I look right at her. "And I wanted you to know something, because maybe no one else will tell you. I looked into what you told me about."

Her eyes squint. She's searching through the files in her dusty cabinets. Finds the one she's looking for. Brightens. "Abijah?"

"She's real, Soph. You didn't imagine her. Her name's Abijah Zurer and she does in fact work for Mossad, in Legacy, and she was indeed recommended by a Mr. Baudelaire of DGSE." She stares at me

349

for a second, her face a mask, revealing nothing. "A friend of mine did some digging on Zurer, and, thanks to you and Zurer's passion, there's been a coming-together of sorts. We're going to get him, Soph. We're going to get Vogel."

I see her nostrils flare just noticeably from the sudden gasp, the barely concealed excitement. She looks away from me. Her hands are in her lap, lightly tapping her thighs. She looks back at me. "Tell me you're not teasing an old woman, giving me false hope."

"I would never do that, Sophia."

She gauges me a moment longer, then nods and looks away. "He's…dangerous, Nathan."

"I know. And his people are highly trained. But I think I can manage."

"He's slippery. His mind is like an eel's, *that's* how he's evaded capture." She looks back at me. "You watch him. Watch out for his tricks."

"What's the deal with you and him, Soph? I mean, you never mentioned him to me before, then suddenly you see his picture and now you're a woman on a mission. You went out of your way to call DGSE and make time for this Baudelaire guy, then Zurer, then me. Who is he to you?"

Oie

How do I explain it to him? Nathan is in a job a lot like the one I was in, yes, but the methods are totally different, as are the settings. And times. How to explain the overall sense of the world in decay, and that you might never rebuild, even after the War was over? How to explain the loss of 73,000 Jews across France is just four years? How to explain the feeling of coming home to neighborless neighborhoods and then trying to recommence life as it was before?

We did not try to pretend that post-War France could ever be like it was pre-War. We did not because we could not. It was simply not possible. Just as easily count the stars as bring back old France. A fruitless exercise. And in the newly-formed intelligence-gathering world, it was a lot like the Wild West, lots of lawlessness, and what rules there were were easily bent.

The CIA was just forming around the same time as SDECE, Mossad, and dozens of other intelligence agencies. The Great War forced our hand. We had to develop new systems for dealing with both our enemies and allies, because it was then clear that we were a world connected, and allies could quickly transition over to the enemies column. We had to interface with each other in new ways, and those ways were being invented as we went along. New techniques were tested every day. That is how you got all the psychics, the groups like the FBI's "Naturals" who tried to divine the location of criminals and dead bodies by communing with spirits, and the enormous budgets spent on developing listening devices.

Entire networks were established just for agent handling, identifying those people in government who could be compromised, and psychologically controlling them over long periods. Channels were opened for easier defection, new laws were drawn up to allow those defectors new lives, and meticulous protocols were implemented to save a defector's whole family if the need came. Lots of bullshit martial arts came and went, our training increasing as our understanding of what worked and what didn't work became more refined.

It was all made up as we went along, nothing was too ridiculous to try at least once. Many things never worked. Some things worked just once, and never again. One of those things that worked just once and never again was *Le Concierge*, a honey trap of such astounding complexity it is almost embarrassing to think of now.

After the Great War, France shifted its focus to concerns other than Germany, which had utterly crumbled. France was soon embroiled in war against the Viet Minh in the First Indochina War. Almost all of these operations involved guerilla warfare around places like Saigon, while French forces slowly took control back over regions in both the north and south of Indochina. Talks were held in France to find a solution to the conflict before it got worse, but Ho was intractable, he fled back to Indochina and went underground. The war would cost us 75,000 French lives, 58,000 Vietnamese, and almost 300,000 Viet Minh. Taking place just a few years after the Great War, France was being hit heavily, we were losing our men again, women were left with children in homes that had only just seen repair.

For Operation *Le Concierge*, SDECE received multiple points of intel saying that the Viet Minh were getting aid from other foreign actors. Ho Chi Minh was vocal in asking for help, and did his best to make French forces sound like butchers who had no right to be operating as they were. In 1948, there was a spate of particularly brutal failings on the part of French forces. The rumor was that Ho had found people that had infiltrated the French government and were helping him to undermine French military operations.

Much of my work during this time was still in training female agents. I had done a few bits of field work, mostly just running agents, nothing too taxing. But as the war with Indochina increased in intensity, many of our jobs became more involved, more around-the-clock, more integral to the safety and security of France. There was rumor that a group of rich socialists calling themselves The Natural Path were working with certain governments to undermine France and her World War Two allies. They had not gained much influence internationally, but in Marseille they had done surprisingly well in setting up a chapter.

At the same time that SDECE heads were contemplating infiltrating civilian social clubs like The Natural Path, Department XV, my old stomping grounds, said that they had found evidence that a few people on the Wiesenthal List were living in Marseille. After an investigation, three of their names happened to pop up on The Natural Path's club membership list. This caused a *convergence*, as we used to call it, an issue that brings together multiple departments and appears to confirm, on multiple fronts, that something suspicious is going on. Convergences are usually a good sign you are on the right track.

And so I tell Nathan about Operation *Le Concierge*, in which I and six other female agents were brought in to talk about a possible approach to this club and its members. It was sickening to think that not even five years since the Nazi scum had fled, we actually had Frenchmen involved in a socialist party that seemed somewhat sympathetic to Hitler's cause. The dead Tyrant's seed still lived, and I agreed to do what I must to make sure France never suffered it again. Whatever SDECE required of me, I would do.

Anything.

My department head was a man named Victor Sartre, a keen man with intelligent eyes and who, incidentally, I had slept with many times to comfort him after his wife's death. When Victor remarried, we remained close friends, and never spoke of our relationship again. In those days, though, he favored me very much, and tried to coax me out of joining the operation and allowing the girls I had trained to take over. *Le Concierge* was going to involve seduction, and Victor very much cared about my safety.

"This is my work," I told him. "I joined for this reason, I will not back down now. I know what I am. I know that my legs and ass and tits are still in their prime, and if my heart can commit itself to France, then those other parts of me can pull their weight, too."

When I come to this part of the story, Nathan smiles his sincerest smile. It looks good on him.

The girls and I were briefed on all the key members of The Natural Path. We drove past their clubhouse at 106 La Canebiere in Marseille, near the old opera house, and staked it out for two months before any of us made our approach. I started by allowing Alice, she of the biggest tits, to strut in and out of the opera house twice a week. She always went alone, unescorted by a man, and usually at eleven o'clock at night, when the mostly male members of The Natural Path were filing out after one of their gatherings. It did not take long for Alice to latch on to two men, Arthur and Louis, and allowed them both to take her back to their homes, where they both fucked her all night. I chose Alice first, because she was much like me, no compunctions about fucking the enemy.

Next, I selected Sasha and Jeanne, a pair that looked so much alike they could be twins, and often passed as such. Together they seduced a man named Albert, an impressionable nineteen-year-old, naïve about the world, looking for his place in it, easily recruited by the socialists and fed their dreck propaganda. Sasha and Jeanne introduced him to the dildo and the concept of submission to women, and made him their lapdog in less than a week. He was smitten, and told them everything that happened at each meeting without thinking twice. They bent him in ways I'm sure he never imagined, and from behind the curtains, pictures were snapped by our agents.

Victor brought me in for weekly briefings, and was surprised at the progress my girls and I were making. His superiors, previously unsure of our approach, were suddenly giving us free reign. "Do whatever it takes," one of them said to me.

So we went further.

One of our main targets was a German named Hans, who, after rebuffing both Louise, who approached him at a theater, and Ines, who all but threw herself at him during a cocktail party on Le Vieux Port, we realized was homosexual. It took a bit of a search to find a man at SDECE willing to take that plunge.

Two other female operatives were sent in, both of them providing only steady companionship to club members without sex. One of my girls, Emma, had her man crawling naked into her lap like a baby and weeping as he offloaded his problems and admitted to all his life's sins and deficiencies. These sessions she recorded and fed to us.

Non-members were not allowed inside The Natural Path's chapterhouse. At least, that was the rule. But almost all of my girls (and my one male recruit) were able to persuade their men into a risqué tryst up on the rooftop, or on a chapterhouse balcony, or in the game room. On each visitation, recording devices were planted by my girls, and slowly a picture began to form of what exactly was happening inside The Natural Path.

Such scandalous use of female agents would never be tolerated today; at least, it would never be officially sanctioned. But in those days we were trying anything, and sticking to what worked. And this seemed to be working. For a time.

In all this time, Herr Vogel was rarely ever spotted coming or going from the chapterhouse. He struck me as a cold man. Distant. I followed him a number of times on foot, then in my car. I found where he lived in a house on the outskirts of Marseille. Watching him come and go, always alone, never with any friends or lady friends or prostitutes, I found him to be methodical. I decided that it was purposeful, this lonesomeness.

My old friends in Department XV discovered he had another getaway home more than an hour away in Uzès, where he walked the streets and spoke to the locals as one of their own. The monster walked among those he had invaded and smiled and waved naturally. Often, I found him outside, walking alone with a cane, setting up a camera on a tripod and taking pictures of the Pont du Gard. He took pictures at sunup, sundown, at night, in the rain, whenever. He was quiet, considerate, even went out of his way to be polite and open doors for people. He was sweet to children that he passed, and complimentary to elderly women in the park. He did not seem the slightest bit interested in torture or rape or vengeance against the French and her allies.

It was perplexing. I tried to match this man with the one Wiesenthal described in his List. It did not fit. Considering all I have learned recently from Abijah, I realize now that this is where I went wrong. This was all obviously an intricate, weeks-long SDR that Vogel was running, allowing people following him to reveal themselves to him, and to contradict the expectations of anyone who thought he might be *the* Wilhelm Vogel of Gestapo fame.

So he knew who I was even before I approached him.

He knew who I was when I flirted with him.

And he knew who I was the eleven times I let him have his way with me.

When Nate hears this, he lifts his chin, but otherwise keeps his expression neutral. Now he begins to see. Now he will understand. Everyone else I used my wiles on, both during the War and after, were undone by my actions. Vogel was the only one who used me and threw me away and I never got anywhere with him. Once he realized who and what I was, he began investigating the rest of The Natural Path's members, and found that all of them had coincidentally recently come across sexually adventurous girlfriends of their own. He found our recording devices, but, clever man that he is, did not remove them. He informed his fellow members and arranged to have false discussions that misled us.

Then, of course, there was the fiasco with Faustine, which nearly destroyed us. But that came to light much later.

What happened next was a six-month-long counterintelligence game that set us all back considerably. Resources were wasted and we had no idea. Meanwhile, the members of The Natural Path were having fun fucking us without us knowing that we were not getting anything real out of them.

"An orgy of disinformation" was how one of our department heads would put it months later, red-faced and screaming about our incompetence. I know the other girls were ashamed, not only for what they had done, but for the fact that they had been used in such a way and nothing came out of it. Years later, when one of the compromised SDECE agents was rooted out, we discovered that he had told Vogel and his people everything. Even our names and codenames. He knew that I was codenamed *Oie*, and that I was the leader of what he called the "Sirens," our little team of seductresses.

Knowledge of these things would come much later. At the time, we were certain things were working out just fine.

Vogel was a cruel lover. He did not spank gently, he slapped hard. Once or twice he slapped my face during coitus. He must have enjoyed himself immensely, the old torturer in him getting what he needed. It must have felt like the good old days of the War, sticking his cock into any place he wanted without fear of being caught. He and his friends must have enjoyed getting back at some of the people who had brought their precious regime to an end. And now I wonder if we only ever fed the monster more, gave him the drive to keep going, made him feel like his efforts could bear fruit. Just as the U.S. intelligence agencies who trained him after the War, perhaps we gave his methods validation, gave him this feeling of superiority.

We had confirmed for Vogel that he was, as he suspected, the alpha and the omega.

All I ever knew was when things went wrong. He became aware that the Goose and her girls were about to make their final arrest. This happened because we thought we had enough information from a Viet Minh defector to tie The Natural Path's members to Ho's counterintelligence teams in Indochina. I was there that morning, at a hotel in Paris, on my knees, performing my work for SDECE when the call came in to his house. An assistant answered, and came rushing in while Vogel was going at me, and shouted that a source said French Police were on their way.

Vogel pushed me away, started getting clothed. It was almost humorous, watching his manhood flop around like that and slowly shrivel as the fear of the approaching arrest set in. I kept my smile to myself, and privately reveled in the fact that soon, very soon, he would be in custody and I would be fully clothed, staring at him from the other side of the bars.

But that did not happen. What happened instead was that Vogel shot two officers as they stormed his house. I got halfway dressed in the time it took the police to get there, so I chased him out of his house. He smiled when he saw me coming after him with the only weapon I could find, a butcher's knife from the kitchen. In that moment, I knew that he knew. That is the *exact* moment when I knew that he had known all along.

It happened to be *la Fête nationale*, Bastille Day, when he fled out into the streets. Crowds dispersing from the parades were a convenient way for him to vanish.

Three weeks later we stormed a hotel in Marseille and caught two of his friends, but once again Vogel slipped away, out a back window. I chased him through the night, through fog-choked streets, pushing aside vendors and darting through multiple lanes of traffic. He escaped again. I cursed at God that night.

It was the last we ever saw of him physically. A month later the famous note arrived at SDECE headquarters, where he boasted and mocked us, called me "that French tart who sniffed my ass as I slipped away." We came across pictures, and in the coming years, we saw video footage of him getting in and out of cars, but it was usually old, outdated. Vogel never again stayed anywhere for very long. He kept moving, never becoming complacent.

It was a marathon for him. He just had to keep doing it for ten, twenty more years, enough that funds and resources were no longer allotted to the hunt. Then it must have become easier. His face changed. His hair turned gray, then white. He probably grew beards, changed his name, bounced around the globe using the skills he had accrued over a lifetime.

"And at some point acquainted himself with computers and the business of running mercenary security forces," Nathan says, looking across at me.

I come back to the present. The warm spring air smells nice. It is bracing. It has been a long run, for both Vogel and myself. I feel like I was an agent just yesterday. Someone must've hit the fast-forward on the movie of my life, and now I'm here. Old. Forgetful. Useless. How did that happen?

"Vendettas as old as ours must seem like a joke," I say, "but only if you were not there. But if you had looked into the faces of Vogel's victims, which I eventually did over the years…"

Nathan nods. "I know. Different story."

"Very different."

"I'm going to get him, Soph. You have to believe that."

"When you do, will you send me a picture?"

"Of course."

"And…give him a message, if you would please."

"What's that?"

"Tell him the French tart sends her regards. Tell *Bite Molle* that the Goose chased as long as he ran."

He promises. At least, I think he does. Hard to say, because the next thing I know I'm lying down in this damn bed and our conversation almost seems like a dream. It never happened. I think it did, though. I believe it. I have to. Time skips again and it is the next morning. A light rain has come in. I look out the window and for a brief instant forget again, then remember what I had forgotten. It is strange, feeling myself going in and out, knowing that I am going in and out. Terrifying at times.

Look at these hands. Shaking. I wonder if Isabella will visit me today…

PART FOUR

The Ghost

28

When Connor comes for me, I'm waiting outside with my single backpack. No other luggage. I hop inside his F-150 and we head east towards Langley Air Force Base. Halfway there, I say to him, "I have a favor to ask."

Connor takes only a little persuading. It's a short pitstop at my home. I don't walk inside. Rather, I make sure no one's looking, and I step around to the back porch. I stand there for a second making kissing noises. I hear a meow. I turn, smile, and kneel when Edward comes trotting up to me. I hand him some tuna I saved from the groceries Connor got for me. "Hey, little man. Good to see you." He purrs and nuzzles me once he's done feasting. "You're welcome. You take care now." He meows again. "I might have a friend for you when I get back. I'll see you then."

I'm in the car and waving off Connor's strange look. He didn't see me go inside and he didn't see what I did out back. He drives in silence. At Langley AFB, I pause before getting on the jet. I take a look around, breathing in the fresh American air, wondering, as always, if this is the last time.

Once again no one asks any questions. I get on board a Boeing C-17 Globemaster III, a massive military transport with weapons and supplies meant for Sweden. Though they have remained mostly neutral, Sweden has requested special equipment when it comes to defending their waters against a possible response from the Eastern Alignment. The U.S. would like very much for Sweden to maintain good control of Gotland, as it is a place of strategic military importance in the Baltic Sea. That may come in handy for the U.S. and its allies down the road, when Sweden may eventually have to pick a side.

I sit in the main passenger area with three grunts, a lieutenant, two CIA officers in pressed suits, and an Army colonel. No one talks to me. They treat me like they treat the CIA guys, probably assume I'm one of them. They're half right, I suppose. I split my time between napping and reading a newspaper (remember those?), and catch up on the chaos that's unfolding in the waters beneath us.

Nine hours later, we land in Gotland. I show my papers to just one French officer at the airport, a guy named Gabriel who I've been assured is one of ours. Gabriel escorts me to a car outside the airport driven by a silent bald man who only ever glances at me through the rearview mirror. He takes me to Visby, to a luxurious Vant 880, a semi-cruise ship for the rich that carries a max of eighty. Once again, I am ushered through without even a glance at my passport. The captain shows me my quarters, where I stay for four days.

I meditate. And when I do, I think of Sophia. I think of how far she's come to see this shit brought to a close. I think of Yarwick, and other missed opportunities. Scott, wherever he is. Harrison Dean, who invited me to take a trip to Australia with him in college. He stayed there. Wonder if I would have.

I think of Zurer, whoever she is, and what vile determination must live in her gut to propel her forward on this kind of operation. I think of Karambit, and the Cosmodrome, and the impending war that may render all of this moot. I think of my part in it all. I decide it's a funny world.

You don't have it, Ares! You don't have what it takes!

Thinking on Karambit's last words, I think I can see why Sophia has a vendetta after all these years. I wonder if it will be sixty years before I get to see Karambit dead.

Then it hits me. All of us in the intelligence world are someone's Vogel. I think of Farooq Salam, and I know that somewhere out there are people who would love to pay me back for what I did to him. But at least I never enjoyed it like Vogel did. At least I have that separating us.

Please. I have children. I have three children.

See these hands. See them. Steady as a fucking rock.

We follow the coast for the entire trip, coming within sight of beaches but we never go ashore. Parties are held on the upper deck, mostly old people, tourists from a dozen nations. No one speaks to me, and I speak to no one. The captain approaches me only twice to ask, "Is everything to your satisfaction?" I nod, and he leaves me alone. I sip a Mediterranean wine and think of the drinks I shared with Yarwick. I wonder who the mole is. I wonder if we'll ever know.

Finally, on the morning of the fourth day, there is an announcement over a speaker that tells all of us that Helsingborg is just coming within view. I go to the window in my room, open it, and look outside at a gorgeous port city lit by a newborn sun. The windows in the towers are radiant and glimmering. The waves sough lightly against the ship's hull. Salty spray comes through the window, misting my face.

When we dock, I shake hands with the captain, thank him, and step off the boat. My limp is a little more pronounced. I take an aspirin to handle it.

At the foot of the stairs I see a familiar tan, bald head. Fardün isn't really smiling, but he isn't really grimacing, either. It's something in between that only he can do. He's dressed casual, khakis and a light jacket. He looks good. You'd never know he'd been shot. He looks like someone's lost uncle, not a trained assassin.

"Well, well, well," he says. "How the fuck did we end up here, Adamson?"

"I'm not sure."

He eyeballs me for a second, then takes out a cigarette and lights it. "How are you?"

Can't tell if he's sincere or sarcastic. "I'm okay. How 'bout you?"

"I hate this fucking place. It's freezing."

Yes, it is cold. Our breath is coming out in white clouds. "You sure about this?"

He knows what I'm talking about. "It's like you said. I tried to kill you, you tried to kill me. Even Steven, eh?" He shrugs and blows out a cloud of smoke. "Besides, you could've left me for dead in Mongolia, but you took the time to get me to a hospital. Even if it was to help capture Matveyev, it was decent of you. I've come to terms with it. I still hate you, but I've come to terms." He smiles that smile.

I don't know if I can trust Innick Fardün any farther than I can throw him, but his reputation has been shattered now that Karambit's been freed and he knows that he's now on CIA's radar, so if he wants to keep us as powerful friends and not powerful enemies he'll go along. Plus, he knows I'm a free agent, still disavowed as far as the world is concerned, handing me over now is meaningless. Plus, he's getting paid. Plus, Yarwick says he's been handed a new set of IDs. It's a bridge he can't burn without losing everything.

That's a lot of reasons to go along. Still, we're both mercs now and we're being utilized like guerilla insurgents, so there's no code of conduct for us. We're disposable. If we kill one another at this point, Langley won't shed much of a tear. I've already got my medal, but I won't get my star on the wall. It'll all be cleaned up. It is what it is.

"Are we cool?" I ask.

"What is this? 'Cool?'"

"It means are we okay to not kill each other."

He looks me up and down. Take another toke. "Your people promised to relocate my family. Which, if I'm being honest, I don't know if that was so much a favor, or a subtle way of letting me know that they know where my family lives. Either way, it worked. My family is being moved someplace safe."

"So, you're ready to do this?"

"I've been waiting here a whole week, Adamson," he says, exhaling a cloud. "The food here is shit. Want me to tell you how bad all my injuries hurt in this cold weather? A fucking lot."

A beat of silence. He takes another toke of his cig and shoves his hands into his pockets.

"Are you going to tell me what it is we're actually doing here? The guy your people sent with instructions wouldn't tell me shit, besides how to get here."

"Well, let's go rustle up some answers, whattaya say?"

He stares at me, ruminating. Thin white clouds roil out from his mouth and nostrils. He shakes his head ruefully. "I can't believe I'm doing this. Lead the way."

We walk off the pier and into a city almost as cold as Ulaanbaatar. I finally turn on my watch and send an e-mail, letting Mossad and OSI know that I have landed and made contact with my first team member. Operation WOLFCATCHER commencing.

*

Next order of business make contact with the Mossad field agents in charge of the local safehouse. Weaving our way through Långa Oton, passing the street vendors fanning the charcoal of their braziers and pushing out smoke fragrant with sausages and shrimp and

363

mashed potatoes, all being crammed together in the ultimate Swedish version of a hot dog called *tunnbrödsrulle*, Fardün and I speak very little.

I blend in just fine here, the fact that I don't speak the local language is irrelevant; virtually everyone here speaks some level of English. There are a couple of shops that even remind me of home. Tattoo parlors advertise Nordic and Viking designs. There's a Burger King that sells meals half the size of Burger Kings back home. A store selling cool T's and jewelry has the front door wide open and I can hear them blasting a techno version of "Tainted Love." I suddenly recall lip-synching to that with Scott, our girlfriends Angie and Rebecca laughing hysterically at us.

Where did everybody go?

"This place gives me the fucking creeps," Fardün says.

"It does? Why?"

"Never seen so many white people in one place. They look pale enough to be dead." He laughs. "Imagine having to grow up in a place this fucking cold."

I glance over at him as we weave our way through a crowd at a crosswalk. "What kind of place did you grow up in?"

Fardün finishes his cigarette and flicks it to the ground. He gets an ugly stare from a woman who saw him do it. "Gödöllő, a town outside of Budapest. First ten years, anyway. My mother was Mexican, but she moved to Hungary chasing a boyfriend who eventually broke up with her. She got a job in the embassies, in outreach. We traveled a lot. She married my father and we stayed in Puerto Rico until I was grown up. Then I went to college in Tokyo, then did a year in California."

"No shit? Guess you really got around."

He nods. "I liked California the best. And Puerto Rico. In those places, the women in the summertime…you never see asses like that in Hungary," he laughs. "I never lost my Hungarian citizenship, though. I returned, and joined the military."

"Which branch?"

"Defense Forces, HDF Twenty-four *Bornemissza Gergely* Reconnaissance Regiment."

"Bet you saw a lotta action."

"Actually," he says, "the Russians were doing a lot to bolster our defenses, and our government cut back on our operations to save on money, diverting funds to feel-good socialist measures." He shrugs. "But I can speak five languages, and I was good at stealth and reconnaissance, and at fixing things, so the Russians we worked with took me and my unit under their wing. They taught us a lot."

"How long did you stay in?"

Fardün chuckles. "Until we started fighting rebel uprisings in three different countries." He fishes around in his pocket for another cigarette. He puts it between his lips but doesn't light it. "When I dropped out, Információs Hivatal came calling—civilian intelligence office. They paid to further my education, and I performed penetration operations for eight years. Then I quit. Had a nervous breakdown. Lost my families."

"Families? Plural?"

"I had two wives. Neither of them knew about each other. Still don't, to my knowledge. Three sons with one wife, a daughter and a son with the other. Both began because of spy work."

Now the conversation moves smoothly. Much better than any other we've had before. We're two ex-soldiers now, talking shop. Both of our careers diverted into clandestine intelligence-gathering work, and both of them led to wildly different results. I have no family, he has two. Strange.

"Each of your wives, they were initially targets for attack vectors?" I ask. Meaning they were targets he was sent to compromise, to spy on them, to pry information out of them.

He's not offended by the wording of my question. "Yes. One was a woman with FSB, the other a spy for Iran's MOIS."

"That's...crazy, Fardün. I hope you don't mind my saying."

"I don't mind. It *is* crazy. It is all craziness. The places we end up..." He sighs and shrugs. "Anyways, both of my wives have since had to flee because of me. Their bosses found out they were compromised. They would have been executed for colluding—even though neither of them had any idea—so they both ran. My Iranian wife is still on the run. Because of me. They hate me and love me."

"Sorry to hear that," I say, and mean it.

"We end up where we're supposed to," he says. "How much farther? Should we grab a cab?"

The coords to the safehouse have been e-mailed to me. I follow the directions on my watch, Fardün and I move with a casual SDR to see if anyone might be following. Not likely, but ever since NARROW VOID I've picked up the habit of always assuming I'm being watched. So we slide through a few shops, exit out the back doors wherever possible. I pause at a Systembolaget, one of the shops in the government-owned chain of liquor stores, and lead my partner inside. We get a taste of the local flavor. Sweden is pretty relaxed on public drinking laws, you can drink your alcoholic beverage as you walk.

Fardün is happy about that. "Once in a while the white people have a good idea," he says, sipping as we make our way across a railroad track.

The main streets are wide open and clean, with plenty of space for both foot and vehicle traffic. The sound of bicycle wheels buzzing is omnipresent. Their riders go zigging and zagging from street to park and back to street. Many of the buildings look like castles, they're shaped like squares with the corners built like tall, Medieval cylindrical towers, often topped by a spire for good measure. And fountains. Fountains everywhere.

As we walk, I give Fardün the rundown on what we're here to do. He's heard only broad strokes, I'm giving him the details, leaving only Sophia's name out of it. He listens like a professional, absorbing it all, only asking brief questions when he needs clarification.

It is just past noon when we reach the safehouse on Kung Kristoffers Gata. The building is innocuous, just one in a series of white apartment buildings. We pause to let two cyclists zip by and then cross the street. We don't go directly for the safehouse in case we're being followed. Instead, we go past it, walk two streets over, and double-back, checking for any familiar faces that keep pace.

When we finally come to the safehouse, I knock once. The door opens and we step inside.

There are two Jewish men who wave us into the living room. They introduce themselves briefly as Saul and Abner. Both are sharply dressed and with short, precise haircuts. They could be brothers. They shake our hands, but cautiously. They don't know that I'm ex-CIA, they just think I'm as much a merc as my companion. All they know is that CIA trusts us to do the job they are too understaffed to do.

After I drop my bag and have a seat, they ask if we want something to eat or drink. I accept a bottled water. Fardün wants another beer. Saul sits in front of us. Seems to be the lead agent. Leaning forward, elbows on knees, fingers steepled, he gets down to business.

"First, we would just like to thank you for helping us in this endeavor," he says. "This has been a matter of great consternation for some of us, but not enough of us. Agent Zurer has done a lot to raise awareness of these issues and keep prosecuting the people who try to outrun their past."

I nod. "Glad we could help." I open the bottle of water but I don't drink it. I accepted it out of courtesy and to seem pleasant, but I've heard of Mossad tracking some agents using Argin-5. No one knows what it is, maybe it's a radioactive isotope, or else some kind of nanomachine—whatever it is, it is believed that they can track any person that has it in their bloodstream. I'm meant to be among friends here, allies, but all of my colleagues have been through the same training I have, so they understand.

Fardün drinks his beer like he's at a stag party.

"We hope your trip was a good one," Saul says.

"Very relaxing, thank you. Hope I didn't miss anything by taking the long way."

Saul glances sidelong at Abner. Seems to check something. Then looks back at me. "Nothing has really changed. We've had soft surveillance on Vogel's estate for the last week, nothing that ought to catch his eye, just drive-bys and a few joggers. We're certain he's still in there. He has had some guests over, though. Not sure who they are, only got a snapshot of one, we're running his face through facial-recognition now."

"Is he entertaining them?" Fardün asks, and belches.

"Satellite shows they're playing golf most days. Seems like a retreat with friends."

I raise an eyebrow. "Vogel plays *golf*? I'd heard his home had a golf course, but he's still playing, at a hundred years old?"

"I don't know how well he plays, but yes, he appears to go out there with his guests."

"Well, I guess it's true what they say about active and sedentary lifestyles."

"He does appear active," Saul says, and gestures over at Abner. "We've spotted him on a few jogging runs. He doesn't run fast, but he does powerwalking, carries one-kilogram weights in each hand. The third hole of the golf course is very flat, and also serves as a gun range. He likes to shoot rifles out there. Occasionally he goes hunting. Once every September he goes to northern Sweden to hunt moose, always with a guide who does most of the work for him, Vogel just pulls the trigger."

Too bad it's not anywhere close to September, it would be easy to grab him out there in the open, away from his home and the city and all law enforcement. Could probably even arrange a helicopter to snatch him up. "Got a layout of his home?"

They take us into the dining room, where they have everything ready. Two maps on the wall show the wilderness surrounding Porjus, and on the dining-room table there is a large blown-up satellite map of Vogel's entire estate, golf course and all. There's another map on the wall that shows only his house, magnified. A two-story monster, a castle with dozens of rooms, left over from the 17th century. Some rich guy back then decided he wanted a brick-for-brick remake of the Bäckaskog Castle. It only got half built, abandoned, then reworked with modern (for the time) accoutrements, and Vogel bought it ten years ago and had it altered further.

"It's a maze," Abner says, speaking for the first time. "Getting schematics on it was next to impossible, and most of what we got is old, and we completed our own versions based on speculation, but *informed* speculation."

"Informed?"

"We had some of the architects who work for Mossad designing hidden rooms in embassies take a look at it. They agree it's…well, it's complex."

"Looks like something out of a fucking storybook," Fardün says. He's standing right next to me, his beer breath wafting all over me.

"Probably one of the reasons Vogel liked it for his purposes," says Saul. "He may be old, but all signs are that his mind is like a steel trap. Just like he's kept his body mobile, so too has he kept his mind. We did some digging, and found that three separate security companies have been hired by Vogel over years to install alarms, sensors, cameras. He also rotates security guards in and out, and never places them at the same post for long."

"Reduces complacency," Fardün says, nodding in admiration.

Saul taps his temple with his forefinger. "This Nazi is still savvy to the game."

"Any taps on this guy?" I ask.

"We have not tapped his phones, but we have some guys in our IT department who managed to get into his e-mails. He writes everything in code, no names, no locations. We did find, to our surprise, that he's the publisher of *Daseinskampf.*"

"What is that?"

Abner says, "It's a newspaper meant to spread propaganda about perceived enemies to the Aryan race—Jews, Slavs, and whoever sides with them. *Daseinskampf* has found its way into many countries, and has decent circulation in the United States among the alt-right, and much of the U.K. The word means 'struggle for existence.' Herr Vogel is still fighting the fight, all these years later."

"Got his fingers in a little bit of everything, huh?"

Saul nods. "Yes, my friend. He has."

*

We get to know Saul and Abner. Both are family men, both are descended from Holocaust survivors. That explains their commitment to Legacy, which they say they've made clear to their children is important. The persecution of those who persecuted so many innocents is paramount to them. Their wives are both very supportive of their work, and Abner's wife has even used her journalism degree to help in some ways, by traveling the world to interview every Holocaust survivor she can find.

They both describe it as a dying art, this Nazi hunting, which is not surprising as the villains themselves are all dying. They describe this as Zurer's crusade, and that she alone has kept interest alive in agencies across multiple continents, and continually forces Interpol to keep operations dedicated to this work. I'm surprised to learn that my own American OSI has pledged to keep hunting Nazis into the 2040s, long past when they all must be dead, and that their pledge comes largely because Abijah and her people have been so adamant.

The quality of their advance work speaks to their qualifications. Not only have the two men been keeping tabs on Vogel since finding him, not only have they mapped out his estate and painted a picture of Arumush's infrastructure, not only have they brought me the gear I need to complete my task, but they've also ran *computer simulations* on a one-man infiltration/exfiltration scenario. It's part of a new program Mossad has, kind of like a video game, like *The Sims*, where the "players" map everything out, place guards, build the landscape, and then put on goggles and step into virtual reality. The AI on the bad guys in the sim is state-of-the-art, and shift changes and general foot patrols serve to give them an idea of problems of cover, concealment, even the differences between a cloudy night and a full moon, and the directions the shadows will lean.

None of this VR sim is conclusive, of course, but it has helped them select the best ingress and egress points, our best points of cover, and gives them an estimate of how many men Fardün and I may have to neutralize in order to reach Vogel and extract him.

Best case scenario, they say, one man dies. In some of the simulations, that one man is me. Fardün will be giving distant cover, doing what he does best with a sniper rifle at long range, so he's mostly safe.

The sim even has a setting that places an Aurora Borealis in the skies. "They shouldn't be happening this late in the year, but they have been. The theory is changes to Earth's poles have altered their schedule. In any case, it is entirely possible for you to encounter them. Should they light up the night, it could be a problem, not the least of which for your night-vision goggles."

When they show me the gear, I'm pretty impressed. Weapons and body armor are optimal, as is the black heat-masking suit I'll be wearing under it all. I pick up the FAMAS-G2, heft it, been a while since I held one of these. The SIG Sauer and its holster are more familiar. The Dragon body armor is a good blend between protection and flexibility. The vest has spare clips and two flash-bangs. Even the boots have a jungle platform outsole for aggressive traction. I suit up, just to test that it all fits.

"Remember, alive to stand trial," Saul says. "But if you have to…"

I nod, and look over at Fardün. "We got it. Right?"

He nods. "Right."

"And here, find a pocket in your gear for this," Saul says. He hands me a flat, rectangular, palm-sized device with a finger-sized wand sticking out of one end.

"What's this?"

"An IR-based hard drive reader/copier. We call it the DIVINER. You can download any hard drives within range via an infrared link. Just point it at any computer's USB port, and it'll do the rest. The light will turn green on the side when it's finished the download." He adds, "If you don't find Vogel there, at least bring back some useful knowledge about his operations."

"Got it. What's the range?"

"Twenty feet."

Later, Fardün gets a look at his sniper rifle. His request went through Yarwick to Mossad, and it appears he got his wish. An exact copy of his personalized Barrett M82, with a long silencer, custom scope, expertly crafted. He disassembles it on a coffee table to make sure all is as he requires.

"You know," he says, peering into the receiver, "I heard on the news that this whole part of the world may soon be contested waters. Gotland being a strategic point in the Baltic Sea, and all."

"Yeah, I heard the same." I'm sitting across from him, screwing on the SIG's suppressor and making sure it's a perfect fit.

"What's it like, seeing the effects of your work ripple across the planet?"

"If it wasn't me, it would've been someone else."

"Would it? Would it, really, Adamson? I wonder, because from what I hear, the mission in Russia was a very tight thing. You barely made it. Five, maybe only six guys in the world could've pulled that off, I'd wager." He points over my shoulder. "And now, that work follows you here."

I look where he's pointing. Behind me, a TV has been left on. It's muted, and much of the subtitles is in a language I don't understand, but I can see the scene on the local news. They're showing a map of Sweden and its surrounding waters and islands. Tiny, red-blinking submarine shapes are peppered all around the waters, with either Russian or Chinese flags hovering over each of them.

"Yes," says Abner, hovering in the doorway nearby. "The EA is rumored to be moving around in these waters. Could be that the war comes here, after all."

I look at Fardün. He looks at me. We return to addressing our weapons.

*

Porjus is a twenty-hour drive north of Helsingborg in their jeep. Saul drives. Abner's in the passenger seat. Fardün sleeps beside me in the back. I watch the cityscape vanish almost instantly and now we're racing across an empty highway through flat pastoral fields, which are broken intermittently by dense green forests. A place where cattle and giant waterwheels aren't just for looks. It's getting colder by the mile. Thick clouds roll overhead. Weathermen are saying they're gonna hang around another day, then it's clear skies.

They bring us to the outskirts of Porjus, population 334, and park us at the edge of a small cluster of buildings. What passes for "town" around here. Verdant green hills surround us. The cool wind blows gently through the grass, carrying the scent of birch and maple and pine and fly honeysuckle. I can see why a hundred-year-old bastard would want to retire here.

They take me inside what is apparently the only inn in all of Porjus. It's empty this time of year, but I'll bet tourists flood it during prime Aurora Borealis season. There's an old woman behind a counter where a mounted moose head looms above her. Abner negotiates us a room. They've brought binoculars and nets, completing our cover as birdwatchers and small game enthusiasts, should anyone ask. Mossad picked a pair of thorough guys.

The room is two-bedroom. Abner doesn't stay. He says something to Saul, then they embrace. He turns to me and shakes my hand and says, "I've got another errand to run." He shakes Fardün's hand. "I'll be there to perform the distraction you need. After that, I may never see you again. Good luck to you. And if I don't see you again, thank you."

"Not a problem, Abner," I tell him. "It's our pleasure."

He heads for the door. Stops. Turns back to me. "For Sophia."

I look at him. Guess Zurer told them the whole story. "Damn straight. For Sophia."

When he leaves, Fardün looks at me. "Who's Sophia?"

Saul rolls out the map again and we get to work, reviewing what we know. Fifteen guards. Always fifteen guards. Two on stationary patrols on the north, south, east, and west sides. Two on the rooftop. Two doing a roving foot patrol inside the halls of Chateau de Vogel. Two supervisors walking or driving around the grounds outside, checking in regularly with each post, making sure no one's asleep. And one personal bodyguard always right next to Vogel.

Saul did some checking into the guards. Three of them came up ex-British military, two of them former Blackwater mercs, the rest are unknowns, but it's a safe bet they're just as professional.

"And they're all killers," Saul says. "Extremely bad people. Guns for hire. Most of them wanted in multiple nations for serious contract killings."

Beside me, I can feel Fardün pointedly not saying a word.

"We will go birdwatching in the forest here," Saul goes on, pointing on the map. "Two kilometers from Vogel's estate. I'll hike with both of you until about halfway, which will take us almost to midnight, then go back to the car and wait for your signal. I'll be listening to your transmissions to the Nest, and when you give the word, I'll drive to either exfiltration point you tell me to. With Vogel or without him, I'll get you out, my friends." He pats his jacket. He's carrying a piece under there, ready to give me cover fire should I need it.

"We appreciate it. Who's in my Nest? Just Zurer and your people?"

"As far as operational assistance, yes, but I have been told that two or three of your people will be listening in, as well, advising as need be."

"Sounds good. What kind of assistance are your people giving?"

"The moment you tell us you're making your final approach, we cut all landlines and an MQ-9 Reaper drone overhead will blanket the airwaves with white noise. If anyone tries to use their radios or make emergency calls to police, they won't get through to anyone."

"Good deal."

Saul looks at me seriously, and claps my shoulder. "Are you ready for this, my friend?"

"Born, bred, and trained to be ready."

"And you?" he says to my companion.

Fardün gives a thumbs up.

"What is it your American military says? 'Hooyah?'"

I snort out a laugh. "That's an Army thing, actually. And I was Navy. But I appreciate the sentiment." I return the shoulder clap. "Let's go bag us a Nazi."

*

The drive is scenic and silent. It's as if the whole countryside senses what we're up to. It's 10 PM on the dot when we reach the roadside rest stop, with just four parking spaces, all of which are empty. There's nothing here but an eight-by-eight shack with nothing inside but two vending machines and a landline phone for people in emergencies. A map of the area is on the wall for birdwatchers and hunters.

Saul takes the lead. Fardün brings up the rear. It's cold, near freezing. We step into the forest and hike until we come to a small rope bridge that Norrbotten County Wildlife keeps up. The bridge is precarious, old, and it stretches the narrowest part of Lule River. We step onto a hiking trail that stretches from Porjus to neighboring Gällivare. We follow the trail a quarter-mile, then turn northwest, into thicker woods. It's here that Saul gives me and Fardün a final clap on the shoulders and says, with white breath-clouds coming out of his mouth, "You're on your own from here on out, but I'll be listening for your signal. Good luck, my friends."

I make a fist. He bumps it. I don't know if he has the gesture where he's from or if he's just seen enough American movies. "Thanks, Saul. See you on the other side."

He turns and heads out.

Fardün looks up at the sky, then at me. "I hope I don't die in this fucking place."

I take a moment to secure all my gear. I pull on my NVGs and kneel. I shut my eyes, meditate for a few minutes, go to the Drifting Place. This time it's the peak of a snowy mountain, overlooking an endless white range. Fardün just stands by and says nothing. When I open my eyes again, all is clear to me. I look up through the forest canopy. The skies are clear, all clouds have dispersed. Once again it's Betelgeuse and Rigel. "Hey boys. Long time no see." They're joined by a faint reddish-greenish glow somewhere to the north. The Aurora is cueing up.

"What?" asks Fardün, looking up at the sky.

"Nothing." I click my teeth. I hear a short beep in my ear. "Nest, this is Gemini. Do you read? Over."

"Gemini, Nest. We read you loud and clear."

My heart skips. "Yar—eh, that you, cat lover?"

"It's me, Gemini."

"Jesus. Good to hear your voice." And it is.

"Good to hear yours, too. I'm here to liaise between all agencies involved. Last-minute decision."

Hearing Yarwick's voice emboldens me in ways I didn't know I needed. "Copy that, Nest. Glad someone made the smart decision of putting you in charge." I sigh. "Well, what's say we get to it?"

"That sounds good to us, Gemini."

I look at Fardün. "You know where you're going?"

"Yes. Don't die. Your people promised me a bonus if you don't die."

"Be a shame if you lost that bonus."

"It would."

He's taking off his thick gloves, leaving only his thin shooter's gloves. He nods. "In case I don't get to say it later, 'Fuck you, Adamson.'" He turns and heads out, leaving me in the dark.

I take one more look around, judging the lay of the land. Then I'm on the move. One foot in front of the other.

29

I've never seen the Aurora Borealis. Never even had an inclination to. But when I peel off my NVGs and see the colors begin to bloom in the sky, green and pink and red, I understand what all the fuss was about. Had a friend named Alan Baxter back in the Navy who had just one dream destination: anywhere he could see the Aurora. Never understood him. Figured it was overblown. Alan, old pal, I can still see you sitting on the edge of the bunk, the acne thick on the right side of your face, your slanted smile and dream-filled eyes as you describe what a religious experience it would be to see the Northern Lights. Jesus, I hope you got to see this, brother.

It's like thin sheets and threads of light are being draped across the sky by the invisible hands of gods. The night is lit up brighter than I would have ever imagined it could be. And with the gibbous moon out, it's like the world is conspiring against my mission tonight.

The golf course begins where the trees end. I move in a low crouch, my FAMAS in hand but kept low. There are a few course lights, I suppose if Vogel and guests ever want to play a night game, but most of them are off. I stop and kneel every hundred yards or so, scan the area, and listen. Saul and Abner said there were no sign of dogs, but that doesn't mean there aren't any.

The large half-castle/half-mansion is framed against the horizon west of me. The red-green threads of light seem to be snaking towards it, leading me right to it. I'm up and moving. Slinking parallel to the forest in case I have to dive into it. The world is tomb-quiet.

"Gemini, Nest," says Yarwick.

I stop and kneel. "Nest, Gemini," I whisper. "Go ahead."

"We may have hit a snag."

Don't like snags. Snags are never good. "What's the problem?"

"We have an issue with the bird overhead." She means the drone, Mossad's MQ-9 that's supposed to blanket this area in white noise so that if anyone sees me my enemies can't call in backup or local cops or sound any kind of general alarm to Vogel's friends abroad.

"What kind of issue?" I ask.

"We have LOS on it." Loss of signal. "Not sure what happened but our friends are working on getting it back online."

I look up at the sky. Somewhere in all that exploding light was a helpful angel, and now it's gone. "Do I wait to see if it comes back online, or keep moving?"

"We're determining that now. Standby."

While they're figuring that out, I step over into the woods and take cover behind a tree. And wait. Two minutes later, I get my response. "Gemini, it looks like the drone issue cannot be determined at present. Our friends are requesting that you move ahead with mission. I'm not so sure. I'd rather have the certainty of total blackout. I leave it to your discretion."

My discretion. I look up at the Northern Lights, leading me on. I look behind me, and consider the retreat. I've never liked going backwards once I've gone so far forward. That's a pet peeve all of us in Special Forces and SOG have. Make progress, cover ground, and don't give up the ground you've gained. It can be a serious problem, that habit, because sometimes you have to be patient, retreat when necessary, give ground to gain more later.

"Nest, Gemini. I'm moving ahead with mission." For Sophia. I don't tell her that, but Yarwick probably gets it.

"Understood, Gemini." Her voice sounds tense. "We've still got you by satellite GPS, we're monitoring you from Among High and we've got real-time vid, so all of that is still on your side. Everything *seems* clear." Emphasis on *seems* is telling. She really doesn't want me to continue. She's got a bad feeling.

"Copy. Gemini is mobile."

I slide out of the forest and move with soft knees across the golf course. I notice my right knee is a bit sore. The more I walk on it, the more it starts to send tiny pings of pain up my thigh. Jesus, tonight of all nights.

I cross the third hole, the one Vogel uses as a gun range. I pass the hole-riddled man-shaped targets and use one of them for cover. I stop, scan the area, look up at the sky. The Northern Lights are leading me. I'm up and moving west, towards the dark castle on the horizon.

*

The first guards I encounter are near the east wall, facing out. The wall is three feet tall and made of solid brick topped with bars that add an extra four feet with sharpened prongs at the top. There are cameras spread every twenty yards or so. I find the blind spots, belly crawl between the cams, and climb the wall. As soon as I land on the other side, I go to my stomach, flat against the well-manicured grass, and check my immediate vicinity. NVGs show me everything. The two guards just on the inside of the wall near a wrought-iron gate, fifty yards to my left, they see and hear nothing.

The castle was built halfway in the image of the Bäckaskog Castle, a monastery, and like many Christian monasteries of the time, there were churches built in the shape of a cross, the long stem of which opened into the nave. The crosspiece always formed the transepts, and out from that was the chancel, or the church proper. There are many reasons to think that the chancel here at Casa de la Vogel has been used mostly for storage, and a variety of game rooms.

I pull the NVGs up on my head to get a true-color image of the world. There are dozens of windows to the castle, but the lights are on in only four. Abner and Saul had a pretty good idea of where Vogel sleeps at night, but as paranoid as the old man appears to be, you have to believe he's smart enough to either have it fortified or change where he sleeps each night. You don't reach a hundred years old, eighty of which you've been on the run, without learning a few tricks.

It's a long crawl across the yard with my knee hurting me like this, and all the while I'm listening to the guards murmuring to my left, pausing to check through my NVGs, inchworming through the grass, waiting to hear the alarm that I've been discovered. It never comes. I reach a garden, do a push-up to kneeling, look around, then move in a low crouch with the FAMAS at low-ready. I pass rows of well-kept flowers, roses and wax plants and smörboll, then sidle up beside a statue of a naked baby angel with wings. "Why is it always a naked baby angel with wings?" my old roommate Danny asked when we were both high one night in college, looking out at the fountain beyond our dorm balcony.

There are glass doors at the rear. Cameras are aimed right at me, but I have no choice but to cross their paths. With any luck they're just there to record, not to enact any alarms. Abner and Saul said they did not think there were any motion detectors, at least none that would set off alarms, since there were steady patrols around the place all day and night, and security guys would just be setting them off all night.

If there are any alarms, however, I'll have to rush the place and hope I can get Vogel out in a hot extraction.

No lights. No alarms. Everything seems clear.

"On your right." Fardün's voice is in my ear. He's broadcasting by radio to Saul, who in turn is sharing the broadcast with the Nest, who in turn relays his transmission along their private connection to me.

I look to my right. Fardün's eyes are sharp. A guard is emerging from a row of trees, having just taken a leak, and now zipping up his pants.

"Got him," I whisper.

The guard is thirty yards away, moving east to west. I wait for him to vanish around the far side of the castle, then I'm on the move again. I check the coordinates on my NVGs, which are sat-linked. When I arrive at the predetermined spot, I give the sign: "Gemini is in position. Awaiting the flat tire."

"Copy that," Yarwick says. "Flat tire en route. ETA, sixty seconds."

The night is so quiet you could hear an elk fart from a hundred yards away. The Aurora shimmers overhead, illuminating the landscape. The moon aids it. This is the worst night for an extraction imaginable.

For a time, I hear nothing but my own pulse in my ears. Then, a snoring engine. It comes from someplace distant. I can just see the headlights in the distance, a pair of glowing white eyes bouncing around. As it approaches, I watch a pair of guards walk out towards it. The vehicle passes by the great castle, and stops about forty yards beyond it. The driver gets out. It's Abner. He's walking around to the front, checking the right tire. Through the NVGs I see him shaking his head, taking out a cell phone, making a call.

Four security guards now walk towards him. I zoom in. As they approach, he looks at them and smiles, and starts talking. He's sharing the woes of a weary traveler trapped outside on a cold night with a flat tire. His story is that he was coming to see the Aurora, got lost on his way back.

Abner is waving his hands, looking stressed. He's telling them he doesn't actually know how to change a tire. They're probably laughing about that. What kind of man doesn't know how to change a tire? Two of them are helping him locate his jack and tire iron. The other two are standing nearby, just watching him.

"Looks like they're buying it," Fardün says.

"I see it. Nest, how's that bird? Got it working yet?"

"Negative," Yarwick says. "The MQ-9 is still showing offline. Reason unknown."

"Understood. Gemini is mobile."

It's a minor thing. A small distraction. But that's four guards I won't have to worry about for the next fifteen minutes. Longer if Abner can soak up some time shooting the breeze with them, or asking them to teach him so that he can use the knowledge in the future, bungle it a few times on purpose.

I approach a low wall around a tiny garden. I'm just peeking over the top when I hear, "Gemini, Nest. The view from Among High looks good. You're clear on Ingress Point A."

"Copy, Nest. Gemini is mobile."

I'm up and dashing across the garden. My knee suddenly screams at me. The pain surges to a six. I make it to a window. I try the door latch. Locked, no surprise there. I use the butt of my rifle to smash it. I reach inside and unlock it, raise it, and climb through. Take one last look outside, making sure no one saw or heard me.

Massage my knee a second. Turn to address the room. A study. NVGs reveal a kidney-shaped oak desk surrounded by tall bookshelves. I tread lightly across the hardwood floors, open the door into a dark hallway, and step through.

The corridor is wide and quiet. The only sound is my boots on cobbled floors. Mounted game hang from walls. Moose, elk, beavers, couple of wolves. I come to a dining hall with large stuffed eagles hanging from the ceiling, frozen mid-attack. The whole room looks like it was once a chapel. There are even stone pews arranged in a circle, with a raised dais at the center, like a cult leader lives and preaches here.

Willing myself to ignore the pain in my knee, I step through a door behind the dais, and into an office. There are two computers in here. I take a moment to point the DIVINER, the IR hard driver reader, at them, and download their hard drives. The light on the DIVINER turns green just like Saul said, and I move on.

I find the eastern stairwell. I walk up it smoothly, the FAMAS's business end looking for work. I step onto the second floor, into another long hall, this one lined with paintings that look expensive. Impressionistic art. Formless slashes of paint with occasional human silhouettes emerging from chaos.

Footsteps. Someone muttering something to someone else.

The first man I kill steps out from an open doorway. It's just bad luck. For him and for me.

He turns and sees me and starts to go for his. A short, controlled, muffled burst rips into his chest. When he drops, I hear someone else yelp from inside the room he came from. It's a small office with a light on. I pull up my NVGs and sweep inside. I find a man in black suit and tie diving behind a desk for cover. I press into the room smoothly, firing short bursts into the desk, keeping his head down until I can round the desk and shoot him point blank. He's got armor, but the Israelis sent me with armor-piercing rounds.

After the chaos is over, I stand there for a moment, assessing everything. "Gemini is red," I say. "I repeat, Gemini is red."

"Copy red," Yarwick says.

"Our friend with the flat tire is still talking to the guards," says Fardün. "One of them is walking back towards the house. They don't seem to know anything's gone wrong yet."

"Copy. Keep watch over him."

More footsteps. Coming from down the hall. I hear someone shout something in English. Sounds like *fuck*. Sounds like they found the dead body out in the hall. I sweep outside, fire into a fat goon's head. My weapon goes dry just as another goon steps out from another corridor. I transition at once to my SIG and fire a shot into his head. The suppressor doesn't quite silence the shot. I take cover behind a suit of Medieval armor hanging on a mannequin. And wait. And listen.

No alarm.

I come to a T junction and turn right, following the only light source I see down a long, dark hallway that is wide enough for six people to walk abreast. More suits of plate armor stand silent vigil against each wall. At the end of the hallway is a tall, stained-glass cathedral window, with rippling light pouring through from the Aurora.

There's an office to my right with the door ajar. I peek inside. It's a small library, with a computer sitting atop a desk. The DIVINER downloads its hard drive, and I keep moving.

I hear voices in a room up ahead on my right. The door is closed. I see light and shifting shadows just underneath it. I don't waste time. I kick open the door and double-tap the armed guard who's rising from his chair, going for his pistol. When he's down, I descend on the shriveled old man at the far side of the room.

It's strange. Anticlimactic.

Vogel. The great monster. Like monsters from most tales, he's tinier in person. He is in boxers and a bathrobe. His skin looks like cracked, wrinkly leather. His hair is in disarray. He's screaming, clawing at air. His dentures are on the bedside table. His mouth is filled with empty blood-red gums.

"Herr Vogel," I say.

He's shaking his head. He's holding up placating hands. He reaches for his inhaler on the nightstand—

He's slippery. His mind is like an eel's, that's how he's evaded capture. Sophia's advice.

As soon as he grabs the inhaler, I grab him by the wrist and break it. He yelps. The inhaler drops to the floor. I pick it up, inspect it. A false inhaler. A button on the side. Sounds an alarm, no doubt. "Yeah, you're him," I say.

Clutching his wrist, he looks balefully at me. And then, the ghost of a smile. He speaks with a harsh lisp thanks to those missing teeth. "You've just made...the *biggest* mistake of your life."

I point the gun at him. "Still. Quiet."

He's not shaking. The pain in his wrist must be awful, but he takes it. He has a defiant look on his face. Even now, he thinks he'll win. Because he always has.

"Nest, Gemini. I have the target. Get ready for exfil."

"Gemini, Nest," Yarwick says. "We copy that. Our friend with the flat tire is almost finished. For the time being, your way is clear, but the opening is closing fast."

"Copy. On my way."

I grab the old Nazi, getting the strange feeling that I'm touching history. He paws at me feebly with arthritic hands. See those hands. See them. Know the lives they've ended. Think of the pain they've inflicted without remorse, with only joy. I throw him over my shoulder. He's as light as a child. But even a child can burden my knee right now. I falter, then regain my balance.

Down the quiet hall, down the quiet stairs, back the way I came. I'm halfway down the hallway where I first entered, and then I see a flashlight coming from an adjoining corridor. I turn quickly away, search for another way out.

Down one corridor and then another, limping slightly, following the general map that Abner laid out in my mind. Through a short open-air courtyard, beneath the Aurora. Crossing over into an aviary. Birds flapping all around. Crossing into a maze of corridors. Into a study. Through a game room filled with animals killed from many continents—tigers and boars and gazelles and an elephant's head. Through a giant ball room with a grand piano and crystal chandeliers twinkling in the spotlights. Through a set of double doors. Now into an entertainment room with a projector and theater seats. Now into a guest bedroom. Now through an indoor pool enclosure and into an adjoining greenhouse. The Aurora is brighter than ever above my head, visible through the glass ceiling.

On my back, Vogel is breathing heavily. I smell piss. And shit. He's emptying his bowels onto me. Is he just that scared, or is he hoping the smell will attract someone? *You watch him. Watch out for his tricks.*

I stop just short of stepping outside through a door at the back of the castle. I open the door, peeking outside. "Nest, I'm exiting the southwest side. How's my way?"

"Your way is clear, Gemini," says Yarwick.

I say over my shoulder, "You make a noise, you try to call for help in any way, I'll just take you back as a corpse. Either way works for me."

He says nothing. I hear him fart. The shit stink increased threefold. I open the door and step out into the night. In a low crouch, I make my way across the lawn. Wielding the FAMAS with one hand, I sweep left and right. I don't see anything that could—

Zip! The bullet cuts the air right beside my head. I hear someone yelp. I turn and see a gun-toting merc flop to the ground about ten yards behind me, clutching at his throat. He fires one wild shot at me as he dies. I turn and keep running.

"I've got you, Gemini," Fardün says calmly. "Keep moving. Don't cheat me out of my bonus."

"Where did he come from?" I ask. "How did he know where we were—"

"Keep moving, Gemini!"

We're at the wall. Can't climb over, not with Vogel, not with this knee. There's a front gate, though. Locked, inaccessible except by the proper code punched into keypad lock. Abner, Saul and I planned for this. I drop Vogel, and he collapses in a wet heap on the ground. I approach the gate.

"You...can still walk away," he whispers.

I point my gun at him. "What did I say?"

Vogel looks up at me. By the light of the Aurora, I can see his gummy smile.

I reach into a right pocket on my vest, produce a strip of thermite and slap it on the gate's lock. I back away, dragging the Nazi away as the thermite ignites brightly in a shower of sparks. A short *pop!* and the gate separates. I kick it open. Collect Vogel. Run through.

The golf course is ahead. Almost there.

*

I've jogged a mile, maybe more. There's a slight *crunch-pop* in my right knee joint now. I hear the alarm going up like it's a prison break. Someone heard the last gunshot and found the dead bodies. They know their boss is missing. I hear more raised voices. Headlights go bouncing off in the north, patrols in search of an errant killer. I'm wide open. One foot in front of the other. No cover for another hundred yards. The tree line. Multiple flares are shot into the air, illuminating the whole world. The Aurora has never been more beautiful. The moon is fat and swollen. It is the brightest night I've ever seen.

Spotlights slash in front of me. Look up. The source is a silent wraith streaking across the sky. The drone is maybe two hundred feet in the air. Doesn't see me. But how did it zero in on this location? Vogel's estate is enormous. That drone certainly did come close…

Watch for his tricks.

I stop, and drop the old man to the ground. I snatch him up by his neck, and stare into his grinning face. "You're going to tell me where the GPS tracker implant is on your body. If you don't tell me, we'll start cutting pieces off."

The smile falters, but then comes back bigger than ever. But he raises his left hand, the one I *didn't* break. I grab his wrist, turn it over, and see a small scar and a teeny, tiny, raised bump under the skin. I grab the tactical knife from my vest, and Vogel stares at me, unblinking, while I carve it out of him. It's half the size of a thumbnail. I throw it to the ground and crush it with my bootheel.

I snatch him up and keep moving. I pray that my luck holds out. When I make it into the woods, I'm only partially mollified.

One foot in front of the other.

Now my knee is really hurting. Feels like I should lay down, rest, quit for a day. I'll quit tomorrow. I cut hard to the southeast, following no trail. Vogel must be completely lost. NVGs give me an idea of the obstacles but not the overall layout. I trip twice, stagger, almost drop my target, recover, and keep moving. Yarwick is speaking calmly in my ear, telling me about the ETA on my extraction. We're all playing it by ear. There's a lot of heat behind me.

I've been running for a while. Haven't come to the road yet. I may have miscalculated the distance. I may have gone in the wrong direction. How would I really know when I'm inside this choked forest?

Suddenly, the foliage gives way. I am in a clearing, splashing through a stony brook. Spotlights glitter through the treetops. I keep moving, back into the woods. It seems like the forest will go on forever. My knee is killing me.

At last, my boots hit pavement, and I'm out of the woods before I even know it.

"Nest, Gemini! I'm here! I'm on the road! Where's my ride?"

"Incoming," Yarwick says. "Thirty seconds, he says."

It is the longest half-minute of my life. I stand there panting in the middle of the road, looking both ways, seeing nothing.

"You're going to regret this," Vogel says.

"Shut the fuck up."

Then I hear it. A low motor. I turn to my right. Still see nothing. Then two bright bulbs flash briefly and I realize he's driving without headlights or taillights. Of course. Smart. The jeep goes to the shoulder of the road and slews to a stop ten feet from me. I run over to him and he climbs out to meet me.

"We gotta move fast," I say.

"How far behind you are they?" Saul asks.

"I don't know. Everywhere. Open the passenger door." Saul is already doing it. He folds the passenger seat forward and I throw the old fucker in the back, then slam the seat back on him. "Drive." Saul is already heading there, too. I shut the door and roll down the passenger window and stick my FAMAS out the window. He keeps the headlights off as he pulls a U-turn in the middle of the road and we're headed south. The Aurora is fading, but there is plenty of light left from it and the moon to see by.

"Fardün?" I ask, massaging my knee.

"Abner's got him," Saul says.

He cuts through a forest on the left side of the road and we go off-roading for five minutes, then emerge onto a small highway with zero traffic. We say nothing as we are jounced around. I keep glancing back at our prisoner, trapped on the floorboard, barely able to lift his head. The entire jeep smells like feces.

For ten miles, we speak little, saying things like "See anything?" and "Negative." We're twenty miles away before I start to relax. We're thirty miles away before we both feel safe enough to turn on the headlights and the interior light. I unstrap the front of my body arm and yank it down.

I hold up a fist. Saul takes time to bump it, but never takes his eyes off the road. I glance back at our prisoner. "Herr Vogel, I have a message for you."

"*Schwein…*"

I look into his eyes, the one drooping looks glazed over. His large forehead gleams with sweat. He looks at me with that gummy grin. A grin that says he's going to enjoy seeing what his friends do to me for this outrage. "The French tart sends her regards, *Bite Molle*. She says the Goose chased as long as you ran. Time's up."

A change in his eyes. The smile wavers. He looks confused. Then, slowly, realization dawns on his face. I laugh at him and turn away, facing the road.

Then, I wince. A sharp pain in my side. I reach down to touch my right side. Something warm there. I look down. By the moonlight, I see the problem. "Might wanna step on it, Saul. I seem to have sprung a leak."

*

Saul called ahead, so Abner is at the cabin with a medical team on standby. They were prepared in case either I or Vogel needed medical attention. They want to make sure the Nazi lives to stand trial, as well, even if it's a secret trial and no one will ever see him again. They want the others in his dark world to get the message that Mossad will chase you forever. The trial says *We do not forget.*

The two teams address us separately. Vogel is screaming and trying to push back against his captors. They forcibly strip him naked and his pendulous scrotum swings as he tries to run, but they effortlessly fling him onto a bed and inject him with a light sedative. Within seconds he is looking around sleepily at all of us. He pisses himself again.

My armor and outfit are both ripped from me, my shirt cut with scissors, and a couple of packets of my blood type are brought in. A doctor and three nurses attend me. A whole other aspect of the operation that was prepared without me ever meeting these people. My part in WOLFCATCHER is over, theirs is just beginning.

It's not bad. The Dragon armor did its job, but the bullet went through a ways and is still inside, just barely beneath the surface. I lost a decent amount of blood. I'm tired. I'm aware of Fardün hovering nearby, smoking a cigarette and watching them work on me.

Once Vogel and I are determined to be stable, they load each of us in separate vans and get ready to roll out. The last I see of Herr Vogel is a frightened, dazed old man, naked and strapped to a gurney, looking around for answers. I think I catch his eye. He seems to be begging me to save him. I'll remember to tell Sophia that later. That ought to please her.

The doctors give me something for the pain, and I spend most of the twenty-hour drive back to Helsingborg sleeping. Wake up occasionally to look around the beautiful green countryside. Slip back into a great soft nowhere. I can see Derek and my mom. They've been lost in black waters recently, but not anymore. Dad is calling to me from somewhere. He sounds healthy and happy. A dog and a son that I never had are running up to me. My son throws his arms around me.

Now I'm waking up inside the Helsingborg safehouse, on the quiet street of Kung Kristoffers Gata. Now I'm getting a full physical from the doc who took care of me in the cabin. Now I'm waiting three days for a helicopter to take me to an airport outside of Malmö. Now I'm falling asleep in a bed. Well-earned sleep. I see darkness, and I'm walking in a black, unending ocean. Above me are spotlights. They're on to me—

I awake with a jolt. A knock at the door. "Come in," I grumble. I speak mostly by reflex, not because of any genuine want of visitors.

Fardün walks in. He's smiling a strange smile. "Wakey, wakey, sunshine," he says.

"Oh, fuck you, Fardün."

"That's my line. Hey, guess what, the world is ending."

"Yeah, well, what else is new?"

"No, I mean, it's actually ending." He picks up a remote from a bedside table and turns on the flat screen hanging on the wall. I see a news report showing a familiar-looking city. Takes me a second to recognize it.

"Is that...Helsingborg?"

Fardün nods. "Wait. It gets better."

The footage changes, showing Steel Octopuses floating over the sea. Cell phone footage shows a submarine surfacing off the coast of some island. At the bottom of the screen, it says it's Gotland. *Gotland.* The same island I passed through to get here. This is happening close to us.

"What's going on?"

Fardün reaches into his pocket, pulls out a sucker. He peels off the wrapper and tosses it in the garbage, and smiles. "Remember the MQ-9 Reaper?"

I nod. "The drone."

"Know why it went offline?" he asks. I shake my head. He puts the sucker in his mouth and smiles. "Because the Russians have been blanketing huge swaths of this region is sensor-scrambling noise. They've invaded Gotland."

"What...?" I swing my legs off the bed. "What're you talking about?"

"The Russians. They're here."

I stand up, massage my side where the bullet was dug out, and waver for a second. My knee is at a three right now as far as pain. Manageable. I look at the TV. It shows Russian troops coming on land via LVTP-7s that land on shore. "Is...is anyone stopping them?"

"This is old footage from this morning. No one's stopping them. A Russian sub is parked off the coast. It's already over. The Russians have a key stronghold in the Baltic Sea now. The Chinese are moving on Taiwan. U.S. and its allies don't know which nation to send reinforcements to first." He pulls the sucker out of his mouth with a smooching sound. "The airports are jammed. People fleeing. We're trapped. There's no way out."

30

Russia's calling it a soft occupation. Not an invasion. They claim it's self-defense, that if they didn't get to Gotland first and claim it, the U.S. would. They claim that this will actually help *deescalate* the Conflict, by ensuring the U.S. and its allies do not overtake the waters on this half of the globe. Journalists are pointing out that even though Sweden famously has a policy of political neutrality in international affairs, they're still participants in the Euro-Atlantic Partnership Council, and have leaned on the U.S. in secret in the past, such as during the Cold War when they were prepping for a possible Soviet aggression. Putin is on TV, saying he has it on good authority that the old Cold War ties between Sweden and U.S. are flaring up again. He means to "soften" them.

"That is all we are talking about," he says in a cold yet passionate speech. "Just softening these tensions, to ensure that American aggressions do not begin to seed hostility towards Russia in the rest of the world. We cannot allow the Americans to control the narrative and turn the world against us while they manufacture a war with those of us in the East."

"Can you believe this guy?" says Fardün, leaning back in a recliner and finishing off his sucker. "I mean, he's a comic book villain. If he wasn't already real, someone would've invented him, had him fighting Spider-Man and the Avengers."

I'm sitting across from him, watching Putin on the screen as he speaks about his reasoning like it is all perfectly logical. Like it's normal to invade a foreign country that's shown you no aggression whatsoever, and land troops with guns on the beaches and send them into the cities. Even now a Russian gunboat is being escorted into the waters by a Chinese submarine, bringing ashore officers at the docks in Helsingborg. The officers do not come to aggress, they say, but to speak with local municipal leaders about proper procedures for allowing shore visits by EA troops and personnel. They make it all seem very formal and polite, as if they were invited here. Not a single shot has been fired. Putin makes sure to repeat that loudly and often.

The rest of the world is scandalized. The POTUS and foreign leaders are admonishing Moscow, some of them being quite excoriating. And this is the very thing President Putin hates the most, to be talked down to, to not be taken seriously, to be scolded like a child. It will only make him madder.

Meanwhile, the situation in Ukraine is ramping up. Death tolls are rising in the hundreds. Mostly near the borders, but Steel Octopuses and tanks and soldiers have pressed deeply into the country. It's a safe bet they mean to keep going until they reach Kiev, and take it.

Saul has returned. He's in the next room, talking on the phone to someone. When he enters the living room, he's taken off his crème-colored jacket and loosened his tie. He looks stressed as he hands me a phone. "Phone call."

I take it. "Hello?"

"Hey" Yarwick says. "Are you watching this?"

"Yeah. I'm seeing it just now."

"Is that Yarwick?" Fardün says. I wave him to shut up. "If it's Yarwick, tell her I want my bonus. Wired to Verdergatten Bank, like she said." I wave at him again. "It's local, right down the street, shouldn't take her long to—"

"Things are escalating fast," Yarwick says. "The Ukrainians are asking for any help we can give. If we do that, we basically declare open war with Russia. The Taiwanese are begging us, too. Something happened out at sea that I can't talk about over the phone. No one died, but it was close. And now there's a rumor that Homeland is on to a couple of Russian spies who were in the country to spy on NASA's launch sites, which are undergoing remodeling."

"A sabotage attempt. Like NARROW VOID. Think they wanted to do it back to us?"

"Maybe. That's a theory."

I get up and walk out of the room.

"Ask her about my bonus," Fardün reminds me as I leave.

I step into a study and shut the door. I turn and face a large paper map of the globe pinned to the wall. "Any news on our mole hunt?"

"A couple things, but it's intensifying. A lot of people at CIA and JSOC that had any ties to NARROW VOID at all, even the most tangential, are having to hand over their e-mail accounts for inspection."

"Any heat on you?"

She sighs. "No more than anyone else. But there's reason to believe it could've simply been a sophisticated spear-fishing attack."

I wince at that. "You mean like those 'Hello I am a Nigerian prince and I have an investment to sell you' kind of e-mails?"

"Yes, but way more sophisticated. There's evidence of high-quality, high-volume attacks from what looked like reputable sources within the government. So far the investigators have identified multiple enemy actors that have been attacking small systems throughout the Department of Defense and all networked agencies."

"But that wouldn't lend any info on NARROW VOID, would it?"

Yarwick gives another exasperated sigh. "Who knows? There's so much up in the air right now..." She trails off. I can hear the stress in her voice.

"So, with all this ramping up, I guess you just got really busy then, huh?" I say.

"Yeah." A palpable silence, during which I can sense her thinking. "How are you doing? I mean, physically, mentally, how are you?"

"Good. Our Israeli friends were more than prepared."

"Good. That's good."

"Is that why you called? To check on me?"

"Not strictly that," she admits. "Remember how I told you I was given the greenlight to begin covert operations in Ukraine?"

"Yeah. Agent-handling stuff, right?"

"Right. Well, there's a series of missions that need talent attached to them. There are pro-Russian Ukrainians causing trouble in Kiev, leftovers from the 2014 uprisings. They are out in force, smashing windows and throwing Molotov cocktails into cars. Russia's propaganda has been prepping Ukraine for this kind of invasion for years."

A great civilization is not conquered from without until it has destroyed itself from within. I remember a college professor telling me that. Who was he quoting? Durant, I think.

"Yeah," I huff. "Well, no one ever accused the Russians of not having the long con in mind."

"This is bad for the Ukrainian government. They've got a large contingent of pro-Russian radicals in the streets, and a lot of Russian haters ready to counter-protest. It's a powder keg waiting to explode. We have intel saying SVR, specifically Karambit's Unit, will be there to exploit it, recruit a bunch of the pro-Russians to help them. But there's also likely to be a guerilla group of rebels, armed citizens fighting back against the invaders."

"There usually is."

"Yes. Especially when that rebel group is stoked."

"Stoked." That's an interesting word.

"Yes," Yarwick says. "Like when they're fed weapons and training? Or when they're taught how to conduct clandestine operations. Sabotage. Spying."

And now it hits me. "You need recruiters in the city," I say. "For when the Russians finally get there."

"We've already been in contact with a dozen local armed militia leaders. They just need to be brought under one roof, one leader. You could help us find the right one, recruit him, feed him information about the enemy. Information we'll collect from drones, wiretaps, satellite surveillance, all that."

Now it all makes sense. Not enough soldiers to go around the world, fighting off China, Iran, Russia, North Korea, and Syria. But if you sow deception into the malcontents, into the rebellious folks already there, you get...well, you get a bunch of Sophias. You get the French Resistance and freedom fighters. Terrorists, rebels, whatever you want to call them. People who will fight back and weaken the overall structure of the military occupiers, leaving them softened for any attack from a major military force.

Yarwick's been tasked with building allies in the region. She says, "I know it's asking a lot, but if you think about it, you won't be as exposed as we initially thought you might—"

"I'll do it."

That gives her pause. "You won't have much backup from us. You're still on the blacklist. We can funnel you supplies, some money, but you and any partners we send in will all be mercenaries. Completely off-the-books."

"I understand."

"And Kiev will probably be under siege eventually, so you'll almost certainly be in a warzone like no other. Not disorganized religious extremists, but a well-coordinated modern army, complete with drones, Steel Octopuses, highly-trained personnel—"

"I said I'll do it. I'll go in there and start recruiting. Just give me the date, and a means to get there. I'll do the rest."

A longer pause this time.

"Nate...I have to ask, as both a friend and your handler now, *why* do you do this?"

"Why did you ask me to do it?" I counter. "Because you knew I would say yes. And the reason you knew I'd say yes is that you already knew why I do this. One foot in front of the other, Tara. What am I without this?"

At first I think she'll push it, but she accepts it. "Okay."

"I guess we should talk about payment. Fardün's asking about his bonus, and I'm sure we'll need to work out cleaner payment strategies for funding Ukrainian rebels."

"Sure. We can work all that out in the next couple of days."

I scratch my chin, thinking. "One thing worries me. The mole."

"What about him?"

Him. She's assuming it's a man. "Well, whoever it is, they may still have connections to you. It may be a colleague. It could be someone at JSOC, someone blackmailing one of your superiors with knowledge of operations."

"You're worried that whatever operations we conduct in Kiev will also be in jeopardy."

"That's a concern, yes."

"I don't think that will be an issue."

"Why?"

"This spear-fishing thing, the investigators are pretty sure that's all it was."

"But if it wasn't? If there's someone around you that's feeding the EA actionable intel?"

Yarwick makes a *tsk* noise. "Well, we can't allow ourselves to be crippled by indecision. We have to make a choice soon. Are you in, or are you out?"

"I told you already, I'm in. We just need to be extremely cautious from here on."

She thinks on that. "You're right. You're absolutely right. Let's keep that in mind," she says. "We'll develop our own codes and passphrases, our own e-mails, shared only between you and me. No one else. Knowledge of your whereabouts and actions will be known only to me."

"Yeah. All right, let's get crackin'. Any details you can clue me in on?"

"I'll send you a list of contacts, pro-Ukrainian militia leaders to start with. Also a target. Just one. A Russian general named Ormav Yevtushenko. Highly skilled, highly experienced. He's led the Russians to numerous victories against ISIS and in parts of Ukraine. He's considered an ace in Putin's camp, a real tactical genius. He's overhauled the SVR, top to bottom, and we think he created the Unit. He needs to be neutralized, and it needs to look like an accident." She's been doing this long enough it sounds like she's ordering a Big Mac. Extra pickles, extra sauce, hold the lettuce.

I've also done this long enough that I receive her orders like the good McDonald's employee that I am. If that's the way you like your Big Mac, lady, I'm here to serve. "All right. What else?"

"There are some listening devices Langley's sending you. Very small. It would be beneficial if, when the Russians reach Kiev, you could plant them in key areas of their encampments, or else on some piece of heavy equipment, like a tank. It'll let us listen to chatter within the units each day."

"All right. Tell me about these devices."

We discuss a few more details. She hangs up after agreeing to get back with me on the exact date of deployment. I walk back into the living room and see Fardün still sitting there. He's eating a reheated slice of pizza and drinking a Dr. Pepper while he watches soldiers on TV landing on shores that are just a couple hours away from us. He looks up at me, and through a mouthful of double pepperoni, says, "Did you ask about the bonus?"

"Yeah, you'll get it. I've got a question. How do you feel about a trip to Ukraine?"

Fardün stops chewing. He points at the TV. "You *do* know what's happening there, don't you?"

"We'll get in before the Russians reach Kiev. It's potentially a long-term thing, though. And you'll get another payday."

He shakes his head ruefully. "Oh, fuck you, Adamson."

"So you'll do it?"

"Yeah."

*

Some wars start with a loud bang, lots of action, lots of battle cries. Others start with a trickle. The Conflict with the Eastern Alignment is still not being called a war, but we are seeing a trickle. We are seeing Australian and British navies deploying into the South China Sea with intentions to support Taiwan. We are seeing more U.S. troops landing in Iraq and supporting troops already in place there to protect the oil fields. We are hearing reports of a few "shots across the bow" being fired out in the Atlantic and Pacific between subs. We are also hearing new talks from Russia about wanting to talk with our NATO allies about arms reduction, proposing that we all play nice and begin scrapping old obsolete bombs and submarines—history tells us that whenever the Russians do that, they are invariably planning for a future war. They want *us* to downgrade *our* militaries, all in the name of peace. They know this age-old *maskirovka* ploy can't work, but it eats up time with the diplomats and keeps politicians busy and talking.

There are reports that British SAS and Green Berets are at the Syrian borders, ostensibly to protect the country from Islamic extremists, but the insinuation being that they're actually staging in case they have to go into Russia. This rumor seems all but confirmed when you hear about how many C-130s are stationed there; those being made specifically for transport of troops, weapons, and vehicles.

And now Russia has given up almost all pretense that they have no major weapons upgrades in mind. There is a military parade down the streets of Moscow, demonstrating their new power. A dozen of the Tianshi platforms float down the main avenues. The Russians are officially calling them the *Khishchink*: the Predators. People in the press have been calling them Steel Octopuses from the start, and I'm guessing that's because it's the term I used, which was given to me by the Tidov family, passed to the ears of CIA, who then briefed the president, who then started tossing the word around.

My actions continue to influence history.

The *Khishchnik* hover over tanks, some rusty and some old, some new and powerful-looking, while Moscow citizens cheer from the parade side. There is footage released to the Russian media of a device that looks very much like the *Kop'ye*, and American newscasters express worry when they see the effect of the invisible beam. In answer to this, the U.S. has released more footage to the press of their new Hammer-1 in action, the tank slashing across lakes and firing its devastating railgun as it goes. And then there are videos taken by the Navy that show even larger railguns on top of the latest warships.

Russia responds by releasing video of the Vostochny Cosmodrome launching a Soyuz 2.1a rocket, and then more footage from space as it releases its payload, some new satellite that is believed to be a hunter-killer, showing the world that they are still moving ahead with space operations. But I notice the satellite is *not* the Great Donut, and I have a smile over that.

North Korea, not to be outdone, has the largest-ever military parade in its history down the streets of Pyongyang. That same day, there is a hack attack against two different power plants in the U.S., and one-quarter of the East Coast goes dark. Three days later, power is restored, but the damage is done and the message is clear.

We're in an epic dick-measuring contest.

*   .

"We found a lot on those hard drives you copied," Saul says, taking a seat across from me in the kitchen. He pops open a beer, a Carnegie Porter, and hands it to me. Beside him, Abner hands one to Fardün, who accepts it graciously and takes a long swig. Abner starts passing around dishes of the local cuisine, nettle soup and Hasselback potatoes. "Enrichment curves for the uranium, as well as supply lines from men that our people in Research say are Russian scientists, probably scientists that Arumush bribed. There are also contact lists, phone numbers and e-mails to people we know have connections to organized crime. Russian mob."

"The feed stocks," I say, digging into the potatoes. "Arumush opened a supply line between compromised Russian scientists and Iran?"

"Compromised? Maybe. They brokered a few deals, at least. Our people have already found code phrases that they think relate to the viability of weaponization, talks of the 'ninety-percent range,' which is the percentage of weapons-grade uranium." He slurps his soup. "Vogel's people even fouled up in one spot in a file marked 'Unilateral,' in which there's a three-hundred-page dissertation on HEU, highly enriched uranium." Saul nods. "You can bet that if it was the mob funneling these materials, they didn't get it through standard means. The Russian government has been using them to give it to Iran as a gift. So, the scientists weren't 'compromised,' as much as they were flat-out told to give the mob the uranium, and the mob sold it to the Iranians with the Russians' secret blessing."

"For how long?"

"We don't know. Possibly years. And one of Arumush's lists indicate they had dealings with people in the IAEA, the International Atomic Energy Agency. Operations meant to find leverage on those IAEA officials."

"Leverage? You mean blackmail."

"Yes. Iran has only been allowed to have 660 pounds of enriched uranium, but they've somehow gone far past that."

I nod, take another bite of the potatoes. Damn good. "If that's the case, they've been planning their Eastern Alignment for much longer than we previously thought."

"That is true," Saul says.

"In exchange for what? Besides the money, but the Russians can't be that strapped for cash, can they? To risk arming a potential future enemy with nukes?"

"God only knows. But international sanctions and embargoes on materials critical to making nuclear weapons has kept Iran from *making* such weapons. Using the mob and Arumush and other go-betweens allows the Iranians to get around such obstacles, and the Russians get plausible deniability if it is ever uncovered."

"Six degrees of Kevin Bacon," Fardün says.

"I'm sorry? Kevin Bacon?"

Fardün points at me. "He can explain."

I wave that away. "What about Vogel himself?"

Saul is about to answer when Fardün shoots to his feet. He takes a vibrating phone out of his pocket and looks at it. "Family," he says, and walks into the next room speaking German into the phone.

Saul slurps his soup, and says, "Vogel's not saying much. When he does, I'm told he issues threats. But Zurer has already begun the process of a secret trial, and she has arranged for two surviving camp victims to say something to him." Another slurp. "She likes to do that, whenever possible. Find the last remaining camp survivors willing to make the trip, and have them face the Nazis before they are condemned."

"That's a lot of work you people go through to see justice done," I say. I admire them. The commitment is tremendous. The glory is virtually nil. You have to do it because you believe in it.

"We do what we can," Saul says. "What is justice if it has an expiration date?"

I nod. "Fair enough."

"So, you're going home after this?"

"I don't know. This 'soft invasion' may prevent any kind of travel. What about you? What do you do now that you've bagged your Nazi?"

"Find another Nazi to bag," he says.

"There's that many?"

"You'd be surprised. Just when we think there can't be anymore, something pops up. A new piece of evidence. An undocumented citizen hiding in South America, a set of fingerprints from a ninety-seven-year-old who got drunk one night and wandered out of his grandson's home and got picked up by police, or just someone manages to recognize their neighbor's likeness in an old photo from Dachau. Anything can launch a new investigation."

"I guess some wars are never really over," I say.

Saul snorts, finishes the last of his soup, and says, "No war ever ends. It just folds over into the next one. We've been fighting the same wars for ten thousand years, they all just splintered off from the first one, I'm sure of it." He shrugs. "We just constantly move the goal line and change sides, that's all."

Fardün steps back into the room, replacing the phone in his pocket.

"Everything all right?" I ask.

"Fine," he says. "Your people moved my family to a nice spot."

I rise to my feet, taking my plate over to the sink. "It helps to have friends," I say, surprising myself by giving him a clap on the back. It feels natural, even though he once tried to kill me. He also saved me that night with Vogel. It's a bizarre world we live in. Even Osama bin Laden was once an ally of the U.S., so I guess it's not too strange to befriend the occasional hired killer. Like Saul said, it's all the same wars, we just change sides. Today, Fardün and I are friends, and tomorrow we may need to kill each other. That is the way of things.

Fardün looks a little awkward accepting the companionable clap, but he lights a cigarette and smokes it, letting the weird moment go. He follows me as I walk out of the kitchen, and pulls me to a stop in the hallway. "Hey," he says, sotto voce. "Your woman Yarwick, did she say anything about Alpha Source? Do they know who the mole is?"

"What does it matter to you?"

Fardün looks at me like I've grown a second head. "What do you mean, 'what does it matter?' It matters a lot to me if your people are moving my family around to a secret location that only *your people* know about. And if your people are compromised, they could spill everything. If Karambit finds out where my family is…"

"He's not gonna find out, Fardün. He probably doesn't even care."

"And why not?"

"Because you and I? We're old news, pal. The world's already accelerated past caring about me. The Unit couldn't give less of a shit about you or me, and the SVR is about to have its work cut out for it. You saw the news."

He takes a long, thoughtful toke, and exhales roiling clouds of smoke. "I just need to be sure my family is protected, is all."

"I know. I get it. But don't worry," I say, giving him another clap on his shoulder. He looks at my hand. "My people have got it covered."

"Good. Because if they don't, I may have to kill Karambit myself."

I nod, knowing that if he goes that route, I might be right beside him. *You don't have what it takes, Ares.*

"We'll cross that bridge if we come to it. It's time to get our head in a different game, though. Yarwick thinks she can get us flights out of here in a day or two. You and I will go separate, meet up there. Make sure you're ready to go."

Oie

They tell me my contributions were essential in finding him. They tell me I might be on the news. They tell me that the details of their operation cannot be made public but that they can give generalities to the media, let them know that justice is still finding Nazis. They tell me Nathan had a hand in that, and that he's safe somewhere. They tell me it's over, Herr Vogel is in captivity. They tell me it was because of me.

That's what they tell me.

But I don't remember. I don't recall any of it. Not right now. But on some instinctive level I know that later I will be able to recall it. I'm inside this dark cave, sensing warmth on my skin, knowing that the light is nearby, but I'm unable to find the source. There's a way out of all this dimness, if I could just...

"Mom? What do you think? The pink one?"

"Mm?" I look up at a face I know I'm supposed to know. And the one next to it. My daughter and granddaughter. And the littlest one, so bright and beautiful. What are their names? Oh, yes. Chloe, Zoe, and Henrietta. But which one's which? They must know that I don't know. I can tell. I think all of us who suffer this kind of slippage can tell when others are humoring us. It's like you've farted in an elevator with only one other person, and they know it's not them. You both share an embarrassing secret.

"The pink one?" the one who I think is Chloe says again.

I look down. The young girl—*Henrietta* is her name!—she's holding out something she made at school. Two somethings. Clay pots. Their art teachers fired them up in a kiln and let the children paint them. Now I remember. There's a blue one and a pink one.

"I like the pink one," I say. Henrietta stares blankly at me. I suddenly realize I said it in German, the language I use when I don't want to be found out. I can't let my guard down. Not here among strangers. Any one of them might notice I'm not a real German, and they'll know I'm one of the French girls they've been looking for who help POWs across the border. They'll tell the orderlies and the orderlies will tell the Gestapo—

Only no one's going to tell the Gestapo, are they? No, Sophia. No, you're getting worse.

"The pink one, yes," I say, this time making sure to use the right language.

Henrietta leaves it with me. I know I will cherish it. Until I forget to. Until I wake up one morning with this clay pot beside my bed and wonder where this useless piece of pottery came from.

Zoe takes Henrietta to visit the little girl's room, and I'm left alone with Chloe. My eldest. No…no, not my eldest. Isabella is my eldest. But she's not coming, is she? No. No, something happened to her long ago. What was it?

"She loves visiting you, *Mère*," Chloe says. "She talks about it every time we leave. You know, she learned about you in school. Not *you*, exactly, but the jobs you and the others did. Then she wanted to watch a documentary about it on Netflix."

I nod. A certain clarity returns. A light in the cave. The darkness and fog all recede and I am once again fully restored to my old self. *Mon Dieu*, what a relief. "That's nice, Chloe. But do me a favor, when you tell her the stories someday, don't tell her everything. I shouldn't have told you what I told you when you were young. You shouldn't have that burden, it should die with me."

"You didn't burden me, *Mère*. I'm proud of what you did."

Not if I told you the whole truth. I never told you the *whole* truth, sweet girl.

"How are things around here?" Chloe asks. "Is everyone taking good care of you?"

"Yes, it's fine."

"Kristin says you're not taking your pills again—"

"Kristin. That Faustine-looking whore. Spilling her secrets, just like Faustine did. They're all the same."

"*Mère*, she's just trying to help."

"I know. And I know you pay for that extra care and that I should be grateful. But I'm old and stupid and bitter."

"Settle down, *Mère*. You're not that bad."

"Tell me about your day. Are you working now?" I know I've probably already asked this and I'll probably forget later. I sense it. I sense that I'm fading from the world, becoming less connected. I'm cogent now, but later? That's a different story. And let later be later, for now there's light in the cave and I'm with my daughter.

As Chloe speaks, I cast occasional glances over her shoulder. The TV is on in the background. Something's happening in China. And Sweden. And other places. It seems to have some of the seniors around here pretty alarmed. Gabe, the Vietnam veteran, seems particularly agitated.

To my right, I see a dozen or so men. Spirits. The dead men who stepped out from their graves. They're waiting for something. I ignore them, as always. They want my attention, but I won't give it to them.

Chloe is still talking. I'm still listening. An orderly comes walking by. It's Orson. Why the fuck do I *always* remember *his* name and not my own children and grandchildren's? I reach out to touch his hand. "Orson, a glass of water, if you would, please?"

He gives a quick smile. "Sure thing, Sophia." He turns to go away. As he does, his jacket brushes me. As my hand falls away from his, it does something. My hand moves and...I'm palming something. What is it? What did I just steal from Orson the orderly? I have no idea, nor do I know why I did it. Chloe is still talking, she didn't even see it. I pocket the item before she notices.

As she talks, I wonder about Nathan. I seem to recall he was going to do something for me. Some errand I sent him on. Or, no, wait...that isn't right...

Henrietta comes running back from the restroom and regales me with a story of how she just met an old man who pulled a coin out from behind her ear. I ask to see this coin. She hands it to me. I set it in the center of my palm. In one motion, I run my other hand over it, and it disappears.

Henrietta's eyes are saucers. "Whoa! Where'd it go, Soso?"

"I don't know, sweetheart."

It's the truth.

31

Fardün is standing at the airport entrance when I step into the fresh, foggy Kiev air. He looks healthy. He even looks in good spirits. He's dressed lowkey in jeans, brown jacket, and white T-shirt. The beard he's grown is almost as thick as mine. Still bald as a rock, though.

"You look hideous, Adamson," he says.

"I'm trying to be more like you," I say. "I like your tactic of looking as ugly as humanly possible, that way no one will stare." I stick my hand out, and I am surprised when he shakes it. "In all seriousness, you look pretty good—"

Fardün waves a dismissive hand, and starts walking away. "Oh, save it. I don't need your pleasantries."

Smiling, I drag my luggage behind me and keep pace with him. We're two killers who shouldn't be alive, much less talking to one another. Now we're companions in an endeavor to undermine the incoming EA military forces. How did we get here, Sophia? Is this what you felt, when the Tyrant began escalating the conflict the world over? Did it feel this out of control? Did you feel this divorced from reality?

Fardün's got a car waiting for us. An Uber. "Been waiting here long?"

"Stationed and waiting," the killer-for-hire says.

Once we get in the back seat, we keep quiet for the first few miles away from Boryspil International Airport. I look out my window. It's a gloomy day on the Dnieper, the fog is draped heavily over the water, like it's frozen in air. I look over at Fardün, who is reading something on a burner phone. I reach into my jacket pocket and hand him a silver pin. It's kind of large, shaped like a falcon.

"For your locker," I say. "I've got my own. Yarwick says to wear the pin when we get to the train station and our guy will find us."

He pins the falcon to his lapel and says nothing.

We remain quiet all the way to the hotel on Strand, when he gets out and makes a quick phone call, then does something on his phone. Looks like texting.

"Who are you talking to?" I ask, as I grab my luggage out of the trunk.

"I'm texting family."

I raise an inquisitive eyebrow. "Family?"

"Yes. And don't give me any of that PERSEC bullshit. Personal security is for you spooks, I have my own brand of security."

"What kind of security allows people like us to text families while on mission?"

He makes no comment on that. I don't pursue it further.

There's a roadblock up ahead, a makeshift checkpoint made by Ukrainian forces. They're all young men in light-green uniforms with dark-green berets. It's the Mechanized Infantry. They are flanked by military jeeps. And, rolling down the street behind them, is a T-64BM tank. Part of the support the U.S. has been giving them since 2015.

The Rosaline Hotel is middle-grade lodgings, not swanky and not a sty. We've reserved a room on the third floor. It wasn't hard finding vacancies in the city. No tourists in warzones, just a few journalists.

Without even thinking about it, we both check the room out before settling in. Fardün walks over to the windows and shuts the curtains immediately. I check the closets and bathroom. He checks under the bed. "Find any monsters?" I ask. He grunts, says nothing else.

I turn on the TV. It's playing a soap opera. I open my laptop on the only desk in the room and send an e-mail to Yarwick saying we've arrived. Fardün switches the channel to BBC, showing reruns of *Fawlty Towers*. He watches it for about a minute, then heads out of the room.

"Where are you going?" I ask.

He stops at the door. "I'm going to check out the escape routes. Just in case."

He doesn't come back for almost an hour, and when he does, he sits on the edge of the bed and takes off his shoes. I've been stretching and meditating with the TV on mute. Fardün turns the volume up, and he's laughing at the hijinks of Basil Fawlty. "British humor is the best, don't you think?" he asks.

"They've certainly got their own flavor," I say, doing a Google search for maps of the area.

"You know, I've read that the big difference between American comedy and British comedy is that American comedians always want to play hero archetypes—you know, people with good intentions and who will ultimately get the girl in the end—while British comedians prefer to play the losers, the downtrodden, or arrogant fools who are oblivious to their own inadequacies."

"Would certainly explain a lot," I say.

Fardün turns to me. "It's weird, isn't it? Sitting here?"

I look up from my computer. "How do you mean?"

"Well, it all seems so peaceful from here. Like there's no war. Like there's nothing of great consequence happening anywhere in the world. You couldn't blame anyone living here for not really believing that war is coming to these streets. You see the faces of the hotel staff? No one's panicking. They're going about their business, even though the Russians are already in the country."

I nod. "People have to go on with their lives, even when the world's going to shit. Plus, they've dealt with Russians before. Not like this, but still."

"It's the two worlds you and I live in. In a tranquil city one day," he uses the remote to change the channel to news anchors discussing footage of new artillery rolling into the country, "and in a warzone the next."

*

Kiev-Pasazhyrskyi Station is busy at just about all times of day. Fardün and I show up at night and go directly to the lockers on the east wing of the station. We are wearing the falcon pins that Yarwick gave us. I see the man approaching us in his black overcoat and carrying a copy of *The London Times* tucked under his right arm. That's our guy. He spots us. Sees our falcons. I signal Fardün, who nods and takes up a lookout position near a large potted plant. I walk right up to the man in the overcoat, barely touch him, and keep walking. Brush passes are old tricks in tradecraft, and no matter how good technology gets, it seems brush passes will never be obsolete.

The keys the guy handed me go to two lockers on the east wing of the terminus. I touch my nose, signaling Fardün that's it clear for him to follow me. He signals back that I'm in the black—no one's surveilling us. I find our lockers and take out the gear bags. They're color-coded: black for Fardün, brown for me. Once we're in the rental car and driving away, I can see Fardün is pleasantly surprised as he rummages through his bag.

"Your people really came through," he says. "These new IDs are better than any I've seen. Flawless." Then he takes out the stock for the rifle. "Superb," he comments. And it sounds like he means it.

"Put it away," I say. "We're coming to another roadblock."

We are stuck in a line of about thirty cars, all slowly trundling through Kyrylivs'ka Street, where men in green berets and with automatic rifles are diverting us around a large group of pro-Russian and anti-government groups. There are three dozen men in armor carrying riot shields that are advancing on the crowd.

This whole place is just a puddle of gasoline waiting for someone to drop a matchstick. As we drive past the protesters, Fardün takes only a single glance and grunts, "Huh."

When we reach the hotel parking lot, we climb out of the car just in time to watch three SU-33 fighter jets go streaking overhead, their combined engine roars drowning out all sound. This is strange to me. I've never been in a city on the brink. I was in Kandahar *after* the fighting started, and we fought nonstop in Korengal Valley, but I was never in any place that was tranquil yet building towards all-out war.

You can feel it in the air. See it on everyone's faces. Even as they go about their lives—shopping, bagging groceries, driving to work—you also see them with an extra pep in their step. *Better get home*, their eyes say. *Don't know when the bombing's going to start.*

But there are other signs that things are about to change for the worse, besides the roadblocks. Shops close early, most pubs don't open at all, and the local police are posted on every street corner.

Back in our hotel room, Fardün and I lay out our gear. Quietly. Not speaking to each other. He assembles his sniper rifle and I try on my body armor, cinching the straps here and there, making it a perfect fit. We've been given twelve miniature listening devices that are about the size of a pinky fingernail, almost as thin, and a dull gray color. Perfect for fitting into tight corners, or onto the inner workings of a random piece of military gear. There's also a photo and full dossier on

General Ormav Yevtushenko, and the highest pieces of tech we have are cell phones that look pretty mundane, but in fact have advanced facial-recognition software built into their cameras, so that we can scan large fields of soldiers and potentially single out Yevtushenko.

I've been told Yevtushenko must die, but that it must appear accidental.

There's also a notebook in this gear, one filled with a list of contacts. Local Ukrainian militia leaders, some of whom were friendly to the U.S. back when we were giving them more support. They've been told to expect my phone calls. I send out texts first. They reply with their all-clear codes, indicating they're not under duress. I send them the locations of future meetings. Some of them are open to it, others are more hesitant.

I sit down on the bed, try on the tactical boots. But when I stand up, I get a catch in my right knee. I hiss through the surge of pain. I try stretching but it doesn't help. I pop an ibuprofen. Take a look in the mirror. I ask the man there if he's sure he's up for this.

When we're all done, Fardün and I walk outside, into the foggy streets—the fog hangs around at all hours—and we grab something to eat from the only café that's open past six for miles.

We see light traffic outside the window. Occasionally, a military vehicle carrying troops goes by, pushing the omnipresent fog around like it's snow. We both regard it the way you might if you saw a fire engine going by. Probably means trouble for somebody somewhere, but not for us.

"So," I say. "This family you've got Yarwick moving around for you. I've never really asked. Is it wife and kids? I mean, I know you were married twice when you were a spy, but what about now?"

I expect him to be a little dodgy, but Fardün surprises me when he's forthright. Looking out the window at another APC grumbling by, he says, "She's remarried. I have a daughter and a son with her. I've never met the boy, he was born after she and I fled and I had to go on the run. I'm told he's mine. Looking at the pictures she sends me, I believe her. He has my chin and my eyes."

"Were you guys in love?" I ask. "Or was it just business for you?"

It's a frank question. And again, he surprises me by answering. "The relationship…it is an artifact from another time, when things might have been different."

"What happened?"

Fardün sips at his coffee, then looks at the cup and makes a face, like the flavor offends him. "You know we cannot shrink all of our experiences into one word, Adamson, or into one sentence. Our lives are a collage of good and bad." He chuckles. It's the same kind of rueful chuckle he gave in that restroom where we first spoke, when his life was in my hands. "You ever watch documentaries on space, on how solar systems are formed?"

I nod.

"It's like that," he says. "Our lives are all this random debris that come together, the sperm and the egg that form us, the proteins and DNA that constructed us, and then we are born into swirling chaos, attracting other people to us. Some random moons will orbit us—in this analogy, these moons are our friends, people you run into—but some of these moons will pick up speed and be flung from our orbit, out into space, never to be seen again. You following?"

I nod.

"All the while, the planets—that's us—we are agglutinating, still forming from all the storms, earthquakes, and volcanic activity in our lives. Eventually, you reach a kind of harmony. Your life is now a complete solar system, in total balance. But occasionally, there are cataclysmic events that tear the solar system apart again. Maybe some asteroid smacks into your planet, or your sun goes supernova."

Fardün shrugs.

"I met a woman. She was my moon. It was quite random. Just like the sun that went supernova in my life, and flung her from my life forever. She's no longer in my orbit, but I occasionally send her messages from far away."

"Can I ask what the supernova was?"

"You can ask," he laughs, and downs the rest of his coffee. "But you can probably guess. This is how the spy game works. This is how soldiers end up if they don't have a family to go home to. Adrift. Without purpose. Excommunicated and friendless."

"You've got me," I tell him.

411

"Fuck you, Adamson," he chuckles. "You and I will keep doing this because we are compelled by forces outside our control. We have skills for this and no other job. If we don't do this, we might as well put a bullet in our own heads."

Fardün's phone buzzes. He looks down at it.

"It's a news alert," he says.

"What's it say?"

He shows me the text. "Eight hundred members of the PLA just landed on the Russia-Ukraine border. The Chinese have sent military support for the Russians. It looks like the invasion is under way."

*

The Octopuses are in full view on the evening news, looks like about ten of them, all hovering twenty feet in the air above the Russian soldiers like angels of death. The tanks are trundling down the streets of Chernihiv, a city in northern Ukraine, close to the border. Hundreds of young soldiers are piled in armed vehicles, dozens more march alongside tanks with heavy rucksacks on their backs. I see Spetsnaz. No obvious signs of the Unit, but of course, they will be moving more clandestinely, probably not even with the main battalions.

For a whole week, Fardün and I have been watching it all unfold from our hotel room. He's sitting on the edge of the bed and I'm sitting in a chair near the TV. Neither one of us speaks.

The news is saying that the Ukrainian government wants to bring more military troops from the borders to reinforce Kiev, but that those reinforcements are already being cut off in the city of Pryluky, near the Udai River. What forces are in Kiev are all that the citizens have got for now.

The Eastern Alignment is full steam ahead in this region now.

The U.S. is said to be sending support, but there's no timetable. I send an e-mail to Yarwick and speak in a pre-agreed code (*Hi, it's your own pal Charles from high school, how've you been and how's your dad?*), in case anybody's monitoring her e-mail. I ask her if she knows anything about U.S. troops. She replies using the same code, which interprets as she has no knowledge of any reinforcements coming anytime soon.

This is it. The endgame that Russia has been playing towards ever since the annexation of Crimea in 2014. Scooping up territory, just like China with Taiwan, and Iran with the Persian Gulf oil fields. Lots of plays being made simultaneously around the globe.

"This is madness," Fardün says, and lights a cigarette.

"We knew this was coming," I reply. "We—"

A knock at the door. My pistol is in my hand. Fardün watches me approach the door, his own pistol out and ready. I wave a magazine in front of the peephole, then open the door and see the female desk clerk, looking a little fretful. "Hello. Something wrong?"

"Nothing wrong," she says haltingly. "Eh...just want you to know...eh..." She struggles with English. "There's a basement. In case you and friend need, eh, protection? From bombs later?"

I nod. "Oh. Thanks."

"Manager say we have food. Eh...stocked up on food?"

"I understand. Thank you. We'll come down to the basement if the bombing starts."

She smiles sadly and walks away to knock on the next door. I walk back over to Fardün.

He points to the television. "They just said that the airport is being shut down, all flights grounded because there are Russian fighter jets and *Khishchink*s all over the airspace." Fardün looks at me. "We made it into Kiev just in time, my friend."

"Let's not waste our good fortune, then," I say, taking out a manila envelope and tossing it onto a table. "Come over here, let's go over this General Yevtushenko and his background."

He takes another toke of his cigarette and then mutes the TV and walks over to the table with me. He lifts a photo someone took of Yevtushenko and takes a few more tokes considering the skinny, stone-faced son of a bitch in the general's uniform. "Miserable-looking prick. Just like all of them."

"Lifelong military man," I say, flipping through his dossier. "One wife who died in childbirth. Ever since then he's committed himself to nothing but duck hunting and reforming Russia's military.

He's big on propaganda, and on being seen among his troops. He was part of the Russian siege of Crimea, he all but executed it himself."

Fardün takes another toke. Says nothing. Just stares into Yevtushenko's eyes.

"Profile says he's a die-hard Putin supporter," I go on. "Has his head way up the president's ass. He's been talking about sieging Kiev like this for fifteen years. He's cutthroat, the Unit was his brainchild, he's a no-mercy kind of asshole."

"That is one *hell* of a high-value target," Fardün finally says.

"That's why we're getting paid the big bucks."

"When *do* we get paid, by the way?"

"Funds should be transferred later tonight," I say. "Half up front, like we discussed, and the rest doled out as our objectives are completed."

We pull out a large paper map of Kiev, and go over the routes we've already marked for quick escape vectors. Red lines are the main arteries, green lines are back-ups, orange lines are culverts or sewers that he and I have been spending days scoping out and walking through the tunnels. Black X's are no-go spots, areas with zero cover or alleys with complete dead-ends. Pink circles are prime sniper locations. This is urban warfare like I got used to in Kandahar, and I suspect Fardün knows this lifestyle well, too, for the more I talk to him, the more our tactics seem to align.

"I can almost guarantee that these two bridges here will be destroyed by the Ukrainian military themselves," he says, putting his cigarette between two fingers and pointing to two bridges we scouted the day before. "They'll do it to keep the Russians and their Chinese friends from advancing too far, too fast."

"Exactly what I was thinking. It'll cut off all heavy vehicles. In fact, I—"

We both hear it. A loud siren. It's going up all over the city, echoing from one street to the next. The warning siren. This is not a drill.

The Russians are coming.

*

There is no mad scramble in the streets. That is, there are certainly people running around, dashing to their cars and leaving work early, but there were also plenty enough people taking the week off from work that the roads are surprisingly clear.

Fardün and I walk down Holosiivs'kyi Avenue at midday. Dark gray clouds loom overhead, casting their inescapable gloom on a ghost town still bathed in frothy fog that just won't clear. We stand at an intersection with a stoplight that is changing from red to green to red without anyone around to obey it. We cross the street on a no-walk sign with no problem. The airhorn siren goes off once every hour.

Once in a while, a car races by. Usually, it's Ukrainian military in a jeep or APC.

Unfettered, Fardün points to a series of low-rises across the Darnytsia District, which we can see laid out before us from the bridge we stand on, and stretches across the left bank of the Dnieper River. "There, there, and there," he says. "Each of those gives a good shot of the main streets, which will become major arteries once the Ukrainians blow up the bridges."

"You have one you prefer?"

He takes out a packet of cigarettes, tosses one between his lips expertly. "The main building of the Business Aviation Center has lots of windows, and an easily accessible roof. The parking garage next door is a good escape route. But all of them are good lookout points."

"They'll be checking them, with drones and with their own counter-sniper teams."

"They will," Fardün admits. "But I'll be sure to keep moving, even more than I usually do."

"The Russians may shell the hell out of those buildings," I say. "Especially if the battle gets pushed this far in. What if you're in one?"

"Then I'll probably fucking die," he laughs. "But that probably won't happen, since they want the infrastructure of Kiev intact when this is all over. That being said, if they feel like it's no longer worth the risk, blowing up a few buildings may seem like it's worth it."

I take out my binoculars. Scan the skyline. "It'll get hot, and Ukrainian snipers will start sending their own snipers up into those buildings. They won't know you from Adam, and if they see you there, you'll just be another enemy combatant to them. They won't know you're there to help them."

"I've done this for ages, Adamson. I think I know the risks."

"All right, then. Let's talk about choke points. We don't want to get trapped in any of those when EA troops start going street by street, closing off escape vectors."

*

When the first sounds of bombardment begin, we're both lying in bed in our hotel room. I'm wide awake, watching a local news station with English subtitles explain how the United States president has issued one final warning. We can all back out of this now, while there's still time to walk to the negotiation table. Fardün is asleep, but comes wide awake when there's a distant whistle followed by a loud *thump!* that shakes the hotel floor and walls.

The bomb hits several blocks away, but I feel the detonation in my chest. Even the pipes behind the wall squeak. It feels so familiar. It feels like coming home.

"Well," Fardün chuckles. "There it is. The beginning of the end." He lays back down, but then sits back up. "Shit, I can't go back to sleep now. What's on TV besides the fucking war?"

"There's a channel that plays American cartoons at this hour," I say. "Want to watch *Samurai Jack*?"

"Might as well. And turn the fucking volume up," he adds, after the next shell hits in the distance.

As we watch the adventures of a time-traveling cartoon samurai, I check my e-mail several times to see if Yarwick makes contact. She doesn't. I watch news of the war's start on the laptop, I see those bits of night-vision footage we're all so used to, from news crews stationed miles away and recording it all. Tracer fire goes lancing out into the darkness as the EA and the Ukrainian military open up on one another. World leaders from every country are shouting that this is an outrage, that there needs to be a stand-down, that we all need to gather our collective heads and talk about this.

But the bombs dropping outside don't hear all that. The concussive detonations resonate throughout the foggy city, rattling pipes and windows.

Fardün lights a cigarette and focuses on the time-traveling samurai. I think of Sophia. And Yarwick. And all those people I grew up with that might have their lives destroyed eventually because of actions I took in Russia on the CIA's behalf, and because the wrong people got voted in as leaders of the wrong nations.

Cooler heads shall not prevail.

*

One of the more peculiar images I have of my time in Kandahar is a woman walking across Myaninshi Street with her two daughters. All three were covered head to toe in burkas, for fear if they removed them the Taliban would find them, rape them, and behead them. Even though they were surrounded by NATO troops and Afghan police that were there to protect them, even though the Taliban had been driven out of the city for the most part, and even though we stood there with guns and promised to kill their enemies. It did not matter, they went about their business and kept wearing the burkas, though all the women there professed to hating them.

The mother was carrying a basket. Her two daughters had plastic boxes with fruits in them. I remember that there were gunshots going off nearby. The woman and her daughters did not hurry. They were seemingly unafraid of the death happening all across their city, and that the rubble they were walking through had been part of their home the night before.

One of the little girls was carrying a small chalkboard, and on it, written in English and in white chalk, were the words AMERICANS ARE CHEAPSKATES. I don't think she really knew what a cheapskate was. Probably some random word she read somewhere, and barely knew how to spell it correctly, but she knew it was supposed to be an insult and so she took the time to show me and my platoon the chalkboard as she went by.

My buddies and I had a laugh. Even as chaos was raining down on parts of the city, we laughed. At this little girl walking among the rubble of her home.

People will go about their business no matter what. Their children will do as their parents do. And soldiers will laugh even as they're scared shitless of what the day may bring. In a warzone, life goes on, almost like it never changed.

Fardün and I are among the few who walk out of their homes to observe the destruction, though we don't go near it, and we do so like two old friends going out for a Sunday stroll. Plenty of others join us. Journalists are out taking pictures and video.

We stand on bridges and look at the columns of black smoke that stretch high into the sky, spread out into thin clouds, dimming the morning sun. There are people with their phones out, taking pictures and sharing on Twitter and other social media. They take pictures of a historical church with its half-obliterated onion-shaped roof. They take videos and they weep as they narrate them for the people watching their livestream.

Fardün and I are taking pictures, too, but not to share on social media. We're tracking the direction of the explosions, because they give us some idea of where the EA coalition forces will start their march into Kiev. The bombings were to clear out Ukrainian tank brigades, snipers, and artillery-covered checkpoints. Some of it will be for misdirection, but the overall pattern should be crystal clear.

"Looks like they'll be coming through Petropavlivs'ka Square," I say. "Tonight or early tomorrow morning. They did a lot of damage and won't want to lose this momentum."

Fardün nods without comment.

"They'll probably set up base around the Square," I add. "At least a temporary point of operations. Might be a good opportunity to check them out." I point to a building we scouted a couple days ago, the headquarters of the Raiffeisen Bank Aval. "Think maybe there's a good overwatch spot?"

Again, Fardün nods without comment. He's humming something. Sounds like the theme song to *Samurai Jack*.

The humming is drowned out when two SU-33 jets go roaring nearby. Then I hear someone gasp. They're pointing to the damaged church. There's something moving in the columns of black smoke. Something coming out of it. Something huge.

I lift the binoculars to my eyes and zoom in on it. At first I think I'm looking at flying tanks, and I feel like I stepped into an episode of *Black Mirror* or something. But then I see what's going on, and it's not much better. Steel Octopuses. *Khishchink*. Tatiana's *Bespre 'del*. Seven of them. A good deal larger than the ones I faced in Amur Oblast. Each one carries a single Russian tank in their steel tentacles. Those tentacles do all the lifting, while vertical thrusters blast towards the earth. Not so silent as the ones I went up against.

"They're bringing in heavy weapons without having to push the tanks through every single street," Fardün says, his voice filled with a tinge of awe. "Saves on fuel, I'm sure. And gets them past any mines the Ukrainians might have set up to stop them."

I nod. "Yeah, and also over any bridges or roads the Ukrainians blew up themselves."

And there it is. Just like that, the true invasion of Kiev has begun.

But the Ukrainians aren't going down without a fight. In the next hour, we hear multiple heavy detonations. Sounds like the sequential *boom-boom-boom-boom* of a controlled demolition.

The Ukrainians did as we predicted, and demolished at least three of their own bridges, still trying to cut the EA's mobility down. But the Steel Octopuses levitate over all this chaos, and float inexorably deeper into Kiev.

*

The bombing carries on every night and most days for the next week. At all hours we hear the *pop-pop-pop* of gunfire in the distance, but neither I nor Fardün go anywhere close to it. Rather, we view it from miles away, taking it all in through our spotter's scopes or binoculars. We watch Russian snipers find their emplacements throughout the city, in church towers, mall rooftops, parking decks, and the windows of skyscrapers.

"Vega Telecomms building," I say. "Fifteenth floor, seventh window from the east."

"Got it," Fardün says, marking it down in his notebook.

"They're facing the Udabenskyi Mall, so I'm thinking that's where the EA troops will head in the next couple days, make their way towards the center of the district. At least one battalion will, at any rate. The others may splash around to the other districts."

"Probably."

The Ukrainian military will be doing the same thing, performing recon like us, but they're not sharing that intel with us. All recon has to be done by Fardün and myself. I scan his notes every night and e-mail the files to Yarwick, who thanks me and says to keep up the good work. She passes them along to CIA, who in turn feeds it to their contacts in the local Ukrainian militias.

*

Our hotel is still quite outside the hot zones, but by the sound of things tonight, you have to believe that won't last much longer. Warning sirens blare at all hours of the night and the walls and pipes rattle like Godzilla is right outside our window, getting ready to smash it down with his tail or atomic breath. Just conjuring up that image makes me remember nights at Sid Baker's house, watching *kaiju* monster flicks all night while he sometimes went into his bedroom with his girlfriend Lacey. Where did everybody go?

While the bombing continues, I unravel our map of the city on the table, using coffee mugs and pistols to hold down the corners of the curling paper. Fardün downs a Sprite he took from a bombed-out clinic he scouted earlier in the day—the closest either of us have come to the hot zone. He said he found it in a smashed vending machine, right beside the smoldering remains of a body in nurse's scrubs.

"It looks like they're keeping to the Petropavlivs'ka Square, like we figured. But you said you saw a fresh battalion around the fringes that didn't seem to be making camp?"

"I did," he says, belching and crushing the soda can and tossing it at the nearest bin. He misses. "I scoped them from a mile away on the hospital roof. Russian tank brigade, with a couple of Chinese techies working on the Octopus drones."

"Then that battalion is probably not staying with the camp. They'll move forward in a day or two while the others stay behind to hold the ground they've taken."

"Agreed."

"Any sign of our general?"

"Not a glimpse."

"You're sure? You used the phone's camera?"

"I'm sure. He's probably at the back of the march, outside the city leading the shelling on the city. He won't be coming into the city until it's all but taken."

I'm about to agree with him and offer a different route for tomorrow's intelligence-gathering foray, when a bomb strikes just outside our window. It's enough to crack our window, in fact, and shake the foundations of the hotel. He and I both drop to the floor as we listen to the boom that echoes across the world. After a minute, we slowly climb back to our feet and look out the window. A shopping plaza that was under construction down the street from us was hit, and is partially collapsed with flames shooting out of its first and second floors.

"It's getting closer to us," I say.

"Closer than I thought it would," Fardün says in awe. "Our General Yevtushenko is moving fast."

"Time to move our operations to Location B?"

"Fuck yes, Adamson."

*

Location B is a bunch of apartment buildings in development ten blocks west of the hotel, we scoped it the first day we were here. It's the kind of place squatters will take up residence, homeless people or drifters who need a place to stay. We select an unfinished flat on the fifth floor, facing east. It's kind of cold since there's no finished air-conditioning system, but we thought of this, too, and a few days ago we bought a space heater, which I now plug into the wall.

We stole the pillows and sheets from the hotel, and lay them out on the floor. Our rental car we park outside beside the bulldozers and cranes the construction workers left behind.

I look out one of the windows. About a hundred yards away, I see a riot happening. Pro-Russian Ukrainians are out in force, smashing windows, setting fires. Russia's propaganda machine has torn this society apart.

Fardün hangs by the main bay window for a while, looking out over the city with his binoculars. Tracer fire etches dotted lines in the sky. We hear an occasional rippling of detonations. The ground shakes, though not much. We hear gunfire in both the north and the south. Probably Spetsnaz units moving clandestinely in ten- and twenty-man groups in different parts of the city, weakening security forces at key intersections with hit-and-runs.

As I lie down, I say, "Wake me if anything changes."

"I will," Fardün says.

I shut my eyes.

For some reason, the first thing I see is Tatiana's face. It's there one second, gone the next. I saw myself handing her the suicide pill. Somewhere, I hear someone weeping. A man. Is it Fardün? Sounds like him.

It also sounds like my father.

*

The next morning there are dead bodies strewn all over Antonovycha Street, mostly soldiers, all Ukrainians. The dead Russians, if there were any, seem to have been taken away. The fact that the dead Ukrainians haven't been cleaned up should be a sign to everyone who now controls these streets.

I snap a couple of pics from a building up the street and e-mail the images to Yarwick, for what good it will do. Maybe JSOC will be able to make use out of the intel we're sending. But now the Russians are in the streets and begin true occupational operations, going building to building, knocking on doors and asking questions and even dragging a few people out into the street.

"Two companies moving east on Dilova Street," a voice says in my ear.

I'm leaning against a wall, eating potato chips. I look across the neighboring rooftops. Fardün is somewhere out there, checking the movements of the ones that did this massacre I'm documenting. The war is getting closer. No longer on the city's doorstep, its foot is now firmly planted in the door and it's coming in. I can hear the squeaking of gears that is the distant song of incoming tanks. Occasionally, I see an Octopus appear in the sky, a large piece of equipment wrapped in its tentacles, as it zips around one building after another.

This is going to be tough, but this is what we've been waiting for. For them to get close. All the recon work has been leading up to this. Now we can really start to operate.

Do. Not. Let. Them. Win, Sophia said to me.

I send the e-mail to Yarwick, letting her know intense operations are about to begin. She sends back her approval.

Looking through my binoculars at the dead soldiers lying in the street, I see a black bird has landed on one of them and started pecking the corpse's face. In the distance, I hear gunfire. A tank lets out a bark. In the street, a teenage girl is walking about the corpses and laying a single white flower on their chests. Warzones are strange, hideous, beautiful places.

I lower the binoculars and look at the noon sky. Somewhere out there, there are thousands of soldiers who are just as I once was. Freshly recruited, handed a gun, and told to kill. It feels the same, yet it's completely different.

That's because this time, I'm the insurgent.

*

The militiamen are called the National Militia. At times, they've been accused of being neo-Nazis. They deny that characterization. I keep that in mind as I go to meet with Zhadan, the local chapter leader. He's been on CIA's radar ever since he led a semi-successful attack against Ukrainian separatists and started making appearances on national television praising the work of his fellow fighters. They've been kind of a vigilante group, but one that CIA has been thinking about putting in their pocket, should they ever need them.

It's dangerous doing a meeting in broad daylight, but that's how Zhadan wanted it. I perform an SDR, over railroad tracks in

Shevchenkivskyi District. No signs of destruction here, but give it a week. There are probably plainclothes Unit operatives already moving through here, operating among the people still hustling to do their shopping or loot destroyed grocery stores, making their own contacts. Even as I'm recruiting local leaders, the Russians are looking to do the same. It's almost funny, like a college where a bunch of sports agents are silently trying to snatch up the best players before anyone else can. Only here, there are clearly two sides, and CIA has fed JSOC and Yarwick all the right names.

I step through a café where the brave owner has decided to keep business going. I move down Volodymyrska Street, double-backing and cutting through an alley, headed towards the Golden Gates of Kyiv, a rebuilding of the fortification that was here in the 11th century, one of three entrances into the ancient walled city. Here, I see a skinhead standing by a giant plaque that tells of the Gates' history.

He sees me.

As I approach, I switch the duffel bag from my left hand to my right hand. That's my signal that I'm clean, no one's followed me. He nods to his left. Two of his guys are sitting by a bench. One gets up to leave. His signal that, as far as he knows, he hasn't been followed, either.

In the faint distance, I hear the crack of gunfire. Then a report. A bomb explodes somewhere, and then all fighting ceases. None of the militiamen around me seem the slightest bit perturbed that the fighting will come this way soon. They all just watch me, silently.

I spot a guy in a black leather jacket hanging out near a closed concession stand. I see the pistol tucked in his waistband. Not too subtle. I've got my work cut out for me, training these assholes. We'll see if they're even trainable, first.

Fardün's voice comes through my Bluetooth earbud. "I see three guys about thirty meters west of you. He brought a lot of people, Hades."

"Copy that, Nemesis," I mutter. We decided to use codenames in case the Russians start picking up our transmissions. Not likely, since it's an army intent on blanketing the area in radio saturation, and not hacking into local phone calls. Still, best to be safe.

Zhadan's got backup, and so do I. Fardün is resting in a perch atop a parking garage behind me, with a clear shot of the street. As I approach Zhadan, he turns and walks away, into a park. I walk on a path parallel to him, until we come to the center of the park. There are sparse trees, it might be difficult for Fardün to get a shot in here if he has to, but I don't think it will be necessary. I've already talked with this guy over the phone, I've got a feel for him, and CIA seems pretty go-ready with him.

We meet at a gazebo, and I'm looking at this guy, practically a kid, with a shaved head and a burn scar on his right cheek the size of a coin. He's tall, skinny, and his eyes are smoldering with youthful resentment. He's a remainder of the Azov movement, and its political spin-off, the National Corpus party. "Well?" he says, in passable English.

I pull the phone out of my pocket. "It's only got one phone number programmed into it," I say, and hand it to him. "It's more secure than any other phone you could use. It'll also make a loud squealing noise in your ear if you're being bugged."

"What do I need this for? I need money, man. Supplies. You want this to work, you're going to have to do better—"

"The person that will call you will tell you about scheduled dead drops, times, and locations. At each dead drop, you'll find supplies of what you need."

"How are you going to arm all of us? You can't get weapons in here. Not now, with the Russkies at the front door."

"You let us handle that," I say. He wouldn't understand it anyway. The complexities of CIA's front companies setting up slush funds and funneling money through everything from local crime lords to sympathizers to the Ukrainian cause, and that money being utilized to purchase any weapons already inside Kiev, then stockpiled at various hidden locations like a dispensary, awaiting their shipping addresses.

"I have to know your people aren't making things worse for us," Zhadan says. "By arming the local drug dealers, the pimps. We're not working with those pieces of shit."

Despite having close ties to neo-Nazis, the National Militia is all volunteers whose goal is to crack down on drugs, public drunkenness, and street crime. If they found out that the tools of their salvation (guns) were somehow financially benefiting the same shitty people they've been fighting, it would be unacceptable. They're willing to kill Russians, but if it means giving money to the people they view as devouring the soul of Ukraine, they'll find some other way.

"You don't have to worry about that," I say, which is a dodge, not an answer.

I think the kid knows the answer. How could he not, being a leader? Leaders have a sense for things like this. But he's also young, meaning he has few, if any, major connections, and he's scared for his people. Those two things make him desperate. My bet is that he's willing to pretend he doesn't know I'm deceiving him, and take the weapons being offered.

It turns out I'm right. "Okay," he says. "When's the first drop?"

"Keep the phone on you. And keep it charged at all times." I turn and walk away.

I perform another dry-cleaning run, both to make sure no Russian operatives are following me, and to ensure none of Zhadan's people try and track me back to my hideout. I have to be a ghost to everyone, including my allies.

Fardün's voice is in my ear again. "Well? How'd it go?"

"I think they'll be up for it."

"That's good. Who's up next?"

"That gunfire sounds like it's happening over near Lukyanivka," I say. "So let's skip that for now. I'll call Pului, let him know it's too hot in that direction to meet. I'll head for Shuliavka, meet up with Mazepa."

"Copy that. Nemesis is changing position to east-facing side of the garage."

Later that night, when we're both fed and bound for sleep in our hideout, Fardün and I look over the street map and decide on tomorrow's work schedule and meetings. I send the day's progress and tomorrow's itinerary to Yarwick, and also tell her that there's been no sign or even rumor of Yevtushenko's presence in Kiev, but we'll keep looking. She responds with a short e-mail:

That's good to hear. You're doing excellent work. You guys are yielding more results than any others we've planted in the region, and much faster. As for your target, we think we've got a bead on him. Satellite images are promising. I'll send you a package in the morning. I hope all is well with you. Stay sharp. And let me know the second you start feeling overwhelmed. We've got two extraction plans for getting you out of there. I'll take you for a ride on the Harley when you get back.

I smile at that, and close the laptop.

The small TV that Fardün stole from a bombed-out electronics store shows almost nothing but static—most TV stations have either been abandoned, destroyed, or had their transmissions interrupted by Russian forces who are blanketing this region in radio-saturation attacks.

Gunfire in the distance. Before I go to sleep, I glance out the window. A Steel Octopus goes gliding across the sky about a mile away, slowly scanning the streets with two spotlights. A helicopter goes streaking past, a Kamov K-52, its red lights twinkling in the darkness. The soft sigh of new rain makes me a little sleepy. Behind me, Fardün laughs at something. He's picked up a channel playing *Dumb and Dumber*. I remember seeing that in high school with Sid Baker. Jim Carrey at his peak.

A missile goes slicing through the air in the distance, arcs towards the ground. I both hear and feel the distant thump of the explosion. Makes me think of German-occupied France. I think about Sophia, and home. It's weird. Whenever I'm at home, I think about the job. And whenever I'm on the job, I think of home. Both Yarwick and Fardün have asked me why I do this. I think it's because I like it. God help me, I love the dichotomy between the two worlds, the dichotomy that Fardün described.

I need the Drifting Place. Haven't been there in a while. I lay down, shut my eyes, and see the sun setting over a field of flowers. It's somehow not enough. It's missing something. Then, Sophia's there. I see her how she was back when she was fighting the Tyrant and killing his Gestapo agents, long black hair rippling in a sourceless breeze, machine gun in hand and a cold stare. She's looking at me. Her lips are moving. I can't tell what she's saying, but I'm sure it's an insult.

Oie

  I look at the clock on the wall. Six o'clock. They will be trying to put us to bed soon. Orson is working tonight, so it will be him that comes and gets me. We have a rapport. A barely friendly one, but it works. I have had a particularly cogent day. I have been thinking about many things, recalling them with the same clarity I did in my thirties and forties. Instinctively, I know this is transient. I am vaguely aware that it is all slipping away, and that today has been a gift, a brief reprieve from the frightening fog that surrounds me more and more each day.

  So I spend it in conversation. I have been talking with Gail and Roy and Alberta, just reminiscing about old times. Each of was born in a different decade—I am the oldest, obviously—and we chat about the feeling of each era. I describe the thirties in Paris, before the bad times. Gail tells us what it was like being a teenager in the fifties, when swing music reached its peek and she was out with a different guy every Friday. Roy describes being a young man in the hippy movement, losing his virginity at Woodstock—to his mother's best friend!—and we all tease him as he turns red. Alberta is closest to me in age at eighty-nine, and recalls the forties and fifties in California, the birth of doo-wop music, and her lifelong obsession with Frankie Valli.

  Chloe and Zoe came by earlier. I think. No, I *know*. Today I know things. I am secure in the knowledge that I am knowing. I never thought that simple act would be all I ever yearned for. Such a simple thing, our sanity. But since I know that my girls came by today, I know that the conversation I had with them was real, and I remember that Henrietta says her hands get cold easily.

  As I sit listening to Gail, Roy, and Alberta, I keep my hands busy with work, knitting a pair of mittens for Henrietta. Summer is around the corner, but she can use them next year. I will make them a little bigger, so she can grow into them.

A tap on my shoulder. I know who it is. I look up and see Orson standing there, but he looks strange. His face. Something's not right. I have known him long enough now and teased him enough to know when he is settled and when he is unsettled. "What is it now?" I say.

"Uh, hey, Sophia," he edges. "You got a visitor."

"My girls already came today. Did they forget something?"

"Um, no, no, it's your daughter or—"

"Abijah? That's strange. She knows that it's well past visiting hours."

"Not the lady, either," Orson says. "A man. He said he'd just like a quick word with you."

"A man? What man?"

His hands are already on my handlebars. He is taking me away from the others and I am not sure how I feel about this. They watch me go. Like prisoners, we must obey the guards, even when we don't want to, even though our caretakers are younger than us. We raised them, we nurtured them, we fed them, and now they control us. "I am talking to my friends, Orson."

"I know, Sophia. But…the guy seems urgent. He needs to talk to you now about something."

"What?"

"I don't know." He glances over his shoulder, looking to see if any of the staff are watching him. "Something important."

"Orson, *sous-merde*, what is going on?"

"It's not a big deal, Sophia. Don't freak out," he laughs. But the laughter is forced.

"Is it Mr. Baudelaire, the man who visited me a while back?"

"Um, no. No, it's…it's just a guy who needs to ask you some questions."

We are moving down an empty hall with locked doors on either side of me. I look for any nurses, any nightwachmen, anyone at all. The hall is devoid of human life. He turns me down another corridor, equally sterile. I think of Nathan. I don't know why, but I do. And I think of Karkus, and Jean-Luc, and Chloe and Zoe and Henrietta. I think of Abijah and Baudelaire. I think of Chloe's father and how he admonished me once for staying out late drinking with my friends and how I walked home one night through dark alleys. For a moment, for just once second, I'm not sure when this is all happening. Am I in a dream, or am I really this old and feeble?

I realize we are headed right for my room. I am only mildly comforted.

Orson stops at the door, reaches to open the door. "Orson? What is this? What is happening?"

"It's okay, Sophia," he says. Another glance over his shoulder. "It's all right."

The door opens. He rolls me inside. He shuts the door behind me. In the room is a man, well dressed. Gray suit, pressed. He is seated with his back to me. When we enter he stands up and turns to face us. He is pale. Extremely pale. And blonde. I know this man. I have never met him but I know *him*. I know his type. I remember this. This feeling. Being in the wolf's den.

Where am I? When am I?

"Sophia de Marenches?" he says.

"Who are you?"

"I'll leave you two alone," Orson says. He holds out his hand, and the tall blonde man hands Orson a large wad of cash.

"Orson…"

"It's fine, Sophia." To the blonde man he mutters, "She won't even remember this tomorrow. Ask your questions and leave, but don't put her under much stress."

"Orson."

"It's okay, Sophia," he says, and pats my shoulder as he steps out. The door shuts softly, leaving me alone with the blonde man.

For the longest time we just stare at one another. I am frightened. I know this feeling. It is a warning, coming deep from within myself. Ringed around the room are the dead men who stepped out of their shallow graves. This blonde man is their messenger, I know it.

"*Bonjour, madame,*" he says, in a faint Russian accent. "My name is Mr. Matveyev, I am a friend of Nathan Adamson. I understand he is a friend of yours, too. Perhaps he's mentioned me?"

A veil of fog falls over me. I feel myself descending into a soft obliviousness.

*

"Is this comfortable?" the man in front of me asks. "I hope it's no problem me visiting like this."

Where am I? What is happening? I do not understand. I...I was...in the TV room with Gail and Alberta and...How did I get here? Oh no, it's happening again. The slippage. Like quicksand, the more I stress, the more I fight against it, the more I sink. I look at the blonde man and I smile. A reflex. I know that I have been doing this a lot lately. Dr. Zaib said people do that when their minds start to slip, they inherently know that something is wrong, and so they smile to make it look like they're fine, like they know everything that's been going on. Like a child caught daydreaming in class, pretending they have been paying attention. I remember that much. Despite the time skip and the stress, I remember that.

My right hand is doing something. Thumb and forefinger lightly rubbing. That means I was just thinking about something. Planning something. That's my tell. What was I thinking?

"Sophia?" he says.

"No," I say, reverting to my training. I smile and sigh and act casual. "No, it is fine." Who is this man? What is happening? Is he a friend of Baudelaire's? Abijah's? "It is no problem at all. Of course, you may visit me." I look at the window. The curtains have been drawn. I didn't do that. I couldn't have. Through the curtains I see a shaft of dying sunlight. Must be past six or seven. Nightfall will be coming soon. Isn't that a line from that song Chloe likes? *Nightfall will be coming soon.* Tom Petty. Yes, that's the one—

"Sophia? I asked you a question."

"Hm? Oh, sorry, I was daydreaming." Damn it. Got caught slipping again.

The blonde man smiles politely. "It's all right. I just asked if you wanted me to fetch you something. I see you have a food tray by your bed with a juice box untouched."

I have to stall. Have to figure out what is going on. "How about some water?" I nod towards the pitcher on the table behind him.

He turns to look at it. He smiles at me. "Sure. Mind if I have a sip?"

"Not at all." He walks over to the table.

My hands do something. What are they doing? I look at them. My right hand is just coming away from my bed corner, from under the mattress. My right hand just exchanged something with my left hand. What just happened? I am lost inside my own body. What's going on?

The blonde man picks up the pitcher, starts to pour.

Then, on a whim, I say, "I'll hold the cups, you pour." I begin to roll myself over to the table.

The blonde man holds up a hand. "No, no, no, I don't want you to exert yourself."

"I insist. I have to do as much as I'm physically able. Keeps me moving."

He smiles at me. "I admire that about you, Sophia."

That smile seems familiar. Or maybe it doesn't? Maybe I've only just met this man and the mind—the foggy mind—is telling me it's familiar. Or maybe it reminds me of someone. Yes…yes, that wolfish smile. I know this man, don't I?

The blonde man hands me two plastic cups. I hold them in two shaking hands while he pours. He turns to set the pitcher down. When he turns back to me, he is smiling that familiar wolfish smile. Where do I know you from, *monsieur*? I hand him his cup of water. He accepts it and never takes his eyes off me as we sip. I look at my hand. It's just done something. What has it done? I do not remember. Like the coin trick with Henrietta, I do not know what I've done. Where am I? Who is this man? I do not know him and yet I do. He smiles at me and I smile back.

"*Tu as de beaux yeux,*" I say.

"That's beautiful," he says. "What does it mean?"

I smile sheepishly at him, and sip my water.

"Can we talk now, Sophia?" He turns a chair around to face me. He takes a seat, and leans forward like a dear old friend. "Can we talk about Nathan?"

Nathan. He's a friend of Nathan's? Is that it? Is that why he's here, to tell me something about Nate? Has he already told me and

I've forgotten? I look to the dead spirits arrayed around the room. They are stoic. They will not give me the answer. I smile at the blonde man and nod like I know exactly what he's saying and where this is going. "Yes. Nathan."

"That's right, Sophia. I'm wondering, do you know where he is right now?"

"Where Nathan is?"

"Yes."

"You want to know where he is?" I am stalling now. I need time. Time to think.

"That's right. I was wondering if you might be able to tell me where I could find him."

"Why? Are you a friend of his?"

"I am," the blonde says, giving a sincere smile. A smile that haunts me. Forces me to recall something else. Some*one* else. But who? I see a face. It's there and it's gone. I can see that wolfish grin looking down on me. I am on my knees, sucking his prick. Did that happen? Did that really happen? Or am I conflating things? Where am I? Where is Chloe? I need Chloe. I am so frightened. This man...his wolf grin...

Get it together, Oie.

Jean-Luc? Pierre? I know that voice.

Get it together. You know what this is. We prepared you for this eventuality. You know where you are. You're in the wolf's lair. He and his friends have you. They're going to coax you, pretend to be your friend. You must resist, Oie. They will pump you full of drugs that will confuse you and they will intimidate you and they will pretend to be your friends. You must resist, Oie! You must resist!

"I'm sorry, what did you say your name was?" I ask.

"Matveyev, ma'am," he says, taking another sip of his water.

"Matveyev. Yes, of course." I shift in my seat. Something pokes me in the leg. Sharp. Like I'm sitting on a needle. What is it? "Yes, Mr. Matveyev. Nathan's friend. Now I recall."

"Yes, that's right. We've been looking for Nathan, my friends and I. We're very concerned he's gotten himself into a lot of trouble, and we just need to know his current whereabouts. You know the line of work he's in."

433

"Oh, yes. Very dangerous," I say. "I'm sorry, but how do you know Nathan? How do you know his work?"

"I got to know him through a mutual friend of ours. A Monsieur Baudelaire. You remember him?"

I do. "I do," I say. "We only met the once, though. A very fine gentleman. Very polite."

"Yes, Baudelaire is a charming man. He introduced me to—"

"How is he?"

"Who? Baudelaire?" Matveyev shrugs. "He's fine. Doing very well these days."

"And how is his wife, Julia?"

"Julia's fine. They're both very happy, Sophia. In fact, they asked me to send their love."

"Well, how very nice of them to remember little old Sophia."

"I'm sure you're a hard woman to forget," Matveyev says. And there's that wolfish grin again. I know you, Matveyev. We met somewhere before, in a different lifetime. *Remember, Sophia. Remember that you are in the wolf's lair.* Yes…yes, you are right. All is not as it seems. In fact, he has already exposed himself. Twice. Does he see it? Can he see it? What are my hands doing now? Thumb and forefinger are rubbing gently together. I must have just been planning something but I've already forgotten what. I shift in my wheelchair again. And again, something pokes me beneath my thigh. "Tell me about Nathan, Sophia. Help us help him. We have to find him if we want to do that. Can you help us find Nate?"

Careful now, careful.

"I think I can."

The wolf's grin brightens. "You can?"

"Yes, I think so."

"Tell me."

"He's working on something."

"Something for the CIA?"

I nod. "Yes. And for Mossad. Yes, I think…for Mossad and MI6." *Blend truth with fiction. Give him a taste and then poison the next morsel. Lead him by the carrot but feed him the stick.* "If I'm not mistaken…let's see…let's see, let me think where it was he said he was going." *Play up your weaknesses, let them be a strength. You're on the table right now and he's pulling out your fingernails and he's going to start on your teeth soon. Then your fingers. Then your eyes. He'll threaten you with rape. Then he'll rape you. You're in the wolf's lair, guide him deeper in. He feels safe here. Guide him deeper.* "It was that woman, Abijah. She was the one who told me."

"Abijah? Was there another name?"

"Let's see. Let me think. Let me think…"

Time passes. I'm not sure how long.

*

We talk plainly, like old friends. We talk in circles. I let him get a bit more information out of me, but then I become vague. Some of it is authentic confusion, I feel my grip on the moment as slippery as a jellyfish in my hands, but try to hang on. I am confident that my instincts are leading me, and I am scared of that. Time has jumped, only a few minutes, and I am unsure of what I have admitted and what I have lied about. The lies compound enough that I am no longer sure what is real. I am terrified. I do not recall how I got here.

I smile, and keep up my end. I am not at all certain I am supposed to be here with this man, but I am also not sure who he is. I keep forgetting his name. I keep forgetting everything. My hands are fretting. Something is poking my thigh, like I sat on a tiny knife. I shift in my wheelchair. The faces of those from the shallow graves look on expectantly, as if they are waiting for me to catch on, like there is something they saw and cannot believe I missed.

The blonde man takes another sip of his water. I take a sip of mine. He compliments me on the attention I have paid to my own health over the years. He talks about how he wishes his own grandparents had eaten healthy, remained ambulatory, like me. He says he wishes he could still speak to them, hear their wisdom. He is very charming.

"I'm sorry, what did you say your name was again?" I ask. "Matt Vev?"

"Matveyev, ma'am," he says politely, flashing his wolfish grin. "Fyodor to my friends."

"Fyodor. Matveyev. Russian?"

435

"Yes, ma'am."

"Your English is very good."

"Thank you." He downs the last of his water. Rubs his right eye, like he's sleepy. Then he looks at me and smiles big. The way adults do to babies. Big expressions to get big reactions from infants. That is familiar to me. For the last twenty years, it has been the look on the faces of everyone new that I meet. Next, he will talk slowly, like a father proud of his big girl. "Sophia, I bet you know all kinds of secrets about Nathan. In fact, I bet you could tell me where he lives, where he hangs out, the friends he has."

"Nathan's only friend is me," I tell him. "Or, at least, I think so." I see him nod, and, gauging his disappointment, I follow my instincts to keep him engaged. "You know young people, they are always keeping things from us old folks. But we are not so stupid as you young people think. We know when you're sweet on someone, for instance."

"Sweet? Ah, you mean when someone has a, ah, crush on someone. A sweetheart, yes?"

"Yes." *What are you doing, Sophia? Why are you leading him on?*

Very good, Sophia, a voice says. Who's voice? *You've given him the bait. Careful now. Careful. Watch how he reacts to it. Watch him closely. Watch him so, so closely.*

"Did Nathan have someone he was sweet on?" Matveyev asks.

"Yes," I say. "In fact, I know her well. Karen. He visits her often. She has an ex-husband, though, that's been stalking her. Giving them trouble. Asshole should leave my Nathan and his Karen alone." Fact with fiction. I used to know a Karen, and her ex-husband was indeed an asshole. *Good, Sophia. That helps sell it.*

Matveyev smiles, and leans forward. Eager. Here's something he can use. "Is that right? Well, sounds like Nathan should teach this guy a lesson?"

"Someone should."

"I think I know a Karen. Where does she live again?"

"Karen? Let me think…" I trail off for a second, thinking. My thumb and forefinger are rubbing together again. I think I just had an idea. It was there and gone. Slipped. Then, Matveyev rubs both his eyes. I look at him. His eyes are bloodshot. Looks sleepy. And then I remember. The fog lifts for a moment and I remember what it was I was thinking. I remember what it was he said. About Baudelaire. And his wife.

Baudelaire's wife.

I smile. The wolf's eyes shift. Does he detect it yet? Does he see it?

Careful. Do not scare him away. Hold him. You are in danger, Oie. When this conversation is over you are dead. He will suffocate you with your own pillow and then leave. And who will believe you died of anything but natural causes? Your only chance is to hold him here, do not give him a reason to leave this room.

"I believe Karen lives on...Belmont, was it? Or no...no..." I look into the wolf's eager eyes. I see him blink. There is confusion there for a moment. He rubs his eyes again. Stifles a yawn. I feel the prick of the pointy object beneath my thigh. And now I remember what it was my hands did when he turned his back to get our water from the pitcher. It's like it happened in a dream, but I still recall doing it. "I forget which city, but I think Karen lives on a street that starts with a B."

"A street that starts with a B," he says.

"Yes, I think so." I sigh. "It has been a confusing time. I am sorry if I am not being very helpful, but I have seen Nathan's face on TV. Now, I'm just an old hen, politics confuse me, but I've been following the story and I worry about him. They say...they say he did something awful. The *president* even mentioned him by name."

The wolf stares at me. "You don't say."

He will not believe you forever. He will not go along with your ruse for much longer. It is time to transition. Change the course of the conversation. Tease him, but not too much. Slowly mete out what you know.

"Yes, I do say. Said he was, eh, doing something or other in another country that Putin was blaming him for." I brighten, and snap my fingers. "*Russia.* They said he was in Russia doing something, some secret thing or other. Russia. Yes. Where you're from."

Matveyev nods. "It is true. Our president and your president seem to disagree on just what he was doing there."

"I understand the Russians want him alive for something. Now, if I'm following all this, and I'm not sure that I am," I laugh, and the wolf smiles with his lips but not with his eyes, "Russia and this, ah, Eastern Alignment are racing towards a war, and they have blamed the U.S. for interfering with their operations. Now," I take a sip of my water and watch as the wolf blinks through bloodshot eyes. "It seems to me that your president would benefit from having Nathan in custody. Torture him for what he knows. Or, at the very least, force him to admit to the world what he was sent into Russia to do."

Matveyev smiles, and shrugs. "Who am I to say what would benefit whom?"

"Just proving that Nathan was alive and well in the U.S. might indicate he's being aided and abetted by the government. You wouldn't even need to kill him or capture him to prove the president lied when he feigned ignorance of Nathan Adamson."

"Who said anything about killing or capturing him? I'm only trying to help him, Sophia."

"And my cunt is as fresh as a spring chicken's," I say. And glare at him.

The wolf stares at me. Blinks. Smiles.

"I'd say that's enough bullshit from both of us, wouldn't you say?"

The wolf tilts his head to one side, curiously. Then he nods. "So," he says slowly, almost dreamily, "the old Goose is still in there, I see."

"*Sous-merde*, this old Goose never left."

*

The wolf smiles. Blinks. Rubs his bloodshot eyes and reaches out to touch my knee. I notice his hand is trembling. Ever so slightly. "Sophia," he says, as gently as a lover. "I don't want to hurt you. Or your family. Chloe, Zoe, and little Henrietta. All very pretty. I'm sure Henrietta would fetch a fine price on certain markets."

I want to vomit, but I smile back at him. "Do you know what never ceases to amaze me?"

"What's that, *mademoiselle?*"

"The tenacity of men like you. We did our very best to wipe the world of your scum. We killed scores. We hanged them, shot them, even boiled a few of them alive to get what we wanted. But it seems the object lesson did not stick. Creatures like you will persevere, won't you?"

"You need to appreciate the situation you're in, Soph—"

"And you need to appreciate yours, Herr Vogel."

He winces. "Vogel?"

I continue on, unfettered, aware that I'm getting confused and yet am laser-focused. "You came here to intimidate me. How very brave of you, scaring a hundred-year-old woman. Do they give out special badges for scaring great-grandmothers? No? Well, maybe they'll make one specially for you."

And then it comes. What I've been waiting for and preparing myself for. His hand moves out, fast as lightning and snatches my left hand and breaks my middle finger in half. The wind is sucked out of me. My heart skips. I look down at the finger, grossly bent, the bone sticking out and dripping blood. Once upon a time I might've been fast enough to stop him, or fight back, but not now. I am old. And I am in the wolf's lair. He makes the rules here.

My hand is throbbing. Shards of pain leak into my arm and my mouth is agape in a silent scream. I look at him. The grin has never been more predatory, more lascivious, more needy.

The men in their shallow graves nod their approval. They are happy to see me get mine.

"Now, Madame de Marenches, talk to me about what a creature I am," he growls. He leans in more. Close enough now that I can smell the onions on his breath, and see the sweat on his brow, and the pallor in his cheeks. "You think I broke your finger just now because I'm insulted? No, name-calling does not bother me. What bothers me is people wasting my time. People who are too old or too slow or too stupid to know that they don't have a choice. I will rape your daughter, your grand-daughter, and your great-granddaughter, then let my men have their turn. They will know nothing else, no other life, but being locked up and made to service men in the lowest fucking whorehouse in Russia! Separate whorehouses, so they never see each other again! And it will be because of you! Do you understand?"

"There…are men…in graves…"

"What? Speak clearly, *madame*, I believe you are fading," he laughs.

And I laugh, too. That startles him. I can tell. "There are men…in unmarked graves. Left where I put them." A jolt of pain travels up my arm. "Their mothers died never knowing what happened to their sons! Sons that I fucked and then killed! One or two I tortured, along with my friends! They are in this room with us, Vogel! They are here with us! I know what this is, Vogel! I know, because I've been on your side of the room before!"

"You keep saying Vogel. How do you know that name? Are the Americans on to Arumush? Did Nathan tell you that?" He reaches forward and grabs my pinky finger. "Tell me, Sophia. For every finger you make me break, that's how many times I fuck your great-granddaughter in the ass!"

"Go ahead and break it, Vogel! I know you! I've seen you!" I throw my head back and laugh. "I know your dick stays limp when you are with women, because you do not feel like a man! I know you pull yourself off while fingering your own asshole because your dick stays soft unless you are raping! I know what you are, Vog*ahhhhhh!*" The bone snaps louder this time, and when I look down, the pink is torn nearly completely off.

"That's two ass-fuckings, Sophia."

The pain shoots up and down my arm, reverberating in my skull and bringing on visions of Jean-Luc. For a moment I am there. I am *there*, and not here in the room. Running through the cornstalks and laughing and wondering what time his mother gets home and if we'll have enough time to go down by the lake and then visit Louise later since she lives so close by—

—and now I'm back where I know I'm supposed to be, looking the wolf in his grinning face. And I'm laughing. And I'm babbling something. I've been out of it, talking out of my mind. How much have I told him?

He's in the middle of making more threats. "—stomp her head into the mud while I shove this blade up her cunt!" He pulls out a small curved blade. A karambit. He holds it an inch from my face. "I'll peel the flesh off her ass after I'm done, but she won't be dead, Sophia. This is your last chance. Where can I find Nathan Adamson?"

"You work for Putin, eh?" I chuckle, battling waves of pulsating pain. My whole left hand is swelling up and shaking like mad. "You work for that *fini à la pisse*. He likes to kill people. Journalists and protesters and ex-spies and anybody that exposes what his regime is up to. I keep up with politics, Vogel. Your boss would like my Nathan as a trophy, wouldn't he? Yesssss, Vogel, I know! And I know you would be his favorite lapdog for bringing back my Nathan! But my Nathan is smart and fast and strong and a killer! He will not bend or break! He's coming for you, Vogel, and when he finds you *he's going to fucking kill you!*"

The wolf reaches out again, stabs my left arm, and starts peeling flesh. Slowly.

I scream.

And that's when my right hand does what it must. It reaches under my seat and grabs the syringe I don't remember hiding there but I must have done because it's there and it's in my hand and now I'm plunging it into his neck and injecting him with whatever clear liquid is in it. I do not even know what it is, but I must have known when I first came in here and had him turn his back to pour the water. I must have known which syringe to grab from my treasure trove beneath my mattress. I must have known, because as soon as I inject him he smacks my right hand away, jumps back, kicking over his chair, and goes stumbling backward, clutching his neck.

He might have been able to stop me if not for Janette Oakes's medication, strong sedatives for crazy people, clear capsules that dissolve almost instantly, two or three of which I dropped into his water before I handed him his cup, along with God knows what else I palmed while he wasn't looking. I cannot remember. But the bloodshot eyes, the pale color of his cheeks, the constant rubbing, and the sweat all told me that the drugs were taking effect.

"Baudelaire had no wife," I tell my enemy. "He had a girlfriend. And her name was Claire, not Julia. You slipped up, Vogel. You slipped! Do you see? I want you to see where you failed."

441

The wolf lunges at me, drops to his knees, and falls forward. He drops his knife, and reaches forward to clutch my ankle and squeeze. Face reddening.

I look at my arm. A slab of flesh hangs off. I'm gushing blood.

The wolf squeezes harder. Tries to climb my wheelchair. I reach down and grab a fistful of his hair and yank his head back so I can look him in the eye. "I found you, *Bite Molle*! My Nathan and I, we found you!" I laugh exultingly. "You thought you could hide, but you couldn't! There is nowhere left to run, and now the Goose has you and you will meet the others. See them, Vogel?" I turn his head to face those in their shallow graves. "Do you see them, Vogel? They're waiting for you to join them!"

Through a foaming mouth, I think I hear him say *My God*. He sees them. I know he sees them.

"No funerals for you creatures! No marked graves, no one to mourn you! Just a spot in the dirt for me to piss on!" I spit in his face as he struggles to stand. "I have you now, Vogel! This French tart has you and you won't escape! I found you! I found you and I fucked you! You thought this was your wolf's lair, but you are in *the Goose's nest*! And now we will all feed on you, *Bite Molle*! We will feed on your soft prick and toss your bones in the dirt for the mice to make homes in you!"

He falls to the ground, convulsing. His grip on my ankle weakens, melts, then falls away. He lays still on the ground. For maybe a minute, I hear wheezing. He's struggling to breathe. Then he stops. I don't know what cocktail I gave him but apparently I knew what I was doing when I planned it, because it was a system overload.

I look around at the men in their shallow graves. They have backed away. So sorry, friends, but you won't get your pound of flesh from me tonight.

*

Wait…wait, what happened? Where am I? Oh, God, who is on the floor? Wait…hold on, Sophia. You remember. Yes, you remember some of it. Think hard. Calm yourself. Calm down. Just breathe and think. You remember the wolf, don't you? Yes, of course, how could I forget? My God...my hand! The pain! Two fingers bent grotesquely in unnatural shapes. It looks like I stuck them in a blender for half a second. *Mon Dieu*, the pain! And I've been stabbed. I'm still bleeding. My arm is going numb.

I look at the man on the ground. Did kill him? Yes, of course I did. But why? I vaguely remember. I recall the wolfish grin and that he hurt me. He smiled while he hurt me. Who sent him? Was it Vogel? Does he know I'm on to him? If so, does he know I sent Nathan to take care of him? *What am I going to do about this dead fucking body?!*

The syringe is still sticking out of his neck and I cannot bend down or crawl over to get it. Everyone will know I tried to kill this man. What am I going to do? He is on his belly but his head is turned, I can see his face, the half-lidded eyes looking across the floor like he's trying to spot something in the distance. I look around the room. Matveyev—yes, that's his name—he's standing on the other side of the bed, along with the others. They see me. They are waiting for me.

"Not today, motherfuckers!" I hiss.

Get it together, Sophia. Think. You have a dead body and you need to get rid of it. Add it to the list of men you left in shallow, unmarked graves. But you can't move this one. You can barely stand up. So, you can't bury it. What *can* you do?

The plan comes to me fully formed. Simple. No need for moving parts or keeping too many secrets.

Blood is spurting from my arm. There is a vase of flowers sitting on the windowsill. I pick it up with my one good hand, quivering with the effort, then hurl it at the window. The vase breaks. The window cracks. Then I wheel over to the other window. Straining, I reach forward and unlock it, then push it open. I wheel myself back over to the door. Crack it open. I summon the courage to give myself the self-inflicted injury I know will result from this. Then, I slide forward. It hurts. I don't think I can do it—

When I slip and fall to the floor, I let out a scream for help that is more authentic than I'm prepared to admit. I push open the door and crawl into the hallway, leaving a crimson trail behind me, as well as a yellow one. I've pissed myself. I scream. And I keep screaming. Until finally I hear footsteps. Two orderlies, James and Orson, come rushing down the hallway. Part of my foggy memory recalls that Orson put me in the room with the wolf, but for the moment I feign ignorance.

"Jesus Christ!" James breathes. "What the fuck?"

"Help me! H-He broke in…he tried to hurt me…I-I-I did what I could…"

"Jesus fucking Christ, Sophia. Look at your arm. Your fucking hands."

Orson looks down at me with supreme fear. I will make him pay another day, in other ways, but for right now it is best that he thinks I do not remember.

"I-I don't know what happened!" I pant. "We struggled and I fell out of my chair and I broke my fingers. He slashed me on my arm. I th-think he tried to cut me. He was looking for drugs…started eating my stash…my fucking pill stash!" Sounds implausible, but for the moment it is going to be far more plausible than an old woman getting the drop on a trained killer.

Orson walks over to the dead man, rolls him over, and checks his pulse. "Fuck me, Jimmy. Fuck me, he's dead."

"No fucking way." James puts his hands in front of the dead man's nostrils, feeling for breath. He looks at Orson, then pulls out his radio. "Haley, this is James, do you copy?" He looks at Orson and points at me. "Orson, stop fuckin' around with that body and put some pressure on her fuckin' arm! Use the bedsheets!" Orson stumbles over to me, rips off my bedsheets, and begins wrapping my arm. "Haley, do you copy?!"

A bit of static from his radio. Then, "I hear you James. Go ahead."

"Call the doc, and call nine-one-one. Now ! This instant!"

"Um, okay."

James stands up and looks around the room, at the cracked window, at the broken vase. Then he turns and looks at the only open window in the room. Putting it together. I left the window open and a burglar got in.

Orson looks me in the eye. "H-Hey, Sophia…it's me. You remember me, don't you?"

I blink. "Orson? That you?" I can see the relief in his eyes. Not that I remember him, but that I only vaguely do. He is hoping he does not have to explain himself to anyone later. No conflicting stories. He just brought me to my room because I looked tired, that's it. And then I must have left the window open. A burglar came in. A psycho junkie looking for drugs, money, whatever he could find. Swallowed my stash, then plunged the needle in his own neck, looking for a fix. A schizo looking for a way out. "You remember what happened, Sophia?"

"What happened?" I look down at my ripped arm, my mangled hand. I am shaking through waves of exquisite pain. I look back at Orson. "No, Orson. I don't remember anything."

Shush, my friends. Go back to your shallow graves. My secrets stay safe another night. Sorry, old friends. So, so sorry. But the old Goose is not yet yours.

32

There is a ghost in Kiev. He is without form or shape, without compassion or constraint. He emerges only at night, moves here and there, clutching the fog to him like a blanket, and he does his ill deeds. Then, as the sun rises, he recedes along with the shadows.

During the day, when the gunfire tapers off and most of the battles cease, the ghost rests. On occasion, he pops up from his hiding place and gazes into the city streets. He tracks pro- and anti-Russian marches, marks the drones hovering in the sky, and communicates with his partner, who is also a ghost.

Then, when nightfall comes, the ghost comes back out. He slinks from building to building, clutching to shadows. The ghost watches which way the shadows move, the way spotlights sweep the areas and push the shadows around like plows push around snow. He uses the fog to his advantage. Once or twice, a Russian patrol thinks they see something moving in that fog, but when they check again, there is nothing there. Only the fog. Only the darkness.

Day comes. The ghost rests. Night comes. The ghost comes out to play.

This ghost rattles no chains. He makes as little noise as he possible. He leaves few footprints. The ghost's only job is to track and observe movements. When helicopters come in to dump troops on the ground, the ghost is watching. When troops are rotated out or a new patrol is set up, the ghost is watching. When nothing particularly special happens at all, the ghost is watching.

Day comes. The ghost rests. Night comes. The ghost comes out to play.

There are more places to hide. New places every day. Buildings turned to rubble provide chaotic scenes of dust and debris that the ghost can meld with.

The ghost watches and he records and he remembers and he feeds the information to his partner, the other ghost. They interact rarely, but their coordination makes each ghost's maneuverings more informed, more subtle, more impossible to detect. The EA battalions have no notion that two ghosts are moving all around them, and neither, it seems, does the ill-trained Ukrainian Army.

Day comes. The ghost rests. Night comes. The ghost comes out to play.

All night long, the city is bombarded from forces both internal and external. Two marketplaces are hit by the Russians, using their TOS-1 "Buratino" launch platforms. The explosions illuminate the night.

Several blocks are destroyed at once.

The Ukrainians really start laying it on. They have to fight for every inch. They can't be worried about destroying their own city, they just have to drop their own warheads, one after another.

The ghost watches as buildings collapse. The ghost watches as people are torn from their homes, some stripped naked and searched. The ghost knows this is when it gets bad, when soldiers no longer care about the dignity of their captors. The ghost knows this. He has haunted other battlefields before.

The ghost notes that it is mostly officers and plainclothes men with black body armor doing these nude interrogations. It is the work of the Unit.

The ghost is almost spotted once. He is trying to maneuver close to a T-14 Armata tank, and plant a device on it. But the patrol stepping away from a nearby jeep, and who was hitherto asleep in the driver's seat, comes walking too close. Just two feet away, about to piss into a shadow. A shadow where the ghost has come to a stop mid-crawl. As the soldier unzips his pants, the ghost rises up quickly, covers the man's mouth, and slits his throat with a Ka-Bar knife. The ghost had to do it. The soldier's nighteyes would have adjusted, he would've seen what, and who, he was pissing on.

Before the body even drops, the ghost melts back into the shadows, but not before planting one of the listening devices onto the side of the tank. Minutes after he's slipped away to safety, the ghosts hears alarmed voices. They're looking for him. But the ghost is blocks away before a flare is sent up and two *Khishchnik*s begin scanning the area from the sky.

Day comes. The ghost rests. Night comes. The ghost comes out to play.

Rigel and Betelgeuse are old friends of the ghost. The stars watch him as he passes through the fog, through the thick smoke of a leveled clinic. Under the watchful eye of his fellow ghost, he is guided safely away from a major tank brigade, and plants another listening device beneath an army jeep. Three soldiers spot him on the way out. They aim their flashlights in his direction, and start after him, moving covertly. Two of the men are killed by whispered gunshots. The third one lives and tells of what he saw.

Day comes. The ghost rests. Night comes. The ghost comes out to play.

*

The two ghosts begin to find their rhythm, and track the movement of the Russians and the Chinese quite logically, almost all of their predictions coming true. They move about in symphony, one ghost keeping to the ground, the other being the eyes in the sky.

The ghost on the ground haunts a Russian camp one night, and the next night he haunts a Chinese camp. Some buildings are being used by the EA for tactical planning. One such building, headquarters of the ASKA Insurance Company, appears to be the main hub. The ghost does reconnaissance on it for three nights in a row before making his approach. He plants a listening device on the chassis of a patrol jeep that has been used by a high-ranking officer, and plants another on the top-left corner of a door leading into the main hall.

On his way out from the insurance building, the ghost is alerted to two men coming up behind him. The ghost's partner tells him they are on patrol, surveying the rubble around the building. They're coming from Taskiov'ka Street. There's no way out, the ghost *must* go that way, so he waits in ambush. As they come through, each one gets a suppressed shot to the back of the head.

Suppressed shots aren't as silent as the movies, and neither are bodies that drop to the ground. Someone comes to investigate, but the ghost is already gone.

Day comes. The ghost rests. Night comes. The ghost comes out to play.

*

The Ukrainians present just as much a problem for the ghost as do the Russians and the Chinese. The Ukrainians don't know the ghost is on their side, and they can't know that, because then they might learn who he really is, and that information could leak to the EA. In fact, the ghost's existence must not even be confirmed.

But it is perfectly okay if it remains a battlefield rumor.

There is talk among the battalions and tank brigades. Someone has been killing their people in the night. A person that is rarely seen and leaves no trace. There is talk that it is a new Ukrainian sniper team in play. However, that story is contradicted by the evidence of bodies found shot and stabbed up close. Battalions assign more men for regular patrol, and less hours for sleep, since all the attacks appear to happen at night.

But then one day the ghost and his partner take out two soldiers on patrol at midday, just to throw them off. And now the battalions are uncertain of many things.

The ghost hides in a roadside ditch and plants three more listening devices on tanks as they go by. Around midnight that same night, he comes across Ukrainian troops installing a bomb in a culvert that runs beneath a road. He is careful to give them a wide berth. One of them hears something, and looks in his direction with a flashlight, but the ghost's partner fires a shot into the ground next to the Ukrainians, and they run for cover, giving the ghost a chance to escape.

Just when things get too hot in the Dniprovsky District, the ghost moves along to EA operations taking place in the Pecherskyi District. Here, the ghost moves among miles upon miles of neighborhoods that hug the right bank of the Dnieper. Some have called this area the very heart of all Ukraine.

Here, the ghost moves from rooftop to rooftop, watching daily as the EA troops make their way slowly over. In the distance is the House with Chimaeras, sometimes called the Horodecki House. It is a large building built in Art Nouveau style. The House with Chimaeras rests in a patrolled pedestrian zone kept clear of all traffic. Not just because the Ukrainians treasure it, but because the Presidential Administration Building is close by.

The last major resistance of the Ukrainian government is here. The military has fallen back all the way to the House with Chimaeras and its surrounding subdivisions, and here they make their stand. Vladimir Putin himself once visited the building years ago. Now he means to demolish it or take it as a prize.

If the EA gets this, it will be a major victory. They will have all of Kiev, and hence all of Ukraine, all of its manufacturing, all of its industry, and all of its weapons.

The ghost sees this. Knows this. Doesn't let it bother him. His objectives are clear.

Day comes. The ghost rests. Night comes. The ghost comes out to play.

*

Four more dead in the night. Only one of them by the ghost's own hand. The other three were taken out by his partner, who felt they were getting a little too close to where the ghost was hiding beneath what remained of a bridge the Ukrainians destroyed.

*Khishchnik*s hover over the residential homes in Pecherskyi, some of them carrying tanks across the unpassable ditches left by the bridge, while others simply scan the rooftops for snipers. As full night comes, each *Khishchnik* retreats back to its main battalions, while the shelling of both sides commences.

The ghost moves among people running from one destroyed neighborhood to the next.

Late at night, he sees three Russian soldiers dragging a woman out of her house, strip her naked, and try to have their way. He calls in his partner for the assist. Together, they shoot all three men. The woman runs away into the night. The ghost wishes he could direct her to someplace safe, but there is nowhere safe and she's already gone by the time the third body hits the ground.

Over the next two days, the stories grow among the EA troops, and the ghost hears it from their own lips as he crawls all around them. Some of their guys are being taken out covertly. Not by return shell fire, but by knives and pistols and sniper rounds.

"Who's doing it?" one of the soldiers asked.

"No one knows," another one says. "Eighth Company says they never even saw anyone, never heard anything, just found the bodies the next morning."

The ghost smiles to himself, and keeps crawling around their camps, planting listening devices wherever he can. He watches the district come apart, day by day. He sleeps in ditches and culverts, eating MREs or whatever he can scavenge. He bears witness to three Steel Octopuses lifting a child, a *boy*, out of a house one night, prying him out like an ant from a hill. They drop him. The boy plummets to his death atop a tiled roof. The ghost can hear the Russian soldiers on the ground nearby, laughing.

The ghost's partner takes a shot at one of Octopuses. His armor-piercing round tears through the center of it, and sends the machine spiraling to the ground. The others disperse and go looking across the rooftops for the shooter.

The ghost smiles to himself, and retreats into shadow.

*

The grenade is from a dead soldier. The ghost hid the body at midnight. It is now 0200, and after a slow, agonizing crawl through rubble and over dead bodies, the ghost has reached the jeep outside of a building the EA troops have been using as a forward operating base. Now the ghost sidles up beside the rear wheel, takes one glance over the hood, pulls the pin and the clip on the grenade, and throws it as hard as he can.

The arc isn't perfect, but the green orb lands in the middle of a group of six soldiers, all peering into the exposed engine of an Armata tank. At the exact same time, someone working on a Kamov twenty meters away gets shot by a silenced sniper round. The dead man's brain matter sprays all over the two engineers working with him on the helicopter's maintenance.

Several things happen sequentially.

The guys around the Kamov scream.

The guys around the Armata look up in alarm.

People start rushing over to help the dead man.

Others dive for cover.

The grenade explodes and all six men around the Armata are shredded.

The ghost has already turned and run away, back to the comfortable shadows. While the troops go on full alert and start firing into shadows, falsely believing they are under an attack on all sides by Ukrainians, the ghost remains ensconced in both shadow and fog a hundred meters away, waiting for the word from his partner.

Finally, his partner informs him that the troops seem to believe all the enemies are stationed to the southeast, so the ghost goes running around the base, and approaches from the northwest. Troops are mobilizing to the southeastern side, providing reinforcements, leaving fewer men on the northwestern side. The ghost moves easily between parked vehicles, taps two young soldiers in the head, and plants two listening devices on military vehicles.

On the way out, he kills another soldier, and his partner snipes two more headed his way. Steel Octopuses descend on the area. They fan out across the area, over the rooftops, looking for the shooters and giving the ghost on the ground a better chance to escape.

*

Now the ghost is real in the minds of the enemy.

The ghost could be anywhere. He could be anyone. Or it might be many ghosts. No one seems to know for sure. From the conversations that the ghost overhears from the Russians over the next week, it doesn't seem like they believe the Ukrainians capable of such tactics. Yes, the Ukrainians can shoot. Yes, they have the hardware that the Americans have been providing them for years. But the Ukrainians do not have the kind of training that American Special Forces or British SAS have. Hit-and-fade attacks are not in their repertoires. And even if they were, it requires experience in the battlefield to tweak one's techniques. The Ukrainians don't have that kind of experience.

So, who is the ghost?

The ghost hears one of these conversations going on one night around the campfire a group of Russians started in an oil drum. He backs away from their camp. Orders his partner to snipe one of them while they're still talking. His partner obeys. The ghost doesn't hear the gunshot, but he hears the screams of the men in camp.

Maybe the Russians aren't superstitious, and maybe they are. Regardless, how could any human being in their position not at least entertain the idea that even mentioning the ghost in conversation might just summon him. Mention death, and its cold hand will find you.

Bombings continue throughout the night. The House with Chimaeras still stands. But it won't much longer.

In separate parts of the city, the ghost can hear other firefights taking place. Small, well-timed, coordinated attacks from militiamen. Some of those attacks were planned by him, and the militiamen took the ghost's advice. Kiev is a stage play starring many killers.

Day comes. The ghost rests. Night comes. The ghost comes out to play.

*

Bombardments shatter Pecherskyi, and the Ukrainian military gives almost as good as they take. They've saved everything for this. It seems they knew they couldn't keep the EA out forever, but instead allowed them to come into the city, sounding the alarms to get citizens to cover, forcing the EA troops to spread themselves thin, having to cover multiple districts throughout the city. Now the EA is arrayed around the main government centers and the upper-class squares, their main artillery and vehicles clustered close enough together that they can be smashed more easily.

But there's the Steel Octopuses. And then there are the soldiers who bring with them *Kop'ye*-like weapons, longer than the pistol-type stolen at the Vostochny Cosmodrome, and they smash through barricades that the Ukrainian military built out of their own tanks and out of civilian vehicles.

The *Kop'ye*-armed troops advance, smash through a barrier, then lay down suppressing fire as main tank groups move forward. The Octopuses scout the areas ahead. Kamovs lend air support, firing relentlessly, their armor-piercing rounds pounding into large civilian homes being used as cover. Jets perform a bombing run, smashing buildings surrounding the House with Chimaeras, while only causing minimal damage to the administrative building itself.

The Ukrainians fight like mad dogs with their backs against the wall. It is vicious and bloody and god-awful. They are plucked off the streets by Steel Octopuses and peeled apart. They fire until their guns are empty, then run forward with knives, some of them diving into the enemy with two grenades in each hand and taking out a dozen or more in the blast.

In all this madness, six men die at the rearmost edge of the last brigade. These six men are killed with Lone Wolf CQB, the shots that kill them never heard, the ghost that slays them never seen.

The ghost moves quietly through the perimeter, until he makes it to the base camp. He plants the last listening device to the upper-right corner of a window on the south side of the base camp building. He sneaks away before the bodies of the six perimeter guards can be found.

*

The surrender of the Ukrainian president takes place at exactly eight o'clock in the morning. Appearing on national TV, he looks dressed for a business meeting as he reads from a prepared statement in his hands. He tells his people to cooperate, that they should have no fear, and that God will do right by the people of Ukraine. He promises "resolution" at some undetermined point in the future. But for now, he tells his people, they must comply and accommodate both the Russian and Chinese occupants.

It took Eastern Alignment forces only a bit more than a month to take over Ukraine and claim it as conquered. The president will remain in office in a non-disclosed political role, governing territories that will soon be formally absorbed into permanent Russian control.

The ghost knows his job is only partially done. It was never likely he and his partner would find General Yevtushenko before the military had advanced this far, nor was it likely that killing Yevtushenko would somehow sway the war. The general is just one component in a global conflict that is escalating quickly.

Now the occupation begins. Now it's time to transition into a different kind of spook.

And as the ghost retreats from the night, he rounds up his partner.

"Nemesis, Hades. Do you copy?" the ghost says.

Fardün responds, "Nemesis copies."

"Time to pack it in. Tomorrow's a new day."

"Copy that, Hades. Meet you back at the ranch."

As he disappears into the night, he can hear the constant rattling of gunfire in the east and west. Militias doing their own work. There are many plays happening across Kiev, and many of them are authored by two ghosts.

33

"Raise your arms," the soldier says. I do so. "Higher." I do so.

The other three soldiers watch with dull expressions while I get patted down. I remain stoic and calm. I look just the right amount of casual and scared.

"ID?" the soldier says. He's young enough to be my son.

"Right here—" I say, reaching into my pocket, but the soldier seizes my hand and another soldier points his AR-15 at me.

I put my hands back in the air and let them take my papers themselves. Together, they look over my passport and driver's license, both of which have me as a Russian citizen working in Ukraine with a visa. They look at the picture closely, which has me with a thinner beard than the thick blonde one I now wear. They put it next to my face, and chatter to each other as they compare face and photograph.

"Where are you from?" asks a husky soldier.

"Originally?" I ask. "Khabarovsk."

"Where? What street?"

"Pushkin Street."

The husky soldier looks at the others. "Any of you know Pushkin Street?"

"I do," says a skinny kid that looks like he ought to be home playing on his skateboard and never here. "What kind of *cheburek* does the vendor on the corner of Pushkin sell?"

I pretend to give it some thought. "*Cheburek?*"

They all stare at me.

"I'm sorry, *comrade*, but there's no pastry shop on the corner of Pushkin, just *The Moscow Times* vendor that's always been there. You might be thinking of Mandelstam, there's a lot of candy stores in the mall there."

The others look at the skinny kid, who only shrugs. "Probably right," he laughs. "I haven't been back to Khabarovsk since I was twelve."

The others laugh. The husky one tosses my passport back at me and says, "What the fuck are you doing here, *comrade?*"

"I've been asking myself that," I chuckle. "Came here chasing a girl, thought I'd stay here after we broke up, go to college. There's a good one here for architects. Cheap." I essay a smile and a shrug. "Pussy, eh?"

They all laugh and nod their understanding at that. Yeah, pussy. I get waved on. It's the third random stop today, and I expect there will be more at the next checkpoint. I walk on, knowing that Fardün still has me in his sights, watching over me like a guardian angel some five hundred meters away.

I make my way down Kazymyra Malevycha Street, where most of the buildings are completely intact, but one, a three-story antique store, is half collapsed by a random shell that was probably meant for the next street over. I see two looters among the rubble.

A truck goes by carrying soldiers in the back. A civilian truck. One of the soldiers must've hotwired and repurposed it for troop transport. As it goes by, one of the soldiers spits on me. The others laugh. I'm not angry. I'll be honest, in Afghanistan I was on plenty of trucks with guys doing shit like this. Spit, throw coins, moon passersby, anything to kill boredom and pretend you're not risking your life every day. Some of the other guys laughed, and some guys, like me, just turned our heads and pretended we didn't see. Almost all these soldiers are young, dumb, and haven't been with a woman in months, if ever. They're bored and a little scared. They're three thousand miles from home and lost and missing their families and being told what to do by a political system they won't understand until they're forty, if ever. I don't forgive them for these horrors, but I understand them.

I hit Butyshev Lane, and here I come to the real devastation. Buildings collapsed on almost all sides. One is even leaning on the building next to it, like a drunkard leaning on a friend to stay upright. It's like out of a cartoon, it doesn't seem possible. Everywhere are the charred remains of…things. Just objects, and maybe even people, that were superheated for a few seconds and then cooled into black blobs when the Buratino warheads detonated in the sky above.

I step across half a hand, with just the ring finger and pink finger attached. No sign of the rest of the body. All around me are the newly homeless, people huddled around the rubble that used to be their homes because they don't know where else to go. Bridges have been destroyed, so they can't cross the river. So, where can they go?

An Octopus zips by overhead. Away in the east, two Kamovs are coming in for a landing on a faraway roof.

I try to keep out in the open where Fardün can keep track of me. I reach my destination at the edge of Preobrazhens'ka Park, where a public bench waits to hold the bus commuters that will never come. I stop there, prop my foot on the edge of the bench, and untie my shoe. Then I tie it back.

Across the street, a man that has been following me for several blocks stops and shifts a bagful of groceries from his left arm to his right arm. He's with the local resistance. I've never spoken to him but he's been countersurveilling me. The shift of the groceries in his arms means I'm clean, no one has followed me.

Now I tie my other shoe.

Right on time, another man steps out from the stone pillar he's been hiding behind about thirty meters away. He's an unassuming man, half past middle age, wearing a black shirt and blue-jean overalls. His hair is thinning and black with flecks of gray. He doesn't look at me at all, yet he walks towards me. I reach into my sock, pull out a small envelope that's been folded twice, and palm it. I start towards him, brush against him, and hand it off.

It's been two months since the Russians claimed victory over Ukraine. And for two months, Fardün and I have been mostly dormant, merely monitoring the movements of troops and artillery from afar, reporting it to Yarwick, and lending intelligence support to Zhadan and other militia leaders. Now, it seems those listening devices we planted have bore fruit. JSOC is getting priceless intelligence about Russian military intentions, and she's been trusted to disseminate some of that intel as she sees fit.

That intel comes to me in the form of e-mails, and I go out twice a day to perform either a brush pass or a dead drop to someone in the militia. The same militia that fought back against pro-Russian forces back during the "stealth invasion" of Ukraine back in 2014, when Putin sent troops as part of a "humanitarian convoy" without permission from the Ukrainian government. The seeds of this invasion may have been planted years ago, but so were the seeds of its undoing.

As I return to the office building in Sviatoshyn District, where Fardün and I have been living these past six weeks, I think of Sophia.

Sophia, if you could only see me now, running the same kind of missions you once did. Nothing high-tech here. Back to old school spy games. Back to basics.

See these hands. See them pass notes. Like kids in school. That thought makes me smile.

*

"I think I've seen this one," Fardün says. He's lying in his makeshift bed with a bowl of Cheetos in his lap, munching loudly, watching some British sitcom.

"Then change it," I say, looking over at the e-mail on my screen. It's another one from Yarwick, and I'm having to copy it onto paper by hand so that I can work out the code. When I'm done, I type it up, then send it to the printer in the corner. The same printer that Fardün salvaged from a destroyed office supply store a month ago.

Fardün sighs heavily and stands up from the bed that he made by pushing two desks together and throwing quilts over them. It's the best we could do considering this sector of the city has been mostly abandoned. Thousands of refugees have left the city and are fleeing to either Romania or Moldova. Apparently, they were not inspired by their president's surrender speech that suggested they be brave and stay the course.

Because of this exodus, Fardün and I have our pick of many luxury buildings in Syiatoshyn. A regular pair of bachelors in our very own bachelor pad. Our base of operations is some senior businessman's former office on the top floor of a seven-story building. The sign on the building says it was once the headquarters of Achta Solutions. Lots of computers, modems, routers, and printers.

After the printer is finished printing our new message, I place the paper in an envelope, fold it twice, and step on it to flatten it out. I then place it in my right shoe.

"Is your contact at JSOC still favoring the one warlord?" Fardün asks.

"For right now," I say.

"You can't trust these warlords to do much."

"You can trust them to create havoc. And Zhadan has shown he's pretty damn good at it."

"Three hundred militiamen armed with shitty weaponry isn't going to push the EA forces back." He tries changing the channel with the remote, but it doesn't work. He shakes the remote, presses the buttons harder, then tosses it. "You want some coffee? I'm going to make some coffee."

"Sure, since you make such a mean cup." I follow him over to the coffeemaker someone was kind enough to leave for us before they vacated the premises permanently. "Zhadan's people have done all right," I say, washing out a cup in the sink of the adjoining bathroom. At least the water's still running and the power's still on. Wonder how much longer that will last. "If he keeps winning the hit-and-fade attacks, he'll keep gaining reputation. That'll help in recruiting people. The underground guys here are big on respect."

"Eventually the Russians will get tired of him and either eradicate his people or run them all out of the city."

"There's still Puluj's people, and Mazepa is gaining some ground in the outer districts."

Fardün yawns as he cleans out the filthy coffee filter. "Warlords like them have no long-term strategies, Adamson. They're all just egos. Most of them are just out for glory or money or both."

"Not that young. That young, they actually *believe*. They're not old and cynical like you and me. Not yet."

"You forget what it was like to be young, to want to make a name for yourself."

I shrug, and lean against the desk with scattered reports still left where their owner left them. I use the desk to press against, arch my back, and stretch. "All we need to do is help destabilize whatever shaky ground the Russians are on here. If the militias keep hitting them, keep weakening their checkpoints, then when the U.S. sends help, they'll hook up with the Ukrainian forces that retreated to the Ukrainian border and come back to Kiev to kick ass."

"Let's not pretend that your American friends will really—"

"Hang on." There's a chime from my laptop. I walk over and check it out. "It's an e-mail from Yarwick."

"That's unusual," Fardün says, opening up the bag of grinds and taking a sniff. "We only ever get two updates a day."

I click the e-mail to open it.

"What's it say?"

I read it twice to make sure I have everything. Then, I turn the laptop so that Fardün can see the screen. "All those devices we planted? Looks like they may have helped us with our target objective. Yarwick's people picked up a bit of audio of someone in the tank battalions talking about Yevtushenko's arrival. He's arriving at the base camp in Shevchenkivskyi District by helicopter. Today."

Fardün hits the start button on the coffeemaker and walks over to have a look at the screen. He nods to himself while humming the theme song to *Samurai Jack*. "Okay, so, we know where he's going to be. I could put a fucking bullet in his brain by sundown tomorrow probably. There's a good angle on that base from the tower at the Toyota dealership, *if* the Russians haven't already claimed it as one of their own sniper nests."

I shake my head. "As much as I would like it to be that easy, it's not. Remember, it has to look like an accident."

Fardün sighs. "Why an accident?"

"We've gone over this. If it's a sniper shot, that'll look too professional, which will make the EA suspect that the Ukrainian military *hasn't truly* surrendered as they've been ordered. Same if I sneak in and slit his throat or double-tap him in the chest. They won't believe Zhadan or his resistance militia could do it."

"And the Americans want to assist Ukraine, but only so far as threatening with troops on the Romanian border," Fardün says. "The U.S. doesn't want it to look like a SEAL team dropped in and did it in the night. Yes, yes, yes, I understand all that shit. But I think your people overthink this shit. Dead is dead, and a dead enemy is always good."

"He has to die in the right *context*," I stress.

"So, what do we do?"

"We start scouting the Shevchenkivskyi base camp tonight."

"That's far from here."

I nod. "Which means we'll have to pack up everything and change locations. Get some rest, my friend. Tonight, we go apartment hunting around the Golden Gates."

*

The scouting is easy, as long as we do it Fardün's way. From very, very far away. Better this way, since my knee has started aching again, just like it did in Beijing that night at St. Joseph's, just like it did in Sweden when I grabbed Vogel. Fardün views the camp through the scope of his Barrett M82. I use a spotter's scope. We select a day with overcast, intermittent showers. It ensures there's no sun glare on our scopes, and our dark clothing helps us blend in with the gray buildings surrounding Shevchenkivskyi. We bounce around from water towers to billboards to the roof of a recently abandoned movie theater. We even approach on foot patrol a couple times, in broad daylight, dressed in ragged civilian clothes and seeing how far we can get before we're questioned and turned back. It helps us get a feel for perimeter control.

At night, we pore over the satellite images that come from Yarwick. She has a team working around the clock on this, and their analyses don't disappoint.

Because the shape of the business center in the district is triangular, it lends itself to a bottleneck, so Yevtushenko wisely avoided that by creating a walled-off area at the end of the street and had his tanks take up guard outside of a three-story office building, inside which he and his senior officers presumably congregate and discuss their theater.

"A shot from far away," Fardün re-suggests. "I'm telling you, it's the only way."

"It can't be that," I tell him, opening a can of tuna. We discuss all this by flickering firelight. The power went out in our building last week. The whole neighborhood has been building fires in their homes, so we shouldn't draw any special suspicion.

I've got a bag of ice on my right knee. Pain's been coming and going these last few weeks. Recently it's been mostly coming and *not* going.

"It has to be that. Adamson, look at it. You can't go into a place like this. It's different than Vostochny—there was military *presence* there, sure, but only as guards. These are active soldiers carrying guns in a warzone. They are shooting and being shot at daily. They've killed. You and I have been hitting them. The militia's been hitting them. They couldn't be any more on edge. What's the expression you have? Trigger happy?"

I eat a spoonful of tuna, wipe my beard, and adjust the ice bag on my knee. "I was told it had to be done a certain way. So that's the way we're doing it."

"An accident." Fardün spits. "You go in there, Adamson, it's likely your funeral. You're being sent on a suicide mission."

I look at him. "What do you mean?"

"I don't think your people like you very much, giving you this. Sounds to me like they want rid of you."

"There are ways these things are done. There are reasons for subtle plays like these."

"Oh, I can understand that. *Of course* it'd be easier to kill an enemy without anyone knowing it was you. But this..." He shakes his head. "This is too far. And after you've been so recently disavowed. If you go in there, and are captured—"

"CIA can still claim ignorance of me, no problem. I'd just be some rogue actor. Crazy ex-SEAL with delusions of being a revolutionary."

He nods thoughtfully. "Who gave you this mission?"

"Who do you think?"

"And her bosses okayed this?"

"Yarwick doesn't have to get an okay for anything involving these kinds of operations. The fewer people know, the better. Especially now."

"You mean with Alpha Source still undiscovered."

"That's right," I say. I decide to pop two ibuprofen for the knee.

Fardün nods again, scratches his chin, chortles. "You know, I had this cousin. Zaz. He got into trouble a lot when we were kids. Nothing too serious. That is, until we became teenagers, and then Zaz went down a different path. Started using drugs. Then selling them.

Turns out, he was really good at distribution, collecting payment from others. Very good. I went to work for him briefly, selling marijuana, no heroin or cocaine.

"Zaz got a real enterprise going. A lot of things seemed to work out for him. Nobody could figure it out, but the cops were never able to bust him. Up and down our street, the cops always raided other people's places, busted up his competition, but never him. I remember a few times, Zaz got stopped on the streets and searched by cops, but they never arrested him, they never found anything, even though I knew he was always carrying an ounce at him, at least, as well as a pistol.

"Some of his competition, when they got out of prison, they had nowhere else to go, no way to make money, because all their contacts got busted, too. So, rather than letting them reestablish themselves through new contacts and become his competition again, Zaz offered them jobs. Most of them took it. But you know what? Funny thing. All those guys ended up getting killed. Even funnier, it was always in the same place. Their bodies were found inside this warehouse in Kukskyi. Every few months, another of Zaz's old competitors, who had come to work for him, wound up dead in the Kukskyi warehouse."

"This story got a point?" I ask, around a mouthful of tuna. In the distance, I hear the product of our handiwork. Guns going *pop-pop-pop!* and someone else returning fire.

"I found out years later through a friend that Zaz had a secret," Fardün says. "Zaz was in with the cops. He was telling them where his competition was, where they hid their stashes, who they got their supply from. He allowed himself to get stopped in the streets, as part of their arrangement, just to keep up appearances. And those competitors of his that he graciously offered jobs to when they got out of prison, the ones who wound up dead in Kukskyi? That was where he sent them to meet with a man named Alexei, who 'retired' people for Zaz. For a price. Alexei was always bad at cleanup, though."

"Your cousin sounds like a real piece of work," I say, massaging my knee.

"He was. Until his girlfriend caught him cheating and blew his fucking head off." Fardün laughs. He stares ruefully into the fire, as if seeing that trickster Zaz in front of him right then. "You had to hand it to him, though. Zaz knew how to control people, how to gather talent. He fucked over his toughest competitors, then put them to work for *him* when they got out of prison, used *their* skills to *his* ends. He gave the cops what they wanted, and he got what he wanted. But before any of those former competitors could figure out how Zaz had fucked them, he sent them to meet with Alexei in Kukskyi."

Fardün looks at me.

"Those people died never knowing what Zaz had done. That he had played them like a fiddle."

I finish up the tuna, and toss the can into the bin beside me. "Why are you telling me this, Fardün?"

"I wonder how often we all get played like that, that's all. Zaz taught me an important lesson. He taught me to think about these things." His eyes bore into mine. "It makes me wonder how disposable I am to you. Or to your people."

"I'm not gonna do you like Zaz did those guys."

"So you say. But walking into this military base camp to go after Yevtushenko? That has the feeling of a date with Alexei."

"We've been doing hit-and-fades for weeks now. How is this any different?"

Fardün's smile fades. He blinks. "My God...you really don't see it, do you? Hit-and-fades around small encampments is one thing. As are the distractions we've caused so that you can slip in and plant those devices. But this...all of these jobs, do they not feel like they're ramping up? And this one...this one..."

"We've been given this job because we're more successful than any other operatives that Yarwick has put in this region."

"Were we supposed to live this long?"

"What?"

"Think about it, Adamson. Were we *really* supposed to have lived this long? I mean, I've been going along because I've got family, and your people are doing right by them, and I'm old and this is all I know. But that doesn't make me glad to be anyone's puppet."

"What do you mean? Who's puppet?"

"Alpha Source," he says, and then looks at me like I should be getting it. "You don't feel it, Adamson? You *really* don't feel it?"

I see where he's going. "Bullshit," I tell him. "Bullshit. If anybody at JSOC or CIA wanted us dead, there are other ways to kill us."

"But none that put our skills to this kind of use, especially after we've been so successful already. Like you said." He smiles grimly. "The world is run by Zaz's, Adamson. They know how to put you to work, even when they're the ones who fucked you. They can find uses for you, keep you busy, so you don't suspect them." He winks at me.

"You're talking out of your ass, Fardün."

"And maybe this is not the first time, eh? Maybe your Kukskyi warehouse was supposed to be along the Amur River, at the Tidov house, only you managed to escape your Alexei. So, they put you back to work."

"Why would they do that? Why would they risk it?"

"Put yourself in Zaz's shoes. What would someone clever like that do if they managed to escape the warehouse? Hm? Would you try and have them killed immediately?"

I just look at his face in the flickering firelight.

"No, of course, not," he says. "Not only would they be on their guard, but others would notice a pattern. An attempt on his life *twice*, and both times it was *after* he was sent alone *by you* on an errand to a mysterious warehouse? Might raise some flags. So…you wait a little while. Keep an eye on him. Put him back into rotation, get some more work out of him, pretend to be his friend. 'Who could've done such a thing? We'll get to the bottom of this.' You assuage his fears. Then, when the time is right, you put him in another warehouse."

"Why would someone that high up be willing to send one of their agents deep into Russia, only to have them set up and killed?"

"Maybe they were manipulated, too. Maybe they were blackmailed or leveraged some other way. And maybe they'll be rolled up one day, too, killed by their own manipulators. Just like Zaz."

"I thought you said Zaz was killed by his girlfriend who caught him cheating."

Fardün snorts. "Who do you think tipped the girlfriend off, Adamson? It was one of his competitors, a guy named Vasily. He called the girlfriend and told her where he was at. Vasily knew she'd shot her last boyfriend for the same thing." He smiles at me. "Everyone has a Zaz, Adamson. Even the Zazes."

*

I usually know when I'm dreaming. This time I'm not so sure. I'm standing on a street corner, waiting for a bus. Fardün is out there somewhere, covering me. A truck full of soldiers is headed my way. Down the street, a woman is crying. She's trying to pull someone out of rubble. Her child, probably. The truck full of soldiers goes grumbling by. Things aren't quite right with them. They're all staring at me.

Nothing is right with the world. When I step off the curb to cross the street, I feel a wrongness to everything. The war's been going on for ages. Years, maybe. I blinked and the rest of my life passed me by. And all I remember is being here. On the battlefield. I know that back home, everyone's dead. There's no one left to mourn me.

I'm aware that someone's following me. I don't turn around. If I turn around, they'll know that I know. It's nighttime. Has it always been nighttime? Feels like I've been walking forever, and that the person behind me has been following me since I was a child.

Up ahead, the side door of a building opens up. A stranger welcomes me in. A stranger that I know. Never seen his face before, but I know him now. He guides me into a smoky room filled with billiard tables. There's a dead body on the floor. Can't tell who it is, if it's man or woman, the face is too mangled. The stranger doesn't acknowledge it, so I don't, either. He steps over the corpse, so I do. He guides me out the back, and says goodbye, but not before whispering into my ear, "You're never going home."

I'm back out on the streets. A woman is walking towards me. She's my contact. She gives me a brush pass. A written letter in my hand. I open it. I can't read it. It's all nonsense, an alphabet I've never seen before.

Feels like I've been doing this forever. Whether it's a dream or not, it no longer matters. I've been here before. A thousand times, a *million* times. On the move. Someone following me. Brush passes.

Secret rendezvouses and secret codes. Warzones. Dead bodies lying unclaimed on the ground. I feel…I feel a tightness in my chest.

I feel myself falling. Except I'm falling upwards, into the sky. A tingling goes from my balls to my spine. Then I sit up, open my eyes. I'm drenched in sweat and staring at the dwindling fire. Fardün is asleep on the floor next to me. I stand up. Stagger. My knee is stiff as hell. See these hands. See them shake. No longer steady as a rock. I rummage through my bag for the water canteen and take four long gulps. I look down at Fardün. Sleeping like a baby.

I massage my knee. Pop a couple ibuprofens. Limp over to the window and look outside. No gunfire right now. Clear skies. A beautiful city, resting peacefully. Filled with dark alleys and schemers. People scheming how to kill one another. How to bomb this person or that person. I walk over to the TV and turn it on. I keep the volume low, so as not to wake my only companion in this world. Surprisingly, it picks up a single channel, though it's a bad reception, all jumpy. Ukrainian News Daily is reporting what's going on outside the city, in the world abroad. Small brushfires, a bunch of almost-battles.

Yevtushenko. One more target. Just one more. I can do it, can't I? Then finish supplying the militias and start training them up, then head home. Job well done.

I look at my hands. Still shaking, though not as bad.

I look at Fardün, my only friend.

I look at the TV. A world on the brink.

For no reason I can tell, the Fermi paradox comes to mind. An old college professor—what was her name? the one with the pink highlights?—she talked about it a lot. Apparently, in 1950, a physicist named Enrico Fermi had a conversation while going to lunch with some colleagues. The men were discussing a spate of recent UFO sightings, mostly joking about them. The others kept talking on it, but at lunch, Fermi suddenly put down his food and exclaimed, "Where is everybody?" When his colleagues asked him to expound, Fermi said that if there was really such a thing as intelligent life elsewhere in the universe, it ought to have been found. Advanced civilizations ought to have to sent out drones a billion years ago, and, according to calculations, those drones would've self-replicated and spread across the Milky Way in less than ten thousand years.

So, the question Fermi was asking was, where the hell is everybody?

There are many theories. One of them is the so-called "Great Filter." The idea that something terrible *must* occur in order to prevent intelligent life from spreading across the universe. Maybe it's the inevitable asteroid collision. Maybe it's disease. Maybe it's a breakdown in the Y chromosome (some biologists theorize that in 100,000 years, human males may cease to exist). But my professor leaned towards one particular filter idea: it is the nature of intelligent life to destroy itself.

We've already had two World Wars. We didn't learn from the first one, who says we learned anything from the second? This could be it. This could really be it. Our own Great Filter, the thing that prevents us from traveling to the stars. And if this is the end? Is this how I want to spend my last years, or the last days of mankind?

You don't have what it takes, Ares.

The words come unbidden to mind. I understand that there is a competition in me. The Unit is here, and maybe Karambit will be, too. Maybe if I find him…maybe justice can be done for Tatiana. I don't want Karambit to become another Vogel. But that's the problem, isn't it? The cycle of violence. Certainly, vengeance is a part of that cycle. Am I a part of that cycle? By being here, now, doing the work I'm doing, am I preventing the Great Filter, or aiding it?

Please, I have children. I have three children.

I took a father away from his children, but Salam was going to kill so many more, or at least assist others in doing the same. But now those children will grow up with a darkness in their heart. Will the cycle continue? I was doing what was necessary. I was doing what I was told, and I'm damn good at that kind of thing. I am now their Vogel. Will they come for me someday?

Everyone has a Zaz, Adamson. Even the Zazes.

And so what if we do? What if we all have Zazes? What if the whole fucking world is nothing but Zazes? Zazes chasing Zazes, like two snakes swallowing each other's tails, around and around we go.

Don't let the darkness win.

My hand shakes as it holds the gun. I'm not even sure when I picked it up. I mean, I kind of recall doing it, but only as an afterthought. See these hands. See them wield the instrument of their trade, the instrument of their liberation. I've been quitting tomorrow a lot. That's all I've done. Maybe sometimes tomorrow shows up in the middle of the night, when you least expect it.

Fuck the darkness.

Come back to me.

The pistol goes back in its holster, where it belongs. "Yes, Sophia," I mutter. I must obey orders. What kind of soldier would I be if I didn't?

Now instead of the pistol, my trembling hands hold the cell phone. I have trouble dialing, but I finally manage it. It's a number I memorized just once. I'm not supposed to use it except in emergencies. When the familiar voice answers, I feel a weight lift. "Nate? What is it?"

"When you said you had planned for emergency extractions, did you mean it?"

Yarwick goes quiet a moment. "Yes. But—"

"I'm coming home." Just like how the pistol wound up in my hand almost without my consent, so too do the words leap from my lips.

"What? Why? What's happened? Is everything all right?" I can tell she just woke up and now she's rising quickly out of bed.

"Everything's fine. I just...I can't do the job anymore."

A long silence. "Why?"

"Every reason you can think of. Do you have the extraction ready or not?"

"Um...well, it'll take a couple days. I'll have to get everything together."

"Just send me the details."

"Sure. Absolutely." More hesitation. I sense it from thousands of miles away. "I...I'm just a little shocked. And worried. This is not like you."

"I know. And that's the problem. I've never had doubts about the job, and suddenly I do. If my mind cannot be fully committed to mission success...well, you know what that means." I'm compromised.

"Okay," she sighs. "If that's really your decision."

"It is."

"Nathan, there's something you should know, since you're coming back." I can hear her moving around, looking for a place she knows she can speak quietly. Something's gone wrong. "It's about Sophia."

My heart sinks. "Is…is she…?"

"No! God no, she's fine. I mean, as fine as can be expected. She was attacked, Nate. I didn't want to tell you, I didn't want it to bother you while you're on mission."

"Attacked? What the hell do you mean?"

"A man came in her room. He attacked Sophia and hurt her. It was Matveyev, Nate. It was Karambit." That doesn't compute. For centuries, it doesn't compute. I feel my heartrate spike. A needle of ice threads through my heart. "I haven't spoken with Sophia, we only just found out about this. Karambit was here in the U.S. about a month ago and we didn't know it—"

"What," I say slowly, through gritted teeth, "did he do to her?"

"He…he broke her fingers, Nate. And he cut her arm. We think he was trying to torture her, maybe? Asking about you? It's unclear if it was personal, just revenge he was after, or if his presence here was sanctioned by SVR."

"Where the fuck is he now?" I'm not off mission anymore. I'm staying. I want reassignment. Wherever she tells me he is, I'm going there. I'm going to kill the son of a bitch. "Do you have a bead on him? Where is he *right now*? Don't hold out on me, Tara! I'm warning you, we're friends, but this is one time you *don't* want to hold out on me—"

"He's in the morgue, Nate. She killed him. Sophia killed him."

Now it *really* doesn't compute. This has gotta still be the dream. I'm dreaming. That's it. "What…what are you talking about?"

"I don't know how she managed it, I don't know what Karambit was doing here, and I don't know even half the details, but Karambit was injected with something. A combination of drugs. Also, part of his jugular was severed when Sophia injected him, he bled internally. They don't know which killed him first, the bleeding or the overdose, but I'm hearing that whichever way he went, it wasn't pleasant. He died in agony."

471

I run a hand over my sweating forehead. None of this makes sense. Absolutely none of it. I don't want to believe it. I want Matveyev to be alive so I can kill him. I *need* him to be alive. I make a fist. Start to scream.

Then I laugh.

You don't have what it takes, Ares. His last words to me. A taunt. No, Karambit, I didn't, but the Goose sure as fuck did. The Goose played you. She had your number. The old fucking hen, she did it!

I'm still laughing and Yarwick must think I sound like a crazy person. "Nate? You okay?"

"Yeah," I say, wiping my eyes. I'm crying for so many reasons I can't even explain. "Yeah, I'm fine."

We both go quiet for a while. A couple of streets over, I hear gunfire erupt.

"I feel like celebrating," I say. "And I also feel like killing somebody. I don't know where to start."

"I'm sorry I didn't tell you sooner. But she's all right now, and it would only have upset you."

"You've gotta get me on the phone with her, Tara. And soon. I need to talk to her directly. I need to hear her voice, make sure she's okay."

"I have it on good authority that she's fine. She's told the nurses that she's fine—"

"She'll lie to everyone else, but she'll tell me the truth. I need to hear she's okay. I need to hear it from *her*."

"Of course, whatever you say, Nate. I can arrange that. And Nate?"

"Yeah?"

"Promise me everything's all right with you. With you quitting, I mean."

"Everything's fine. I just…I just can't do it anymore. Not the op. Not the job. It's time to call it a day. And I need to see Sophia. I need outta this hellhole and…I just need to talk to her, make sure she's okay."

"Okay," she says. "I'm about to hang up and make some calls. Last chance to back out--"

"I'm not backing out."

A moment's hesitation. She really seems to be fighting this. "What about Fardün?"

"Fardün?"

"Is he out, too?"

"I don't know, I haven't asked him."

From the floor, Fardün grumbles, "If you're leaving, Adamson, I am too." Guess he's awake, after all. Been listening this whole time.

"He just said he's coming, too."

"Okay, that can be arranged." Yarwick sounds strange. Somewhat relieved, and a little unsure. "Can you make it out of the city on your own?"

"I think so. We made it this far."

"Where will you be? I need to know where you'll be, so I can send some people to pick you two up, and hand you your new IDs."

I give it some thought. "How about this? We make it out of here, someplace safe like Hungary. We'll head for Budapest. You call me when you have Sophia on the line with you, and by that time Fardün and I should be somewhere we can talk safely."

"All right. I'll make some calls, get the rendezvous ready. Then I'll check in on Sophia, see if she's up for a phone call with you."

"Thank you. And Tara?"

"Yeah, Nate?"

"I'm sorry. I didn't see this coming, either. I'll be glad to hand over operational details to our militia contacts, see if they can nab the target."

"Of course, Nate. No problem. Don't worry about it." But I can tell that it *is* a problem. She wanted Yevtushenko gone. She's disappointed in me. Even if she doesn't know it yet, she's disappointed. "Just take care of yourself until I get back with you."

"You bet. Goodbye."

I hang up, and look over at Fardün, who rolls over and looks at me. "Finally had enough, Adamson?"

One trembling hand reaches down to massage my knee. "Yeah."

He yawns. "Good," he says, and rolls back over. He pulls the blankets high around his head. "Good."

Oie

The last indignity. Not being able to ease myself on and off toilets, or even wipe my own ass. I don't know why I should have such shame over it. I once allowed two very lucky and handsome men access to that part of my body, and without shame, but for a while in my eighties there was nothing but shame when a nurse had to wipe me. I suppose it's the surrender to time. Time. It removes all dignity. And while two orderlies hold me up, Orson finishes cleaning me and pulling up my diaper. They lower me back into my wheelchair. A woman comes and does my hair, prepping me for my visitors.

Today is a good day. Today is a clear and lucid day. I almost wish it wasn't. It might make today easier. My hand and arm are both wrapped tightly in thick casts, so I can't even wheel myself to see the women waiting on me. Orson is pushing me. I don't know if he can feel the vindictiveness radiating out of me, I've tried hard to keep it concealed. Shouldn't be too hard with an idiot like him, and I've had lots of practice feigning ignorance to the enemy. But I'll pay him back for allowing that man in to see me. *Fini à la pisse.*

They wheel me out to the gazebo by the lake. Two women are waiting there for me. I know one of them. Abijah. She's as stony as ever, with only a perfunctory smile. Cold and professional, with respect for her elders but no need to indulge them. My kind of bitch.

The other woman is American, or I'm Eleanor Roosevelt. She has that look. A white woman with a false brightness to her. Congenial. Also, professional. Wearing a black suit like she's going to a fucking funeral. If she waits a few minutes, she may go to mine. Auburn hair, long and pulled back into a bun. She looks at me nervously, and with some familiarity. She's been told about me. She has that look. She has an expectation in her mind and I'm probably a disappointment to her. Big, bad French Resistance lady, all shriveled up, body torn asunder.

Surrounding both women are the men from the shallow graves. They are faint, but there. I can smell their corpses, their decay.

"*Bonjour*, Sophia," Abijah says, and extends a hand.

I shake it with my one good hand. "*Bonjour*, Abijah. Good to see you." It's no lie. I rarely feel good seeing anyone. To Orson, I say, "Leave us. I can shit my diaper just fine on my own."

Orson shakes his head and leaves. Abijah keeps her normal stoicism. The woman she brought with her looks to Abijah for support on what to say.

"This is a colleague of mine from American intelligence, her name is Tara Yarwick. She helped with the operation that stemmed from our discussions."

"*Bonjour*," Yarwick says.

I take her hand. Hold it. Gaze into her eyes. I've seen her somewhere before. Or have I only seen others like her? So hard to tell. Probably not the one I'm thinking of. Still, there's something about her. "So, you would be one of those who sent my Nate to do the deed."

"Well, I can't really discuss that openly right now," she says, glancing over at Abijah. "But I can tell you that it was thanks to you that Wilhelm Vogel was—"

"Fuck all that, I know Vogel's shitting himself in a dungeon somewhere. You can let me know when the fucker's dead. I want to know about Nate. Where is he? The operation with Vogel was months ago. I want to see him."

"Well…" Another glance over at Abijah. I hate it when people do that. Like two teachers silently communicating how to talk to a troublesome child. "He's…sort of on assignment at the moment."

"Is he coming back? Of course, he is," I say, waving off their answers before they're spoken. "He's a survivor. *When* is he coming back?"

"We're looking into facilitating that—"

"When? I want to see him."

"Well, it's a matter of juggling—"

"Oh, for fuck's sakes, Abijah! Why did you bring this one if we aren't able to talk straight?"

"Ms. Yarwick wants to talk to you, Sophia. She thought it best if I make introductions. She and I worked together on your Vogel problem, and I wanted to see you again anyway."

"What does she want to talk about?" I ask, scratching at my cast. It's been itching like an unwashed cunt for days.

"About what happened last month," Abijah says. "The man who broke into your room. Do you remember?"

"I remember just fine," I say. "But why is *she* interested?"

Yarwick speaks for herself. "The man who broke in was here under an assumed name. It didn't reach our ears until just recently, but he was someone we had past dealings with. It's strange that he came here for you."

"Yes, it was strange."

"Do you have any idea why he'd want to do you harm, Sophia?"

"This is about Nathan, isn't it? You're wondering if the man was here asking about Nathan."

Yarwick nods. "Yes, I am. Do you remember what the man said?"

"I remember everything. I remember what he said about Nate."

"Did he say anything else?"

"Like what?"

Yarwick looks at me, then over at Abijah. "I'm sorry, Ms. Zurer, but could you give us a minute? Some of the things I'd like to discuss may include operational details."

"Certainly. I'll be just inside when you're ready. It was good to see you again, Sophia."

"Keep fighting the good fight, Abijah." I watch her go, and as I do, I feel myself slipping a little into the fog. Just for a moment. I kind of have this sense of disconnect. Not quite myself. But then I'm right back and smiling up at Yarwick. "You have me intrigued, young lady. I wonder what it is that an old fart like me could know that interests you."

"There are operational protocols that have to be handled carefully, I'm sure you know."

"Yes, of course."

"So I can't ask this question in front of just anyone. This question is only for you. Did Matveyev—that is, the man that attacked you—did he say anything about who he was working with?"

"No. I can't imagine why he would."

"Did he mention anyone? Any names at all? Or maybe a code phrase."

I scratch at my cast some more. "Such as?"

Yarwick appears to hesitate. Can she trust me? "Did you hear any mention of the name Alpha Source, or anything about people here in the U.S. that might have helped him?"

"No, Faustine, I did not." She flinches when I say her name. Did I mispronounce it? This little tart wants to play her games, I remember her. I remember her just fine. It's in the eyes. Ancient as Eve's first sin, and as red-hot as magma. "Is that all?"

"Not quite." Faustine reaches into her pocket. I go still. Very still. What's she playing at? She withdraws a device. Takes me a second to remember what it is. A cell phone. She dials a number, and says, "Hey. Is your connection good? Can you hear me? Good. Here she is." She hands me the phone, smiling that smile of hers. "Here, Sophia."

I take it and hold it to my ear. "Hello?"

"Hey there, old hen." The voice of an old friend. It's like a warm blanket.

"Nathan?"

Chad Huskins

PART FIVE

The Mole

34

Leaving Kiev was not nearly as difficult as staying inside Kiev and remaining unnoticed. The roads exiting were largely open, Fardün and I drove a stolen Volkswagen right up to a checkpoint at Holosiivs'kyi Avenue, where we had to get out and let the dogs sniff around. Russian troops did the pat-downs, asked us questions, examined our IDs, all while Steel Octopuses glided overhead. From there, we made our way out of the city's nucleus, passing heaps of rubble and bored-looking soldiers that reminded me of my first two tours. Highway M06 took us west, all the way to the city of Chop, right on the Hungarian border. All along the way, we saw small encampments of troops. And food lines. Lots of food lines. Convenience stores closed for good. We saw one police car off in a ditch, burned to a crisp.

Being mostly Hungarian, Fardün navigated and got us through the city and its softer border patrols. He knew two of them by name, paid them something, whispered something. They gave us a ride across the border in their jeep. I think they wanted to hear all the gossip, what we'd seen in Kiev, since Fardün let it slip that that's where we'd come from.

Mile after mile, the farther we got away from Kiev, from the battlefield, the more I felt a great weight lifting from me. A weight I never knew was there. These last several months I've been doing nothing but looking inward—or, at least, I thought I was—and I've been operating on automatic pilot, following old habits, even as one part of my programming was becoming corrupt and starting to contradict old programming. Who knows exactly where it came from? Just like with every mile we drove away from Kiev I felt exponentially better, year after year I've been feeling worse about decisions made.

Where did everybody go? Scott and Dan and Jamal. Kirk Lipscomb and Sid Baker. Derek and Mom and Dad. Jesus, if they could see me now, what I've become, they probably wouldn't recognize me. If I told them what I've done, some of them might never speak to me again.

I don't want it to be that way. I don't want to be that guy, controlled by just a bunch of Zazes, told where to go and who to kill. Not when I'm old. Yarwick asked why. Can't that be the reason? That

I'm just tired of running around, taking out targets, training the next generation of killers?

It was a spur-of-the-moment thing, calling her. Fardün says he'll leave with me, but only to take a sabbatical. He'll be back. He doesn't say that, but he will. It's been a good run. I think it's surprised us both how well we worked together. We didn't talk much on the drive away from Ukraine, but we stuck together out of instinct. Our extraction will happen together, and until that moment, we will have one another's back. It's funny, the friends we make in this field of work.

Now we sit outside the Hadik Café on Bartók Béla Boulevard, a thousand miles from the warzone in Kiev. A thousand miles away from the gunfire and occupational forces and grumbling tanks and secret meetings with militiamen. I sip my coffee and look out across sunny Saint Gellért Square. It's fast-paced here. No one really seems concerned about the war happening a thousand miles away. Why would they be?

"It's strange, isn't it?" says Fardün.

I don't have to ask. I know what he's talking about. "Yeah, it is." He and I have had this discussion before. We've walked between worlds. Not too far away, the world is coming to an end. But not here. Here, there's fresh coffee in cafés and tourists on holiday. "What're you gonna do when you get home?"

"Home? Where's home?"

"When you get wherever, then."

"I don't know." He sighs, runs a hand over his gleaming scalp. "I haven't been to the beach in a while. I think I'll go to the beach."

"Which one?"

"I don't know. What's a good one?"

I try to think. Then I realize I haven't been on a beach since maybe SEAL training. I've been on the ocean, but not the beach. Not in a while. "Myrtle Beach was a nice spot when I was a kid. Gets kinda crowded, though. You need to plan for certain weeks, towards the end of summer."

"Eh, I hate making plans for vacations. I prefer to go somewhere nobody's ever at."

"When's the last time you took a vacation?" I ask.

He thinks. "Five, maybe six years ago? I went to Scotland to look at some castles. Actually...no...no, I went there to do some work. The target I was sent after, he was a tour guide. Forget why someone wanted him dead. After I was finished with him, I went on holiday in the country, just driving around. *Hmph*. I forgot all about that."

I nod. I've kind of forgotten the order things happened in, too. "What castles did you see?"

"A few different kinds. I forgot most of their names. I do remember this one, though. Dunnottar Castle. An old medieval fortress. They hid the Honours of Scotland there—the Scottish crown jewels—from Oliver Cromwell's invading army in the seventeenth century. It was a strategic location during the Jacobite uprisings in the eighteenth century. It was so quiet."

I take a sip of coffee. Nod. "Maybe I'll check it out sometime."

"It was very beautiful. I remember the stone floors and walls...they looked so old, you know. This castle, it was once very important in many wars. Now? Tourists visit it. It sits on a cliff that drops straight down to the North Sea. You can hear the waves crashing at all hours. Just beautiful." He nods, remembering. "I'd like someplace like that to retire someday."

"What, a whole castle?"

"Just someplace out in the middle of nowhere like that. Did you know—"

"Hang on. A call." I reach into my pocket and take out the vibrating phone. I check the phone number. "It's Yarwick." Fardün nods and waves me away. I stand up and limp a few feet away from the table to answer. The knee is still bothering me. Probably a good thing I decided to retire, and not risk going after Yevtushenko. "Hello?"

"Hey. Is your connection good? Can you hear me?"

"Yeah, I can hear you."

"Good. Here she is." I can barely hear her say, "Here, Sophia."

Then, an old, tired voice comes on the line. "Hello?"

A great weight I've been carrying is suddenly lifted. "Hey there, old hen," I say.

There's a long silence. It worries me a little. Does she remember me? How bad has it gotten for her since I left?

"Nathan?"

"Yeah, it's me, Soph."

"Nathan…"

"You doing okay? Tara tells me you had a scare."

"Tara?"

"Yeah, the woman there with you. The one that just handed you the phone."

A long beat of silence. "How are you, Nathan?"

"I'm fine, Soph. I'm just fine. I would've checked in sooner but I didn't know anything had happened to you."

"Yeah, well, we got the cocksucker, didn't we?"

I don't know if she means Vogel or Matveyev or both. So I just agree. "Hell yes, we did."

"Are you coming back soon?"

"I am, actually."

"Good," she says. "That's good." There's something in her voice. Distant. Probably the dementia. It's finally caught up to her. Before it was just a mild forgetfulness that could mostly be ignored, but I hear the exhaustion in her voice now. "Nathan?"

"Yeah, Soph?"

"I think…you're in trouble."

"What do you mean?"

There's a moment of silence, and I think she might've hung up on accident, or dropped the phone. "You need to look out for yourself. I think you're not out of the woods yet. Be careful."

"Well, don't worry about me. I'm leaving today. I'm coming home."

"No," she says.

"What do you mean, no?" Silence. "Soph?"

"I'm giving the phone back to Faustine now. Don't come for me. You need to run."

"Sophia, I told you, I'm fine, I'm coming home."

"Run."

I'm about to ask her what she means when Yarwick comes back on the line. "She's kind of fading, Nate. I...maybe I need to find an orderly. I don't know about taking care of people like this."

"What's she doing?"

"She handed me the phone and now she's just staring off into space."

The relief I felt is gone. I'm a little panicked now. "All right, get one of the orderlies. Maybe she's just having an episode."

"Will do," Yarwick says. "Are you guys heading for the rendezvous now?"

"Yeah. We still on for the fountain?"

"My guys said the embassy fellas should be there," she says.

"Good. We should be there in half an hour," I say. "Hey, did I hear Sophia call you Faustine?"

"Yeah, she did that once before. I think she's confused, scared."

"Shit. Have the orderlies call her daughter and granddaughter."

"You got it. And Nate? Be careful."

"Will do."

I hang up and look over at Fardün. A little girl in a pink dress has wandered up to him and is playing a game of peekaboo. The killer-for-hire is playing right back, chuckling lightly to himself, hiding his face with his hands while the girl's mother watches on, smiling. I put the phone back in my pocket and try not to worry about Sophia. I try not to think about how she's slipping away, lost inside herself. Not for the first time, I wonder what it must feel like to be adrift inside one's own mind.

Faustine.

That name sticks. I remember it vaguely. The only conversation I had with Sophia's daughter, Chloe, ages ago. I had just visited Sophia when she mentioned the name in passing, but with a dose of vinegar. When I asked Chloe about the name later, she said, "*Mère* mentioned her only a few times when I was growing up. Faustine Dubois. *Mère* despised her more than almost anyone. She was a traitor, selling the secrets of French intelligence, got some agents killed."

Strange. Sophia's mind is now in and out of the present, hopping back and forth. Like she's a time traveler without control of her time machine.

You need to look out for yourself. I think you're not out of the woods yet. Be careful.

Run.

"Adamson?"

I look over at Fardün. "Yeah?"

"Well? Are we on?"

I nod. "Yeah. We're on. Good to go."

The little girl he was playing with waves at him as we walk away. "She reminds me of a niece I had. Very pretty. Always smiling, and very friendly to strangers, always assuming friendship with everyone she met."

"Yeah? Where is she now?"

"She passed away. An 'ascending aortic aneurism' is what they said."

"Sorry."

Fardün shrugs, takes out a cigarette, and lights it. We cross the street, Fardün walking a little slower so I can keep up. I pop an ibuprofen for the knee.

Run.

We stop for a crazy bus driver who goes speeding through a stop sign. Fardün yells at the driver. He starts telling me about the differences between drivers in different countries that he's seen over the years. "The people in Puerto Rico, they drive like the stop signs are merely suggestions. Seriously, the whole country is like that. Just madness. They get around by honking horns and letting others know, 'Ready or not, here I come.' It's like that American cartoon, with all the clowns in the cars. Which one is that?"

Faustine.

"I don't know, you tell me," I say. "You're the one with the obsession with American cartoons." I'm still thinking about Sophia. I hate what's happening to her. But she lasted a long time. She retired a bit older than me, but she spent longer in the "work" of clandestine operations. I was ten years in the military, then ten in CIA. Twenty years. That's a long time. Sophia nearly doubled that, if you count her years in the Resistance. She had a bit of a break between the Resistance and SDECE work, but not too long.

That's a long time to stay in the zone.

Faustine.

"—you'd think some of them might be worried," Fardün says, as we move across a crosswalk.

"What?" I say, only now realizing he's still talking.

"These people. You figure with all the refugees coming over, it might start becoming real. Like maybe they don't smile so much? But look at them. All of them are just fine." He points at all the pedestrians swirling around us. Then he points to a food stand. "Oh, hey, let's get a pastry. We've got time, right?"

I shrug. I check the time on my phone while he negotiates with the stand owner, and buys some *lángos*. Fried dough glazed with something. While he's searching for napkins on the other side of the stand, I bend down to massage my knee. Glance over my shoulder. Checking my six. I wonder if that instinct will ever go away. I wonder if Sophia ever stopped looking. Maybe that's why she called Yarwick by that name.

Faustine.

I wonder if she's still searching for that traitorous woman, despite the fact that Faustine Dubois was killed by firing squad, moments after Sophia spat in her face. How many dead enemies are still floating around inside her mind? How many? Will that be me in thirty years? Will I still be expecting to hear from Tatiana? Will I still be hunting Karambit? Will I even remember all these victories? If not, was it even worth it? What good are deeds you can't even remember doing?

And how many relationships has she had? How many have ended in her hundred years on Earth? That must be exhausting, getting to know dozens of people intimately, watching them die or become other people, drifting away. So many enemies coming and going.

I think you're not out of the woods yet. Be careful.

"You want one?" Fardün asks.

He offers me a pastry. "No, I'm good. You ready?"

"As ever." Fardün glances over his shoulder. He's watching, too. Always monitoring. Always searching. Looking for repeats.

People that have been following for blocks, repeatedly crossing our path. People who might've been clever enough to change their jacket, put on a hoodie, roll up their sleeves. We've been on the clock for weeks in a fucking hellzone, it's going to be hard to turn it off.

Our rendezvous is near the terminal for Red Line 2 of the Budapest Metro, at Keleti Railway Station. The people we're meeting are supposed to be officers of the local American Embassy, and they'll escort us to a place just outside the city where a small airfield and a CIA pilot are waiting to fly us over to France. From there, friendly DGSE operatives will assist us in going our separate ways: me to the U.S., Fardün to wherever. We have to do it this way, rather than taking a commercial flight, due to my face. My beard and fake ID might've been enough to get me into Kiev, but now the EA is in Kiev and may have aims towards Budapest. Probably not, but it's safer to go this route, keep my face out of airport computers.

Faustine.

Fardün finishes his pastry, wipes his hands, and tosses the napkins into a bin. He forgets to walk slowly, so I have to speed up a bit to keep up. Jesus, this knee. Think maybe I'll end up needing some kind of surgery.

We pass underneath a few public security cameras. I glance at them. Make sure to keep my face mostly turned away from them. Never know who might get a hold of that footage. I glance behind us, to our right at a meal-delivery cyclist, across the street at a cab moving slowly and parallel to us.

Run.

Ahead of us is an open courtyard with a large fountain. The rendezvous point. I glance to our right. There's a bakery selling Hungarian desserts.

"Hey, you want a chimney cake?" I ask.

Fardün looks at me. "Are you kidding me? I asked you for a pastry back there and you said no. We're almost to the rendezvous."

I'm already headed that way. "It'll just take a second." I pause for someone stepping outside of the bakery. I look around. The cyclist slowed down, almost to a stop. A woman suddenly paused to check her high heels. The cab keeps on driving, but remains slow.

When we step into the bakery, I get a baseline. Eight customers; five seated, three standing in line. Two employees. One of the sitting customers has a laptop out. It's quiet. Mild chatter at one table. Laughter at another. I get in line and look at all the *kürtöskalács*, all the variety of chimney cakes. There is a menu on the wall behind the counter. Beside that menu, a back door. Bathrooms to my right. I have Fardün translate my order for me.

"Never knew you to have a sweet tooth so fast," he chuckles. "What happened? You see me eating my pastry and it made you hungry?"

"Stay calm and do as I say."

Fardün looks at me. It's only a flash. He looks back at the menu. "Oh, fuck you, Adamson. What have you done?"

"You have a 'bug-out' code for your family, I take it?"

"A 'bug-out' code?"

"Yes, a passphrase to let them know you're in danger and they have to get out of their house quickly."

"Yes. Why?"

"Call them."

"What?"

I look at him, smiling, pretending to be in friendly conversation. "Call them right now. Tell them to get the hell out of there."

He stares at me a beat longer, then smiles and takes out his phone. After a few seconds, he starts talking. I can hear a woman's voice sounding very serious on the other end. While he talks, the door to the bakery opens and two people walk inside; a young man and a woman, arm in arm, laughing at some inside joke. The woman is short and blonde with dark streaks in her blonde hair, wearing a skirt but with tennis shoes. Her boyfriend is tall, well built, square-jawed, wearing jeans and a black jacket. I check the SIG Sauer tucked in my waistline, hidden by my jacket.

Fardün sees this motion, sees the newcomers, and looks at me. He becomes forceful with the woman on the phone, then hangs up abruptly. "Okay, she's pissed at me but she's leaving. Now, what did I do that for?"

"Grab something for yourself, then join me over at the table by the bay window," I tell him.

Fardün glares daggers at me but then surveys the restaurant as I turn away. I limp over to the window, keeping the newcomers in my periphery. I take my seat and have a bite of my tall, cylindrical cake. Chocolate and cinnamon. Very rich. I glance out the window on my right, across the street at a car slowing down, letting someone out. Not a cab. An Uber, looks like. The person getting out is a woman in a jogging suit, very baggy. I don't see the cyclist.

Fardün slides into the seat across from me with a glower. "What are we doing, Adamson?"

"How did she sound? On the phone."

"Fine, until I told her to leave."

I nod. "Then they've got time."

"Time for what? What's going on?"

I nod towards the street. The lady in the baggy jogging suit has lingered by a no-parking sign and has her phone out. She's casting occasional glances across the street in our direction, and nowhere else. I see her lips moving. She's got a Bluetooth in her ear. Fardün follows my gaze, looks at her. Then he turns and surreptitiously scans the bakery.

"We've got people on perches?"

I nod. "You got your Bluetooth?"

Fardün nods.

"I'm gonna go to the bathroom. See if anyone watches me, or makes a phone call while I'm gone."

"Okay."

"Eat slower. Get a coffee if you need to. We need a reason to hang out in here longer."

I get up and go to the bathroom, exaggerating my limp quite a bit, looking to see if anyone watches me. I can't tell. I go into the bathroom and lock the door. I check my SIG, make sure it's easily accessible, then run the faucet a second and the hand dryer. I put in my own earbuds, and dial Fardün. "Well?" I say.

His voice is a low mumble in my ear. "The man and woman who walked in. The woman watched you go. Her boyfriend sent a text."

"Where are they now?"

"Ordering a cake in line."

It worked. We outed them. Two of them. There will be more.

God damn it. God *damn* it! This can't be happening. This can't be.

But it is. Deal with it, soldier. And as soon as I recognize the reality, many things start falling into place. Too many things. Missing puzzle pieces that slip right into their awaiting holes. I suspected it many times, but always dismissed the possibility. Until Sophia gave me the final nudge over the phone.

My pulse quickening, I close my eyes and briefly visit the Drifting Place. When I return to reality seconds later, I flush the toilet and limp on out. I make sure not to look anywhere in the couples' direction. When I return to the table, I see that Fardün took my advice and got a coffee. I take a bite of my cake, and look out the window and pretend to admire the gorgeous day. The woman in the jogging suit is still standing across the street by the no-parking sign. I look for any other repeats. Can't see any at the moment.

"What's going on, Adamson?" asks Fardün.

I take another bite. "We're being swept," I say.

"What are you talking about?"

"Drink your coffee and look at your watch." After he's done this, I take another bite, smile, and chuckle as if he's just said something funny. Then I lean in over the cake, use my fork to carve off another slice. "An old friend sent me a warning."

"A warning? About what?"

"I don't know. Maybe she didn't even know. But her instincts and training are solid." I take another bite. The cake is almost gone. We'll have to leave soon or else look suspicious for not making the rendezvous. My heart is beating a little faster.

"Is this the Unit?" asks Fardün.

"No," I say. "This is worse. This is the advance team for the people we're supposed to rendezvous with."

"Advance team?"

"I told you, they're sweepers. We're in their nest. They'll be at least seven of them. Probably more like a dozen, since there's two of us."

"Who the fuck would be sweeping us?"

"Zaz," I tell him. He looks the question at me. "Yarwick."

He shakes his head, not understanding.

"Didn't you try to warn me?"

"I was talking out of my ass that night, Adamson. And I thought maybe somebody would want us gone, but...she's our main contact to your people."

"Our only contact."

"That doesn't make any sense. Not at this point. Why *now*?"

I take another bite. In my periphery, I see the man and woman get up to order coffees, then they take a seat in a different booth, fifteen feet to our left. They've got a wide view of us, they can see if we head towards the front door or the back door or the bathroom.

"She's the one who helped get you into Russia," Fardün says. "Isn't she?"

"She is. But she's also one of three people that survived the raid on the Nest in China," I tell him. I take another bite. "She even warned me to get out of the Tidov's place just before it all went to hell. But why wouldn't she? She had to make a show out of it, in case any of her team survived, which they did. So it paid off. It looked like she was warning me. Unlucky for her, I survived."

"But she helped you escape. She helped you out of Mongolia. She *warned you* about me."

"She was part of a larger team. If any intel came in about Innick Fardün trying to kill me, she would be expected to pass it along," I say, and take another bite. One bite left. We have to leave soon. The jogger across the street still hasn't moved. The cyclist returns, swishing by the bay window. "She was in on the setup, letting the Russians know about NARROW VOID. Maybe they blackmailed her. Maybe she felt threatened. But she told them about it."

Fardün sips his coffee, and takes a bite of his own cake. "But this woman helped you out of China."

I look at him. "No, she didn't. She responded when I showed up at the embassy spilling my agent code, and when the intelligence community became aware we had Karambit in custody. When it reached her ears, she came to see about me. In person. She wanted to feel me out, see what I knew, whether I'd figured it out, or if Karambit had told me anything about the real Alpha Source."

I take the last bite of cake.

"And then I started looking into Vogel. She was glad to put me to use on that one. Maybe she'd even get lucky and I'd die going after the Nazi prick. But that didn't happen. And she had a need for agents in Ukraine. So, she put me to work. And you with me." I add, "Just like your buddy Zaz did. Put the people you betray to work for you, and they'll thank you for it."

"But if she's serving the Russians, she could've told them where you were at any time."

"No. If they'd just so happened to turn up in Sweden or Ukraine, and scooped me up, that would've been *two operations* that Yarwick had knowledge of that I got ambushed in. Too much of a coincidence. She couldn't risk that."

Just like the Brits who cracked the German's Enigma code. They couldn't act on every single message they decoded, or the Germans would've known Enigma had been broken, and they would've scrapped it and switched to something else. So, the Brits had to allow some German operations to be successful, even if it meant the deaths of innocent British lives. The long con.

"She had to choose carefully which operations to compromise for the Russians, and which ones to keep secret," I say. I look down at his coffee. Almost done. "Finish up. We need to start making moves."

"What's the plan?" he says, taking his last sip.

We both stand up and take our trash over to a bin. I notice that the couple is wrapping up their meal, as well. They're pretty good, laughing and flirting like a real couple. Perhaps they even are.

As we step out the door and onto the sidewalk, I surreptitiously call Fardün on the phone. I leave my earbuds in. When he accepts my call, we can both hear each other's voices through the Bluetooths, in case we get separated. "You keep track of the ones we've already outed," I tell him, as we begin making our way towards the Keleti station. "I'll keep scanning for any new ones. There'll be an A and a B team. The A team are the ones closest to us, and the B team will stay far ahead and behind, ready to close the gap if we slip away from the As."

"Do we make the rendezvous with the embassy guys?" He's walking right beside me, but mutters just loud enough for me to hear him over the earbuds.

"They're not embassy officials," I say. "And no, we're not doing the rendezvous."

"If we go past that fountain and into the station without meeting them, they'll know something's up."

"If we go to that fountain we're going to be tased and dragged into a van that's waiting around the corner. We'll be injected with something and never wake up."

"I know. Just making sure you know how this is going to look," Fardün says.

"I understand." I glance across the street. "By the way, the cyclist? He's one of them."

Fardün glances. "Got him."

We approach the fountain of the rendezvous. I take the lead and Fardün follows. We've developed a chemistry, one alternately guiding the other, depending on the situation. Kiev taught us to do that. When we're within thirty feet of the fountain, I turn to the right, and start heading around it, still exaggerating my limp. "Let's keep chatting," I say. "So that they think we've only made a mistake, that we're lost in our discussion, ignoring the rendezvous instructions."

"All right. Then let's talk. Why are these people sweeping me, too? What have I got to do with anything?"

"Because you're with me. It's all gotta be cleaned up. Anything I might've told you, any suspicions I might've shared."

"And how do you know I'm not in with them?" He looks at me.

"You had plenty of opportunities to kill me in Kiev. My guess is, she probably considered asking you to do it, but was afraid it would go wrong, afraid you might feel you owed me for sparing your life in Mongolia. It had to be someone unconnected to her. Like these mercs."

"How long you think they've been following us?"

"They were waiting for us to come near the rendezvous, they saw us when we came to the street, then tightened the net as soon as they spotted us."

"Okay. Speaking of that net, how are we getting out of it?"

"I'm thinking of taking a train."

"We'll need tickets," he says.

"Ahead of you." My phone is in my hand. As I've been limping along, I've been doing a Google search. Now I'm making the purchase online, using my set-aside funds that Yarwick gave me for the mission. If she's smart, she hasn't frozen any of my assets yet. That would only raise my alarms. She'll do that if I slip free, though. I log into the Keleti station's website and find two tickets for the 4:35 to Pillangó Utca, a station two stops down the Red Line, close to the outskirts of the city. I get the QR code sent to my phone, and check the time: it is now 4:24. "All right, stick close. Once we're inside, be ready to fan out."

"How do I know you won't leave me? How do you know *I* won't leave *you*?"

"Because we're better off together." I glance sidelong at him. "Still, if you find an opportunity to make a run for it, you should take it. Get to your family. Fuck all this. Find that beach you were talking about."

He gives me a look, then goes back to scanning the crowds. "The cyclist double-backed at the end of the street. He ditched the bike and took off his jacket. He's approaching us. About forty feet away, at our eight o'clock."

I glance up at the sky. I don't see any drones.

As we approach the steps of the terminal, a dozen pigeons scatter in front of us. I pause to look at the fountain, about fifty feet away from us now. Any of the teams watching us will see me hesitate. It'll confuse them. They'll wonder if I've just realized we missed the rendezvous. Fardün stops, too. I see the couple from the bakery, they're twenty feet behind us. The cyclist takes a seat on a bench thirty feet away, facing the fountain. He takes out a bag of seeds, starts feeding the pigeons. Taking up his perch.

"All right," I say. "You ready?"

"I don't see any other choice," Fardün says.

Up the steps and through the glass doors. We don't even look behind us, we know that they know something is up now. They'll be scrambling, ditching their preplanned routes and perches. There might

493

be one or two sets of eyes in here already—if the grab teams were smart, they would've seen this as a possible exit for us, in case we got spooked.

"This is your home turf," I say. "What're we dealing with?"

"No metal detectors, but ever since the 2016 bombing there's security everywhere," Fardün says. "Cameras all over the place. And not just in the terminal, in the trains, too."

"What's the layout?"

"Wide. About seventy meters, end to end. Main exits are to your right, about twenty meters. Restrooms on the right and left. Gift shop over there. Information center and ticket counter over there." He gestures casually. "Four escalators up ahead. Stairs right beside them, with a mid-level landing. Glass elevator over there, takes people to a little café on the roof." I glance at the elevator taking people up.

"Best way to split them up?"

Fardün thinks for a second. "Think maybe you should go left to the bottom of the escalator, towards the restrooms. I'll take the stairs, hang out on the mid-level landing as a perch. That'll help me get a wide view."

"All right. Keep in touch. I'm texting you the QR code for our tickets. If I can't shake my tails, and you find a way out, just go for it."

"Understood. Good luck, Adamson."

"Same to you, Fardün."

We hit a crowd of people headed towards the escalators, and another group coming up them. I cut right, hunch my posture. Fardün disappears to my left. On the escalator ride down, I take off my jacket and turn it inside-out. It looks a little strange, but from afar the gray flannel ought to throw off searchers.

When I get to the bottom, I move immediately to a kiosk with paper maps and a touch-screen computer for general inquiries. I try to minimize my limp now, so as to confuse their search—they'll be looking for my wobbly gait. It hurts to walk normally, but I force myself to do it. "I'm at the bottom by the kiosk."

"Copy. I just reached the landing. The cyclist and the guy from the bakery are coming down the same escalator you took."

"His girlfriend?"

"I don't see her."

I peek out from the side of the kiosk and scan around. I see the mid-level landing of the stairs. There are potted plants there, and I can just spot Fardün among them. He's also turned his jacket inside-out. If I didn't know he was there, I never would've spotted him. Then I look just above him. The glass elevator is going up. I see a familiar blonde in a skirt inside. "Found her. She's going up the glass elevator behind you."

"Good eye. I see her. Any eyes on the jogging suit lady?" he asks.

"Negative. Am I clear to move?"

"Hang on…they're reaching the bottom of the escalators. There's a cluster of people coming up on your right I suggest you utilize." A beat. "Okay, now."

Grinding my teeth against the pain in my knee, I move out from cover and merge with a family of six. I bend slightly at the knees and hunch my shoulders. Up ahead are the turnstiles. People insert their tickets or rake their phones over the scanner. I get my phone ready. Glance to my left. I see the jogging suit lady. Whoever she is, wherever Yarwick found her, she's damn good. I don't know how she made it this far without either of us seeing her, but she managed it.

"Found the jogger," I say, running the QR code over the scanner. A green light and a chime, and I'm through the turnstile. I chance another glance at the woman. She's headed right towards me, though she's not looking at me. "Pretty sure she's on to me. It'll take her a second to buy a ticket, so I've got a lead. Think I can lose her."

"Copy. That's all four of them. I'll keep looking for others."

I check the time on my phone. "Better hurry. Train leaves in three minutes. If you're coming, better get a move on."

"Copy. Nemesis is mobile."

I reach the rail platform. The train hasn't arrived yet. It's a pretty busy time of day, lots of people heading home from work. There are tall marble columns spaced every twenty feet. I slip behind them, maneuver through the crowd. Now I ditch my jacket entirely, let the flap of my shirt conceal my pistol, and keep my back facing the turnstiles. The jogger will be coming from behind me. As long as she doesn't see my face, it'll take some luck for her to spot me. Still, she knows where I'm going.

"You've got the cyclist and his buddy coming through the turnstile," Fardün says. "I'm right behind them. Your jogger must've tipped them off."

"Copy. The woman in the elevator?"

"I see her coming down the steps now. I don't think she's spotted me. I don't think anyone has. I'm clean so far."

I hear the faint roar and moan of a train approaching. I pop another ibuprofen while waiting, replace the bottle in my coat pocket. The throng of people scuttle forward just a little, in that eternal jockeying for position that people unconsciously do. I fight the urge to look around for the jogger. The train comes screeching up to the platform, comes to a sighing stop. The doors open. We all rush in like cattle. I don't get there in time to take a seat, so I stick close to the door, in case I have to bail before it closes.

"I'm inside the train," I say.

"Copy," says Fardün. "I saw you getting on. I'm two cars back from you."

"What about the two you were following?"

"I took care of them."

That sounds ominous. "What do you mean, 'took care?'"

That's when I look out the window and see two security guards rushing across the platform, headed for the turnstiles. Outside the train, I hear shouts of alarm.

"What did you do?" I ask.

"I had no choice. The cyclist turned around and checked his six. He looked right at me."

Fardün must have equipped his silencer, because I didn't hear any shots. Of course, over the roar of the oncoming train and the general chatter of the crowds, that's not so surprising.

The doors start to close just as the passengers around me begin to realize something is going on. As the train starts to move, I reach for a handhold over my head, and look around for the jogger and the woman in the skirt. I'm sure they're on the train, and if they are, they must know something's wrong. At least two of their team isn't responding anymore, and they had to see the upset before the train got moving.

I look around the train car. It's a motley crew of suited businessmen, girls with purple mohawks, quiet nerds playing games on their phones, and almost everyone texting or talking on a phone.

The train moves into the dark tunnels that run under the Danube. There's some light chatter. Most people keep inside their own private bubbles. I scan the lightly rocking crowd. That's when I spot her. The jogger. She's stepping into my car from the next one over. She sees me. I look away, making her uncertain whether I know she's a threat or not.

"I've got the jogger coming into my car," I mutter.

"Copy. I've got someone blocking my way. A new tail. Never seen him before, but I'm pretty sure he's one of them. Short guy, bald, brown leather jacket."

"Copy." I glance at the jogger. She's walking towards me. Stops ten steps from me, then finds a spot by the door and hangs on to a handle with one hand, and texts with the other. "I've got the jogger on me, so I can't come towards you."

"Shit."

"They can't make a move on the train, that'd make a scene."

"They have to know what happened to their friends," Fardün says. "That might push them over the edge."

"How far to the next stop?"

"Pillangó Utca's not even eight minutes by train."

"Well, I'm sure there must be a B team. What are the roads like this time of day? Do you think B team will have time to drive from the rendezvous point to Pillangó Utca?"

"It's possible. But these guys won't know which station we're getting off at. So we have that advantage."

I check the jogger in my periphery. The train jostles us all gently side to side.

"I'm thinking we've only got one option," I say.

"I know what you're going to say."

"One of us gets off at Pillangó Utca, and one of us stays on the train after it leaves."

"Well, we can't do rock-paper-scissors," Fardün chuckles.

"I'll get off at the next stop, lead the jogger away. Her B team probably won't have time to buy a ticket and get on, it'll be just you and your guy." I feel the train start to slow down. "Are you okay with that, Nemesis?"

"Copy, Hades. Nemesis will stay on the train. Watch your ass. Be ready to draw that pistol and give them hell."

"Will do. You do the same."

The train comes to a moaning halt at Pillangó Utca, and a few people stand up to get off. I try to look far too eager, and rush towards the door like I'm going to bolt. The jogger steps quickly to another door, and texts something on her phone. When the doors open, I step out quickly, and walk with my normal limp, and merge with the crowd eager to get in. They have proper etiquette, leaving room for people to leave the train, and I make my way directly to an escalator, looking around for perches.

"I don't see anyone here yet," I say. "No obvious perches. I think you should be good on the train."

"Copy."

At the top of the escalator I find a similar layout to the Keleti station. I make it to the street, and find myself facing not a fountain, but a tiny street, one lined with small shops, tattoo and ice-cream parlors. I cross the street, step into a small park. I keep my head facing straight ahead but my eyes are sweeping, looking for B team. Think I might've spotted them. A black van comes to a quick halt a hundred yards to my left, at the edge of the park. If it's them, it means the jogger is close behind, watching me, guiding them to me.

Sirens. A couple of squad cars go screaming by, followed by an ambulance. I wonder if they're heading for the Keleti station, to the two dead bodies Fardün left there.

Four people hop out of the black van at the same time. Only the driver stays inside. Definitely B team.

I keep walking until I step out of the park and cross another street to an outdoor café. I make a show of looking left and right, but nowhere near my pursuers. They know that I know they're on to me, but I can at least fool them into thinking I haven't pinpointed them. Now I'm on cruise control, walking at a brisk pace but not in panicked flight. I'm on a public street, very busy. Safe.

For the moment.

I have to look for an opportunity. A cab dropping someone off, perhaps, so that I could quickly slip inside and disappear. I don't see any of those. Lots of cyclists go by, lots of foot traffic, plenty of cover. I weave through them, make it over to a delivery truck parked at the side of the road. I notice the driver's busy loading something at the back on hand trucks. Once I've used the bulk of the truck to break line-of-sight, I open the passenger door and slide inside the truck's cab. I lie down in the seat, massage my knee, go to the Drifting Place, and count to sixty.

When I peek my head up, I look through the windshield, side windows, and rearview mirrors. B team has gone past me, moving up the sidewalk on the opposite side of the street. The jogger has also passed by, but she's on my side of the street now. I see her looking around confused. She steps slowly into a clothing store. I see her lightly touch her jacket, checking her pistol. I check the rearview mirrors on each side of the truck, making sure the truck driver isn't around before I slip out.

After a quick glance across the street to the four team B'ers, I follow the jogger into the clothing store. It's small inside. Quaint. A little Asian mandolin music playing. The front door closes behind me. I scan the store. No other customers besides the jogger, who I see slipping around one of the aisles, looking for me. There's a large, round, female clerk folding clothes and placing them on a shelf.

There's a turn lock on the door, so I lock it and take cover behind the first clothing rack I see. And I wait. Twenty seconds later, the jogger walks right by me. Doesn't even see me. Her eyes are fixed on the bay window facing the street. She goes to the door, tries to open it, finds it locked. Just as she goes to unlock it, the cold barrel of my SIG is at the nape of her neck.

"Don't move," I say.

"You say something?" Fardün asks. At least he's still alive. I hadn't heard anything in a while.

I pat the woman down, checking where I saw her touching before. I find the Glock and stuff it at the back of my waistline. "Phone. Now. Slowly." She hands me her phone. "Back of the store. Let's go." I touch her shoulder and she goes rigid, but follows.

She does as I say. I can see the smoldering look in her eyes, though. She's not scared, she's furious. She can't believe I got her like this.

As I lead her into the back room, the store clerk sees us walking there. We step through a doorway into the backstock area, and the clerk hollers something in Hungarian. But by the time she's chasing us down, the jogger and I are already stepping out the back door and into an alley that leads to an open street where two trams are approaching.

"Just stay calm and do as I say, and you won't get hurt. Make a sound, try to call for help, and I shoot you where you stand and take my chances running for it. Do you understand? Say you understand."

"I understand," she says in accented English. A local.

Pedestrians and cyclists are rushing to get ahead of the tram, or to hop onto it. I keep the jogger in front of me, hand on her shoulder. We look like a couple, maybe like my girlfriend is a little pissed at me and I'm trying to comfort her. The hand also keeps her from running, because with this knee, I wouldn't be able to catch her. I look around for the rest of her team as we make it to the parking lot of a shopping mall.

In my ear, Fardün says, "I'm clear. Lost my guy."

"Copy that," I mutter. "I've got my jogger, we're moving away from her team. Stand by."

When we get to the mall, I guide her into a picture booth, where couples sit and pose behind a curtain. I close the curtain and press her face against the wall. "How many others are on your team?" I ask her.

She hesitates only a second. "Just two."

"Wrong. I saw at least four." I press the gun to the back of her head. "That was a test. Fail again, and your life ends in this shitty booth. Understand?"

Less hesitation this time. "Yes."

"My problem is not with you. Just give me a name."

"What name?"

"The name of your contact. Who handed you the job? Don't lie to me, because I'm about to make you call him."

"His name is Yevgeny. Yevgeny Ponomarenko."

I hand her her phone. "Make the call. Tell Yevgeny you got me and my partner both. And no codes. I've got a friend on the phone here who speaks Hungarian, and I'm putting him on speakerphone. If he hears anything suspicious, you die. Fardün, you hearing this?"

"Yes, I'm listening."

I tap a button on my phone. "You're on speakerphone." To the woman, I say, "Make the call. And put it on speakerphone."

She takes her phone, and starts dialing. After a few rings, a man picks up. "*Helló?*"

The jogger talks in clear tones. She doesn't sound like she's being held at gunpoint at all. There's a quick back-and-forth, during which Fardün remains quiet on the phone. When the woman is finished, the man on the other end hangs up.

"Fardün?"

"Nothing she said sounded suspicious to me," he says.

"Good. Now text your friends," I say. "Tell them you've caught me and to meet you behind the mall. And before you hit send I'm going to take a picture of your text with my phone, and show it to my friend. If he sees anything suspicious, I'm going to kill you. Understand?"

"Yes," she says, and slowly starts texting. When she's done, I take a picture of the text and send it to Fardün.

"Looks good to me," he says. I hit send. Wait for the reply. When I get it, I take another picture of it and send it to Fardün. "They say they'll meet her there in five minutes, they're coming from the postal office up the road."

"Good," I say.

I put one finger in my left ear so as not to totally deafen myself, and pull the trigger. The shot rings out in the close confines. Her body drops to the floor and brain matter leaks down the wall and I put the pistol back in my waistline. I step out of the booth and close the curtain. All around me, I hear people talking excitedly, shouting, some of them alarmed by the gunshot, but nobody knows where it came from. I look for the nearest exit that will take me to the back of the mall and go limping that way.

In the back of the mall is a large parking lot that's half filled with delivery trucks—supply trucks for the clothing stores, food supplies for the food court, and so on. I find a truck about midway across the lot and hunker down behind one of the giant tires. I take deep breaths, and visit the Drifting Place. A nice beach with white sands, the water sighing up onto shore, the sun just beginning to set. I peek underneath the truck and look for four sets of legs moving fast.

When I see them, I move around to the back of the truck, and listen for their footsteps and slightly hushed voices. When they pass the front of the truck, I walk slowly around it. There they are, all four of them, their backs to me. Is this it for B team? Are there more that I missed?

I don't have time to wonder. I take quick aim, fire into their center mass, into their spines. The shots ring out as only one of them manages to turn and face me, taking it in his chest. I hear screaming. I tuck the gun back in my waistline and head across the street. My knee is singing now. I should be sitting down with ice on it, not walking all over the goddamn city.

Shouts. People crying out. Someone knows there's been a mass shooting. Police will be called soon. Don't hear sirens yet.

I check my six. Look for any repeats. Don't see anyone. I spot a tram at the middle of the street, just getting under way. I run after it, grinding my teeth against the pain, and climb on board.

"Nemesis, Hades," I say. "I'm clear." No response. "Nemesis, this is Hades. I'm clear. Fardün?"

No answer.

I look at the phone. There's still a connection, he hasn't hung up.

"Fardün?"

No answer.

*

When I'm three blocks away, I hear sirens. I spot a beauty supplies shop and jump off the tram, then slip inside and pay cash for an electric razor. Ten minutes later I'm limping into a hipster's clothing store, buying tan khakis, a black leather jacket, and a *Star Wars* T-shirt with Chewbacca and Han back-to-back, firing their blasters at no one. Scott was really into *Star Wars*. He went as Han two Halloweens in a row. I was Chewie one of those years, can't remember which.

"Fardün, you there?" Still nothing.

I step into a public bathroom two blocks up, shave my beard down a bit, just so it's not so bushy. I shave my head down a lot, almost to the scalp. I strip off my clothes and check on my knee. Slightly swollen. I can feel and even faintly hear the crunching sounds when I move it. I change into my new clothes, and step back out, just in time to see an ambulance go racing by, headed for the mall, I'm sure. All in all, my change in appearance took less than five minutes.

I cross the street, passing in front of a tram to break line-of-sight with anyone that might be following behind. A cop car goes screaming by, following the ambulance.

"Fardün?" Nothing.

I don't want to admit what happened, but I have to. There was another team, or maybe only a single operative. Langley trained such people, we called them nomads. Operatives whose job it was to stay way, way back from the chase, listen to all the feedback from A and B teams, remaining at distance in case the target pulled a trick and double-backed. Such a person would remain in wide orbit around the chase, with an overview of everything, and would only close in if the other teams went offline. That's what happened to Fardün. He's gone.

Yarwick didn't send just any team. I should've known. As she told me in our first meeting, she only likes to work with the best.

I'm moving through Orczy Garden, a park covered in jogging courses and ponds and gazebos and flowers. I'm looking around for my nomad. I watch the joggers and the tourists snapping pictures and the cyclists zipping by. I'm looking for repeats. Don't see any.

The limp is getting worse. Very pronounced now. I pause by a pond, lean against an iron railing to compose myself, and stare at the ducks.

"Fardün?" Nothing.

I need to sit down. There's a bench behind me, facing the pond. I limp over to it and have a seat. Massage my knee. I'm alone. Adrift. Nowhere to go and no one to turn to. Maybe the call from the jogger to her boss Ponomarenko will trigger a bit of confusion. Maybe it'll reach Yarwick's ears that I'm dead, and whenever this Yevgeny

Ponomarenko figures out his teams have been nearly wiped out, it'll be too late. I'll have made enough distance.

A small drone goes drifting through the sky, nearly silent. It hovers for a second, then disappears over a row of swaying willows. I watch it go. Wondering. Could be a hobbyist out flying his drone today.

I take out my phone and find that I still have a connection open to Fardün. Whoever got him, they've left the channel open. They're probably listening in, hoping I'll reveal my location. I decide to throw them off. "Fardün, if you're still listening, I'm at someplace called Rákóczi Avenue," I say, recalling a street name he and I discussed as a possible rendezvous if we ever got split up in the city. "I'll wait here for you twenty minutes, after that, I have to bail. Out."

I hang up. I stare at the phone and consider calling Yarwick, giving her a piece of my mind. No. Let it play out. See where it goes. I remove the phone battery, toss it, and smash the phone on the ground.

I massage my knee. The pain is subsiding a little, thanks to the pills. I can't help but think about Sophia and her last warning to me. Whether she knows it or not, she helped me. I hope to make it back one more time. Just to see her. Even if she doesn't remember me. I imagine she's—

The drone peeks over the top of the willows. It's just hovering there.

My hand reaches inside my jacket. On my right. Movement. Someone stepping out from behind a tree. I turn, draw the gun, stand, wavering on my leg. Me and the bearded man both fire at the same time and we both miss. I hit the tree, and he takes cover behind it. People scream. I'm backing away, squeezing off rounds at his cover, keeping him hidden. He fires blindly around the side. I keep limping away, firing until my pistol is dry. I drop it, and pull out the jogger's pistol, and keep firing until I've disappeared around a group of pines and move onto a jogging path.

All around me, I hear people screaming. Up ahead, a woman runs away from me with her child in her arms. I come to a small garden of roses, turn left on a gravel path, and take cover behind a pine tree. I visit the Drifting Place. Sophia is there. Not as she is now, but as she was when she crossed the French mountains, long brown hair, machine gun in hand. She nods at me, telling me to keep my game face on.

I bolt away, moving as fast as I can through a patch of woods, crashing through briars and brambles, until I emerge on a sidewalk where people are evacuating the park. I hide the pistol in my waistline, and take off my jacket and toss it in a ditch.

Crossing the street, I look to the sky. The drone is there, but it's moving away from me, scanning the trees to my right. I look to my left. The black van. I see it. Parked on the curb. The driver is just getting out and scanning the crowd. I look around for a taxi to disappear into, a large truck to hide behind, anything. But there's nothing.

Except a trash bin that's overflowing with cans, bags, and plastic bottles. I walk directly over to it, grab a bottle, and unscrew the top. I jam the bottle's top to the end of my pistol's barrel, and keep limping along. There's a lamppost up ahead. I take cover behind it, peek around for the driver. He's a large blonde man, jogging through the street, saying something into a phone, looking for me. All around him, people are shouting, I imagine they're warning each other about a gunman in the park. The driver starts running right towards me, looking all around.

He suddenly locks eyes with me.

He drops his phone at once and goes for his gun.

I fire.

The muffled pop alerts a couple of people nearby, but for all the screaming and car engines it's mostly lost. At the very least, no one can place the sound. However, they can certainly see the big blonde guy dropping dead in the center of the road. I drop the plastic bottle, replace the pistol in my waistline, and keep going.

The drone has disappeared over some trees. No sign of the bearded guy from the park. I'm clear. I think I'm clear.

I turn down another street and head towards an outdoor café. I step inside and, just so I don't look suspicious, I stand in line for whatever they're serving. I look out the bay window, looking for the bearded guy or any repeats. Sirens. They sound pretty far off. I turn and head for the back of the café, looking for another exit. When I find it, I peek outside, into a side parking lot filled with cars. Before stepping out, I check the skies for the drone. All clear.

I limp out and make my way across the parking lot. Sirens are closer now. I need to make space, get beyond the search area. Budapest has a mass shooter today, and it's me, though they'll be getting conflicting descriptions, it doesn't look good for Hades. God knows how many cameras my face passed by from the Keleti station to now.

Jesus, my knee. It's singing right now. The limp makes me look like I've been shot in the kneecap.

I'm on the open street now. Another tram is headed my way. It slows down enough to let new passengers on. I limp up to it, barely make it in time before it shoves off. There's nowhere to sit. I hang on to a metal bar and try to disappear among the passengers inside. No one around me seems to think anything about me is unusual. In the distance, the sirens are fading.

The tram goes for two blocks without stopping. Slow and steady. Passengers get off, passengers get on. The buildings all around are getting lower and lower. The roads more pocked with holes. Fewer trams and more automobiles. We're leaving the nexus of the city behind, coming to the fringes. I keep looking around the tram, checking out the passengers, the conductor, the people jumping on board.

That's when I see him. All the way at the back. He must've been hiding well. The bearded guy from the park. He tracked me to the tram, whether by the drone's assistance or some other alchemy. However he did it, he's here. He's maneuvering his way from the back to the front. So why hasn't he tased me, or shot me, or knifed me? He had the drop on me this whole time, so why?

I look around and find the reason. Between him and me, there's an armed security guard, one hand on a handlebar and the other holding a Kindle. Looks like he just got off from work, just getting in some leisurely reading. If Mr. Beard attacks me now, he has to explain himself to the armed guard. He's likely to get shot.

I look right at Mr. Beard. He sees me. He sees me seeing him. He glances at the security guard standing ten feet to his left. He mutters something. He's got a Bluetooth in. Calling in the last of his backup.

The tram slows down. I move like I'm going to get off. Mr. Beard does the same, watching me. But the security guard doesn't get off, so I stay on. A few passengers hop on, a few more hop off. There's now a man carrying a baby in a chest harness standing between me and Mr. Beard, as well as three chattering teenage girls.

The tram picks up speed, and away we go. Me and Mr. Beard hold on to our handlebars and stare at each other.

Two more blocks. He and I don't move. The tram comes to a stop this time, letting another tram pass up ahead. The security guard takes this opportunity to go ahead and get off. I hide my movement behind the teenage girls, adjusting the Glock in my waistline, make it easier to draw.

The tram keeps going. The next time it slows down, a host of people get off near an outdoor market. I decide to get off with them, dropping a couple inches at my knees, ducking my head. I'm sure Mr. Beard is right with me.

I weave my way through the crowd, moving fast, bumping a couple people to one side until I reach an office building with glass doors. All the while my knee is screaming. Look up. See the drone. I walk up the steps to the office building, hustle inside to the lobby, and face the glass doors. I can see Mr. Beard approaching, but he turns away, knowing that I can see him, and because of the reflective glare outside he can't see inside to me.

He backs off, walks across the street, and takes up a perch between a mailbox and a newsstand. Just watches the front door. Waiting. The drone will be circling around the back of the building, watching to see if I go out the emergency exit.

I look around the lobby. There's a woman at the large kidney-shaped desk, fielding phone calls. The place looks nice, like some kind of insurance company's offices. I walk right over to her, and say, "Excuse me, ma'am?" She looks up at me helpfully. "Um, do you speak English, or Russian?" I say it in both languages.

"I speak Russian," she says.

"Ah, good. I need your help. Listen, there's a man across the street—you see him there?—yes, he's been following me for many blocks. I just came from Keleti station, I'm sure you've heard of the mass shooter that's going around?"

"Oh, yes, of course!"

"Well…I don't want to sound too alarmist, but…well, he's been following me since I left Keleti. And I took the tram away from Orczy Garden. He was there also, jumping on the tram after we heard the shots. I…I think he might be the shooter. Can you please call someone? I'm very frightened."

The woman stands up, looks across the street worriedly, and picks up the phone. She starts dialing. "Of course," she says. "I'll call 112." I'm assuming she means the local number for emergencies.

"Thank you. Thank you so much."

For seven minutes, we wait in the lobby. We watch Mr. Beard stand there, barely moving. The sirens approach. I watch Mr. Beard look a little uncertain as they get louder. I smile to myself when I see him suddenly realize what this is. He turns and starts walking away quickly, which only makes him look more suspicious. A squad car pulls up and two officers get out, and immediately start chasing him.

I walk out the front door. The woman at the desk calls out, "Are you sure you want to go out there?"

"I want to see if they catch him."

"Are you sure that's a good—"

I'm out the door and limping across the street. I don't see where the cops or Mr. Beard went. I head in the opposite direction of the chase. Two blocks up, I see a taxi pulling up to the curb, depositing a passenger on the sidewalk. I head straight for it. Home free, Soph. Home—

I see the movement in my periphery a second before it's too late. On my right. A tall man, black jacket, stepping out from behind a work truck stacked with ladders. This city doesn't want to let me go, the hunters can't let me go.

I turn and aim my gun, fire, but he's already wrapped my arm and pulled me in close, wrenching my wrist until I drop the pistol. He kicks it away, it goes skittering into a storm drain. I see nothing by stars for a second and hear ringing in my ears—his fists have hit me two or three times before I register the first one, rocking my equilibrium. He delivers a knee to my stomach. All the wind leaves me. I try to recover. My knee fails me. I stagger backwards, unable to stand up.

I do the only thing I can. Put my arms in front of my head in a boxer's block, absorbing the rain of fists and elbows he sends into me. Again I try to stand up straight, and again my knee buckles. I'm too old. Too old and too slow. He's a young buck. The deck is stacked in his favor.

Another punch makes it through, connects with my jaw. I stagger back until I hit a wall. Above the ringing in my ears I can hear a woman's high-pitched scream. I take a hit to the gut, another to the temple. I swing wildly, miss, take another hit to my left eye. The world goes spinning and I crumple to one knee. My good knee. I put up my hands because I know what's coming next. He tries kicking me in my face while I'm down, I barely absorb that one—

I step inside the Drifting Place. White shores. Brilliant sunrise.

—the next shot I absorb, then clutch his leg, start to climb him like a monkey, clawing at his clothing—

Sophia is standing on the beach. Her eyes are burning into mine. *Do. Not. Let. Them. Win.*

It's a commandment.

—wrap my arms around his waist, pinning one arm to his side, holding on for dear life—

Other people are there on the shore. People both alive and dead. Mom, Dad, Derek, Scott…Karambit. *You don't have what it takes, Ares.*

—my left foot searches for one of his feet, stomps it, pins it down, keeps him from moving—

This should be you, Derek said to me, when he was stuck in bed, his body paralyzed by Guillain-Barre. No, it shouldn't be, Derek, and here's why.

—hammer fist to his groin, then another, and another, and another, trying to make one of his testicles hemorrhage—

Now everyone's gone, and it's just Sophia on the shore, waiting for me. Young and beautiful and fierce and deadly and inviting me to join her on her quest.

—my enemy snakes loose of me and I drop to one knee again but now I'm level with his legs and I deliver a hammer fist to his sciatic nerve. Both his knees buckle and he drops to the ground, putting out his hands to keep himself from face-planting—

The sun sets lower and the stars are coming out. They're spinning fast overhead. Rigel and Betelgeuse are there, brighter than ever. Hey guys, long time no see.

—leap on top of him and sink my hands into his collar, but he's punching me and I'm burying my head in his chest and shutting my swollen eyes tight—

you don't have what it takes, Ares

—push my knuckles into his throat for a squeeze-the-bread choke and I feel his body convulsing—

Fuck the darkness. Come back to me.

—squeezing and squeezing and squeezing and waiting for his body to go still.

When it finally does, I'm still latched on. I feel people trying to pull me off of my enemy but I'm like a pit bull with its jaws clenched on its dead prey. Then, through the ringing in my ears, I hear voices. People all around me. I look around at the feet, at the cluster of people. Three guys are trying to pull me off of the corpse.

All energy is drained from me. I suddenly go limp as a noodle and they drag me off of him. I see a woman kneel beside the dead guy and try to give him CPR. I try to stand, but my knee completely gives out. I look at the crowd all around me.

A face emerges. A serious-looking face. A man coming right for me in a brown jacket. I know who he is before he even draws his pistol. Another sweeper, come to kill me. I know that I'm dead before I even hear the gunshot or the screams around me. I'm prepared to die. I had a good run. See these hands. See them. Solid as a fucking—

BANG!

The assassin's head cocks sideways and he drops. The people all around me flee. All except one. A man comes racing over to me, kneels, and grabs me by the arms. "Get up, Adamson." He helps me to my feet. I stagger. I look at him, dazed, knowing I've seen him somewhere before. Through one swollen eye, I see the tanned bald head, and the angry face.

"Now we're even," Fardün says. He leads me down an alley.

I'm limping along, barely able to stand, keeping an arm wrapped around his neck. Everything's a blur. Now we're cutting through a parking lot, now we're take cover around the back of a church, now we're smashing the window of a parked car, now he's throwing me into the passenger seat while he hotwires it. Time jumps. I don't remember how we got so far away, but now there is no more city, just endless rolling hills and an orange sunset happening on the horizon.

My hands tremble as they reach into my pocket for the ibuprofen. I don't find them. Oh, right, they were in my other pants. Forgot them when I changed clothes.

I shut my eyes, and fade.

Oie

"You sure you don't want me to stay, *Mère*?"

We are in the clinic. The nurse is standing nearby, taking my blood pressure. I shake my head. "No, Chloe. You go. I'll be fine."

"You're sure? You're sure you're okay?"

I take her hand and squeeze it. "Don't waste any more time on me, dear."

Chloe squeezes back. "You're not a waste, *Mère*."

"I am if I say I am. Now go. I'm going to visit with Abijah a minute. She and I have unfinished business."

Chloe smiles at me and kisses me on the head. I used to do that to her. I give her hand a final squeeze, unsure if it will be the last time. Or just the last time I will remember. She promises she will be back next week and bring Henrietta. "She misses her Soso already," she says. I smile and wave as she walks away.

Abijah has been waiting a respectful distance away while my family was here. She's been discussing something with the orderlies. Chloe gives Abijah a brief hug, and leaves. Then Abijah walks over to me and pulls up a chair.

I look at the nurse to my left. "Shoo."

She smiles and obeys.

It is just me and the Jew woman now. "Well," she says. "I'm glad you're all right."

"You stayed to make sure?"

"I did."

"How nice of you. And where is your friend?" I almost say Faustine, but I know that's not right. Or is it? Seems appropriate somehow.

"She's waiting outside in the hall. She's anxious to hear if you're okay."

I nod. "Listen to me, Abijah. Nathan…you never met him."

"I know him by reputation," she says. "I wasn't allowed to know who it was that Yarwick sent on WOLFCATCHER, but after it was done, my people and I worked it out."

I nod. "My Nathan is a special man. Cunning. He's got the grit. That's what Pierre called it. The thing you need to keep going when others would have given up."

"I'm sure he's very special, to have won the respect of a woman like you." She smiles. It is not a cold smile for once.

"When this is all over, he may need some help," I tell her.

"When what is all over?"

"Promise me, as one woman in the intelligence field to another, as one Nazi hunter to another, that you'll take care of him. Things…they may not work out for him here. I can't say why. He may not be able to come home. At least, if he does, I don't think he can stay. Not for good. Promise me you'll offer him safe harbor somewhere."

Abijah nods. "If it is in my power, Sophia, I will do it. It's the least we can do to repay you for your life's work."

"Thank you. Now, roll me down to the game room. There's Bingo tonight. I despise bingo, but I do so relish watching Gail Abernathy lose and accuse the gamerunners of cheating. It's always a good show."

35

When I wake up, I keep my eyes shut, making sure I haven't been taken prisoner. I listen to my surroundings, trying to determine who is around me. I don't feel any handcuffs, twine, or rope around my wrists or ankles. I'm definitely in a bed. I smell cigarette smoke. I hear a TV on somewhere, with low volume. Sounds like a sports game going on. I peek one eye open. This is harder to do than I would've thought. One of my eyes are nearly swollen shut. When I finally pry it open, I find myself on a small one-person bed.

"Don't worry, I paid cash for the room," a voice says. I turn and see Fardün sitting in an old Naugahyde chair, the color fading. He's got the cigarette between his fingers, and he's facing the old TV on the table at the foot of the bed. "They don't ask for IDs around here. Or, rather, they ask for them, but if you put enough cash down they stop asking."

Slowly, I swing my legs over the side of the bed. My right knee crunches. The pain shoots up my thigh, up my spine, causes my hair to raise. "Painkillers," I say.

Fardün nods. He walks over to a backpack on the floor, opens it, and pulls out a bottle and tosses it at me. "Advil. It's all they had."

I pop three of them, swallow them dry. I look around the room, dazed, yet accepting it. I'm alive. Don't know which gods smiled upon me for that to happen, but here I am. "So..." My mouth is dry. I swallow, and try again. "So, what are we doing? And where are we?"

"Kecskemét," he says. "A nice enough place to lay low. Which we'll have to do from now on, I assume. That is, unless you know some other way to get fake passports."

I test the tender flesh around my swollen eye, by far the most swollen, and shake my head.

"Then you are still a disavowed American agent and I am still Innick Fardün the assassin that the SVR wants dead, so traveling under our real names can't work. And the fake IDs your woman Yarwick gave us will just help her track us better."

I nod. "I know that."

"So, what do we do now?"

"Got an icepack?"

513

He rummages in his backpack, pulls out a large Ziploc bag filled with ice cubes, and tosses it to me. I fumble it, drop it on the floor, pick it up. Pressing it to my eye is both painful and the most exquisite relief ever. "How did you find me?"

Fardün takes a long drag, exhales a huge cloud ostentatiously. "I thought I had them shook, but there was a man that closed in on me out of nowhere. I made a run for it, bumped into some woman pushing a stroller, and my Bluetooth fell out." Another toke, he exhales from his nostrils like a dragon. "I managed to shake him, double-backed, and began to follow him. Imagine my surprise when he closed in on you. The man you were fighting must've been his partner. They lost me and went right for you."

"You arrived just in time."

"I saw that. I considered letting him kill you."

"Why didn't you? You don't owe me for saving you anymore."

Fardün takes another toke, and shrugs. "At the chimney cake store, you were thinking of my family. You had me call and warn them."

"Don't get all sentimental on me."

"It's my family."

I nod. Fair enough. I try to stand, and test my knee. Hurts like a son of a bitch. "So what's your plan now?"

"I don't know. Nothing concrete. I have people in Slovenia who could maybe help us. Right now we need new IDs. They don't make passports, but they do forge basic papers, work visas, things like that. Slovenia doesn't look too hard at people crossing the border without IDs, not on the east side, anyway."

"Slovenia it is, then," I say. Then something occurs to me, and I laugh.

"What's funny, Adamson?"

"I was just thinking. You were an enemy, now you're my friend. Yarwick was a friend, now she's an enemy." I laugh again. "We just keep switching sides."

He snorts out a plume of white smoke. We sit in silence for a moment before he says, "You want something to eat?"

"Hell yes. And I'm thirsty as hell."

"I'll run out and get us some burgers. There's a McDonald's up the street. The TV's on a soccer channel, but I can't find the remote or any buttons to change it." He heads for the door. Pauses. Turns back. "What are we going to do about all this, Adamson?"

"I don't know yet," I say, pressing the ice to my face. "Just get me a goddamn burger."

*

Dusk. Driving in a rented vehicle through the rising foothills of the forested mountains of Bükk, then into the green valleys and passing the vineyards of the Tokaj wine region. Fardün is driving. Not just because I'm injured, but because I'm furious. I reckon he can sense it, after spending a couple months with me. He can probably feel it roiling off of me like heat radiating from pavement on a summer day.

"You're going to go back to the U.S.," he says.

"Yes," I say. It's the first word I've said in the two hours since we left the hotel in Kecskemét, and my lips say it before my brain processes it. It's a truth I've been working on without even knowing it.

"You're going to confront her."

"Yes."

"I'll say that's a bad idea."

"She can't hire a death squad back home," I say. "Out here, she has operational control, because JSOC gave her this region to deal with because of the Conflict, the War, whatever. She was able to utilize assets from CIA. The agency probably had no idea she was using their mercs to sweep me up. Her JSOC bosses probably thought she was going to use them to pick up some Russian spies scouting the region."

"Still, she'll be waiting for you to show up."

I nod. "I know that."

He controls the steering wheel with his knees for a few seconds while he reaches into his coat pocket, and pulls out a strip of nicotine gum. I look at him questioningly. "What?" he shrugs. "I stopped by the store when I got us food."

"And you decided to kick the habit. *Today* of all days."

"It's never too late to quit," Fardün says, and smiles at me. We drive on in silence for a bit longer, passing through a small, nameless settlement. Then he says, "How will you get back to the States?"

"I don't know." I look at him. "Where will you go?"

"My family and I had an agreement on a backup spot. Some friends in Costa Rica. I'll make my way there somehow." He rolls down the window and spits the gum out. "I hate spearmint."

"Then why'd you buy it?"

"It's all they had." He looks over at me, watching me fume. "You're still thinking about her, aren't you? Not just about what you're going to do next. *Her.*"

"Yeah."

Fardün sighs. "It's not the first time I've had an employer do this to me. You get used to it."

"That's the problem. No offense, Fardün, but I don't want to become you. I don't want to get used to it." I shake my head. "More than anything, I'm mad at her for proving me right."

"Right about what?"

How to express it? "It's this feeling I've had for a while now. Something I've learned while talking to a very old friend. It's what happens after we spend all our time making and breaking relationships. It's not the years put on us that ruins us, it's the mileage."

"What do you mean, making and breaking relationships?"

"The thing about relationships is that when one ends, you throw a little less of everything into each relationship after it. Less trust, less devotion, less love. That's why your last love is never like your first love. That's why your last friend is never as good as your first friend." I apply the ice bag, now mostly melted, to my face again. "I had too many friends die on the battlefield, and too many women not willing to wait for me when I got back. Too many relationships…never a good thing. And now the professional relationship I had with Yarwick…it's going to be difficult ever trusting someone like that again. I hate that she's made me into a person who will never be able to trust like that again."

"I see your point. But while every new relationship is maybe 'less' than the last, it's also a lot stronger. Made that way by experience. Like tempered steel."

"I don't know if I agree with that," I say, thinking of Sophia's first child, Isabella, and how she died soon after birth and to this day Sophia sometimes still calls for her. What about all the loves she's had come and go. All the sex. All the joys. Are we diminished by experience, or heightened by it? Does each experience dilute the next one? Does each new experience pale in comparison to the last? Is that what getting old is?

Is this the darkness setting in?

Fuck the darkness. Come back to me.

"Yes, ma'am," I mutter.

Fardün glances at me. "You say something?"

I shake my head. "No," I say, and give my right knee a testing squeeze. The countryside goes swirling by as night falls.

*

We sleep in the car two nights in a row. Parked off the side of the road at rest stops. We keep moving west, following the M70 expressway towards Slovenia. We speak very little. We left our phones at the hotel and have picked up prepaid burners. We ditch the rental car at the border and take a bus across. Now we're moving across the A5 motorway, still pushing west. Three days riding across Slovenia, stopping at hotels here and there, paying cash. We toss the old IDs Yarwick gave us off a bridge.

We come to a tiny seaport on the west coast of the country. We stay one night, during which Fardün steps out to go and visit his "people." He returns after midnight, with very basic papers that have no photographs on them. Work permits with immigration forms we have to fill out. "It doesn't have to be ironclad," says Fardün. "Not since we're just hopping over the pond."

The next morning, we cross into Italy, then step on a boat that rocks gently in the glittering waters of the Adriatic Sea. We head northwest across the waters. The ferry carries about fifty people, mostly sightseeing tourists. People on the boat look at my eye, now not so swollen, but still slightly purplish. Three hours later, we come to the docks of Venice. I maybe haven't seen a more beautiful city in all my life. It's near sunrise when we arrive. I limp off the boat with Fardün right beside me, and we make our way through the crowd and on to the not-so-crowded piers. Long, slim gondolas glide down the narrow canals, carrying sleepy lovers. Candles float on the water. Stepping into this place is like stepping into a dream. Buildings that were here when da Vinci walked these streets stand on either side of the canals.

"I had a friend in college who always wanted to come here," I say, when we find a café to have a sit. It's outside facing the canal, surrounded by docks and piers. "Said she saw it in her favorite movie."

"Which movie?" Fardün says, around a mouthful of crêpes.

"I don't remember." I snort. "I told her I'd never come here, not ever. I don't like stuffy cities like this. I said I thought it was one of those pretentious cities, where it's all supposed to be beautiful because we're *told* it's supposed to be." I look around at the buildings seemingly floating on water. Some of them are, from what I understand. "I kinda see what she meant, though. A person could get lost in this fairy-tale city."

"Look her up. Who knows, she might just be here."

I shake my head. "She got married and moved to New York. She was doing good up there until her husband got ALS. I meant to send flowers at the funeral."

"Why didn't you?"

"I got deployed. I'd just gotten in with the SEALs. I got so amped to go…" I trail off, remembering her. Rebecca Hawke. Cute freckles, amazing smile, loved *Monty Python*. I remember toying with the notion of asking her out. Should have. Wonder where she is now. Wonder where everybody is. "By the time I came back, months had passed, and I felt weird about sending the flowers so late."

"So you never sent them at all?" Fardün says.

"That's it."

He nods. "It's weird how saying nothing at all feels better than actually saying something too late."

"It is weird," I agree. I look over at him. "Where are you going from here?"

He finishes the last of his crêpes, wipes his mouth, and leans back in his seat. "You mean after I see my family, I take it?" I nod. "I suppose I'll find my way back into the work. You know how it is. Try and stay out, it only draws you back in. Why fight it? Why pretend we have a choice?"

"I say we set up a couple of fire-and-forget e-mail addresses and check them at least once a day to make sure each other's still alive. But besides that…I guess we're good?"

The assassin-for-hire nods. He takes out a pen and scribbles an e-mail address on a napkin. Hands it to me. "It's been a strange few months, Adamson."

"It has. Thanks for coming back for me."

"Thanks for ensuring my family was safe." He stares at me a beat longer, then pushes himself away from the table and stands up. He offers me his hand. We shake. "I can't tell you how to get home from here, but I'm sure you'll figure it out. Good luck to you, Adamson." He shoves his hands in his pockets and heads off towards one of the piers. I watch Fardün walk away, blending in with the crowd, and glancing over his shoulder to check his six.

I look across the table at the empty plate he left. I stand up and turn my back to the dock. Then, I pause. I turn back to face the piers, and the waters gently flowing down the canal. I look at the buildings floating on twinkling water and listen to the soft chatter of other café patrons. This would make a nice Drifting Place. When I'm done with my work, I think I'll come back here.

But the work is not yet done. Not quite. I head up the cobblestone street, looking around, checking for repeats, and clinging to the lengthening shadows.

36

Do they know? That's always the question, and it's with me all the time. It's there when I wake up, carries me through the day, and is baked into every decision I make. Do they know? And when I go to bed every night, it follows me into my sleep. Do they know?

And another question. How long? How long will this go on? Is it possible that it will never end? How long do I have to carry on this charade? A reoccurring dream I have is that someone always catches me, and I'm forced to make a decision: allow myself to be caught or kill them. In the dream I always kill them. When I wake, though, I feel instant regret, knowing I could never kill anyone. Or could I? Which one is the real me, the one in my dreams or the one when I'm awake? There's another question.

Life has become questions. Never any definitive answers. All of them are open-ended. All paths splinter off into more paths, never ending at a door or a destination. All these lies, they just continue on. One lie carries me into the next one, and the next one, and the next one. And all paths lead back to the central one, all questions lead back to the first one.

Do they know?

"Ms. Yarwick? You have anything?"

I look up at the sound of my name. Doesn't feel like it belongs to me. Looking across the table at the seven faces arrayed there, I feel ashamed. Do they know? If they did, they sure as hell wouldn't tell me. Like they did with Hanssen, they gave him enough rope to let him hang himself. Some of the people in this room were actually around back then. They know a breach is possible. They've learned the hard way that a friend can betray them. Hanssen wasn't the first, he won't be the last.

"No, Madam Director," I say. "There's nothing more to say than I already have. I should have more for you by Friday, that's when I usually touch base with my contacts in Kiev." My voice never catches. Give credit where it counts, my voice never catches. I wasn't taught to lie, I'm just a natural. Don't know which side of the family I got that from, Mom and Dad were always so honest. Or were they? Maybe they were like me. Naturals.

"That sounds good," says Susan Halbach, Deputy Director of Operations for CIA. She and I have been working together for a while, ever since JSOC sent me to develop something for NARROW VOID. It's been a pleasure working for her, and a terrible burden to undermine her work at many turns. "We want to thank you, Ms. Yarwick, for these past few months' work. Your performance has been exemplary. I've spoken with Alison over at JSOC, and I've let her know I'd like you to stay on as liaison for the time being."

I smile. I was hoping she wouldn't say that. I was hoping for a way out, one that I could explain to my New Masters and they would have to accept. I nod appreciatively, and say, "Thank you very much, Madam Director. It's been a pleasure working with you all." I look around at all the faces I've betrayed and smile. This isn't how it was supposed to be.

"Well then, I think we are adjourned here, folks," says Halbach, and stands up. Everyone files out. Halbach hangs back, though, and catches my arm as I'm about to leave. "Ms. Yarwick, a moment." She turns to her assistant. "We'll just be a second, Charlie. Please shut the door."

"Yes, ma'am," he says, and steps outside, closing the door lightly.

I look at Halbach expectantly. But I know what this is. I know what she's going to ask.

"Thank you for all your hard work," the director says. "I know you put in more hours than Noah on the ark, everyone knows, and I know this job can be thankless work, so thank you."

I nod. "You're very welcome, ma'am. I appreciate that." Here it comes.

"Listen, I know I'm not meant to be privy to any operations involving...*him*. But can you at least tell me...how is he?"

I give a brave smile, and sigh. "We put him in the field six months ago. For the first two months he was reporting just fine, doing exceptional work, as you might expect. We gained a lot of ground intelligence from his work. A lot of what you've heard me reporting in all these meetings—all the advances we've made with Ukrainian militias? —that's been virtually all him."

She nods, bracing herself. "And now?"

I put on my most concerned face. "The agent is not responding. We don't know what that means just yet, he might've only had to make an emergency SDR, and found too many tails. He might've had to ditch all his covcom equipment, might've gone deep underground."

"But you haven't gotten a sign from him," she clarifies.

"No, ma'am," I say regrettably. And mean it. "But he's a survivor, I'm sure he's hunkered down somewhere, just like after Amur Oblast. He'll find his way clear."

Halbach nods, but she looks unconvinced. "Yes. I'm sure you're right." She gives me a pat on the shoulder. "You will let me know if you hear anything at all."

"Yes, ma'am."

I don't vomit until I'm in the restroom. That's another thing I've been able to control since I was a kid. My nervous stomach. Sometimes it comes in the form of an emergency bowel movement, other times it's vomit. Rarely is it both. It usually hits me after a meeting. During the meeting I'm strangely calm, like a cow being led into a slaughterhouse, just kind of not seeing the implications of what it could mean for my safety. Mild butterflies during the meeting, nothing else. Then, as soon as I reach safety, the shakes begin. Hands trembling. Then the waterworks. The tears flow and I get a mild panic attack. I usually get that under control pretty fast. Then, like clockwork, I have to rush to the bathroom and empty my belly. Just like when I was in those theater groups in college—I could perform on stage for a time, but as soon as the curtain fell, straight to the toilet.

JSOC has a few offices reserved for them at Langley. That's where I go to shut myself in. I tell my secretary to hold all calls for half an hour. I need that time to decompress. I usually check my phone while I'm in the bathroom, looking to see if my New Masters have sent any new messages. I should be relieved when there are none, but somehow the absence of any messages at all only makes me more nervous.

My stomach stays in knots. Some days the knots are tighter than others. Today is not one of those days. My stomach was in knots leading up to Nate's deployment, and it remained in knots while I received his daily updates in Kiev. And on the day I arranged for his retirement, my stomach had never been clenched tighter. I had to stay home, not go into work, claim I had the flu. I was sick while waiting for updates from Yevgeny. CIA had recommended Yevgeny Ponomarenko to me two months before, when it became clear I was going to be working with them closely in Kiev, liaising between them and other agencies. They didn't know they'd fed me a weapon to use against one of our own.

I had contingency plans. I had all sorts of them. I tried to work out a way that Nate got to live. I worked really, really worked hard on that one. I spoke with my New Masters. I held off on telling them where he was. I feigned ignorance. "I'm not sure, he could be anywhere."

But they have ways of finding out. As soon as Karambit was free of the Embassy, he reported back that Adamson wasn't dead. The Unit wanted him badly, not only as proof of the U.S.'s meddling and sabotage, but for the deaths of multiple agents and soldiers. They wanted him more than anything.

In my office, I walk around on the carpet barefoot. The carpet is soft. Crinkling my toes on it somehow soothes me. I turn on the TV and see CNN reporting American and Australian naval forces are approaching Taiwan, but so far showing no outward sign of aggression. MSNBC is interviewing someone in Kiev via Skype. Looks like a woman protesting the Russian occupation. They cut to nighttime images of battles happening in the street, and missiles flying through the air. American troops have now landed in Hungary and are expected to cross the border into Ukraine if the Russians don't stand down from Kiev.

It's strange to think of myself as part of the war machine I see being built up on TV. It almost doesn't seem real. Like it's a video game.

I look down at my hands. They're shaking.

I need to go home. The office reminds me of everything going wrong in the world, both abroad and in my own set of circumstances. Home feels better. It was once just a place where I put my stuff, but now it's comfort, a nest that offers the temporary illusion that none of this is really happening.

The drive is scenic. Summer-green fields roll on forever. There was a heavy rain last night, and the steam coming up off the pavement gives the ride home a dreamlike quality. Tomorrow is supposed to be clear, and a little cooler. A good day for a ride on the bike. Haven't had a chance to do that since the Ukrainian operations began. Maybe I'll dust the Harley off, see if she's still purring like she should. If not, a little maintenance will take my mind off of things.

When I get to the house, I once again feel a knot in my stomach. I park the car at the end of the driveway and shut the engine off. I approach the house slowly, looking around, happy to see that my neighbor Mr. Gibson is outside. Up the steps, I check the front door. Seems okay. I unlock it and step inside. The alarm goes off and I go to switch it off. Then, I reset it for STAY.

I relax by a few degrees, then go around the house making sure the curtains are drawn close.

The house is thankfully clean. I left it a mess, but it looks like Agatha was able to come by today. I need to remember to write her a check and leave it on the counter. I relax, have a sip of wine. Not too much, just enough to take the edge off. I turn on the TV and switch it to the first channel that doesn't have the war on. It's HGTV, that renovation show *Fixer Upper*.

Do they know?

The question follows me even here. Here, in my house.

I hear a faint, pining meow. Out of the bedroom saunters Persephone. She wraps herself around my feet as I take off my clothes. I pet her, then go and refill her food and water bowls. I put on some light jazz, some Charlie Parker and Herbie Hancock mixes, and do some yoga while I watch Chip and Joanna Gaines tear into a two-story family home that's not been updated since the 1980s. It still has cast-iron sewer lines. Jeez.

The nest feels comfortable. Here, I'm at ease. The problems of the world bleed away and become almost entirely forgettable. Almost.

When I'm done with yoga I switch off the TV and take a nice hot bath, then dry off and put on a robe. I put my hair up in a towel and curl up on the couch with Persephone and a book. *Sense and Sensibility*. Never read any Jane Austen, but it's always been on my to-do list. Persephone sits on my belly and purrs lightly, sleeping. I stroke her head.

Do they know?

The thought interrupts my reading about once every page or two. I try to deflect it. Swat it away like a fly. It keeps buzzing.

The book is good. Never read a voice quite like hers. When I'm a quarter of the way through, I look up and realize it's getting late. The sun is dimming through the curtains. I'm feeling a little sleepy, but it's not yet time for bed.

I stretch, and as I do, Persephone's head snaps up. I smile at her. But then she lets out a low, guttural moan. Almost a growl. "Hey, what's the matter?" I go to pet her, and the hairs on her back rise up. She comes up slowly on her haunches and looks behind me.

I rise up and look around. The bedroom door is halfway closed. It's dark in there. The house is suddenly very small and confining. Not a nest at all. Too quiet. A hear a pop from the house settling. It makes me jump. Where's my pistol? In my purse. Where's my purse? I think I put it on the dining-room table.

I slowly stand up, and Persephone jumps off me and hides under the sofa. I start for the dining room. I don't make it three steps when I hear the low, quiet voice that makes my bones want to leap out of my skin. "Tara."

I go rigid. A faun locked in the eyes of a predator.

"Hands up. Turn around. Slowly."

When I do, I see what I've been waiting to see for several months now. The man I knew is gone. I knew a man who was professional, with a touch of humor and sadness to him. I've never been on this end of his professionalism, or his sadness. It's different. The pistol aimed at my body somehow paints a cold spot on my chest where I imagine the bullet will go.

My lips try to move. I want to beg. But that's not what happens.

I wait for him to kill me. But that's not what happens.

Nothing happens. Not for a while. We're just...here. In my nest. It's all come around. No more questions to ask. No more going into work and wondering *Do they know?* It doesn't matter if they know. It's all come around. It was all carefully constructed, this house of cards. Just like that, none of it matters. All the dead drops to my New Masters, all carefully written e-mails, all the meetings in malls and parks. None of it matters. Because it's not the Russians who get me, and it's not the people at CIA or JSOC who find out. It's all come around.

"I tried to put you out of harm's way." The words leap unbidden from me. And they're honest. "I swear. And I tried to keep you happy. I knew you were depressed without work, I tried to keep you in the loop on things and keep you working, while keeping you out of danger. And your skills are too good to go to waste, and I needed—"

"My skills produce results," Nate says. His voice sounds different. How long has it really been? "And that's what you needed to keep the illusion alive. Your work had to be above reproach."

I nod. "That, too. Yes, I admit it. Putting you to work served many functions. It kept you going and it kept me above suspicion. I tried to find a way to keep both you and I alive. I tried…everything."

"But when you found out I was coming home?" he says. "When you found out I was leaving Kiev, and that my use was up?" He trains the gun on my head. "Don't bullshit a bullshitter." His tone is colder than I've ever heard.

I've never had a gun pointed at me before. I swallow the lump that's been growing in my throat. Fuck it, out with it. "They were pressuring me. I had stalled them too long, pressing my luck. They were getting ready to out me to my superiors, and I believe they would have. You know what treason means." I heave the heaviest sigh of my life. Telling the truth like this feels both terrifying and euphoric. God, what a relief. God, I don't want to die. "They knew I still had you in the pocket somewhere, they just didn't know where. That's why they came for Sophia—they weren't just sending a message to you, they were sending one to me. They demanded I hand you over, but I wasn't going to do that. They would've tortured you beyond anything you can imagine."

"So you sent people to kill me as a mercy?" A smile touches his lips. The coldest humor.

I try to think of another way of putting it, some other way to stall him. Why fight it?

"Yes," I say bluntly.

He stares at me. I wish I could read that mind. But I never could, not completely. "Was it...was any of it ever *real*? When you and I chatted, we were like friends. Was it real, Tara?"

How best to answer that? "I wanted it to be, Nate," I say honestly. "I hoped that one day, once we were done with all this, once *I* was done, we could be..." I give a shrug. "I don't know. Friends. Something."

"How were you planning to 'be done' with this? You know once they get their claws in, they never let go."

"It was all nebulous. I was making up both long-term and short-term plays as I went along, stitching things together, hoping that it all worked out in the end. I was always looking for ways out, testing them by giving them some half truths and lies. But they know how that game is played."

"Yeah. They do." He snorts. "Were *all* my operations for you meant to benefit them?"

"No. The operations you've done for us did benefit the country, and you did great work, Nate. I just...I compromised NARROW VOID, but only *after* we'd already planned it."

"And when did you tell them about NARROW VOID?"

"They needed something from me. Anything. They'd been pressuring me for a while and I'd been stalling. If they didn't get something from me, they were going to out me. And it couldn't' be anything small. I had to give them something big."

"So you tried to play both sides."

"Yes. I'd hoped to be able to both give them what they wanted and yet keep everyone alive. I gave you the warning in Russia so you could escape. I was hoping you would. I knew the Unit was planning on closing in on our Nest in Harbin, but they came earlier than we agreed on."

The gun stays trained on me, but it has lowered a couple degrees. Maybe there's still a chance. "Nate, you know I'm telling the truth. You know I didn't want you dead because I brought you *back* from Beijing. I helped secure your ticket back home, so you wouldn't be *persona non grata*—"

"You could've done that to put me somewhere you knew I'd be, back home, and eventually let the Unit know where I was. But CIA put me in a safehouse and you couldn't risk having them kidnap me from there, it'd focus the mole hunt on just you and a few others."

"That was *never* my intention, Nate! I swear it wasn't—"

"How did they get to you? In the beginning."

I sigh a quivering sigh. "Remember my sister, the one who never visits her son, the one who's in and out of jail?" I say. "I told you nobody really knows where she is. That's not true. Three years ago, she killed someone. She was prostituting. Her and her pimp killed a john. The pimp fled, she never saw him again. The john died in her home. There was blood everywhere. She called me. And I'm such a fucking idiot that I helped her hide the body."

He shrugs. "How did the Russians know about that?"

"Because they were surveilling numerous CIA, JSOC, and NSA personnel at the time, looking for ways to infiltrate. They call it Operation DEEP SEER. They had me under surveillance because they thought they could honey-trap me."

"A honey trap? On you?"

Never thought I'd have to confess this. "They…hacked my computer. They saw I visited a few kink sites."

"Kink sites."

"S&M. And they knew my…purchase history. A couple of different vibrators, and a sex doll. They had this 'Romeo spy' who was good at seduction, and they knew I was a lonely bachelorette, living a sexless life. The idea was to have him get very close to me, so that I'd give him a key to my house eventually, and he could root around my place at his leisure, maybe drop a compromised USB in my briefcase, have me accidentally infect a computer at Langley, things like that. They were tailing me the night I helped my sister. They saw everything and recorded it. I'm sure they couldn't believe their luck. They ditched the Romeo approach and went straight for the golden ticket. Blackmail."

He takes a step towards me, and I take a step back. My hands are still up in the air. I think about leaping at him. Wonder if I could reach him. He's a trained fucking killer, but even killers get unlucky sometimes. But I'm scared. I don't want to kill him any more than I want to be killed. I don't know what to do. I don't know which way I should—

"Because you compromised me, Sophia was nearly killed."

I swallow again. "I know."

"He broke her fingers, Tara. He filleted her arm."

"I know. Nate, I'm sorry. I...I really thought I could manage all this."

"And then you sent me the last job," he says. "Yevtushenko. I almost didn't see it."

"See what, Nathan?"

"You know, I was so blind, I almost didn't see it. I was so used to winning, to coming out on top, that I was starting to believe I was invincible. It was Fardün who noticed it, he warned me something didn't smell right. You used me, built up my confidence. Between that and befriending me, you had me ready to say yes to anything you asked." His nostrils flare in anger. "Yevtushenko was a suicide mission, and you knew it. And you knew that I *wouldn't see it*."

"Nathan, no—"

"I'm ready to kill you right now," he says.

A tear falls on my cheek, goes into my lips. Tastes salty. Such a strange thing to be focusing on before you die.

"Nate...Nate, please—"

"But, as it stands, it's not up to me." He raises his other hand. In it, he's got a phone. "Goose, you hearing all this?"

"I hear it," says an old, craggy voice. He's had it on speakerphone this whole time, and she's been listening in.

"Sophia?" I say.

"Yes, Ms. Yarwick. I told you, my Nathan is a survivor."

"Yes. I've always known he is." My voice is quivering. Feels like I'm inside a nightmare.

Nate looks at me. "I came here to kill you, but maybe I'm not thinking clearly," he says. "Right now, I don't trust you or anyone else. For all I know, more people at Langley and JSOC could be compromised. If I turn you in, it might not have the desired effect. This might still come back on me. And killing you just feels right, Tara. It feels *right*." He sighs. "But I need a second opinion, and there's only one person's opinion I trust right now. Sophia?"

The old woman's voice comes through waveringly on the phone. "You could check and see if she was lying about the vibrators and sex doll," she says. "But my guess is, if she's lying, she knows to blend truth with fiction. You'll find all the evidence to back up her story, but it doesn't mean it's the truth."

"It is the truth, Nate! I swear!"

"You could tape her confession," Sophia goes on, as though I haven't spoken. "But she could argue later it was given under duress. Meanwhile, her SVR friends could be maneuvering against you. They might even plant evidence in your home that *you* were the mole, to deflect suspicion from her. If you burn for her sins, she gets to go free, and keep spying for them. That's a strategy they might consider."

The old woman is strangely lucid right now. She sounds like she's still in the game, and not decades removed from it.

"Nate," I say, "I will walk right into Langley and confess. I'll do it with you right beside me. I swear. I'll confess—"

"Her only motive is to stay alive," Sophia continues, "so I'm inclined to believe she *would* walk into Langley and confess. However, follow that to the next logical step. If her only priority is to stay alive—not duty, not patriotism, not a sense of what's right and wrong—if her *only priority* is to live, then once she's in custody she might have second thoughts—"

"I won't have second thoughts, Nate—"

"—and she knows that treason carries a possible death sentence, especially in cases where agents' lives were lost," Sophia finishes.

"Nate, listen to me," I say, taking a step towards him. The pistol's barrel looks enormous from this angle. "Nate, I won't change my mind. I won't send the SVR after you."

He stares at me. He doesn't even blink.

"That's not up to you, though, is it, *amoureux*?" Sophia says. "Once you're in custody, the SVR runs the risk of you outing their operation. They won't be able to reach you in CIA custody, but they *will* be able to begin campaigns to smear Nate's name further. And you might convince yourself to go along with such a smear job."

"I won't!"

"But, darling, you've just confessed that you will do anything to save your own life. You will lie, you will manipulate, you will even put the lives of your colleagues in jeopardy if it means protecting your own skin."

Nate glances at the phone. Then looks at me.

"Nathan," I say slowly. "Listen to me. Please. Even if she's right, what use is it killing me? I'm just a dead body at that point. How does that possibly serve you?"

"Because he can come back to work for the agency if he wishes," the old woman says. "You'll just be a missing persons. Maybe a random mugger killed you on a jog. Maybe you collapsed under stress from the job and killed yourself, lonely, unloved, sexless girl that you are. With you out of the picture, there's no reason for the SVR to keep probing for Nate, or to frame him for your work."

To hear myself talked about like this...so disposable...

"Nate. No. Please, just...don't. Don't."

He looks at me. I can barely speak.

"Don't."

"Sophia?" he says.

"Nathan," I say, "don't put your trust in a woman with dementia. She doesn't know what she's saying. Trust me. Just trust me. I brought you back home. I brought you back from disavowal—"

"Sophia?" he repeats.

My heart won't stop pounding. My hands...they're not my own. They hang numbly in the air beside my head. I'm outside of myself. Where do I go? Where is Persephone? How did I get here? God, what have I done?

"Do it," Sophia says.

"Nate! N—"

I don't complete the word. I don't know why. Something weird is happening. I saw a flash, my head twitched, and now I'm crumpled to the floor. This...what is this? I can't even move my head, it just stays turned to the right as something warm spreads across my scalp. My fingers grip the carpet. Soft. Agatha did a good job cleaning up today. Things look dark. I can just barely see underneath the sofa. Persephone. There she is.

Do they know?

37

The park is lovely today. Clear skies. Lots of families out. I see the Rose Lawn van pulling up. All the old folks need help getting out. A side door opens on one van, a ramp comes down, and an orderly slowly rolls Sophia down it. There's a crafts show today. I checked Rose Lawn's event calendar online and gave Sophia a call last night. She knows what to do and where to meet me.

The rest of the seniors take their time walking or rolling around to see some of the crafts. Sophia requests a spot by the duck pond, surrounded by trees. She's got her cell phone on her, and I send her a text. I watch from twenty yards away behind the basketball court bleachers. She gets the text and shoos her orderly away. The guy is hesitant, Sophia is extremely old and recently suffered a physical attack, but she gives him an earful and he goes a respectful distance away, managing the other seniors, and keeping a distant eye on her.

I've grown my hair out a bit, let the beard grow some, too, and dyed it all blonde again. I approach Sophia, but don't go right up to her, in case the orderly is watching. I stand by the pond, just another gazer enjoying the day. I talk to Sophia without looking at her. "How's it going, old hen?"

"I think I'm shitting myself as we speak." She glances sidelong at me. "You look like a fucking hippy."

I snort out a laugh. "We'll probably have to meet secretly like this for a while," I say. "I'm still technically disavowed. Spoke with Halbach. She was happy to hear from me. CIA can't claim me, but they might still have use for me in the future."

"That's good. I spoke with Abijah, she should have work for you if you need it."

"Thanks."

"Did she mention Faustine?"

I'm pretty sure the old hen knows that's not Yarwick's real name, she's just speaking in code in case others are listening. I'm not sure about that, though. Her mind comes and goes. Even on the phone last night, I wasn't sure she understood me when I instructed her on how to meet me. "No," I say. "Nobody's mentioned her. I don't think anybody's missing her yet."

"It was for the best, Nathan. Exodus 22:18. The only part of the Bible I ever had any use for."

"Which one is that one?"

" 'Thou shalt not suffer a witch to live.' Faustine was a witch. All such Faustines are. *Fini à la pisse*, the lot of them." That curse always threw me for a loop. I read that it means "finished by piss," meaning someone who was conceived with not just sperm, but with piss mixed in. The French are a very colorful people. "She had to go. It was the only way to be sure justice was done and you were safe."

I give it some thought. "Yeah." Seems about right, sure. Still, though…it hurts.

"From time to time, we have to weed our gardens. We have to rip out the weeds, wherever we find them. We have to do it without bias. A weed is a weed, it must go, no matter the attachment."

I look over at her. Stone cold bitch, this one. Had sex with Nazis and killed them. Spat in the face of a fellow agent and friend, seconds before a firing squad took her out. I always knew she was relentless, her need to find Vogel was proof enough of that, but I didn't realize until just now that she doesn't do half measures. Not at all. For Sophia, there is no compromise on morals—tactics and methodologies, sure, but not the core principles of the game and why you're playing it. For her, it's not about self-preservation, it's about *winning*. At all cost. Even at great personal loss. Yarwick gave me up to SVR with just the *threat* of violence. Sophia accepted the torture of Karambit's knife and welcomed death if it meant protecting me. Two different animals entirely.

I know I chose the right one to listen to. Still…

Nate. No. Please, just…don't. Don't.

"Do you have any more of those Fiones coffee grinds?" she asks, as though we weren't just talking about killing someone.

"No, I don't."

"Next time we meet, you'll bring me some."

"Yes, ma'am."

"How are you feeling?"

I know what she means. I shrug. "I reckon I'll quit tomorrow."

"That's my boy."

My phone vibrates in my pocket. I check it. Got an e-mail from Fardün, he's still doing okay. I send a quick reply, letting him know I'm clear, too. It's important to keep up these check-ins. The Unit is still probably raw about him helping me set up the ambush on them. We'll be checking in on each other for years to come.

"How's Chloe and the girls?" I ask.

"Chloe's good. Zoe's the one I'm worried about. She's still single and complaining about men. You need to fuck her soon, maybe that'll settle her down a bit. And give Henrietta a stepfather."

"A family all packaged and ready to go, huh?"

"You need it," she sighs. "Oh, yes, before I forget! Do you have any more of those Fiones coffee grinds?"

I look at her. "No, Soph, I don't."

"Hm. Bring me some the next time you visit?"

I muster up a smile. "Sure, Soph. You bet."

Out of my periphery, I see one of the orderlies approaching.

"Looks like it's time for me to go," I say.

Sophia glances at the orderly. "Oh, shit, it's that fuckwad." She looks at me and sighs. "You keep in touch, Nathan. I need to know you're all right."

"Sure thing, Soph."

When the orderly comes over, he grabs her handlebar and says, "Okay, Sophia! There's a puppet show going on. Pretty funny. The others are asking me to invite you over."

"The others can suck my dick," she says. The orderly shakes his head ruefully and carries her away. As he does, Sophia waves over her shoulder at me.

I watch her go, and smile to myself. Despite all the darkness, I smile. I turn back to face the pond, and watch some kids feed the ducks for a while. Then I turn and walk way. I cross the street, check my six, double-back at the end of the street and use a slow-moving bus for cover. I cut through a restaurant, step out the side door, cross the parking lot and check the skies for drones. I cut around the corner of a building and then look back around, check for repeats.

All clear.

I head down the street and find myself walking past a group of about thirty people with signs protesting the war. They're chanting that the U.S. is only making things worse by meddling in China's affairs with Taiwan and Russia's beef with Ukraine. Police in riot gear are forming at the fringes of the protesters.

Check my six again. All clear.

I pull out my phone and look for any good grocery stores in the area. I find one called Darby's. Website says they do healthy and high-quality foods. I set the destination in my GPS and head that way. Wonder if they have Fiones coffee there.

I'll find out tomorrow.

THE END

If you liked this story, please let us know (editor@9dusks.com). And if possible, leave a review on Amazon.

If you are looking for more books by Chad Huskins, check out our website at:

www.9dusks.com

Be sure to become a subscriber and get updates and free early releases of new stories and material.

Afterward by the Author

As we get older, we will notice the gap between those that we know and those that we knew getting wider. The seemingly everlasting summer of our childhood comes to an end, causing a branch in the river of our lives, a splintering, and we all go in so many different directions. Friends promise they will stay in touch. Some few stick around, but most become the casualties of new jobs, new families, suicides. Some end up in prison. Some lose their minds. Some simply move to a place in Montana no one's ever heard of, and are never seen again.

We make new friends. We hang out with people in our chosen profession. We date coworkers. We get fired or quit or get promoted out of state, and the river grows more branches. We make new friends again. We adapt, creating new social structures, hugging close to the ones that feel more familiar, reminiscent to the relationships that worked in the past.

But it gets harder to adapt and make new friends, because we've had to start and stop so many times before. We've been through this countless times, earning the trust of new friends, giving them our trust in return, feeling betrayed, then earning newer friends. This goes on for decades, until our tank seems to be running empty. It becomes harder to make new friends, because you know they'll just be added to the tally of those that came and went. Funerals are regular enough that they become routine. We may begin to picture the day we'll be inside the coffin, inconveniencing other people who have to miss work or a football game in order to dress up and see us off. It will be easy to see it all as being so pointless.

It takes an effort to stay attached to the world. It takes real effort to stay committed to the outcome. We've seen so many leaders come and go, so many societal changes, so many movements, so many good and terrible ideas. How many politicians have we seen get away something? How many times have we seen a good man or woman never get what they deserved? These things are like raindrops, small and not very noticeable as the years go by, but slowly erode mountains. Erode our hearts.

Chad Huskins

No one is immune to this, it just depends on when the realization dawns on you, and when the melancholy sets in, and, of course, what antidote you have prepared to combat it. Good habits can save you, I've learned. Bad habits will mean your doom.

In this book, there are two spies who dealt with this knowledge in their own unique way. One flowed with the coming changes, adapted to new technologies, to new friends and family, even as her body and mind withered. The other spy, much younger, was just entering into the phase of his life when he noticed the erosion to his heart. A few too many raindrops.

Often, a story is just a means for a writer to have an argument with himself, or with others. It might be an internal debate that needs working through. Like therapy. Characters can teach the author as much as he or she can teach the reader. While writing Sophia and researching the women of the French Resistance, I learned something about resilience. While writing Nathan, and keeping in mind old people I've known who despised the graying of age, I learned a little about self-reliance, and reminded myself to be vigilant against the melancholy. I've been fortunate enough to have never felt depression before, but I've noticed the raindrops, and writing these characters helped me see things from a perspective I found surprising.

My thanks to you, dear reader, for your time and attention. I hope you found some entertainment in this story, and that you will continue to grow and adapt in the downpours to come. One day at a time. One foot in front of the other.

About the Author

Chad Huskins' debut novel 'Khan in Rasputin's Shadow' won the 2009 EVVY Award for fiction. He is a self-defense instructor, has trained SWAT and bodyguards, and worked private security for various television shows. He lives outside of Atlanta, Georgia.

He has published over fourteen novels and many short stories over the last decade, mostly in the SciFi, Fantasy and Horror realms, but is always experimenting with narrative styles and crossing genres.

Made in the USA
Middletown, DE
22 September 2020